MONSTER CASE FILES COMPLETE

ADVENTURES WITH URBAN LEGENDS AND MYSTERIES

CRAIG MARTELLE

KATHRYN HEARST

Monster Case Files (and what happens within / characters / situations / worlds) are Copyright (c) 2019-20 by Craig Martelle
Cover art by "The Cover Designer", Ryan Schwarz. www.thecoverdesigner.com
Pen & ink drawings by Sumit (Scorpy)

Monster Case Files is published by LMBPN Publishing

First US edition, May 2020
eBook ISBN: 978-1-64202-882-9
Print ISBN: 978-1-64971-024-6

DEDICATION

We couldn't do what we do without the support of great people around us. We thank our spouses and our families for giving us time alone to think, write, and review. We thank our editor (Lynne Stiegler) cover artist (Ryan Schwarz), insider team of beta readers (Micky Cocker, Kelly O'Donnell, Dr. James Caplan, and John Ashmore) and the last line of defense, our proofreaders (Linda McCarthy, Tom Nye, Rob Kerns, Arthur Fortune, Jr, Adena Lee). It's not who we are as authors, but who we are surrounded by that makes this all happen. Enjoy the story.

REAL GHOSTS
MONSTER CASE FILES BOOK 0

Adelaide, South Australia—the Old Jail, or Gaol, as They Say…

"What better way to kill some time than to spend it with killers? Come on Grace, lighten up," the young man quipped. At seventeen, he was tall, dark, and invincible.

His twin sister was unimpressed.

"Rundle Mall is just as close, Henry!" she countered, pointing in the opposite direction. The Cumberland Arms Hotel loomed behind them, a colonial backdrop in a modern city. Grace smiled as she pulled up the map on her phone. "There's a Krispy Kreme right around the corner."

Henry looked over her shoulder. "And a Ferrari dealership!" He pointed in the direction of the Adelaide Gaol. "It's on our way." He took two steps, but she didn't follow.

"A high school is right across the street." She pointed ahead.

"We have a great life, Gracie, getting to travel with Mom and Dad while they lecture," he countered, trying to focus her on what he wanted.

"But not being strapped down like children. If we go to the Gaol," she looked sideways at her twin, "what do you think you'll get out of it?"

"If I'm going to study law in college, I want to see these things. That way I know what I'm recommending in the way of punishment, should it come to that. And who knows, maybe there's a mystery in there that needs to be solved." Henry pulled his phone from his pocket and typed in Adelaide Gaol to see what else he could find. Grace expanded her map to show more of the city center.

"I'm glad we don't have to go into lockup for eight hours a day like everyone in that school," Henry countered without looking up. The twins were home-schooled by their parents: their mother Faith, a professor of engineering, and their father Ethan, a lawyer and former judge.

"There's a museum, an art gallery, a botanical garden, and a zoo." Grace pointed up the street, opposite the direction Henry was facing.

"Gaol," he said with finality. "You can study the engineering they put in place to keep the prisoners inside. The self-guided tour shouldn't take long. It's a small place. It'll probably take us longer to walk there than we'll spend inside, then we'll make a gastronomic exploration of the city."

"After looking at where they executed people, you think you'll be hungry?"

"No," Henry stated sadly, dramatically throwing the back of his hand to his forehead. "I *know* I'll be hungry!"

Both their phones buzzed at the same time. "We have to meet Mom and Dad for lunch at one." Grace tapped the address, and it showed on her map as the University of Adelaide School of Law. "It's just past the museum."

"The Gaol opens at ten. We can be standing there when they unlock the doors, but we need to start walking." Henry put his words into action, and without looking back, took off at a good clip. Grace hurried to catch up.

"Fine, but after lunch, we're going where I want to go."

"Deal. If Dad's buying lunch, I might be hungrier than usual. After a good meal, I might need a nap."

"Since you're always hungry, I can't fathom what 'hungrier than usual' looks like. Maybe you should look into Pilates?"

"What does one have to do with the other?" He looked down the street and started to step off the curb, but Grace grabbed his arm. A scooter raced by from his right.

"They drive on the other side of the road here. Look right, then left, then right again."

Henry scowled at the hand on his arm but quickly turned it into a smile. "Thanks, Grace. Dad would be so mad if I got clocked by a scooter. If it had been a Ferrari, maybe, but not a scooter." Grace laughed at her brother's remark as they ran across the street, stopping by Krispy Kreme for a couple of quick donuts and coffee before continuing to the Gaol.

The twins had misjudged how close the Gaol was and underestimated their good fortune at getting greenlighted through the crosswalks. They arrived ten minutes before it was to open. Without any cars in the parking lot or people walking around, it appeared as if it wouldn't open at all. They walked along its imposing entrance and around the corner, where they found two cars, warm from being recently driven, suggesting that those running the museum had already arrived.

They returned to the entrance. A picnic table sat under a massive tree that dominated visitor parking. They took seats, pulling their windbreakers tighter around their shoulders.

"It's winter here," Grace commented needlessly. "I understand the planetary tilt and all that, but it's still weird to fly for a day and leave summer behind. But if this is the worst they have, it's not bad."

"I like the weather, but I hear it gets hot in the summer. Like, brutally hot. Hey!" Henry pointed at a guard tower overlooking a corner wall. "Did you see that?"

Grace rolled her eyes and looked where Henry was pointing. "What am I supposed to be looking at?"

"I swear there was somebody looking at us."

"Probably a worker checking the area."

"But the towers are off-limits," Henry replied.

"Not for the workers." Grace stood up as the front door opened and a kindly-looking woman waved to them.

"It's go-time," Henry intoned in his deepest voice.

"Dammit! If you try to creep me out during this tour, I'll leave you here!" She gave him her best withering glare.

Henry had seen it before—maybe too often. He snickered but nodded. "Fine, but I *did* see somebody in the tower." He started to sulk as they entered the Gaol, casting furtive glances back toward the tower with each step.

"G'day and welcome to Adelaide Gaol!" The first woman beamed at them infectiously from behind the counter, her short hair tinted a light shade of purple.

"Is there anyone in the tower over there?" Henry asked, gesturing in the general direction.

"'Strewth, you're a keen one." She shot a glance at the two men outside who were on their way to unlock an exhibit. "Darl', no one has been in that tower for months. The Gaol's a big place, and it's just us—" she nodded at a younger woman in the gift shop and the two men outside, "running the show. Here you go, love. Get yourself a free map, and you can buy your tickets at the counter."

Grace nodded and headed into the gift shop. Henry poked his head outside to get a better look at the guard tower. When he returned, scowling, Grace shoved a ticket into his hand. "Stop goofing around. It was probably a bird, or maybe a bat. I hear they have flying foxes down here that are as big as squirrels."

He pursed his lips and stared at her.

"Don't tell me you're *that* spooked?"

"I hate it when things don't have an explanation. Let's go look for ourselves." Henry urged Grace to follow as he rushed through the door that opened into the small area between the entry and the main guard shack, staffed only by mannequins now. He took a sharp right and started jogging between the outer wall and an inner cell block. When he reached the end, he found the door to the tower locked. He pulled on the handle anyway.

"That's off-limits to tourists," a young man's voice said in a distinct Australian twang.

Grace caught his eye and smiled. He looked barely older than the twins. The young man tossed his head, clearing a shock of hair from in front of his eyes.

"I didn't hear you say it was off-limits to the staff. We really want to see what's up there. Maybe you can help us?" Grace bit her lip and looked down. Henry stepped away from the door.

"Americans? What brings you this way?"

"Dad's lecturing at the law school," Grace replied, holding the Gaol employee's gaze.

"Isn't school in session for you guys?" Henry countered, standing close to his sister. He was as tall as the Australian stranger.

"It is, but I mostly have night classes. Is your father Professor Warner?"

The twins did a double take.

"Are you in law school?"

"Bugger I couldn't make his lecture. Sucks being stuck at work."

Grace and Henry smiled and nodded as one. Henry laughed. "We come all the way to Australia, and people still know our parents."

"Is there any way we can get up there to take a look?" Grace asked smoothly, eyes sparkling with their elevated status.

The young man looked both ways. "I don't see why not," he replied and pulled a ridiculous ring of keys from his belt. He fumbled through them until he found a series that were shaped for the tower padlock. The third one popped the massive shackle free. He pulled it off the hasp and opened the door. "I'm Simon, by the way."

The twins introduced themselves. Henry checked to see if there were footprints in the dust, but the area was as clean as if a crew had just swept it. He hurried up the steps. The tower was austere. If there had been any equipment, it had been removed. Grace found Henry at the top, standing where he could see the main entrance to the Gaol.

"He would have been standing right here," Henry said.

"Who?" Simon asked. He looked around and checked through the windows but stayed back as if trying to avoid being seen.

Grace saw his hesitation. "Are you going to get in trouble for letting us up here?"

"Maybe. We should probably go." He motioned toward the stairs. "Did you find what you were looking for?"

Henry shook his head. "The only thing I found was more questions."

Simon ushered them from the tower and relocked the padlock. "I've gotta get a move on. So much to do, so little time."

"Thank you!" Grace blurted, thrusting out her hand. He shook it gently, smiling.

Henry shook Simon's hand, frowning with the thoughts of the tower.

The young Australian man hurried away.

Henry pulled out the map and unfolded it. "So many executions," he muttered.

"We aren't going to talk about the tower and Simon?" Grace asked.

"What's there to talk about? We're never going to see him again. Let's take a look at this Elizabeth Woolcott, the only woman executed here." Henry started walking, but Grace grabbed his arm. He continued talking. "You know, this place was in use until 1988! All the way from 1841. Three hundred thousand prisoners! That is crazy. And they executed a total of forty-five people, right here."

Grace was shocked by the stupid grin on her brother's face.

"That sounds awful." She crossed her arms and looked down her nose, giving him her best judging face. "The tower. Nobody up there. Simon. Will any of these things elicit a response?"

Henry looked over the walls and took a deep breath. He pointed at a flock of birds. "Probably a magpie flying at just the right angle, creating a reflection in the window." He shrugged. "There's more to see and if we doof around, then we won't get to what *you* want, like the museum."

"Sometimes you make too much sense," she agreed.

They walked toward the next tower in the wall along the gap between the inner yards and the outer wall. The first tourist attraction held the improved hanging chamber. Henry headed in, but Grace remained outside. Henry was inside for a total of five seconds. When he came back out, he was pale.

"It's like the full weight of anger and despair descends on you the second you walk in the door."

"That's enough of that!" Grace declared. "You and this stupid jail. We didn't come to Adelaide to get bummed out."

"We came because Mom and Dad brought us," Henry countered, hoping his indomitable wit would lift him out of his new-found Gaol funk.

"You know what I mean." She pushed Henry aside and walked quickly around the next corner. Placards set into the prison wall memorialized the remains of a number of executed prisoners.

"E.W.," Henry read. "This is where she's buried." A simple plaque set chest-high into the wall designated her as the third prisoner executed. It happened on December 30, 1873. On the ground, flowers were arranged in an impromptu memorial. Behind the twins, a museum picture showed where the temporary gallows had been erected.

"I've seen enough," Grace said sadly. "I think we'll go shopping at the mall instead of visiting a museum. That will make me feel better." She checked her Apple watch. "It's almost time to go."

"It was a different era, Gracie." Henry started tapping on his phone. "There was an attempt just a few years ago to get her a posthumous pardon, but it was denied."

"People want to forget, just like me. Are we done yet?"

"Let's check out the other Woolcott displays and then we'll go."

Grace trudged along behind Henry as he circled back the way they'd come. When they rounded the last corner, they almost ran face-first into Simon.

"Dude!" Henry stopped, holding out his arm to keep his sister from colliding with the law student.

"Oh, hey! I was looking for you," Simon said casually. "There's a ghost tour tonight. Show up 'round seven and bring your parents. I think you'll get a kick out of it. I won't be here because I have uni, but my mate Sarah will be running it, so you'll get the full monty."

"The full monty?" Henry asked.

"The full show; everything bared before your eyes. If you're lucky, you'll see a ghost. There are at least fourteen unique spirits who haunt this ground."

"Fourteen?" Grace wondered aloud. "And it's okay to be here when they're out and about?"

"Of course," Simon replied, shaking his head. "Despite what you see on the telly, spirits are harmless. They may scare you, but that's it. They aren't like poltergeists, where they pull people between the dimensions."

"You believe there are multiple dimensions?" Henry asked.

"I believe, and we'll leave it at that." He waved and continued around the corner.

Henry watched him go, staring at the empty space where he last stood.

"*Now* do you want to talk about it?"

"No, not until after we're out of here. I want to get a picture of Mrs. Woolcott's cell before we leave." Henry consulted the map and strode boldly in the wrong direction. Grace waited. He stopped, checked his surroundings, consulted the map, turned back, and pointed to the side, smiling. "That way."

"I'm ready to go,' Grace insisted.

"Investigating things which are hard to investigate is the best practice for someone who wants to be a lawyer. And for an engineer-type like you, imagine what you'll learn from the problem solving of figuring this one out?" Henry pleaded, edging slowly in the direction he wanted to go.

"This once, but don't think we're going to make a career out of this." With a final smirk, Grace followed her brother.

Grace and Henry walked along North Terrace, the main drag between the Gaol and the university. Despite Grace's worrying, they were over an hour early. They stopped by the National War Memorial to appreciate the artistry and message. They continued toward the university, their eyes drawn to the magnificent chrome ball in front of the art museum. From a distance, it looked to be covered by raindrops. Up close, the drops were holes. A sign on the front of the museum said Free Admission.

"We have some time to kill," Grace said, nodding toward the museum.

"My payback for an hour and a half in the Gaol is forty-five minutes? Deal!"

"Not quite, young man."

"We're technically the exact same age," he countered.

"That's not what our birth certificates say," Grace replied smugly. They laughed as they entered.

"You make a cute couple," the woman at the counter told them.

Henry stopped and made a face. "My sister and me? I pity the man who gets this one."

The glares that both women gave him suggested he had stepped over the line.

"Check our backpacks over here?" he asked and hurried toward the coat check, breaking eye contact.

"He's normally a decent sort," Grace told the attendant.

The other woman laughed. "He has learned a valuable lesson about what not to say."

"Maybe, but probably not," Grace agreed before following Henry to check her backpack and explore the museum.

"A diner?" Henry asked. Ethan Warner looked distinguished in his suit and the stylish hat that Faith had purchased earlier in Rundle Mall. The Australians liked their hats much more than Americans, it seemed.

"Is this how one dresses to eat in a fifties diner throwback?" Faith replied, purposely not looking at the open entrance of the diner. Despite her attempt to distract her children from their desire to eat there, her mouth watered at the aroma coming from the grill.

"Smells pretty good," Ethan admitted. Henry nodded vigorously while Grace shrugged her indifference.

"We can look at the menu to make sure there's something for all of us," Faith suggested.

"Chicken sandwich, salads, fries, fries, and more fries. Oh, man, look at those!" Henry pointed with his chin as a server walked by.

"Fine," Faith conceded. She held up four fingers to the maître d. Ethan winked at the twins.

"You showed five, Mom," Grace said. "The thumb counts as one here."

"He speaks American," she countered without hesitation. They were shown to a booth and quickly gave their order. Henry unashamedly ordered double fries to go along with his two burgers. He only ordered one shake, though.

"You are incorrigible."

"I'm hungry." He smiled at his sister, and she smiled back but shook her head. "The Gaol," Henry started. "We want to do the Gaol ghost tour tonight, which starts at seven. Can we? And would you like to come along?"

Ethan and Faith looked at each other. "We do have the night free..." he started.

"I see that Grace is as amused by this as I am," Faith replied, her expression telling the full story.

"I think it's an exercise in seeing what is not to be seen. You two are hard-pressed because you believe in the physical world and empirical data. Henry and I believe we should look at all the evidence presented before making our judgment."

"Always the judge." Faith leaned toward her husband.

"Always the engineer." He kissed her quickly while the twins looked away.

"Fries!" Henry cheered, breaking the lovers from their moment. A small bucket appeared with mayo on the side. "Ketchup?"

"Of course," their server answered, soon returning with a small dish of Henry's preferred fry-dipping sauce.

Grace snagged the first French fry and stuck it into the mayo. She put it on her tongue and rolled it around before eating it.

"Gross!" Henry exclaimed, jamming a handful of fries into the ketchup and stuffing them all into his mouth.

"Gross!" Grace replied.

"Fine," Faith Warner interjected. "We'll go to the Gaol and see what there is to see. Now, you two need to stop being disgusting. Eat like normal human beings and make reservations for us when you're done."

Henry started to object, but Ethan held up his hand to stop all arguments. "It's lunch with our family. That is the most important thing. Enjoy your meals." Faith squeezed his hand.

The twins never took their parents' relationship for granted. It was a gift to be in a family where people genuinely cared about each other. No sores were allowed to fester, and no grievances went unaddressed. At the end of the day, each of them was at peace.

Unless they went on a ghost tour right before lights out.

"You'd think the architecture would be more austere," Faith Warner pondered.

"I read that the governor at the time had a lot of problems because of grossly overspending to have the Gaol built," Henry replied.

"Where politics and engineering collide. They want more for less." Ethan was happy making his point.

"That goes for just about everything, Dad. I remember you negotiating when you bought the truck. It wasn't pretty." Grace crossed her arms and challenged her father with her gaze.

"I guess not. We still spent a small fortune on that truck!"

"But it's our life, dear," Faith replied. The Warners had a heavy-duty truck with a fifth-wheel hitch so they could pull their forty-nine-foot trailer around the United States. Ethan and Faith had been lecturing for years, collaborating on academic topics and living their lives as nomads in high demand. They always had a gig the next week. When they had to go, they needed their truck and trailer to work. It also meant the twins had to be homeschooled since they were always on the road. Their truck was comfortable and filled with the latest gadgets, which made studying while driving feasible.

"And maybe the governor saw that Gaol as not just a place to put criminals, but as a symbol to the law-abiding citizens that evil would be contained," Henry interjected. "The populace would be able to live their lives in relative safety."

"Nice conjecture on the relative safety. The crimes were committed out here in the city," Dad replied. "Any facts to back up your premise?"

The lawyer and judge in him always pressed for more than pure speculation.

"No facts, but he was willing to risk his political future over something like the Gaol, where they could treat prisoners as harshly as they wanted. If they were out of sight, would anyone care? He could have cut corners, but he didn't. I think it would be hard to prove that he wasn't making a statement, but the people he made it to weren't listening."

"I could buy that as a closing argument...if I hadn't read Batchelor's report that called the prison a hotel in the early days. Ashton's hotel, because the governor lived in that wing to the right."

Henry's eyes jumped to the tower where he'd earlier seen the shape. It was at the very end of what would have been the governor's residence. "I didn't know," he stammered.

"And that is why a lawyer must always be reading and always learn a little bit more than his opponent. Knowledge is the key to legal success."

Faith could only shake her head. "Henry is not your opponent, Ethan."

Henry continued to stare at the tower, rethinking what he'd seen. It had looked like a person, not a magpie's reflection or a flying fox.

A small group had gathered near the entrance to the old Gaol. A young woman with a clipboard appeared and waved her arm.

"Are you here for the ghost tour?" she shouted. Henry replied with two thumbs-up as the four Warners approached to gather in a small circle around their host and tour guide. The closer people mumbled something in reply to the woman's call.

Her face dropped, and she twisted her mouth sideways. "Really?" She took a deep breath, gave the group her biggest smile, and tried a second time. "How about a ghost tour?"

"WOOHOO!" Henry bellowed, shocking the people in front of him.

"Ten points to Gryffindor!" the woman replied. "My name is Sarah, and my American friend can be my special assistant. Come closer, please. What's your name?"

"Henry," he told her boldly as he worked his way forward. She took his arm and gave him a peck on the cheek before turning him toward the door.

"Follow us to the mysteries and terror of the Adelaide Gaol, the most haunted place in Australia. I say the whole world!" She laughed heartily, setting the stage for her role as ringmaster.

Henry looked over his shoulder at his sister. His expression said it all: *I hope this isn't just a show.*

Sarah opened the front door of the Gaol and stopped where she could account for everyone on her list one by one as they walked through. When the group was ticked off and was assembled in the courtyard, she closed and locked the main door.

"It's only you?" Henry asked.

"Simon had school, so yeah, just me."

"You're not kidding, are you? Is someone hiding inside to shine lights or make spooky noises?"

"We have our first skeptic!" Sarah declared, her Australian accent becoming heavier as if part of the presentation. "There's always one. No, there is no show. We don't have anyone hiding, waiting to shine a light or press a button to create the impression of a ghost. This *IS* the most haunted place in Australia. Terrible people came here to pay for their crimes. If you don't believe in evil, you should. It is real, and the finality of death cannot stop it. There are stories of the innocent jailed and executed. Their spirits lurk in between with those who refuse to die because their evil hasn't been spent. Follow me as we stop by the gallows, both permanent and temporary, where their condemned souls screamed their last."

Sarah took Henry's arm and guided the group around the perimeter.

"Stay close, please," she warned, checking behind her often to make sure she didn't lose anyone. She whispered out the side of her mouth to Henry, "If you want to see someone terrified, let them get lost and trapped in here. This place ain't somewhere you want to be alone."

"I'd be manly and say that I'll protect you, but it's probably the other way around. Please don't let one of your snakes, spiders, or bats bite me."

She laughed. The musical sound of her voice quickly faded in the dimly lit Gaol's interior. It was a mirthless place; the darkness hung over it like a physical presence.

No wonder people think it's haunted, Henry thought.

"First stop is the Hanging Tower, where those who were condemned to death danced their last. It was only used a few times. It's not well lit, but you can go inside if you like. Please let us know if you see a ghost," Sarah intoned in her well-practiced guide voice.

Henry was the first to go in. Having been there earlier, he expected to see nothing new. In fact, he saw nothing at all. The courtyard lighting had been too bright, and his eyes were slow to adjust to the darkness. He stopped one step inside the front door. Someone bumped into him, screamed, and ran over someone else on her way out.

"It's just me!" Henry called. The place was dank and cool, the air heavy. Henry coughed so those behind him knew where he was as more people came in.

There was a figure in the doorway. "Coming through." The shadow stepped aside, and Henry walked out.

He chuckled lightly when he saw his parents, Grace, and Sarah standing together. "After the bright lights of the courtyard, can anyone ever see anything in there?" he asked.

"No," she replied softly, biting her lip to keep from laughing. She sobered before continuing, "There has been a ghost sighting in there, but not by a tourist. It was by a groundskeeper during the day. He quit right after that. It scared the bejeezus out of him."

"No!?" Henry challenged.

"Yeah," Sarah replied, before taking his arm and directing the group to follow once she had verified the headcount. "Next stop is the temporary gallows where Elizabeth Woolcott was executed in 1875."

"We've been researching her. I think she's innocent."

"She wasn't pardoned when the governor had the chance just a few years ago," Sarah shot back. "Although I think the general consensus is that she was not guilty. At least now, we no longer have capital punishment in Oz."

"Just ghosts from Adelaide's past?" Grace suggested.

"Nice!" Sarah replied, nodding.

"You had to have heard that one before. You've probably heard them all," Henry said.

"Not that one. Not like that." They were the first around the corner, and Sarah pulled up short. Henry followed her gaze. He closed his eyes and reopened them. Ethan, Faith, and Grace were right behind them and craned their necks to see a wisp of white disappear into the stone of the interior Gaol wall.

"No way!" Henry exclaimed. He turned to find Sarah staring, a vein throbbing in her neck and her pulse racing. He shook her gently. She blinked but kept looking ahead.

"They say she's the most common of them—Elizabeth, stalking the grounds, unjustly condemned to death. She felt she was a sinner and that she deserved it. Her purgatory is that she is caught between worlds. I've never seen her before, or any of them."

"Was that..." Grace stammered. The rest of the group filled in around them.

"I saw it," a tall man said from the back. "A ghost."

"That's not possible," Faith replied.

"But you saw it," Henry whispered to his mom. "Just like I did."

"Yes," she agreed, barely loud enough to hear.

"Tour's over," Sarah said, twirling her arm over her head and pointing in the direction she wanted them to go. She hurried to the front of the group and power-marched to the exit, counting heads on the way out and locking the Gaol behind her. Then she ran to her car.

"I wonder if *that* was part of the show?" Ethan asked.

The twins reclined in their hotel room, with their parents in the room next door.

"Why did you recommend a ghost tour right before bed?" Grace complained.

"So many questions," Henry mumbled.

"Since I have no hope of sleep, have at it. Start asking."

"Ignore everything that was emotion-based," he started, staring at a spot on the wall. "What could we have seen?"

"Besides the obvious?" Henry gave her the side eye, so she straightened up. "Smoke. Fog. A reflection."

"A reflection... We didn't get to walk down there, but maybe this is an upgrade to the tours. A quick interactive in-and-out. Maybe they change it up. Pictures from other tours show they go into the cell blocks and through the graveyards, which have been moved into the prison walls. There isn't a single review that talks about anything like this."

"All those tours and no one has seen a ghost before?" Grace started tapping on her laptop computer. "Nope. Lots of people *thought* they saw something, but I would chalk that up to the power of persuasion or the influence of the location touted as the most haunted, or maybe even post-dinner drinks."

"How about a weather anomaly? There *is* a bit of a chill in the air, and the back of the prison is what...a hundred yards from the river?"

"Googling ghostly fog..." Grace replied, typing furiously. She scowled at the results and typed something else. She tossed her hair and looked at her brother, tucked under his covers and typing on his own laptop. "Sounds like a will-o'-the-wisp, but those are caused by gases escaping the marshy moors."

"And that sounds like Sherlock Holmes," Henry said laughing. "Can you imagine us sleuthing?"

"No. Like Donnie and Marie, you're a little bit country, and I'm a little bit rock and roll."

"I like rock," Henry shot back.

"I like hard engineering, and you like the touchy-feely side, like the law."

"The law has rules. Lots and lots of rules." Henry studied his sister. "I get what you mean, though, especially when it comes to this. I wonder what Mom and Dad thought it was. I bet we get two wildly different answers."

"Dad will waffle and ask questions we can't answer before he won't take a position, and Mom will be a definite 'no.'"

"That she will," Henry agreed. "I'm like Dad, but I will commit. I think we saw Elizabeth Woolcott."

"I think what we saw can be explained by something that doesn't include the word 'ghost.' I'm thinking it is more physics based than otherworldly."

"Then we need to find out what that is, so I can be proven right!" Henry declared.

"What?" Grace wasn't sure that he knew what he wanted to find. "Definitely no sleuthing for us."

"What are you two going to do today?" Faith asked.

Neither of the twins spoke.

"You're going back to the Gaol, aren't you?"

"We have questions..." Henry let it linger since he didn't want to explain further.

"As you wish. Anything that engages your mind is a good thing, don't you think?"

"I agree completely, Mother," Grace replied with a smile. "Is there any way we can get a couple of dollars to tide us over for the day? It's expensive here."

"It's not bad at all," Ethan replied before looking at the ceiling as he did when he told stories of the good ol' days. "I remember when we were in Reykjavik..."

"Time!" Faith interrupted. "Would you look at the time? We better get going. It wouldn't do at all to be late."

She tossed a couple fifties on the table and hurried her husband away, winking over her shoulder at the twins.

"Money!" The twins cheered. Henry took one and Grace took the other.

"What are we going to do?" Grace asked, turning serious.

"Are we looking for Elizabeth, or are we trying to find out how someone spoofed us into thinking we saw her?"

"I see you're taking my side."

"As Dad always says, a lawyer needs to be able to argue both sides using the same facts with equal vigor. I think we should explore the more plausible options first because I have no idea how to research whether a ghost is real. And if she is, what would we do about it?"

"Nothing?" Grace offered with a one-shoulder shrug.

"Exactly. I'd rather deal with something actionable since we don't have the Ghostbusters' firehouse and arsenal of tools." Henry pantomimed firing the ghost-catching nuclear discombobulator.

"We need to study the ground where we saw the...where we saw the..." Grace stopped.

"Apparition?"

"Something like that." The two left the hotel lobby, Henry holding the door for his sister. She didn't hesitate walking through. She'd get the next one. They took turns that way.

"Motive, means, and opportunity. We'll do a little amateur forensics exam to see if anything jumps out while discussing the motive. I think we need to talk to Sarah. We'll have to gauge her truthfulness through observation and cross-examination during the interrogation," Henry suggested.

"We're not interrogating anyone. How many police dramas have you been watching?" Grace considered what was ahead. "Remember the part where we aren't sleuthing? I thought we agreed on that."

"Isn't it exciting, though? I want to be a lawyer because the law fascinates me. I love seeing it in action. You want to be an engineer because you can construct things in your mind and see how they work, then build them for real. Investigating this appeals to both our natures, don't you think?"

She nodded begrudgingly. "Where do you want to go? I know you've been thinking about it."

"I don't know. Stanford Law is right up there. I think I'll like that part of California. What about you? Stanford has a great engineering program too."

"I like the sound of MIT," she replied slowly, not looking at her brother.

"It looks like a great school for engineers. Lots of prestige, but I hear that the Colorado School of Mines has the highest starting salary for its graduates."

"Do I look like a miner?" Grace wondered.

"You look very much like a minor," Henry agreed, using his definition of the word.

"Maybe I'm an emancipated minor?"

Henry pulled the fifty from his pocket and waved it in front of her. "Emancipated minors don't need to beg money from their parents. Wait. I'm sure some think they are adult, but they aren't quite ready yet, even if they are on their own." Henry gave up since he had talked himself in a circle. "No matter! Apparitions in Adelaide. Let the sleuthing begin."

Grace rolled her eyes closed, but never hesitated in joining her brother.

"Blimey, you're back!" the elderly lady with the purple hair greeted them. "I'm not sure we've had back-to-back visits before; you two are the first. Must really like history and the legal system, huh? Good to see. You young whippersnappers are our future. It's in your hands."

The twins smiled. She sounded like their parents with an Australian accent, which made her words seem more philosophical.

"Thank you," they replied. The woman beamed warmly at them as they passed through the entryway into the Gaol.

Making a beeline for the location of last night's encounter meant following the interior side of the outer wall. They hurried down it, almost running to be the first ones there. They passed a Chinese family reading the plaque outside the Hanging Tower. The twins nodded and headed to the corner, where they stopped and started taking pictures. Once that was done, they studied the scene.

"Limited locations for projectors or a fog generator of some sort because of the high walls." Grace pointed to the walls. She walked her eyes across the scene, taking in one piece at a time and building a catalog of angles and possibilities. To the right of where the apparition had appeared were two security cameras on a chest-high pole.

The family approached from behind them.

"We better check the ground before anyone can disturb it, if no one has already." Henry rushed forward to stoop and study the grass between the sidewalk and Elizabeth Woolcott's tombstone in the prison wall.

Grace stood beside him, blocking the way as she expanded the search.

"Here!" she declared triumphantly, then stepped to the side and knelt. Red dirt had been dug up and replaced. She took a closeup, then angled back. She took pictures of the security cameras, too, and the pair on the other corner, positioned inside the wall to show the walkways coming and going.

The family stayed on the sidewalk as they strolled by, looking strangely at the twins.

"Beautiful day to study the flora!" Henry told them. Grace gritted her teeth.

The family hurried away.

"You need to work on that. Could you be any more obvious?"

"Obvious about what?" he asked.

"Being weird and seeming like you're doing something you shouldn't."

"But I am, and we are." He stood and joined her. "What do you think these are?"

"This could be anything." Grace pointed to the ground. "Like a battery-operated vaporizer with a small remotely-activated fan, or, you know, something like that."

"Looks like they dug out a weed. Do you always think like that?" Henry replied. He leaned down to look in the lens of the security camera. He used the flashlight function on his phone to see past the glass of the huge 1970s-style camera housing.

"What do you think this is, Mademoiselle Engineer?"

She smiled and scrutinized it, her smile quickly fading. "That doesn't look like it belongs there. We probably need to ask someone about it." Grace took a picture while Henry adjusted the light to get a few different angles. They took closeups of the housing as well. "Screws look new on this one, but not the other one."

"It's also been adjusted. It looks toward the wall, not down the walkway like its brother." The two cameras were stacked on top of each other, intended to face opposite directions.

"Not quite a smoking gun, but that suggests something's afoot."

"The game, perhaps?" Henry quipped, enjoying the Sherlock Holmes banter. "Or maybe 'afoul' is the right word." He returned to the wall and put his hand on the stone plaque with the initials E.W. "I'm sorry we can't save you, but if you are at peace wherever you are, we can at least put to rest the ugly rumors that you're a ghost."

"I don't think these things work anymore. They look like they still have the original cameras inside," Grace stated after finishing her examination. "There's a spot to signal that the camera is on. I wish I had a voltmeter to check if there's any power in these cables."

"Just lick your finger and touch it," Henry suggested.

"I think not," Grace replied, used to her brother's attempts to get her to take senseless risks. He wouldn't let her get hurt. He only wanted to see her try something without thinking.

That wasn't her way.

"We need to talk with Sarah," she proclaimed.

"Agreed." Henry turned from the wall and almost ran into Simon. "Dude! You move like a ninja."

"I'll take that as a compliment, mate! Can't stay away, eh?"

"We saw something that required more research, as in something that needed to be followed up in daylight."

"I heard! It was a once-in-a-lifetime opportunity, and you two are now part of the storied history of the Adelaide Gaol," he deadpanned as if trying to convince a jury, complete with hand motions and big eyes.

Grace and Henry regarded the man skeptically.

"Who is responsible for maintaining the security cameras?" Henry blurted, almost taken aback by the ferocity of his own question.

The whites showed around Simon's eyes as he looked unblinkingly at Henry, then his face returned to its normal jovial expression. He whispered conspiratorially, "Those things haven't worked in years."

"I didn't think so. Those are old-school, for sure. But who would open them up to keep the bugs out and stuff like that?" Henry shrugged disarmingly.

Simon pulled a small Philips-head screwdriver from his coveralls. "That would be me."

"Have you ever been killed by one of your venomous creatures?" Henry asked, pinching Simon's arm as if checking to see that he was real.

"Good try, buddy! I thought I'd heard them all, but that's new!" He clapped Henry on the shoulder, making the young American stumble.

"We need to get going," Grace interjected. "Our parents are expecting us shortly. How was your class last night?"

"I didn't have class," Simon started, his expression turning cold. "I had to finish a paper that is due today. I was at the legal library. I need to go, too. They already think I'm a bludger; you know, a slacker. Can't give them proof. Innocent until proven guilty, am I right?"

He belly-laughed as he walked away.

The twins looked at each other once he was gone.

"What's his relationship with Sarah?" they asked at the same time and chuckled.

"That obvious, huh?" Henry asked.

"Let's have a casual chat with the nice lady at the entrance." The twins left Elizabeth Woolcott to rest in peace as they worked to solve a different mystery.

The twins smiled as they found her on a chair reading the latest thriller from the English author Mark Dawson. Grace smiled. "Can we ask you a question?"

"Of course, you can, darl'."

"We'd like to talk to Sarah about something from last night's ghost tour," Grace started.

"Crikey! Did something go wrong? What is it?" the woman asked quickly, eyes wide with surprise and tension.

"We thought we saw a ghost and wanted to know what she thought," Grace clarified, watching closely for any indications that the woman was hiding something. Henry stood to the side, looking for outward signs of stress from a different angle.

She relaxed. "You thought you saw a ghost?" she replied skeptically.

"I think she saw it too. She canceled the tour after only fifteen minutes and left without a word."

She frowned, and a crease appeared on her forehead.

"You sure? Cuz, darl', those tours usually take about two hours."

Henry bit back a retort and settled for watching his sister engage.

"Quite sure. We were back at the hotel well before eight, and we walked."

"Flamin' heck." The woman chewed her lip. "Would you like a refund?"

"No, thanks," Grace replied quickly. "How many ghost tours do you actually get to see a ghost on, as opposed to someone telling you that ghosts have been seen?"

"In those terms, yes, that is different. Maybe we should charge double?" the woman joked, her smile returning.

"When will Sarah be back?"

"She'll be running tonight's tour as well. You can see her then."

"She's already called and bailed," a voice from the gift shop advised them.

"I better call her." The woman tapped the address book and pulled up the number. Grace surreptitiously tried to see but was stymied by the way she held her phone. "Sarah? Hi! This is Mrs. Handley from the Gaol. Did you end the tour early last night?"

Not how I would have phrased it, Henry thought. Grace made eye contact, obviously having the same thought.

"You were crook? I can understand that. You get some rest, and drink plenty of fluids." She looked at her phone for a moment before tapping End.

"She was sick, that's all," the woman remarked. "Sorry, guys, it's time for my break. Gotta have a cuppa and a bikky to keep this darn blood sugar under control." She walked away before they could reply. The twins thanked her despite the fact that she kept walking away. They headed into the gift shop but stopped when they heard the woman call Simon's name.

"What did you do?" she said, louder than intended.

Henry continued into the shop after a nearly imperceptible signal from his sister. He engaged with the clerk quickly before checking out the clothing sale rack, where they would make no noise. Grace sat on the chair in the entryway and listened intently.

"Nothing," came Simon's muffled reply.

"She quit!" Mrs. Handley expressed her outrage. Grace thought she heard a foot stamping.

"Why do you think I had anything to do with it?" Simon demanded.

"Didn't you?"

"No." His voice receded as if he were walking away.

"We should have fired you both. No dating between employees!" the woman shouted after him. Grace couldn't hear his reply. She hurried through the gift shop and gathered Henry up, and they headed outside.

"We need to be here when he gets off work. He said nine to five, which means we need to be standing right here at four thirty." Henry pointed at the ground while clenching his jaw resolutely.

"Yes, we do," Grace agreed, believing they were on the way to finding the answer.

The twins could think of nothing else the remainder of the day. A light rain interrupted their afternoon and almost made them late getting back to the Gaol.

"Is that who I think it is?" Henry asked and started to run.

"If you think that's Sarah's car, you'd be right." Grace sprinted after her brother. The driver had disappeared through a side door into the Gaol. The twins slowed as they got closer. "I think we'll wait right here."

They lingered behind Sarah's subcompact, trying to look like they belonged. Henry walked to the side, his eyes never leaving the tower that had caused him so much grief and started this adventure which was turning into something far different. "I'll be damned."

"Of course you will be, but why this time?" Grace taunted.

"There's a magpie nest on the roof beyond the tower. It *was* their reflection I saw in the window of the tower."

"Uh-huh," Grace mumbled. "But why was it clean in there?"

"We'd need to check the others to see if anything is less than clean here. This is a historic site. I expect it has a certain budget for maintenance. It's kind of anti-climactic. I think we're back to just one ghost."

"And I suspect it won't be long before one becomes zero." Grace tapped her temple with a finger as she looked at her brother. He nodded and half-smirked in reply.

Henry moved to the wall next to the door, leaning his back against it while he accessed his phone.

He jumped when the door opened, and Sarah stormed out with Simon right on her heels.

They stopped when they saw the twins.

"We know what's going on," Henry said, having only a half-formed idea.

"Yeah?" Sarah challenged. "Like, my boyfriend is an idiot?"

"How so?" Grace asked sympathetically.

She crossed her arms and glared at Simon.

"Say it out loud," Grace rolled her hand as if calling a puppy, "how you projected the image."

Simon threw his hands down in exasperation. "I did it! All right? It was me, but I only wanted you to get a glimpse of what I saw for real. Honest."

Sarah leaned against her car and started to tap her foot. Her expression softened. Henry didn't understand. If her boyfriend had lied to her, why would she be sympathetic? *I have a lot to learn.*

"So we could have more in common." He approached slowly and held out his hands to her. "I don't want to lose you."

"Getting us both fired is your great idea for both our futures?"

"I'll see Mrs. Handley and make things right." Without hesitation, he turned and stalked back inside the Gaol.

"How did you know?" Sarah asked.

Grace leaned on the car next to her. "We started with the premise that it wasn't real. We looked at the ways it could be faked and checked the grounds for physical evidence to prove or disprove our theories. It didn't take long to find his projector."

"Sounds simple once you say it." She snorted and shook her head. "He had me, that's for sure. I was ready to bugger off for good."

"I'm not sure there's any call for that," Henry said. "I don't know if he's a good guy or bad. I *do* know that he spoofed us all, which was pretty amazing. He has a career in making the tour more ghostly if you need it, or maybe he could be a part of Disney Down Under."

"They'd put it in Sydney. Everything cool is in Sydney," she lamented.

"The Gaol isn't there, and you know what's coolest about this?" Grace leaned against Sarah. "It's not in use anymore. It's a monument to a past we don't want to duplicate."

Sarah nodded. The door opened and Mrs. Handley leaned out. "Sarah," she said, the corners of her mouth twitching upward. "Come on in and let's have a chat."

"You two be good," Sarah advised. "And thanks."

"They didn't get fired?" Ethan asked.

"Nope. And he got the job of adding spice to the ghost tours," Grace explained.

Henry shook his head. "I wouldn't believe it if I hadn't heard it for myself."

"*I can't believe* you kids solved a mystery." Ethan beamed at his children.

"You shouldn't be surprised, dear. Now, let's talk about where these two are going to make their marks in college. They have their senior year coming up, and we don't want them to waste it by not doing the *right* things to get into the *right* schools."

"Oh, man!" Henry cried. "Can't we have *one* night to celebrate before you give us the heavy 'future is now' talk?"

"But it is," Ethan deadpanned.

MONTAUK MONSTER

MONSTER CASE FILES BOOK 1

CHAPTER ONE

Twilight found the couple strolling the beach, hand in hand. Rheinstein Estate Park, popular with surfers in the daytime, popular with lovers all the time. The two let the water lap to their knees, and it foamed as something moved through the rolling breakers.

"OW!" the woman shrieked. She jumped and dashed out of the tide, then hopped on one leg where the hard sand turned soft, the moon's light showing the dark of a gash and blood streaming down her leg. "I'm bleeding."

The size of a medium dog, it thrashed ashore, a shadow, but more. The man held up his cell phone and tapped the flashlight icon. Red eyes flared above a beaked snout. It crouched in the light, opened its mouth and hissed.

The man stumbled backward and would have fallen if not for his companion. She yanked his arm and pulled him away, limping from the pain of her wound, but energized to escape. Together they ran.

Away from the creature. As far away as they could go.

A dark shadow at the beach's edge moved against the breeze and disappeared into the bushes beyond.

"A senior project?" the seventeen-year-old complained. Her twin brother rolled his eyes and then his whole head as if in mortal agony. The bounce of the big truck made the exaggeration even worse.

"Yes. You think you're going to do nothing this next year?" Doctor Faith Warner was a relentless taskmaster. "Your college applications are incomplete."

"Only mostly incomplete," Henry offered in a weak attempt to change the course of the conversation. Grace elbowed him in the ribs.

Ethan and Faith Warner had both had wildly successful staid careers but decided to uproot their lives by moving to a lecture circuit. Ethan had been a lawyer turned judge and Faith had worked in research engineering. And then they found they were most gratified in teaching what they had learned. They preferred life on the road, homeschooling their children, and seeing the world.

They wanted an incomparable education for their teenagers.

The twins had inherited their parents' desire to learn and share. With curiosity came acceptance of risk. They wanted something a little more. Faith wanted something more process oriented, developing a hypothesis and either proving or disproving it. Ethan wanted them to dig deep into the facts and examine how a problem fit within the world's greater structure before finding a solution. Research. Analysis. Conclusions. Despite the genes and the education, the twins were not their parents.

"Senior project. Ideas?" Faith Warner pressed.

Henry frowned and stared out the window. Since they'd crossed the Verrazano Narrows Bridge, the scenery had changed from the New York City skyline to trees and subdivisions. In other words, boring.

If the navigator's calculations were correct, they would arrive in Stony Brook in an hour.

"I always enjoy being *there*, but sometimes *getting* there is a trial," Ethan remarked to no one in particular. The corners of his eyes crinkled when he spoke. He turned onto a two-lane road, and they started traveling north.

After forty minutes of silence, Faith shifted in her seat. "Well? Senior project ideas?"

Henry groaned.

"It's our last year." Grace hadn't meant to speak aloud or in such a needy voice. She hurried to cover her mistake. "We should work on something together. Fewer politics and less science; something different."

Her brother pressed his hand to his chest. "No politics or science? Who are you, and what did you do with my sister?"

"Ha-ha." She tapped her lips. "I'm serious. Admissions counselors give extra points for creativity."

Ethan nodded. "She's right. Not every student can demonstrate practical applications of academic skills. If done correctly, it will prove you have what it takes to survive college outside of the lecture hall."

"We should take advantage of our travels and study something universal, but unique to each area. A phenomenon that happens everywhere." Grace came up blank with the rest of the words. She had an idea but hadn't properly vetted it within her mind.

Henry wiggled his fingers like an evil supervillain—a sure sign he was thinking. "I'd rather not spend the entire school year in a library. I'm ready for some adventure. We could study the effects of extreme sports on the teenage body."

Faith's brows climbed into her hairline. "I'd rather not spend the entire school year in the emergency room."

"Adventure? You mean living the life of nomads isn't an adventure?" Ethan liked to pretend their custom-made fifth wheel trailer was one step up from a covered wagon.

"You could take another self-defense class." His mom winked at Henry.

"Please, never again. I'm the only male in there."

Grace pulled out her phone and was scrolling through a website listing activities near Stony Brook University. "Does surfing count as an extreme sport?"

Henry leaned in to get a better view of her screen. "Surfing's a start."

"We're here." Her mother blew out a breath. "And we're late. You guys are in charge of setting up the rig while your father and I get dressed for the reception."

Ethan eased the truck onto a drive beside a massive Cape Cod style home. "Preston said the RV pad is alongside the house."

"You mean alongside the *mansion*." Grace gawked at the impressive structure. "They have—"

"—a view of Smithtown Bay," Henry completed her sentence. "How does a college professor afford a house like this?"

"His wife Dianna was an Astor before she was a Prescott." Her father spoke as if they rubbed elbows with the richest of the rich every day. "Relax.

They're RV people just like us. I knew Preston before he was somebody, and I have stories." Ethan chuckled lightly as one does when remembering the good old days that people are happy to relive only when ribbing each other.

Ethan expertly drove the truck nose-in, delivering the trailer perfectly in one shot, and motioned to electric and water hookups, something the usual home did not have.

Henry nudged his sister, eyes wide at their residence for the next week.

"Ethan Warner!" A man appeared, his arms spread and smiling even wider. "Good to see you."

Ethan exited the truck and embraced his old friend in a guy-hug, complete with back slaps and laughter. "Preston 'the Prez' Prescott!"

Preston wrapped Faith in a bear hug before making a beeline for the twins, hugging each of them.

The professor tilted his head, but his smile didn't falter. "I can't get over how much the twins have grown. They look just like you, Faith."

"What can I say? Dominant genes," Faith replied, a good-natured poke at her husband's blonde hair and blue eyes. The children were both dark-haired and brown-eyed.

"I'll get our things. The kids will handle the setup." Ethan turned toward the trailer.

Professor Prescott shoved his hands in his pockets and rocked back on his heels. "That's an amazing rig, but are you sure you don't want to stay in the house? Dianna's out of town, and we have plenty of room."

Faith spoke quickly. "Thank you, but you know how it is. You always get more rest when you sleep in your own bed."

Ethan jogged back to the truck and retrieved their overnight bag. "We'll see you in a couple hours. Order a pizza and stay close."

"We know the drill. Have fun tonight,"

Faith and Ethan disappeared inside the house to change, but Professor Preston Prescott joined the twins, still smiling. "You can go ahead and plug in. The box is on its own circuit, and the water is set to fifty psi."

"Too bad everywhere we stay isn't this nice." Henry connected the power cord. "I know the white hose is potable water, but what are the others?"

"Green's your garden-variety garden hose." He paused as if to give them time to laugh. Unfortunately for the professor, the twins were immune to dad jokes.

Grace eyed the wider, heavier brown hose. "That looks like a sewage connection."

The professor pointed toward the flower beds lining the walkway to the

bay. "It's one of my own inventions. Hook it up to your grey tank. It deposits the wastewater in a Roman-style impluvium, where it's filtered and used to water my wife's roses."

Grace gazed over the lawn. Somewhere beneath the perfect green blades was a basin with layers of sand and gravel resting above a holding chamber. Her father had mentioned that Professor Prescott was an environmentalist, but he hadn't said the man was a genius.

"Impressive. Do you have an RV?" Up close, what Grace had thought was a plastic upper-class smile made his eyes twinkle.

He glanced to the side in that dreamy way people did when recalling happy memories. "Not anymore, but we do get quite a few traveling lecturers for Stony Brook. It's nice to be able to accommodate them."

"You went to Stanford with my father?" Henry asked.

"That's right. We're fraternity brothers and played on the soccer team together."

Henry perked up at the mention of the school. "I'd like to speak with you about..." he glanced at Grace, "...fraternities. I haven't decided if I want to join one."

Her heart sank. Sure, she didn't want her brother to attend college on the other side of the country, but she hated the weirdness between them. "I'll make sure the rig's level."

Not wanting to interrupt Henry's conversation, Grace continued the setup without him. She shoved wooden blocks behind the tires, engaged the electric jack, and leveled the rig. With hookups complete, she was ready to settle into the trailer for the evening, maybe stream a movie or two.

Henry hopped into the truck bed and disconnected the tow harness. "Sorry about that."

"Are you applying for Stanford or not?" Grace blurted.

"Probably, but I haven't yet. If we're to have any chance getting in somewhere, we need to have a killer senior project. It always pains me to say it, but Mom's right. *But,* I have an idea for our independent study project."

"Yeah?"

"Urban legends." Grunting, Henry struggled to disengage the lock mechanism from the hitch. "It's stuck. Too much pressure. Inch the truck forward."

She climbed into the cab and started the truck.

The vehicle rolled forward almost imperceptibly, and Henry shouted, "Got it."

Urban legends? Has he lost his mind? She doubted the admissions officers at MIT would approve of her spending her senior year hunting down Big Foot.

Then again, every region had some sort of local lore, ranging from ghost stories to mysterious creatures.

Henry knocked on the back window. "I'm clear."

Grace moved the truck from under the gooseneck and parked it.

Her brain kicked into overdrive. Some of the places they'd visited had made a tourist industry off their urban myths. One only needed to visit New Orleans to know ghosts, vampires, and other things that went bump in the night made money. Heck, even the most magical place on Earth had its own set of myths. Anyone who'd grown up in Orlando would tell you that some guy had been decapitated on Space Mountain, and they kept Walt Disney's cryogenically frozen head in Cinderella's castle.

But how can we turn it into a senior project? After locking the truck up, Grace joined her brother inside the fifth wheel.

"You're thinking about the project and planning to argue that it's not academically rigorous." When Henry pressed the kitchen slide button, a mechanical grating sound filled the air, and the living room wall moved out several feet.

Mind-reading—one of the coolest, and at times most annoying, things about having a twin. "I suppose you have a rebuttal already planned out?"

"As a matter of fact—" He pressed another button. Of course, he knew she couldn't hear him, but he kept talking.

She waited until the opposite wall, couch, and dinette had moved into position. "You're *almost* as funny as Dad."

"It's brilliant, really. Think of it as one big research project. We focus on the—" He opened the sliders containing each of their twin beds, talking as they moved. In less than five minutes, he'd doubled their living space. "Not even MIT could turn their noses up at it. We start with the Montauk Monster."

She placed her hands on her hips and prepared to launch into a lecture about humor and how he needed to take a class or something, but then it hit her. *What the heck is the Montauk Monster?* "Start explaining, and don't you dare press another button."

Grace pulled her laptop out of her backpack.

"Preston gave us the wifi. Link to DoctorPsInternet with password TravelersUnite-CardinalsRule."

Grace disappeared into the Google search engine as soon as she was connected.

CHAPTER TWO

At seventeen, Henry considered himself an expert at two things—role-playing games, and his twin sister.

He'd known he had her the moment he'd said the word "monster." Grace had a mind like a machine, but mysteries put a steel bar in her spinning wheels. He'd seen the exact moment her brain had switched from "older-sister-lecture mode" to "tell me more."

Henry plopped onto his bed and pulled his notebook from its hiding place. "I forgot the year, but somewhere around 2007, a creature washed up on the shore near Montauk. Some girls took photos of it and sent them to the media. It became an internet sensation."

Grace tapped her lips. "Wait, are you talking about the decomposed raccoon?"

He shrugged because he knew it aggravated her and to keep her thinking. He went with the tried and true double question. "Was it?" He paused dramatically before increasing the volume of his question. "*Was it?*"

Her thumbs flew over her keyboard, paused, scrolled, and typed some more. "It was 2008. There's been little written about the Montauk Monster since 2009."

"Which is why we should do it." He drew a rough sketch of the beaked mammal and showed it to her. "What does this look like to you?"

She gave him a dubious look. "A chicken with ears."

He glanced at the drawing and frowned. "Look again. Think 500 to 300 BCE Iran."

Grace squinted. "Is that supposed to be the Persepolis Griffin?"

Henry tossed his notebook aside. "Look up images of the Montauk Monster."

She typed, furrowed her brow, and looked at him again—only this time, she'd lost her smirk. "You're right. There *is* a resemblance, but do you actually believe an animal from ancient Iran found its way here?"

"No, but it's no more ridiculous than some of the other theories floating around." He'd expected less skepticism from his sister. At the very least, he'd expected her to jump on the research train and help him come up with a project proposal their parents wouldn't veto.

Staring at her phone, Grace giggled. "Are these people serious? Ancient alien washes up onshore. There was a television special about it."

"There are conspiracy theories that it was a mutant from the Plum Island Animal Research Facility." His hope that they'd have a little fun their senior year wilted. He'd seen her expression when Preston had mentioned Stanford. If Henry didn't do something drastic, they'd spend their last year together being miserable. "Think about it. How does something like a decomposed raccoon on a beach turn into an urban legend? What impact does that have on the community? On the people involved?"

"Or the economy. I immediately thought of vampires in New Orleans when you mentioned your idea."

He had her on the line. All he had to do was set the hook and reel her in. "How would all of that change if the myths were debunked?"

"Conspiracy theorists and true believers ignore science and logic. We could produce the carcass, and they would still find a way to cling to their beliefs." She stretched out on her bunk. "I'm not sure your idea is strong enough to impress college admissions officers. We need something with more hard science."

You *need something with hard science. I need a clever idea that can prove why the jury system is inherently flawed. Something like, "people will believe anything if they hear it enough times."* "I'm starved. Did you switch over the fridge from gas to electric?"

Grace opened the panel and hit the switch. She leaned close to the refrigerator to make sure it was humming. She opened the door slightly. "Nice and cool."

"Sorry, Henry. It's a compelling idea, but there isn't enough there." She turned her attention back to her computer. "Pepperoni extra cheese or the works?"

"Everything except green peppers. They give you gas." He stood and turned on the television.

"They do not." She tossed a pillow in his direction. "Fish and pineapple on pizza should be illegal."

"Obviously." He plopped into his dad's overstuffed recliner.

Grace sighed and seated herself on the couch. "Mom didn't seem herself," she remarked.

Henry mentally rolled through likely scenarios. *Intimidated by the vulgar display of wealth? No, that didn't make sense. Faith Warner didn't care about the size of a person's bank account. Old crush on Dad's best friend? Possible, but unlikely. The guy seemed too pretentious.* Then it clicked—the most obvious reason for a man's wife to dislike his best friend. "I bet Preston didn't agree with Dad's decision to give up his career to follow her on the lecture circuit."

Grace considered his theory but shook her head. "Professor Prescott is a scientist. He has to understand the importance of her work. Lecturing and consulting are part of it."

"Oh, he understands, but who better than a fellow scientist to know that a position on the right court bench is more lucrative." He motioned toward the enormous house. "The guy obviously enjoys money."

She made a face that told him she'd bought into the professor's blue eyes and John F. Kennedy smile more than his theory.

Two hours later, they'd polished off an extra-large pizza and the latest sci-fi on Netflix. Neither twin had paid much attention to the movie. Henry had booted up his laptop and searched for project ideas, and Grace had evidently surfed the web for memes. She hadn't stopped snickering since she'd picked up her phone.

Headlights illuminated the inside of the fifth wheel. Henry peeked out the side window. "It's a car. Must be the professor."

"Mom and Dad are probably right behind him." She plugged her cell into a charger and wandered toward the bathroom.

"He's coming this way." Henry glanced around the room to make sure they'd cleared their dirty dishes. Not that he felt the need to impress the professor, but his parents wouldn't appreciate returning to a mess.

Wide-eyed, Grace stood in the narrow hall leading to the front bedroom. "Why?"

"How would I know?" Henry enjoyed living like a gypsy, but he'd never understood why people would knock on an RV door much more freely than a regular house. In the previous ten years, they'd had more strangers banging on their door "to introduce themselves" than a turnstile at a theme park.

The professor rapped twice on the metal frame and peered through the screen. "Hi, forgive the intrusion. Your parents said it'd be all right if I took a look inside the rig."

Grace glanced at Henry and shrugged.

"They're on their way. Should be here any minute." Preston seemed to realize how creepy he sounded and backed down the steps. "You're right to be cautious. I'll wait for them to return."

"It's okay. Come in." She turned the lock and opened the door.

The professor stepped inside and gazed at everything from the solid wood cabinetry to the granite countertops. "This is as nice as my kitchen."

"You seem surprised." Henry folded his arms. Something about the guy started to bother him, but he couldn't quite put his finger on it.

"I guess I am. I've been inside quite a few of these, and this is by far the nicest." He glanced at the twins. "How do you like living on the road?"

"It's amazing. How many kids our age have seen the entire United States and most of Canada?" Grace motioned to the sofa.

Preston parked his butt on the couch and spread out like he owned the place. "Don't you miss going to school? Your friends?"

They'd fielded this type of question so often, the twins responded in unison. "Not at all."

Henry continued, "Traditional schools have some things we don't, but they can't compare to the education we've received."

"From your parents?"

Grace sat at the dinette. "We've taken most of our courses online since eighth grade. We prefer dual enrollment through Duke University."

"And how are you socialized?" He flashed them his blinding smile.

"For starters, we aren't puppies in need of socialization so we don't bite the neighbors." Henry mimicked his hey-I-meant-no-harm expression.

Grace, always the peacekeeper, said, "Honestly, I find people my own age befuddling. Most girls are wrapped up in fashion, prom, and boys. But I do have a few close friends I met in virtual classes."

Preston chuckled. "I'd have to agree with your assessment. My undergrad students are quite immature at times."

The roar of their dad's truck cut the awkward conversation short.

Henry forced his voice to a normal level. No sense in coming off as gruff to their host. "Would you like to see the rest of the rig?"

He stood. "Thank you. I have to say, I'm twice as impressed with the two of you as I am with your home."

Ignoring the compliment, Henry led the way to the back, where his and Grace's beds were half-made. "We have storage above and below the bunks."

The professor nodded.

They returned through the living room and kitchen. Henry opened the door to the full-sized bathroom.

"This is larger than most apartments."

"With four of us, we need it." He moved to the end of the hall and into the master bedroom. "My parents sleep here. It's a regular-size mattress. Dad's too tall to fit on the typical RV queen."

Ethan's voice echoed through the rig. "That's not something Preston has to worry about."

The men laughed, but when Henry returned to the living room, his mother looked like she had had enough of the evening with her husband and his fraternity brother.

"Thank you for the tour." Preston turned to his parents. "Would you mind stepping outside for a moment? There's something I need to discuss with you."

Henry met Grace's eyes.

Faith nodded, and she and their dad followed the professor out.

Henry hustled to the open window beside his bed, and Grace crowded in. With the lights off in the back, the adults couldn't see them eavesdropping.

Preston went straight to the point. "Are you aware of the lawsuit that has been filed to prevent the sale of Plum Island?"

"I read something about it months ago." Faith had used her patient-yet-encouraging tone—the one she used on the rare occasions he and Grace were in trouble.

"There are countless species of rare and endangered plants and wildlife on the island. Congress plans to sell it to the highest bidder to pay for a new animal research facility in Kansas, of all places."

"Kansas? Doesn't the Department of Homeland Security study foot and mouth disease there?" Faith's voice rose in pitch and volume.

"Among other things, yes."

Ethan said, "Is it a good idea to move the labs to an area where the test animals could escape?"

The professor barked a laugh. "One would think not. An outbreak of hoof and mouth could potentially wipe out the beef and pork industries and devastate our food supply. However, the lawsuit isn't to prevent the move. It's to protect the other eighty percent of the island from development."

"I see." Faith had gone back to her patient voice. "Didn't they do an environmental impact study?"

"Not an adequate one. Several congressmen from New York and Connecticut agree, and are working to block the sale." Preston lowered his voice. "Something's off with the entire thing."

Henry and Grace pressed closer to the window.

"Normally, when federally-owned land is vacated, it's handed over to another government agency. This time, Congress decided to auction it off to pay for the move."

Ethan whistled. "Land like that has to be worth billions."

"That may explain the urgency to sell. Any idea who wants the island?" Faith sounded unhappier by the moment.

"Besides all the corporations?" Preston gave the same bitter laugh again. "The lawsuit is moving forward. In the meantime, the Town of Southold has rezoned the island so only nature preserves, parks, and museums can be built."

Faith said, "It sounds like a mess, but what does this have to do with us?"

"I'm the board chair of one of the organizations that brought the lawsuit. Not everyone at the university agrees with it. In fact, the entire ordeal is splitting the faculty in two."

No one spoke for a long moment.

"We'll be here a week, ten days at the most," Faith said.

"I'm not asking you to take my side, but you should know that some people will assume you have." Preston paused and faced Ethan. "You, on the other hand, I want on my side. We could use a legal mind like yours going over the government's case."

Henry met Grace's gaze and mouthed, "He wants Dad."

She nodded.

Their father's voice had lost its usual humor. "I'll think about it."

Pulling Henry to her side of the room, she whispered, "Plum Island is part of one of the conspiracy theories about the Montauk Monster."

"I know. *I'm* the one who told *you*, remember?"

She shook her head. "I read up on it while you were watching that ridiculous alien movie."

That *was what she had been doing?* "What did you learn?"

"Besides that you have terrible taste in movies?"

He nudged her shoulder. "You already knew that."

Her expression grew more serious. "In the early fifties, the Army Chemical Corps owned the island. There are no records of any testing being done there, but the president shut it down without explanation in 1954. Shortly thereafter, the Department of Agriculture opened the research facility to study infectious diseases in animals. Until recently, they allowed tours to the island, but that stopped...also without explanation."

"It all sounds a little fishy, doesn't it?"

"Very much so. I'm not ready to buy into the idea that a dead raccoon is a mutant escapee from the Plum Island Animal Disease Center, but I'm willing to investigate it."

Henry's heart raced at the possibility of uncovering a government conspiracy. He also smiled at the first chapter of their senior project. "How do we get to the island?"

"We don't." She unlocked her phone and opened a link on her browser. "But this is a good place to start."

CHAPTER THREE

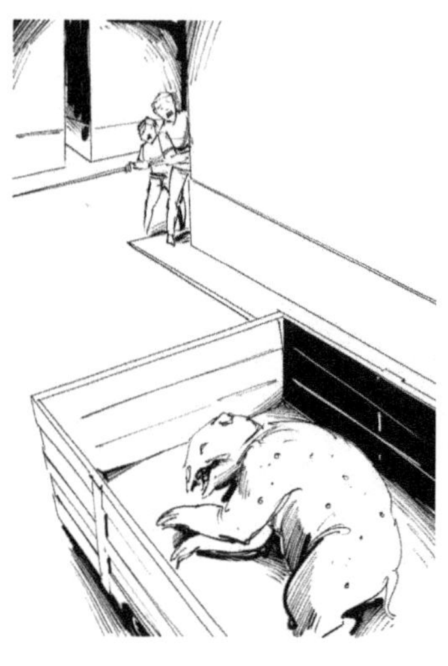

Grace huddled at the dinette over a cup of coffee. She'd done her best to ignore the fat envelope addressed to Henry, but the darned thing mocked her.

Get a grip. It's not like it's a Stanford admissions packet. She nudged it closer to the edge of the table. *It'd be a shame if it fell and became lost.*

Her brother zombie-walked into the kitchen. His dark hair stood up at various angles, making him look like one of those freaky troll dolls. He smacked his lips, scratched his butt, and poured himself a cup of coffee.

Grace watched in quiet fascination as the steaming-hot liquid sloshed around, but by luck or a trick of physics, stayed in the mug. "Good morning."

Henry grunted and plopped down across from her.

She hadn't had the most restful night's sleep either, but unlike her twin, she would put effort into behaving like a human being.

Professor Prescott knocked on the screen door. "Good morning, Warners."

Ethan emerged from the bathroom with his hair still wet from the shower. "Come on in. I'm getting a bit of a late start."

The professor flashed a grin, which was too bright for first thing in the morning. "It's Labor Day weekend. There's no such thing as a late start unless your father and I miss our tee time."

Tee time? Since when does Dad play golf? Grace stood. "Would you like some coffee?"

He shook his head. "Never touch the stuff."

She couldn't help but stare. She'd heard of the mythological creatures known as morning people but had always assumed they were mere humans hopped up on caffeine.

Ethan sat down and was tying his sneakers. "What do the two of you have planned for today?"

Henry hadn't said a word and had only made it through half his mug.

Crud. With her brother in his current state of undeadness, asking permission for their plans would fall on her shoulders. "There's a powwow on the Shinnecock Reservation. It's one of the largest Native American gatherings on the East Coast."

Ethan ran his hand over his freshly shaved jaw. "Southampton is a good forty miles away."

"Thirty-seven." Grace smiled and hoped her dad was in a generous mood. "Three hours by bus or eighty dollars by Uber."

He glanced over his shoulder, likely hoping his wife would appear and make the decision for him.

"They can borrow one of my cars." The professor reached into his pocket and produced a key ring.

"That's a generous offer, but I have to decline." Ethan nodded to Grace. "Uber there, bus back."

"The buses are running on a holiday schedule and will be packed. It's not a problem. I have good insurance."

Grace glanced at them. Even Henry had woken up enough to show some interest in the conversation.

"All right." Ethan stood and turned to the twins. "Make sure you have your licenses on you. Drive safely and be home by ten."

"Yes, sir," they said in unison.

The professor handed Grace two keys on a slim ring. "Black M3. It's in the front drive."

Her eyes widened. *A BMW sports car? Is he serious?* "Thank you."

Henry, on the other hand, hopped up from the table. For a split second, she thought her brother would hug the man. Instead, he stopped short and grinned.

"Thank you. We'll be careful, drive the speed limit, and replace the gas we use."

Ethan clamped a hand on the young man's shoulder and lowered his voice. "I'd be out of here before your mother wakes up."

The twins exchanged looks and shot into action.

Less than an hour later, they sped down Sunrise Highway toward the Shinnecock Indian Reservation. The sun warming their skin, the radio filling the air, and excitement pumping in their veins, the day promised an amazing adventure.

"I could get used to this." Henry caressed the soft leather console.

"Uh huh." Grace would never admit it, but she'd fallen in love with the car the second she'd heard the engine's throaty growl.

"Beats driving Dad's beast of a truck." Henry turned the music down to listen to the GPS.

Grace nodded at the exit. "Look, there's a sign for Stony Brook University. This must be where the School of Marine and Atmospheric Science is located."

"Too bad Mom's not lecturing there. It would have saved us a lot of driving."

"Yeah, but then we wouldn't have met Professor Prescott—"

"—and his sweet ride." Henry glanced around. "I always thought the Hamptons would be nothing but big houses and money."

"I think it's that way on the water. Besides, we're on reservation land now. You can always tell."

Being one-eighth Seminole, their mother had made visiting Native American cultural sights and museums part of their education.

"There's the turn for parking." He pointed to what seemed like acre upon acre of cars. "I bet the powwow generates a fortune."

"They don't have gambling here. The event is probably the majority of the reservation's income for the entire year." She followed the directions of the attendants in orange safety vests to an empty spot.

At ten-thirty sharp, Henry and Grace entered the gate and followed the crowds to an area where several men danced. Grace closed her eyes and focused on the drums until her heart beat in time with the *thump, thump, thump* of the music. Someone bumped into her.

"Excuse us!" Twin girls all of seven, maybe eight years old, cried. They were decked out in full ceremonial regalia and spun in circles.

Grace couldn't help but smile. They were adorable, with their braids and fringed dresses. "I love your beadwork. It's beautiful."

They giggled and ran away.

"Oh, to be young again." Henry slung his arm over her shoulder. "Where should we start asking questions about our monster?"

Grace glanced around. A line of vendor tents bordered one side of the field, and tables and chairs were set up on the other. "It's pretty crowded. I'm not sure the crafters will have time to speak to us."

He rubbed his stomach. "We could grab some food. People with full stomachs are more likely to talk."

"You ate a half-dozen breakfast sandwiches and two orders of hash browns on the way here."

"So? It's time for second breakfast." Henry turned to go, but Grace stopped him.

The drumbeat had slowed, and a wooden flute had replaced the singing. Women in colorful dresses moved to the center of the clearing. Long ribbons hung from their shawls and flared like wings as the women spun in graceful circles. Their steps were so light that they appeared to float over the ground.

"Wow." Henry seemed to have forgotten about food.

The twin girls who'd bumped into Grace joined the adults in the dance, clumsy, but no less mesmerizing.

"Look at their shoes." Henry grinned.

One of the Shinnecock twins wore beaded moccasins, but the other wore light-up sneakers that flashed pink with each step.

"They're so cute."

"My granddaughters." The gravelly male voice sent a shiver down Grace's spine.

She turned to find an older man in full regalia and face paint standing beside her. With feathers and shells woven into his greying hair, he looked as if he'd stepped out of an old photograph.

"Didn't mean to sneak up on you." His smile creased his face and showed every tragedy and joy he'd experienced in his long years. "It's the shoes."

"Your grandchildren are beautiful. Is your daughter dancing with them?"

His eyes grew distant as if the question had brought back a memory. "Daughter-in-law."

Her brother stuck out his hand. "I'm Henry. This is my twin sister Grace."

The man sandwiched Henry's fingers between his. "*Wingapo.*"

"I'm well, thank you." Henry grinned. "We're visiting the area with our parents."

"Your coloring... You are Indian?" He glanced at them.

Grace nodded. "One-eighth Seminole."

His posture softened as if their heritage had marked them as something other than strangers. Perhaps to him, they were. "Not many your age would come to a powwow while they were on vacation."

"We're not like most kids," Henry said. "We're working on our senior project. Would you be able to answer a question or two?"

The man narrowed his eyes.

Grace panicked. This was their first conversation with a local, and she had a feeling this one wouldn't appreciate an interrogation. "My brother and I are homeschooled and travel a lot. We try to find a gathering or museum or cultural site in each place we visit. Our mom's a professor. She's lecturing at the university next week."

The older man nodded and turned his attention back to the performance.

Henry elbowed her side.

She ignored him.

When the dancers exited the field, the man turned to go.

Henry said, "We're trying to find information about the—"

"—Congress' plans to sell Plum Island to the highest bidder." Grace spoke over him before he dropped the Montauk Monster bomb. She had agreed to investigate the creature but wasn't quite ready to speak to strangers about it. She flushed slightly with the diversion.

His shoulders tensed. "I don't know anything about it."

"Do you know anything about the Montauk Monster?" Henry spoke loud enough that several people turned and stared.

Grace had seen cartoons where smoke came out of a character's ears, but she'd never witnessed the human equivalent until then. The old man's eyes bulged, and his face turned deep red. Balling his fists at his sides, he shouted, "Ten years! Ten years, I have worn this like an albatross around my neck!"

She opened her mouth to apologize, but he stormed away.

"What the heck was that about?" Henry stared after him.

Grace huffed and turned to go, but the little girl with the light-up sneakers stepped in front of her.

The child planted her fists on her hips. "Are you from the news?"

Surprised by the question, she recoiled. "No."

"The internet?"

Grace shook her head.

"Government?" The girl gave her the same look her grandfather had moments before.

What's with this kid? "No. I'm not with anyone but my brother. We're high school students." She knelt. "We didn't mean to upset anyone."

"Well, you did." She spun on her heel and walked away.

Unwittingly, they'd robbed the child of her smiles and giggles. Grace turned to Henry but found him speaking to the moccasin-wearing twin.

Nodding and whispering, he seemed engrossed in the conversation.

"Kylie, time to go!" A dark-haired woman gave Henry an odd look and ushered the girl away.

Her brother grinned like he'd just consumed a tall stack of pancakes. He was satisfied and quite pleased with himself.

Grace whispered through gritted teeth, "What did she say?"

"I'll tell you in the car."

For the third time in five minutes, someone had walked away from her. Although she stood five feet five inches tall, Grace struggled to keep up with her longer-legged brother. By the time they'd reached the car, she wanted to clobber him. "*Now* will you tell me what's going on?"

"Zion, the man we were speaking to, was accused of stealing the Montauk Monster back in 2008." He flashed her a triumphant grin.

The urge to clobber him increased. "That's great, but you scared him away."

"Shhh." Henry pressed his finger to his mouth and pulled out his phone.

Grace counted to ten and then to twenty, but Henry continued to type and stare. Type. And. Stare. "What are you looking for?"

"I skimmed an article about an artist who claimed to have had the carcass but reported it stolen by a taxidermist." He paused and read something.

"Is Zion a taxidermist?"

"Don't know, but I'm sure we can find out. He has an unusual name."

Grace's head spun. "Next you'll tell me Professor Plum hid the monster in the conservatory behind the candlesticks."

Henry either hadn't heard her or was ignoring her. He slid his phone into his pocket. "Let's go."

She froze. They'd flipped a coin to determine who took first shift driving the BMW. *Did he forget it's his turn? Is he that distracted?* "Where are we going?"

"Ditch Plains Beach for surfing lessons." He winked and grinned, which meant mischief with an extra helping of trouble.

"Dare I ask why?" Grace pressed the unlock button on the key fob and slid onto the steaming-hot leather seat.

Henry cranked up the air conditioning. "A surfer by the name of Martin Miller was the one who reported the creature missing from the art studio. He owns Miller's Killer Waves Surf School."

"Can this get any weirder?" She maneuvered the car through the busy parking lot.

"I have a feeling we're about to find out." Henry patted her hand. "By the way, I didn't forget. We're still heading east. I'll take my turn driving when we head west."

His logic made her eyes cross.

"We have to hurry. I booked surfing lessons for one thirty, and we need to make a couple of stops on the way."

Grace nodded; she'd given up trying to figure him out. "And?"

"We need bathing suits and burgers."

Only a boy would use those words in the same sentence.

CHAPTER FOUR

"That's it, dude! Paddle. Harder. Yes!" Marty Miller, self-proclaimed surf instructor extraordinaire, cheered from Henry's right. On his left, his twin sister caught the wave and zoomed to shore.

I really stink at this. Henry sat upright with his legs dangling on either side of the board. He hadn't struggled this hard to learn a new sport since he'd attempted to ice skate.

Marty paddled next to him. "Dude, I thought you said you were from Florida?"

"I am. The Gulf Coast. No waves in Tampa." He rolled his head from side to side.

Between the instructor's solemn expression and deep nod, he'd acted as if Henry had shared a personal tragedy. "I feel you."

Henry had things to discuss besides waves, but this time he'd try a different approach. "This is the beach where they found the Montauk Monster, right? I bet it was gnarly."

Marty ran his hand over the back of his neck. "Bro, you have no idea. The place was overrun with looky-loos and paparazzi."

"Bet it was good for business."

Grace paddled toward them but turned and caught another wave. The girl was a freaking natural. She'd probably figured out the physics involved before they'd even hit the water.

"Sure, sure, but that was before my time. I was still in college. Funny story

—" Marty's eyes widened, and he nodded to a swell forming several yards behind them. "Give this one a go."

Henry pressed his chest to the board and swam a few feet away.

"This time, stay in front of that beauty. Let her do the work."

The ocean moved around him, drawing him back as the wave gained strength. Working at a slight angle, Henry paddled for the shore. The closer the swell came, the greater the drag, until in one magical-stars-aligned moment, the force shifted from pull to push.

The power of the rolling water intimidated him. For one gut-wrenching second, he feared the sea would chew him up and swallow him into its depths. Henry pushed past the fear, gripped the board, and planted his feet. A wobble to the left, another to the right, before finding his balance.

"Wooo-hooo!" Marty, or maybe it was Grace, called to him.

Heck, yeah! He'd heard the term "one with nature" forever, but he'd never experienced it until that moment. The wave at his back, the wind in his face—the water filling his lungs, and the rocks and sand peeling his flesh from his bones.

As he'd feared, the sea chewed him like a wad of gum, but rather than swallow, it spat him out near the shore.

"Are you okay?" Grace sloshed through the water toward him.

"Dude, that was righteous...until it wasn't." Marty helped him to his feet.

Coughing and laughing, Henry took a mental inventory of his aches and pains. *Nothing broken.* "That was awesome! I want to go out again."

Grace gave him a look that would have made their mother proud: one-part annoyance, one-part concern, and a dash of disbelief.

"Whoa, there. Let's take five and make sure you don't have a concussion." Marty raised his hand as if to pat Henry's back but seemed to think the better of it. "You're pretty banged up."

He grabbed his board and followed Marty and Grace to the beach. Once out of the water, a dull ache began in his head, and pain flared in his shoulder.

The instructor guided him to a cabana and parked him in a chair. "I'm medically trained. Mind if I do a quick assessment?"

"I'll be okay. Just thirsty."

Marty dabbed something cold on Henry's shoulder. The smell and sting of the antiseptic reminded him of skinned knees and elbows from his childhood.

Grace handed him a bottle of water, recoiling after leaning too close. "You're bleeding."

"You should step out, or Marty will have two possible head traumas to assess." No one liked the sight of blood, his sister included, although she could handle it just fine. He just liked to tease her.

She nodded and hurried away.

"This's gonna hurt a little." The surfer held a bottle of orange-colored liquid in one hand and a bandage in the other.

Henry had an idea so brilliant it made him doubt he'd had a concussion. "Don't suppose you could distract me with the story about the Montauk Monster?"

"Totally." Marty moved closer and inspected the abrasion. "So, like I was saying, I was in college when The Hound of Bonacville was found."

"The what?" Fire erupted in his shoulder, and Henry sucked a breath between his teeth. Marty hadn't been kidding when he said it would hurt. "How exactly are you medically trained? First aid and CPR?"

"I'm a doctor, dude. Medical school, residency, license, the whole nine yards." He continued to clean the wound.

Did I hear that right? Maybe I do have a concussion. "No offense. How does a doctor end up teaching surfing lessons?"

"After my father died, I realized I didn't want to work in a hospital or office or indoors." He shrugged and doused Henry's shoulder again. "Took my inheritance and came here for a girl. It was her idea to start the surf school."

"Sorry about your dad." Henry's eyes welled with tears, although he couldn't say if the fresh coat of antiseptic or the thought of losing his father had caused it.

"Don't be. He was a tyrant. Hunch over a bit." He eased Henry forward. "So yeah, 'the Hound of Bonacville' is a nickname. We call East Hamptoners 'Bonackers,' and the creature was a mystery—"

"The Hound of Baskerville. I get it." Whatever the guy did to his shoulder sent a shot of pain through him that curled his toes. Henry bit his lip to keep from crying out. "How bad is it?"

"Looks like you scraped it on a rock. Probably could use a stitch or two, but there's not enough skin to pull it back together."

"Oh, eww." At some point in the conversation, Grace had returned. "Mom's going to flip out and insist you go to the emergency room."

Marty said, "Nah, no need. Just keep it clean and change the bandages every day until it stops oozing. You can take ibuprofen for the pain."

Grace went from red-faced to white to an odd shade of green. "He should see a doctor."

Henry nodded toward the surfer. "He *is* a doctor, and he's telling me about the Montauk Monster."

She gawked at Marty but took the hint and sat.

"By the way, what do your folks do for a living?" The surf instructor glanced at the twins.

"Our father's an attorney." Grace stiffened her spine and gave him a wide-eyed stare—her "I'm just an innocent kid" look.

"Of course, he is." Marty ran his hands through his sandy blonde hair.

"What were you saying about the creature?" Henry gave his sister the side-eye. Discussing lawyers usually stifled conversations about a potentially liable injury, especially when the man was just starting to open up.

Marty taped a bandage over the wound. "Right. So, the monster... One of the Shinnecocks took it from the beach."

Henry and Grace exchanged looks. It was too much of a coincidence. He had to be talking about Zion.

"The dude says nothing to no one, just walks up and carries it off." The doctor-turned-surf-instructor moved his chair in front of Henry and shined a light in his eyes. "After all the hubbub, an artist friend of mine decides he's going to capitalize on the publicity. He goes to the reservation and finds the creature."

Grace cleared her throat. "How exactly did he *find* it?"

Marty shrugged. "No idea, but that's not the strange part. A couple of days later, someone stole the carcass from the artist."

She met Henry's gaze and grinned. Another clue.

He did a mental fist pump. Marty's story matched the article almost word for word, except for the reference to the Shinnecock. In the article, they had called him a taxidermist. The twins hadn't gotten that from their time on the reservation.

Now to find the artist. "Does your friend still live around here?"

"Lancaster? Yeah, he's in East Hampton." The surfer checked the reflexes in Henry's arms and legs.

Grace said, "I read the creature was a raccoon some college kids found while camping."

Marty's shoulders tensed. "I... Uh... There was a lot of speculation about the monster back then, but I haven't heard that one."

Grace laughed. "It's a ridiculous story. They were drinking and found a dead raccoon. One of them thought it was a great idea to give it a Viking funeral—"

"Stand and walk a straight line." Marty's surfer accent had vanished.

Henry did as he was told. "Is Lancaster his first or last name?"

"Lance Lancaster." Marty motioned for him to come back. "Any headache, dizziness, nausea, blurred vision?"

"A little nausea, but I swallowed five gallons of seawater."

"You're probably fine, but to be sure, you should see your own doctor."

"Thank you. I think I'm okay. I don't remember hitting my head." Henry and Grace shrugged as if they were mechanically connected. Marty raised one eyebrow and chuckled.

Grace stood. "Yes, but you didn't know you were bleeding, either. We should tell Mom what happened. Head injuries are tricky. Symptoms can pop up days or even weeks after an accident."

It was Marty's turn to go from red to white to green. "Here, take my card. I'll take care of the bill if your parents decide to have you checked out."

What the heck is she doing? We have enough info. Henry shot Grace a warning look and slid the bright blue card into his wet pocket. He opened his mouth to apologize, but then it occurred to him. Marty's story matched the statements he'd made for the article almost word for word. From watching his father, he knew that witnesses had trouble recalling details of crimes weeks later, and he'd described an event that had happened over ten years ago.

Is he lying? "It's almost five. We should get going. It's an hour drive back to Stony Brook."

"Drive safe." Marty turned and headed toward the surf shop.

Grace eased her arm around Henry's waist and guided him back to the car. "Nice job fake-limping."

"Nice job intimidating the witness." He held out his hand.

"Uh-uh. No way you're driving with a bruised brain." She slid a t-shirt over her head.

He had looked forward to driving the BMW ever since the professor had handed him the keys. "My shoulder feels like road rash. Otherwise, I'm fine."

She pulled on a pair of shorts and snatched her cell phone from their bag. "Let me call and check in with Mom."

"Fine. You win." Henry covered the seat with a beach towel and eased into the car. He'd never admit it out loud, but he felt like he'd been put through the spin cycle of the world's largest washing machine.

She put the phone back, started the car, and pulled out of the parking lot. "What did you make of his story?"

"I'm not sure. He's either hung up on his fifteen minutes of fame or—"

"—he's lying." Grace adjusted the air conditioner vents and fiddled with the temperature. "Are you cool enough?"

"Yes, *Mom*." He leaned his head back and closed his eyes. "Sorry. Thanks for looking out for me. This case doesn't add up. Marty never claimed to be on the beach the day the monster washed ashore."

She frowned and tapped the steering wheel. "Nor did he mention the girls who found it by name. How does he know so much about it, and where does the artist fit in?"

"Maybe Lancaster was on the beach?"

"Maybe, but Marty said he became interested in capitalizing on the publicity. The news stories came later." She huffed. "Maybe he's told this story so many times he's simply reciting. This is almost as strange as a doctor-turned-surf-instructor, but it was kind of romantic, the way it happened."

"Did you notice his shoulders tense when you asked about the campers and the Viking funeral?"

"No. I was too busy watching him beat you with a tiny rubber hammer." She tightened her grip on the wheel. "Are you sure you're okay?"

"Yeah, at least until Mom finds out." He found out that laughing made his shoulder throb. He shifted sideways to face his sister. "I could use some water and ibuprofen."

"I'll find a convenience store."

"What do you say we skip the whole doctor thing when we see Mom and Dad?"

She eyed him. "I don't think that's wise."

"We can't find Lance Lancaster if we're in an emergency room—"

"—or grounded." Grace nodded. "Okay, but if you start acting strange, I'm going to sing like the Colossi of Memnon."

He chuckled and then winced. "Ouch. Stop making me laugh with nerd similes."

"Are you calling me a nerd?"

"Considering 99.9 percent of the population would have said 'sings like a bird,' and you chose to reference ancient Egyptian statues...which, by the way, haven't sung since 199 CE."

"Now you're just showing off." Grace rolled her eyes. "That you know the year they stopped singing out-nerds me by light years."

"Hey, I had to do something to make up for my complete failure on a surfboard."

"You did stink at it." She wrinkled her nose. "But you nailed that last wave for a good thirty seconds before you crashed and drowned."

The mere mention of it made his body ache. "Speaking of which, I could use some ibuprofen."

"Right, sorry." She slowed and pulled into a convenience store. "When do you want to visit Lancaster?"

"Tomorrow. We're covered in sand and salt." Henry ran through the growing list of potential witnesses. "We also need to find the woman who took the photos of the monster, and the names of the campers who gave the dead raccoon a Viking funeral."

"Let's hope the studio's open tomorrow. It's Labor Day. Don't forget, our regular classes start on Tuesday." She climbed out of the car. "And we still have to convince our parents this is an academically rigorous research project."

"Yeah. There's that, too."

Besides, we're probably going to be grounded tomorrow and/or without a car. Henry grabbed their bag from the backseat. "We should clean up."

"Why? We'll be back home in an hour."

"Because we can't go to an art gallery in swim trunks."

CHAPTER FIVE

Gas station bathrooms were a bit like drinking water in a third world country. Sometimes they were clean and fresh and safe. Other times, one came away praying they hadn't contracted any diseases. Unfortunately, Grace found herself in the scariest type of all—the middle-ground restroom, just enough grossness to make her wonder if she was current on her vaccines.

She tossed damp paper towels into the trash. They'd proven worthless at removing the residual sand from her skin, but twelve years on the road had taught her a trick or two. She had managed to rinse the salt and grit from her hair by using a thirty-two-ounce fountain drink cup and some yoga positions over the sink.

Grace emerged from the convenience store feeling half-human.

"Took you long enough." Henry glanced at the sky as if to gauge the time by the angle of the sun.

"Sue me." Other than a sprinkling of sand on his tanned legs, no one would ever guess Henry had spent the afternoon at the beach.

He sat in the passenger seat and set up a smorgasbord of junk food. Beef jerky, cheese sticks, and crackers rested on the console and his left thigh; chips in the middle, and a chocolate bar and gummy bears on the right.

Grace reached for a cracker, but he slapped her hand away. "Are you serious?"

"Dead serious. You're going to mess up my filling-to-cracker ratio." As if to demonstrate his genius plan, he stacked meat and cheese between two generic Ritz crackers and shoved the whole thing in his mouth.

"You're not going to share?" She turned onto the highway and headed west.

Henry reached into the bag and pulled out one of her favorite energy bars. "I also bought you a banana and a bottle of water."

"Thanks." He tore off the wrapper for her, and she finished the bar in three bites. "What's the plan?"

"I say we go with the school project angle. Drop Marty's name and see what happens."

Grace mentally compared the surfer's story with the articles she'd read about the Montauk Monster. "I know we're just getting started, but Marty's story bugs me."

Henry washed his chips down with an energy drink. "Wait, didn't we have this conversation before?"

"We did, but there's more. Let's start at the beginning. A girl finds the creature and takes pictures. Then a man, presumably Zion, removes the carcass from the beach."

He nodded.

"How did Zion know it was there? How long had it been there?"

"No idea."

Grace drummed on the steering wheel. "That's not the part that's bothering me. How did Lancaster know where to look for the carcass? What are the chances someone on the beach would recognize a Shinnecock taxidermist?"

"We don't know who else was there that day. For all we know, Zion's next-door neighbor could have been catching some rays." He tilted his head back and dumped the cheese dust and chip crumbs into his mouth.

"Okay, fine. Let's say someone called 'the taxidermist' introduced himself to the crowd. Do you think he would just hand the monster over to Lancaster? Think about it. Stuffing a creature that by all reports looked like a mutant alien could be huge for business."

"Only if the exchange happened after the creature went viral. Look. Maybe he gave it to Lancaster, maybe he didn't. We need facts, not speculation."

Grace groaned. "Yes, we need facts, but we may not get them. All I'm saying is, why would you give something away, only to steal it back?"

"Relax. I agree with you. I'm just trying to do things by the book."

"There *is* no book. We're making it up as we go." She poked his side. "With all the back and forth, how did an actual scientist examine the creature?"

"From what I read, they came to their conclusions based on the photographs." Henry moved on to his dessert course. "Want a gummy?"

She waved her hand. "I'd have to look again, but I'm sure I read something about DNA evidence in one of the articles."

Her brother crammed the chocolate bar into his mouth, closed his eyes, and chewed slowly. Lucky for her, he did his best thinking while eating. "We should print the articles, create a timeline, and make a list of everyone involved, including the reporters."

"Good idea. We need to find ways to separate the facts from the nonsense."

"Take the next exit." Henry shoved the empty wrappers into the plastic bag and brushed the stray bits from the seat. "We're going to need to clean the car before we return it."

"You think?" Grace eased to a stop in front of Lancaster's Gallery. Other than a handful of lights illuminating sculptures and paintings in the windows, the studio was dark. "Looks like we missed him, and they're closed tomorrow." She pointed to a hand-painted sign in the window.

"Stay here." Henry hopped out of the car and walked to the door.

She glanced up and down the street and tightened her grip on the steering wheel. They weren't doing anything wrong, but she couldn't help feeling like the getaway driver at a bank robbery. Any of the men strolling the quiet East Hampton sidewalks could be Lance Lancaster, one of two people who claimed to have had possession of the creature.

Henry rapped on the car window.

Grace started with a shock before lowering the glass. "You scared ten years off my life."

"Get a grip, will you?" He pressed his lips into a thin line. "I called the number on the door. Lancaster's meeting us in five minutes."

Her stomach did a somersault. *This is a bad idea. A very bad idea.* "How did you get him to agree to come?"

Henry looked away and grinned. "I told him we were interested in buying the mermaid sculpture in the window."

"I don't like lying to people."

"Me either, but it had to be done."

None of this had to be done. They could forget about it and come up with another idea that didn't involve lying. "I'll park the car and meet you back here."

"No, leave it. It'll make us look more legit." He opened the door and slid into his seat.

"We're dressed like boxcar kids and smell like saltwater—"

"Or, we appear to be teenagers who are looking to spend their parents' money after enjoying a day on their yacht." He typed into his phone and turned the screen toward her. "This is Lance Lancaster."

Grace stared at the image of a thirty-something, hipster-ish man with thick glasses and a soul patch. "He looks harmless enough, but he's not going to be happy when we don't buy anything."

"You look at the statue. I'll strike up a conversation."

"Henry and Grace Rothschild?" An older and slightly rounder version of the man in the photo waved from the sidewalk.

Rothschild? Henry's taking this undercover detective thing too far. Grace remained rooted in the driver's seat.

"That's us." Her brother climbed from the car and shook Lancaster's hand.

The man looked him over from head to sandy toes.

Blood whooshed behind Grace's eardrums. *He's not buying it. I knew this was a bad idea.* Keeping the keys in her hand and adopting a casual expression, she joined her brother.

"Funny. Martin Miller said your last name was Warner." He folded his arms. Though Henry stood several inches taller and was twenty pounds heavier, Lance Lancaster seemed to take up more physical space than the younger man. Angry people had a way of doing that.

Henry must have felt it too because he took a step back. "I'm sorry I lied to you. My sister and I are working on a school project. We really need to get a good grade to get into college."

"We didn't mean any harm," Grace said. "Would you mind answering a couple of questions?"

He scowled and glanced up the street. When he turned back, he pegged her with a glare. "You have thirty seconds."

Her heart battered against her ribcage, but she persisted. "Mr. Miller said you had the Montauk Monster, but someone stole it. Do you know who took it or why?"

"My money's on the Shinnecock taxidermist." The muscle in Lancaster's jaw bulged, and the right corner of his mouth turned down. They were running out of time before he left or lost his temper.

"Were you on the beach when the monster was found?" Henry, the picture of calm, folded his arms.

"Nope."

"Do you have the name of the taxidermist?" Her voice came out in a squeak.

"Look it up, kid." He shook his head, threw his hands down as if brushing away a mosquito, and walked away.

"He needs a hug, or maybe anger-management classes." Henry opened the car door.

Grace narrowed her eyes. "You *lied* to him. Of course, he's upset."

As usual, her brother had a different take on the situation. "Yeah, but why bother to meet us? He knew I'd given him a fake name *before* he agreed to meet us."

Her brain stuttered. "That's true, but from now on we stick to the plan and tell the truth."

"Agreed. Let's go. I have a theory."

Back in the car, Grace locked the doors just in case Lancaster returned. Until then, she'd thought of herself as worldly, but despite all the travel, she realized more and more they'd led a sheltered life.

"He wants us to find the taxidermist." Henry seemed completely unaffected by the encounter. "I'm unsure of his motives. Revenge, maybe. Marty and the artist are still close friends. That's interesting, too. I say we find Zion."

She wanted to go back to Stony Brook, take a shower, and put the entire day behind her. "The powwow runs into the night. I doubt anything will be open, and we don't know if Zion is the taxidermist."

"We won't know until we try." He pulled his phone from his pocket. "There's only one shop listed near the reservation. No mention of the owner."

"I'm going to say, 'I told you so' every day for the next twenty years if things go bad." Grace put the car in gear and headed back to the Shinnecock Nation.

"Stop worrying and live a little." Henry rolled down his window and closed his eyes.

She pinched him on the soft spot on the back of his arm. "I'll stop worrying when you stop acting like Detective Dimwit."

"Ouch, that hurt." He rummaged through the plastic bag and retrieved the gummy bears. "I know what's really bothering you."

Refusing to take the bait, she stared straight ahead.

He popped several candies into his mouth. "I'm better at this than you are."

"Better at lying?"

"Better at thinking on my feet. You're good at facts and figures, but I have more street smarts."

Street smarts? Is he kidding? "Whatever." She maintained a straight line with the car through multiple eye rolls.

The last remnants of color splashed across the darkening sky. Much to Grace's delight, a handful of stars twinkled overhead. She'd assumed the light pollution from New York City would make the night sky a blur. At any other time, she would have pointed the constellations out to Henry. They hadn't bickered like children since...well, since they were children.

The drive was quick. The phone's map made short work of the directions.

She followed Henry to the small building nestled in the trees. "There aren't any lights on downstairs. We should go."

"The sign on the door says Open."

She squinted at the rectangular cardboard. "They probably forgot to turn it over."

He pointed to the second story. "I bet they're on break or something. Looks like an apartment. I can smell dinner cooking."

"We shouldn't interrupt." She stopped walking a couple of yards from the porch. It was quiet; so quiet she could hear the ceremonial drums beating in the distance. "Let's go home and come back in the morning. Didn't you see the huge envelope for you on the table? I bet it's feedback on your research paper."

"I saw it, but I want to read it when I have time to myself." He avoided her gaze. "And no way are we going home now. Like you said, we'll probably be grounded. Come on, Grace. This is our senior year; our last chance for adventure before we split up for college. I intend to make every minute count."

She sucked in a breath. He'd given her a verbal gut-punch and hadn't bothered to look her in the eye when he'd done it.

Her brother turned the doorknob and laughed. "I told you they were open."

"You can't go in there."

Of course, her brother didn't listen. He seemed to have left his common sense in Stony Brook. *He doesn't need it. He has "street smarts."*

"Come back," she whisper-shouted, and glanced from the upstairs windows to the dark storefront and back again.

"Hello? Anyone here? The door was open," her brother called from inside the shop.

The lights in the apartment went off, and the exterior floodlights came on. Grace froze like a wild animal caught in oncoming traffic. A human-sized shadow moved behind the upstairs blinds and her throat tightened.

Get out of there, Henry. She dove behind a tree. Pressing her back to the rough bark, she struggled to remember how to breathe.

"Who's that?" The child's voice seemed to come from her left, not above as she would have expected.

She peeked around the tree and caught sight of a large figure with a smaller one disappearing into the forest. Grace counted exponents of three until she reached 59,049, or three to the tenth power, and nothing happened.

I'm going to drag him out by his ear. She eased from behind the tree and took two steps toward the porch.

The unmistakable racking of a shotgun stopped her in her tracks.

"Who are you, and what are you doing on my land?" He sounded like she imagined a talking grizzly bear would sound.

Her hands flew up on instinct. "Grace Warner. We're looking for the taxidermist."

"We?" The man, who looked exactly like he'd sounded, stepped in front of her.

Grace was no shorty, but this guy's height and width eclipsed her. And there was the gun. The thing looked like it'd fire cannon balls, and it was pointed at her chest.

He glanced at the open front door and swore beneath his breath. "You robbing me, little girl?"

"No!" The trembling started in her fingers and worked its way down to her toes. She opened her mouth to explain but couldn't manage to form a word.

"I have your girl. Come outside," Shouting, his gaze moved from the door to her to the door and back again.

"Whoa." Henry stepped onto the porch with his hands in the air.

CHAPTER SIX

They say your life flashes before your eyes when faced with certain death, but all Henry saw was an enormous gun aimed at Grace's heart. *This can't be happening.*

The man motioned toward him. "Come here. Nice and slow."

"Let her go." His voice sounded much more confident than it should have, considering his legs had gone rubbery. He moved to stand between Grace and the shotgun.

"I'll let the police sort this out." The guy patted his pockets with his free hand and let out a few choice curse words before shouting, "Kylie, Kara, bring me my cell phone!"

Kylie? Oh, please let it be the same girl. "We meant no harm. The sign said Open, and the door was unlocked."

Grace whispered something, but he couldn't make it out over his pulse beating in his ears.

The guy narrowed his eyes, but he lowered the barrel a few inches. "Like I said, we'll let the police sort it out."

Sure enough, the little girl he'd met at the powwow came outside.

"Where's your sister?"

"Kara's...um..." She took one look at Henry and grinned.

He didn't like the look in her eyes. He knew self-preservation when he saw it.

"You're the cute boy from the powwow. Henry, right? Did you follow me home?"

The gun snapped higher.

Oh, crap. Henry opened his mouth, and too many words fell out. "I'm not a creeper. My sister and I were talking to Zion. The girls were performing. Afterward, we talked. She told me about the Montauk Monster. I swear. We came to ask some questions. That's it."

"Uh-huh." He looked down the sight and raised his aim a fraction of an inch.

"The sign said Open, and the door was unlocked." Henry's voice cracked.

"Look, Daddy. He's telling the truth." Kylie waved her hand like a miniature Vanna White.

The man glanced at the door and cursed again. "You look like a smart kid. Too smart to think a dark shop was open for business. Kylie, call 911. Tell them we had a break-in."

Grace eased from behind Henry. "Please don't call the police. We just wanted to speak to Zion about the creature for a school project."

"That *creature* ruined my father's reputation and my family." He lowered the gun. "Zion doesn't live here anymore."

She swallowed hard. "We didn't realize..."

"Leave, and don't let me catch you back around here."

Henry grabbed Grace's hand and tugged.

She didn't budge. "How? How did the Montauk Monster ruin your family?"

"Girl, I suggest you get in that fancy car of yours and go before I change my mind."

"Grace, please." Henry would have gone to his knees and begged if it meant getting his sister out of there.

"Okay." She nodded to the guy with the gun. "I'm sorry for disturbing your dinner."

Back at the BMW, Henry took the keys and slid into the driver's seat, but not even the fine leather or the growl of the engine could snap him out of his mood. He'd messed up big time and nearly gotten himself and Grace hurt, or worse. "I should have listened to you."

"I can't talk about this yet." She drew her knees to her chest and stared out the window. Knowing his sister, she was replaying the events of the day, scrutinizing each detail, and identifying her mistakes.

Although it killed him to keep quiet, he owed her that much. The drive back to Stony Brook dragged on and on. Henry had nothing to do but think. He couldn't put his finger on what exactly she'd done, but Grace had grated on his nerves most of the day. She'd argued and tried to wuss out at every turn, but that wasn't it. It'd irritated him that she'd been right.

"You should pull into a gas station. We need to top off the tank and vacuum the sand out of the floor mats." Grace continued to look anywhere but at him, but at least she'd spoken.

That's a start. "I'll stop at the next place."

"I was thinking. Back at the powwow, I asked Zion if the girl's mother was performing and he got this sad, lost look. Like my question had hurt him." She picked at the hem of her shorts. "Did you notice how Kylie avoided telling her father where her sister was?"

Heck, yes, I noticed. "She threw me to the wolves."

Grace sighed and met his gaze for the first time since they'd gotten in the car. "I think Kara was with their grandfather. I saw a man and a child coming out of the forest. I thought they saw me and turned back, but maybe they were avoiding Kara's father."

"You're telling me Zion saw that maniac hold a gun on you and did nothing?" For all he knew, Zion could be as crazy as his son, but he'd played the role of the doting grandfather at the powwow. Why hadn't he at least tried to help?

"Maybe, but it doesn't matter." She turned to him.

The look in her eyes brought back painful memories. She'd worn the same expression when their dog had passed away, and again when she'd overheard him tell their parents he wanted to apply to Stanford. "Grace, I—"

"He said the Montauk Monster destroyed their family. I want to know how." After reaching the auto-wash, she stepped out of the car to stuff quarters into the vacuum.

Henry spent the remainder of the drive in a clean car with a silent sister and a guilty conscience. Debunking urban legends had seemed like a fun project, but he had gotten carried away. Grace had been at the wrong end of a shotgun. He vowed to himself to be a better brother. If there was a next time, it couldn't be her in the line of fire.

Once again, Grace leapt from the car the moment it came to a stop.

He hustled to catch up to her but slowed when he spotted his parents and the professor sitting beneath the awning on the fifth wheel. *Doesn't that guy have decks made of rare African Blackwood to lounge on?*

"You're late." Faith stood and set her hands on her hips, the universal body language for "I'm angry, and you're the cause."

Luckily, Grace chose that moment to break her silence. "We forgot to allow time to gas up and vacuum out the car."

The wrinkles between his mother's brows deepened to form an eleven. "And why did you find it necessary—" Time slowed. Her eyes widened, and she marched toward Henry.

His breath caught, his stomach twisted, and his pulse raced. Every kid who'd ever been caught doing something stupid knew the feeling.

"You're bleeding." The lift in her voice made the statement sound like a question, but he doubted she wanted an answer.

"We went surfing. Henry fell. Our instructor was a medical doctor and patched him up." Grace spoke too quickly.

"What's all the fuss?" Preston strolled closer. He might have tried to play it cool, but his voice was strained.

"The car's fine. We cleaned out the sand." Henry handed him the keys. "Thank you for it. That is one sweet ride. Gives me something to aspire to."

"Surfing? I was told you were at a powwow. And why didn't this *doctor* obtain permission to treat a minor? Take off your shirt."

Henry and Grace exchanged glances.

"Don't look at each other. *I'm* talking. Do as I asked. You've bled through the bandage." She huffed and pointed at the trailer. "Go inside."

Preston turned as if to follow, but Faith stepped in front of him. "We should call it a night. Ethan and I need to speak to our children."

He opened his mouth as if to argue.

"Thank you for allowing us to use the car. It was a lifesaver." Grace smiled, or tried to, at least. She looked as miserable as Henry felt.

"*Now*, Henry." Faith's voice rose to a dangerous level. "You too, Grace."

Knowing better than to push their luck, they crossed the lawn as if going to the executioner. In a way, they were. Their freedom would likely die within the hour.

"I'll get the first aid kit." Ethan gave them a disappointed headshake and followed them inside.

Faith came inside and shut the door harder than necessary. His mother's anger made it hard for Henry to breathe; like a fire, it seemed to consume the room's oxygen.

She's overreacting. Sure, they'd gone surfing without permission, but they'd done similar things in the past. Henry feared his shoulder made a good scapegoat for whatever was really bothering her.

"Start explaining." She flipped on the overhead lights and motioned to a barstool.

Henry sat and hunched forward to give his mother access to the wound. "We went to the powwow, but on the drive back, the ocean looked so inviting. And we saw the sign for a surf school. We decided to go surfing."

"I gathered that much." She pulled the bandage from his shoulder and hissed. "This should have been treated in an urgent care clinic."

Ethan leaned in for a closer look. "It's not that bad. Whoever patched him up did a good job cleaning out the sand."

Henry found himself in a conundrum. He could admit he'd forged the online consent forms and almost gotten Grace killed, or he could lessen his prison time by whining about the wound. One tack was riskier than the other.

Somewhere behind him, Grace sucked in a breath. "We've decided on our senior project topic. We haven't written a proposal yet, but we intend to investigate urban legends in the places we visit over the school year."

"Did you hit your head?" Faith's hands went to her hips again.

He needed to speak fast before she poo-pooed the idea. "Urban legends impact everything from the culture of an area to the economy. Debunking these myths will involve science, journalism, research, and analytical skills."

"Take the Montauk Monster, for instance. Did you know that a local Shinnecock family was personally impacted to the point that they think it ruined their lives?" Grace spoke matter-of-factly.

Good plan. Emotion would have been like waving a red flag in front of their mother.

Ethan said, "How does this relate to the law?"

"I intend to illustrate a flaw in the jury system by proving that people are susceptible to believing the improbable if they're exposed to the information enough times. Media coverage of the Montauk Monster was widespread. It was covered on local news and in the papers, and it became an internet sensation. So much so, documentaries were made about it."

His parents stared.

Behind their parents, Grace winked. "Big Foot is big business. People have formed secret societies with the sole goal of finding proof of his existence. Every area has legends of creatures, unexplained phenomena, or ghosts. Some have all three."

"I'm impressed." Ethan glanced at them.

"Grace, your part in this needs to focus on the science. Henry, I like your idea to apply the research to jury trials." Faith folded her arms. "I expect a written proposal by the weekend."

Wait, had she given her approval? Henry's head spun.

Grace squealed. "Absolutely."

"Now, tell me how you two managed to take surfing lessons without parental consent?"

When their parents announced the twins would spend the day in the university library as recompense for forging the consent forms, they hadn't realized that most of the campus was closed for Labor Day. For one brief shining moment, Henry thought they'd be pardoned. Unfortunately, Professor Preston Prescott came through with an eleventh-hour stay of execution—the keys to an empty classroom.

As far as prison cells went, this one wasn't half-bad, but it would have been better if the coffee cart in the lobby had been open. As it was, Henry had to rely on vending machines for nourishment. Three sodas and six bags of chips later, his stomach protested.

"Here it is." Grace angled her laptop toward him. "Doctor Frank Fluke from Plum Island Research Facility wrote a piece claiming to have examined the DNA of the creature. I'm going to email him."

"Give me the website." He pressed a hand to his gut, rethinking his dietary choices.

She rattled off a thirty-character web address.

"Never mind. I'll google it." Henry typed the search criteria into his computer and gasped. "Holy smokes. There was another one on Friday night."

"Another what?"

"Sighting. Listen to this. A couple reported being attacked by a beak-nosed creature with glowing red eyes at Rheinstein Estate Park." He minimized the window and searched for the location. "It's less than a half-mile from Ditch Plains Beach."

"Does the article give their names?" Grace moved to his side and hovered over his shoulder. "That doesn't look like a reputable source."

Henry pinched the bridge of his nose. "We're searching for monsters, not the atomic mass of selenium. There are no scholarly journals on urban legends."

"True, but I'd feel better if the author had legit credentials."

"We need to get ahead of the media on this. I'm going to email him for more info."

Grace added a circle to their investigation diagram. "I'll check the surface currents and winds between the new location and Plum Island."

"What's this about Plum Island?" Preston stood in the doorway with what smelled like a sack of seafood.

Henry closed the notebook containing their version of a detective's string board. "There was another Montauk Monster sighting," he blurted.

The professor grinned and set the food on the table. "I remember when all of that started in 2008. You're wise to check the currents. Most people believe the original creature was a dead raccoon from Shelter Island, but I've always wondered..."

"You think it was some kind of mutation?" Grace gawked.

"Not after the first discovery, but there have been others." His tone grew ominous, cartoonishly so.

Henry rolled his eyes. "I don't suppose you can get us a pass to Plum Island?"

He chuckled. "Considering I sit on the board of one of the organizations suing the government over the sale of the island, no. I don't think so."

"What sale?" Henry pretended not to know what Preston was referring to. No sense alerting the professor that they'd spied on his conversation with their parents.

He motioned to the food and took a seat. "I thought you two might be hungry."

"Thanks," the twins said in unison.

"You're very welcome. Now, about the Plum Island debacle..."

They ate their fish sandwiches and fries while the professor went into great detail about Congress' intentions, the history of the island, and the environmental impacts—all of which they'd either heard or read before.

"I believe the media attention put a kink in their plans in 2008."

Grace perked up. "Their plans to relocate the Animal Disease Center to Kansas, or did they intend to sell the island that far back?"

He gave her an appraising look. "Officially, Congress approved an unfunded plan to move the facility."

"But you think they intended to sell the island even then?"

"I do. That is, until the Montauk Monster washed ashore and the internet went crazy. There was too much scrutiny at the time to move forward unnoticed."

Henry crumpled his wrapper and tossed it into the bag. "You wouldn't happen to know anything about the Viking funeral guys on Shelter Island?"

He glanced away. "No, but I know one of the women who found the original creature."

Grace folded the paper over her half-eaten sandwich. "Do you know how we can reach her?"

"Let me make a call. She's more likely to speak to you if she knows I sent you." He stood but hesitated. "Be careful around the reservation. Not everyone there is friendly."

She nodded. "Thanks for lunch."

Henry waited until Preston left the room before grabbing the remainder of his sister's food. "Okay, that was weird."

"I'd say it was enlightening." She drew two more circles on their diagram, one for Professor Prescott, the other labeled Mystery Woman with a question mark.

Henry shoved the last of her sandwich into his mouth and chased it with half a soda. "Come on."

"We can't leave. Mom's orders," she protested while shutting down her laptop.

"I have a plan. Show her our work and explain the urgency of following up on the new sighting. It's too good an opportunity to miss." Henry packed his computer and notebook.

"And if she disagrees?"

He wrapped his arms around his middle and made a sour face. "Did that fish taste funny to you?"

Grace narrowed her eyes. "Lunch was delicious, and you know it. No more lying."

CHAPTER SEVEN

Not only had their mother allowed them to visit Rheinstein Estate Park, but she also agreed it would save time if they drove the professor's car. However, she'd expressly forbidden them from entering the water or participating in anything more than fact-finding. The twins were comforted that not telling their mother about the taxidermist incident had been the best choice.

"I'm worried about Mom." Grace struggled to focus on the road instead of the dozens of questions bouncing around in her head.

Henry glanced up from his phone. "She's been acting strange since we got here. I'm telling you, it has something to do with Preston."

"Maybe." She turned on the radio to drown out her thoughts, but song lyrics added to the clutter between her ears. "I think you should drive."

Henry's expression brightened but immediately turned skeptical. "Why?"

"I'm distracted. I need to put my thoughts on paper to sort them out."

His phone rang.

"It's a blocked number." He pressed the Answer button and put the call on speaker. "Hello?"

A female voice came across the connection. "Is this Henry Warner?"

"Yes."

Losing hope of paying attention to anything other than the conversation, Grace pulled into the closest parking lot.

"Preston asked me to give you a call. To be honest, I don't think I can help you." The woman had spoken too fast and was too breathy and too nervous.

"I understand, Ms...."

"No names."

He glanced at Grace and frowned. "I understand. Any information you can give us will help."

After a couple of seconds, she said, "My friends and I found the creature on the beach."

Grace motioned for him to continue the conversation.

"Do you believe it was a raccoon?"

"It's possible."

A non-answer. What was it with people agreeing to speak to them, only to refuse to answer simple questions? She wanted to join the conversation, but Henry hadn't introduced her. Another person on the call might spook the unnamed woman.

"Do you know who took the creature from the beach?" Henry persisted.

"No, but he looked Native American."

"Any idea what happened to it after he took it?"

"No."

He pinched the bridge of his nose, a habit he'd picked up from their father. He'd lose her if he didn't come up with something more than the basics.

Grace mouthed, "Plum Island."

"Can you tell me anything about what was happening with Plum Island at that time? How much did the general public know about the Animal Research Facility's planned move to Kansas?"

She hesitated for a long moment. "There were rumors the government planned to close that horrible place, but nothing concrete until that summer. I remember hearing about developers showing an interest in building luxury resorts on the island. Some students at the university organized a petition to turn it into a nature preserve, but their efforts didn't last long. A week or two, maybe."

Grace gave him a thumbs-up.

"Do you know why they stopped?"

"You know how it is. Students are busy and impatient."

Henry laughed a game-show host's ha-ha-ha. "A story surfaced back then about a group of guys who claimed to have held a Viking funeral for a dead raccoon. Do you remember that?"

"I don't recall..." The hint of uncertainty in her response made Grace suspect she was lying.

"Did the land developers back off after the creature was discovered?"

"I don't know. Maybe? I didn't really follow. I don't know."

Something in the caller's tone made Grace uneasy. She nudged Henry.

He gave her another wide-eyed look and shrugged. "I read reports of a similar creature washing ashore a year later. The people who found it described a sweet smell. How would you describe the odor of the one you found?"

Grace's mouth fell open. Of all the questions he could have asked, he'd chosen that one?

Henry held up a hand.

"It smelled sweet." She sighed. "Things were crazy back then. People came out of the woodwork with stories about the monster. You need to be careful. Better yet, find another topic for your project."

Grace pressed Mute and whispered, "She seems more sad than worried."

He nodded and unmuted the call. "Did something else happen to you?"

"No," she said on an exhale.

"How can I get in touch with the women who were with you that day?"

"You can't." She sighed and hung up.

Henry stared at the phone. "That was—"

"—odd."

"This doesn't prove anything, but there was an inconsistency in her story. The girls originally reported the creature smelled like rotting fish. Olfactory impressions stay in the memory the longest."

"But she was the definition of an unreliable witness." Grace rested her forehead on the steering wheel. "We're missing something. I can feel it, but I don't know what or where to look."

"You think better on paper. Why don't I drive while you take notes?"

"Sure, why not?" Back on the road, Grace jotted down a rough transcript of the telephone call. "The conversation was odd. She was uncomfortable, but she called anyway."

"Like Lancaster"

"Yes! I hadn't thought of it, but you're right." She wiggled the pencil between her index finger and thumb until it blurred. "Was it me, or did she seem sad?"

"I read her as spooked." Henry scratched his head. "These things happened ten years ago. I understand it was bizarre—downright gross—but finding a dead animal on the beach shouldn't have caused her to have such a reaction."

"Maybe the media coverage traumatized her?"

Henry shrugged. "Maybe."

Grace tried to imagine how she'd react in the same situation. "It's all too disjointed, like we're missing the first floor of a one-story building. We have the foundation, and the roof is built, but there's no structure to connect the two."

He stared, smirked and shook his head, in that order. "We're looking at this the wrong way. What is our hypothesis?"

"Good question." She ran through the facts as they understood them. "We can't prove any physical properties of the original creature except what we can determine from the images."

"Which could have been manipulated."

"Right. We should focus on another angle." She flipped to the page containing the diagram of people involved in the case. "How about the conflicting stories? Could we prove that someone is lying?"

Henry opened his mouth to speak, but she interrupted.

"No, that would take too long. We're leaving in a few days." Grace paused and followed the logical pattern of their data. "I know. We could prove or disprove that a person or group benefitted from the existence of the urban legend of the monster."

"I like it, but we have to narrow the list of suspects. To me, the most obvious choice is the Save Plum Island folks."

"You're not suggesting Professor Prescott had anything to do with it?" As soon as she spoke, a piece of the puzzle snapped into place. "We need to find out who was in charge of those student petitions, as in, who arranged the protests."

"Good idea. How do we go about it?"

"I'm sure the university has records of the group and their events. Student organizations have to register."

"You're assuming they were an official organization." Henry frowned. "While you're at it, find out where Preston was in July of 2008."

"You can't honestly believe he has anything to do with this?"

"I don't like the guy."

She leaned close and stared until he glanced her way. "I thought we were going by the book? Facts, not speculation."

"We are, but the best detectives know when to follow their gut. My gut says that Professor Preston Prescott isn't as squeaky-clean as he wants everyone to believe."

"You're crazy." Grace's phone dinged to alert her she'd received a new email. "Doctor Fluke replied. It says he's willing to discuss his findings face to face at Orient Point County Park. He says it's adjacent to the ferry terminal."

"That's on the North Fork of Long Island. It's at least an hour away."

She did a quick search for the park and sucked in a breath. *Bingo! Another clue.* "You're not going to believe this. Orient Point has the only ferry to Plum Island in New York. He's a—"

"—scientist. Which means there's a very high probability he works at the Animal Research Center." Henry laughed and slapped the steering wheel. "I'm turning around."

She changed the destination address in the GPS app and replied to Dr. Fluke. "This could be our big break."

"We should ask him for a tour of the facility." His stomach growled as if to agree.

"It's worth a shot." Grace finally had more hope than at any previous point in their research. Fluke had claimed to have examined and run DNA tests on the creature. He could put an end to their speculation. Surely a fellow scientist would share his research findings?

As predicted, the twins arrived a little over an hour later. Orient Point Park turned out to be the worst rendezvous location in the history of rendezvouses. The holiday weekend had brought hordes of people to the beach. Cars lined both sides of the road and spilled out of the parking lot.

"This stinks. There's no open spots, and Mom is going to kill us if she finds sand on our shoes." Henry's head moved as if it were on a swivel.

Grace pointed to a grassy area. "Looks like overflow parking."

"Yeah, and it's already flowed out onto the road."

Ten minutes later, they still hadn't found a safe place to leave the car.

"Let me out. I'll go meet him. You can catch up once you find a parking place." Grace slung her bag over her shoulder.

"No way. We aren't splitting up."

She rolled her eyes. "I'm meeting a scientist, not breaking into a taxidermy shop. I'll be fine."

Henry stopped the car. "Keep your phone in your hand."

"Will do." She climbed out and made her way across Point Road to the wooded park entrance.

A small man with thick glasses and thinning hair stood at the entrance to a hiking trail. He glanced from his cell phone to his surroundings and back at a rate of once per three seconds.

That has to be him. Grace pasted a smile on her face and waved. "Frank Fluke? I'm Grace."

Eyes darting from side to side, he pressed his index finger to his lips.

They were meeting in broad daylight in a public place, albeit secluded, but still. What had him so nervous? For a split second, she debated returning to the car.

He nodded toward the trailhead and started walking.

Grace worried she'd spook the guy if he saw her make a call, so she dialed

Henry's number and slid her phone into her pocket. Trying not to move her mouth, she said, "I'm going into the first trailhead. Stay on the line, but be quiet."

He replied, but it came out like an unhappy version of Charlie Brown's parents' *wah-wah...wah-wah-wah.*

"Pssst. Over here."

She fought hard not to roll her eyes and turned toward the voice. The man had a Ph.D., but he was behaving like a double agent in a B-rated spy movie.

He popped his head out from behind a tree. "Did anyone follow you?"

"No." The closer she came, the more he freaked her out. *This is a bad idea.*

"Good. Good." The man seemed to be on the verge of a heart attack. Sweat dotted his forehead and upper lip, red cheeks were the only color in his otherwise pallid complexion, and his hands shook more than the leaves above them. "We don't have much time."

Grace got straight to the point. "Did you examine the Montauk Monster?"

She wouldn't have thought it possible, but he paled even more.

"Before I answer..." He pulled a crumpled piece of paper and pen from his pocket. "Sign this."

She skimmed the document. "A non-disclosure agreement?"

"Sign it, or I walk away."

It was her turn to tremble. Grace couldn't imagine what would drive a scientist to behave in such a way and frankly feared learning the answer. Kneeling, she scribbled her name. Not that she planned to rat him out to the world, but the document was worthless. She was a minor. It would never stand up in court. It helped to have a father who was a lawyer and loved talking about his work.

Dr. Fluke folded the NDA and shoved it in his pocket. "I was paid to release a statement."

Grace hoped Henry could hear the conversation, because she finally understood Fluke's paranoia. Every snapping twig or rustling branch made her want to run. "But you didn't examine it, did you?"

"I did not."

"Who paid you to lie?"

"You don't need to know that. My employer wanted to put an end to the rumors."

Holy smokes! Her heart battered against her sternum. "Rumors that the creature had escaped the Animal Disease Center?"

He nodded and took a step closer. "You need to stay away from this. It's dangerous."

She had no reply other than a gasp. *The woman who called Henry had said the same thing.* "Are you afraid the government will hurt me if I continue?"

"The government wants the money. Developers want the land. Environmentalists want to protect the plants and animals. It's only a matter of time before someone else gets hurt." He turned to go.

"Wait, who was hurt?" Grace followed, but the man quickened his pace. She could shout or tackle him, but not without drawing attention—something she didn't want to do.

Her phone buzzed in her pocket, and her heart palpitated.

"Hello?"

"Are you okay? Are you finished?" Henry sounded as frantic as she felt.

"How much did you hear?" Her knees felt as if they'd lost their connective tissue.

"Just the first few minutes. I had a call from the Rheinstein Estate Park blogger. He's contacted the couple who saw the creature Friday night. We're going to join them on a stakeout tonight."

"Where are you? I want to get out of here. Now."

"Still looking for a parking spot."

Two men in dark matching outfits walked toward her. Between their all-business expressions and gloved hands, they looked as if they'd graduated from knee-breakers' boot camp.

"I think I'm in trouble." Adrenaline pumping, she veered off the trail.

"Are you there? Grace? Hello?" Henry's voice rose. "Answer me."

She ran.

CHAPTER EIGHT

Henry made it to the trailhead in a matter of seconds. Throat tight, chest heaving, he came to a dead stop at the sight of two men standing over Grace. The girl sat on the ground with her knees pulled to her chest. Judging by the way her shoulders shook, she was crying.

She must have twisted an ankle. It was the only plausible explanation he could come up with. "Are you injured?"

She snapped her head in his direction and gave him a watery smile. "Only my pride."

One of the men turned toward him. "You must be Henry."

"I am." He looked from the park ranger to his sister. "What happened?"

"I almost stepped on a snake and freaked out."

"She bolted into the forest like the devil was on her tail." The ranger's southern accent seemed woefully out of place.

"It was probably more afraid of you than you were of it." Henry grinned and played along, although he knew she'd lied. One, there were no poisonous snakes on Long Island. They'd looked it up before they'd arrived. Two, Grace would never freak out about a snake. Their father, on the other hand, would scream like a little girl and head for higher ground.

"We didn't mean to scare her. We thought she ran when she saw us and pursued." The other ranger spoke with a thick Bronx accent. "Occasionally, we find kids using drugs out here."

"May I go now?" She glanced at the men.

The southern gentleman offered his hand and helped her to her feet. "We had you sit because you were upset. You were free to go at any time, miss."

"Thanks." Grace speed-walked to Henry and grabbed his hand. "I want to go home. Now."

He nodded to the men and guided his sister to the park entrance. "What really happened?"

"I caught Dr. Fluke's paranoia." She sighed and wiped her face. "I saw two men in dark clothing coming toward me and thought they were there for me. I ran. They followed, which only made it worse."

"I bet." He didn't mean to laugh, he wasn't that big of a jerk, but the mental images proved too much.

"It wasn't funny." Grace pinched the back of his arm. Hard.

"I know. I know. But you have to admit, it is a little." He pulled her in for a hug. "Do you really want to go back to Stony Brook?"

"No. I want to solve this case." She broke the embrace. "Where's the car?"

"Over here." The car was angled behind an end spot, blocking two other cars in, but the owners had not returned, and the rangers had been with Grace and not on parking patrol. They quickly jumped in and drove off.

On the way to Rheinstein Estate Park, Grace filled him in on her bizarre conversation with the scientist.

"No wonder you assumed the worst when you saw the rangers." Henry wanted to hug her again, but he was driving, and their mother would kill him if he caused an accident.

"I always thought they wore khaki." She turned to face him. "I'm not sure what to make of Dr. Fluke. He believed he was in danger."

"Or he's lost it after spending too much time on Plum Island." He laughed, but it sounded hollow. "I can't believe he had you sign a non-disclosure agreement. He must not have realized you were a minor."

"I had the exact same thought when I signed it." She grinned. "It's scary how much we think alike."

"Are you up for the stakeout? I don't think we'll find the creature, but I'd like to interview the couple."

"As long as we make curfew, I'm game. Tell me more about this blogger." Grace pulled her notebook from her bag.

"Not much to tell. His name is Danny Darnell. He's a local, and he wrote quite a bit about the original sighting."

"And the couple who saw the monster are meeting us there?"

"Yep. Evidently, their friends and family are giving them some grief. They're on a mission to prove they aren't nuts."

"That must be how Zion felt. I can't imagine." Her voice trembled.

"I'm worried about you." He squeezed her hand, something he hadn't done in quite some time. Sure, they poked and shoved and pinched when goofing around, but tender sibling moments were few and far between.

She returned the squeeze. "I'm good. I promise."

"All right, then. As long as we're getting mushy, I love you, Gracie."

"Love you, too." She turned her attention back to her notes.

"We have a little time. Mind if we get some dinner?"

Grace tapped her pen on the paper. "I was wondering how long it would take you to bring up food."

Danny Darnell looked exactly the way Henry had envisioned him. Six feet, messy hair, glasses, a little extra weight around the middle, and a sense of humor that drew people to him. They'd hit it off with a series of one-liners that had Grace groaning.

"I hear the Improv offers comedy classes. Maybe you two can get a BOGO?" she quipped, relaxing as the day's events faded with the daylight.

"Hey, we can refine our comedic geniuses, but you can't buy a sense of humor." Henry motioned for Danny to pass him on the path leading from the cliff to the water.

Grace, who was sandwiched between them, stopped and sucked in a breath. "It's beautiful."

"Wait until you see the hoodoos." Danny flashed her a smile.

"The what?" She sounded intrigued. Then again, it wasn't often that either of the twins heard a new word.

"Erosion carvings in the face of the cliffs. They remind me of something you'd see out west in Utah."

"I can't wait." The girl practically bounced on the balls of her feet.

A weight lifted from Henry's shoulders at seeing his sister acting like her normal self. *She's really okay.*

"I see them." Danny bounded down the last few yards of the incline and joined a couple on the beach.

Hanging back, Henry lowered his voice. "We stay together. No splitting up."

"Agreed. And we keep an eye on the time."

"Yeah, I don't want to risk another day locked in an empty classroom."

Danny smiled as they approached. "Henry, Grace, meet Jack and Samantha."

The dark-haired couple looked a few years older than the twins. Both wore shorts and t-shirts and sported deep tans. Unlike Henry and Grace's naturally darker skin, they had freckled, sunburned glows.

"Nice to meet you both." Jack shook their hands. "I'm glad to have a couple extra sets of eyes. That *thing* moved wicked-fast."

"I suggest we keep away from the water." Samantha shrugged, looking excited and nervous at the same time.

Henry noted the bandage on her leg. For some reason, seeing the white gauze made his shoulder ache. He rolled his head from side to side to relieve the growing tension.

"Can you describe it?" Grace glanced at them.

Jack held his hand three feet from the sand. "It's about this tall. The size of a spaniel, but huskier. More like an English Bulldog. It had a beak, and its eyes glowed red."

Samantha smirked. "Yeah, that sounds about right."

Henry didn't have much experience with dating, but these two seemed as mismatched as a couple could get. "Glowing eyes? Was it a reflection from a flashlight?"

"They glow-glowed like lightbulbs or demon eyes." Jack shrugged. "It couldn't have been mechanical. It crawled out of the ocean."

The twins exchanged looks.

Danny nodded toward the setting sun. "I'm thinking we split up into two groups to cover more ground. One person in each group should have a cell phone ready to record any sightings. Since I'm the fifth wheel, I'll be the go-between."

Jack rubbed his hands together. "I like it. We need a way to alert the other group if we see something."

Grace said, "There are a lot of rocks. We should probably use our flashlight apps. We could signal by waving them overhead."

An ear-piercing whistle tore through the roar of the surf.

Everyone turned to Samantha.

"I coach cheerleading at the local high school. I have an extra for the second group." She pulled one arm across her body and stretched. "We're going to catch the monster and go freaking *viral*.

Henry doubted the sound would carry any farther than a human scream, but the whistle would save someone's vocal cords. "I'll be the whistle-blower."

"Hey, that's my job." Danny gave him a mock glare.

Samantha wasn't entertained. "On that note, we should split up. Jack and I will start. Wait about five minutes, then follow us."

Grace shifted her weight from one foot to the other and glanced around.

Henry couldn't blame her for being anxious, not after the events of the last two days. "Let's get some photos of the hoodoos before we lose the light."

"Great idea. Follow me." Danny led them east. "By the way, I searched through my notes for the names of those bozos out on Shelter Island."

Henry hadn't heard anyone refer to another human as a bozo since he'd last visited his grandfather in Florida. "Did you find anything?"

He shook his head. "Nope. No mention of Lancaster or Miller in my notes. I checked my journals and my hard drives. I hate to say it, but this isn't going anywhere. Jack and Sam are looking for their fifteen minutes of fame. They probably made it all up."

Grace caught sight of one of the rock formations and darted ahead.

"Maybe, but I intend to finish my research." Henry ran his hand over the back of his neck. "Does Prescott ring a bell?" He used his phone to take a picture of the formation.

"No. I'll...I'll check my notes and get back to you if I find anything." He pointed to Jack and Samantha. "They're pretty far off. We should start monster-hunting."

The trio walked along the water's edge. Despite the dying light, beachgoers lingered on the sand, and a few people remained in the water. Not the smartest move; many species of sharks came closer to shore at dusk to feed.

They spent the first pass of their stretch of shoreline discussing everything from climate change to superheroes. While they hadn't spotted a beaked creature with red eyes, they had decided that Batman was the baddest of the good guys.

On the second pass, Danny left them to join the couple, and Henry's stomach began to growl.

On the third pass, Grace began to growl. "It's too dark to see past the flashlight. This is a waste of time. We have all the information we're going to get from Jack and Samantha."

"I agree. It's unlikely we'll find any clues here, but it was fun." He nudged her shoulder.

"Until it wasn't." Grace signaled to the others.

Farther down the beach, someone responded with an arc of light, a scream, and the same ear-piercing whistle as earlier in the evening.

Squinting, Henry tried to make sense of what was happening. The illuminated cell phone was bouncing like a sing-a-long ball. The whistle went off in a series of short bursts, and it appeared Danny and the couple were heading toward them.

But there was something else.

Something glowing red and moving fast.

"Is that..." Grace shouted over the rolling surf.

Henry took three long strides toward the strange object, motioning at Grace to start the video.

"Wait." Grace grabbed his arm. "Don't spook it. We'll never find it if it crosses the bluff."

Right. Makes sense. He shifted his weight from side to side. "What do we do besides wait for it to attack us?"

She tugged him to the sand. "Lay low until we can get a better idea of what we're dealing with."

Crouching, Henry watched in horror as the creature barreled in their direction. The closer it came, the more distinct the twin dots of glowing red light became. His mouth went dry. "What if it attacks? Who knows what sort of diseases that thing is carrying?"

Grace gasped. "The eyes...they're not bobbing."

"What?" He whipped his head in her direction but snapped it back to the creature just as fast.

"It's moving at a good clip, but its head is stationary like a cheetah." She readied her phone. "I'm going to wait until the last second, so the video light doesn't alert it to our location."

"Cheetahs are deadly."

"I said, *like* a cheetah."

Henry's heart beat fast enough to burst the blood vessels in his brain. Poised like a sprinter waiting for the starting gun, he dug his fingers into the sand. "Now, Grace!"

The cell phone illuminated the darkened beach.

Beaked snout and mottled fur and glowing eyes. The creature opened its mouth, hissed, and headed for the vegetation.

"Are you seeing this?" Grace shouted.

Henry bolted after it with his twin on his heels. The creature darted left, then right, and back again, more like it was trying to escape the light than the humans pursuing it.

"I lost it. Do you see it?" she called from in front of him.

How did she get ahead of me? Henry glanced around, trying to orient himself.

Red eyes blared to life as if the thing had laid in wait for the right moment to strike. It made a shrieking sound and charged Grace.

To her credit, she didn't scream, nor did she take the camera off the creature.

"Run!" He sprinted after the creature. "Circle back toward me!"

As far as he knew, animals, even mutant ones, didn't speak English, but this one seemed to understand him. Running in an arc, it managed to keep itself between him and Grace. He'd read about wolf packs performing similar maneuvers, but the creature was alone. *Please be alone.*

"Good job! Keep it between you." Jack's voice had risen several octaves. The man was freaked out, but he joined Henry anyway and stood at his side.

"I'm not doing anything. *It* is!" He had turned one hundred and eighty degrees, and still the creature circled. "Grace, stop running."

She stopped, and so did the creature.

Danny came out of nowhere and inserted himself between the beast and the girl. "That thing doesn't move like any animal I've ever seen. I say we let it go. Someone's going to get hurt."

"No way. Fan out." Arms wide, Jack lunged to the left several times.

In any other circumstance, Henry would have laughed. As it was, he fought the urge to high tail it back to the car.

Her eyes focused on the creature, Grace eased from behind Danny.

They had the thing surrounded.

"Move forward. Nice and slow," Jack said.

A cornered animal should have looked around, taken stock of its enemies, searched for an escape route, or attacked. This one seemed frozen in place.

"What's it doing?" Danny sounded as if he'd come out of his skin. "I don't like this. We should run."

"Keep moving forward." Jack took a couple of steps closer to the creature.

Henry widened his stance. Sooner or later it would attack, and he'd be ready.

Grace swept the beam of light over the sand. "Um, guys. There aren't any animal tracks."

The creature screeched and surged forward.

CHAPTER NINE

Grace dodged to the side, catching her foot and taking a dive.

She hit the sand face down. Gasping for breath, she pressed her hand to her solar plexus. Her chest burned, her lungs felt squeezed, and spots danced in her peripheral vision.

A woman screamed, high and loud and steady like a human air horn.

"Sam!" A man, probably Jack, called into the darkness. "Are you hurt?"

Grace doubted the other woman could hear him over her hysteria. "Henry?"

"Stay put. I'm okay." He flashed his cell on the couple. "Did it attack you?"

"She'll be okay," Jack called over Samantha's wailing.

Grace hadn't realized Danny was close until he squatted beside her. Somehow, having another human being within arm's reach made her feel safer. Safe enough for her emotions to push through the surge of adrenaline. Tears stung her eyes, but she blinked them away. Unfortunately, she couldn't do the same to her racing pulse or trembling hands.

"Are you all right?" The dry, heavy sand squeaked beneath Danny's feet.

"Will be. Where is it?" She didn't dare raise her head to look.

"Don't know, but that thing's dangerous. I think it's time to let our investigations go."

Grace agreed to a point, but she found his behavior odd. Danny had covered the first Montauk Monster sighting. *Why isn't he more excited to have seen it?*

To her left, Jack murmured, and Samantha cried. Otherwise, the beach had grown quiet.

"It's long gone. No way is it coming back." Danny spoke as if to convince himself. "We should *all* leave."

Henry made a sound that could only be described as a yelp. "Dang rocks."

"Use the light on your phone." She pushed herself upright.

He cried out again, this time higher and louder.

Danny shot into action. The man was on his feet and moving quicker than Grace would have thought possible. "Is it back?"

"Yeah, you could say that." Henry's tone made the hair on the back of her neck stand on end. "But it seems to have lost its mojo. It looks dead."

The long chain of curse words Danny uttered didn't help matters.

"What's wrong?" She drew a breath. Bad idea. The coughing started and didn't stop until she expelled gobs of sand and mucus.

"I'm okay, but you don't sound good." He seemed to be avoiding her question.

"No biggie. I puked sand."

Danny said, "We should take some pics and leave it. I don't want to be anywhere near the media circus this thing will bring."

"We should call the police." Samantha choked back a sob.

"No. They'll take it away. We need to examine it first," Henry said.

"We should leave it and go." This from Danny, who refused to let go of his singular focus.

The argument continued, with no hope of resolution.

Jack put an end to the debate. "The police are on the way."

"We have to hurry." Henry finally turned on his phone's flashlight.

The blinding beam illuminated a lump of sandy fur and flesh. He toed it once, twice, three times, and knelt beside it.

"It's not real, is it?" Grace edged closer.

"What do you mean?" Jack stood several yards from the creature as if afraid it would awaken and slaughter them all.

Henry leaned over the thing. "I'm not sure. Give me a minute."

"That's why you said there were no animal tracks?" Danny spoke in a low voice, though there was no point. No one was listening.

"I suspected. I could clearly make out human footprints, but there were two ruts where I estimated the creature had passed."

"I'm telling you, it's real." Jack said, "There have to be tracks. It's a moonless night. You probably looked in the wrong place."

"Give me a break." Samantha's voice sounded like she'd smirked, rolled her eyes, and thrown up her hands. "It's sand. Sand is bumpy. Of course, you can't see tracks."

"Maybe." She didn't have the energy to explain they'd run in a semicircle, so eventually, she would have crossed the path. "It didn't move like an animal. It only turned its head when it was sitting still."

"She's right. It was running straight for me, but the eyes didn't bob." Henry grunted, and a cracking sound followed. "This is definitely artificial, and a very impressive creation, at that."

"No freaking way." Jack elbowed his way forward and inspected the creature. "It can't be. It was in the water."

"The Navy has used remote-controlled mines and vehicles for decades, and NASA has used similar technology to collect rock samples from the moon." Henry paused as if thinking. "I bet the university has a robotics team."

Jack smirked. "I'm sure they do, but I doubt they're building monsters to terrorize beachgoers."

Henry prodded the belly area. "Check this out. It has the same configuration as those robot dogs they sell at the mall, but it's much more sophisticated. This is cutting-edge robotics."

"You have got to be kidding." Samantha joined the group. "I was attacked by a fake monster?"

Ignoring the now-bickering couple, Grace knelt and pushed aside the outer casing. "This reminds me of the prosthetic limb prototypes we saw at Walter Reed."

Danny glanced at them. "It's probably some student's idea of a prank. I'll blog about it tomorrow and end the mystery once and for all."

Jack interrupted the party. "If it's a robot, who has the remote control?"

The twins locked eyes. They'd been so distracted with the technology, they'd missed the fact someone had tried to scare, if not hurt, them.

"There are cameras in its eye sockets." Henry pried open the mouth and exhaled through gritted teeth. "Ouch. Sharp protrusions beneath the skin to inflict damage by bumping someone. It's also wired to bite. Whoever made this meant business."

Grace had no concept of how much time had passed since the creature had attacked. Nor did she know the area well enough to anticipate East Hampton PD's response window, but time was running out. "What did you say to the emergency dispatchers?"

Jack shrugged. "They laughed when I called the first time. Rather than mentioning the Montauk Monster, I told them an animal was attacking tourists on the beach."

Danny swore under his breath. "We should get it out of here while we have the chance."

Flashing lights on the cliffs cut the conversation short.

"Looks like the cavalry has arrived." Samantha blew the whistle again.

"Stop that." Grace's eardrums ached. She had a theory to run past Henry, but she didn't want to share it in front of the others.

"Uh-uh. No way. We're turning it over to the police. I want to find out who did this so I can sue the pants off them."

"Leave it. I've seen enough." Henry yanked something out of the creature and shoved it in his pocket. "If we stay, there could be a great number of unintended and unpleasant consequences."

She'd thought the same thing, but rather than complaining, she'd devised a solution. "That's a good thing."

"I fail to see how—"

"Not even Mom can argue with the police." Grace surprised herself with the deviousness of her plan. "Follow my lead."

"Wait. Tell me what you're going to do."

She ignored him and called their mother's cell.

Faith picked up on the second ring. "Hi, Grace. Is everything all right?"

"We're at the beach. Don't freak out, but we found the Montauk Monster. It's robotic and designed to hurt people."

"What! Are you injured?" Faith Warner never yelled. She didn't have to. Her death-stares were legendary. "Tell me exactly where you are. Dad and I are on the way."

Uh-oh. I shouldn't have mentioned it was quasi-weaponized. She hadn't planned for *that* reaction. "There's no need. We're fine. Besides, the police are here. I doubt they're letting anyone into the area."

"I don't like this. Not at all. This senior project has been nothing but trouble, and you've only just begun."

"This was a random wrong-place-wrong-time situation. There's no way whoever made this knew we'd be here tonight." Grace gave her brother a wide-eyed stare.

Henry replied with an I told-you-so look, although he didn't say a thing.

"We will discuss this when you get home." The note of finality in her mother's voice worried her.

"We're going to be late. We have to give our statements to the police, and it's a long drive back."

"One moment." Faith's muffled voice filled the line. When she came back on, she seemed marginally calmer. "Drive safe."

"We will." Grace disconnected the call.

"Well?" Henry stared.

"She said to drive safe."

He quirked a brow. "No 'come straight home or have one of the nice police officers contact me?'"

She shook her head.

"You're a miracle worker." He ran both hands over his head for the hundredth time that day. If they didn't solve the case soon, he'd likely go bald. "What's the plan?"

"We're going to speak to Lance Lancaster."

This time Henry dragged his hands down his face. "Why him?"

"Because that creature's a work of art." She opened the video she'd shot on the beach. "Let's hope I managed to get a decent shot of it."

The group gathered around her phone and watched. Most of the video was sand and darkness, but she'd captured several seconds of the mangy beak-nosed robot.

Grace hit pause and zoomed in on its feet. "The way it moves... It really is impressive."

Henry took the phone. "It is."

Danny took a turn examining the still frame. "I'm coming with you two. This is too big to miss. My audience will eat this up."

Henry lowered his voice. "Sure, but you have to get us out of here now."

Danny turned to the couple. "Can you guys handle the police? I'm putting my money on these two to find out who to sue."

Samantha's eyes lit with dollar signs. "Only if you feature us as the people who stopped its rampage."

"Deal."

Henry and Grace nodded.

A half-hour later, Danny dropped the twins off in front of Lancaster's Gallery. They'd agreed he'd drive to the back of the building and serve as the criminal equivalent to a pinch hitter. In other words, he'd mitigate the unexpected risk by creating a distraction, driving a getaway truck, or calling for backup—whatever they needed.

Henry met her gaze. "Any weirdness, and we run. We don't know if Lancaster was the one controlling the creature."

"Agreed, but it's unlikely he was at the beach. He answered the store phone, remember?"

"You're good at this detective thing." He cracked a grin.

"So are you. Did you dim the light and silence the phone?"

"Yep."

"Call Danny."

He dialed the number. "We're going in."

"Ten-four. Delta Dawn is in position," Danny's disembodied voice crackled through the phone.

Henry set the cell to mute and opened his door. "Roger that. Hotel and Golf going dark. Over and out."

Grace fought the urge to groan and followed him to the glass door.

Lancaster glanced up from his computer. He took one look at them and appeared to mutter something beneath his breath.

She chewed her lip and waved.

"He doesn't look happy to see us." Henry pointed to the lock.

Lance Lancaster strode to the door and shouted through the glass. "Let me guess, you're the ones who called and hung up on me?"

"Sorry, but we really need to speak to you." Henry gave him a wide-eyed-little-boy look.

They'd debated how to handle this moment on the drive over, but rather than playing the scared high schoolers they'd agreed upon, Grace went with brutal honesty. "The police have a robotic replica of the Montauk Monster."

Henry sighed.

Lancaster, on the other hand, laughed. "What does that have to do with me?"

"Maybe nothing, but the creature...it was a masterpiece." She gave a genuine smile. "I immediately thought of your work and wondered if someone had stolen your sculpture."

He unlocked the door, then turned and walked back to his desk.

Henry hesitated. "Do we follow him?"

"Yes." She pressed her lips together and entered the gallery.

"You're right, my sculpture was stolen, but after the way I was treated the first time, I didn't bother to report the second break-in." Lancaster continued to type on his laptop. "Was that the East Hampton Police Department or the Sheriff's Office?"

It took her a minute to understand the question. "East Hampton."

He nodded. "Perfect. I'm writing an email to a friend of mine over there. If you two connected the sculpture to me, I'm sure the professionals will, too."

"Happy we could help." She smiled, but her stomach churned. The workmanship on the robot was amazing—too amazing for someone to have implanted the technology into an existing sculpture, which changed the dynamic from the way Lancaster was trying to shape the impression.

"Do you have any idea who took it?" Henry leaned his hip against a display case.

Lancaster motioned to him. "I just cleaned that, and yes, as a matter of fact, I do. The same individual who took the actual creature."

Grace's mouth fell open. "Are you sure? We saw it in action. The technology reminded me of the Defense Advanced Research Projects Agency prosthetic limbs."

He eyed her as if seeing her for the first time. "Color me impressed you know about DARPA, but if you'd done your homework, you would have connected the dots."

Henry folded his arms. "Why don't you connect them for us?"

"Our Shinnecock warrior is a genius."

She glanced at Henry, who seemed as surprised as she was.

Lancaster stood. "Now, if there's nothing else you wish me to explain to you, I have work to do."

Grace caught sight of the artist's sandy shoes and turned for the door. "Thanks. There's nothing else. After you helped us the other day, we thought we should warn you about the robot."

Normally, the twins could practically read each other's minds. In reality, it had nothing to do with extra-sensory perception. Grace believed the ability stemmed from understanding each other's nonverbal cues. However, Henry had completely misinterpreted her body language.

"Did you make the first creature too?" He folded his arms.

"I most certainly did not." The man's voice deepened.

She tugged his arm. "Where are your manners? Come on. We've bothered Mr. Lancaster enough."

Her brother didn't move. In fact, he stood straighter and planted his feet farther apart—the real-life equivalent of digging in his heels. "How could someone dismantle your creation, shove a robot in it, and put it back together? There were no rough seams. No zippers or glue."

Grace pinched the back of his arm and didn't let go until he looked at her. She widened her eyes and said, "We. Have. A. Curfew."

Lancaster moved behind the counter Henry had leaned on and reached down. In the movies, store owners kept shotguns under counters. She didn't want to stick around and find out if they did that sort of thing in the Hamptons.

"You're right. Let's go." Henry snapped out of his bad-cop routine and headed for the door.

Grace pushed on the bar, but nothing happened. She stared at the sign that clearly read Push and tried again. *He's locked us in.*

"On second thought. I think I'll keep you here until the police arrive." He folded his arms.

Her throat tightened. "But we haven't done anything wrong."

"Not yet." He nodded toward the back of the gallery. "Let's go."

Grace and Henry didn't budge.

Lancaster reached beneath the counter again. This time he pulled out a shotgun. "I won't ask again."

CHAPTER TEN

"Is that a shotgun?" Henry carefully articulated every syllable while speaking loud enough for Danny to hear.

"It's not a stage prop." Lancaster nodded to the back of the gallery. "Move it."

"The police will sort this out." Henry motioned for Grace to go first.

She rolled her lips in and shook her head. "I'm not going anywhere."

She's right. We should stay near the windows. Better yet, we should throw something through them and get the heck out of here. Before Henry could do anything useful, Lancaster racked the shotgun.

"Why are you doing this?" Although she kept her head high, Grace's voice quivered.

"You were repeatedly warned to stop snooping around, but you couldn't let it go." The artist ground his teeth. "There's more at stake here than a high school research project."

Heart in his throat, Henry stepped in front of his sister. If the guy planned to kill them, he'd at least give Grace a chance. Or maybe he was a coward and wanted to die first. Either way, he blocked the other man's view of her. "Like Plum Island?"

Lancaster dipped his chin in acknowledgment. "Among other things, yes. Now, get moving."

"Not until you call 911." Grace sidestepped her brother.

Where the heck is Danny? "We don't want the government to sell the island any more than you do. Let us go. We'll drop our investigation, and we won't say a thing."

"Backroom. Now." He moved from behind the counter.

Pivoting with every step, Henry kept his eye on the other man and Grace behind him. "So you can shoot us without making a mess in your gallery? I don't think so."

Lancaster lunged forward, spun the shotgun, and slammed the stock into Henry's stomach.

Henry doubled over, wheezing. The blow hadn't surprised him, but the way the artist handled the gun had.

"Henry!" Grace blurted and caught her brother to keep him from falling to the floor.

Gasping, he tugged her closer. He had a handful of seconds at most before Lancaster grew tired of waiting for him to catch his breath. Henry twisted his upper body and fumbled with his cell phone. As he'd feared, his connection with Danny had failed.

"Stop stalling." This from Lancaster, who sounded closer than he should have.

Henry kept his hand in his pocket and pressed what he hoped was redial. 911 would have been infinitely better, but beggars and choosers and all that.

Music came from the back of the gallery, and not just any music, a grungy guitar riff from the nineties—Danny's ringtone.

"Ah yes, that reminds me. Put your cell phones on the counter." Lance grabbed Grace and jerked her forward. "You might as well come out. I could use some assistance."

Danny, the traitor, stepped around a hideous sculpture of a pirate merman sitting on a cresting wave. He took one look at the situation in the gallery and froze. "Whoa. You never said anything about guns."

Grace went slack-jawed, blinked, and did the last thing in the world Henry would expect his sister to do—she *fainted*.

Henry took a step in her direction, but Lancaster pointed the barrel at his chest. Until the previous couple days, he'd never experienced mortal peril. He was instantly struck by remorse at his choice for a senior project, but only because of putting his sister at risk. If they didn't find the truth, then it would remain hidden, and others would get hurt, like Zion and his family. Henry clenched his teeth and glared.

All he had to do was think. He needed to find Lancaster's weakness, or a devise a distraction. *Why do people faint? Shock. Illness. Low blood sugar.* "She's diabetic. She needs an injection."

The men exchanged looks.

Danny shrugged.

Think, Henry, think. "Her medication is in the car."

"Nice try." Lancaster smirked. "Danny, take the girl to the storeroom."

The blogger went pale. "No. Uh-uh. I'm out. I'm not going to be an accessory to child murder."

Lancaster nudged Grace's still form with the tip of his boat shoe. "No one said anything about murder, you idiot. I need to contain the situation so I can contact Prez."

Henry exhaled as if struck by an invisible fist. *Prez? Preston Prescott?*

Danny continued to shake his head.

They're distracting each other. This is my chance. To do what? He couldn't make a break for it with Grace unconscious on the floor, nor could he leave her behind. Then it hit him. Lance hadn't actually taken his phone. Henry darted behind a statue of a giant butterfly, pulled his cell from his pocket, and attempted to dial. If his hands hadn't been shaking, he might have pulled it off.

"Stop!" The artist aimed but hesitated. "I'll shoot your sister."

Chaos ensued.

Grace performed some sort of ninja move. One minute she was on the ground out cold, the next she flipped around, sprang to her feet, and landed a size-nine Converse sneaker in Lancaster's groin.

The man howled high and loud until the shotgun blast drowned it out. The thunder reverberated through the store.

Plaster rained down from the ceiling where the blast had gone. Grace ran for the door, slammed into it because it was still locked, and bolted to the side. In his haste to join her, Henry knocked the butterfly from its stand.

Lancaster shouted something, but Henry's hearing hadn't recovered.

Danny seemed to have had a change of heart on the whole child-murderer thing. He dove for the discarded shotgun.

"Grace!" He grabbed his sister's arm and jerked her behind a partition holding several paintings.

Covered in debris, wide-eyed, and open-mouthed, she threw her arms around him. Her lips moved. She was speaking and pointing, but he couldn't hear her over the constant ringing in his ears.

Bright light filled the front windows of the gallery. Now deaf and blind, Henry squinted at the door. A man stood in the entry with a set of keys in his hand.

Grace tugged at his shoulder. His bad shoulder. Pain raced up his neck and down his arm, but it helped to clear his head.

He stared, unable to make sense of what he saw. A pickup sat with its grille inches from the gallery's front window. Henry couldn't identify the man over the glare of the headlights, but his sister continued to point and shout. The door opened, and the Shinnecock taxidermist stepped in. He jerked Grace to him and clamped a hand over her mouth.

"Let her go!" Henry took a step forward but stopped short when the taxidermist raised a pistol.

Lancaster shouted from somewhere in the gallery, "What are you doing?"

"Taking these two to Prez," the native replied.

"How did he know they were here?"

Henry picked up on two things. The doubt in the artist's voice, and a flash of fear in the taxidermist's eyes. Dissension in the ranks did not bode well for the twins. They needed to get far away from these three and their guns.

"I followed them from the beach and checked in when I heard the gunshot. What are you, stupid? This is East Hampton. How long before the police arrive?"

Lancaster apparently bought the guy's story. "Take them. I'll handle this."

The man whispered something to Grace.

She went wide-eyed but nodded.

"Let's go." He motioned to Henry.

His feet and his brain seemed to have lost communication. The artist was a threat, but he had nothing on the Shinnecock. "Okay, but don't hurt my sister."

He led them outside and opened the passenger's side door. "Get in."

Henry hesitated. "Grace first."

"I'll put her in on my side. Insurance, in case you try something stupid."

He climbed in and watched as the man walked Grace to the other side of the vehicle.

Tears streaming down her face, Grace slid across the bench seat and wrapped her arms around Henry

The taxidermist started the truck and backed out. "Are you two okay?"

What kind of question is that for someone taking us to our deaths?

"Look, I just saved you from... I'm one of the good guys." He glanced from the road to them and back as he accelerated away from the gallery.

Grace whispered, "I'm not hurt."

Henry took a mental inventory of his aches and pains. Other than the surfing injury, he felt great. Too great. Once the adrenaline spike wore off, he'd crash and burn. "I'm fine, but I'd like some answers."

"How about a name? I'm Zeek, and you two are the trouble twins. Henry and Grace, right?" He glanced in the rearview mirror, checked the surviving side mirror, the road, and the rearview again.

"Yes." Grace grabbed Henry's hand and didn't let go. "I don't understand what's going on. Are you working with Lancaster?"

"Yes and no." His frown deepened the lines around his eyes. "I broke ties with them years ago, but they dragged me back in. We have a history. They know things about me and threatened to turn me in if I didn't help them."

It was Henry's turn to frown. He could only imagine the dirt Lancaster had on Zeek: misappropriation, grand theft, murder? "What were you doing at the beach?"

"Operating the creature. It wasn't supposed to go down the way it did. Lancaster screwed up and misidentified the other couple as the two of you." He tensed as a police car passed. Zeek slowed to the speed limit and kept his truck pointed straight ahead.

"That was you?" Grace edged closer to Henry.

"Relax, it was never meant to hurt you. We've been trying to scare you off this 'project' of yours since the day you stumbled onto Marty Miller."

Another piece of the puzzle clicked into place. "That was why Lancaster told us about your father, knowing full well we'd follow up and find you. You left the door unlocked on purpose."

"Correct."

Grace sighed and settled against Henry's side.

Henry had more questions. "Where are you taking us?"

"My father's place. You'll be safe there."

She bolted upright. "We need to go home. Our parents—"

"Not an option." He stopped at a light and tightened his grip on the wheel.

A handful of police cars, sirens wailing and lights flashing, crossed through the intersection in front of them. Zeek leaned closer to the windshield and stared after them. The light turned green, and he hit the gas.

"Look, we appreciate you saving us, but we just want to go home. We're leaving Long Island in a couple days." Henry noted that the door was unlocked, but he didn't have the guts to jump. Nor would he risk injuring his sister. *I should have jumped out and waved down the squad cars. Good going, Henry.*

Zeek met his gaze over Grace's head. "She won't be safe until *I* put an end to this, and I can't do that with you two in the way."

The she in question bristled but remained quiet.

Henry worried they'd gone from one homicidal maniac to another. Henry didn't have any choices left.

"I'll take you to your folks if you promise you'll lay low. No more poking around. Lancaster's small potatoes compared to the others who'll be looking for you."

"We promise. We're staying at a friend of the family's place near Stony Brook U's main campus." He'd had enough guns pointed at him to last two lifetimes. Enough was enough, but they had a problem. A huge, expensive problem. "The BMW's at the beach. We rode with Danny to Lancaster's."

Grace sucked in a breath. "It's not ours. We have to go back."

Zeek looked at the two of them as if they'd spoken in Swahili. "Tell the owner it wouldn't start."

Their parents would flip when they learned they'd hitched a ride instead of calling home. "That won't work."

"It has to." Grace lowered her voice. "Mom might be tough, but she won't shoot us. Priorities, Henry."

"True. Very true."

After another mile or so, the man turned onto a side street marked with a short, squat beige sign. Although it was too dark to read it, Henry recognized the shape. It was the same as the state park they'd visited earlier in the day.

"Where are we going?" Grace leaned forward and squinted.

"My father's place. I need to drop something off before I take you home." He drove past several campsites and parked near a pop-up camper that looked like it'd been through the zombie apocalypse. "Home, sweet home."

The twins exchanged glances and piled out of the truck.

Zeek nodded to his right. "There are bathrooms and showers down that path. You should clean up. The fewer questions you have to answer, the better."

"Thanks. I feel like I've been coated in flour." Grace shook plaster from her hair as if to prove her point.

He held out his hand. "Phones, and I'm going with you."

Henry began to doubt his gut. "Why? I thought you were one of the good guys?"

"Good guy or not, I'm not risking kidnapping charges."

Grace kept her mouth closed and handed over her cell.

Henry tossed his phone into the truck and followed Grace and Zeek to the facilities.

Ten minutes later, they were as clean as they were going to get and ready to go home.

Zeek pulled something wrapped in a tarp from the bed of his truck.

"What's that?" All sorts of images ran through his mind, from a body to a deer to one of Lancaster's ruined sculptures. It turned out he was two-thirds right.

He lifted the material to reveal the beak-nosed robot.

Grace's eyes bugged. "What? How?"

He shrugged. "The young couple you were with got tired of waiting for the police to come down to the beach. They left it unguarded."

"Figures." Henry hadn't considered Samantha or Jack overly intelligent, but leaving the creature on the beach had been downright foolish.

Zeek carried the robot into the camper. He returned a moment later and pulled what looked like a garage door opener from his pocket. It beeped and was answered by a series of three chirps. "Alarm system."

The twins frowned at each other and followed Zeek to the pickup.

"Who created the robot?" Grace asked the question before Henry had the chance.

"I made the machine. Lancaster sculpted the covering. Prez bought a ridiculously expensive battery pack."

Henry gave him a slow nod. "I thought you were a taxidermist?"

"I am now, but I had high hopes of working for DARPA when I was your age."

"What happened?"

"I guess you could say I fell in with the wrong crowd."

"I don't understand." Henry pressed his hand to his pocket. The battery pack he'd ripped from the robot was safe and secure, and hopefully still contained fingerprints.

"I met Lancaster and his friends while I was home on summer break in 2007. They seemed like nice guys. Privileged, but decent. Had I known then..." He cleared his throat. "They were involved with an environmental organization."

"The Save Plum Island Coalition?" Grace's frustration with the situation seemed to have vanished. She turned and gave him her full attention.

"It was called something different then, but yes." Zeek shook his head as if to clear his thoughts. "The next school year, my sister started classes at Stony

Brook. She became involved with the organization. *Too* involved. The term that applies is 'radicalized.'"

Henry grew impatient. Try as he might, he couldn't connect the dots. "Who were the other guys?"

"Martin Miller, Danny Darnell, and Prez. To this day, I don't know the guy's real name."

"Lancaster told Danny he had to call Prez for help dealing with us." Grace's spine stiffened. "Could it be Professor Preston Prescott?"

"Like I said, I don't know his name."

Henry didn't buy it. "How's that possible?"

"We were young and stupid. I stopped hanging out with them after 2008."

He reached for his phone and realized it was somewhere on the seat. "Let me find my cell. I'll show you his picture."

Grace sighed. "What exactly are Lancaster and the others trying to do?"

Zeek shifted like a caged lion. The truck was too small to pace, and he needed to work out his tension. "They've been trying to prevent the sale of Plum Island for years."

"Them, not you?" Grace spoke in a less-than-friendly tone.

"I'd hate to see the island developed, but I don't like their tactics."

Having located his cell, Henry found a recent photo of Preston and held the screen so Zeek could see it while driving.

The truck swerved to the right.

The man cursed. "That's him."

She hung her head. "You were right about him all along."

"I really wish I wasn't." Henry gave her a half-hug. "Prescott is an old college friend of our dad's. Our fifth wheel is on his property."

"That's convenient." Zeek's grin reminded Henry of the big bad wolf right before he ate the grandmother.

He ran through every possible scenario. Did they plan to renew interest in the legend to help bolster the lawsuit against Congress? It seemed almost childish.

Grace cleared her throat. "Lancaster said your father took the original monster from the beach. Is that true?"

"Yes."

"Was it real?"

Zeek chuckled. "It was a real sculpture made out of rubber and molded foam."

Henry's eyes widened. "The same stuff they use on movie sets and for make-up?"

The man nodded.

Grace gave her brother a dirty look and turned the conversation back to the creature. "Did Zion steal it back from Lancaster?"

"No, but rumors spread that he was involved. He never denied it. He was trying to protect my sister and me." Emotion choked his voice.

She swallowed hard. "From what?"

"Zoe was involved in the scheme from the beginning. I didn't know what they were doing at the time, but I knew it was wrong when she started researching media outlets. Too many secrets. I was worried about her."

Another piece of the puzzle fell into place. "She's the one who sent the photographs to the reporters."

He nodded.

Grace lowered her voice. "At the powwow, when I asked Zion about his daughter... Where is she now?"

"She died in a car accident in August of 2008." Zeek squinted as if fighting back his emotions.

"What was she like?"

"Zoe? She loved nature and the ocean. The girl could surf before she could walk." His smile faded as quickly as it'd come. "I've tried to get the details of her death for ten years but have gotten nowhere. The police reports are missing. Someone covered it up."

"That's awful."

Henry's heart ached, but he couldn't help but marvel at his sister. Unless he was mistaken, she'd guessed that Zoe had passed away.

Zeek glanced at them. "It's my technology. It can be traced back to me. We have to stop Prez and Lancaster before..."

"Before Kylie and Kara lose their father to a prison cell or worse." He hadn't meant to speak the words aloud.

Grace shook her head and gave him a Mom-look. "We can go to the police. Lancaster tried to kill us tonight. No one needs to know about the robot. His arrest would put a stop—"

"No. It won't matter. Lancaster's a pawn."

Henry perked up. "We can help. We have access to Stony Brook's library system, and—"

"No! No more snooping. He knows who you are and what you're up to. You two are going to get yourselves killed." Zeek shook his head and turned on the radio. Loud.

Evidently, no more snooping meant question-and-answer time had ended.

CHAPTER ELEVEN

Grace typed Preston Prescott into the search bar. Entry after entry of environmental research articles and professional accolades populated the screen.

"Any luck?" Whispering, Henry glanced from her screen to Zeek and back again.

"Not what we're looking for." She tapped her lips. "You try 'Prez Preston' and I'll see what I can find on the others."

The twins worked in silence for quite a while and found nothing. Grace glanced at the clock on the dashboard. "We have twenty minutes."

"Bingo." Henry glanced at Zeek again, and slumped as if that would provide privacy. He handed her the phone and grinned like the kid who won the golden ticket to the candy factory.

The headline read, *Congressman's son involved in automobile accident on Long Island. One fatality.* It was dated August, 2008.

Grace skimmed the article. Zoe Zion, nineteen, had died at the scene. Unconfirmed sources claimed romantic involvement between Prescott and Zion.

She swallowed the lump of emotion in her throat and typed Zoe Zion Stony Brook into her phone. An image of a smiling brown-skinned girl with dark hair and eyes caught her eye. When Grace clicked the link, a university newspaper article came up, including a photo of Zoe and a blond man with a killer smile.

Leaning closer to Henry, she whispered, "Did you see this?"

"Is that?"

"I think so." She sighed. Marty had his arm slung around Zoe's shoulder. The couple was smiling at each other, their lips only inches apart.

He frowned. "I can't find any listing of a Prescott in Congress. I'm missing something."

Grace fell down the research rabbit hole investigating the environmentalist activities at Stony Brook University and the surrounding areas. It seemed Plum Island wasn't the tip of the iceberg, it was the gigantic part hidden beneath the water. "Almost every environmental initiative from SBU relates directly or indirectly to Plum Island."

Henry made a low humming sound that sent a shiver of fear down her spine. "Congresswoman P. Beckham was up for re-election in 2008. Get this: she's an outspoken critic of the EPA."

"Who?" Grace looked over his shoulder. "Holy smokes. Is that Prescott's mother?"

"Sure is." His thumbs flew over the phone. "What did Dad say the professor's wife's maiden name was?"

"Astor." Her heart raced. They were finally seeing the big picture, but nothing they'd found would implicate the professor in a crime. More troubling for Grace, she wasn't sure she wanted to find the missing link. *This is going to crush Dad.*

Zeek grumbled, "You two can stop trying to whisper. I've heard everything you said. What did I tell you about snooping?"

"We're not home yet. I figured as long as we're with you, we're still involved." Grace smiled.

The man tightened his grip on the wheel.

Henry fist-pumped. "Preston's in-laws were the top bidders on the Plum Island sale."

Zeek whipped his head toward the younger man. "What did you say?"

"Prescott's wife is an Astor. Her family owns one of the corporations trying to buy real estate on Plum Island."

"That SOB." He snickered and slapped the steering wheel. "Kid, you don't know how happy I am to hear that."

Grace rubbed her forehead as she worked through the facts as she understood them and came up with one huge question. "Which side is Prescott on?"

Zeek laughed and looked past Grace to her brother. "You're too young to know this, but a smart man is always on the side of his wife, even if he pretends otherwise."

Henry shrugged. "Preston enjoys his money."

"They all enjoy their money." Zeek turned onto the long drive leading to the mansion.

"Stop here." Grace motioned for Henry to get out. "You don't want him to see you with us."

"The he—" He glanced at them. "*Heck* with that. I'm taking you straight to your parents."

It sounded like a foolish idea, but Grace was relieved. She doubted Prescott would pull anything in front of her father.

Zeek parked behind the fifth wheel and they piled out. It took Grace a half a heartbeat to realize something was awry. A half a heartbeat too long.

Their parent's truck was missing.

Worse still, the Prez was smoking a disgusting cigar beneath the rig's awning.

She wanted to march up to him and punch him in his smug face. "Where are they?"

"They went to find you, of course." He nodded to Zeek. "Nice of you to bring them to me."

"We need to talk." The larger man folded his arms.

"Yes, we do, but not in front of the kiddies." Prescott nodded toward Zeek's vehicle. "You're dismissed."

"I'm not leaving until their parents return."

Who does he think he is? She'd heard enough. "Why are you here?"

"Straight to the point, just like your mother." The professor rested his ankle on his knee. "Relax. If I wanted you dead, you'd be dead."

"Thanks for the consideration for our lives." Henry pointed to the envelope on the table. "What are you doing with my research article?"

Prescott grinned his politician's grin. "Do you know how much money my family donates to Stanford?"

"You mean your wife's family?" Grace gave him her own version of a plastic smile.

He ignored her. "One call from me, and your admissions packet would be rejected. Think about it, Henry. You yourself told me how you'd dreamed of attending your father's alma mater."

"You're trying to bribe me?" Henry patted his pocket as if looking for his phone, but it was in his other hand.

She stepped forward. "Too bad MIT only accepts legacy students on merit. You have nothing to hang over my head."

Prescott nodded toward her brother. "Don't I?"

She sucked in a breath. Until that moment, she would have done anything to convince Henry not to attend college so far away. The idea of separating from him had terrified her, but that was before she'd faced down bad guys, had guns pointed at her, and understood that family was family, no matter what or where they roamed.

Prescott had her, and he knew it. He'd exploited her weakness before she'd realized it was a thing.

"I didn't think so." He stood and tucked the envelope under his arm. "So what's it going to be, kids? You go inside and forget everything you *think* you know about this, or I ruin Henry's future?"

"I'm not going to let you do that to another kid." Zeek positioned himself between the twins and the professor.

Prescott sighed deeply enough to make a southern belle green with envy. "I wanted to do this the easy way. I really did."

Zeek drew a breath and raised his hands.

Grace didn't need to see the gun to know what the professor had done. She grabbed Henry's hand and tugged him toward her.

"Marty, please join us. It seems that Zeek and I are going for a boat ride." Prescott took a step forward, forcing the other man and the twins to take a step back.

Marty Miller, surfer, doctor, and as suspected, Prez's lackey, walked down the steps from the fifth wheel.

The fact that the man had been inside her home made Grace's blood boil. Who else did he have in there going through their things?

"How's the shoulder, kid?" Marty could have modeled his smile in toothpaste commercials. Broad. White. Fake.

Henry glared. "It's healing."

"Glad to hear it." He removed a gun from the back of his waistband and nodded toward the water. "Start walking. No funny business. It'd be a shame if I had to sully the perfect lawn."

She rolled her eyes despite the seriousness of the situation. "Where are you taking him?"

"It doesn't concern you. Now, go inside and get ready for bed. Be sure to brush." Preston smiled.

"You'll have to take us, too." Henry inserted himself between the professor and Marty.

"You're determined to die tonight, aren't you?" Prescott shook his head. "Move."

They marched toward the water like good soldiers—except Grace. She sidestepped her way to the professor's side. Thankfully, he'd holstered his gun. She just had to keep it that way.

Grace had a question. It'd needled her since her meeting with the scientist at Orient Point, and more importantly, she needed to catch him off-guard.

He made a tsking sound. "The company you keep needs improving."

"Obviously." Grace lowered her voice. "I'm pretty sure I have this all sorted out. You're pretending to be an environmentalist but secretly feeding the opposition information and/or sabotaging the cause."

He clenched his jaw but didn't deny it.

"Who does Frank Fluke work for?"

A flash of emotion crossed his expression, and he tried to cover it with a chuckle. "Fluke? Never met the guy, but I've heard the name. He's one of the top scientists at the Animal Research Center."

"Interesting. He didn't mention that when I met with him earlier today." She tapped her lips. "I'll have to check my notes. I wrote them on my phone and emailed them to myself. One can never be too careful."

The professor stumbled over a divot in the yard.

Grace smiled to herself. She started to get inside his head and had made him nervous. Now was the time to push his buttons. "You blackmailed Zeek into creating the robotics for your fake monster. I haven't figured out the specifics, but I have a hunch it has something to do with Zoe's death. Right?"

The professor's eyes widened a fraction of an inch. "Enough talking."

She raised her voice enough for the others to hear her. "For the life of me, I can't understand why *he's* not blackmailing *you*. You were drinking the night Zoe died."

"Enough!"

Zeek roared, and a scuffle broke out between the Shinnecock and Marty. Grace would put her money on Zeek any day of the week, but she didn't trust Prescott to stay out of it.

"You caused the accident, didn't you?"

Prescott shoved her hard enough to throw her off balance, but she'd seen it coming.

It was the break she'd hoped for. Grace grabbed his arm as if to steady herself, but instead, she used his momentum to pull him down. One well-placed punch to the throat left the professor on the ground clutching his neck.

Grace leaned in, snatched the gun from his side, and chucked it into the darkness. For the second time that day, she silently thanked her mother for insisting the twins take self-defense classes.

"Didn't you hear what the girl said?" Zeek shouted. "Prescott was driving the car the night Zoe died. You and I both know how much he had to drink."

Grace blinked not believing her eyes. The larger man had disarmed Marty, but the surfer continued to throw punches.

Her throat tightened. *Where's Marty's gun?*

Henry pulled her away from the fray. "Are you okay? I saw you fall."

"I'm fine. Where's Marty's gun?" She pulled free of her brother.

"Relax. I hid it." He gave her a sheepish grin.

Grace sighed, unable to take her eyes off the fight.

Marty stopped moving and stared. "Zoe was driving."

"You honestly think his parents would have covered it up if a Shinnecock had been behind the wheel?" Zeek stomped over to the professor and hauled him to his feet. "Tell him the truth, or I'll beat it out of you. For my sister."

Prescott coughed out the words, "It was me."

"Tell him why you wanted the robotic monster." Zeek shook him as if to make the words fall out.

"To discredit the organization." The professor hung his head.

Marty took several steps forward, turned back, and ran his hands through his hair. "Years of work to stop the sale, and you'd sabotage it? For what?"

Zeek nodded toward the mansion. "Why do you think? A woman. Money."

Prescott remained quiet.

Henry furrowed his brow. "He's on the board of directors. It'd ruin his reputation."

Grace rested her hand on her brother's good shoulder. "Not if he threw his three oldest friends under the bus."

"What do we do with him now?" Marty sounded breathless. "We can't take him to the police. We have no proof."

"Actually, you do have some potentially incriminating evidence." Henry stepped forward and pulled something from his pocket. "This is the battery pack from the robot. It may have his prints. If not, the purchase can be traced back to Prescott."

Zeek took it and nodded. "It'd mean incriminating myself, but maybe I could strike a deal."

Marty stared at the twins. "What about you two? You have enough dirt to bury us all."

They exchanged looks.

Henry shrugged. "We're leaving soon, and I'd rather our parents not find out about all of this until they read our paper at the end of the school year."

Grace shook her head. Sometimes Henry *did* have more street smarts than she gave him credit for. "He's right. We accomplished our goal by solving the mystery. You two suffered because of his dishonesty." Grace stabbed a finger in the professor's direction. "You should be the ones to decide. Lancaster, on the other hand—"

"Is a jerk." Her brother smirked. "Whatever you decide, leave our names out of it."

"Take him inside and keep an eye on him. I'll get Lancaster over here. It's time the four of us had a chat." Zeek handed Prescott over to Marty and walked to the twins.

Grace gasped when the big guy drew her into a hug.

"Thank you. You have no idea what you did for me tonight." He released her. "But how did you know he was drinking?"

She rolled her lips in and looked at Henry for back up.

Her brother laughed. "She didn't."

Zeek's jaw fell open.

"Oh, before I forget—there's a gun in the impluvium."

"And another one somewhere in that direction." Grace pointed to where she thought she'd thrown the gun.

He furrowed his brow but didn't ask. "It's been a pleasure meeting both of you."

"There is something you can do for me." Grace had no right butting into his personal business, but after everything they'd been through, manners didn't seem to matter. "Your daughters love their grandfather. Mend the rift between the two of you. If not for your sake, for theirs."

He stared at her as if she'd sprouted wings and a halo. "I'd ask how you knew that, but I'm not sure I want to know. My father and I are making amends. He's babysitting my creature, remember?"

Headlights flashed at the far end of the drive.

Henry glanced toward the fifth wheel. "I hate to cut this short, but we need to go."

CHAPTER TWELVE

"Kids, breakfast!" Ethan called from the other room.

Henry closed his laptop and stowed it beneath a light blanket. They'd been lectured enough the previous night. The last thing they needed was for their parents to find out they'd stayed up all night writing up the exploits of one of their father's fraternity brothers.

He'd understood their mother's meltdown. The woman had every right to worry about her children, especially when they'd broken curfew to give police reports and hitched a ride home with a stranger. But that wasn't close to what had really happened. Henry felt guilty for lying, even by omission. However, Faith Warner would ground them until they were forty if she ever found out the truth.

"We're getting good at all-nighters." Grace nudged his shoulder. "I bet they'll come in handy at Stanford."

"If I get in."

"You'll get in." She grinned and opened the accordion door.

Ethan stared at the television. A blonde reporter held a microphone with the call letters of a local station. "Authorities are asking the public's help in locating the perpetrators. Lance Lancaster, the gallery owner, was reportedly working at the time of the break-in..."

The old photo of Lance that Henry had shown Grace a couple of nights earlier flashed on the screen.

Henry stood rooted in place, afraid to move or speak or breathe.

Grace made a choking sound beside him.

Their father glanced between them and frowned. "What's gotten into the two of you? It's a sad state of affairs when something like that happens in a town like East Hampton, but you look as though you've seen a ghost."

Grace plopped onto the couch. "It's shocking. First a robotic monster, and now this? I always thought the Hamptons were swanky."

"They are, but every place has crime." Ethan grinned. "Your grandparents preferred to vacation in the Adirondacks, but I went to school with kids who spent their summers here." He shook his head and drew a finger across his throat.

Henry could count on one hand the number of times their father had mentioned his parents. He'd never met them. There had been a falling out before his dad married his mom. "Do our grandparents still live in New York?"

Ethan scratched his head. "That is a conversation for another day. You two have to get dressed."

Henry groaned. "Aw, really? Another day of solitary confinement in an empty classroom?"

He folded his arms. "It's not solitary if you're with your sister, but no. We're leaving this afternoon. I thought we'd spend some time with Preston on his boat before we go."

In books, authors often describe fear with terms like icy-cold tendrils and frozen blood. In reality, Henry experienced a wash of heat that started in his face and ended in his stomach.

Grace just sat there and stared. The color had drained from her face and her breath came in shallow huffs, but she didn't so much as twitch.

She's gone into shock. I have to do something.

"Can we bail? We're both feeling under the weather." To his surprise, his voice came out almost normal. His insides, on the other hand, felt like someone had shoved an immersion blender through his belly button and hit puree.

"Nonsense. The fresh air will do you both some good." Ethan pulled two bowls from the cabinet and filled them with apple spice oatmeal, which was Henry's favorite. "Besides, we won't be out long. We have to leave after lunch. Your mom's standing in for a colleague in New Hampshire tomorrow."

He choked down his breakfast. All he could think about was what the professor would tell his parents. *Why do they bother giving death-row inmates a last meal when they can't taste it?"*

Faith walked into the kitchen in her traveling clothes, yoga pants and a t-shirt. "I agree with the kids. I'd like to bail and get on the road early. We've hardly had any family time since we arrived."

Ethan glanced at each of them and finally settled on Grace. "Come on, Gracie. What do you say? You've always loved the water. Prez has a pocket yacht."

"We're not really yacht people, Dad. Pocket or otherwise."

"You're right. I've fallen right back into the blueblood trappings of my youth, but Prez is an old friend..." Ethan tilted his head as if waiting for someone to concede.

Faith's phone rang. She listened and nodded. "Thank you for letting us know."

She disconnected the call. "That was Dianna Prescott. Seems Preston has come down with something and can't take us out on the water after all."

Henry and Grace exchanged looks. Was the man ill or in jail? Hard to say.

"You don't have to sound so happy about it." Ethan turned his attention to the pot of oatmeal on the stove.

Faith rested her hand between his shoulder blades and lowered her voice. "I'm not exactly his favorite person."

"It's nothing personal. He disagrees with our lifestyle choices." Ethan's tone softened.

"That's a nice way of saying he thinks I ruined your career." Faith kissed his cheek and turned to the twins. "About this independent study project. When will I see what you have on the Montauk Monster?"

Henry paused with the spoon halfway to his mouth.

Grace said, "We're collecting data and recording our thoughts. It won't be completed until the spring."

She rested her hip against the counter. "I see. And you two believe you have enough information? We were only here a few days."

Henry choked on his orange juice.

Grace saved them both. "More than enough."

Faith narrowed her eyes and stared.

The twins knew the routine. They faked smiles and refused to flinch.

Their mom nodded once. "Very well. Finish your breakfast so we can pack up and get on the road."

"I'm telling you, something is up with them." Grace put her bag in the back seat of the truck.

"You're being paranoid." Henry had said the same thing three times, and she continued to insist that their parents were up to something. "Any idea what needs to be investigated in New Hampshire?"

"I'll research on the way. I'm sure we can find something interesting near Manchester."

Ethan came around the corner and grinned. "Grace, you're in charge of making sure everything's secured. Henry, double-check the locking mechanism on the hitch and pull up the wheel chocks."

"Yes, sir." They spoke in unison.

He turned to go but stopped and wiggled his brows. "Don't waste your time on research just yet."

"Why?" Grace stretched the word into a whine.

"No reason." He clasped his hands behind his back and walked away —whistling.

"Okay, you're right. Something's up." Henry hopped into the truck bed to double-check the gear.

Rather than doing her chores, Grace loitered. "I bet they've come up with another research topic. They were really freaked out when they came home last night."

"Grace! Less talk, more prep." Faith placed a Styrofoam cooler on the rear floorboard.

The girl frowned and stomped away.

Not thirty seconds later, she popped up again. "Bet me."

Henry tightened the connection to the trailer's light cord. "I'm not going to bet you."

"Chicken."

Leaning close, Henry whispered, "It's not going to work. Get the chocks up. I, for one, am ready to get out of here."

"Nice try. Dad told you to do that." She smirked and walked away.

Packing up was Henry's least favorite part of living in a fifth wheel. Besides the yuck factor of disconnecting the sewage and grey-water tank lines, the work was tedious. Setting up, on the other hand, meant a new beginning. New places to explore. New adventures. *That* he could get behind.

What felt like hours later, Ethan fired up the truck, tested the brakes, tested the connections, and with a fist pump as if tugging a train's whistle, he pulled the trailer out of the driveway into the lane behind the house, turned wide using the large parking pad, and continued toward the main street.

Grace bobbed her knee and chewed on her fingernail.

"Will you stop?" He waved the hand-graded research article. "I'm trying to read."

Ethan, still grinning, looked in the rearview. "Don't make me stop this truck."

No one laughed.

Henry cringed at red blobs noting incorrect punctuation. Of course, he'd missed several commas. Only English professors and fifth-grade teachers understood the rules of commas. He worked his way to the last page and sighed. "You have got to be kidding."

Faith whipped around in her seat. "What grade did you receive? Is it a C?"

He snapped his mouth shut. *She honestly thinks I earned a C?* "I got an A, but I'm missing the comments page."

"What do you mean? Let me see." She thrust her hand into the back seat.

Ethan had stopped grinning. In fact, the muscle on the side of his jaw bulged, a sure sign he was grinding his teeth.

"Henry, it's right here. The professor found your research to be sound, with minor corrections as noted." She paused and flipped through the paper. "Mostly commas. He recommends you submit for publication."

"That's it? That's all the feedback I get?" Henry leaned his head back and stared at the headliner.

"You submitted to a professor who's used to grading graduate-level work. You should be proud of yourself, son." Ethan was back to grinning. "Mom has some news that'll cheer you up."

Grace shot Henry a nervous look.

Their mother shook her head. "Honestly, Ethan, you're worse than the kids when it comes to keeping secrets."

This earned a chuckle from the twins.

If she only knew. "What is it?"

"Your father and I were talking, and we've decided on your—"

Grace reached forward and squeezed her dad's shoulder. "Please, no. I know you both were worried last night, but Henry and I are committed to this project."

Their mother cleared her throat. "As I was saying, we've decided on your next urban legend."

She sat back. "What?"

"Mom, Grace and I would rather—"

"We're sending you to the Curse Isles for three nights!" Ethan blurted the words out so fast, Henry wasn't sure he'd heard him correctly.

Grace pulled out her phone and typed. "The Isles of Shoals are a group of islands six miles off the coasts of New Hampshire and Maine. It says there are no full-time residents on any of the islands."

"You'll be staying at the Oceanic Hotel on Star Island." Faith turned and smiled. "Blackbeard had his honeymoon on Smuttynose, one island over."

"Sounds...interesting." Henry had yet to recover from the lack of praise for his paper. Staying anywhere that Blackbeard had frequented didn't exactly improve his mood.

"Oh." A slow smile spread over Grace's face. "It's allegedly haunted by the ghosts of shipwrecked sailors, pirates, and Blackbeard's wives,"

"And two murdered Dutch girls." Ethan said, "Plus, the Oceanic Hotel is reportedly haunted."

This caught Henry's attention. "What happens at the hotel?"

"Guests report hearing someone rummaging through their drawers late at night." Ethan made ghost sounds.

Grace giggled. "The only person rummaging through Henry's drawers is Henry before he's had his coffee."

"Ha-ha. You might have inherited your hair from mom, but you got your sense of humor from—"

"Don't say it." Ethan chuckled.

"Thanks, guys. You're the best. Most parents wouldn't send their teenagers off to a haunted island."

"We aren't most parents," Faith and Ethan said in unison.

THE CURSED ISLES

MONSTER CASE FILES BOOK 2

CHAPTER ONE

Eight-year-old Emily wasn't allowed to go to the beach alone, but everyone knew midnight was the best time to spot a ghost. Besides, she had the full moon to light her way. Not that she needed it, she'd spent every summer on the Isles of Shoals for as long as she could remember.

The girl tiptoed out the backdoor and hurried to the rock at the edge of the path where she'd hidden a snack, her walking stick, and her pink and green light-up sneakers. She should have stashed her water shoes, but her mother had already packed them for the trip home.

Everyone's asleep. No one will see my blinking feet.

Emily glanced back at the building one last time, turned, and made her way down the path toward the far side of the island. She had found the perfect spot to wait: a rock, higher than the rest, just past the children's cemetery where she liked to play.

She sat and pulled a roll of candy from her pocket. There were forty wafers in a pack, and the longest she could last before biting into one was five minutes.

That gives me three hours or so. If I haven't seen the ghost when I run out of Neccos, I'll give up and go back.

Emily had made it halfway through the candy when she noticed a fine white mist drifting over the shallows. She shot to her feet and squinted through the fog. The closer it came, the more it looked like *her*—the Lady in White.

Heart racing, Emily took a step back before she gathered enough courage to move forward. "Hello? Mrs. Blackbeard?"

"He will come." The spirit drifted over the seaweed-shrouded boulders. "He will come."

"Wait!" The girl darted after the ghost.

Emily felt her mistake right away. A skid followed by a wobble, followed by fear. She pinwheeled her arms, but it was too late. She fell between the rocks and didn't stop falling until she landed in a sandy puddle.

Her head pounded, and her knees and elbows felt like they were on fire. Above her, the sky had turned black as if someone had switched off the moon.

"Help!" Emily screamed, but there was no one to hear her. No one to help her.

"There's no such thing as ghosts." Grace grabbed her twin brother's arm and dragged him to the side of the travel trailer they called home.

Henry glanced over his shoulder to where their parents were unhooking the fifth wheel from their pickup truck. "Maybe, maybe not. But I want to investigate something that doesn't involve people pointing guns at us this time."

"That part sucked, but what about that thrill when we solved the mystery?"

"You're right. It was amazing when the pieces fell into place, even though Zeek had to fill in some of the blanks for us."

"Why isn't the electricity connected?" Their mother's no-nonsense tone put an end to the twins' debate, at least temporarily.

"I'm working on it, Mom." She locked eyes with Henry and pointed to the back of the trailer.

He nodded and hurried in the opposite direction.

Doctor Faith Warner, their mother, had two sides—scientist and drill sergeant. That afternoon, she was all about accomplishing the mission of setting up camp. The twins, on the other hand, hadn't stopped debating the islands' supernatural history since their parents had announced they'd booked the twins into a hotel on Star Island, the largest of the Isles of Shoals—otherwise known as The Cursed Isles.

"Whoa, there." Ethan's voice snapped her back to the present.

Grace pressed her hand to her chest. "You scared the daylights out of me."

He motioned to the electrical outlet. "You were about to put a 220-volt plug into a 110-volt socket."

She gave her father a patient smile. "I think I would have figured it out when the prongs didn't line up."

"Yes, but mistakes lead to injuries, and injuries can lead to death." Ethan Warner, Esquire, mimicked her expression. As if that wasn't bad enough, he'd put his hands on his hips and imitated her voice.

"You're pretending to be me quoting Mom? Nice." Grace put the plug in the proper outlet and flipped the breaker.

"I'd ask where your head is, but I already know." He connected the pressure regulator to the water hose. "You two have spent more time talking and researching on your cell phones than on chores today."

Living on the road meant every family member had certain responsibilities when it came to setting up and tearing down. Distracted twins meant more work for their parents.

"Sorry. We're trying to decide which mystery to research. It's not our fault you're sending us to a place with such a rich history."

Ethan grinned. Not a happy sort of grin. This one told Grace he had a surprise or two in store.

She narrowed her eyes. "What aren't you telling us?"

"Nothing, other than that your mother and I are looking forward to a few nights alone."

"No way. I'm not buying it. You're keeping something from us." She entered a staring contest with her father, neither willing to blink or look away.

Henry joined them. "Grace is right. You haven't stopped grinning since you told us about Star Island. What gives?"

Ethan raised his eyebrows and his shoulders simultaneously in a Gallic shrug and backed away.

"Are we clear?" Faith shouted from the front of the rig.

"One minute." Henry measured the distance from the side of the trailer to the trees surrounding the pad. "Clear, with half a foot to spare."

"Opening the slides." She pursed her lips and waited for the three of them to move out of the way.

"Did you double-check that we're level?" Ethan jogged to the side door.

"Of course." Faith blocked his path and slid her arms around him.

Henry blanched. "What's gotten into them?"

Grace nodded to the picnic table, which was well out of range of the sliding sections. "I think Mom's happy to be away from Long Island, and Dad's happy because she is."

"Speaking of husbands and wives, why are you dead-set against investigating the Lady in White? Legend has it she was Blackbeard's fourteenth or fifteenth wife."

"We only have three nights on Star Island. The chances of debunking a centuries-old ghost story in such a short time are slim. It makes more sense to investigate the Smuttynose Murders. Do field research while we're there and follow up with more once we're back in Portsmouth." She tugged the power cord from its storage bin.

Henry pulled his cell from his pocket and focused on the screen. "There does seem to be disagreement about the killer's identity. This case would fit in nicely with my research on jury behavior and mob mentality, but—"

"It's not as fun as ghosts and pirates." She bit back laughter.

"Exactly." He plopped down on the bench.

She sat beside him and stretched out her legs. The mid-September sun seemed to burn less bright than it had a day or two ago. She intended to enjoy every last moment before it turned cold. "I wouldn't mind investigating something easy. It'd give us more time to enjoy the beach."

Henry turned his face toward the sky and closed his eyes. "You don't want easy any more than I do. You want the challenge, but there *is* something to be said for beach time."

"I looked at Mom and Dad's schedule. We won't see a warm climate until January."

"I'd like to migrate south for the winter once before we graduate." Henry rolled his head in her direction. "As for the project, if you're anti-ghosts, how about we focus on the buried-treasure angle?"

"You're suggesting we look for evidence that pirates left their treasure on one of the islands?" She'd likely read the same websites he had. How had they come to such different conclusions about which legend to research?

"There's some dissent among historians."

"Probably because it's impossible to prove." Grace hated the early stages of any project. She much preferred to get to work, but before they could do that, they had to nail down a topic.

He pinched the bridge of his nose. "We could wait until we get there to decide."

She nudged his shoulder. "This must be what it's like doing group projects in regular school. Think of our debate as practice for college."

"You mean we won't be collaborating on every assignment when you're at MIT and I'm at Stanford?" Henry smirked.

"Nope. You'll be forced to work with lesser beings." *And I'll be forced to do the same.* They bickered, like most siblings, but between the twin-bond and being raised on the road, Grace believed they were closer than a typical brother and sister.

"I'm starved. Let's go check out the camp store. You'll be more amenable to ghosts and pirates once you've had some sugar and caffeine." He stood, stretched, and strode in the direction of junk food with Grace on his heels.

As camp stores went, it was nice. Besides the regular equipment, they had a small snack bar, a soft-serve ice cream machine, and an outside seating area. They also had a selection of candy bars that would make Willy Wonka jealous.

"I've died and gone to heaven." Henry filled his basket with chocolate.

Grace turned her attention to the television behind the counter. A sobbing woman held a framed photograph of a little girl. The scroll across the bottom of the screen read, "Emily Blanchard, missing one year today. Presumed drowned off the Isles of Shoals."

"Sad story. It was all over the news last year." The man working the cash register pointed a remote control at the TV and turned up the volume.

The girl's mother stared into the camera. "Please. If you have any information about our Emily, contact the police. She's out there somewhere. I just want her home. Her birthday's coming up. She'll be ten. She loves the beach, pirates, and ghost stories. Her favorite foods are Necco wafers and French fries. Please help me find my baby," the woman pleaded, despair tugging at every word.

Henry set his basket on the counter and typed into his phone.

Grace stared until they cut to another story. The woman's emotional plea had stunned her, but the details of the lost little girl's life had stolen her breath.

"You two must be the Warners. Nice rig you have out there." His smile revealed a missing front tooth, and wrinkles stretched from the corners of his eyes to his neck.

"Henry and Grace Warner, and thank you. Our parents are quite proud of the trailer." Henry pulled his wallet from his back pocket.

"What happened to her? The reporter said she drowned, but her mother seemed convinced she was still alive."

The man hitched a shoulder. "The family was staying out on Lunging, and her mother reported her missing. Said someone had stolen her from her bed. The authorities found no sign of forced entry or any trace of the girl. About two months after she vanished, a shoe like the one that's missing from the girl's room washed up on the shore."

Henry furrowed his brows. "Her kidnapper took the time to grab her shoes?"

"Not likely. That shoe's what made the police believe she'd snuck out in the middle of the night and drowned in the ocean."

Henry and Grace exchanged looks.

"What other evidence did they have?" She knew something didn't add up but couldn't guess what. It sounded like the perfect mystery to research.

"Nothing they reported in the news. Details were scarce." The man spoke between ringing up candy bars. "There was a storm off the coast that night, and the seas were high. Too high for anything smaller than a ferry to dock."

Grace tapped her lips. "What was the family doing on Lunging Island? I thought it was privately owned and closed to tourists."

His smile wilted. "Visiting, I suppose."

"Were there any other guests on the island? What about the girl's father? He wasn't on television. Is he in the picture?"

The man stared.

"Sorry. She's a huge fan of crime shows." Henry paid for his snacks and pressed his hand to the small of her back. He spoke over his shoulder as they walked out. "Thanks. It was nice meeting you."

There were two things Grace despised above all others—Lima Beans and feeling foolish. Outside the store, she sidestepped her brother. "I don't watch television, let alone crime shows. And why did you interrupt me?"

"Because you were badgering the witness. Or just bugging a guy who got all his information from the same program you just watched." He unlocked his phone and handed it to her. "And he had one *major* detail wrong. The family spent their last night in the Shoals on Star Island. The storm made the seas unsafe for small craft. They'd planned to take the morning ferry to the mainland."

"That makes even less sense. A kidnapper could have braved the elements. Did they question every hotel guest? How could the police decide she drowned without a body? Why not leave her listed as a missing person?" She needed more information. Copies of police reports would be great, but she doubted they'd closed the investigation. *Or had they?* "I wonder if they officially ruled it a drowning."

"It makes perfect sense to rule it a drowning. She disappears, and the only evidence is a shoe that washes up on shore. She goes into the ocean and doesn't come out. No one knows why she was out there, but without a reason, and with no other way off the island, ergo, she left on the tide and maybe fell in by accident."

"What about the shoe? Most of the island is surrounded by open water. The current would have washed it out to sea. I mean, it's possible it floated near the shore if she fell into the harbor, but then why didn't they find her body?"

Henry grabbed her shoulders and squeezed until she met his gaze. "Slow down. Take a breath."

She nodded and attempted to rein in her racing thoughts, but it was no use. Memories of Emily Blanchard's freckled face and her mother's tears were already haunting Grace.

"I know that look. It's a sad story, but a missing girl isn't an urban legend."

"Not yet, but she'll be just another ghost on the Cursed Isles in a few years. We have to find out what happened to her." Her voice came out two octaves too high, like a twelve-year-old boy singing the National Anthem.

"Why are you so upset?" He stepped back as if afraid he'd catch her crazy.

Much to Grace's surprise, she couldn't come up with a logical explanation. The story had hit her on a purely emotional level. She sucked in a breath and hoped he'd understand. "Because I like the beach and ghost stories, and..."

A hint of a smile tugged at his lips. "And?"

"I thought I was the only other person in the world who loves Necco wafers."

"All right. We'll investigate her disappearance." Henry regarded her with an expression that reminded her of her father's courtroom face. "You shouldn't get your hopes up. We may not find anything on the girl, and we still have to investigate an *actual* urban legend."

Grace threw her arms around him. "Thank you!"

"Don't thank me yet. Since you insisted on looking into Emily Blanchard's disappearance, I'm going to insist on looking for buried treasure *and* the ghost of Blackbeard's wife. We have three whole days to do all that."

CHAPTER TWO

The triple-decker ferry chugged under the Piscataqua River Bridge. Henry couldn't see much through the dense fog and rain, but he didn't need to see the ocean to know when they'd reached open water. The plastic chairs on the decks toppled, and his stomach started churning with the rough sea.

The abysmal weather turned out to be a blessing and a curse. The water reminded him of a line from Hemmingway or Melville, or maybe it was George from *Seinfeld*. Whoever said it had gotten it right: "The seas were very angry, my friend."

As for the blessing, most of the tourists had opted out of a day trip to the Isles of Shoals. Great news for Henry, who already regretted the enormous breakfast he'd eaten in Portsmouth.

Grace eyed the waves splashing the boat. "This can't be safe. If the swells get any higher, we'll capsize."

"It's fine. The captain would have canceled the ferry service if the weather conditions were unsafe."

"Oh, man. This is..." She pressed her hand to her mouth.

Henry forgot about his nausea and went into panic mode. "Don't throw up out here! Go to the restroom."

She groaned. "Way to be supportive."

"We have about an hour to go." He patted her back.

Grace lurched forward and hung her head between her knees.

"I know what might help." He took her hands and pressed on the insides of her wrists. "Sit up, stare at a fixed point, and tell yourself—"

"—I'm not going to hurl?" She may have mocked him, but she didn't pull away.

"Yes, exactly that. Studies show seasickness can be cured by using mind over matter." Motion-sickness bands operated under the same principle as acupressure. "Besides, it worked for me. I was feeling queasy until you started gagging and took my mind off it."

Grace muttered an apology.

"I found quite a bit of information online about Emily's disappearance. Emily's father is deceased, and her mother is an elementary school teacher in Connecticut. Lunging is owned by her uncle. The family spent summer vacations on the island. They had booked rooms in a cottage on Star Island the night she went missing. Her younger brother was sleeping in the same bed but didn't hear anything."

She sat back and rotated her hands to get the blood flowing to her fingers. "How old is her brother?"

"He's eight now."

Grace pulled her notebook from her backpack and skimmed a page of notes. "The mother said she'd locked up for the evening, but the backdoor was open in the morning."

"You mean unlocked?"

"No, I mean, whoever went through the door left it slightly ajar." She gave him a crooked smile. "Does that sound familiar?"

"Yeah." Henry resisted the urge to sigh. They'd done the same thing when they'd snuck out of the trailer after their parents went to bed. A partially-opened door made less noise and was less likely to set off their mom's internal security system. "Doesn't her sneaking out make sense with the drowning scenario?"

She turned and stared out the window. "Maybe. Especially if the surf was rough, but she'd spent every summer on the island. Wouldn't she know to stay away from the water?"

"Do you know what kind of exterior lighting they had?" He recognized the absurdity in the question a second too late.

"Nope, but we'll soon find out." Grace drummed her fingers on her chair.

"Are you feeling better?"

"Oddly enough, I am."

He leaned closer. "Are you sure you're going to be okay if we prove she's dead? It's not like you to react on such an emotional level."

His sister tensed and opened her mouth as if to argue but nodded. "If it gives her family some peace, yes."

"And if we don't find anything?"

Grace rubbed her earlobe like she used to do when she was little and stressed out.

Henry couldn't help but smile. No one else on the planet knew her the way he did, and vice versa. He figured that she wouldn't be okay, but after a good cry, she'd reconcile herself with the truth. They only had to find it.

"They won't be any worse off than they are now. It's not like they know anyone else is looking for her, right?"

"Right."

They spent the remainder of the ferry ride in silence, Grace writing in her journal and Henry staring out at the slate gray sky and darker gray water. He'd conducted other research the previous night as well, but he kept his findings to himself. His sister wouldn't appreciate hearing tales of an illustrious pirate burying treasure on the tiny islands. And she'd downright hate the rumors that Blackbeard had left not one but several wives behind to guard it.

Maybe we'll find some doubloons while we're searching for the little girl.

By the time the ferry arrived on Star Island, the winds had calmed. Unfortunately, the rain continued. The Oceanic Hotel looked like it belonged on the cover of a gothic romance novel. Mist shrouded the imposing white structure and surrounding buildings.

Grace gasped. "It's beautiful. I half-expect to see women in turn-of-the-century dresses strolling the veranda."

Henry hiked his backpack higher on his shoulder. "Let's get out of the rain."

"If we must."

"You've read *Anne of Green Gables* one too many times."

"That you'd make the connection means you had the same thought, and maybe you have found culture and are good at hiding it." She laughed and sprinted past him.

They reached the enormous front porch at the same time, both drenched and laughing. Henry would never admit it out loud, but he looked forward to spending some time in one of the many rocking chairs. A man and his laptop, writing about the legend of Blackbeard.

Ready for a hot cup of coffee and a shower, Henry walked into the lobby. As far as hotels went, this one struck him as homey. Round tables with wooden chairs filled half the space, and mismatched couches and chairs the other.

Someone was cooking what smelled like chili nearby. The aroma mixed with the scents of oil soap, sea air, and chalkboards.

"I've never seen wood floors shine like that. I hate to drip on them." Grace chewed her lip and glanced around.

A blonde who couldn't be much older than them stood behind the desk speaking to an older man. She turned to them and smiled. "You're a little early for lunch, but you're welcome to look around."

"We're checking in. Henry and Grace Warner." He walked to the counter and spoke to the gentleman.

"I'll check you in." The girl grinned, not seeming to mind that he'd made the wrong assumption.

Ignoring the twins altogether, the man shoved his hands in his pockets and turned.

"Dr. Jaffrey, before you go, I need your signature on that bill of sale." She motioned to a piece of paper on the desk.

The man pulled a pen from his pocket, placed his elbow on the paper, and scribbled his signature.

Henry kept his expression neutral, embracing his new hobby of people watching.

"Don't mind him. He's not the social type." She rummaged through an old-fashioned file folder, pulled out a card, and frowned. "My manager mentioned we had two personal retreat guests arriving today."

"Personal retreat?"

"Most of the people who stay here are conferees."

He'd never heard the term "conferee," but assumed it meant conference attendees. *Did they make it up, or is it a real word?*

"It's an actual word." Not only had Grace read his mind, but she'd also saved him the time of looking it up.

"I'm surprised they put you on the fourth floor. It's mostly staff up there." She pulled a few more cards from the file, likely checking the availability of other rooms.

Henry asked, "Could it be because we're seventeen?"

"Ah, yes. That explains it." The blonde nodded to a row of bulletin boards. "Feel free to check the schedule of classes and seminars. Some are open to guests."

"Thank you. We're here to work on a research project. We'll be pretty busy." Grace took a couple of flyers from the counter. "We'll need the Wi-Fi password."

She cocked her head. "Wi-Fi is available in the Business Center in Cottage

D. You may be able to hit it from your phones, but it can be spotty. The same goes for cell reception. The side of the porch closest to the mainland is your best bet...once the weather clears."

Henry froze in place. No Wi-Fi in the rooms? Spotty cell reception? What kind of place was this?

Grace seemed to have taken the news in stride. She smiled and nodded as if this sort of thing happened every day. "We understand. It's pretty remote here."

The young woman slid a map of the island in front of them and marked the main hotel with an X. "We're here. Your room is on the fourth floor of this building. Cottage D is here."

Henry ran his hand over his head. "Thanks."

"I'm Jessica, or Jessie. I'll be around during your stay. My room's two doors down from yours. Let me know if you need anything." She turned her attention to Grace. "There are restrooms on each floor. They're clearly marked."

His sister's mouth fell open. "Shared bathrooms? With everyone on the floor?"

The blonde nodded and continued, "The showers are on the basement level. Shower days are Monday, Wednesday, and Friday."

"Excuse me?" Grace gasped.

Their parents hadn't sent them to a beachside resort. They'd sent them back in time to the 80s...the 1880s.

"We're only allowed to bathe every other day?" Grace's voice came out in a squeak.

Jessie nodded and smiled the sort of smile that said she'd answered the question a few million times. "We provide a basin of warm water every morning for hygiene. Our goal is to be a self-sustaining community, so we conserve our resources. Solar electricity powers sixty percent of the island during peak season, and a hundred percent during the winter. We use filtered rainwater for drinking, laundry, and showers. Our toilets are saltwater. We also recycle as much as possible. That flyer in your hand will become chicken bedding when you're finished with it."

The twins nodded, but otherwise, neither responded.

It wasn't that Henry had anything against the green movement. In fact, he appreciated their efforts, but a little warning of what they were walking into would have been nice. *No wonder Dad couldn't stop grinning.*

Grace rolled her lips in, drew a breath, and squared her shoulders. "That's terrific. I can't wait to learn more about it. We just need our room keys. I need to charge my phone."

"Oh, we don't have locks on the doors." Jessie sighed a little deeper this time. "Or outlets in most of the rooms."

Grace made a sound like her heart had broken and the end of days had descended like a guillotine. She turned to go but paused. "Are there locks on the doors in the guest cottages?"

Jessie's shoulders tensed. "No."

Henry picked up his sister's likely train of thought. "What about the exterior doors?"

The girl shook her head and refused to meet their eyes.

Henry glanced at his sister and back to the blonde. "How do the cottages work? Are they like renting a little house?"

"No. They contain six to eight guest rooms, and most have shared baths." Her voice had an edge to it.

They marched upstairs. To say their moods were somber would have been an understatement. Heck, Henry had seen more festive funeral processions.

"Did you see the way Jessie's demeanor changed when we asked about the cottages?" Grace turned the corner and headed up the third flight of stairs.

"I did. I can't decide if she lost her patience with us because of our reaction to the accommodations or if she was uncomfortable discussing security."

Walking down the hall, Grace checked the number on each door. "Either way, it was weird."

She stopped and walked into their room. It had two twin beds, a small desk, and, as Jessie had forewarned, a washbasin.

Henry dropped his backpack and plopped onto the bed. "At least this is comfy."

Grace stared out the window. "The view is amazing. It's stopped raining, and the sun's coming out."

"See? Not so bad." He tried the mind-over-matter-positive-thinking routine. "This'll be good for us. Unplugging. Focusing on the case. It's like camping, only indoors."

She rolled her eyes. "Haven't you had enough roughing it? We live in a trailer."

"Yes, but it's a forty-nine-foot luxury rig. It's hardly rustic."

"You're right. We're not here on vacation. We have a case to solve." She slid her bag onto her shoulder. "Lunch is in a half-hour. I'm going to find the bathroom and change into dry clothes."

Henry leafed through the information Jessie had given them, including a list of house rules. It surprised him to learn that because the Star Island Corporation owned the hotel *and* the island, they could expel guests for a variety of reasons, most of which wouldn't apply to the twins. However, their parents must have pulled some strings for two unaccompanied minors to come for a personal retreat.

Grace barged back into the room waving her hairdryer around like a weapon. "Did you know *this* is *contraband?*"

"As a matter of fact, I did." He snickered.

She tossed the illegal appliance into her backpack. "After three days here, we're going to stink and have frizzy hair and nervous ticks from technology withdrawal."

He shrugged because he knew it annoyed her. "It's different, but I'm looking at it as an adventure. Give it a chance, it'll be fun. Let's check on lunch. It smelled ready."

He stood, stretched, and headed downstairs, with Grace on his heels. The twins entered the dining room and paused.

Voices and long tables arranged cafeteria style filled the space. This was as close to a school lunchroom as either had come. Sure, they'd accompanied their parents to countless universities, but most had food courts that would make the Mall of the Americas jealous.

Grace took a step back. "Where do we sit?"

"Pick an empty table."

A guy wearing a Star Island polo approached. "Hi, welcome. I'm Jonathan. Follow me."

They obeyed, but Henry's pulse sped up the deeper into the room they went.

Grace must have felt the same because she touched Jonathan's shoulder. "Excuse me, but we'd prefer to sit alone. We have work—"

"I understand, but please consider joining others at a table. Part of the Star Island experience is making new friends over shared meals." He flashed his pearly whites.

It wasn't their first choice.

CHAPTER THREE

Following Jonathan into the belly of the cafeteria made Grace more nervous than speaking in front of an auditorium full of people. At least when she'd given presentations, she'd known where to sit and where to stand. Where she belonged.

Each time they passed a table, a person or two would glance up. Some would smile, but others would look away as if mentally chanting, "Keep walking."

Thankfully, Jonathan moved on.

"Jon! There's room for them here with the Pels." Jessie, the girl from the front desk, waved. She'd done her hair in a French braid and had changed into a pink button-down shirt with the hotel logo and her name embroidered on the pocket.

A handful of young people wearing different-colored Star Island polos turned and stared.

"Looks like you've already made a friend." Jonathan motioned to the table.

The twins exchanged a quick glance.

"Henry and Grace, meet everyone. Everyone, this is Henry and Grace." Jessie moved her chair down to make more room. "Did you get settled into your room?"

Grace sat beside the blonde. "Yes, thank you."

"What's a 'Pel?'" Henry took the breadbasket from a guy in a green polo. "Thanks."

"The Pelicans are the heart and soul of Star Island." Jonathan sat at the head of the table, likely to keep an eye on the entryway. "Otherwise known as seasonal employees. Most of us are in college or getting ready to start. We live and work here over the summer."

Grace took the basket from Henry and pulled out a huge hunk of cornbread. "Sounds...fun."

Jessie laughed and spoke to the others. "They're still in culture shock."

Several of the male Pelicans nodded, and two snickered, including Jonathan. However, the women glanced at a blue-eyed girl with a name tag that read Miranda.

Miss Blue Eyes ignored everyone except Henry. "Where do you go to college?"

"We're high school seniors, but I plan to attend Stanford." He filled his bowl with chili and passed the dish to his sister.

"Impressive. Do you think you'll get in? Not many do."

Jessie gave Miranda a mom look. "What about you, Grace? Have you decided on a school?"

"MIT."

The guys at the table nodded or gave her an appraising look or both. However, the girls kept their heads down or glanced at Miranda. The interactions between the others intrigued her.

It was obvious there was a pecking order. Jessie wore a different uniform than the others, so she held some authority over them, but why did the rest of the girls seem to defer to Miranda?

"I'm a junior at MIT, but I took a leave of absence until January. Once the resort closes, I'll be interning with the environmental scientists on the island. We're testing a new desalination system."

Grace's stomach did a somersault. She'd stalked on-line forums for incoming freshmen, but she'd never had the opportunity to speak with someone face to face about the university. "I have so many questions."

Jessie leaned in and lowered her voice. "And I have so many answers. We'll definitely talk before you leave."

Miss Blue-Eyes set her elbows on the table and batted her lashes. "What brings you to Star Island, Henry?"

He swallowed the food in his mouth and washed it down with lemonade. "We're working on a research project. Debunking urban legends."

This grabbed everyone's attention. Forks paused midway to mouths. Others put down their silverware altogether, but everyone stared at the twins.

Miranda blinked. "Like what? Ghosts? Bigfoot? The Loch Ness Monster?"

"Among others, yes. We're interested in learning the facts behind the legends and their impacts on the local cultures, and in some cases, the economies of the regions."

Grace had finally made contact with someone who could give her the inside scoop on MIT. The last thing she wanted to do was to blow it by coming off juvenile. "There are no such things as ghosts or monsters."

Miranda snickered. "You might want to tell the spirits who haunt the attic they don't exist."

The female Pelicans nodded.

Jessie rolled her eyes. "It's an old building. It makes all sorts of noises."

"I've seen the ghost of a girl in a white nightgown in the gazebo." Miss Blue-Eyes turned to Henry. "I could show you tonight."

Jonathan scowled and shifted in his seat as if he couldn't decide if he wanted to go or stay.

Jessie cleared her throat. "Miranda, that's enough."

"Whatever." The girl huffed.

Henry lowered his gaze to his food.

A boy in a dark blue polo said, "I've seen her, too. On the emergency staircase."

Two sightings of a girl in two different places? Grace didn't believe in coincidences, especially with a missing child to investigate. "What did she look like?"

Miranda blatantly ignored the question. She seemed to be engaged in a silent conversation with Jonathan.

Blue Polo furrowed his brow as if trying to recall.

Not a good sign. I doubt I'd forget the details if I'd seen an actual ghost.

"Light-colored hair, like a dark blonde. Long white nightgown, the old-fashioned kind."

Jessie went stock still and glanced at Jonathan.

"Could it be the spirit of Emily Blanchard?" Grace cringed as soon as the words fell from her mouth.

Jessie dipped her chin, Jonathan sucked in a breath, and the table went quiet.

Miranda frowned. "Not all of us were here last summer when the girl went missing, but those of us who were are still traumatized. Like, we don't want to talk about it. M'kay?"

"I apologize." Grace set her napkin on the table. As delicious as lunch tasted, she'd lost her appetite.

"It's okay. You didn't know." Jessie squeezed her shoulder. "The Shoals is a small community. Some of us know Emily's family. Her uncle still lives on Lunging."

Henry drained his glass and set it on the table hard enough to take the attention off his sister. "Actually, we're more interested in learning what we can about Blackbeard and the other pirates rumored to have visited the islands."

Jonathan chuckled like a game show host—forced and phony. "I'm sure many pirates passed through here. Back in the day, the islands were busy fishing villages. But It's highly unlikely any of them buried treasure here. The ground is solid rock."

Grace saw her chance to redeem herself and jumped in. "That's exactly the sort of thing we want to investigate. It's all but impossible for a bunch of pirates to smash through solid granite and bury gold without someone noticing them, but people ignore the evidence and cling to their beliefs."

Henry said, "I intend to prove how this form of 'group-think' can influence juries in high-profile cases with intense media coverage. It's a potential flaw in our judicial system."

Jessie glanced at the twins. "You really should visit more than one island while you're here. A few of us are assigned island cleanup on Smuttynose tomorrow afternoon. We make it fun. Pack a picnic, bring music. You two should come."

Grace turned to Henry. "What do you think?"

"That sounds great. Do you think anyone would mind if I tested the depth of the topsoil and pick-axed a couple of rocks?"

The blonde laughed. "Not at all. I'll be sure to bring a ruler, a shovel, and a pickaxe."

Miranda wore a fish-eating grin—smug and self-righteous.

Wide-eyed, Jonathan held up his hands and stopped the conversation before it took a wrong turn. "Let's everyone simmer down. We can learn much from each other by listening instead of judging."

Miranda shot him a glare that melted into a moon-eyed smile. He returned the affectionate expression and leaned closer to the table as if drawn to her by an invisible string.

"It's been fun. Thanks for lunch." Henry stood. "We should get going. This island isn't going to explore itself."

On the one hand, Grace wanted to hug her brother for giving them an exit, and on the other, she desperately wanted to groan. She said a quick goodbye and hurried after her twin.

He all but jogged from the room and didn't stop until he reached the veranda. "That was *interesting*."

"Which part? The blue-eyed witch flirting with you or the way they stared at us like we were freaks?" She leaned against the railing and hung her head. This so-called vacation had gone from bad to worse over cornbread and chili. They could have taken pictures, but only until their phones died and couldn't be recharged.

"She wasn't flirting with me. She and Jonathan are dating or will be soon. Her behavior had more to do with her being intimidated by you."

"Me? You're kidding, right?"

"She was making sure you knew she was the queen bee."

Grace pinched the bridge of her nose. "I'll never understand the pack behavior of teenage girls."

"When I said it was interesting, I was referring to the way they reacted when you mentioned Emily Blanchard." He glanced over his shoulder at the after-lunch crowd on the porch and motioned to the stairs. "Let's take a walk. And for the record, the food was good. More of that and it'll be a great stay, no matter what we uncover."

Grace gawked. She hadn't noticed anything other than shock and anger when she'd mentioned the little girl. "What do you mean? They reacted like people who'd witnessed a family's grief first-hand instead of on the five o'clock news."

They made their way down the boardwalk to the western side of the property. A thick fog had replaced the rain. She would have preferred a sunny day, but the dreary weather matched her mood.

Henry walked toward the backs of the cottages. "Everyone at the table had the *same* reaction."

She waited for him to continue. When it became clear he had nothing else to say, she sighed. "And?"

"It may be nothing, but Miranda said they weren't all here last summer, including her, but her initial reaction was the same as the others'—nervous."

"And she seemed the most offended." Grace hated that she'd missed it, but the girl had gotten under her skin. "You think she knows something?"

Henry's lips curled in the same slow smile he wore when he won at chess. "I don't think so. But she knows the others do, and it eats at her. She seems like a girl who likes to know everyone's secrets."

Okay. That makes perfect sense. "You're right about that. The question is, how do we find out who knows what when they obviously don't want to talk about it?"

"It's going to take luck and patience."

"Great. We don't have much of either."

He pulled the map out of his pocket, glanced up, and pointed to the second floor of a smaller building. "There are Cottages A through D. Notice the floodlights? The entrances are on the boardwalk side."

He turned and nodded toward a detached structure, also with the front door facing north. "That's Cottage E. More lights.

Grace followed him to the back of the two-story building. "More lights."

He scratched his head. "We should check tonight, but the area appears well-lit."

They continued on a southerly path, and the buildings changed from whitewashed wood to stone. Other than a couple of dozen seagulls, the twins seemed to have the property to themselves. Most of the conferees had stayed under cover on the veranda or in the dining hall.

The island had a certain draw. Time seemed to move slower, and for the most part, the guests smiled and appeared friendlier.

Henry stopped outside Vaughn Cottage, the home of the island's library, museum, and archives. "What do we know so far?"

"They aren't overly concerned about security here. At least two of the Pels have seen a girl in a white gown on this island." She refrained from adding her thoughts on Miranda. "Oh, and Jessie seems to be the real leader. She also has an in with the environmental research team."

"Then that's where we should start. Ask her about MIT. Toss in another apology for mentioning Emily. Maybe she'll open up when it's just the two of you."

"I'll try." Grace hated the idea of risking a potential friend at MIT, but they had nothing else to go on.

"We need to find transportation to the other islands." Henry glanced back toward the hotel. "They have kayaks and rowboats..."

"Uh-uh. No way. They'll throw us off the island if we take them outside of Gosport Harbor."

"I'll ask around. There has to be a way. Smuttynose is a great start, but I'd rather conduct our pirate research alone."

"I agree, especially if Miranda's going to be there. Let's go inside and check out the exhibits. Given the local lore, I'm sure they have information on Blackbeard and the Lady in White."

"We only have three days." Grace led the way inside.

A Beatle-haired boy in a light blue polo glanced up from his book. "Welcome. I'm Dylan, let me know if there's anything I can help you with."

Grace wandered to a series of framed maps. Judging from the yellowing of the paper, they were old. "These are amazing."

The Pelican set his book aside and joined the twins.

She leaned closer to inspect a sketch of a neighboring island. "I didn't realize the Appledore Hotel was so massive. It's a shame it burned down."

"It is. Fire is still a threat. We don't have a fire department out here."

"Ah, *that's* why my hairdryer is off-limits."

Dylan laughed. "It may seem like overkill, but we take safety seriously. Every time there's a renovation to one of the buildings, management has firebreaks installed."

"That's reassuring." She made a mental note to research firebreaks once they had internet access. "I'd like to see Appledore. Is there a tour or boat rental that would take us there?"

"There aren't any this late in the season." He scratched his jaw. "You might be able to find a local willing to take you out on the water. Check with Jessie at the front desk."

Henry nodded. "We've met her. Is she the head Pelican?"

"You could say that. She's more like management than a regular Pel. She's worked here since her freshman year of high school, and she comes from a long line of Shoalers."

A collection of hand-painted vases and plates caught Grace's eye. "These are pretty. Is the artist local?"

"Most were hand-painted by Celia Thaxter, the writer." He brushed his hair from his eyes.

Grace had only read the author's work after learning they'd be visiting the islands. Unlike her contemporaries Emerson, Hawthorne, and Longfellow, her work seldom made it onto required reading lists. However, her paintings were in high demand among collectors, fetching exorbitant prices.

Henry leaned closer to the map. "Lunging is where they think Blackbeard left his treasure, isn't it?"

"Some folks say so, but I've heard the same thing about Appledore, Smuttynose, White, and even Star Island." Dylan walked to a shelf and pulled two books down. Both were missing their dust jackets and had thread-bare hardcovers and yellowed pages. "You can borrow these if you'd like. They're ancient, but they contain histories of pirate activity in the Shoals."

"Thanks." Henry flipped to the table of contents of the first book and disappeared into the text.

A series of black and white photos lined the far wall. Each image featured a young man or woman and appeared to have been taken on the island. They were eerily captivating.

"Those are photos of staff from the Forties and Fifties." The young attendant perked up. "Early Pelicans. I guess you could say they're our ancestors."

She nodded and leaned closer to read the descriptions. The man in the picture had a James Dean look to him—dangerous and handsome.

"That's Brad Blanchard. Interestingly enough, he's well-known for insisting the hotel install firebreaks, only to die in a fire a few years later."

"Why does that name sound familiar?" She'd tried to play it cool, but the words came out rushed and breathless.

"Because you just asked about his granddaughter an hour ago." Miranda appeared in the doorway, glaring.

CHAPTER FOUR

"You should have seen your face." Henry knew better than to laugh at his sister's misfortune. Karma would undoubtedly reverse the situation in the near future, but he couldn't help it. It was as if the entire thing had happened in slow motion. Miranda entering the cottage. Grace's eyes popping out of her head cartoon-style. Hasty excuses and apologies, and a hastier retreat.

"Laugh it up. You're the one who agreed to sneak out to go ghost-hunting with her tonight." Grace threw herself on her bed and covered her head with a pillow.

"I'm not going alone. You're coming with me."

"No way. I've had enough humiliation for one day. I'm staying right here. I'm not even going down for dinner."

He checked his phone battery and frowned. Two percent, and no outlets in the room. "I wonder if there's anywhere I can charge my phone in the dining hall."

"There were outlets near the beverage table. I'm sure Jessie would allow us to use one." She yawned and rolled to her side. "Turn the light off."

Whether it was their early start, the ocean air, or the laid-back ambiance of the hotel, Henry had wanted to curl up and snooze since they'd arrived. "That's a good idea. It's going to be a late night."

"For you." Grace nuzzled into her pillow and closed her eyes. "I have no desire to spend time with someone who obviously hates my guts."

"I'm telling you, she's harmless." He sniffed his armpits. "I, on the other hand, smell."

"Same here. I may as well have gone for a swim in the ocean. I can *feel* the salt on my skin."

He dipped a washcloth in the water basin and wiped the sweat and sea air from his face before stretching out on his bed. "Set an alarm on your phone for eleven-thirty, just in case."

She mumbled something under her breath and grabbed her cell.

<hr>

A banging noise woke Henry from a dead sleep. At first, he thought someone had knocked, but when he checked, the hall was empty.

He closed the door, and the racket started again.

"I'm going to strangle someone." Grace threw her blanket to the side.

"There's no one—"

The door smashed into Henry. Before he could make sense of what had happened, Miranda and four of her posse burst into the room making ghost sounds.

His sister balled her hands at her sides. "Very funny."

Miranda glanced at Grace, smirked, and turned to Henry. "We gotcha, didn't we?"

"Not really." He ran his hand through his sleep-rumpled hair. "What are you doing here?"

She stomped her foot like a spoiled toddler. "It's almost midnight. Ghost-hunting, remember?"

"Right. Give us a minute." He motioned for them to leave.

"Us?" Miranda and Grace said together.

He motioned with his head that she was going. She wouldn't be so cruel as to send him out alone with a rabid pack of girls.

Grace frowned but acquiesced. "I want to go, too," she said flatly.

"Fine. Whatever." Miranda turned on her heel and walked out. "Meet us by the outside stairs in five minutes, and don't get caught. Curfew was ten o'clock. I mean it. I'm not going to get fired because there's one too many—"

He smiled and nodded and eased the door closed. "For someone who doesn't want to get caught, she sure made a lot of noise."

Blinking and breathing deeply to kickstart her brain, Grace put on her sneakers. "I give you permission to shoot me if I act like them when I'm in college."

"I sure hope not."

It seemed as if the entire island slept. Only a handful of lights remained in guests' windows, and the grounds were eerily still. Even the wind that had torn across the lawn for the better part of the day had quieted.

Henry couldn't shake the feeling that this was a bad idea. "I'll get us out of this."

"It's a little late," Grace whispered. "In for a penny, in for a pound."

Miranda and the girls stood in the shadows on the side of the building. She made a sound that vaguely resembled an owl and waved them over.

"Oh, brother." Henry shoved his hands in his pockets and slumped his shoulders.

Grace giggled.

"We're going through Caswell Cemetery to the summer house." She rubbed her hands together.

"You mean the gazebo?" He'd seen the name on the map but couldn't be sure.

"Yes. We call it the summer house." She huffed. "Never mind. Just follow me."

He glanced at Grace and shrugged.

She shook her head and trudged after Miranda and the nameless girls. The smell of the sea air was strong without the breeze. Somewhere a salt marsh stagnated.

Without trees or the cover of the buildings, they were running in the open. Had anyone glanced out their window, they would have seen the group crossing the lawn. A shiver ran down Henry's spine. He risked a look back at the hotel, half-expecting to see someone watching him.

Grace tugged his arm. "What's wrong?"

"I'm not sure."

The ground sloped upward, making them even more conspicuous to onlookers, and the sensation that someone was watching them increased.

"Miranda, is anyone out here?" Henry glanced back toward the hotel again.

She grinned and wiggled her fingers at him. "Spooked already?" Her blue eyes sparkled in the night as if filled with stars, and her teeth shone white as her lips parted in a smile.

He did his best to ignore her *and* the smattering of headstones in the small cemetery, quickening his pace to the gazebo.

They took up positions in the four corners of the summer house, each person looking in a different direction. Unfortunately, Miranda and the girls had a different concept of ghost-hunting than the twins. They chatted nonstop about topics so random Henry had a hard time following the conversation.

Grace whisper-shouted, "Get down."

He crouched and followed his sister's gaze to a light on the water.

Miranda barked out a laugh. "Seriously? It's just a boat, and it's going away from the island. They can't see us from up here."

"No, but *they* can." Grace pointed to two figures making their way up the rocks.

"Oh my God." Miranda flattened herself on the floor.

One of the girls who'd accompanied them curled into a ball in the corner. Smart move. She'd all but hidden in the shadows.

Henry tugged his sister down. Crouching, he peeked over the railing to get a look at the people. "What's someone doing out here so late?"

"They're going to see you. Get down." Miranda waved and pointed to the ground.

Grace scooted closer to the corner.

Henry continued to stare at the pair. He couldn't see their faces, but they were tall and thin. One appeared to wear her hair in a ponytail, and the other carried a bag. Their voices confirmed his suspicions that one was a female, although he couldn't make out their words.

He waited until they'd passed the cemetery to whisper, "They're heading for the hotel. Do you recognize them?"

Miranda slunk to his side and peeked over the railing. "It's Jonathan. I'd know that walk anywhere."

"Who's he with?"

She frowned. "I don't know."

One of the girls said, "It's probably Jessie. She has family in the Shoals."

Everyone turned and stared, but it was Miranda who spoke. "What is Jonathan doing with Jessie? And why aren't they using the pier?"

"We should go back." Grace ran her hands over her arms.

"I couldn't agree more." Miranda marched from the summer house without a backward glance.

Henry grabbed his sister's arm. "We should hang back. She's angry, and liable to get caught stomping around."

"Good idea."

The twins followed at a slower pace. Once again, the hairs on the back of Henry's neck stood up. He glanced over the lawn, back toward the water. Although he didn't notice anyone else nearby, he couldn't shake the feeling of being watched.

Grace whipped her head to the right and stopped walking.

"What is it?" He followed her gaze.

"I don't know."

A gull cried overhead, and something moved in the darkness. Silence returned.

She laughed and shook her head. "I've had enough ghost-hunting."

"Me too."

While they hadn't spotted any ghosts, they'd stumbled onto another mystery. Henry couldn't care less about Jonathan and Jessie's relationship, but he wanted to know where they had gone.

They reached the top of the stairs, and Henry cracked the door enough to make sure the coast was clear. He nodded and ushered his sister to their room.

Henry closed the door behind him. "Let's hope she doesn't throw us under the bus."

"I think she's overreacting. Besides, we can't get into trouble when four of the staff were out, too."

"True." He kicked off his shoes and stretched out on his bed. "Why wouldn't they use the pier?"

"Jessie's a supervisor. She probably has fewer rules than the rest. Maybe she didn't want Jonathan to get into trouble." Grace sat to remove her shoes.

"Maybe. But why take the risk? She has an internship on the line."

"Good question."

Staring at the ceiling, he put Jessie's behavior out of his mind and ran through what they'd learned about Emily Blanchard's disappearance. Other than learning that some of the Pels knew the family, they hadn't accomplished much on their first day. "Mind if I read?"

"Go ahead. I can't sleep either. That nap messed up my circadian rhythm." She removed her journal from her bag and began writing.

Henry opened the book he'd borrowed from the museum and lost himself in the history of pirates in New England.

Halfway through the sixth chapter, wood scraping against wood sounded from overhead.

"What the heck?" He checked the time on his phone—three in the morning, which was a little late for construction.

"What's that noise?"

"Sounds like someone's moving furniture." An alarm bell went off in his head. Moving furniture. Tourists had reported the same types of sounds coming from the attic for years. According to his research, the space was empty. "Holy smokes."

His sister must have had the same aha moment because she hopped out of bed and stuffed her feet back into her sneakers. "Let's go."

"We'll have to be quiet. Curfew, remember?" He double-knotted his laces. No sense in face-planting while ghost hunting.

Grace cracked the door open and peeked into the hall. "It's empty."

A similar noise came from overhead, only this time it sounded more like cardboard tearing.

She stared at the ceiling and smirked. "I'll bet you fifty bucks this is the Pelicans pulling another prank on us."

"Could be." He reached for his phone, but it died when he hit the flashlight function. "How much battery do you have left?"

Grace pressed the power button several times. "None."

"Great. Okay. I'm down to nothing. We'll have to do this without light." He stepped into the hall and motioned for her to follow.

They took each step painstakingly slowly, stepping on the sides closest to the walls, testing the floorboards before putting their weight on them. Henry strained to listen for more noises from the attic but heard nothing except their breathing and the occasional squeak from the old wood beneath their feet.

Henry opened the door and stepped into the stairwell.

Grace pushed past him but hesitated when the wood on the first step groaned. She pressed her finger to her lips as if to shush him even though she'd made the noise.

They took each step slowly, staying to the outside to limit the squeaks, creaks, and groans.

He reached the top of the stairs and pressed his ear to the door. "It's quiet."

"We're pretty far from our room."

The attic door creaked like every creepy door in every horror movie ever made.

"Shhh." She nudged his shoulder.

"Stop shushing me." Henry eased through the opening and squinted into the darkness. He would have loved to have a moment to give his eyes time to adjust, but his sister pushed him forward.

"It's so dark," she whispered.

No kidding! He took a step forward and stumbled. "There's no floor."

"What do you mean there's *no floor?*"

"Hang on." He bent down to examine what he could see in the near darkness. Joists and boards. There was no floor in the attic. The area consisted of two by eights a couple of feet apart.

"That makes zero sense. How can someone move heavy objects over beams?"

"It's probably just this section." Scraping noises stopped Henry cold. That they were farther away made sense, but they seemed to be emanating from below. "Where's that coming from?"

"I don't know." He inched forward on a joist. The moonlight trickling through gaps in the roof glittered off a line of small objects on a joist a few feet away.

"What are those?"

"Gold, but I can't tell if they're coins or jewelry." Henry crept forward and picked up a shiny coin.

Grace attempted to follow, but her foot slipped off the edge of the joist and came down hard on what he assumed was the ceiling plaster in the room below. "Ouch."

Before he could ask if she was okay, a flashlight crisscrossed over the space and landed on his face. Henry shielded his eyes, but he couldn't see past the glare.

CHAPTER FIVE

"What are you two doing up here?" A male voice, somewhat familiar, echoed through the empty attic.

"We heard scraping noises like we were talking about at lunch. Ghosts moving furniture." Grace stepped toward the door.

The light lowered enough for Henry to make out Jonathan's angry expression.

"Is there actual floor on the other side closest to our room?" She smiled like they were strolling in a garden instead of getting caught in a forbidden place after curfew.

"No, and there's nothing up here for anyone to move around." He shined the light on Henry again. "I should report this to management. They'll put you on the first ferry back to the mainland."

Henry's pulse raced. The last thing he wanted to do was explain to his parents why they'd been kicked off the island. "Don't do that. We heard noises and came to investigate."

"Out! Now."

Even though he was not much older than them, the twins followed him like scolded puppies.

Jonathan paused before opening the door to the fourth floor. "I'll let you off with a warning this once, on one condition."

Grace nodded. "Anything."

"What condition?" Henry had no idea why he'd decided to push his luck, and he couldn't say no to whatever the other guy asked of him. However, he wasn't in the habit of agreeing to terms before he heard them. It was like signing an unread contract—not smart.

"No more paranormal investigations. You two stick to history books and sightseeing."

They exchanged a quick glance and nodded. Judging by the twinkle in his sister's eyes, she had as much intention of dropping the investigation as he did.

"Do we understand each other?" The young man widened his stance and tensed his jaw as if trying to look menacing. He had about as much success with that as a Ken doll trying to pass as GI Joe.

"Yes," they said in unison.

"Good. Go back to your room and *stay* there."

Grace made a show of yawning by stretching her arms over her head. "I'll sleep like a baby once I brush my teeth and get into my PJs."

"What part of 'stay in your room' didn't you understand?" Jonathan followed them to their door and clasped his hands behind his back.

Grace pouted, but Henry dipped his chin to hide his expression. It wasn't that he had a problem with authority, but this guy seemed to enjoy bossing people around.

Staring at the ground turned out to be exactly what Henry needed to do. Jonathan's boat shoes were covered in a layer of milky-white dust. *Interesting.*

Grace closed the door and put her finger to her lips. She listened for a few heartbeats and giggled. "He's gone."

"That was—"

"—weird."

"Did you notice his shoes?"

She gave him a strange look. "Preppy docksiders? Yes, why?"

"It looked like they were covered in drywall dust."

Her brows rose into her hairline. "It did sound like someone was ripping something heavy off the walls."

He knocked lightly on the wall. "The only problem is, this sounds dense like plaster. Concrete doesn't tear."

"Drywall is unlikely in a building this age, but they've done construction as recently as 2008." She took off her shoes and sat on her bed.

Henry thought back to something he'd read. "You're right. The workers found dishes, an old hairbrush, and a shoe in the walls."

"Why would Jonathan be tearing down drywall in the middle of the night, especially after getting back to the hotel so late? Maybe it's dust from the rocks?"

"Good point." He added walking along the shore to his mental to-do list.

"I don't understand the beams in the attic. I know what I heard. There has to be a floor and something heavy up there. The way he tried to intimidate us was over the top. My guess is, he doesn't want us to know what's really going on up there."

"I agree. I'm no expert on mid-nineteenth century architecture, but I find it odd there's only one way into an attic that size." His stomach growled almost as loud as the noises that'd gotten them into trouble in the first place. "Stand guard in case he comes back."

She stood and leaned against the door.

Henry pulled the coin from his pocket and examined it under the light. "This looks old. Do you think it's real?"

"May I see it?"

Henry handed it to her.

Grace peered at it. "They sell these in gift shops everywhere from Florida to Maine."

"You're probably right. It's odd that they were laid out like that." He slipped it into a small tear in his backpack liner that served as a secret compartment.

"Who knows how long they were up there?"

"We need to go back up in the daytime. In addition to the missing floor, I'd like to see what else we can find." He sighed and rolled his head from side to side to loosen the tension. "I'm starved."

"What happened to the snacks you bought at the camp store?"

"I'm rationing them. Besides, after that ferry ride and the scares tonight, I need real food." Henry plopped down on his bed. "It's like my stomach is cannibalizing itself."

"I promise you'll live until morning." She stretched out and tugged her blanket to her chin. "I have an idea. You go down for breakfast first thing. Stay and eat if Jonathan's working in the dining room. I'll wait for ten minutes. If you don't return, I'll assume the coast is clear and sneak upstairs and check it out."

"No way. You almost broke your neck up there."

She sighed loudly. "It'll be easier to see in the daytime."

"*I'll* investigate the attic. *You* go down for breakfast."

Grace grew quiet for so long he thought she'd fallen asleep. "On second thought, it's best if we stay together."

Grace entered the dining room with her hair in a French braid and a lump of fear lodged in her throat. She stunk at lying. If someone really questioned her, they'd know something was up.

Henry whispered, "Relax. We'll make sure Jonathan's busy and grab a quick bite while our phones are charging."

Jonathan walked toward them with a coffee pot in one hand and a basket of pastries in the other. Before he could give them a hard time about the previous night, an elderly woman stopped him. He smiled and leaned closer, most likely to hear her over the din of the crowd.

Grace saw his momentary distraction as an opportunity to escape. She glanced around and decided to join an elderly couple wearing business suits. They looked out of place in a room full of people wearing casual attire. "Let's sit with them. He wouldn't dare harass us in front of witnesses."

"Good plan." Henry walked to the table. "Good morning. Would you mind if we join you?"

Grace smiled and forced herself to keep her gaze on the couple rather than checking on their new nemesis.

They nodded to the empty chairs. "Go right ahead, but we're a couple of old farts. I doubt we'll be much fun."

"Honestly, sir, as long as you share the food, I don't care what we talk about." Henry sank into a chair.

"Man after my own heart." The gentleman passed a plate of scrambled eggs.

"I'm Henry, and this is my sister Grace."

"Nice to meet you. You can call me Mort, and this is my lovely wife Esther."

"It's our pleasure to meet you," they said in unison.

They seemed taken aback.

Henry grinned. "We're twins. It happens a lot."

"Excuse me. I'll be right back." She glanced across the hall and locked eyes with Miranda. Thankfully, the electrical outlet was on the other side of the room. She pulled the phone and charger from her pocket and knelt.

Miranda chose that moment to make her approach. She loomed over Grace and lowered her voice. "Don't tell a soul about last night."

"I hadn't planned on it. We heard you when we came in. Did you confront Jonathan?" She plugged it in and waited until the screen showed a big red battery icon.

Her frown deepened into a scowl. "Yes. He denied it was him and gave me a lecture. Don't worry, though. I didn't tell him about you and Henry."

"Thanks." She stood, which put the other girl in her face. "The person was pretty far away, and it *was* dark."

Miranda leaned closer still and whispered, "I've been watching him all summer. He has a slight limp, like his right hip is higher than his left. I *know* it was him."

"You and Jonathan would make a cute couple."

She gawked. "What are you talking about?"

Grace dipped her chin. "Sorry. I thought I picked up on a vibe between you."

A flash of emotion crossed her face. "Staff aren't allowed to date."

Oops. "I didn't realize. I won't mention it again."

"We're both leaving soon. I'd hoped we might keep in touch, but now..." She shrugged. "By the way, you're not supposed to charge your phone in here."

Jessie joined them. "She's right. You can use the outlets at the front desk or in the Business Center."

Miranda folded her arms and glared at Jessie while she wasn't looking.

Grace worked to keep her expression even as she unplugged the phone. "I'll do that."

"You're twenty minutes late opening the Kiddie Barn. I told the parents to bring the children here." She nodded toward a cluster of kids near the exit.

"You work in the daycare?"

"Kiddie Barn, and yes, I do. I'm an early education major." Miranda smiled at the children. A real smile, not the thinly-veiled annoyed expression she normally sported.

What happened next made Grace fear for the younger generation. Miranda strolled over to the group of kids. "All right, Munchkins. Follow me for arts and crafts!"

The children fell into line behind her and marched out of the dining hall.

"Weird, isn't it?" Jessie whispered, nodding at Henry and the others at the table.

"I can't help feeling like someone put Cruella Deville in charge of puppy adoptions."

Jessie choked back laughter.

"I should eat while the food's hot."

"I'll go say hi to Henry."

Grace internally cringed and crossed the room to rejoin her brother.

Jessie smiled at the older couple. "Good morning, Mr. and Mrs. Montgomery. How's your breakfast?"

"It was wonderful, but it's time for me to retire to the veranda." Mort stood to pull his wife's chair out.

Esther rose to her feet. "And I have a seminar starting soon. It was nice to meet you both. Perhaps you'll join us for dinner soon."

"Absolutely." Henry downed half his coffee.

"I'd like that." Grace sat and placed a pastry on her plate. They had a limited amount of time to explore the attic, but first, they needed to get rid of Jessie.

"You're both still coming to the Smuttynose picnic this afternoon, right?"

"Looking forward to it." Henry smiled and put his napkin on his empty plate.

"What happened to you two last night? I didn't see you at dinner." She glanced at her watch and frowned.

"We went to sleep early. It was a really long day. I was seasick on the ferry, and we explored the island. Plus, you know how it is with fresh air. I mean, sea air. It makes me sleepy." Grace would have continued to ramble had Jessie not laughed.

"Your middle of the night trip to the attic probably didn't help."

Grace choked on her breakfast.

Thankfully, Henry had his wits about him. "Either the chili was coming back to haunt us, or there's an apparition up there moving nonexistent furniture."

She pressed her lips together and gave him a quick nod. "I heard. Listen, Jonathan can be intense, but he takes his job seriously. I'd hate to have to ask the two of you to leave for going where you're not supposed to."

Grace's cheeks burned. She had no reply, nor did she trust herself to speak.

"A bunch of us are getting together for a bonfire after dinner. You should come." Her tone had changed from conversational to bossy.

Henry glanced at her and Grace. "We really do have work to do."

"You're only here for three nights. You can work when you return home." The blonde smiled and walked away.

Grace watched her go. "It's like we woke up in an alternate reality. Miranda was quasi-nice to me, and Jessie—"

"—was pushy. Why do I get the impression she's going out of her way to keep us busy?"

"She's a supervisor. She's used to bossing people around." Grace took a bite of the pastry, but it tasted like ash on her tongue. "Speaking of that, she made me unplug the phone. It's still dead."

"Great." Henry glanced over his shoulder and turned back to Grace. "Let's go while they're all still here."

CHAPTER SIX

Although the sun had risen an hour before, only slivers of light seeped through the gaps in the plywood covering the attic windows. Thin lines of dusty light crossed the attic at irregular intervals. The rest of the planks that created the walkway across the attic joists remained cloaked in shadows.

Standing on the small platform inside the attic door, Henry whispered, "We took too long in the dining hall. We have to hurry."

"Sounds good to me." Her eyes rounded and her voice thinned. "We're looking for the source of the noise. Don't get distracted by anything else."

"But...clues!" Henry replied in a laughing whisper. He shook his head and started across, trying to step only where he could see. If he had to feel his way with a toe, it slowed him down.

Creak.

They froze. "Step only where the boards cross the rafters," Grace cautioned. Henry looked back. He had been. The twins had a tendency to tell each what they wanted to remind themselves, like Henry encouraging them to hurry. He knew that he could spend all day in the attic, searching and discovering. Grace was looking everywhere except where she was walking because she wanted to solve the riddle.

"Coins?" she asked, referring to the one they'd found on their first trip up. She was convinced there were more. Henry thought so, too.

Money was a prime motivation for crime.

"After we've reached the other side to see what they were moving up here."

"Follow me." Staying close to the wall, Henry stepped where the planks crossed the joists and worked his way across the attic. Thankfully, the joists running lengthwise were a bit wider and less bendy beneath his weight.

"Not so fast. I don't want to fall and alert anyone we're up here."

"Sorry." He slowed his pace. "Watch out. I felt nails sticking through a couple of these boards."

"Lovely." *Creak. Groan.* Grace whispered, "Sorry."

Henry came to a wall far too soon to have reached the end of the building. When he knocked on the smooth surface, it sounded hollow. "I doubt this is part of the original construction."

"It's probably one of the firebreaks the Pelican in the library mentioned."

"Stay close." Keeping one hand on the wall, he carefully maneuvered toward the center of the building until he found an opening. "Do firebreaks have doors?"

"I don't know why not."

He walked through and ran into the angled roof, then continued his trip toward the far end of the attic. At approximately the halfway mark, they came to another wall, and again at the three-quarter mark. "Our room is below this section." Henry pointed at his feet, but they were in a shaded area and his gesture was lost in the darkness.

Henry skimmed his fingers over the surface of the barrier. "Be careful here. The boards are exposed."

"That could explain the sounds, but why would someone tear apart a wall in the middle of the night?" Grace ran her fingers carefully across the structure in front of them. "Only the bottom two-thirds has been removed."

"They could be replacing electrical wiring or pipes. The restroom is in this area," Henry noted.

"Rather than missing something, we should cross back and forth from the front to the rear of the building in a grid pattern," Grace suggested. Henry took two steps toward the center of the attic, stepping only where the walking planks crossed the joists.

Creak. Groan. He stopped and backed slowly to where Grace stood. "I'm too heavy. I sound like somebody walking across the attic. They're going to know we're up here. You go. You're lighter."

Their plan to cover the area was easier said than done. Once she left the security of the wall, she had nothing to hold onto for support. "This is like walking a tightrope over an alligator-infested pond while blindfolded."

Henry didn't reply, but he could hear her heavy breathing.

After several passes, Grace's footstep made a hollow sound near the center of the space. She crouched and patted the plywood until she reached the edges —a cutout in the middle of the attic floor.

"What was that?" Henry whispered.

"A floor? A door?" Henry crawled along the flat surface until it widened. He felt his way around the edges of the larger platform. *Six feet long and four feet wide. Why would someone put this here? It can't be random.*

He followed the narrow strip again. Several feet later, he jammed his knuckles against what he thought was a pile of two by fours. Upon closer inspection, he realized he'd found a drop-down stair. "It's a drop-down staircase. There's a secret way into the attic."

"Where are we in relation to the fourth floor?"

"I'm not sure. This place is massive." He squinted at the slivers of light around the windows. "We have to be near our room."

Grace took one slow step at a time until she knelt by his side.

"Be careful. I can't see well enough to understand how the ladder works. If I put my weight on the wrong spot, it could open."

She crouched beside him. "Which room does it open into?"

"There's one way to find out." Heart thumping, a warning he chose to ignore, he pressed down on the stairs folded within the door, Henry and Grace determined the top and the bottom. Henry balanced over the section that would swing downward and began to push.

Grace put her hand on his arm. "Wait, what if someone's below us?"

"Besides ours, the fourth floor is mostly staff rooms. They should be working." He continued to push. The contraption moved three or four inches before catching on something. "It's stuck."

He pushed again, harder. This time the springs screamed in protest, but the door refused to budge. The twins froze before realizing the screech was loud in the attic but may not have carried into the room below.

Grace shook her head and pulled his hand back. "We're making too much noise."

"I bet this thing hasn't been opened in decades." He sat back, wobbled to the side, and slammed his hand down to catch his balance. His palm landed on something sharp. The pain was instantaneous, as was the sound of metal clanking against metal. "Ouch."

"Are you okay?"

"I cut myself." Henry rubbed the injury to check for blood and cringed when his thumb came away wet. *Rusty nails? Broken pieces of springs? When was my last tetanus shot?*

Grace sighed. "I've seen enough. Let's get out of here."

"Hold on." He fished around the area, sliding his hand sideways to determine what he'd impaled himself on and found something metallic, but this was smooth and shaped like a silver dollar, only thicker and rougher. "Coins."

"Henry, I really want to leave." She stood.

He explored the cubby hole again and found three more coins, and two similarly-shaped items that felt like chalk. With very little light, he had no way of knowing for certain, but he thought he'd found a broach. Whatever it was, it had a sharp pin attached to it. "I found what stabbed me."

"Okay. Let's go," Grace whispered.

When Henry stood, the access door sprung open with a squeal and the uncoiling of rusty springs.

Grace gasped and grabbed Henry's arm. He put his hand over hers, and they stood as still as statues.

They had no idea what or who to expect to crawl up the ladder, and they weren't sure they wanted to find out.

The wood creaked, and the top of someone's head appeared in the opening. They couldn't see much other than light-colored hair on the back of the person's head.

Henry held his breath, but he could do nothing about the twitchy feeling in his legs. They were telling him to do something. He argued with them, his mind telling him that stealth was the best choice. The muscles in his legs vibrated with tension. Grace's grip tightened on his arm until the blood pounded in his fingers.

The person dropped what looked like a small bag into the space where Henry had found the coins.

A beeping sound and radio static crackled through the air. A disembodied voice said, "Problem with the first-floor water reclamation system. 10:25 ferry, ETA fifteen minutes."

The man backed down the ladder and let the pull-down door swing back into place.

Three things occurred to Henry. One, the room must not have had windows, or the blinds were pulled. Two, the guy had worn latex gloves. And three, the door seemed to have opened fairly easily. Maybe four, there was a beeping that might have been from a low battery. He thought he had heard it on Jonathan's radio in the locker room.

There's probably a lock on the latch. Which made sense; the ladder was meant for people to enter the attic from the fourth floor, not the other way around.

They waited and listened and waited some more before Henry reached for the bag. It had some weight to it, along with the tell-tale jingle of coins.

"What are you doing?" Grace whispered close to his ear.

Henry wasn't a thief, but he had a feeling the man who'd left the loot was. Curiosity got the better of him, and he took one of the rough metal objects out and stuffed it in his pocket with the others. "We need to know what he's hiding up here."

"He was wearing gloves. Whatever it is, it isn't good." She sounded as if she would come out of her skin at any moment. "Let's go!"

"Yes, but quietly." Henry could feel Grace's hand shaking as she let go. He found that he was shaking, too.

They made their way back to the stairwell without incident, but once again, they'd taken longer than they'd planned—which meant the Pelicans could be anywhere.

The color had drained from Grace's face, and a layer of sweat had formed on her forehead. "Just to be safe, we should take the stairs to the first floor."

"Good idea. The radio call mentioned something about a water system and the ferry," Henry recalled, before adding, "We need to figure out who dumped the bag in the attic." He turned and eased down the stairs.

When they reached the fourth-floor landing, they picked up the pace.

Grace stopped and stretched, trying to relieve the tension in her body. Henry did the same thing, finding that he was as tight as a coiled door spring. When Grace righted herself, she grinned. "That was intense."

"That's an understatement." Henry laughed, but it came out higher and more breathy than normal.

Grace shook her arms out and bounced on the balls of her feet. "We have a fifty-fifty chance of getting it right unless we split up."

"You take the ferry. I'll look for the desalination system."

"Sounds like a plan. I'll meet you by the dining hall when I'm done."

"Okay." Henry had no clue where to look, so he started in the most logical place—the basement.

Locked doors labeled *Employees Only* blocked off both ends of the hall, and other than the hum of machinery, the place seemed deserted. Henry walked through the door labeled Men's Showers, the only place on the basement level he could explore without picking a lock or breaking down a door.

He found himself in a locker room with no lockers. White shelves with cubby-hole-sized openings sat in three rows with benches between them. Henry listened for voices or the sounds of workmen, but like the rest of the basement, the place was silent.

He went out the same way he'd come in and ran into Jonathan in the hall. "Good morning."

The Pelican narrowed his eyes. "The showers are closed today."

"I know. I thought I'd get a look at them. Jessie said they used filtered rainwater. I was curious to see how it worked."

"The plumbing and other facilities are off-limits to guests." He tucked what looked like a rectangular tissue box under his arm. "One more strike and you're out of here. I suggest you find a book and a rocker and stop going where you don't belong."

Henry understood they'd irritated the guy the previous night, but his lack of hospitality was getting on his nerves. "That sounds great, but Grace and I have plans to visit Smuttynose with Jessie today."

Jonathan stepped into his path. "Where were you this morning after breakfast?"

"We went for a walk." He nodded toward the stairs. "And now I'd like to grab a snack."

"The kitchen is closed."

Henry sighed. He knew for a fact the snack bar was open but saw no reason to argue. "Have I done something to offend you?"

"Besides sneaking around in the middle of the night?" Jonathan smirked. "Let's see. You and your sister continued sticking your noses into my cousin's disappearance after you were asked to leave it alone. Now I find you coming out of the *closed* showers?"

Hold the phones. Did he just say Emily Blanchard was his cousin? Henry worked hard to keep his expression neutral. He shoved his hands in his pockets, and the coins jingled. Unlike quarters and dimes, gold had a distinct melodic *ping*.

Jonathan narrowed his eyes.

Luckily, the radio on Jonathan's hip crackled and beeped. The same disembodied voice came through the connection. "10:25 ferry departed. Twenty day-trippers incoming. Ten for guided tour."

He pulled the walkie-talkie from his belt and pressed the button. "Jessie, what's your location."

"The pier. Can you cover—"

Jonathan dropped the box of tissues. No not tissues, *surgical gloves.*

He's the guy in the attic. Henry didn't stick around to hear the rest of the conversation. He pushed past Jonathan and hurried to put as much distance between them as possible. His chest tight and mind spinning, he didn't dare continue the conversation. The Pelican would notice the change in his demeanor. Henry could feel Jonathan's eyes boring holes in his back as he made his escape.

No sense in searching for the desalination system. I've found our culprit. He doubted Grace had made it back from the pier in such a short time, so he went in search of her.

He stepped onto the veranda and spotted Grace, Jessie, and an older man making their way toward the hotel.

As if she sensed his presence, his sister glanced up and frowned.

He smoothed his expression and walked down the steps.

"You don't look well. Are you sick?" Jessie had such a maternal expression, he half-expected her to press her hand to his forehead.

"I'm feeling a little under the weather." He pressed his hand to his gut and met Grace's gaze.

She smiled, but it seemed forced. "This is Jessie's father, Dr. Jacob Jaffrey. He's the head scientist on the Gosport Green Initiative, and an MIT alum." She turned to the man. "This is my twin brother Henry."

Head scientist? No wonder Jessie planned to intern on the island. Their relationship explained the scene from the night. Jessie had probably taken Jonathan home for a family dinner.

Henry offered his hand.

"Nice to meet you. You're not feeling well. Forgive me for not shaking your hand."

"Of course."

"I offered to give Grace a tour of the desalination system and recycling center." Dr. Jaffrey curled and flexed his fingers several times.

Henry chalked the strange gesture up to a nervous habit.

"Would it be possible to see it tomorrow?" Grace moved to her brother's side. "I should take him upstairs."

Jessie tilted her head. "But we're leaving for Smuttynose Island in a half hour. Are you sure you can't manage without her?"

"Nonsense, let the boy rest." Dr. Jaffrey nodded to Grace. "I'll be on the island tomorrow. Have Jessie radio me."

"I'll do that, thank you."

"You really do look awful." The blonde frowned and guided him back to the veranda. "Have a seat out here. The fresh air will help, and I'll be right back with some antacids from the kitchen."

"Thanks." He eased into one of the rockers.

Jonathan loitered a few chairs down. Although he spoke to another guest, he continued to glance at the twins.

"Jessie was telling me about MIT." Grace plopped down beside him and spoke in a loud, clear voice. More than likely, she intended for Jonathan to overhear her. "Her father is amazing. The science behind the green initiative is state-of-the-art."

"That's great," he said aloud before mouthing, "I need to speak to you *alone*."

"It's nice to have someone with inside information about the school. I haven't been able to find any real answers online. Did *you* find any decent forums for Stanford?"

Ah, she's speaking in code. "Yes, as a matter of fact, I did. I was able to get answers to quite a few questions."

As if she'd smelled blood in the water, Miranda strolled toward them.

Henry's shoulders slumped.

The girl glanced between him and Jonathan and cut a path to the Pel. The two seemed downright chummy considering the argument yesterday.

Grace leaned close and whispered, "Now that he's occupied, let's go."

"Here you are. I hope you don't mind ginger ale and toast." Jessie set a tray in front of him. "I couldn't find the—"

"This is fine. Thanks." He hadn't meant to come off as gruff, but he'd explode if he didn't get his sister out of there soon.

"You're welcome." The young woman gave him an odd look and turned to Grace. "Do you have any other questions about MIT?"

"A few hundred, but I'll catch up with you later. I think Henry needs to lie down."

"Don't be silly. You're coming with us to Smuttynose, and I won't take no for an answer." She folded her arms as if to prove her point. "Henry, I'm sending you to the First Aid Station for an evaluation."

He didn't want to see a nurse or go to the island, but if he had to choose, he'd make a miraculous recovery and go on a picnic.

The twins continued to make inane small talk while in the public eye, Henry eating his toast and downing the ginger ale. A half-hour later, the twins made their way to a line of rowboats on the beach.

"You're going to need to paddle." Henry glanced around before holding out his palm.

"Ouch. Is that where you stabbed yourself?" Grace winced. "Do you know who the man in the attic was?"

"Jonathan."

She nearly dropped one of the oars. "How? I mean, are you sure?"

"He was in the basement when I came out of the showers. He was carrying a box of latex gloves, and his radio beeped in the same odd way as the one we heard in the attic."

"Incriminating, but the kitchen staff wears gloves, and quite a few of the staff carry walkie-talkies. It's not out of the realm of possibility that more than one needs new batteries."

"You have a point, but I'm telling you, the guy's up to no good." He pulled the items he'd collected in the attic from his pocket. "The coins jingled, and the look he gave me? I think he recognized the sound."

"That makes him the most likely suspect, but for what?"

She must have caught his paranoia because she was too busy looking over her shoulder to notice the objects in his hand. When she finally returned her attention to him, she blinked. "Are those Neccos?"

"What?"

"The candy. Are they Neccos?"

"I'm holding what could be pirate treasure, and you're asking about candy?"

"A certain missing little girl happens to love Necco wafers." Her expression looked pinched or pained or frustrated, or maybe all three.

He set the broach, coins, and what had felt like chalk on the bench beside him and examined all three. "They look like Neccos, but I'm not about to eat one to find out."

"Let me see it." She took one from his hand and held it up to the light. "It was humid in the attic. The moisture would have made these dissolve, which means these aren't too old."

"Everything up there was covered in dust, but these have the normal chalky coating."

"Once opened, the sugar will start to separate from the other ingredients, and they will taste off. Stale." Grace bit off a small chunk of the candy.

"They always taste stale, like eating a flat piece of chalk soaked in licorice juice."

Grace popped the remainder of the wafer into her mouth.

Henry watched in horror.

"They taste as if they came from a newly-opened roll. These were left in the attic recently. The sightings of a little girl in a white nightgown on the island? It's Emily!" Grace stated, firm in her resolve. "Is that crime enough for further investigation?"

He leaned into her line of vision. "Other people eat Neccos, but if there is a reason to believe that kidnapping and theft have taken place, then yes. That's a crime worth investigating. And if our perpetrator is using the little girl as part of the urban legend to deflect attention..." Henry's eyebrows pinched together as he concentrated. He glanced around to make sure no one was watching before continuing. "Jonathan let it slip that he's Emily's cousin. She could have gotten her love of bad candy from him."

"Her cousin?" Grace furrowed her brow. "Both Jessie and Jonathan have family living in the Shoals?"

"They could be related."

"I doubt it. You saw how jealous Miranda became after she saw them together." She drew a deep breath and motioned to the coins. "Emily's mother said she loved pirates. What if these are her pretend pirate treasure?"

"They must be real. Why else would someone hide them?" He furrowed his brow. "The stones in the broach aren't plastic and don't look like glass."

"I'm sure there's some way to tell the difference. We need time alone to research it, but we're stuck with the Pels for the afternoon."

Henry looked out over Gosport Harbor. "The others are already on Smuttynose. You should paddle before Jessie swims out to see what's taking us so long."

"Why can I see her doing that?" Grace put the oars in the water and got to work—turning the boat around.

Henry glanced toward the shore. Jonathan stood with his hands on his hips like some sort of monolith warning travelers not to enter. "He looks angry. What are you doing?"

"I'm going back to Star Island. We have a mystery to solve."

CHAPTER SEVEN

Back in their room, Grace grabbed her notebook and phone charger. "Jessie's going to be upset we turned around. She may come looking for us when she gets back."

"The Business Center is the first place she'll look." Henry pulled his clothing and toiletries out of his backpack and shoved the coins, broach, and his computer inside.

"This is a conference center. There have to be rooms with Wi-Fi and electrical outlets. I say we ask at the front desk."

A pretty girl with dark skin and a riot of dark curls sat behind the reception counter. She glanced up and smiled when they approached. "Hi. How can I help you?"

Grace smiled and forced herself to speak at a normal rate. "Is there a place we can plug in our computers besides the Business Center?"

"You're welcome to work in the lobby."

She glanced over her shoulder at the growing crowd. "It's pretty busy in here. We're working on a project for school, and our mom is going to flip if we don't have it completed by the time we return home."

She removed a key ring from beneath the counter. "I have just the place."

The twins followed her to a large empty room. Stacks of plastic chairs rested against one wall, and a chalkboard hung on another. If it weren't for the view of the ocean through a series of plate glass windows, it would have been a boring classroom.

"The room's empty until seven o'clock yoga. There's an outlet behind the long table."

Grace took in her surroundings. "This is perfect. I'm going to have to focus to keep myself from staring out at the water."

The girl smiled. "No food or drinks, except water. If you need to leave for lunch or the restroom, just pull the door closed behind you. Your belongings will be safe in here."

"Thank you. We shouldn't need more than an hour or two." Henry plugged in his laptop and attached a phone charger to the USB port.

The young woman wished them well and pulled the door closed on her way out.

"Where do we start?" Grace pulled up a chair.

"How to identify gold from other metals." He typed the words as he spoke.

The do-it-yourself techniques required magnets, acid, scales, or ceramic plates, and even then, they weren't conclusive.

Grace took notes, but judging from her sighs, she'd come to the same conclusion he had. The at-home tests wouldn't work until they were actually at home.

"Let's try to identify the coins." He opened another browser window.

She nodded and flipped to a clean sheet of paper.

After nearly two hours of digging, they found an image of a Spanish gold escudo with the same images of a cross and shield as the coins from the attic. The website dated the coins between 1516 and 1556.

He sat back and rolled his head from side to side. "That's two hundred years before Blackbeard's time."

"Could the pirate have recovered these from a shipwreck?" Grace tapped her pen on the table.

"It's possible. I'll search to see how long these coins were in circulation."

She grinned. "Spanish and Portuguese coins were the most popular form of currency in the early Colonial Period."

"How do you know that?"

"I was curious why we have dollars instead of pounds. 'Dollar' is an alternate term for Spanish pieces of eight."

"Nice. Okay, let's see if we can date the broach." Henry searched antique jewelry for the same time period. Though he couldn't find any similar pieces from the 1500s, he located several comparable items from the 1600s.

Leaning over his shoulder, Grace whispered, "Holy cow. I thought it was cheap painted metal and fake stones."

He nodded. "I've never heard of enameled gold. It says here it was popular during that time period."

"Not conclusive evidence, but too much of a coincidence to ignore."

"Speaking of coincidences, let's see if we can find anything on Jonathan." He entered various search terms and came up empty. "We need his last name."

"Try searching for Jessica Jaffrey."

Evidently, Jessie didn't have social media accounts or much of a digital footprint. They found one article that mentioned her working with her father on the Gosport Green Initiative.

"Well, that was a bust." Grace stood and stretched.

"Dr. Jaffrey looks familiar, but I can't put my finger on it."

"I thought the same thing. I figured I'd seen his picture when researching the island."

"That's probably it." Henry googled the shelf life of Necco Wafers.

Grace looked at the screen and laughed. "What are you doing?"

He read three websites. "It turns out you were right. The candy should have dissolved after as little as two weeks in the humid environment."

She pumped her fist in the air. "Neccos. Not only are they delicious, but they're also awesome clues."

He wanted to say something, but the words wouldn't come to him.

She ruffled his hair. "Your strengths compliment my weaknesses and vice versa."

"To quote Aristotle, the whole of the Warner twins are far greater than the parts." He couldn't stop grinning. This was the thrill she'd mentioned while setting up the RV. They were getting closer to solving the case.

A lady in stretchy pants and an oversized t-shirt walked into the room and stopped short. "Oh! I thought this was the yoga class."

He glanced at the time on his computer and frowned. "It is. We lost track of time."

As if on cue, Grace's stomach growled.

Two more women entered the room before the twins had packed their gear and headed for the dining hall.

Henry blew out a sigh of relief when the wonderful sounds of voices and clanking dishes filled his ears. The aroma of something beefy and warm hit his nose and made his empty stomach sit up and take notice. Not even Jonathan's glower from the entryway could ruin his sense of contentment. *This is what heaven smells like. Beef stew and fresh-baked bread.*

"It was rude to turn around without telling anyone where you were going." He used the same superior tone as he had the night before and that morning.

Grace raised a single brow. "Jessie knew Henry wasn't feeling well."

The Pelican eyed her for a moment and then turned back to him. "Where were you all afternoon?"

"In a classroom researching pirates, if you must know." He walked past him and waved. "We'll find our own table."

"Should we sit with the Pels?" Grace chewed her lower lip.

"Not a chance." He spotted Mort and Esther Montgomery and waved. "Hello, would you mind if we join you again?"

"The more, the merrier." Esther motioned to the empty chairs beside her.

The twins filled their bowls with beef stew.

Mort passed the breadbasket. "Are you in college, son?"

"I'm a senior in high school, but I hope to attend Stanford next year."

"Good school. I went to Cornell myself." He turned his attention to Grace. "And you, young lady?"

"I plan to attend MIT, my mother's alma mater."

"Ah, very good. Very good indeed." Mort winked at his wife. "My Esther was one heck of an engineer before she quit to take care of me."

"I took a leave of absence to raise our children." The woman slapped his arm. "Now I'm an antique dealer."

"How did you make that transition?" Grace sipped her tea.

"I realized I had an eye for it while traveling with Mort. I liked my work as a civil engineer, but antiques are my passion." She waved to the twins' food. "Go ahead and eat before your supper gets cold."

Henry shoveled a spoonful of stew into his mouth and sighed. It was almost as good as his father's. He turned to Grace. "I'm still hung up on authenticating coins."

The older couple exchanged a glance.

"Any ideas?" Grace turned to face Henry.

"Hard to tell without the proper equipment. Maybe we could ask for a bottle of vinegar?"

"All right, All right. You two can stop now." The older man sighed.

Esther chuckled.

Henry glanced at the couple. "I'm sorry, I don't understand."

"Mort's a retired jeweler with an old coin addiction." The woman winked. "But you knew that already, didn't you?"

Henry took a sip from the water glass in front of him. *This could be good or very, very bad.* "No, actually. I had no idea."

"You're kidding." Mort's bushy eyebrows rose. "Of all the gin joints in all the towns in all the world, you happened to sit at my table?"

"Appears so." Henry's surprise morphed into caution. *It could be a coincidence. Mort could be on the island to attend a conference, or maybe he was vacationing with his wife. Or he could be here to evaluate Jonathan's treasure trove.*

The old guy's eyes lit up. "What sort of coin do you have?"

"My grandfather gave me an 1870 two pesetas coin." He lied. "First, I thought it was a fake, then I thought it might be worth something."

Mort chuckled. "About ten dollars."

"Great." Henry made a show of grumbling and returned his attention to his dinner.

Grace patted him on the back. "It's the thought that counts. Besides, you can't put a dollar figure on sentimental value."

"Truer words have never been spoken." Esther raised her glass.

Mort pulled a business card from his wallet. "Look me up the next time your grandfather gives you an old coin. I give preliminary appraisals from photographs."

Grace took the card, read it, and slid it to Henry.

Jonathan stopped at the table and flashed his made-for-television smile. "Mr. Montgomery, sorry to interrupt your dinner. Might I have a word with you?"

The older man pushed to his feet and followed the Pelican to the back of the room. Every now and then Henry would glance in their direction and find one or the other staring back. Call it paranoia, but he had the distinct impression they were discussing him and his sister.

Grace set her napkin on the table. "Do you want to go to the bonfire tonight?"

The *last* thing he wanted to do was go to the bonfire. "We should stay in and work on our report."

Mort returned to the table. "Homework? Here? You kids should have some fun. Go ghost-hunting."

Esther gave him an odd look and turned back to the twins. "What sort of report are you working on?"

Henry snatched a brownie from the dessert plate and laughed. "Actually, we are researching ghosts. Specifically, the Lady in White."

This seemed to catch Mort's attention even more than the coin had, likely because searching for spirits had been his idea. "I saw a ghost here when I was in my twenties."

"In the hotel?" Grace leaned in and gave the man her full attention.

"I'll let her tell you. She has a far better memory than I do."

Esther's expression took on a dreamy quality, and she gave Mort's hand a squeeze. "It was our first date. We were both working at the hotel, and we hiked to the uninhabited side of the island. There's an old cemetery over there where the Beebe sisters are buried."

"I didn't see the ghost. I was too busy tripping over my tongue and staring at her." He kissed Esther's cheek.

The twins exchanged a glance.

Henry knew how he'd be spending the next few hours the moment he caught the glimmer in his sister's eyes. "Too bad we don't have flashlights."

"You can borrow some at the front desk." Mort lowered his voice. "Just don't tell them where you're going. That area's off-limits at night. Hotel policy since that little girl fell off the rocks and drowned last year."

Grace gasped. "Are you talking about the Blanchard girl?"

He nodded. "Terrible thing. We've known her family since we were kids. Isn't that right, Esther?"

She glanced in the direction of the Pelicans' table. "Good people."

Mort tossed his napkin on the table. "Be careful if you go out there. The rocks can be slick, and the paths are covered with poison ivy."

CHAPTER EIGHT

A dense fog hung over the island. Miles from the mainland, and yards from the hotel, the night seemed darker than any night she could remember. Grace loved it.

"This is perfect weather for ghost-hunting." She aimed her flashlight at her brother.

Henry groaned and shielded his eyes. "Cut it out. Are you sure this is the path Mort told us to take?"

"Absolutely. He said there'd be a fork. One side led to the Tucke Monument, and the other to the Beebe gravesites." She'd replayed the dinner conversation over and over and had come up with nothing but questions. "I can't figure it out. How did the police determine Emily came out here the night she disappeared?"

"No idea."

"I read everything I could find about her case. There was no mention of her wandering to a remote part of the island. How's that possible?" She tapped her lips. "Maybe they found some of her belongings out here?"

"The police withhold details from the media in cases like these." He stopped and turned in a full circle. "We've been walking too long. Did we miss it?"

"It can't be much farther. It's an island. Sooner or later we'll fall into the sea." Grace trailed behind him. "Are you going to have Mort authenticate the coins?"

"I'm not sure. I find it too much of a coincidence that he's here on the island as well as someone stealing treasure and stashing it in the attic. He's friendly with Jonathan, who is stashing the coins, so I can only conclude that he already knows about them. If we show him coins that he's already seen, we can assume he'll tell Jonathan."

"You may be right. Mort can't be the only person who does that sort of thing. Maybe we can find another dealer who can tell you if it's real from a photo?"

"Unless I catch a fatal case of poison ivy and never leave the island."

She rolled her eyes, although he couldn't see her. "Look. That has to be it. They said to look for low stones where the iron fencing used to be."

The twins made their way closer to the white rocks surrounding the cemetery. In the center sat a short obelisk, and to the side were three small headstones.

Grace shined her light on the memorial and read the inscription under the name of one of the girls out loud. "I don't want to die, but I'll do just as Jesus wants me to."

"That's—"

"Horrifically sad." She knelt to clear away debris from the bottom of the monument and froze. "Neccos."

"What?"

She plucked several black wafers from the ground. "Someone left a stash of licorice Neccos here."

"Are they melted?"

Grace shined her light on the candy. "Some are, and some look like they were left here tonight."

"That's just...creepy. Didn't Emily's mother say she liked ghost stories?"

"Yes." Grace returned the wafers to the base of the monument and rubbed her upper arms to chase away a chill.

"Are there any ghost stories related to this cemetery?"

"I'm not sure, but we should do a stakeout here. If it *is* Emily, maybe she'll come back tomorrow night."

"Good idea. Even if it's not the girl, the person leaving the Neccos will know something." He bent and scratched his ankles. "Where do we go now?"

She dearly wished Mort had never mentioned poison ivy to Henry. He'd have red welts all right, but not from the plants—from all the scratching. "We're supposed to follow the path to the rocks above the shore. Esther said the Lady in White appeared at the highest point."

He grumbled about not having calamine lotion but made his way out of the tiny graveyard.

Grace lingered. The oldest of the Beebe sisters had been seven when she'd died of scarlet fever, a year younger than Emily Blanchard had been when she went missing. She pressed her hand to the monument and whispered, "Where are you?"

"Holy smokes! Grace! You need to get up here," Henry said too loudly.

She moved as quickly as she dared. The path leading toward the water seemed far less traveled than the one from the hotel. The stones were larger, and less packed down. She moved clear of the trees and stopped dead.

Henry stood on a boulder with his light shining toward the sky. A few feet away from him, thick white mist in the shape of a human appeared to hover above the ground.

A cold sweat broke out across her entire upper body. *That can't be real!* "Turn off your flashlight."

Henry's light went out, but whatever the thing was didn't.

Okay, not a trick of the light. She inched closer, and the apparition or whatever it was drifted farther out onto the rocks.

She couldn't see more than a faint outline of her brother's body, but she caught his movement. "Henry, don't!"

The sound of sliding rocks told her he hadn't listened.

Grace trained her flashlight in front of her and moved forward one careful step at a time.

A short scream tore through the night air, and her heart stopped beating.

More rocks and sand fell, along with something heavier; she could only assume it was her brother. "Henry!"

Grace shined the light over the area, but he'd vanished. Slowly, testing each space before she put her weight down, she moved forward. In the movies, people rushed to the edges of cliffs when someone went over, but this was no cliff. It was a series of craggy, weather-worn boulders that appeared to have swallowed her brother whole.

"Henry?" She strained to hear over the pounding surf.

"I'm okay." He didn't sound okay. In fact, he sounded the opposite of okay.

"Are you hurt?" She swung the light back and forth over the area and found cracks and crevices, but none appeared large enough for a five-foot-eleven-inch boy to have fallen through.

"I'll live."

"I can't find where you fell. Do you still have your flashlight?"

"Yes. Lost my backpack, though."

She took another step forward, and a flat rock the size of a pizza box shifted beneath her foot. Grace froze, afraid to move or even breathe. "I have to go back and get help."

"There's water. Walk out here."

"Stay put!" She barely recognized the sound of her own voice. They'd been through a lot together, but this terrified her.

He said something she couldn't make out.

"I can't hear you!" Grace went to her hands and knees, held the flashlight between her neck and shoulder, and crawled forward in hopes of finding where he'd fallen. "Henry?"

No reply.

Emotion threatened to swell her throat shut. She blinked several times to clear her vision and inched closer to the edge of the rocks. *This is madness. I should go for help.*

She caught sight of dark-blue fabric and scurried closer. Henry's backpack had caught between two boulders, and just beyond it was an opening large enough to have swallowed her brother.

"Hello? Can you hear me?" Grace stretched out on her belly and shined the light into the crack.

She heard something, but couldn't tell if it was him or a gull. "Answer me!"

The sound came again.

Frustration, fear, guilt, and several emotions she couldn't quite name threatened to overtake her. *He said he was okay. He'd spoken after he'd fallen. But what if he'd passed out? He said there was water.*

Pulse racing, she tugged the backpack. It didn't budge, but a pink light flickered. *What the heck?*

She wiggled the bag again. The light blinked on and off, but she couldn't free it. Grace gave up, backed off the loose rocks, and stood when she reached solid ground. She turned toward the path back to the cemetery when she heard the sound again, only this time she knew it was no seagull. Her brother's pain-filled cry hit her like a gut punch.

She swept the light over the area.

A skid, a thump, and more earth falling came from the left.

"Henry?" She rushed toward the sound and skidded to a stop at the edge of a boulder. A few yards below, water crashed against the steep edge of the island.

"Grace." More rocks slid, and a young man groaned.

She followed his voice to what she could only describe as the aftermath of a rockslide. Halfway up the C-shaped slope, a flashlight bobbed as Henry struggled to find his footing. "I'm coming down. Stay put."

"No. Too dangerous." He took several steps and slid again.

Hands trembling, she shined the light at the space directly in front of him and prayed the dark spots on his shirt were seawater.

After what felt like an eternity of three feet forward, two back, Henry made it to the top of the slope. He dropped to the ground and rolled to his back. "Need a minute."

Grace knelt beside him and surveyed the damage. Blood covered his hands and knees, and he'd scraped his forehead—probably on the way down.

"I know you want to go for help, but don't." Despite his condition, he grinned. "Minors aren't allowed to go past the boundaries of the hotel property without adult supervision."

She wanted to smack him, but he'd taken enough of a beating. "You need help. I don't care if they send us home tomorrow."

"The initial fall wasn't that bad, but the rocks on the way back up were slick and covered in barnacles." Henry sat upright and sucked in a breath. "My knees feel like hamburger."

"There's a lot of blood. You're probably going to need stitches." The thought of it made her stomach hurt. In fact, her entire body hurt. Call it twin weirdness, but Grace always seemed to suffer from sympathy pains when Henry injured himself.

"Add that to the list right after a tetanus shot." He glanced at his hands and frowned. "Did you see the ghost?"

After everything that'd happened, she'd forgotten all about the strange figure. "I saw something, but I'm not sure what it was."

"You're going to think I'm crazy, but I swear it was a woman. She looked right at me."

"It did have a vaguely human shape…"

"And we did just visit a cemetery. I suppose it's possible I imagined her, but I'm telling you, she had distinct facial features."

Grace nodded unsure of how to respond. She wanted to believe him. But a ghost? "I'll do some research on weather phenomenon in case there's a rational explanation."

"Like what?"

"I don't know. A mirror effect?"

He turned his face toward the sky and stared as if he expected the answers to fall from heaven. "Did you find my backpack?"

She debated denying she'd seen it but figured he'd insist they search for it. "It's stuck between two boulders."

"My computer's in there." He raised his hand as if to run it over his head but seemed to think the better of it.

"I think the laptop's toast. A pink light came on every time I tugged on the bag."

He furrowed his brow. "Pink?"

"Red? I don't know. I was too busy freaking out about you falling to your death to worry about the color."

He stood, staggered, and grabbed her shoulder for support. The move must have hurt because he hissed. "Show me where it is."

"Nope. No way." She pushed to her feet. "The rocks are loose. We'll come back tomorrow when the sun's up."

"If it's not dead now, it will be after it gets rained on in the morning." He turned toward the treacherous rocks. "Where is it?"

She folded her arms.

Henry narrowed his eyes. "The coins are in the pocket. I'm going out there."

Grace closed her eyes and counted to ten. "Stay here. I'll do it."

"I'm stronger. If it's wedged in, I'm more likely to be able to get it out."

"Not with your hands all chewed up." She walked as far out as she dared, then dropped to her knees. Rather than holding the flashlight in the crook of her neck, she secured it to her shoulder by twisting it in the top of her shirt and bra strap.

"What are you doing?"

"MacGyvering a flashlight holder."

"Sorry I asked."

She ignored him and crawled out onto the loose rocks.

"Do you see it?"

"Not yet." Grace twisted from side to side to sweep the light across the area before moving forward again. She repeated the process three more times before she found the backpack.

The closer she came, the more the earth shifted beneath her, but she managed to reach Henry's precious laptop. Like before, she pulled and it blinked. "It's stuck."

"Let me try." Henry spoke from a foot away.

Grace yelped and scrambled to the side. "Not cool."

"Sorry." He crouched beside the crevice. "Shine your light on the backpack. I need both hands."

She bit back a few choice words and did as he asked.

Her brother, the jerk, assessed the situation, looped his arm through the strap, and pulled the bag from the opposite direction. It wiggled and blinked several times. Henry leaned over the gap between the boulders. "What the heck is that?"

Her heart leapt into her throat. "Please back up."

"I'm being careful. Trust me, I have no desire to climb back up here." He reached into the opening and pulled out his backpack, along with a light-up sneaker.

Grace's throat went dry. "That's Emily's."

He glanced from the pink-and-green shoe to her and back. "How do you know?"

"I saw a picture of her wearing it in a photo online." She swallowed past the lump in her throat. "It's the mate to the one found in the water. It's a size two, right?"

He checked the inside of the tongue and nodded.

That's it. She's dead, just like the police said. She fell into the ocean and drowned. Grace rarely let her emotions rule over common sense and science, and this was why. Emotions clouded one's judgment.

What was I thinking? An eight-year-old little girl could never have survived on the island for a year without anyone spotting her.

"Do you know what this means?" Henry enjoyed being right, but it wasn't like him to gloat.

She glared.

"Gracie, it's high tide."

"So?"

He laughed. "The water was only ankle deep, and the fall wasn't that far. Plus, the space was pretty small. I would have found her remains as I was looking for a way out."

"She could have washed out with the tide."

"It's not a cave. It's a gap between two boulders. The front one blocked the waves." He wrapped his arms around her. "There's a very good chance Emily Blanchard didn't drown."

CHAPTER NINE

Henry sat on an exam table in the First Aid Station while a Pelican in her last year of nursing school scrubbed the cuts and scrapes on his knees with enough force to remove skin. Jonathan and Mr. Smith, the hotel manager, stood outside the door discussing putting the twins on the first ferry out in the morning. Grace, uncharacteristically silent, stared at her shoes.

And all Henry could think about was finding Emily Blanchard. He had no idea who had her or why, but he was convinced the girl was out there somewhere.

The soon-to-be-nurse placed sterile pads over the wounds and wrapped them with gauze. "You're lucky the cuts don't require stitches, but marine injuries tend to get infected. You should see a doctor when you return to the mainland."

"I will, thanks."

"Take these and change the dressings in the morning." She slid several bandages into a paper bag and handed them to Grace. "Try to have a good night."

His sister nodded.

She left the room and closed the door behind her.

"Can you hear what they're saying out there?" Henry strained to listen to the muffled voices.

"Not really, but it doesn't sound good." Grace leaned over and brushed her fingers over the tops of her shoes. "It's not plaster or drywall dust."

It took Henry a moment to understand she'd referred to the white powdery substance on Jonathan's dock shoes the night before. *Had it only been twenty-four hours?*

"We no longer have a suspect." She sighed and cradled the bag to her chest.

He refused to believe that. "I'm willing to concede on the shoes, but let's not forget the box of gloves."

"True, but we still need to know what they are for. Those are a clue without a crime unless we can find there has been a theft." She met his gaze with a heartbroken expression. "And then there's Emily."

"The evidence we've seen suggests the girl's alive, and we know she likely visits the cemetery."

"We won't be here tomorrow night to find her." Grace's voice cracked.

"You're right." He motioned to his backpack. "But don't give up yet. We have something to take to the police when we get back to Portsmouth."

She nodded, but it seemed nothing he could say would cheer her up.

Mr. Smith, a tall man with salt and pepper hair, stood in the doorway. "You're fortunate you weren't more seriously injured."

Henry nodded, because what else was there to say? He'd taken a risk and gotten hurt.

"I'm required to contact your parents and tell them what happened."

He nodded again for the same reason.

"Were you aware that area of the island is off-limits to minors?" The manager glanced between the twins.

Grace drew a breath and stood. "Another guest mentioned it might be the case, but none of the staff told us we weren't allowed to visit the Beebe Cemetery."

"Was it not in the information you received during check-in?"

"I read the house rules. There wasn't any mention of restricted areas." Henry swung his legs over the edge of the table and cringed. *Ow.*

The man turned to Jonathan. "Make sure it gets added before next season."

Grace saw a ray of hope in their situation. "We left right after dinner. We would have made it back before curfew had it not been for the accident."

"I intend to personally see the two of you onto the 10:25 ferry to Portsmouth in the morning. Although Jonathan assures me you have been up to mischief since your arrival, you're not being asked to leave due to your conduct." He motioned to the bandages. "Your injuries require evaluation by a physician."

"And that's what you will tell our parents?" He cocked his head to the side.

"Yes. Now see to it you don't find yourselves in any more trouble before your departure." He turned and walked out.

Jonathan gave the twins a dirty look and loitered in the doorway. "I radioed Jessie. She's bringing a clean pair of shorts for you to wear."

Henry was a far cry from a germaphobe, but the idea of wearing someone else's clothes bugged him. "I'd rather Grace go to our room and bring my things."

The Pelican tensed his jaw hard enough to crack teeth. "Jessie *is* getting *your* clothes."

"Right. No locks on the doors." He glanced around the room. "Mind if I charge my cell while we wait?"

"Not a chance."

Grace cleared her throat. "My phone is dead in our room. Our parents are going to want to speak to us after Mr. Smith calls. I don't know if you remember, but our father's an attorney."

"Go ahead, but she'll be here any minute." He'd taken her not-so-veiled-threat better than Henry would have expected.

Henry worked with his phone, which was sporting a fifty percent charge after time plugged into his laptop while they were in the classroom, but he didn't have a signal. He moved around the room holding the phone over his head.

"Jonathan, forgive me for asking, but are you Emily Blanchard's cousin?" Grace chewed her lower lip.

The Pel's eyes widened. "No. Why would you ask such a thing?"

"Because you told me you were when you were harassing me outside the showers." The phone came to life. Henry opened a browser window and searched for antique coin appraisers.

"You must have misunderstood me. She was *like* a cousin to me." For the first time since they'd met, Jonathan seemed unsure of himself.

"I see. You were close to her, then?"

He glanced between Grace and the door. "I wouldn't say close. Her family vacationed in the Shoals every summer."

Grace softened her expression and lowered her voice. "Why did hotel management make Beebe Cemetery off-limits to minors after her disappearance? Did she drown out there?"

He took several steps in her direction. "You were asked to leave this alone. Why must you persist in bringing it up?"

"Jon, that's enough." Jessie stood in the doorway, clenching Henry's clothes.

Miranda glanced around the other young woman, met Henry's gaze, and frowned.

His sister sidestepped Jonathan and went to Jessie. "I apologize. I didn't mean to bring up painful memories, but—"

"It's to be expected, I guess. I just wish..." Her voice trailed off, and she turned her head.

Henry cleared his throat and willed his sister to look at him. *Not the time or the place. Please. Please. Please. Let it go.*

Grace didn't look anywhere except at Jessie. "We saw her mother on the news the day before we arrived. We had no idea anyone here knew the girl, let alone was related to her."

The young woman's eyes widened. She glanced at Grace and Jonathan and pressed her lips into a thin line. "I don't need or want your sympathy. Emily is...*was* more like a little sister to me than a cousin."

Whoa. Henry admired his twin, but in moments like these, she left him gobsmacked.

Grace whispered, "Is there any way Emily's still out there somewhere alive?"

He held his breath and waited for the others to react.

Miranda gasped and covered her mouth with both hands.

Jonathan cursed under his breath.

And Jessie? She stared straight ahead as if she'd stepped out of time and space. Not a muscle twitch, a blink, or a visible breath.

"Why would you ask such a thing?" Jonathan's voice rose breaking the silence.

"Emily's mother believes she is still alive."

"Betty Blanchard is a horrible person. She's responsible for everything that —" Jessie covered her face and ran from the room.

"Jessica?" Jonathan hurried after her.

Miranda watched him go with a look that could only be described as pure confusion. She marched over to Henry. "Start talking. What's going on?"

He sat back to put some distance between himself and the girl. "It's a long story, one I'm not ready to share."

Grace started to speak, but Miranda cut her off.

"Let me guess... This is part of your research project, isn't it?"

She sighed. "Yes and no."

"Honestly, I don't understand the two of you." Miranda's face turned as red as the biohazard box. "You both seem really nice, and then you go and do something like this."

"It'll all make sense soon." He pushed off the exam table and stood. The jolt of pain when he put weight on his left leg surprised him. It hadn't hurt when he'd walked from the rocks to the hotel. Then again, he'd been juiced on adrenaline.

"Are you okay?" Grace moved to his side.

"Stings a little. I'll be fine." He bent to pick up his backpack, but his sister took it from his hand. "Let's go. There's no sense in sitting here waiting for Jonathan to come back."

His sister paused at the door. "Miranda? Are you coming?"

"Why not?" She moved to his other side.

They walked to the hotel lobby in silence. Henry could all but hear the questions pinging around in his sister's head all the while feeling the nervous energy coming off Miranda.

The Pelican stopped near the door. "You two go up without me. I'll come check on you later."

Much to his surprise, the girls embraced.

Grace turned to him and smiled. "Ready?"

"Let's hope so." Henry stood at the bottom of the stairs and bit back the urge to ask for a room reassignment. He wanted to be nearby in case the attic apparition made a cameo appearance.

By the time they'd reached the second floor, his knees had loosened up and the pain had dulled. "How did you know Emily and Jessie were cousins?"

"Educated guess." She hovered around him like a mom with a toddler. "When I asked Jonathan about it, he kept glancing at the door like he was afraid Jessie would overhear the conversation. I had a hunch it had less to do with him worrying about hurting her than saving his own hide."

"There's something strange going on between them, but I can't figure it out."

"Partners in crime?"

"Maybe, but I doubt Jessie knows anything about the girl."

Grace nodded.

He slowed a bit on the last flight of stairs. They were happy to make it to their room without running into Jonathan.

"I wonder if they'll allow us to shower before we're banished from the island?" Grace kicked off her dusty sneakers and grabbed her toiletries bag.

"I hope so." He glanced around for his shorts and realized Jessie had taken them with her when she'd run off. "Go ahead and get ready for bed. Just knock when you come back."

"Okay." She walked into the hall.

For the second time in as many nights, it sounded as if someone tore something above his head. Henry froze and listened. A tapping sound replaced the tearing, followed by a bang. He grabbed his cell and hit record.

Five minutes later, Grace knocked on the door. "It's me."

He lunged to open it. Big mistake. The bandages tightened, and his knees roared in protest. "Come in."

She took one step into the room and the tearing sound returned. "You've got to be kidding me."

He pointed toward the ceiling and pressed his finger to his lips.

Grace rolled her eyes. "It's not like whoever it is can hear us over the racket they're making."

"The way I see it, we're out of here in the morning no matter what we do."

She gave him a conspiratorial grin. "Let's go."

"One sec. I recorded it. I want to email it to myself, so we have a backup copy." He glanced at his phone. "Forget it. No signal."

"Look on the bright side. We have a legitimate excuse for not answering Mom's and Dad's calls."

"Excellent point." He put his soggy shoes on and shoved the phone in his pocket.

Three quick bangs sounded overhead.

Grace frowned. "Whoever this is, they're asking to get caught."

"Or they're in a hurry because the jig is up."

The twins left their room, and the noises stopped.

Henry motioned for her to wait and opened the door again.

A faint tearing sound echoed from inside.

He shut the door, and it stopped.

"Okay, that's just weird," Grace whispered. "Maybe it *is* a ghost."

"After my run-in with the Lady in White, I'm not ruling it out." He hurried to the interior fire escape and walked up the stairs without bothering to check for squeaky floorboards.

Grace tugged the hem of his shirt and whispered, "Shouldn't we be quiet?"

"They're sending us home tomorrow either way. I'd like to solve the mystery of the noises in the attic before we go." Armed with the flashlight app, Henry didn't bother hugging the walls. He used the joists like stepping stones and made it to the first firebreak.

Grace used more caution, then caught up and grinned. "Haven't you had enough of falling through things tonight?"

"Come on." He crossed the second section of the attic, paused at the door, and lowered his voice. "Our guy may be on the other side. Be ready for anything."

She pressed her lips into a line and nodded.

Henry pressed the phone to his thigh to kill the light and cracked the door open. The tearing noise sounded far off and seemed to be emanating from the floor. He took a step, lifted the phone to illuminate the next joist, and took another step.

Grace followed close behind.

Bang. Bang. Bang. The sounds grew louder.

Where are they coming from? He stopped, listened, and pointed down.

Grace nodded.

They crossed four more joists, and the hammering and ripping started again.

He lifted the light higher and scanned the next firebreak. The wall was solid.

"Other side," Grace whispered.

Pulse racing, Henry set his hand on the knob at the same time the hammering started. He felt the vibrations from his finger to his elbow.

Grace pulled on his arm and pointed behind them.

Springs groaned.

He stared, unable to move.

The attic access door opened, light flashed, and a person stood in the opening.

"Henry and Grace Warner! You just can't stay out of trouble, can you?"

CHAPTER TEN

Grace recognized the young woman instantly, but that didn't stop her central nervous system from kicking into overdrive. Heart racing and palms sweating, her mind searched for the right thing to say or do. Her senses became hyper-aware, and the world seemed to slow.

Jessie hopscotched across the joists like she'd done it a thousand times.

A rustling noise drew Grace's attention. Before she could make sense of it, Henry grabbed her arm and pulled her against the firebreak.

Is he in the wall?

The rustling stopped, and heavy footfalls echoed on the other side of the break.

Grace crouched. She wouldn't go down without a fight. She'd be ready for whoever or whatever came through the door, but nothing could have prepared her for what happened next.

A loud bang filled her ears.

And the wall erupted where she'd stood only seconds before. Drywall dust and bits of debris rained down on her head.

Jessie screamed and her flashlight fell, wedging into the gap between the joists.

A second bang came from overhead.

Henry jerked Grace forward without warning, causing her to stumble and fall.

She turned her head but couldn't make sense of what she saw. An ax blade protruded through the wall. Then the person on the other side pulled it free and smashed through again.

Henry yanked her to her feet and dragged her toward the attic door.

"Here!" Jessie waved to the folding ladder.

Grace scrambled down, Henry made it three rungs and jumped, and Jessie followed.

The Pelican slammed the door closed and turned a metal latch to keep it from opening. "Who is that?"

"No idea." Henry glanced from the ceiling to the door to his sister and to Jessica in rapid succession.

"Go to your room and stay there." Jessie grabbed a radio from the dresser and hurried down the hall.

Grace knew she should do something, but the connection between her body and her brain had short-circuited as her existence returned to real time.

Henry gripped her shoulders and met her gaze. "Are you okay?"

"He could have killed me." She didn't recognize the sound of her own voice.

Her brother drew her into a quick embrace. "We need to go with her."

"Okay." Her knees had turned to rubber, but she managed to make it to the hall.

"Security, fourth floor," Jessie shouted into her radio. "Need someone in Room 90 to monitor the Warner twins."

Grace set her hand against the wall for support. "Does she think the person's coming after us?"

"She's probably trying to keep us out of the way." Henry motioned at Jessie's retreating form. "Come on. She's not safe up there alone."

They'd made it halfway down the hall when several Pelicans stepped out of their rooms.

Miranda took one look at Grace and turned to the others. "I've got them."

Dylan, the young man from Vaughn Cottage, said, "Want some help?"

"We have to find Jessie. She's in danger." Henry tried to push through the growing crowd, but they blocked his path. "There's a guy with an ax in the attic."

Some gasped, some bristled, but no one moved.

Henry motioned to his sister. "This is drywall dust from where the maniac hacked through the firebreak."

Miranda nodded to the others. "Go. I'll take them to their room."

The group of six staff members hurried down the hall.

The last thing Grace wanted was to be directly below an ax-wielding madman. "No, not our room. Take us downstairs."

"You're serious, aren't you?" The white showed all the way around the girl's irises.

The twins nodded.

The Pelican glanced at the ceiling and pointed in the direction opposite the one the others had gone. "Go."

Henry hesitated. "Shouldn't we take the main staircase?"

"No. If we run into management on the way down, they may send you to your room." She took Grace's hand and half-dragged her to the exterior fire escape.

The wind had picked up considerably since the twins had returned from the cemetery. The scent of ozone on the air told Grace a storm was coming.

Jonathan met them near the second-floor landing. "Where do you think you're going?"

She did a double take.

"How?" Henry moved in front of his sister. "How are you here?"

"What do you mean, how am I here? I'm answering Jessie's call." He folded his arms and stared at Miranda. "Why aren't they in their room?"

"They didn't feel safe. I'm taking them to the lobby."

Grace leaned over the railing and counted the flights of stairs above her. *Two.* As she had thought, this fire escape didn't reach the attic. "There must be another access door."

Henry motioned to the young man. "Move into the light."

"Look, I don't know what's going on, but you two need to come with me." He shot Miranda a hard look. "*Go to your room.*"

The twins moved up a couple of treads.

"What's wrong with the two of you?" He stepped onto the landing beneath the flood light.

Grace gasped. He didn't have as much as a speck of dust on him—even his shoes were clean. "It's not him."

"What's not me?" He ran his hand over his head. "Never mind. Go!"

Grace pushed past him on her way down.

"Uh-uh. Someone is supposed to monitor you, which means you're going to turn around and go back to your room."

"There's no way I'm going back up there," she called over her shoulder.

Henry shrugged and followed his sister, with Miranda on their heels.

Jonathan pulled his radio from his hip. "I have the twins. Heading to the lobby now."

"Ten-four," a male replied.

The gleaming floors and homey atmosphere of the first floor did nothing to calm Grace's or Henry's nerves. With their primary suspect cleared, anyone and everyone else was a suspect. Grace turned to Jonathan. "Did you change the batteries in your radio?"

Jonathan opened his mouth, snapped it shut, and folded his arms. "No. Why do you ask?"

"It was beeping yesterday." Henry glanced between the young man and his sister.

He stepped closer and lowered his voice. "Why do I get the impression you two are keeping tabs on me?"

The twins exchanged a look.

Miranda set her hands on her hips. "So, what if they are?"

Henry tightened his jaw and shook his head a fraction of an inch. She received the message loud and clear. He still didn't trust the guy.

"That's how it's going to be?" Ignoring Miranda, Jonathan motioned to a table. "Sit down."

A category-five hurricane had nothing on the tempest growing inside Miranda. Red-faced and hands balled at her sides, she stepped in front of Jonathan. "There's a man with an ax in the attic. That's drywall dust in Grace's hair."

Henry muttered under his breath.

The color drained from Jonathan's face. "Where's Jessie?"

"She went up after him." Grace couldn't decide what to believe about his motives. He'd either reacted out of fear of being caught or fear for the girl, but either way, the news had shaken him.

Jonathan ran for the stairs.

"Well, that settles that. He's clearly in love with her." Miranda sighed and sank into a chair. "What happened in the attic? Tell me everything."

Henry nodded his approval.

Grace leaned forward and narrated the story, starting from the first time they'd heard the noises. She'd gotten to the part where the ax came through the wall over her head when the Pelican stopped her.

"You honestly believe Emily Blanchard's alive?" Her words came out breathy.

Grace hesitated to answer the question, but they needed help, and Miranda was all they had. "Maybe. Do you know of anyone on the staff who likes Neccos?"

"Yuck. No. None that I know of." She narrowed her eyes. "You think Jonathan has something to do with this?"

"We did." Henry lowered his voice. "He didn't have any dust on his clothes, nor did he have time to run downstairs, change, and meet us."

Miranda sighed. "Maybe, but who knows what he's capable of?"

Her radio chirped, and a male said, "The attic's clear."

Grace's heart skipped a beat. "He got away? What about Jessie?"

Miranda pressed the talk button. "Jessie, are you all right?"

The radio crackled. "No sign of her up here."

"Jessie, what's your location?" Another voice came through the connection. "Anyone have eyes on Jessie?"

Silence stretched on for what felt like minutes.

A female shouted through the walkie talkie, "We've found her radio."

"He's taken her." Grace shot to her feet, but Henry grabbed her hand before she could go too far.

"We don't know who it is or where they may have gone."

She wrapped her arms around her midsection. "We can't just sit here. We have to do something."

"Unless..." Miranda's lips twisted into a grin. "Unless she's in on it."

"We don't even know what *it* is," Grace snapped.

Henry seemed lost in his thoughts. He pressed his lips together and tilted his head to the right and then to the left—the same move he had made when he was five and learning his multiplication tables. "She might be right. Think about it. The attic access was in her room."

She couldn't wrap her brain around it. "Right, but she's not the one who put the bag in the attic."

Before they could sort it out, Mr. Smith and Mort Montgomery came through the front door.

"That's him. That's the kid who has my coins." He pointed a boney finger at Henry.

Grace's brain skidded to a halt. *This can't be a coincidence. Mort's involved somehow.*

Henry stood and faced his accuser. "What are you talking about?"

"Don't play coy with me, boy. You know what you did." Mort lunged forward, but the manager stepped in his path. "Calm down Mr. Montgomery. We'll get to the bottom of this. It is, after all an island. If he has your property, we'll find it."

As if on cue, several of the Pelicans who'd searched the attic came down the main staircase.

Miranda pushed to her feet. "Sorry to interrupt, but Jessie's missing, and there's a guy with an ax running around the hotel."

The manager's eyes bulged. He glanced from her to Mort and chuckled. "I can assure you there's no armed man in the hotel."

Grace and Henry said, "He was in the attic."

"Jessie went after him. Some of the staff found her radio up there, but there was no sign of her." Miranda glanced at the others for confirmation.

Dylan pushed his hair from his face. "I don't know about a man with an ax, but Jessie's radio was up there."

Mort turned beet-red and shouted. "This is preposterous. Can't you see it's a ploy to distract you from the matter at hand?"

Mr. Smith squared his shoulders and pointed at two male Pels. "You two, come with me to search the Warners' room. Miranda, escort the twins to room 11 and don't let them out of your sight. The rest of you, search the grounds for Miss Jaffrey. And someone check in with her father."

Grace's stomach fell. Not only did her brother have several coins in his backpack, but he also had Emily's shoe. "You can't search our rooms. We have an expectation of privacy."

"This is a private establishment on a private island. Had you read the information provided to you when you checked in, you would know we reserve the right to inspect guest rooms if given cause." He drew a breath. "And this, young lady, is *cause*."

Henry hung his head. "He's right. It was in the orientation paperwork, but cause requires more than a blind accusation."

"What is your room number?"

Neither twin answered.

Mort smirked. "What did I tell you? This only proves their guilt."

The manager turned as if to go to the reception desk.

"They're in room 79," Miranda said too quickly. She'd given the wrong number, and judging by the glint in her eye, she'd done it on purpose.

"Thank you."

"You're welcome." She pasted on a sticky-sweet smile. "Mr. Smith?"

"What?" He seemed to realize he'd shouted at a staff member and blanched. "What is it?"

"Might I suggest the Warners are moved to Cottage E? It's empty, and far enough away that any future shouting won't disturb the other guests." She nodded to a handful of pajama-clad conferees who'd undoubtedly come out of their rooms to see what was going on.

He stiffened his spine. "Very well. Take them to E. They're not to leave the premises until I say so."

She nodded. "Will you have their things sent to them? After everything is searched for the stolen property?"

The guests who'd gathered whispered.

Mr. Smith and the twins cringed.

Gee, thanks, Miranda. Grace wanted to scream. They were about to be found guilty for something they didn't do, and they had a second missing girl and a crazy person with an ax to find.

The manager's face scrunched in concentration for a moment before he answered. "Yes, of course. Now go."

She wiggled her fingers at him in a sort of wave and motioned to the door. "You heard the man. March."

Outside, Henry spoke through gritted teeth. "Was that necessary?"

"Yes, and you're welcome." She nodded to two Pelicans coming toward them. "We'll talk once we get to your new digs.

They continued down the path toward the cottage. A call came over Miranda's radio announcing the twins' new location, and requesting all available staff search for Jonathan and Jessie.

"I wonder why they're searching for Jon?" Miranda frowned.

Grace's voice thinned. "He just told everyone where we're going. What if the guy with the ax..."

Henry slung his arm around her shoulder. "I understand you're scared. I am too, but we don't know if he meant to hurt us. He could have been trying to frighten us so we'd leave, and he could escape."

She nodded in general agreement. If only she could convince herself.

The staff they passed along the way stared. Some offered weak smiles, others openly glared.

"This is bad," Henry whispered.

"Mom and Dad are going to freak." She could only imagine the looks on her parents' faces when the manager called to tell them the twins had stolen valuable coins. If they were worth what the twins' thought, the crime would be a felony.

Miranda opened the door to the cottage and ushered them into a plain white hall with two doors on either side and another behind a flight of stairs. "Rooms 1 and 2 have twin beds, but I'd suggest you stay together in room 3. It's at the back of the building."

Henry looked as if he'd explode at any second. "You're awfully pleased with yourself," he blurted.

"I got you access to a first-floor room with a *window* and bought you some time. A manager must be present when a guest's property is searched or when it's packed."

Henry stormed ahead several paces, then turned and walked back. "Montgomery's involved in this."

"I had the same thought, but we have bigger problems." She sighed and turned to Miranda. "You have to get upstairs and stop them before they find Emily Blanchard's missing shoe."

The girl's mouth fell open. "Omigod! I didn't think about that."

"No, this may work in our favor." Henry looked away and bit his thumbnail —a sure sign he was forming a plan. "How well do you know Mr. Smith? Do you trust him?"

She shrugged. "I guess, but after the entire Jonathan thing, I don't think I'm a very good judge of character."

"Good point." He sighed. "Unless the manager's in on whatever it is going on around here, he'll do the right thing and turn the shoe over to the police."

"If he recognizes it." The initial shock had worn off, leaving Grace antsy. "What'll happen to us when they find the coins?"

"We don't have a jail or dungeon if that's what you're asking." Miranda nudged her shoulder. "Relax. The police will get to the bottom of all of this."

"I'd rather it not come to that," The twins said.

The girl seemed to rethink her words for half a second before she grinned. "We'll figure something out."

Grace cocked her head. "You gave them the wrong room number."

"I know." Miranda's grin widened to rival the Cheshire Cat's. "I sent them to Jonathan's room."

CHAPTER ELEVEN

Henry plopped onto the double bed and attempted to calm his nerves by focusing on the facts. "What do we know?"

Miranda glanced at them.

"We're in big trouble." Grace leaned against the wall for a split second before going wide-eyed and stepping to the center of the room. She met his gaze and frowned. "It's going to take me a while to get over having an ax so close to my head."

"I understand. It's going to take *me* a while to get over it, too." He rested his elbows on his knees and clasped his hands. "My working theory is that Mort is here to appraise or purchase the coins. We need to figure out who he's purchasing them from, and most importantly, where did the coins come from?"

Miranda held up her hand as if in a classroom. "But isn't it like Mel Fisher finding sunken treasure? Finders, keepers. Why all the secrecy?"

"Actually, I believe this falls into the same situation as mineral rights. The Star Island Corporation owns the island, which means they have a claim to anything found here. In theory, the coins should be given back to Spain, but that almost never happens in cases like these," Henry suggested.

Grace tapped her lips. "And we've crossed Jonathan off the suspect list."

"Not crossed off yet. He wasn't the guy in the attic, but that doesn't mean he's not involved, since he put at least one bag of coins up there." Henry mentally ran through the people they'd met on Star Island. "It could be anyone, or a group of people."

Miranda laughed. "Except me. I would have gone on the six o'clock news or run away to Paris if I'd found gold coins."

Henry didn't doubt that for a second. "As for Emily, the only way she would have survived a year without being discovered is if someone hid her."

"Jessie's her cousin, but I don't think she'd hurt—" Grace turned to Henry. "Jessie said Betty Blanchard was a horrible person and was responsible for everything. Everything like Emily's disappearance?"

"And the deaths of Betty's husband and Jessie's mother." Miranda folded her arms. "I don't know the details, other than they drowned. I swear the Blanchards are cursed."

"They've had more than their fair share of tragedy." Grace hugged herself. "If Jessie believed she was protecting Emily from her mother..."

"She has a strong motive." The puzzle had potentially come together for one mystery, but he had too many missing pieces to see the full picture of the other.

Dylan burst through the front door of the cottage, looked around, and all but ran into the guest room. "You're not going to believe what's happened now."

"At this point, I'll believe just about anything," Henry muttered.

"After you sent us to the wrong room..." he glared at Miranda, but his smile ruined the effect, "we found a stash of original Celia Thaxter paintings in Jonathan's quarters and in the firebreaks in the attic."

The twins glanced from Dylan to each other and back.

Miranda's hand flew to her mouth. "Jonathan's been stealing?"

"Looks that way. Mr. Smith thinks Brad Blanchard hid the items in the walls during construction."

Henry ran his hands over his head. Despite what they'd found, he didn't believe Jonathan had been in the attic that night. "Brad is Jessie's grandfather?"

"Yes." Miranda flashed Dylan her mean-girl smile. "I knew there was something going on between Jessie and Jon! Miss High-and-Mighty, always preaching about staff fraternizing."

Grace sighed loud enough to draw everyone's attention. "That's great and all, but it doesn't help us. Maybe you could talk about it in the other room?"

"Yeah, you two are in serious trouble. I mean, what kind of morons steal a coin and leave it on the wash basin?" Dylan smirked. "The police will be here in the morning to question you."

"What?" Henry had done no such thing. The coins and the broach were in his backpack, along with Emily's shoe.

The Pelican hitched a shoulder. "We didn't even have to search for it."

Grace sat on the edge of the bed. "You didn't go through our things?"

"They'll get around to it, but since nothing else has been reported missing, Mr. Smith's more concerned about finding Jonathan." He shook his head and walked out.

"I'll be right back." Miranda followed him out.

As soon as the door closed, someone tapped on the window.

Henry turned and could not believe his eyes. The last person he'd have expected to see stood outside—Jonathan.

The Pelican motioned to the lock.

Henry hesitated for a moment before turning the latch and opening the window. The idea of secure windows given that there were no locks on the door would have been odd, but that was to protect them from flapping in the wind and breaking the glass. "What are you doing here?"

Jonathan glanced over his shoulder and locked eyes with Grace. "You believe Emily's alive, don't you?"

She took a step back. "Yes, why?"

"I may have seen her. Tell me what you know." He shoved the screen into the building as if he planned to crawl through the window.

Henry stepped in front of his sister.

Unfortunately, Grace didn't seem to want his protection. She rushed to the window. "Where?"

"Out by the Beebe Cemetery."

She gasped. "We found the match to the shoe that washed up a year ago. It was wedged between the boulders where Henry slipped. We think she could have survived the fall and crawled out."

"My God, could it be?" Jonathan's jaw dropped. "That's near the cemetery, right?"

She nodded. "Come on, we have to find her."

Henry grabbed his sister before she climbed out. "Wait. You said you were close to her. Why didn't you call her name?"

He sighed. "I thought I was seeing things. I just caught a glimpse of her, and just as quickly, she was gone."

Henry wasn't buying it. "So you came here to find *us*?"

Jonathan produced a small pistol and pointed it at Grace. "Scream or make a move and she dies. Got it?"

His sister had frozen in place with her hands on the sill.

Henry raised his hands. "Got it."

Jonathan yanked Grace through the window and pulled her to his chest. "Crawl out."

The grounds had to be swarming with Pelicans looking for Jessie and Jonathan. Someone could come around the corner at any moment, but that wouldn't help. Grace and Henry needed to see it through.

I can't risk her life. Henry crawled through the window. Jonathan gestured that Henry was to stay to the side where he could see him. They headed off the path and out of the light.

Jonathan led them around the backs of the buildings toward the monuments.

He's taking us to the cemetery. Henry had walked this area before and devised a plan. "I need to slow down. My knees—"

"Are fine. I saw you running downstairs a couple of hours ago." Jonathan jerked Grace hard enough to make her cry out. "Keep up."

Henry's throat tightened. "Okay, just don't hurt her."

"I'm okay." The strength in her voice reassured him.

They continued until they reached the boundary of the hotel property. Rather than entering the path leading to the cemetery or the obelisk, Jonathan skirted the dirt road and backtracked toward the hotel. They passed the vegetable garden, and the ground changed from grass to stone.

Henry had no idea where he planned to take them or what would be waiting for them once they arrived. He lost his footing on the loose rock, and blood roared behind his eardrums. "Hey, let her walk on her own. The ground isn't safe."

The Pelican shoved Grace ahead of him but kept the pistol trained on her back.

"I don't get it. I know you weren't the one with the ax, and I doubt you're stupid enough to keep stolen goods in your room. Did someone frame you?" Henry edged closer, waiting for an opportunity to act. *Come on, fake a fall, trip —anything, just get out of the way.*

As if she'd read his mind, Grace stumbled and went to one knee.

"Nice try." Jonathan yanked her to him, turning to put her between him and Henry. He pressed the gun to her head. "You two put the stuff in my room."

Henry raised his hands. He could barely make out her face in the dim light, but he thought he saw tears. "We found coins and Neccos in the attic. We didn't know anything about the Thaxter paintings."

"Shut up and walk."

"Whoever it is you're working with can't be trusted." Grace softened her voice. "We're all in the same boat. We'll vouch for you if you vouch for us."

"I said shut up." He tightened his grip until she grunted.

They walked between a cliff and the backs of three buildings before the main hotel came into view. *Is he taking us to the hotel?*

Jonathan pulled Grace in the opposite direction—toward the water. It was as if the guy was trying to confuse them.

"There you are. What took so long?" Jessie stepped from behind a boulder and grabbed Grace.

She made a sound somewhere between a gasp and a sob. "You? Where's Emily?"

"Safe and sound." Jessie motioned to Jonathan. "Give me the gun and get his phone. Type a suicide note from both of them—something remorseful about not wanting to go to prison."

"That's ridiculous. We'd hardly go to prison for stealing a single coin. You two, on the other hand... Those Thaxter paintings are worth a fortune, and that's not even considering the rest of the Spanish gold. There's more, isn't there?" Henry took a step forward and his foot sank into sand.

"Yeah, there's more." Aiming the gun at Henry's chest, Jonathan backed up toward Jessie.

Grace asked, "Why do this?"

"I didn't want to. I tried to keep you busy. When that didn't work, we had Mort send you to the rocks to get you kicked off the island. We all know how *that* turned out. You two left us no choice."

"It's not our fault your accomplice decided to tear apart the attic above our room. You have the coins. Every minute you spend here is one minute closer the police are to finding you." Her voice warbled. "Please let us go."

Jessie snatched the gun from Jon's hand so quickly Henry feared it'd go off by accident. "And spend the rest of my life looking over my shoulder? No thanks."

The light went on in Henry's mind as a puzzle piece fell into place. "Aren't you going to do that anyway? Jonathan's wanted for questioning, and you're presumed missing."

"Shut up and walk." The young woman pointed toward the water. After Henry passed them, she turned and half-dragged Grace down the rocky embankment to the beach.

Henry squinted at what looked like a small beach and thought he saw a boat floating near the shore. He had to keep them talking.

"I'd like to hear your answer." Jonathan flipped on the flashlight app and shined it on the girls.

Henry's lungs squeezed. Once again, they'd stumbled onto something that ended with guns pointed at them, only this time, he wasn't sure they'd survive it.

A man called from the boat. "We need to go."

Jessie released Grace and shoved her into the water. "Move."

His sister glanced over her shoulder.

Nodding for her to go was the hardest thing Henry had ever done. Had he not, Jessie would have killed her on the spot. *Or would she? The hotel's not far. Would they hear the shot?* "Grace, run!"

Jonathan turned and slammed his fist into Henry's stomach.

Henry grunted as he doubled over, pain filling the dark space between the stars flashing before his eyes. He could barely hear the splashing and sounds of a struggle over his wheezing breaths.

Grace screamed, but it was cut short by a meaty thud.

Henry had no idea what'd happened to his sister, but Jessie trudged toward him.

Jonathan hoisted him up by his shirt and pushed him into the water. "Don't be a hero. Your sister's waiting. It'd be a shame if she watched you die here instead of with her. Twins share everything, right?"

Between the two of them, they managed to half-drag, half-carry him onto the swimming platform at the back of the boat. Jessie gave him a shove and he landed next to Grace.

Jessie shouted, "Get in the boat, Jon."

"I'm not going anywhere until you answer some questions." Jonathan turned and sloshed back to the shore, with Jessie on his heels.

Henry took in his surroundings. The boat reminded him of one his family had rented one summer. Bench in the back. A four-seat configuration that included the driver's seat, two forward and two rear-facing.

He recognized the man sitting in the cockpit as Dr. Jaffrey. It didn't surprise him to learn Jessie's father was involved. What *did* surprise him was the little girl staring at him from the seat behind Jaffrey. *Emily Blanchard.*

Grace moaned and bent at the waist. "The rocking."

"Deep breaths." He rubbed her back. When he glanced up, he made eye contact with Emily.

The girl wiped tears from her eyes and forced a smile.

Jonathan shouted. "You're my fiancé. How could you set me up like that?"

Jessie aimed the gun at his chest. "Get in the boat, Jon."

"So, what? You can toss me overboard in the middle of the Atlantic with those two?" He shook his head. "Why, Jessie? I love you."

"This wasn't the plan, but Dad and I need a clean get-away. You'll be blamed for my disappearance. Dad will leave in a week or so, too distraught over my death to remain in the Shoals."

"It'll be good to have him with us, Jess. We'll come up with a new plan once we're underway." Dr. Jaffrey took off his gloves and snatched a clean pair from the box beside him.

Click. Another piece fell into place. Jessie's father was a germaphobe. He was the one who'd stashed the coins in the attic and wielded the ax. It made sense now why Jessie had run into the face of danger—she hadn't been in danger at all. She was helping her father escape the attic.

The couple continued to argue.

Grace grappled for his hand. "Seasick."

Whispering, Henry hoped she'd understood him and that she'd forgive him for what he was about to do. "Aim for Dr. Jaffrey and then get down." He leaned forward and made the most heinous retching noise he could muster.

Dr. Jaffrey shot to his feet but stopped a foot or two away from the gagging twins. "Not on the boat! Stand up! Lean over the edge!"

Henry whispered, "Sardines, milk and OJ, liver, lima beans."

That was all it took. Grace lurched forward, grabbed the man's shirt, and vomited down the front of him.

The scientist screeched like a cat with its tail stuck in a turbine.

Grace moved past him toward the control panel.

Henry rammed his shoulder into Jaffrey's mid-section. The large man stumbled back and grappled for him, but he'd anticipated the move and ducked. Wrapping his hands around Jaffrey's calf, Henry lifted with all his strength.

The man toppled backward into the water.

Jessie shouted from the shore as she started to run toward the boat, "Emily, get the keys!"

The girl curled into a ball as if trying to make herself disappear.

Grace started the engine but hesitated, her hand hovering over the knobs and switches. "What do I do?"

Henry lunged toward the cockpit, but Emily beat him there. The child pushed up on the throttle. The boat shot forward straight toward the rocks along the side of the cove.

Grace grabbed the wheel and turned hard enough to throw her brother and

Emily off balance. He grabbed the girl, and they both fell to the deck so they wouldn't be thrown overboard.

"Sorry," Grace yelled over her shoulder as the boat sped toward open waters.

Henry set Emily on her feet and stood. "Just be thankful they hadn't dropped anchor."

"What do we do now?" She pushed a button, and the lights came on. "We can't go to the pier. That's the first place they'll look."

Emily hopped up and took the radio receiver from its cradle. "Call a mayday."

Henry turned and guesstimated their distance from shore. "She's right. This area's full of submerged rocks. We should drop anchor and call for help."

The girl's face brightened. "Can I do it?"

He nodded. "Sure."

"Hello, Mayday. Mayday. This is Emily Blanchard. I need help, and I'd like to talk to my mom. Mayday."

Grace turned her head and sniffled.

CHAPTER TWELVE

The sun crested the horizon as the Coast Guard vessel moored to the Star Island pier. However, Emily and the twins weren't permitted to leave the boat until the police gave the okay.

Grace tucked the girl's blanket tighter around her shoulders. "Are you warm enough?"

"Yes." Emily sipped her cocoa. "I saw you guys before."

Henry glanced from his sister to the child. "You did?"

She nodded. "Twice. Once in the cemetery, and once near the summer house."

"That was you watching us?" His brows disappeared beneath his shaggy hair.

"I wasn't supposed to be out of Uncle Jake's cottage, but I got bored." She dipped her chin. "I wonder if my mom will come."

"Of course, she'll come. They're flying her in on a helicopter. She'll be here soon." Grace met Henry's gaze and mouthed, "What the heck?"

He leaned into Emily's line of vision. "You know how you said you'd seen us before? We've seen you, too."

The girl gave him a dubious look. "Where?"

"Your mom was on tv a couple of days ago. She showed the world your picture and asked for help finding you."

Emily glanced at Grace as if for confirmation.

"It's true. She inspired us to find out what happened to you."

"But..." She furrowed her brow. "Uncle Jake said she left me here with him because she was angry that I snuck out."

Grace glanced toward the hotel where the police were questioning Jake Jaffrey, Jessie, and Jonathan. She knew better than to speak poorly of the girl's family, but she had a few things to say to Uncle Jake if she ever had the chance. "I don't think that's true, but you should talk to your mom about it."

The girl nodded. "Darn it. I left my Neccos on the boat."

Grace's big goofy smile warmed Henry's heart. He said, "They're her favorite too."

"Really?" Emily stared with an expression that could only be described as hero-worship. "I love them. Except for the black ones. I leave those for the Beebe sisters."

Grace poked her side. "And in your uncle's things. And in the attic."

A man in jeans and a sports coat boarded the boat. He flashed a badge to the Coastie before heading in their direction. "I'm Detective Giacomo. Mind if I ask you a few questions?"

Emily burrowed into Grace's side.

Henry said, "Sure, but you should know we're minors, and we didn't steal anything from Mort Montgomery."

"Relax, kid. You're not being charged with anything. Montgomery's a known black-market dealer of jewels, art, and antique coins." The detective cocked his head. "I'm curious how you knew the girl was alive."

Grace grinned and did her best imitation of Miranda on a sugar high. "A few of the Pelicans reported seeing the ghost of a little girl in a white nightgown, then we found black NECCO wafers in different places around the island, and Henry found the mate to the shoe that washed up on the island last year."

The detective turned to Henry for further explanation.

"It was a short fall, and the space was protected from the surf. Since I didn't see any..." he glanced at the child, "sign that she was still down there, I figured she'd walked out the same way I did."

Emily peeked at Henry. "Did you see the Lady in White?"

All eyes turned to the child.

Henry ran his hand over the back of his neck. "I saw *something*."

"Me, too. I ran after her and fell through the crack." She dipped her chin. "She was guarding Blackbeard's treasure, but Uncle Jake took it when he found me."

The detective's eyes widened. "Do you know where it is now?"

"On the boat. Jessie said we were going to the Caribbean to give it back to the bank Blackbeard stole it from."

Grace would have bet her right arm the bank Jessie had referred to was located in the Cayman Islands. "Detective Giacomo, is there any way Emily can speak to her mother?"

"Absolutely." He pulled his cell phone from his back pocket and pressed a few buttons before handing it to the girl. "Press the green circle when you're ready."

Emily wasted no time. She jabbed her finger onto the screen and held the phone to her ear.

The detective motioned for the twins to follow him. "We're charging Montgomery, the Jaffreys, and Jones with a long list of crimes. They won't bother anyone for a very long time."

The twins nodded.

"What I can't figure, is how the two of you ended up on that boat."

Henry sucked in a breath.

Grace shrugged and did her best to avoid outright lying to an officer of the law. It wasn't like she had a choice. Their parents would never let them out of their sight if they learned the truth. "We saw Jonathan sneaking around outside."

"And we followed him." Henry folded his arms. "We'd heard he'd been accused of stealing some artwork and put it together. He and Jessie are engaged."

"And Jessie is Emily's cousin." Grace glanced at her brother. "Jonathan led us straight to her."

The detective scratched the side of his head. "You snuck onto the boat?"

"Kind of. Jonathan and Jessie were coaxing us with a gun, but then they got into a lover's tiff—something about Jonathan not wanting to die. We pushed Dr. Jaffrey overboard and took the boat." Grace pressed her hand to her chest. "Sorry. I know that's illegal."

"Yes, but in this instance, I'm willing to overlook it." He glanced at them both. "Anything else?"

The twins exchanged looks and shook their heads.

"All right. Let's get you three inside. They'll be bringing the others out soon to take them to the mainland for processing." He turned and smiled at Emily, who was happily chatting with her mother. "You two did good. Real good."

Grace held Emily's hand as they walked up the pier. The child hardly seemed to notice when Jessie and her uncle passed them in handcuffs, but Henry did.

He stopped as Jessie approached. "There's one thing I don't understand. How did you make the ghost appear on the rocks?"

She looked at him as if he'd sprouted horns. "I don't know what you're talking about."

The officer escorting her gave her a nudge. "Keep moving."

Jessie hung her head and continued doing the perp walk.

The remainder of the day went by in a blur of questions and accolades. Mr. Smith allowed them to shower as a token of his appreciation for the twins finding the missing girl. Henry assumed it had more to do with the media swarming the property and the twins' newfound fame than appreciation, but that didn't stop him from enjoying the hot water.

He changed into semi-clean clothes and met Grace on the veranda.

She stared at the lawn, so transfixed, she didn't notice his presence until he placed his hand on her shoulder. "Look how happy they are."

He followed her gaze to a group of reporters surrounding Emily and her mother. The woman knelt on the grass and wept into her daughter's hair. "Happy tears?"

She nudged his side. "Yes, and *we* did that."

He slung his arm over her shoulder. "Was it worth the danger?"

She turned to him and stared.

Chuckling, he held his hands up and backed away. "Kidding."

Mr. Smith cleared his throat. "I've taken the liberty of having your things packed."

Miranda stood beside him with a backpack in each hand and one on her shoulder.

With everything that'd happened, Henry had forgotten about the coins and broach he'd stashed in his bag. "One second. I have something that belongs to you."

Mr. Smith watched noncommittally.

"Or I should say, they belong to the Star Island Corporation." He removed his laptop and reached into the split in the lining of the cushioned section. After some fishing around, he retrieved three coins and the antique broach. "We found these in the attic."

"Thank you. That you returned these further proves you're a young man of integrity."

"There are more coins in a pouch to the left of the attic access door in Jessie's room." Grace took her backpack from Miranda and embraced her. "I'm going to miss you and this place. It grew on me."

The Pelican quirked a brow. "Like a barnacle?"

Mr. Smith bristled and turned on his heels. "If you'll excuse me, I have guests to attend to."

"You two better hurry or you'll miss the ferry." She threw her arms around Henry.

He froze with his arms pinned to his sides. He didn't have anything against hugs, but it'd taken him completely off-guard.

"Safe travels."

The twins hurried through the crowd of shouting reporters. They'd given a brief statement at the press conference held by hotel management and the police department, and there was nothing else to say. Besides, Henry hated the attention.

He followed Grace onto the vessel and stopped her. "I have something for you."

"What?" She set her hands on her hips. "Please don't tell me you kept one of the coins."

"Cursed pirate gold? Are you kidding?" He pulled a small pill bottle from his pocket. "For motion sickness. Take one now so it has time to hit your bloodstream."

"You're a life-saver."

They spent the first half of the ride back to Portsmouth in silence. Grace took copious notes in her journal, but Henry took in the scenery and enjoyed the warm sea air. It'd been a whirlwind three-day adventure, but it was time to move on. Next stop, Westfield, New Jersey.

He nudged Grace's shoulder. "Which mystery do you want to tackle next?"

"Jersey, right?" She tapped her pen to her lips. "The Jersey Devil's the obvious choice, but I was thinking we could look into their version of the Lady in White."

Henry had zero interest in investigating another ghost, not with their first one unsolved. "I'm telling you, she was real."

"You know. Evolutionary scientists have a name for seeing faces in ordinary objects."

"Pareidolia. I'm familiar with the phenomenon, but how do you explain Emily seeing the same thing?"

Grace bit her lower lip. "I saw her too."

Henry raised a single brow and gave her his best The Rock imitation. "Are you a true believer?"

"I haven't given up on finding a rational explanation, but it freaked me out. I don't like things I can't explain with good old-fashioned science."

The ferry came to a bumpy stop, and a static-filled voice announced they'd arrived in Portsmouth, New Hampshire.

Henry stood and slung his backpack over his shoulders.

Grace muttered under her breath and ran to the railing. "Oh, no."

"Holy smokes." He stared at the crowd on the pier. Beyond the well-dressed reporters and their camera crews stood Ethan and Faith Warner, and neither looked happy.

Grace frowned. "Looks like we have our very own Lady in White to deal with."

Their mother, wearing a white sweatshirt and jeans, pushed her way through the gathering and positioned herself at the foot of the gangway.

"We'd better go. The longer she waits, the more upset she's going to be." Henry fell in line with the other passengers and made his way to the exit.

When they reached solid ground, the reporters shouted and pushed forward, but his mother wrapped her arm around Grace, and his dad did the same for him. NFL defensive linemen had nothing on the elder Warners. They blocked and shoved their way to the truck.

Ethan pushed the unlock button on the key fob and they piled inside.

"Vultures." He started the engine.

Henry glanced over his shoulder. "I can't believe you brought the fifth wheel to the port."

"There's plenty of room and I'm a master driver!" Ethan Warner claimed.

Faith turned in her seat and flashed her children a huge smile. "First off, Henry, how are your knees?"

He'd taken the bandages off in the shower and hadn't bothered to replace them. "Fine. Scabbing over."

Faith made a tsking sound. "What were you thinking, going out on the rocks?"

Henry glanced at Grace, who bowed her head, ready to submit to their punishment.

Ethan cracked up. "She's joking. Mostly we couldn't be more proud of you two."

Henry sputtered in surprise. "Thanks."

Faith's eyes grew watery, and she shook her head. "We saw the news conference this morning. We want the inside scoop, but the two of you look like you're about to collapse. Why don't we book a hotel—"

"No," the twins said in unison, then glanced at each other and laughed.

Grace reached forward and took their mother's hand. "What we mean is, we'd rather sleep in our own beds. Sit on our own couch. And watch a movie as a family."

"That can be arranged." Ethan glanced at them in the rearview mirror and passed back their spare phone chargers. "So...how was the Oceanic?"

"It took some getting used to, but I liked it." Henry met his father's gaze. "I think you two should go next summer. Stay for a week or two."

"We'll have one week in New Jersey. Choose an urban legend that doesn't involve falling through rocks this time, and don't forget your other classes." Faith's prompt change of subject meant she wouldn't be visiting the Isles of Shoals anytime soon.

Henry laid his head back and closed his eyes.

Faith continued speaking words like "textbooks" and "required reading" and "exams," but he couldn't help but smile.

Resting her head on his shoulder, Grace whispered, "It's good to be home."

"Yes, it is."

THE WATCHER

MONSTER CASE FILES BOOK 3

CHAPTER ONE

Timothy Templeton stood on his front porch and smiled like a man who owned the world. He had it all—a beautiful wife, two kids, and a brand-new million-dollar home on the best street in Garwood, New Jersey. Life was good.

An older lady walking an even older poodle waved. "Welcome to the neigh borhood!"

"Thank you." Tim pulled his bathrobe tighter to ward off the early autumn chill and strode to his mailbox.

A middle-aged man jogged by. "Good morning."

"'Morning." He couldn't help but grin. Where he'd grown up, neighbors peered from behind barred windows and ran only when something was chasing them.

You're not in the hood anymore.

Tim opened the door and retrieved a letter addressed to New Homeowners. The scrolling handwriting reminded him of a wedding invitation—formal, precise, and expensive.

New Neighbor,

Please allow me to welcome you and your lovely wife to 100 Avenue E. You have purchased a wonderful home. I daresay the property holds a special place in my heart. For a century, the house has called to the men in my family. It now calls to me. You must understand that I have no choice but to obey.

100 Avenue E is unhappy with you and wishes for you to leave. Should you choose not to accede to this request, the house will become angry. Remove yourselves and your belongings immediately. You have been warned.

The Watcher

Is this a sick joke? Tim reread the letter.

The skin on the back of his neck prickled as if unseen eyes glared at him, and he surveyed the stately homes surrounding his property. No draperies moved in the windows. No blinds snapped shut. The sensation of prying eyes only intensified.

He shoved the envelope in his pocket and hurried inside.

Henry let his foot off the brake and waited for his twin sister to shout. They'd disconnected the fifth wheel from the truck countless times. It should have been easy, but the equipment refused to cooperate.

Grace knocked on the rear window. "The kingpin won't budge. Rock it back."

He put the truck into reverse and eased back an inch or two.

"Got it." She hopped down and came to the driver's side. "Go ahead and pull forward. You're clear."

"About time." He parked the truck at the edge of the campsite and stepped out.

Grace wiped her hands on her jeans. "Is it me, or is it one of those days when nothing works?"

"It's not just you." He nodded toward the rig. "Let's get her level."

Normally, setting up was a four-person job, but their parents had taken a rideshare to Kean University shortly after they'd arrived. Ethan Warner, the twins' father, was contracted to give a series of guest lectures to pre-law students starting as soon as he was able.

Grace checked the level mounted on the side of the trailer and adjusted the landing gear. "I don't know about you, but I'm hungry. We should drive to the university and grab some food while we wait for Mom and Dad."

"You read my mind." Henry connected the electricity. "We're live. Finish it up so we can go eat!"

An hour later, the twins headed for Kean U.

Henry, for one, was glad to be finished with the setup. "How do you feel about a drive-through burger?"

"Ugh, not again. We're only seventeen, but I bet we have the arteries of seventy-year-olds." Grace typed into her phone. "There's a healthy sandwich shop in the student union."

"That'll work, as long as they serve some sort of meat. I'm too hungry for a salad on artisan bread."

"There's a Smashburger in the food court," she allowed, grinning and shaking her head before changing topics. "We should nail down a mystery to solve today."

"There's an alleged sea serpent in Sandy Hook Bay. It's about an hour away." *She'll never go for it. It's likely unsolvable.*

Grace focused on her cell for a few minutes and nodded. "Looks interesting. Let's do it."

"Are you sure?" He half-expected her to smirk or roll her eyes.

"There haven't been any recent sightings, but we can focus on the lore and the history." She pointed to the exit for the university. "It fascinates me how these legends take on a life of their own."

"People love the mystique." Henry followed the signs to a visitor's lot and pulled their father's parking pass from the glovebox.

"There's the place." Grace stuffed her phone into her bag. "Mom and Dad always run late. We may as well do some research."

"Or homework. I don't know about you, but I'm already behind in math."

She cocked her head. "I'll help you with calculus tonight if you proofread my English paper."

"Deal."

They hiked halfway across campus to the student union. Visitors' parking was great, but it almost always sat next to the administration buildings rather than anywhere they wanted to visit.

"I'm going to grab a burger. If you get your food before me, find a table." He moved toward the aroma of grilled beef and grease.

Grace headed for the Green Zebra.

After what felt like an eternity, Henry joined her at a corner table. He took one look at her salad-stuffed pita and blanched.

"It's a Roasted Veggie Delight, and it's delicious."

"I'll take your word for it. You'll be hungry again in an hour."

She ignored him by opening her computer and getting to work.

Henry pulled his laptop from his bag but left it closed. He'd boot it up once he'd eaten his triple cheeseburger and double order of fries. "I say we visit Sandy Hook Bay tomorrow and interview a few locals. After that, we might be able to track down some of the bloggers who've written about the sightings."

Grace's fingers flew over the keyboard. "There really isn't much to go on. A handful of top-ten creepy stories, and a reprint of an old New York Times article from the 60s. What if no one we question has heard of the sea monster? It's not like the creature ate anyone."

A lady in an adjacent booth stared. Judging by her expression, she'd either overheard their conversation or didn't approve of using laptops while eating. She muttered something to the man with her, and he turned and stared too.

Henry leaned across the table and lowered his voice. "We should hold it down a little."

Grace glanced around, locked eyes with the woman, and smiled. "School project. Sorry if we disturbed you."

The stranger's face lit with recognition. "You're those kids who found the missing girl, aren't you?"

Henry cringed. They'd uttered a few sentences at a press conference, which started the clock ticking on their fifteen minutes of fame.

Grace's cheeks flushed. "We might be."

The woman came to their table. "I'm Trina Templeton. It's an honor to meet you both."

"Henry and Grace Warner." Henry did his best not to squirm. Being recognized by the press was one thing, but having a random person come up to them was disconcerting.

Mrs. Templeton laughed. "Forgive me. I'm an old friend of your parents. They put me up to teasing the two of you, but it *is* amazing that you were able to save that girl."

The twins should have known.

Henry ran his hand over his head and forced a smile. On the one hand, he was relieved, but on the other, he wanted to crawl under the table. He looked forlornly at his burger and fries. "That sounds like something my dad would do."

The man stood and rested his hand on Trina's shoulder. "I'm Tim Templeton. Mind if we join you?"

Henry motioned to the empty seats. Trina pointed to Henry's burger and nodded. He took that as approval and quickly took a bite before Grace could stop him.

Grace moved her tray to give them more space. "How do you know our parents?"

"Your mom and I interned at the same firm right out of college." Trina smiled. "You look just like her."

"I get that a lot." She closed her laptop as if embarrassed by the photo of the alleged Sandy Hook Sea Serpent.

Mr. Templeton said, "Your folks told us about your research project this morning. We have a potential case for you."

"What sort of case?" Henry popped a bundle of fries into his mouth. He'd have preferred to take another bite of the burger but didn't want to seem rude.

"Go ahead and eat." Trina motioned to Henry's tray. "This might take a moment."

Tim set his elbows on the table. "Are either of you familiar with The Watcher?"

Grace said, "Are you referring to the person who sent the creepy letters to the new homeowners in Westfield?"

"Yes, that's the one." Trina took her husband's hand. "We believe we are the victims of a copycat. We recently moved into a new home, and we have received three threatening letters so far."

Henry swallowed after minimal chewing and washed it down with a swig of Pepsi. "What sort of threats?"

"They're cryptic. The first letter said the house wanted us to move." Tim's jaw tensed, giving Henry an idea of how deeply the letters had shaken the man. "The others threatened my wife and me and suggested the house will punish us if we do not do as The Watcher says."

Grace drew a deep breath and exhaled through her mouth. "That must be terrifying."

Trina nodded. "We figure it's a neighbor or a buyer who lost out on the house, but yes, it's a bit unnerving."

Henry had read bits and pieces of the articles about the original Watcher but couldn't recall any mention of the author directing the homeowners to do things. "Have the letters included any instructions?"

"Other than telling us to move out, no." Tim's voice rose as he spoke.

Grace sat back and folded her arms. "How can we help?"

Henry recognized the look on her face. She hadn't quite made up her mind, but their story intrigued her. Heck, it intrigued him, too. The sea monster was a dead end in his mind, and he was happy to have an alternative. "Yes, what can we do?"

The Templetons glanced at each other.

Trina said, "Your parents suggested the two of you could house-sit for a few days."

The news took Henry by surprise. He could see their father volunteering them for mystery-solving duty, but their mother? She leaned more toward sealing them in bubble wrap and locking them in a library.

Mr. Templeton said, "I would never suggest such a thing if I thought the two of you were in actual danger. This person's a coward trying to scare us out of our home."

"Tim's right." Trina turned to Grace. "We've spoken to three different police officers and a detective. They all agreed that the person writing the letters likely presents no real threat."

She nodded. "You said house-sit. Will you be out of town?"

"I have meetings in New York City for the next four days," Tim said. "We'll stay with Trina's mother in White Plains. That's an hour or so from here, depending on traffic."

Henry glanced at Grace to gauge her reaction.

As if feeling his eyes on her, she turned her head and gave him the hint of a nod.

"We'll need to speak to our parents before we can give you an answer." Henry pulled his phone from his backpack. "May I have your contact information?"

Mr. Templeton rattled off his cell number and home address.

While Henry typed the details into his phone, Grace turned to Trina. "You understand that we aren't trained to do this sort of thing. We'll probably speak to your neighbors and do some looking into the others who were interested in purchasing the house, but we may not find anything."

The woman smiled. "We know, but four brains are better than two. You may see things differently because you aren't emotionally involved."

Tim stood. "Even if you don't learn the identity of the person writing the letters, you'll have access to a great house for five days, and another chapter to add to your research project."

The guy had a point. Investigating a copycat Watcher beat the heck out of a sea monster that hadn't been spotted since the sixties. Henry stood and shook Mr. Templeton's hand. "We'll let you know what our parents and we decide."

The twins watched the couple exit the building before turning to each other.

Grace's brows rose. "What do you think?"

"It's intriguing, but it's not an urban legend."

She tapped her lips. "True, but we could argue it's close enough to the original case to be relevant."

"I'm not sure how I feel about our parents renting us out as amateur sleuths." He finished the lukewarm burger in one bite.

"I honestly don't know." She nodded toward the entry to the food court. "Speak of the devils."

Ethan and Faith Warner smiled when they saw their children.

Faith raised a brow at Henry's Smashburger container.

Ethan sank into a chair and grinned his I-know-something-you-don't-know grin. "Did you get the trailer set up?"

"Yes, and I want to apologize for all the times I slacked off. It's a lot of work for two people."

"Mmmhmm." Ethan seemed pleased with the admission.

Grace sat up straighter. "We met the Templetons."

Faith seated herself. "And? Are you going to help them?"

Henry met his sister's gaze and shared a look that only they knew. While he appreciated the fact their parents cared enough to support their research, he feared they'd set a precedent of parental interference in future cases.

She ignored him. "We're considering it."

Henry sighed. "I'm surprised you two are on board with Grace and me spending five days in a strange house with a potential sociopath running around."

Ethan clamped a hand on his shoulder. "Son, if I thought you and your sister were going to be in danger, I wouldn't have suggested it."

"Your father and I are going to be busier than usual for the next few days. We thought this would give you something to focus on..." Faith seemed to realize she'd tipped her hand and went quiet.

"Ah *ha*! This is less about solving the case and more about keeping Grace and me out of trouble?" Henry chuckled.

His mom pressed her lips together. "If you must know, yes. There are no rocks to fall through in Garwood, nor is there a beach where you can injure yourself surfing."

It was his turn to go quiet. It was a good thing his mother hadn't insisted on reading the actual accounts of their cases before the end of the school year. Even after the fact, the woman was likely in for a meltdown of epic proportions. *We should tone it down. Leave out the guns and kidnappings.*

"How are your lectures shaping up?" Henry asked his dad.

"I met the class today and will start tomorrow with a four-lecture series. I'm looking forward to discussing English Common Law with this group and clarifying that the majority of law in the US is made by judges, contrary to popular belief."

Henry nodded and tipped his chin toward his mother.

"I have this week off. No lectures for me, but I'm finalizing the contracts for the next few. I think you'll be pleased with what we have coming up, even though I always find it amazing how universities embrace us and what we do. I would have never thought we could make a career out of a lecture circuit, but here we are."

"You guys are good at what you do," Grace said matter-of-factly.

"There are lots of smart people out there who are good at what they do. Maybe we're better at marketing. I don't know, but we'll keep doing it as long as they let us." Faith Warner beamed at her husband, and they clasped hands in quick appreciation of their lives before turning back to the twins.

Grace glanced between Henry and their parents, sighing at the good life they had. "We'll help them, but this is an *independent* research project. Henry and I need to do this on our own."

"Of course." Ethan stood. "But I wish I'd been here to see your faces when Trina pretended to recognize you, and I wish I'd thought to paint the RV psychedelic green and call it the Mystery Machine 2.0."

There was a limit to how much interest the twins wanted their parents to take in their senior research project.

CHAPTER TWO

Grace stood on the sidewalk and stared until her parents' truck disappeared around a corner. Her chest and throat tightened. The moment reminded her of the time they'd dropped her and her brother off with her maternal grandparents in Florida for two weeks.

Henry glanced up from his phone. "What's wrong?"

"It dawned on me they have lives apart from us. I mean, they're more than just our parents. They're people with friends and jobs and stuff that we aren't part of." She huffed and waved her hand. "Forget it. It sounds ridiculous when I say it out loud."

He paused, likely trying to make sense of what she'd said. "I understand what you mean. It's weird to think about them as anything other than 'Mom and Dad.' Does it bother you?"

"In a way, it's good. Their lives won't change much when we go to college."

Henry slung his arm over her shoulder. "I don't think that's true. They'll miss us."

"I know." She pulled away and grabbed the handle of her small suitcase. "But I miss them now."

"I do, too. Between our visit to Star Island and five days here, we'll have spent more time away from them than we did all of last year." He nodded toward the house. "But Gracie, look at this place. We're going to have a blast!"

100 Avenue E was a gorgeous two-story Tudor on a tree-lined street full of

beautiful homes. It was hard to imagine anything bad happening in the quiet neighborhood.

As if on cue, a blonde woman pushing a baby stroller smiled and waved. "Good morning."

"There you are! I was beginning to think you'd changed your minds," Trina Templeton called from the front steps.

"Good morning," the twins said in unison and walked up the drive.

"Your mother mentioned you two finished each other's sentences, but she didn't warn me about talking in stereo." Trina pressed her hand to her slightly protruding tummy.

Grace hadn't noticed the woman's pregnancy when they'd first met. *No wonder she's eager to put an end to the bizarre letters.*

Henry grinned. "We read each other's minds sometimes, too."

The woman's smile brightened. "Tim and I are expecting twins. You two are the first people I've told."

"Congratulations." Grace couldn't imagine taking care of two infants. Unlike most girls her age, she'd skipped the part-time job babysitting. Moving from town to town every couple of weeks had seen to that.

She gestured for them to go inside, glancing across the neighborhood while holding the door before talking in a low voice. "I'll show you the house and then bring you up to speed." Her expression changed as she spoke.

The twins entered the foyer and stopped. The interior was more stunning than the outside. Hardwood floors, beamed ceilings, and an ornate staircase. The home looked like it belonged in a magazine.

"That's the same reaction I had the first time I walked through the front door." Trina laughed. "You can leave your things here. I'll show you around once we've had a chance to chat."

Tim entered the foyer, and with one arm, hugged his wife. "Welcome. It's such a nice morning, I thought we could talk on the back porch."

"That'd be great." Henry followed the couple down a wide hall toward the back of the house.

Grace took a moment to view the family photos on the walls before hurrying to catch up.

"How old are your other children?" she asked before finding a cushioned deck chair and taking a seat.

"Three and five. They're staying with my mother until we can sort things out here." Trina went back inside, returning shortly with a plate of croissants, a carafe of coffee, and two mugs.

Grace reached for a pastry but stopped short. "That must be difficult for you."

Tim told her, "We miss them, but they're enjoying the extra time with their grandma."

If she had any doubts about solving this mystery, they'd vanished somewhere between Trina's nervous glances at her neighbors and her concern for her children. "I'm sorry. That must make the ordeal you're going through even more frightening."

Henry poked his sister in the ribs. They needed to sound confident, not descend to the depths of doom and gloom.

Turning her back to the others, Trina dipped her chin and sniffled.

Tim rubbed his wife's shoulder. "We love the house, but after the last letter and the stress this is putting on our family, we're considering moving."

Henry opened his mouth to ask if they were aware of the real estate disclosure laws in New Jersey but decided now wasn't the time and that his father, as a lawyer would have broached the topic if it applied. In researching the original Watcher case, the twins had learned that the other family had been unable to sell their property because the law required them to tell prospective buyers about the threatening letters.

"We'll do our best to solve this mystery." Henry sounded sure of himself, but his bouncing knee betrayed his nerves. "You can be sure that we'll give it one hundred percent, and then some."

Tim lifted a manila folder from the table top and handed it to Henry. "I've made copies of the letters. There's a list of the neighbors, contact information for the realtor who sold us the house, and the names and numbers of the previous owners. With the exception of the neighbors, we've spoken to everyone listed and have gotten nowhere."

Grace chose her next words carefully. "Mr. Templeton—"

"Please. Call me Tim."

She nodded. "Tim. Why haven't you talked to the neighbors?"

Trina sighed. "Besides the couple who lost out on the house, they're the most likely suspects. Who else would want to scare us into moving?"

Who else indeed? "Henry and I will do our best, but I can't guarantee that we can find the person who's terrorizing your family. Perhaps you should consider hiring a professional."

Trina turned back to them and offered a watery smile. "That's our next step, but we thought we'd give you two a crack at it first. Your parents believe in you."

"We know it's like looking for a needle in a football field, but don't underestimate yourselves. You have two things we don't—a fresh perspective and emotional detachment from the situation," Tim added.

Henry tapped the folder. "The neighbors aren't aware this is going on?"

"No, but we have no problem with them finding out."

Good to know. "What do we tell them when they ask who we are?"

"You're friends of the family who are house-sitting while we're in New York." Tim smiled for the first time since they'd arrived. "I find it's better to stick to the truth as much as possible when you lie."

While Grace understood the sentiment, she found it an odd thing to say to a couple of teenagers he'd just met.

Trina's spine stiffened. "He's kidding. We don't advocate lying." She followed her statement with a sharp look for her husband.

"I'm an investment banker. Stretching the truth comes with the territory, but lawyers? You need to watch those guys. You'll have to ask your dad about that!" He turned for the door. "If you'll excuse me, I need to make a call before we leave."

"I'll show you around the house once you've had your coffee." She followed Tim inside.

Henry leaned close and whispered, "That was interesting."

Grace nodded but kept her opinions to herself. They'd have plenty of time to talk once the Templetons left.

Henry opened the folder and skimmed the first page. "Whoa. He congratulated them on Trina's pregnancy."

The hairs on Grace's arms stood up. "How does the Watcher know? Trina said we're the first people she's told."

"They must be close enough to see her on a regular basis." He offered her the letter.

She shook her head. "I'm not in the right frame of mind to read those now."

Henry flipped through the other documents. "They're disturbing and seem to be escalating."

Someone close. Someone who sees Trina on a regular basis. "We should include people she works with and her students on the list of possible suspects."

"I agree. I think this is a copycat case. It makes sense to focus on motive in addition to a link to the house."

Trina returned to the patio more flustered than when she'd left. Wiping her damp eyes, she forced a smile. "Sorry about the tears. Pregnancy hormones. Are you ready for the tour?"

"Sure." Grace picked up the plate of croissants. "We ate before we left this morning. Can we save these for later?"

"Of course. We can start in the kitchen."

Henry stopped at the doorway and took in the room. Some restaurants had smaller kitchens than the Templetons'. Beyond the marble-topped island, a massive gas stove was set into a brick alcove that reminded him of a pizza oven.

"Are you sure no one else knows you're expecting?"

The woman's shoulders tensed. "Besides my doctor and Tim, you two are the only ones. Why do you ask?"

Henry opened his mouth, but Grace set her hand on his arm to stop him.

"We're thinking outside the box." She had a hunch Trina hadn't read the letters, at least not the latest one. Fearing upsetting a pregnant lady, Grace chose her words carefully. "Is there anyone at the university, a student or co-worker, who has an issue with you? Someone you interact with on a regular basis."

"The police asked the same question. I have healthy working relationships with my colleagues. A couple of summer-semester students weren't happy with their final grades, but I doubt they'd do something like this." She dumped the pastries into a baggie. "I'm certain the person writing the letters is tied to the house somehow."

Tim poked his head into the kitchen. "Are you ready to hit the road?"

"I haven't shown the twins around yet. Oh, and I forgot to pack my toiletries."

He narrowed his eyes and sighed, but his playful grin ruined the effect. "Baby brain?"

Trina tossed a dishtowel at him.

Tim rushed in, wrapped his arms around her waist, and lifted her a foot off the ground. "I'll give them the nickel tour. You make sure you have everything you need."

The couple stared into each other's eyes, and it seemed to Grace that they had an entire conversation in a matter of a few seconds.

Henry flushed red while Grace smiled.

Mr. Templeton set his wife on her feet. "Okay, Warners, this is the kitchen. You're welcome to any of the food in the fridge and pantry. There are takeout menus in the drawer if you feel compelled to act like teenagers."

The tour continued with the laundry room, den, library, and formal living and dining rooms.

"Anything we should know about in the basement?" Henry asked.

"Nothing but old junk, damp air, and cobwebs. You're welcome to explore it if you'd like."

"We will." He winked at Grace.

Upstairs, Tim showed the twins the two guest bedrooms with a shared bath, their children's rooms, and the master. They climbed a third set of stairs and entered an attic filled with boxes, trunks, and old furniture.

Great, another dusty, creaky attic. At least this one has a floor.

Tim folded his arms. "Most of this stuff was here when we bought the house. We haven't had a chance to go through it yet."

Grace lowered her voice. "Has Trina read the latest letter from The Watcher?"

"No. I didn't want to upset her." He glanced between them. "You didn't tell her—"

"We didn't." She closed the door to avoid being overheard. "The Watcher knows she's pregnant. He has to be familiar enough with her to notice the changes in her body."

"You may be right." The man shuddered. "Her co-workers respect her, and most of her students love her."

Henry folded his arms. "Speak to her. Get a list of anyone she failed during the summer semester and any co-worker who might be jealous."

"What about you? Do *you* have any enemies we should know about?" Grace held the man's gaze.

He flinched and ran his hand over the back of his neck. "Too many to count, but it's unlikely any of them would know my home address."

Henry said, "You'd be surprised how easy it is to pull up property records. If someone wanted the information, they could find it."

Tim leaned against the doorframe. "I've been so focused on the neighbors and the other buyers, I haven't considered anyone else."

"Can you afford a private investigator?" She stilled, cursing herself for asking the question out loud.

"We're cash-poor after purchasing the house. Now, with Trina pregnant..." He hung his head. "I'll find the money when we return from New York. In the meantime, I appreciate you two looking into this. Anything you can do for us..." He let the second thought drift off, distraction pulling the corners of his mouth into a deep frown.

"We're happy to help." Henry gave her a thumbs-up behind Tim's back.

Grace walked downstairs, feeling heavier than when she'd gone up. She'd asked the right questions—questions that led to a better understanding of the situation. However, she couldn't shake the feeling she'd pried too deeply into their personal lives. The Templetons loaded their car and didn't waste any time leaving.

The twins waved from the front porch as the couple pulled out of the driveway.

Once the car disappeared from view, Henry turned to her. "What's wrong?"

"This mystery's different from the others. They aren't strangers. They're Mom's friends."

"It does add some pressure, but think how amazing it'll be *when* we find the Watcher."

Grace caught movement from the corner of her eye.

An older man with a stocky build and graying hair stared from a neighboring window.

She locked eyes with him, and a chill ran the length of her spine. Whether it was his unfriendly expression or his folded arms and wide stance, the man gave off a menacing vibe.

Henry turned to the house next door, but the neighbor had stepped away from the window and closed the blinds. "What did you see?"

CHAPTER THREE

Henry opened the front door and ushered his sister inside.

Pale-faced, Grace mumbled, "The man next door was watching. He didn't look happy to see us."

"We have to keep level heads about this. Unfriendly or nosey neighbors are common. Someone stalking a family and writing threatening letters is not."

"I know, but the way he was...glaring." She ran her hands over her upper arms. "Where's the folder Tim left for us? I'd like to see what he knows about the guy."

Henry walked to the screened patio and stopped short. He knew he'd left the folder on the table, but it was gone.

Grace furrowed her brow. "Tim probably picked it up. I bet it's in the kitchen."

The file wasn't in the kitchen. Nor was it in the office, the den, the living room, or the master bedroom.

"Okay, I'm officially freaked out." He pulled his phone from his pocket.

"What are you doing?" She widened her eyes. "You can't call them so soon. They're liable to turn around and come home. Trina needs a break."

His sister had a point, but he didn't like it. Had someone been brazen enough to sneak into the porch and steal the file while people were in the house? He walked back outside and checked the patio door. "It's unlocked."

"Lock it. I'll go check the front."

Henry dialed Tim's number.

"Hello? Did we forget something?" The man's voice sounded lighter than it had before he'd left.

"I can't find the folder you left for us."

Tim grew so quiet Henry thought he'd dropped the call. When he finally spoke, the levity had left his voice. "Isn't it on the porch?"

Okay, if he didn't move it, who did? Henry steadied his nerves and faked a laugh. "Yep. There it is. It must have fallen when we cleared away the food."

"All right." He sighed. "If you two get spooked, you don't need to stay at the house."

"Thank you, but it takes more than a misplaced file to scare us away."

"Call if there's anything else." Mr. Templeton disconnected.

Grace stood in the doorway shaking her head. "You shouldn't have lied."

"I know, but he sounded so defeated that I panicked." Henry rolled his head from side to side. "I hate to say it, but you're right. This is more personal than the other cases."

"We should recreate as much of what was in the file as possible, starting with speaking to the next-door neighbor."

"Good idea." He grabbed the keys from the kitchen counter and followed his sister out. After the third key didn't fit the lock, Henry said, "I hope they left us the right ring."

Grace leaned over his shoulder and inspected the dozen or so keys. "Are those all for this place?"

"I don't know." Henry jabbed another key into the lock. "This is the one. We should mark it."

She nodded and walked across the front lawn toward the neighbor's house.

"Wait up." He jogged to her side and caught movement out of the corner of his eye. The draperies in the first-floor window shifted as if someone had pulled them closed.

Spine stiff and head high, Grace rang the bell.

After a minute or two with not so much as a creaking floorboard from inside, Henry knocked.

"Maybe he's out back?" she whispered.

"I saw the curtains move. He's in there, and he knows it's us." He knocked again, louder this time.

"You're wasting your time," a woman wearing a pink jogging suit and pushing a baby stroller called from the sidewalk. "Mr. Davenport doesn't like visitors."

Henry glanced between his sister and the mother. "We're housesitting for the Templetons and are having some trouble with the gas stove. Would you mind showing us how it works?"

"Sure, but can it wait until I walk Little Miss Cranky Pants?"

The toddler grabbed the edges of the stroller, pulled herself up, and grinned. She didn't look cranky at all.

"We'll walk with you if that's okay." Grace headed down the porch steps.

The woman in pink waved them over with her entire arm. "Sure, the more, the merrier."

Henry joined them. "You're obviously not from New Jersey."

"Amy Anderson, Miss Georgia Peach 2010, and this here's Abigail," she stated in a pleasant southern drawl. She offered her perfectly manicured hand palm down.

He didn't know if he should shake it or kiss it. After a moment's hesitation, he clasped her hand. "Henry and Grace Warner. Nice to meet you."

His sister quirked a brow but remained quiet.

"You, too." She gave the stroller a nudge and started walking. "Now, about that range. What seems to be the trouble?"

Grace said. "We've only ever used an electric stove. Do we need to use less heat to warm soup? I mean, I cook it on medium high at home. Should I use medium to account for temperature variations?"

He couldn't help but grin. She needed to break her habit of saying too much too fast.

"The temperature settings are the same on gas and electric." Amy's expression reminded him of someone looking at two abandoned puppies.

"Good to know, thanks." Henry motioned behind them. "What's the deal with Mr. Davenport?"

The woman sighed. "There's loads of speculation, but no one knows. He's kinda the Boo Radley of Avenue E. I suspect he's harmless but has enough weird habits to make people whisper."

Grace lowered her voice. "Does he ever leave his house?"

"Not that I've seen in my five years on the block. He has his groceries delivered, and he doesn't answer the door to visitors other than the nurse who calls on him once a week." She stopped and handed the toddler a sippy cup.

Henry made a show of sighing deeply and shaking his head. "Say, for instance, someone was sending threatening letters to the Templetons—"

"Is that why they left so soon after moving in? I offered to keep an eye on the house for them, y'know. Those poor people. It's like that house in Westfield." She gasped and pressed her hand to her chest. "My stars, we have our very own Watcher on Avenue E!"

Grace widened her eyes and mouthed, "Do something."

Oh, ye of little faith. He'd anticipated the woman's reaction and the fact the entire neighborhood would know about the letters before sundown. Leaning close, he whispered, "Mrs. Anderson, please don't repeat any of this. Tim and Trina are family friends. We're trying to help."

She nodded, pressed her lips together, and mimed turning a key. "Their secret's safe with me."

Grace said, "Do you think Mr. Davenport is capable of sending the letters?"

"I'd have to see them to know for certain." The woman might have pretended to be peaches and cream-sweet, but the look in her eyes was anything but.

"Unfortunately, we don't have copies." Henry ran his hand over his head and glanced back toward the house. "But we'd appreciate any information you can give us about the neighbors. Specifically, anyone who might have a problem with the Templetons."

"I'll need pen and paper. This might take a while. Follow me."

Little Abigail Anderson squealed in delight when her mother made a one-eighty with her stroller and all but ran back to her house.

Narrowing her eyes, Grace whispered, "What are you doing?"

"Recon. Trust me, if everyone around here is like her, people will come to *us* with information."

"I hope you're right." She followed Mrs. Anderson.

Amy led them to her side door and freed the toddler from her restraints. "Come on in."

Henry hesitated at the entry. The absolute last thing he wanted to do was spend valuable time listening to the woman explain everything as she wrote. "Actually, we have a mountain of homework to do."

"Sure. That'll give me more time to think it over." Amy deposited her daughter in a play yard that reminded him of a contraption people used to contain a litter of puppies. "By the way, is it all right if I call a friend to get her input as long as I don't mention the you-know-whats?"

"That's fine." He bit the inside of his cheek to keep from grinning.

"Okay then. I'll stop by in a little while." She all but shooed them away.

Grace made it to the end of the drive before she burst out laughing. "I have to hand it to you. That was brilliant. Risky, but brilliant."

The twins walked through the front door, paused, and stared at the empty place where their luggage had been before they'd left.

"Um…" Grace glanced around the empty house. "Are you sure you locked up?"

"I believe so." He opened the door and tested to make sure the key turned the deadbolt. "It works."

"Mr. Templeton?" She walked further down the hall. "Trina? Anyone home?"

"Maybe Tim took our stuff upstairs before they headed out." He bounded up the stairs and found their suitcases sitting outside the guest rooms. "Found them."

"Where?" Grace joined him in the hall. "I'm certain they were in the foyer when we left."

"I thought so, too." Henry refused to let the displaced luggage change his attitude. "We need to be more observant. I think our luggage was here. But I'm not positive. We need to be positive because the differences are clues. I don't think we're in the little league anymore. We should make sure the windows and the other doors are locked."

"Good idea. I'll figure out the mystery of Tim's keys while I'm at it." Grace stopped and secured Henry with a mature look. "For the record, we've had guns pointed us. Little league cases don't seem to be in our portfolio."

Ten minutes later, the twins had checked every possible point of entry. The house was locked up tighter than a bank vault.

"There's no way someone got inside." Grace sounded sure, but her fidgeting told another story.

"The most logical explanation is that Tim took them up before he left."

"Right." She turned for the stairs. "I'm going to unpack."

"I'll make you a deal. You put my things away, and I'll make us lunch."

"You got it." Grace cast one final glance at the empty spot in the foyer before heading upstairs.

Henry debated texting Tim and Trina but decided against it. They already thought the twins were spooked. If Tim hadn't moved the luggage, he'd have Trina calling their parents to come pick them up.

First a missing file, now this. He pulled sandwich fixings from the fridge. *There's no way someone got into the house, but what if they were already inside?* His heart skipped a beat. "Grace!"

Henry rounded the corner and took the steps two at a time. "Grace!"

She stepped into the hall, pale-faced and wide-eyed. "What happened?"

"There's no way someone got into the house, but what if they were already inside?" His words came out rushed and breathless.

She dropped the sweatshirt she was holding.

Henry paced away three steps, turned, and walked back. "We need to check the attic and basement."

"But they still would have had to lock up on their way out, wouldn't they? We need to stick together." She snatched the shirt from the floor and went into the bedroom.

"What are you doing?"

Grace emerged with two golf clubs. "I found these in the closet. Not as good as baseball bats, but they'll do the trick."

Henry rested the nine iron on his shoulder and crept up the attic stairs with his sister following close behind.

The large room looked the same as it had when Tim had shown them around. A fine layer of dust covered the trunks, boxes, stacks of chairs, and other furniture.

"Look." Grace grabbed his arm. "The floor's dirty, except for this spot near the door."

"Is there a light switch?"

She pulled a cord near the entrance, but nothing happened. "It's missing the bulb."

"Great." He squatted to get a better look at the creaky floor, using his phone as a flashlight. "You're right. I don't see any footprints leading into the room."

"It's strange. I would have thought the Templetons would have come up here at least once or twice since buying the house."

He frowned. "You have to have a home inspection before purchasing a home. That would have been weeks ago, or a couple of months at the most."

"It's pretty dusty. Maybe the footprints are already covered."

"Maybe." Henry motioned to the door. "Either way, it doesn't look like anyone's been up here today except us."

Grace tucked the golf club under her arm and walked to the first floor. "Have I mentioned that I hate basements?"

"How do you know you hate them? We lived in Florida until we were five and in an RV since, and neither have basements." He chuckled.

"Yes, but every scary movie has a creepy basement." She opened the door and jumped back. "After you."

Henry held the nine iron like a Louisville Slugger and took one step at a time—sideways. If The Watcher was living in the basement, he'd swing first and ask questions later.

When the overhead light came on, Henry yelped and nearly lost his footing, his heart beating a staccato in his chest.

"Sorry!" Grace snickered. "I thought it'd be easier with the lights on."

"Thanks," Henry deadpanned.

"See anything?"

Stone walls, musty smell, the sound of dripping water, the basement wasn't anything like the upstairs. It seemed to be a leftover from a previous era. Slivers of light filtered into the room from a series of long rectangular windows at ground level. One was not only open, but it also didn't appear to have a screen.

"Those are behind the hedges on the side of the house facing Mr. Davenport's property." He dragged a chair beneath the window and climbed up. "But it looks like the glass is missing."

"Be careful." Grace set her club to the side and held the chair steady on the uneven floor.

"I was right. No glass, not even shards."

"How could someone have crawled out without standing on something?"

"Good point." A patch of blue cloth caught his attention. "Give me a boost."

"You can't be serious. You weigh a ton."

"Okay, then move the chair out of the way." Henry put down his golf club, grabbed the outer edges of the window frame and half-crawled, half-pulled his upper body through the opening. Resting his gut on the metal, he snatched the piece of fabric from a shrub and dropped back into the basement.

"What is it?" She crowded closer.

He held the scrap of cloth up to the light. "It looks like the same material as those light-blue oxford shirts Dad wears. What color was Mr. Davenport wearing?"

"Blue or gray. I'm not sure." Her voice thinned.

"Come on. We need to find proof someone was down here." Henry stuffed the scrap into his pocket, picked up the golf club again, and headed to the other side of the basement.

Grace sighed. "Times like these are when we need a fingerprint kit and access to the criminal database."

"Agreed." Henry stopped and looked at the floor. "Urban myths don't leave fingerprints. Criminals do."

Like the attic, boxes, old furniture, and miscellaneous stuff filled the majority of the basement. Shelves lined a quarter of the space and overflowed with yet more containers. None of it appeared to have been moved in the last decade.

"My goodness, don't people take their things with them when they move?" Grace lifted the lid on a box and peered inside. "Dishes."

"I bet they're antiques."

She wandered farther down the wall and froze. "Holy smokes."

"What is it?" He wove his way around a stack of chairs and an old-fashioned loveseat.

There, on the cushion of a tattered orange and brown recliner, sat a manila folder.

CHAPTER FOUR

Every fiber of Grace's being screamed for her to run and never look back. They weren't alone in the house. The Watcher had stolen the file and was hiding in the basement. Worse still, he'd moved their things.

"Did you see a drill on the shelves?" Henry rummaged through a rusted toolbox.

"A what?" Blood rushed behind her eardrums, making it hard to hear over her pounding heart.

"A drill. We need to put plywood over the hole."

He can't be serious. One, what do we know about hanging plywood on concrete? Two, we aren't staying here. "I'm calling Dad."

"Good idea. Have him bring his drill." He dumped a coffee can of screws onto the floor. "And a concrete bit."

"Fine. You two can fix the window, but after that, we're going home." She folded her arms.

He whipped his head in her direction. "What? Why? We're making progress. We know how The Watcher got in, and how he learned about Mrs. Templeton's pregnancy. Plus, we have a very good idea of who it is."

"Yes, but he was *in* the house."

Henry pushed to his feet and walked to her. "I'm going to make sure that doesn't happen again. We can't quit now. Think about Trina and the kids. You saw how scared she was when we first arrived. She's afraid to bring her children here."

"With good reason."

"Grace, imagine if Trina had found a stranger down here? We can do this. Give them their house and their lives back."

She sighed because there was nothing else to say. Her brother was right.

The chiming of the doorbell hade Grace jump out of her skin, but the creaking of the front door made her heart stop beating.

"Yooohooo! Warners!" The sticky-sweet Southern Belle accent echoed from directly above them. "It's me, Amy Anderson."

Henry grabbed the manila file and headed for the stairs. "The door was locked!" Henry hesitated. "Wasn't it?"

"Don't show her that."

"I'm not, but I'm not leaving it down here either. Cover me while I stash the folder."

"Coming! One second." Grace took a moment to slow her breathing before stepping into the foyer. The last thing they needed was for Miss Georgia Peach 2010 to start mother-henning them.

She plastered on a smile and reached for the knob, but Henry skidded to a halt beside her and flung the door open.

"There you are. I'd like for you to meet Gary Grossman." Amy motioned to the twins. "Gary, this is Henry and Grace Warner."

"It's a pleasure to meet you. I took the liberty of googling you when Amy told me your names. You two are heroes." The rail-thin man smiled and thrust his hand out toward Henry, and his thick-lensed glasses slid sideways. He pushed them back in place, wiped his nose, and tried for another shake.

"Nice to meet you, but we aren't heroes. We just happened to be in the right place at the right time." Henry stared at the man's hand for half a second, before taking it.

Grace folded her arms and tried not to snicker when her brother covertly wiped his hand on his jeans.

Amy looked as if she'd smelled something foul but smoothed her expression. "Gary knows the house better than anybody. He's a realtor."

"Were you the realtor who sold the Templetons—"

"No." The man smoothed his wrinkled shirt and adjusted his tie. "No, I represented the Blairs, the previous owners, for a period of time."

The twins exchanged a glance. Not that Grace had any experience with realtors, but the guy didn't strike her as a smooth-talking salesman.

Henry said, "Mrs. Anderson, would your husband happen to have a drill, concrete bit, and screws? One of the basement windows is missing."

Grossman sputtered. "You aren't suggesting drilling holes into a historic home?"

Amy said, "Pshaw, don't mind him. He's a member of the historical society."

Grace grinned. The only other person she'd ever heard use the word "pshaw" was another Southern woman, her maternal grandmother.

"At the very least, call the homeowners and ask them to send a repairman." Gary glanced between the twins like his life depended on their answer.

"Sure. I guess we should ask before we board the window." Henry folded his arms and stared at the visitors. It seemed he'd given up on politeness and gone straight to gruff.

Gary blew out a breath and wiped his brow. "And they say the younger generation has no respect for history."

Grace glanced at the ceiling for a three count before meeting Amy's gaze. "We're really busy."

The woman gave Gary the side-eye and handed Grace a stack of notebook paper. Large bubbly letters filled both sides of a dozen or so sheets. "I know you're busy, but we should go over my notes. You know, in case you have any questions."

"Go ahead and start without me." Henry pulled his phone from his pocket and walked away.

"We can sit in the living room." Grace motioned for them to follow her.

"The *parlor*." Gary sniffled and blew his nose into a cloth handkerchief. "It's not a living room in a house this old."

Grace had never taken such an instant dislike to another human being. Considering she'd met some rather unsavory sorts since starting the urban legends research project, that was saying something.

Amy seated herself on the couch and patted the space next to her.

Gary took a step forward, but Grace managed to get there first.

"Okay. We all know Mr. Davenport's the obvious suspect, but I'd also look into Mrs. Perez at the end of the block. She's on the PTA, and has been on a power trip since moving in. Plus, she has a juvenile delinquent of a teenaged son." Amy took the papers from Grace and ran her pink fingernail down the page. "Oh, right. I almost forgot. Mr. Perez moved out last year. Since then... Well, let's just say Mrs. Perez has been very busy."

Gary nodded and glanced around. Judging by the curl of his upper lip, the Historical Society member didn't approve of the sleek leather couches and pops of color throughout the room.

The beauty queen continued to spill dirty secrets about nearly every neighbor on the block. She'd even included a hand-drawn map, complete with color-coded icons. Red for a definite suspect, yellow for a maybe, and green for the residents who should be nominated for sainthood.

They'd made it through five double-sided pages before Henry returned.

He leaned against the arched wall and folded his arms. "Thank you for your help, but we have an appointment. Our rideshare will be here any minute."

As far as Grace knew, they didn't have anything on their agenda, but she'd do anything to put a stop to the neighborhood gossip. She stood and pulled the papers from Amy's hands. "Is it that late already? My goodness. Time flies."

Gary looked down his nose at the twins, skepticism furrowing his brow. He was not buying their story. "I'm at 201. Stop by if you have any questions."

"Thank you." Henry gave him a tight-lipped smile.

Amy, seeming flustered, stood and smoothed her blonde hair. "You two should join my family for dinner tonight. I'd love to hear all about how you rescued that little girl, and I can finish filling you in on the neighbors."

"We'd love to, but we have homework." Grace held her arms out at her sides and walked to the door, essentially herding Amy and Gary in the right direction.

"Maybe another night, then." The woman hesitated on the front steps. "Look into Mrs. Perez. I'm telling you, she is up to no good."

"Will do." Grace smiled and turned to Gary.

The man took one last look around and walked out without another word.

She shut the door, turned the lock, and hung her head.

"Nice work in there, using Mom's move to get them out the door." Henry snickered.

"Thanks for abandoning me. It was your idea to have her give us the dirt on the neighbors."

"Sorry about that." He glanced at his phone. "Our ride will be here in five minutes."

The thought of leaving the house without boarding the window sent a chill down her spine. "Shouldn't we take care of the basement window?"

"Tim's sending his contractor over to board it up while we're gone. He'll make sure the house is empty before he leaves."

"Where are we going?"

"To meet the couple who didn't get the house." Henry rubbed his hands together.

"You still think they're suspects?"

He shrugged. "Hard to tell until we meet them, but I doubt they're involved."

"Then why are we going?"

"Because we needed an excuse to get rid of those two. Besides, we're meeting them at a place called Great Grounds. I could seriously use a cup of coffee, and the Staudingers seemed eager to speak to us."

That tidbit piqued Grace's curiosity. "Really? What did you tell them?"

"The truth. Someone had been sending the Templetons threatening letters, and we'd like to ask them a few questions." He ushered her onto the front step, locked the door, and tested to make sure it was secure.

"That's it? Exactly like that?"

Henry nodded.

"And they agreed to meet us?" It didn't make sense. Why would people who'd lost out on a house want to talk to a couple of teenagers who'd basically accused them of threatening the homeowners?

"They're either a couple of good Samaritans, or they like to write creepy letters."

Mind racing, Grace slid into the backseat of the rideshare.

Henry gave the driver the address and pulled the manila folder from beneath his shirt. He caught her stare and grinned.

Henry checked the time. Three minutes had passed since the last time he'd looked at his phone. "They aren't coming."

"You're sure they said five?" Grace finished her second cappuccino and drummed her fingers on the table.

"I'm sure." He dialed the Staudingers, and the call went straight to voice-mail. Rather than leave another message, Henry disconnected and ordered a rideshare. "What do we know?"

"The next-door neighbor is the obvious suspect, but I can't figure out a motive. Unless he doesn't like kids. Do we know if the previous homeowners had children?"

He flipped to Tim's notes on the Blairs. "Three kids between the ages of eleven and sixteen."

"We need to find a way to speak to him."

Henry leaned across the table and lowered his voice. "We should have held off on calling the Templetons about the window. We could have set a trap in the basement."

"Holy smokes, no. What would we do if we caught someone down there?"

"Call the police." He stood and dumped their empty cups into the trash.

Grace shook her head. "Before or after he kidnapped us, locked us in a hole, and made us put lotion on our skin?"

Henry laughed and slung his arm over her shoulder. "Every once in a while, you're actually funny."

She elbowed his side. "I have a great sense of humor. You just don't recognize it because your idea of funny is Dad jokes."

"All kidding aside, I doubt The Watcher is dangerous. We're looking for someone who's comfortable hiding behind a pen and paper, not Hannibal Lecter."

"Buffalo Bill was the character who made the skin suits. Lecter was the incredibly smart cannibal."

"That reminds me, I'm starving. Let's order a pizza when we get back." Henry waved to the same rideshare driver who'd dropped them off two hours earlier.

"Anything other than dinner at the Andersons."

The ride back to 100 Avenue E gave Henry time to consider the logistics of setting a trap in the basement. Grace had made a good point. They'd need to ensure that the perpetrator couldn't escape or harm them. The basement door was easy. It opened into the kitchen, and the Templetons had enough bulky furniture to block it. However, the window presented a challenge. Would they have enough time to replace the board? Would it hold?

The sun had set and the exterior lights had come on by the time the twins returned, but Henry recognized the shape of the envelope taped to the front door instantly. It matched the three in the file he'd hidden beneath his sweatshirt.

"Is that..." Grace stopped walking halfway up the drive.

"I think so." He hurried past her and tore the letter free.

"No, wait to read it until we get inside," she whispered, glancing around much like Trina had done that morning.

Henry handed the envelope to Grace, unlocked the door, and went straight to the basement. Halfway down the stairs, he stooped to check the window. As

Mr. Templeton had promised, the opening was covered with a piece of plywood.

When he returned to the kitchen, it seemed as though Grace had turned on every light on the first floor.

She frowned at the envelope. "It's addressed to us."

"Okay." His voice came out in a croak.

She shoved the letter at him. "You read it."

Henry compared the scrolling handwriting to the letters in the file. "It looks the same."

"What does it say?"

Dearest Warner Twins,

1oo Avenue E does not take kindly to intruders. The house doesn't want you here. Leave before it's too late.

The Watcher.

Grace stared at the letter like it was a snake coiled and ready to strike.

He tossed it on the counter and turned her to face him. "I meant what I said before. I don't think this person is a physical threat."

She shook her shoulders as if to snap herself out of the trance The Watcher's words had caused. "You're absolutely right. What kind of person threatens a couple of teenagers?"

"If you want, we can go home tonight and come back in the morning. We don't have to sleep here to solve the mystery."

"Uh-uh. No way. I'm not going to let this guy win." Grace smiled her first real smile of the day, now that she'd convinced herself of the necessity in trying to solve the case. She didn't take kindly to being threatened. "Didn't you say something about pizza?"

Henry rummaged through the drawer of takeout menus. "Pepperoni extra cheese?"

"Pineapple, ham, and onions."

"That's not only gross, it's illegal in twenty states." The familiarity of the old argument gave him a sense of hope. If they could debate pizza toppings after a maniac had sent them a creepy letter, they could do anything.

Grace rolled her eyes. "I would point out that twenty isn't a majority, but I'm too tired."

"It's been a long day. Go take a shower. I'll order dinner."

She chewed her lip. "Would you think I was a total wimp if I asked you to check the house one more time?"

"Not a *total* wimp." Henry started in the basement. The plywood remained on the window, and there were no signs of anything out of place other than some concrete dust the handyman left behind.

"All clear?" She shifted her weight from one foot to the other.

"Yep. Nothing but junk and dust."

She followed him around the first floor, double-checking the locks on the windows and doors. They reached the second story, and Grace turned lights on in the guest rooms, bathroom, and hall. "We should double-check the attic."

"Hang on." Henry grabbed a flashlight from the hall closet, trudged up the final flight of stairs, and shined the light around the room.

Grace trailed behind him. "I feel foolish doing this, but—"

Fresh footprints led from the doorway into the interior of the attic.

Henry's pulse quickened. "There has to be an explanation that doesn't involve The Watcher."

"Maybe the handyman needed something up here." She took the flashlight from him. Boards creaking with each step, she walked deeper into the room. "There's a sheet of plywood on the back wall."

"Where do the footprints lead?"

She shined the light over the floor and frowned. "In the opposite direction of the plywood."

So much for a logical explanation.

The doorbell rang, causing the twins to jump.

Henry pressed his hand to his chest to make sure his heart hadn't stopped. "Whoever it was is long gone."

"You're probably right, but how did they get in?" Grace looked around one last time.

The doorbell chimed again.

"It's probably Amy Anderson making sure we're properly fed." Henry hurried downstairs and peeked out the small window on the front door.

A pizza delivery girl stood on the porch.

"What's wrong? Who is it?" Grace whispered, resting her hand on his shoulder.

He swallowed hard. "Pizza, but I never got around to ordering it."

CHAPTER FIVE

Grace steadied her nerves and opened the door. "You have the wrong house. We didn't order a pizza."

The delivery girl leaned back and checked the house number. "100 Avenue E. Last name Warner?"

"That's correct, but we didn't order a pizza." She'd heard of this sort of thing. Usually, it involved bored teens ordering dozens of pizzas to be sent to their high school enemies, another joy of adolescence she'd skipped thanks to her nomadic parents.

The girl narrowed her eyes. "Half pepperoni extra cheese, half pineapple, onion, and ham?"

Holy smokes. That's the exact order we'd discussed. Grace wrapped her arms around herself.

Henry muttered under his breath and opened the door wider. "Do you have the phone number the order was placed from?"

"It was an online order." She rolled her eyes. "Look, it's paid for. Do you want it or not?"

"No," the twins said.

Henry ran his hands over his head. "Sorry. Someone's been pranking us all day. Can you tell us the name on the credit card?"

"This is all I got." The pizza girl ripped the receipt from the top of the box and handed it to him.

The receipt had his name, the Templetons' address, and a code he couldn't decipher. In other words, nothing useful. "Does your manager have access to payment information? I'd really like to know who sent this."

"Don't know. You're welcome to go in and talk to him. I doubt he'll tell you anything over the phone." She smacked her gum and smirked. "You might as well take the pie. I'm just gonna' throw it in the garbage. I don't do pineapple on pizza. It's gross."

Grace pressed her hand to her churning stomach. "I don't want it."

"I'll take it. Just a minute. I'll get your tip…" Henry patted his back pocket and furrowed his brow. "I must have misplaced my wallet."

The pizza girl huffed, shoved the box into Grace's hands, and stormed away.

Grace glanced at the darkened windows of the houses surrounding her, and the sensation of someone staring sent a shiver down her spine. She hurried inside and locked the door. "I'm not eating this."

"It's not like the pizza place poisoned it," Henry called from upstairs. "Have you seen my wallet?"

"Not since the coffee shop. You paid the rideshare driver with your phone." She set the box on the island and opened the lid. *No obvious signs of tampering. A little cold, but that's to be expected.*

He grabbed two slices, folded them into a makeshift sandwich, and took a bite. "I can't find it."

"Maybe it fell out of your pocket when you got out of the ride-share. Check outside. If it's not there, you should contact the driver." She picked a piece of pineapple off the pizza and popped it into her mouth.

"Be right back." Henry had made it halfway to the door before she stopped him.

"I'm coming with you." Grace snatched the flashlight they'd used upstairs. She'd put on a brave face, but she'd be darned if she wanted to stay in the house alone. The Watcher was getting inside their heads. Grace didn't like being threatened but being tormented was something else entirely.

Outside, they combed the porch, driveway, and sidewalk. They found an embroidered cloth handkerchief, but no wallet.

Grace wrinkled her nose. "I'd bet you a month's allowance the initials are GG."

Henry gave her a dubious look. "You're on, but only if you pick it up and verify."

"Yuck. No way."

He nudged her side. "Come on, Gracie. I had to shake his snotty hand. It's the least you can do."

"That," she pointed at the stiffened fabric, "is not a clue."

"I don't know. It's full of DNA."

"Gross." She rolled her eyes and turned to go inside. "Or should I say, 'Grossman.'"

A dark figure darted from the side of the Templetons' toward Mr. Davenport's house.

"Stop!" Grace took a few steps after the man or woman or Watcher.

Henry sprinted past her in a blur.

"Wait!" She took a second to gather her courage and followed.

Her brother rounded the corner and disappeared into the shadows.

Running as if her feet were on fire, Grace sped up.

The sound of bodies colliding, a grunt, and a thud urged her on. She reached the neighbor's side yard and found Henry wrestling with a man. One moment he had the man pinned, the next, he lay flat on his back staring at the sky.

Mr. Davenport stood, brushed himself off, and glared at one and then the other.

Grace glanced between them trying to decide what to do. "Henry, are you okay?"

He gave her a thumbs-up but didn't move.

Dearly wishing she'd brought the nine iron, Grace set her hands on her hips and tried to act tougher than she felt. "What were you doing on the Templetons' property?"

"I saw an intruder." The man's voice sounded like an old engine, wheezy and rumbly.

Henry pushed himself upright. "We had the window boarded up."

"Correct. The contractors arrived five minutes after you vacated the premises and departed at eighteen hundred hours."

She cocked her head to the side and studied Mr. Davenport. In addition to his vocabulary screaming military, he wore his hair in a buzz cut and stood ramrod-straight. It wasn't until he turned to go that she noticed his limp. "Wait. Did you get a look at the burglar?"

Mr. Davenport kept walking.

She followed. "Sir, please. We believe someone has broken into the house at least twice today."

He stopped walking and flexed his fingers at his side. When he turned to face her, his expression hardened, but something else rested beneath his anger. "What do you expect me to do about it?"

Is he in pain, or frightened? She motioned to his leg. "Did my brother hurt you?"

His entire body went rigid. "Hardly."

Keep him talking. "You're obviously keeping an eye on the place. You must have seen something. If not today, then another time."

"Don't want to get involved. Not my problem." He winced and walked to his side door.

Henry stood and brushed himself off. "You involved yourself when you decided to go after the intruder."

"A mistake I won't make again." Davenport slammed the door behind him.

Grace refused to let him off the hook so easily. They needed to know what he'd seen today, and in the time since the Templetons had purchased the house. She banged on the door. "I'm not leaving until you talk to me."

No reply.

"Let it go." Henry shook his head. "How do we know he wasn't trying to sneak in again and got caught?"

"You heard him. He knew the handyman was here. It stands to reason he knows what they were doing." Grace knocked again. "Mr. Davenport, please open the door. Would you send two kids alone into a house with a madman on the loose?"

A shadow moved behind the window. He was listening, even if he wouldn't open the door.

"Someone is trying to scare us. Our things were moved. Someone was listening while we discussed dinner and ordered us a pizza." She banged until her hands throbbed. "There have been scary letters taped to the door. Please, tell us what you know."

Henry tugged her away from the door. "Forget it. He's not going to help."

Tears stung her eyes, but she wiped them away with the back of her hand. "He may be our best shot at stopping this guy before someone gets hurt."

"I know. Let's give him a chance to cool off." He pressed his hand to the small of her back and guided her to the Templetons' front door.

Grace stopped on the steps and stared at what most would consider a dream home. "Why would someone want this place to be vacant?"

"Because they want it for themselves?" Henry mused.

"Or they dislike the Templetons." *No, that's too easy.*

"Let's go inside. Standing out here gives me the creeps." He held the door for her.

She shambled in and glanced at the sleek leather couches and whimsical accent pieces. "The hanky."

"What?" Henry turned the deadbolt and checked to make sure it'd engaged.

"Gary Grossman. When he was here earlier, he looked at the furniture like it was something on the bottom of his shoe."

"The guy was a snob, but that's a fairly weak motive." He pointed in the direction of the Davenport house. "Him? Him we caught in the act."

"Maybe, but I don't think he's doing this." She couldn't explain why, but she had a hunch the recluse next door had tried to help them—at least until Henry had tackled him.

Grace pulled out her phone. "Text the rideshare driver. I'll call the coffee shop."

He nodded and pulled up the app.

She plopped down on the sofa and dialed.

An overly perky or overly caffeinated woman answered. "Great Grounds."

"Hello, this is Grace Warner. My brother and I were in earlier tonight, and he's lost his wallet—"

"Hang on." Muffled voices filled the line. "Sorry. No wallet, but someone came in asking for you after you'd left."

It had to be the Staudingers. We must have just missed them. "Did they leave a name or do you know what they looked like?"

"Nope. Sorry."

"Thanks." Grace slid her phone back into her pocket. "I think the Staudingers came to the coffee shop after we left."

"Darn it." He dragged his hands down his face. "And?"

"No luck with the wallet."

"It wasn't in the car either." Henry's frown deepened. "I have a feeling it's going to be a huge pain to get a replacement license."

"And your debit card. You should call Mom."

"I'll do it later. Right now, we should check the house again."

Grace drew a deep breath through her mouth and exhaled through her nose. "Lead the way."

The twins started in the basement and worked their way up floor by floor. Thankfully, nothing appeared out of place. No more strange footprints. No broken windows. No mysteriously reappearing wallet, file, or suitcases.

"Want to watch a movie?" Henry grinned, but she knew he'd done it for her benefit. He looked as exhausted as she felt.

A comedy sounded wonderful, but she didn't have time. "As much as I'd love to, I need to complete at least two assignments, or the professors are going to send Mom an email telling her I'm off-pace."

He sighed so deeply it seemed to come from his soul. "Same here, but I'm going to polish off that pizza while I work."

"You do that. I'm not hungry, but I do need a toothbrush and PJs." She headed for the bathroom. "And call Mom."

He groaned. "I knew you were going to say that. I'll call her in the morning."

They set up their laptops in Grace's room, her on the bed and Henry seated at the desk because red sauce and white comforters didn't mix. Despite their chaotic day, Grace found a certain peace in her thermodynamics textbook. Science was based on rules and logic and tested theories. Even when the outcome was unknown, there were processes and procedures to follow. In short, no one broke into a science experiment and hid in the attic.

The doorbell broke Grace's concentration.

She cast a weary glance at Henry. "Now what?"

He hung his head, sighed, and brushed the crumbs off his lap. "No idea."

The twins came downstairs in their pajamas. Grace's extra-fuzzy socks slid on the hardwood floors, but she managed to grab the handrail and keep herself from falling.

The bell chimed again.

Grace peeked out the little window and furrowed her brow, then opened the door. A middle-aged couple stood on the front steps. "Yes? Can I help you?"

The woman said, "We're the Staudingers. We were supposed to meet Henry and Grace Warner tonight at the coffee shop."

Henry eased her out of the way and peered at the couple. "That was hours ago."

"We had car trouble," the man said.

"Give us a minute." Henry closed the door and walked far enough down the hall to avoid being overheard. "I don't like it. Someone was out back. How do we know it wasn't one of them?"

"We don't." She glanced toward the door. "But it's not like they showed up out of the blue. You called them, remember?"

"True, but it's eleven o'clock. What kind of people show up at other people's houses this late?"

"I don't know, but there's only one way to find out." Grace walked back into the foyer and opened the door. "We just have a couple questions for you. Would you mind if we talked out here? Our parents are sleeping upstairs."

Henry smirked and motioned over his shoulder. "Pssht, parents sleeping. Trust me, you don't want to wake them."

Mrs. Staudinger's expression hardened. "You expect us to stand on the stoop while you grill us about the letters?"

Between the look in the woman's eyes and the size of her husband, Grace regretted opening the door. "We should reschedule our meeting. My family is house-sitting. I don't feel right about inviting you in."

Mr. Staudinger stepped forward. "We're here now."

Henry pushed past Grace and put himself between the man and his sister. "I'll keep this short and sweet. Are you the ones sending the letters to the Templetons?"

Mrs. Staudinger held up her hands and sighed. "Let's start over. We're sorry to come by so late. We thought if we stopped by, we could see the house. I fell in love with the kitchen and wanted to take some photos to show the designer we hired to remodel our new place."

"You bought another house?" Grace eased from behind Henry.

"We closed on it last week." Her voice softened. "It's not as nice as this one, but we're fixing it up."

"Like I said, I don't feel comfortable having you inside, but if you'd like, I'll snap some pictures of the kitchen for you."

"That'd be great." She reached into her purse and pulled out her cell. "Be sure to get a close up of the decorative tile behind the stove."

"My pleasure." Grace took the phone and hurried into the kitchen. She took several photos before opening the woman's call history. One stood out— Tim Templeton.

Heart thudding, Grace pressed the home button and took one final picture from a few feet back. She returned to the foyer and handed Mrs. Staudinger her phone. "Here you go. You might want to check to be sure the lighting was right."

The woman scrolled through the half-dozen images and nodded. "Thank you."

Mr. Staudinger hadn't stopped frowning since the twins had opened the door. "I'd look into the seller's agent. He seemed like the type who'd hide behind a pen and paper."

Henry stiffened. "He? I thought the realtor was a Melissa Meadows?"

The Staudingers exchanged glances.

"What are we missing?" Grace asked.

"We were dealing with a man." The woman rolled her lips in. "Gary something."

"Grossman?" Grace's mind reeled. The dirty looks. The condescending attitude. The handkerchief.

"That's him. Thank you for taking the pictures." Mrs. Staudinger turned to go, and her husband followed.

The twins watched from the doorstep until the couple pulled out of the drive.

Henry ran his hand over his head. "Gary Grossman, huh?"

"He mentioned he'd worked with the Blairs, but it seemed like it was some time ago."

"Add him to the list of suspects."

"At this rate, we'll need a spreadsheet to keep up with them all." Grace sighed. "There's something else you should know. I checked Mrs. Staudinger's call log while I had her phone. She spoke to Tim Templeton tonight."

Henry stared for a couple of heartbeats. "She probably called to check my story before meeting us."

"Maybe."

CHAPTER SIX

Miss Georgia Peach 2010, otherwise known as Amy Anderson, sat at the kitchen table wearing a baby-blue jogging suit and a bright smile. The beauty queen had another stack of papers in front of her, and this time she'd written in hot pink. "Good morning, Henry."

"Hi." He winced against the sun shining through the windows and her way-too-perky-for-seven-AM voice.

Grace, looking both sleep deprived and rumpled, offered him a steaming cup of coffee. "Mrs. Anderson brought us a quiche and more information on the neighbors."

Henry would eat almost anything as long as it fell into one of the four food groups. However, he had his doubts about the jiggling faintly green goo in a pie shell. "Thanks."

Amy stood and brandished the pie slicer like a weapon. "Sit down. I'll cut you a piece."

While he was curious to see exactly how one went about cutting a substance that fell somewhere between gelatin and liquid, he didn't dare risk it. "I'll have some later, after I've had my daily dose of caffeine and a shower."

The woman arched a brow. "Your sister said the same thing."

"We're twins. It happens a lot." He sipped his coffee.

"Oh! I didn't realize. How fun is that? Twins house sitting for a family expecting twins." She sat and ruffled her papers.

Grace shot him a quick glance and looked back to Amy. "Trina told you?"

Pink spots, the same shade as the woman's nail polish, formed on her cheeks. "Not exactly. I overheard her and Tim talking about it while they were moving in. I'd stopped by with a plate of brownies..."

Henry had watched a documentary on beauty pageants once. The competitiveness and underhanded tactics the contestants used to win had surprised him, but he couldn't imagine Amy Anderson writing those letters. For one, her handwriting looked like it belonged to a middle-school girl, and two, whoever had broken into the house had been quiet—something this woman was not.

As if to prove his point, she squealed. "I was thinking of ways to help the two of you find The Watcher and came up with a doozy!"

Grace downed her coffee and set the mug on the counter. "That's not why we're here. We're house-sitting and catching up on homework."

"I was going to ask why you two weren't in school, but I thought it was none of my business." She rested her chin on her palm and stared.

"We're homeschooled." Henry had no idea why he'd blurted it out, but he would make it a point to avoid the woman's gaze in the future. She was better than a cobra dancing in a wicker basket.

"Oh, how...sad." Amy sighed. "It must be hard only having each other for friends. I mean, what about sports or extracurriculars and *prom?*"

"We manage." Grace folded her arms. "You were saying you had an idea?"

She shook her head the way people do when they learn of an untimely death. "Right. I've put together a block party for tonight."

Henry blinked. "What?"

Amy went back to staring at them like they were abandoned puppies. "Oh, you don't know what that is, do you?"

Grace sucked air between her teeth and turned her head.

Henry intervened before his sister said something she would regret. "We know what block parties are, but how did you plan one in less than twenty-four hours?"

She pretended to buff her nails on her jacket. "I'm a pro."

"Great. Well, thanks for stopping by. We'll be sure to make an appearance at the party." Grace attempted to reuse their mother's trick to get the woman out of the house, but this time it didn't work.

"It starts at six. Dress is casual. Everyone's expected to bring a dish to share, but I'll whip something up for the two of you." She leaned forward and gave them a conspiratorial smile. "We should go over my new notes before tonight."

"Actually, there *is* someone I'd like to know more about." Henry took a seat next to Amy. This seemed to simultaneously thrill the beauty queen and tick his sister off. "What's the deal with Gary Grossman? He was working for the Blairs, wasn't he?"

Amy nodded slowly and picked imaginary lint from her sleeve. "He was their listing agent for a little over a month. They had a difference of opinion, and *he* referred *them* to someone else."

Grace leaned against the counter. "It must have been a serious disagreement to lose a commission on a house like this."

"Gary's a professional. He has several multimillion-dollar listings." She smiled, but it seemed forced. "All the same, it's probably best you don't bring it up with him. You saw how persnickety he gets when it comes to historic homes."

"Of course." Grace made a show of looking at the clock.

Amy stacked her notes into a neat pile and stood. "I should get going. Abigail will want her pancakes soon."

"Thanks for breakfast. I can't wait to dig in." Henry followed her to the kitchen door.

"You're welcome. Now don't forget. Six o'clock." She tried for another smile, but it'd lost its luster.

"We'll be there." He watched her pull her cell from her pocket as she walked across the lawn. "That was weird."

"Very." Grace poked the quiche with a butter knife.

He stared in horror as the surface of the egg mixture wobbled. "What do you make of it?"

"I think she may be trying to kill us."

He nudged his sister's shoulder. "Oh, she's definitely trying to kill us, but what did you make of her reaction to my question?"

"As Grandma Atwell would say," Grace mimicked a southern accent, "She let her mouth get ahead of her good sense."

"Agreed. But what difference does it make if we know Gary worked for the Blairs?"

Grace tapped her lips. "None, except I have a sneaking suspicion they fired him, not the other way around. Maybe she was protecting his pride."

"That makes sense, but I'd like to have a chat with Mr. Grossman." Henry motioned to the quiche. "What do we do with this?"

Grace picked it up, dumped it into the sink, and turned on the disposal. "I'll return the pie plate tonight."

He risked a peek at the waterlogged concoction. "Oh man, is that kale?"

Grace giggled. "Showers, then homework. You promised to proofread my English paper."

Six o'clock came quicker than Henry would have liked. Between their school-work and the case, the twins had barely come up for air, let alone food. He pulled on a pair of jeans and a light sweatshirt and followed the scent of grilled meat.

Grace glanced up from her novel and sighed. "Is it time already? I'm just getting to the good part."

Henry arched a brow. "There's a good part in Hobbes's *Leviathan*?"

"Ha ha." She bent to tie her shoes. "What's the plan tonight?"

"Food first, then we get to know the neighbors."

"I'm half-tempted to bring along Amy's version of *CliffsNotes* for refer-ence." Her wicked grin made him more than a little nervous.

"Horrible cooking aside, she's our only ally. It's best to keep on her good side. Besides, you saw that documentary about pageant queens. I don't think I'd want that woman as an enemy."

Grace rolled her eyes and marched to the door. "We stay together tonight."

Henry nodded.

"I mean it. Don't you dare leave me alone with any of these people."

He held up his hands. "I wouldn't dream of it."

They stepped onto the front sidewalk and into a miniature carnival. Amy Anderson had filled her front yard with not one, but three bounce houses. Tents decorated with fairy lights and balloons lined the street. And the people! Miss Georgia Peach 2010 must have invited half the county to the block party.

"Where do we start?" Grace turned to him with wide eyes. "They can't all be neighbors, can they?"

"Depends on your definition of neighbor." Henry steeled his resolve and entered the fray.

Walking close beside him, Grace whispered, "Is this what we missed by not living in a normal house?"

"I don't think this is normal." He followed his nose to a line of grills outside one of the tents.

Men, dressed in the suburban uniform of khakis and polo shirts, tended every imaginable cut of meat. Most held cans of beer or red plastic cups in one hand and tongs in the other, but the weird thing wasn't their matching outfits. It was the way they moved like synchronized swimmers. Turn the meat. Nod. Sip. Chat. Repeat.

A guy in a coral-colored polo smiled at them. "Burger?"

Henry glanced over the carnivore's smorgasbord. "That's a good place to start, but those ribs are calling my name."

Grace offered the man two plates. "I'll have one, too, please."

"Adam Anderson. You must be the Warners?" He flashed a superhero smile.

He grinned, imagining Mr. and Mrs. Anderson standing side by side like living, breathing Barbie and Ken dolls. "That's us. Henry and Grace."

"Nice to put faces with the names." Mr. Anderson pointed at the tent with his tongs. "Condiments and potluck dishes are inside."

The twins took their burgers inside and stopped short. The cavalcade of grills was only the beginning of the feast. Crockpots and platters filled every square inch of three ten-foot-long tables. The mingled aromas of baked beans, mac and cheese, and spices too numerous to count made Henry feel as if he'd died and woken in food nirvana.

A dark-haired woman glanced between the crowd and a red crockpot, frowned, and looked around again.

Grace leaned closer and breathed deep. "What is that? It smells amazing."

"Paella." The woman motioned to the various salads and more traditional American dishes. "It's spicy. You might want to try some of these instead."

"Are you kidding? Why try something I've had a million times when I can sample this?" She scooped a heaping spoonful onto her plate.

The woman beamed. "It's an old recipe from Cuba. *Mi abuela* brought it over when she came to Florida."

Henry scooted his burger over to make room for the paella. "We're from Florida too," he casually added before inhaling deeply of her *abuela*'s recipe.

"It's not often I meet other Floridians. I'm Paulita Perez." She offered her hand.

They shook firmly. "Henry Warner, and this is my sister Grace."

Grace's eyes lit. "Will you join us? Have you eaten?"

Ms. Perez glanced over the crowd, wrung her hands, and nodded. "I would love to."

This woman was nothing like the image Amy Anderson had painted of her. *I wonder what Miss Georgia Peach says about us?* Grace thought.

Once seated and halfway through the paella, Henry said, "This is amazing."

Grace nodded. "My parents would love this. Would you mind sharing the recipe?"

"Only if you promise never to post it online or open a Cuban restaurant."

She smiled, but it wilted around the edges. "You two are the only ones who've tried it tonight."

"More for me." He shrugged. "I'd be happy to take the leftovers off your hands." He shoveled in another mouthful.

She chuckled. "My children will thank you. They've eaten a dozen hamburgers and twice as many hot dogs between them."

Grace lowered her voice. "Ms. Perez, we're housesitting for the Templetons. They've had some...issues. May we ask you some questions?"

"What sort of issues?"

Henry leaned closer. "They've received threatening letters, similar to those written by The Watcher in Westfield. Are you familiar with that case?"

"Yes, it was on the news." She looked around as if expecting to be interrupted.

Grace said, "Can you think of anyone who might want the Templetons to move?"

"I've only met them once. They seemed like a nice family. I can't imagine anyone on Avenue E would want to scare them away..." Once again, she searched the crowd.

Is she looking for her children or someone else? Henry pushed his empty plate away. "It may not be anything personal against them. We received a letter from The Watcher, too."

The moment his words sank in, the mom switch seemed to flip on inside Ms. Perez. "*Dios mio.* And you're staying in the house? Alone? Where are your parents?"

Grace cringed. "The Templetons are my mom's friends. They're aware of what's happening. We aren't in any real danger."

The woman sighed. "I will ask my son Pablo to keep an eye out for the two of you. He's your age."

"Thank you," the twins said in unison.

"Now, now, there's no need for that. Not with me right next door." Amy Anderson's sticky-sweet accent curdled the food in Henry's belly.

Ms. Perez stiffened her spine and stood. "Excuse me. I should go check on my daughters."

Amy plopped into the chair beside Grace, glanced at her plate, and wrinkled her nose. She must have caught the twins watching her because she smoothed her expression. "So, what do you think? Is she a suspect? Did you meet her oldest son?"

Grace drew a deep breath. "She seemed like a nice lady. A little lonely. Maybe you should reach out to her. I'm sure she'd appreciate it."

"While you're at it, you should try her paella. It's out-of-this-world delicious." Henry added.

Amy ignored their comments and gave the twins a patient smile. "Might I ask a favor of you two? Could you run down to the Grossmans' and see if Gary needs a hand? He's bringing his world-famous red velvet cupcakes."

"Sure." Grace stood. "But first, I think I'll take Mr. Davenport a plate of food."

"Him? Really? Why?" She stretched the last word into three syllables.

"Everyone needs to eat." Henry winked at her on his way to the line of grills.

CHAPTER SEVEN

Balancing a plate in one hand, Grace knocked on Mr. Davenport's door.

"Is it me, or are most of the people on this street jerks?" Henry stepped back enough to watch the windows.

"Not most, just one or two, but what they lack in quantity, they make up in quality." She knocked again. "Hello? It's Henry and Grace from next door. We brought you some food."

"Curtain moved," Henry whispered. "Remind me why we're doing this again?"

"Because it's the right thing to do, and as a bonus, it irritates Amy Anderson." She knocked a third time. "Open up, Mr. Davenport. Don't make me shove your dinner through the mail slot."

No reply.

Grace turned and plucked a roll from the plate in Henry's hand.

"You're not going to do what I think you are?" His eyes widened. "I already tackled the guy."

"I most certainly am." She bent and pushed the bread through the slot. "Ms. Perez's paella's going to make a terrible mess on your floor."

Grumbling came from inside a split second before the man cracked the door open. "What's with the two of you?"

Grace flashed him a grin and held the plate higher. "We brought you dinner."

"And beer." Henry wiggled the can in his right hand. "A peace offering for the misunderstanding last night."

He looked past them to the party. "They let you leave with alcohol?"

"We told them it was for you." Grace offered the food again. "We figured it was the least we could do since you're being subjected to all the noise."

He folded his arms. "I don't drink."

"Do you eat?" Henry shoved the can in his jacket.

"Hand it over."

Both twins offered plates ready to crack under the strain of food, but he ignored them.

"The beer. Something tells me you aren't of legal age."

"Oh, right. We don't drink either." Henry removed the can and placed it in the man's hand.

Grace saw her opportunity and took it. She walked into Mr. Davenport's house without so much as a backward glance. Heart pounding, she took in her surroundings. The place wasn't as grand as the Templetons, but it was orderly—exactly what she'd expected.

"What do you think you're doing?" the man roared.

"Serving you dinner." She squared her shoulders and marched toward what she hoped was the kitchen.

The furniture sat in straight lines at equal distances from the walls. Even the coffee table seemed like he'd measured exactly ten inches from the couch before placing it. She wouldn't have been surprised to see X-shaped pieces of tape to mark the precise location of each leg.

The kitchen counters were completely empty. No toaster, no coffee pot, no canisters, nothing but clean white marble beneath plain white cabinets. The only personal item in the room was a photo of two small children held on the front of the refrigerator by a magnet.

Grace placed the plate on the counter and motioned for Henry to do the same.

"Are you finished?" Mr. Davenport's voice had gone from bark to growl.

"Unless you'd like me to bring you a red velvet cupcake for dessert?" She had no idea where the bravado had come from, nor did she know how she managed to keep her words steady with her lungs squeezing shut.

His brows rose. "I don't eat sweets."

Henry dipped his head to hide his grin.

"Have a good night." She turned on her heel and walked back toward the door.

"Wait." Henry grabbed her arm and whispered, "We should ask him some questions."

"No, you shouldn't." Mr. Davenport glanced over the food, and for a microsecond, Grace saw a ghost of a smile.

"Not tonight. We have to see about the cupcakes." She hurried across the room and stopped at the door. "Good night, Mr. Davenport."

"Grace." He nodded.

On the sidewalk, she exhaled and bent at the waist. "Holy smokes. I can't believe I did that."

"No kidding." Henry risked a glance back at the house. This time the curtains remained still.

"He's not so bad."

"That's like saying a hungry grizzly bear would make a good snuggle-buddy." His hand started heading for his hair when he caught himself and stopped. He was trying to undo that habit, but most of the time, he needed his fingers combing through it. The motion helped him think.

She rolled her eyes and strolled toward 201 Avenue E, the home of Gary Grossman.

The Victorian house was easily the smallest on the block, and also the most well-kept. The lawn was as immaculate as Mr. Davenport's living room. The leaded glass window panes had a blurred and bubbled quality to them that reminded her of some of the houses she'd seen in Ireland. What else would she expect from the historian besides glass original to the time period?

Henry knocked.

An elderly woman with the same small brown eyes as Gary opened the door and glanced at them. "May I help you?"

"Mrs. Anderson sent us to help Mr. Grossman with his cupcakes." Henry shoved his hands in his pockets.

"I see. Come in." She smiled and stepped back to allow them in.

Grace felt as if she'd stepped back in time. Every detail, from the crown molding to the ornate fireplace, screamed original to the period the house was built. That room deserved to be called a parlor.

"Wait here. I'll let him know you're here to help deliver *my* cupcakes." The woman she assumed was Gary's mother tottered down the hall.

Henry whispered, "He lives with his mom?"

"Maybe he's taking care of her?" She remembered Amy mentioning that

Gary had several multi-million-dollar listings. With that kind of commission, he could afford a house like this. However, the more she glanced around, the more she doubted the house belonged to him. "Come on."

"She said to wait here."

"Did she?" Grace pressed her lips together and hurried after the woman. She rounded the corner into the kitchen and frowned. No sight of either Grossman, but several dozen cupcakes sat on the counter.

"Gary? Some children are here to see you." Her voice quivered with age. "Gary?"

Grace followed the sound to a door and crept down a flight of stairs. Unlike the Templetons', this basement was finished, sort of. Shag carpeting covered the floor in colors that reminded her of a can of mixed vegetables—orange, green, white, and possibly some yellow, although it was hard to tell if it'd started out that color. Adding to the weird seventies decor were orange pleather couches and dark wood paneling.

Once again, Grace felt as if she'd entered a time warp.

"Oh, dear." The woman pressed her hand to her chest. "You scared the dickens out of me."

"Sorry. I thought you said to follow you." Her cheeks heated. Lying was bad but lying to a little old lady was just plain wrong.

"I did?" She laughed. "I supposed I must have."

Grace glanced at the space again. Three items piqued her curiosity: a jar of what looked like the stuff from inside a vacuum cleaner bag, a framed piece of wood with several rows of keys, and a wallet suspiciously like Henry's.

"What are you doing here?" Gary's voice boomed from behind her.

She started and turned to face the red-faced realtor.

The elderly woman shouted, "Gary Eugene Grossman, is that any way to address our guests?"

He widened his eyes. "No, ma'am."

Mrs. Grossman nodded once. "Apologize to the nice girl. She's come to help you carry the cupcakes to the party."

Grace stared at the woman, unable to wrap her brain around her transformation. In the span of fifteen seconds, she'd gone from a dear-sweet-grandmother type to Miss Hannigan from *Annie*.

"I'm sorry I raised my voice." Gary's tone softened to contrite.

He won't do anything crazy with his mother here. For the second time that night, Grace took advantage of the situation. She hurried to the table and picked up the wallet. "You must have forgotten this. It's never good to leave home without identification."

"Give me that." He tried to snatch it from her, tottered, and fell into the bookcase. The jar of dust bunnies fell beside Grace.

She opened the wallet to find Henry's hideous driver's license photo staring up at her. "Why do you have my brother's wallet?"

"Answer the girl!" For such a tiny lady, his mother had a voice that would stop a pack of stampeding bulls.

"I found it on the street. I'd planned to return it today." The man stammered.

"Thanks, but I'll save you the trouble." Grace forced a smile and made her way to the top of the stairs.

"What was that about?" Henry stared from her face to her hand. "Whoa! It was here?"

"Yes. Let's go."

They'd made it halfway across the room when the Grossmans emerged from the basement.

Mrs. Grossman said, "Aren't you going to help carry the cupcakes?"

Gary folded his hands and made a pleading gesture behind his mother's back. The man seemed genuinely terrified of his mother.

Rather than upsetting the tiny woman further, Grace nodded. "Of course."

The three walked down the street, each carrying several containers of Mrs. Grossman's world-famous red velvet cupcakes. No one spoke. Not that Grace knew what to say to him. She needed time to process what had happened first.

Gary stopped before entering the tent. "Thanks for not distressing my mother. I...I can explain."

Henry walked inside, set the containers down, and returned. "The letters stop now, or your mom will be more than a little *distressed.*"

His eyes widened. "I didn't write the letters."

"Right. And you haven't been breaking into the house?"

The color drained from his face. "No."

Henry pushed into Gary's personal space. "I suppose you didn't eavesdrop on our conversation and send a pizza last night either? Or move our luggage? Or the file?"

"I don't know what you're talking about." His Adam's apple bobbed like the balloons on the tents.

Grace was no expert when it came to detecting lies, but she thought he was being honest. "What was that board of keys hanging on your wall?"

"It's...uh... Every time I sell a house, I add a key."

She blinked. "You *keep* keys to the properties you sell?"

He shook his head hard enough to unbalance his cupcakes. "No! Not the actual keys. They're symbolic."

Henry took the containers from Grace's arms and set them on the table inside. "Let's go. We'll let the police sort this out."

"No. There's no need to do that. This is all a huge misunderstanding."

By now a crowd of neighbors had formed around Gary and the twins. They watched the exchange like spectators at Wimbledon.

"Is there a problem?" Amy Anderson came forward. Judging by the look on her face, she didn't appreciate the disruption to her party.

"No. We were just leaving." Grace tugged her brother's arm.

Henry followed for several steps before turning back and filling a plate with a half-dozen cupcakes. He caught Grace staring and winked. "What? We helped carry them. We might as well get to enjoy them."

They hurried back to the Templetons' house and let themselves in, locking the door behind them. They listened carefully for any sound of someone inside before they started breathing normally again.

She shook her head but ran her finger through the icing.

Grace pressed her back to the door. "What a night!"

Henry toed his shoes off and tossed them aside. "What's your read on Gary Grossman?"

"It's weird. Heck, *he's* weird, but I believed him."

"Me, too." Henry sighed and consumed half the dessert in one bite—the iced half.

"Give me one of those." Grace walked into the kitchen and pulled a plate down from the cabinet. Splitting the cake part in half and cramming it on top of the glob of icing still on her finger, she asked, "What do we know?"

"Grossman had my wallet, but I doubt he's the person writing the letters. Ms. Perez is off the list too."

"And Mr. Davenport." She took a bite of the cupcake and sighed. Hands down, it was the best she'd ever had.

"I don't know. There's something off about that guy." Henry smirked. "What about Amy?"

She hadn't considered the beauty queen. "What's her motive?"

He shrugged.

"I hate it when you do that." Grace chuckled and slid onto a barstool. "Something's been bothering me. Hear me out, okay?"

"Sure." He went to the fridge and returned with a jug of milk.

"Gary had a framed board full of keys in his basement. It reminded me of Tim Templeton's key ring. What do all of those go to?"

Henry's shoulders lifted a quarter of an inch before he stopped himself. "No clue, but you aren't seriously considering Tim?"

"They bought a really expensive house and then found out Trina's expecting twins. He admitted they were short on cash. Maybe this is his way of convincing Trina to sell?" She hated that it made sense and hated the implications for Trina if it turned out to be true.

"It won't work. First, selling right before building any equity would result in a huge loss. Second, the couple terrorized by the original Watcher tried to sell for over a year."

She'd forgotten. "Right. They'd have to tell prospective homebuyers about the letters."

"And like the other couple, they'd have a difficult time finding a buyer without losing their shirts." Henry filled two glasses and slid one to her. "Besides, you saw the two of them together. Do you honestly think Tim would put Trina through something like this?"

"No, I guess not." She chewed her lower lip. "What about the comment he made about sticking with the truth as much as possible when lying?"

"It was off-color but think about it. He's an hour away with his family—"

"Working. He's not with them all the time. He could have come back."

Henry bobbed his head and considered her theory. "We should talk to Mom about this."

The idea of broaching the subject with anyone except Henry made Grace's stomach hurt.

"See? If you're not ready to ask Mom about it, you still have doubts." He nudged her side.

"Of course I have doubts, but let's face it. None of our original suspects seem to fit the bill."

"Maybe we haven't found the right group yet?"

"Maybe." She tapped her fingers on her lips. "Or maybe we have, but we aren't seeing the whole picture."

Henry sighed. "I don't know about you, but this experience has taught me one thing."

"What's that?"

"I never want neighbors."

"I agree one hundred percent. I'm going to read for a while." Physically exhausted but too keyed up to sleep, Grace wandered into the den.

"Shower and bed for me."

She chewed her lip. "Would it be weird if we used the baby monitor upstairs to communicate?"

"A little, but I promise not to tease you."

Henry went into one of the children's rooms and brought both parts of the monitor downstairs. He clipped the portable piece to his pants and plugged the stationary unit into the wall.

"Thank you." Her cheeks heated.

"Don't mention it." He gave her a quick hug. "Don't worry, we'll solve this mystery, and I promise that we'll solve it without getting hurt."

"You can't promise that, but I hope so." She tossed a throw pillow on the plush area rug and stretched out.

Grace's brain strayed between the text and The Watcher for the first few pages. She shoved the stray thoughts out of her mind and reread the section. A chapter in, she found herself making connections between Hobbes's view of human nature and government to the social order in the neighborhood. Old Hobbes would have had a field day studying the Leviathan ruling Avenue E. Amy Anderson presided over the neighbors with absolute power and fear. Grace had seen that much in her short conversation with Ms. Perez. In one day, Amy had put together a massive party with people filling the street.

This is pointless. I'm not comprehending any of this, nor am I going to solve this case tonight. She closed her eyes and hovered in the gray area between waking and sleeping.

Sometime later, Grace sat up and caught movement from the corner of her eye. Her breath caught.

Someone had been outside the window—*watching her sleep.*

CHAPTER EIGHT

Henry woke to Grace screaming his name over the baby monitor. He threw his covers off and leapt out of bed.

Grace burst into the room, wide-eyed and pale. "Someone. Window. Downstairs. Watching."

It took his brain a few ticks to make sense of the situation. "Show me."

Grace turned and stared at the door as if expecting The Watcher to appear.

He took her by the shoulders. "Which window?"

"The den, closest to the fireplace."

He slid his feet into his sneakers. "Stay here."

"No." She stiffened her spine as she summoned what courage she had left—courage to not be alone. "I'm coming with you."

He wanted to argue, but every second they wasted allowed their suspect to get farther away. "Get your golf club."

She hurried out of the room.

"I'm going to kill the lights." He flipped the switch in the upstairs hall and the one on the staircase. Grace shut off the downstairs lights. It would be much harder to see into a dark house.

Grace joined him in the downstairs hall.

"Be careful," Henry whispered as he made his way into the room where she'd been reading.

Whoever she saw had probably left when she screamed, but Henry didn't want to take any chances. He eased to the window. Not only was the space empty, but it was a half-story from the ground.

Just to be sure, Henry opened the window and popped out the screen. *Someone would have had to stand on a step ladder to look in.*

Grace gasped. "What are you doing?"

The thought of telling her she'd imagined the person made him cringe inside. "This is the window, right?"

"Yes. Now close it and make sure it's locked."

"Gracie, it's at least five feet from the ground."

She rushed to the window. "I don't understand. I know what I saw."

He stuck his head out of the opening. "There's no trellis."

"Come on." She tugged his shirt. "We're going outside. I'm telling you, someone was there."

"I believe you—"

"Don't you dare say you believe that I believe I saw *something*! I didn't imagine it." She grabbed one of the Templetons' jackets from the closet and the flashlight from the hall table.

"Grace, wait."

She opened the door. Once confronted by the empty yard and dark sky, she hesitated. "Are you coming?"

"I'm right behind you." He picked up her golf club and followed her to the side of the house.

A short hedge of holly lined the side of the house. As he'd suspected, the window was almost exactly five feet from ground level.

She shined the light on the wall and pointed. "There! See?"

Henry squinted at the markings on the wall. Unless the person pulled a Spiderman and walked up the stones, the scuffs weren't footprints. "How much of the person showed through the window? Was it just the top of their head?"

"Upper torso and head." Grace aimed the beam at the window. Oddly enough, the staggered markings continued to the third story window.

His heart broke into a gallop. "May I see the light?"

She handed him the flashlight and folded her arms.

Henry craned his neck up to the uppermost window. "Does that look open to you?"

She squeaked an affirmative answer and ran for the front door.

Inside, Henry followed her to the attic entrance and shined the light on the window in question. Sure enough, someone had opened it. "This is really starting to tick me off."

"Same here." She sounded more frightened than angry, but she was determined to end this. She didn't like being afraid.

Henry wove his way through the mountains of stuff left behind by previous owners and stopped short. Gouges and scratches marred the window's frame and the surrounding wall.

"What caused that?" She inched closer.

He ran his fingers over the marks, stood, and resisted the urge to kick something. "My guess is a grappling hook or some type of climbing equipment. This explains how the person was able to look through the window. You probably didn't notice the line because the lights were on."

"I didn't notice the line because I was too busy staring at the person." She sat on the edge of a steamer trunk. "Funny thing is, I didn't see more than an outline. I couldn't tell you what they were wearing or what color hair they had."

"Let's try to get some sleep. We'll call Tim and Trina in the morning and tell them what we've learned so far." He locked the window, for all the good it would do. The person either had a key or could move through walls.

Grace sighed. "If the break-ins stop, we'll know it's him."

He hated to admit it, but she had a point. Then again, why would Tim sneak around his own house? *Who else would have a key?* "We need to get a better look at Gary Grossman's key collection."

"You saw how he reacted tonight. He's afraid of his own shadow. Do you really think he's capable of this?" She stood, and something metallic skittered across the floor. "What did I kick?"

Henry shined the light around her feet and found a broken lock. "Hold the light."

Grace took the flashlight. "What's wrong?"

"The lock. It's old, but doesn't appear to be rusted through." He placed the broken shank into the beam. "The inside is still shiny, and the edges are even. It's been cut."

She moved the light onto the trunk where she'd sat. "What's inside?"

He opened the lid and removed several shoe boxes of old baseball cards. While he'd never collected them, he'd heard some were worth a great deal of money. Next, he removed several personal journals. "It looks like old keepsakes."

"Why would someone lock a trunk of old books in the first place?"

Henry reached into the trunk with trembling hands. *This can't be what I think it is.* "Holy smokes, Grace. Shine the light on this."

Inside a plastic bag was the unicorn of comic books. The rarest of the rare: *Action Comics Number One*. Henry almost fainted.

"What's the big deal?"

"It's...it's the comic that introduced Superman in 1938." He motioned to the book. "It's worth millions."

Gasping, she juggled the flashlight.

Henry caught it before it could touch the precious item. "Careful!"

"You think someone's breaking in looking for antique comic books?"

He shined the light on the comic. "Maybe, maybe not, but they're looking for something. If this is here, can you imagine what else might be hidden in one of these trunks?"

"The Watcher. He's not a psychopath, he's a thief."

Henry returned the items to the trunk. "We need to call Tim and Trina tonight."

"It's well after midnight." She giggled. "Then again, I'd want to know if I'd hit the comic book lottery no matter what time it was."

Downstairs, someone banged on the front door.

The twins froze.

"We can't let anything happen to it," he whispered, setting two plain cardboard boxes on top of the trunk.

"Do you think The Watcher saw the light in the attic window?" She inched closer to him.

"Maybe. Let's get downstairs."

***

The banging increased in frequency and volume, as did Grace's heartbeat.

"Open the door. Police."

"Police?" Grace covered her mouth.

Henry opened the door and took a step back. Two uniformed Garwood Police Officers blocked the view of the outside world.

In situations like these, people in the movies always asked, "Is there a problem, officers?" However, this was no movie, and Grace knew there was a problem—who called himself The Watcher.

The larger of the two men said, "We have reports of squatters on the premises. Can I see some ID?"

Oh, crud. This isn't good. Grace cleared her throat. "Mine's upstairs."

The officers looked appropriately skeptical.

"Mine, too. Please, come inside." Henry stepped back. "We're Henry and Grace Warner. We're housesitting for the Templetons."

The men stood in the foyer taking up more room than their physical bodies.

If Grace didn't know better, she'd have sworn they'd sucked all of the oxygen out of the air.

Afraid to move, she said, "May I go upstairs?"

"Go ahead." The officer turned his attention to Henry. "One at a time."

Henry said, "My wallet is on the nightstand."

"I'll get both." Grace moved as quickly as she could without actually running. Criminals ran. She didn't want to give them any reason to think she'd broken the law. Upstairs, she rummaged through her backpack and her suitcase, but couldn't find her purse. *Oh no. No. No.*

Think, Grace, when was the last time you had it? She tapped her lips. *The coffee shop.*

Her breath caught. There was no way they'd both dropped their identification. Had Gary Grossman taken her purse too?"

She did a quick search of Henry's room and came up empty. Had someone snuck into the house while they were outside or in the attic? The thought sent a shiver down her spine.

Grace made her way back downstairs, read the officer's name tag, and looked him in the eye. "Sergeant Baker, my purse and his wallet are missing."

The men shared a knowing look.

Henry scowled. "Again? How? When?"

"We're going to take you two to the station and sort this out." Baker gripped the radio on his shoulder, likely to report the situation.

"Wait. Can't you call and verify our story with the Templetons?" Grace spoke too loud and too fast. "We're minors. Our parents are nearby. Ethan and Faith Warner. My dad's an attorney lecturing at Kean University. They'll tell you the same thing."

"Sorry, kid. We have to follow procedure."

Henry sighed. "Mom's going to freak out."

Sergeant Baker must have taken pity on them because he softened his tone. "If your story checks out, you have nothing to worry about."

Evidently, Henry hadn't given up hope of avoiding a trip downtown. "The police have been called here recently. The Templetons reported receiving letters from someone calling himself The Watcher. We can't leave. There are priceless...*items* in the attic. We believe The Watcher is getting into the house somehow and trying to steal them."

Grace felt as if the ground had opened beneath her feet. She tried to get his attention to tell him to drop it, but he was too focused on the other officer.

"Did you *report* the break-ins?"

"No, sir. I did not. We found a broken window in the basement and—"

"Okay. That's enough. You probably shouldn't say anything else until your parents are present." The officer set his hand on Henry's shoulder and turned him toward the door.

The physical contact seemed to snap him out of his panic, and the more logical Henry emerged. "Are we under arrest?"

The officers exchanged another look.

"We're responding to reports of squatters on the premises and found the two of you with no IDs."

Henry sidestepped the man. "Yes, but if we aren't under arrest, we're not required to go anywhere with you."

Baker frowned. "Then, yes, you're under arrest."

Grace appreciated what he'd tried to do, but it'd backfired big time. She folded her arms. "Not another word, Henry. Not another word."

Thankfully, her brother seemed to comprehend the error of his ways. "Fine. We'll go with you *voluntarily*."

"I'm afraid the time for that has passed." Sergeant Baker read them their rights.

This is a disaster. Grace closed her eyes and waited for them to slap cuffs on her and shove her into the back of a squad car. She told herself to be brave and keep her head high, but when the cold metal bit into her wrists, her eyes stung.

Neighbors had gathered on the sidewalk by the time the officers led the twins outside. Amy Anderson stood with her hand pressed to her heart, shaking her head. Mr. Grossman smirked and blew his nose. Even his elderly mother had come to see what all the fuss was about.

Others Grace hadn't met stared. Some whispered, and some chatted loud enough to make out words like "delinquents," "robbery," and "runaways."

A male voice rang out from the other side of the yard. "I'd like to make a statement!"

The small crowd gasped, and the whispers grew louder.

Mr. Davenport stopped several feet away—and he was holding Grace's purse and Henry's wallet in his hand.

CHAPTER NINE

How did he get my purse? Grace's chest tightened. *Have I been wrong about him?*

Henry shot her a quick glance and opened his mouth as if to ask.

Grace clenched her jaw and waited. If he accused the next-door neighbor of theft, Davenport could tell the police Henry had tackled him the day before. He might have bruises. People believed adults more readily than smart-mouthed kids. Grace and Henry were at the older man's mercy.

Mr. Davenport pointed at the twins. "Those two young people are house-sitting for the Templetons."

Sergeant Baker tilted his head a fraction of an inch. "And you are?"

"Lieutenant Colonel Davenport, US Army retired. I live next door, and I personally witnessed Tim and Trina Templeton welcome these two into their home yesterday. What's more, I can attest to the fact someone has been playing tricks on them since they arrived."

Davenport's choice of words intrigued Grace. He hadn't mentioned seeing an intruder. That would require a formal statement—something the reclusive man would probably want to avoid.

"Do you know where the Templetons are at the moment?" Baker released his grip on Grace's shoulder.

"They are vacationing in New York." Davenport nodded to Henry as if to confirm his words.

"They're staying with Mrs. Templeton's mother in White Plains," Henry added.

Baker pressed his lips into a thin line. "What sort of pranks?"

The crowd, who'd gone quiet once the recluse spoke, started whispering among themselves.

Davenport's lips curled on one side in what could almost pass as a grin. "Kid stuff. Moving their things. Hiding in the basement to scare them. Ordering pizzas. I found these in the bushes on the side of the house. I believe they belong to the Warners."

"Yes, that's my purse. My ID should be inside." Grace glanced at Henry through narrowed eyes.

Her brother pointedly stared at Davenport and raised a brow.

Grace shrugged. Until then, she wouldn't have thought the next-door neighbor had stolen their things, but now she wasn't so sure.

The officer's jaw hardened. "I assume these items were inside. Entering a home without permission is illegal. Did you see anyone entering or leaving?"

"I did not," Davenport said.

Baker's frown deepened. "You have identification?"

The other man reached into his pocket and produced a wallet. "I do, but what do you say we take this inside? The kids have been traumatized enough for one night, eh?" He nodded toward the gathering of nosy neighbors as he handed over his retired military identification card.

Grace wanted to hug Davenport. She'd had more than enough attention for one evening. However, him showing up in the nick of time with their IDs seemed odd—too much of a coincidence, and too perfectly timed.

Sergeant Baker turned his dark expression on the crowd. "You folks can go back to your homes now. It seems this was a misunderstanding. Rest assured, we will find the person responsible for the false report."

Grace caught Gary Grossman's eye. He wore the same expression he had when his mother had yelled at him—like he might faint, or vomit, or both.

Of course, Amy Anderson took it upon herself to shepherd the spectators toward her lawn. A few went their own way, but most followed her, including the Grossmans. In fact, the elderly Mrs. Grossman had extra pep in her step. The woman seemed downright giddy.

I guess it's not every day someone's almost arrested on Avenue E.

With the lieutenant colonel on one side and Henry on the other, Grace tottered back toward the house, her mind swirling so much it made her dizzy. With the handcuffs off and the threat of spending time in jail behind her, the only thing she wanted was her dad. "I'm calling our parents."

Baker opened his mouth as if to argue but snapped it shut and waved her off.

She hadn't realized her hands were trembling until she attempted to dial her phone. On the third attempt, the call went through.

"Grace? Is everything all right?" Ethan Warner's sleep-thickened voice calmed her nerves.

"Yes. We're fine. I just..."

"One second." It sounded like he put his hand over the phone and spoke to her mom.

She leaned against the wall and hung her head. The muffled sounds of her parents' voices pulled at her heartstrings, but she promised herself right then and there that she'd solve the mystery. The Watcher had messed with the wrong kids. "I just miss you."

One of the men in the other room laughed.

"Who's there with you?" Dad's tone grew more serious.

"No one. Henry's watching a movie." She hated lying, but it was strange how good she was getting at it. She sighed. "I'm sorry I called so late."

Her brother took her hand and pulled her into the living room, away from where the police were speaking to Davenport.

"It's okay, Gracie-bug. We miss you, too. Mom and I have a huge surprise for you when you get home."

She smiled, despite everything that had happened. "Is it a pony?"

"Better than a pony." He chuckled. "Sweetheart, there's no shame in getting a little homesick. Say the word, and I'll come pick you up."

"I'm better now. Thanks, Dad."

"You're welcome." He yawned. "Try to get some sleep. I love you."

"Love you, too." She disconnected and slid the phone into her pocket. She looked at a spot on the wall as she corralled her fear.

Henry arched a brow. "You didn't tell them."

"I wanted to, but then I realized I wanted to solve this mystery more." She forced a smile. "Dad says they have a surprise for us, and it's not a pony."

Henry ran his hand over his head. He was not doing too well at breaking the habit. "Last time they had a surprise for us, we ended up on Star Island chasing kidnappers and treasure hunters."

Sergeant Baker cleared his throat. "We're finished here. I meant what I said out there. If the caller knowingly provided false information, I will find them and charge them accordingly."

"You saw the neighbors. I wouldn't be surprised if one of them thought themselves a Good Samaritan by reporting strangers in the house." Grace silently congratulated herself on not overtly lying to an officer of the law.

"Be that as it may, you need to report any *additional* suspicious activity." He folded his arms and gave them a stern once-over. "Are your parents on their way?"

She shook her head. "I thought I'd save you an hour or so of your night. Our parents are professional lecturers, after all."

He cracked a grin and handed her his business card. "Should either of them have any questions."

"Thank you."

Davenport waited until the officers left before he came into the room. "Want to tell me what's really going on?"

Henry nodded to Grace's purse on the table. "Would you?"

"Like I told the police, I found them in the bushes."

Grace hated to ask, but she had to know. "Mr., I mean, Lieutenant—"

"Please call me Davenport or Dave. I left that life behind years ago."

"Dave, were you injured during your service?"

His expression hardened for a fraction of a second, but then his eyes widened. He pulled his pant leg up to reveal a prosthetic leg. "You could say that."

Henry seemed unconvinced. "You ran when I spotted you outside last night."

"I did." He seemed to chew on his words before finally spitting them out. "And I'm still sore today. Look, you two have no reason to trust me, but I'm telling you I'm not the one breaking into the house."

Grace rested her hand on her brother's arm. "We believe the person calling themselves The Watcher wants the house empty because they're looking for something left behind by previous owners in the attic or basement."

"Do you have any idea what they're looking for?"

Henry said, "It's hard to tell. Both are full of old furniture, boxes, and trunks."

"And you're certain there are valuables in the house?"

Henry glanced at her as if to confirm he should share the information.

Grace said, "We found a comic book we think is worth over a million dollars."

Davenport scratched the side of his head. "And you two intend to stay here?"

"We do," Henry said.

Grace saw the doubt in the man's eyes and went for a preemptive strike. "We've handled far scarier people than a copycat Watcher."

"I don't doubt that, but if that comic is as expensive as you claim..." He tightened his jaw. "That kind of money can make even good people do bad things. You should call the Templetons tonight. Get them home ASAP."

Henry seated himself on the couch. "That was the plan, but now I think we need to catch this guy first."

"Henry's right." Grace sighed. "Besides, I'm not one hundred percent sure we can trust Tim Templeton. He's obviously not crawling in and out of windows to steal property that came with the house, but something feels off about him."

Henry hung his head. "Grace..."

She ignored her brother. "Can you think of any reason Mrs. Staudinger, the other home buyer, would have his telephone number?"

"It's unusual." Davenport eyed Henry. "You disagree with her?"

"We set a meeting with the Staudingers yesterday. I'm assuming she called Tim to check our story."

"That's understandable."

She nodded, but her gut told her there was more to it. "Maybe I'm reading more into it than is there."

"It's generally a good idea to focus on one enemy at a time." Davenport stood and rubbed his hands together. "I should get home, but we should exchange phone numbers. I don't sleep much. I'll keep watch and call if I see anything."

Grace's chest tightened. While she appreciated him saving them from a trip to the police station, the idea of him skulking around outside concerned her.

Henry said, "We appreciate the offer, but—"

"I wasn't asking for permission." Davenport clamped a hand on his shoulder and chuckled. "Your sister's the first person to show me kindness in a very long time. I would never forgive myself if something happened to her. Besides, this is the most fun I've had since I left the Army."

She couldn't help but smile. Two days ago, the guy wouldn't open his front door, and now they couldn't get rid of him. Shows what a little kindness could do.

Pacing his room, Henry ran through the facts as he understood them. When he finished, he had more questions than cosplayers dressed like Spiderman at Comic-Con *and* as many suspects. He glanced at the clock and groaned. Four-thirty in the morning—too late to go to bed and too early to start the day.

He slipped into the hall with every intention of finishing off the red velvet cupcakes, but music from inside Grace's room stopped him. Knocking softly, he asked, "Are you awake?"

"Yep. Come in. You're going to want to see this."

He opened the door and found his sister sitting in the center of her bed with her laptop open and notebook beside her. "Have you slept at all?"

"I tried, but I couldn't turn my brain off." She motioned him closer. "Remember Mr. and Mrs. Staudinger?"

"Yeah?" He craned his neck to better see her notes.

"There's no record of them purchasing a house in Union or the surrounding counties." Grace clicked on her browser icon. "Before you say it's too soon to show up in property records, here are the listings for the Templetons. They bought the house around the same time."

He held up his hands. Grace had the biggest heart of anyone he knew, but lack of sleep hardened her.

"We need to find their realtor, and I know just the person to ask." She snarled, "Gary Grossman."

Her idea was solid, but he had two problems with it. One, he doubted Grossman would help them, and two, the guy's mother gave him the creeps. Had he not seen her Dr. Jekyll-Mr. Hyde routine for himself, he would never have believed it. "You're suggesting we go to a suspect for information on another suspect?"

"Yes, that's exactly—" She sniffed, climbed over her stuff, and sniffed again. "What's that smell?"

The strange odor caused his nose to wrinkle. "No idea."

Grace scrambled from the bed and opened the door. "Fire!"

Smoke billowed into the room. Henry turned and did the worse thing a person can do in a smoky room: he drew a breath. The contaminated air hit his lungs and sent him into a coughing fit.

"Downstairs." She covered her nose and mouth with her arm.

"The comic."

"We need to go!" Grace grabbed his arm and attempted to pull him toward the stairs.

He jerked free and headed for the attic. "Go. I'll be right behind you."

"Don't be stupid." She crouched low to the ground.

Between the smoke and his watery eyes, Henry could barely see. However, after the first breath, he hadn't kept coughing. More perplexing, the air had a powdery chemical odor somewhere between drywall dust and gun powder. It didn't smell like anything was burning, and it didn't burn his lungs.

"It's a smoke bomb," Henry declared. He would have laughed, but he didn't want to breathe in any more than he had to. "Come on."

"What? No!" She shot upright and tried to grab him to shove him toward the stairs. "We're getting out."

Henry caught his balance and widened his stance. "That's exactly what The Watcher wants us to do!"

She squinted through the smoke. "You think he's..." She didn't need to finish her thought.

Something heavy thumped overhead.

Henry pointed at the ceiling, turned, and ran for the attic stairs.

"No!" she called after him.

The smoke thinned as Henry climbed the stairs. He couldn't see. Flipping the switch for the attic lights accomplished nothing. He had forgotten that the Watcher unscrewed the bulbs.

A hazy mist filled the dark space. The slight glow of the street lamps provided the only light. Henry shielded his eyes trying to see. He turned his head one way and then the other to catch a hint of movement or a stray sound.

A second thump, followed by a crash came from his right—the opposite side from the *Action Comics Number One*. Henry jumped into action. He took two steps and yelled, "I know you're up here. You might as well come out. My sister's already called the police!"

He couldn't make out the figure behind a stack of boxes.

Grace eased up beside him.

"Go!" he told her, but she was riveted to the floor.

Henry caught movement, and his natural instinct took over. He ducked into a crouch, shielding his sister with his body.

A second later, a chair crashed into the wall inches from where they had been standing.

"I've had about enough of you!" Henry surged forward, stumbling as Grace grabbed the only thing she could reach—his back pocket. It tore as he lunged and started to fall.

Time seemed to slow. A dark figure appeared from the smoke. Henry pulled free and went to one knee. Grace screamed. The Watcher swung a huge candlestick like a Louisville Slugger. The metal whistled through the air over Henry's head.

The momentum was too much, because he lost his grip on the candlestick. It flew from his hands and bounced across the attic. The Watcher took one step and kicked Henry while he was down. Air exploded from Henry's lungs, and he rolled into a ball, gagged, and tried to see past the shooting stars before his eyes.

The Watcher regained his balance and ran for the door—and Grace.

CHAPTER TEN

The sound of Henry's pained grunt tore through her. Grace had taken several steps in his direction when a person dressed in black from head to toe bounded over trunks and boxes. She had no time to think or look for a weapon, so she turned and ran.

Grace made it into the hall before The Watcher caught up to her. She braced for impact, but it never came. The person pulled some sort of parkour-ninja move—a hand on one wall, a foot on the other, a flip, and a perfect landing.

Unharmed and stunned, Grace stared as The Watcher vanished into the smoke.

A crash and a groan inside the attic snapped her out of her daze. Grace felt her way through the antique obstacle course to her brother.

"Where is he? Are you hurt?" Henry squinted toward the door.

"Gone, and I'm fine. What happened?" She wiped her stinging eyes.

He motioned back the way he'd come. "Boot in the gut. I'm okay. It'll hurt more tomorrow."

She eased beneath his shoulder and wrapped her arm around him. "Did you see the way The Watcher moved?"

"Other than swinging like a Major League batter and then kicking like a mule?" Henry coughed.

"Yeah. Whoever it was used the boxes and walls like springboards. He went *over* me and down the stairs."

He gave her a dubious look.

"I'm dead serious. There's no way that was Gary Grossman or a housewife. I think we're dealing with a professional." She stopped a few feet from the door and picked up a black sack. "I don't remember seeing this before."

He shook his head. "Me either. The Watcher must have dropped it on the way out. What's inside?"

"We should get someplace safe with clean air before we open it."

"Good idea."

Sirens wailed nearby, and for the second time in as many days, someone banged on the front door.

"Henry! Grace! Open up!" Davenport pounded again.

The twins exchanged a quick glance.

"Coming!" Grace held her arm out to her brother, but he waved her off. "Let me help you."

"Get downstairs before he decides to break a window." He gripped the banister and eased to the next step.

"We're okay!" She hurried past him, took the stairs two at a time, and flung open the front door.

Davenport's face had gone pale, except for the red splotches on his cheeks. "There's smoke pouring out of the basement window. Where's Henry?"

"It's a smoke bomb. Henry took a kick in the gut, but he's okay. Just moving slowly."

The man's expression could only be described as gobsmacked. He snapped his mouth shut, opened it again, and shook his head. "Fire department is on the way. We should let them inspect the house to be sure."

"The Watcher was trying to steal this." She handed him the bag.

Davenport pulled out a handful of jewelry and fumbled with a delicate white figurine. It fell onto the welcome mat.

He cringed. "Did I break it?"

Grace inspected the statuette. "I don't think so, but we should be careful. This looks old and expensive."

Henry's hacking cough announced his presence.

"You two need to get out of the house." Davenport put the items back into the bag.

"It's the dust from the attic more than the fake smoke." He cleared his throat and ended up coughing again.

Davenport pointed to the yard. "Wait out here. I'll open some windows."

The twins moved away from the house.

Grace lowered her voice. "We're too close to let a smoke bomb derail us. We need to be careful what we say to the authorities."

"I agree." He folded his arms and stared at the smoke billowing from the open windows. "We're going to finish this."

An hour later the twins, Davenport, the fire chief, and Sergeant Baker stood on the driveway. They'd found three smoke bombs in the air handler in the basement and no sign of forced entry. Thankfully, no one accused Henry and Grace of setting off the bombs.

That hadn't stopped a gaggle of neighbors from gathering on Amy Anderson's front lawn. At the rate things were going, Miss Georgia Peach 2010 could make a fortune selling popcorn and sodas.

Baker left a second message for Tim Templeton and put his phone in his pocket. "I'm going to need the two of you to make an official statement."

Henry frowned at his cell. "I can't reach my parents. Dad must have had an early lecture. Mom probably turned her phone off and sat in."

"I want to see you at the station before five today."

The twins nodded.

Two firefighters emerged from the house. "Chief, you're going to want to see this."

They filed into the house to find a firefighter standing on a ladder in the living room. Above him, a smoke detector hung from an electric cord.

"They didn't go off," Henry said.

"That's because someone took the alarm mechanism out and replaced it with a camera." The guy gave the device a tug, and it came free.

Sergeant Baker took it and furrowed his brow. "None of the alarms sounded?"

"No." Grace ran her hands over her arms. "Are the cameras active? I mean, has someone been watching us inside the house?"

The firefighter avoided her gaze, but the tightening of his jaw answered loud and clear.

Baker nodded to the fire chief. "I'd like to get my men on this. We may be able to pick up a latent print."

"Have at it. My team is done here." He turned to face the twins. "Generally speaking, smoke bombs of this nature aren't toxic, but as I'm sure you know, they can irritate the eyes and lungs. It's best if you two allow the house to air out before returning."

Davenport folded his arms. "They can stay with me until it's safe to return."

Grace wanted to argue, but at the same time, she doubted The Watcher would be stupid enough to come into the house with the police inside. "I need to get a few things from upstairs."

Sergeant Baker nodded. "We'll let you know when we're done here. In the meantime, keep calling your parents."

"Will do." Henry glanced at the hidden camera and Baker. "Is there any way to tell where the feed is going?"

"To tell you the truth, I'm not sure. I'll have someone with technical knowledge look into it."

"Thanks." He followed Grace upstairs and shoved a change of clothes into his backpack, along with his wallet, laptop, and calculus textbook.

"It's awful to think that someone was watching us." She glared at the smoke detector in the hall. "Maybe still is."

Henry ran his hand over his head. "At least now we know how he knew what we liked on our pizza."

She narrowed her eyes.

He waved her into the room and closed the door. "It's best not to talk here. We don't know if there are other cameras."

The skin on the back of her neck prickled.

———

The twins showered to get rid of the powdered chemical smell, dressed, and scarfed down a quick breakfast, courtesy of Davenport.

Henry glanced out the window to make sure the police hadn't left the Templetons' home unprotected. "I'm going to try Trina's cell phone again."

"Hello?" The woman's voice sounded raspy, as if the call had woken her.

"Mrs. Templeton, this is Henry Warner. I'm sorry to call so early, but there's been an...incident."

Grace eased beside him so she could hear both sides of the conversation.

"Did you receive a letter? Are you and Grace all right?"

He drew a breath and gave it to her straight. "We're fine, but someone set off smoke bombs in the air handler. The neighbor called the fire department. The police are in the house now."

"What? Oh, my God." A rustling sound filled the line. "Are you sure no one was hurt?"

"I'm sure. Grace and I are at Mr. Davenport's while your place airs out." Searching for words, Henry frowned. "Someone's been breaking into your house and searching through the things in the attic, and possibly the basement, too."

The woman gasped.

"We found a comic book in one of the trunks. It's worth a lot of money."

She sniffled. "A comic book? I don't understand. Are you saying someone was looking for it?"

Grace took the phone. "Hi, Trina. No, I don't think they know about the comic. We found a bag of jewelry and a figurine. My guess is they were looking for something specific."

Henry hung his head. The Watcher might not have known about the comic before, but if he'd been listening to their previous conversations, he did now.

"Tim's not here. He's already left for the office." She drew a breath. "When you say a lot of money, what exactly do you mean?"

"Henry said one sold for over a million dollars last year."

The line went quiet.

"Are you there?"

"Yes. I'm...I don't know what to think. You two shouldn't be there. It's not safe, but do you think you could—"

Grace said, "We'll bring it here. A person would have to be nuts to mess with Davenport."

A chill raced up Henry's spine. He liked the man, but they hardly knew him. Twice he'd been nearby when The Watcher had struck. His mouth went dry. *Where's the bag with the jewelry?*

"Thank you. I'll call Tim's assistant and have my husband return to Garwood today. Please be careful."

"We will." She disconnected the call.

He leaned close and whispered, "What happened to the Watcher's bag?"

Grace jerked as if he'd slapped her. "Davenport has it."

"What? When?"

"I handed it to him before he went inside to open the windows."

He closed his eyes for a moment and sighed. They had too much ground to cover before Tim Templeton returned. "We need a plan, and we need to determine what Davenport's motives are once and for all."

"We should speak to Gary Grossman while the police are still in the house."

Dave Davenport knocked on the wall before entering the room. "Baker says it's going to be at least another hour."

Grace forced a smile. "Would you mind keeping an eye on things? We need to have a chat with a realtor."

"No problem." He reached behind the chair closest to the door and produced a black cloth sack. "Don't forget about these."

The twins blew out a breath.

Davenport arched a brow. "You didn't think I took this, did you?"

Grace dipped her chin. "Sorry."

The man chuckled. "Not a problem. In fact, I would have thought less of you if you didn't suspect me."

"If we aren't back in thirty minutes, send the police to the Grossman's basement." Henry headed for the door.

"Uh..." The retired soldier stared at Grace as if waiting for an explanation.

"He's mostly joking." She sighed.

Henry nodded toward the house. "I know the police are there, but could you please make sure no one else goes in or out?"

The man nodded. "Of course."

The twins walked down Avenue E in silence. The mystery had them stumped. They had many suspects, but none of them fit the bill. Perhaps Grace had been right when she'd said the burglar was a professional, but would a pro write creepy letters?

The scents of bacon and freshly brewed coffee drifted around the Grossmans' front porch, but Henry's stomach lurched. The last time they'd visited had spun into something straight out of *Twilight Zone*.

Grace rang the bell.

A moment later, Mrs. Grossman opened the front door. She looked them over from head to toe and frowned. "Yes?"

"Is Mr. Grossman home? We need to speak to a realtor." Henry congratulated himself on sounding coherent even though the woman made him nervous.

"Looking to buy a house, are you?"

Grace hugged herself. "No. We think we know who's been causing all of the trouble at the Templetons, and hope Gary can tell us about the other buyers who missed out on purchasing the house."

The old lady's eyes widened. "I see. Come in."

The twins followed her to the dining room where Gary Grossman sat at a table set for a king. Silver, china, and crystal covered the linen tablecloth, but Henry found himself staring at the hardboiled eggs perched on decorative stands. *Awful fancy for a weekday breakfast.*

Mrs. Grossman said, "These two have some questions for you."

He glanced at them before tossing his napkin on the table. "What sort of questions?"

Grace shifted her weight from one foot to the other. "Do you know anything about the Staudingers or their realtor?"

Gary sat back. "They submitted an offer on the house, but the Templetons beat it. Why do you ask?"

"Mr. and Mrs. Staudinger came by the other night. She asked if she could take photos of the kitchen to show her designer. She said they'd purchased another home, but there's no record of it online."

"You searched the Clerk of the Court's website?"

Grace nodded. "There's no record of a mortgage, settlement, or Deed in Union in this or any other nearby counties. How long does it usually take for the information to show up?"

"The sale is recorded with the court the same day. Takes two to three business days for it to become searchable." He pursed his lips. "I can give their realtor a call after nine."

"Thank you." Henry pulled out a chair and sat. "In addition to the threatening letters, someone has been breaking into the Templetons' home. We believe it may be them."

"Where are my manners? Sit, my dear." Mrs. Grossman smiled at Grace.

"Why on earth would they do that?" Hand shaking, Gary took a sip of water.

Grace sat on the edge of the fancy chair. "We were hoping you could tell us. You're familiar with the house. There's a lot of...stuff in the attic and basement."

Mrs. Grossman moved closer and lowered her voice as if sharing a dirty secret. "When Widow Penneyman passed away, there were no surviving children. Rumor has it her things were stored in the attic."

Henry caught himself leaning away from the woman. "Do you have any idea if any of it was worth stealing?"

"Oh, yes. The Penneymans were, as you kids say, *loaded.*" Her grin put crocodiles to shame. "Why, when I was a child, I had the pleasure of seeing her Lladro collection. It was exquisite, and quite extensive."

"Lladro?" Henry asked.

"Porcelain figurines from Spain."

"Ah." He glanced at Gary, who'd gone quite pale.

Grace flashed the woman a bright smile. "It stands to reason that the Staudingers were in the house before they made an offer. Maybe they came across some of Mrs. Penneyman's things in the attic. That would explain how they knew where to look."

"Yes." Gary cleared his throat. "Yes. Most people spend hours in a home before they purchase it, especially one as old as the Templetons.' Things go wrong, like plumbing and electric. Buyers want to be sure they know what they're getting."

"Wouldn't any personal belongings transfer via probate?"

"Yes, but she was estranged from her son, who said he didn't want anything to do with his mother and ordered her belongings to be sold with the house. It was a bit odd. If he had only known. But that's a different issue."

"It all makes sense now. After the smoke bombs went off this morning, we found a bag with a white porcelain statuette inside. We left it in the kitchen, but now I think we should have given it to the police." Grace stood. "Thank you for your help. We should get back before something happens to it."

"You two are quite amazing. I'd say you have a bright future in criminal investigations." Gary pushed to his feet.

Mrs. Grossman gave her son a quizzical look before patting Grace's shoulder. "I'll show you to the door."

Henry followed. He couldn't help but notice how the older woman's shoulders slumped. *She must know her son's involved.*

CHAPTER ELEVEN

Grace forced herself to walk and not run to the Templetons'. She'd managed to dangle the bait but had sent her central nervous system into overdrive in the process.

"That was brilliant." Henry hadn't stopped grinning since they'd left the Grossmans'. "Now all we need to do is set the trap and see who shows up to steal the bag."

Grace gave him the side-eye. "*If* anyone shows up. I'm ninety-nine percent sure Grossman isn't the parkour-ninja from the attic, but he's definitely involved."

"I intend to find out, and this is how we're going to do it..."

She listened as her brother outlined his ideas for capturing The Watcher. She had to admit, he made a compelling case, but they couldn't do it alone. They'd need Davenport's help, patience, and a truckload of luck. "That just might work."

"It'll definitely work." Henry's grin faltered. "Who's that leaving the Templetons'?"

A small tan sedan backed out of the driveway and sped off.

"I don't know, but the police are still there." She quickened her pace.

Amy Anderson pushed little Abigail's stroller on the other side of the street.

The twins waved.

The woman locked eyes with Grace and walked by without a word.

Henry whispered, "She's probably upset about the party."

"Or police activity on Avenue E for the second time in as many days. It's her problem, not ours." Grace had far more important things to do than worry about Amy.

Sergeant Baker met the twins in the Templetons' foyer. "You just missed a Mrs. Staudinger. She left you a note. It's on the kitchen counter."

"Did she come inside the house? Grace peered into the living room and gasped. Between the firefighters and the police, the place was a mess. Black fingerprint powder marred Trina's white leather couches. Someone had walked through mud and cleaned their shoes on the area rugs. Worst still, every square inch of the house was covered in smoke-bomb dust.

"No civilians have been inside." He folded his arms. "We're finished here. Were you able to reach Tim Templeton?"

"We spoke to Trina this morning. She said she'd get word to Tim through his assistant. We're expecting him home this afternoon," Henry said.

Grace chewed her lower lip. "Is it okay if we close the windows and clean up a bit?"

"Go ahead. The smoke's gone." Baker rubbed his jaw. "Crime scene investigation is a messy business. Do yourselves a favor and don't try to wipe away the black powder, use a vacuum."

"Thanks for the tip." She walked into the kitchen and pulled the yellow Post-It note from the counter.

Henry glanced over her shoulder and made a sound in his throat.

"What?"

He glanced toward Baker before opening the drawer and slipping one of The Watcher letters out of the manila file. "Look at the handwriting," he hissed in a hushed tone.

Grace's knees threatened to buckle. While the two weren't identical, the scrolling swirls and dips of the letters were too similar to ignore. "*She's* Gary's accomplice?"

"We're still missing a piece of the puzzle, but I'd bet my right arm she wrote the letters."

"Okay, we're leaving," Baker boomed into the kitchen.

The twins startled. Henry folded the letter, and Grace palmed the Post-It.

"You two all right?" He studied one and then the other like he would suspects trying to not look guilty.

Grace's laugh came out in a nervous twitter. "Yes, sir. It's been a long couple of days."

"You have my direct number. Call me if you have any more trouble." He turned and left.

Letting his head fall back, Henry stared at the ceiling.

She poked his side and read the note aloud. "Have Tim call me the minute you see him. It's urgent. Sarah Staudinger."

"Should we check in with Trina? I'd like to know exactly where Tim is, and where he was at four-thirty this morning." He folded his arms.

"Not yet. We have a trap to set." She tapped her lips. "Close and lock the windows and be sure to close the drapes. I'll call Davenport."

"Are you absolutely sure we can trust him?"

She'd asked herself the same question too many times to count. "I think so, but we'll know soon enough."

"I'll get the comic. We shouldn't leave it here," Henry whispered heavily into his hand, hoping that it masked their planning should the video and audio feeds continue to broadcast.

"I'll meet you up there. Don't forget the baby monitors." Grace dialed the neighbor's number. It took less than a minute to relay their plan to Davenport, and another five to convince him it was the only way to catch The Watcher. By the time she'd made it upstairs, Henry had retrieved the *Action Comic Number One*.

"We need a way to sneak this out without anyone noticing." He held the prized book like it would disintegrate in the slightest breeze.

"Can you hide it under your shirt?"

He looked at her as if she'd suggested they club baby seals. "And risk wrinkling it?"

Grace rolled her eyes. "We'll put it between my textbooks when we leave."

"Good idea." He glanced around the dusty attic. "I think we should start the search near the window where he climbed in."

"But not too close. The Watcher is smart. He wouldn't be obvious." She wove her way through the antiques to the window where they'd found the gouges.

The twins searched boxes and trunks nearby and came up empty. An ornate wardrobe cabinet that reminded Grace of the talking furniture from Beauty and the Beast caught her eye and she tried the door, but it was locked.

"We probably won't find a grappling hook. The thief would take it with him when he leaves." Henry opened another box. "But we may find bolt cutters or other equipment."

"This is big enough to hold all sorts of hardware." Grace stood on top of a trunk and ran her fingers over the curved top of the wardrobe. She brushed what felt like a silk tassel. "I found the key."

Henry stood, stretched, and moved to her side.

Inside the wardrobe, they found bolt cutters, an extra grappling hook, and a rollup emergency escape ladder.

"Pay dirt." He pumped his fist in the air but stopped mid-victory dance. "What the heck is that?"

Grace pulled a jar from the cabinet. "I've seen one like this before in Gary's basement."

"It looks like someone captured a dust bunny, but why bother poking holes in the lid—" His mouth fell open. "Holy smokes! That's why we never saw footprints."

Grace turned the jar upside down and shook it. Sure enough, dust peppered the floor. "This is ingenious."

"If The Watcher can use it to cover his tracks, so can we."

"We have to hurry. Help me move the equipment first."

The twins carried the tools into the master bedroom and returned to the attic. Starting at the window, Grace shook the dust-shaker as she backed out of the room. "I'm only covering our prints near the wardrobe. We don't want to tip him off too soon."

"Good idea." Henry turned on the baby monitor, stepped out, and locked the attic door.

"Warners? You shouldn't be here alone." Davenport's voice filled the house and probably the yard. "You heard what Sergeant Baker said. No one's to be here until the Templetons return at sixteen hundred."

Grace rolled her eyes, and Henry groaned.

"At least he stuck to the script." She giggled.

Henry ducked into her room, grabbed her navy-blue backpack, and rushed downstairs.

"Where do you want this?" Davenport pulled the cloth sack out of Henry's dark-green backpack. Whatever he'd stuffed inside it jingled and clanked. It didn't sound like a porcelain figure and jewelry, but it'd have to do.

"Kitchen counter," she whispered.

Henry took a moment to slip the comic book inside his textbook. "We don't need your backpack now, unless you'd rather not leave it in the house."

She considered his words.

Henry laughed softly. "Relax, no one wants to steal your homework." He slung his bag over his shoulder, leaving Grace's on the floor against the island. "Are we ready?"

Davenport folded his arms. "You sure I can't talk you out of this?"

"Positive," the twins said.

"Okay, let's rock and roll." He set his jaw and followed them outside.

Speaking louder than necessary, Grace said, "This isn't fair. I don't know why we have to leave."

Davenport set his hand on her shoulder. "Sergeant Baker's orders."

The twins slumped their shoulders and made a show of trudging across the lawn to Davenport's house. Once inside, Henry handed off the backpack and headed for the side door.

"The board's unscrewed. I'll cover you." As planned, Davenport walked out front to water his hedges.

Grace giggled. "It's hard to imagine him on covert military missions."

"No kidding." Henry waited a few moments, opened the door, and glanced at the street. The retired soldier had provided a fairly heavy spray of water, but it'd only do so much. If anyone was *really* looking or had a vantage point other than the street, they'd see the twins cross the side yard back to the Templetons'.

"Let's go," Grace whispered.

They'd made it halfway across when Davenport called, "Mrs. Anderson! Good to see you! Is that Abigail? She's getting so big."

Amy's voice drifted over the yard, but he couldn't make out what she'd said.

Grace dove for the bushes and pressed her back against the basement wall. Henry, on the other hand, dropped to the ground and low-crawled the remainder of the distance.

"Did she see us?" Grace squirmed and shifted her weight as if she wanted to peek around the corner.

"No. He would have signaled to abort." He removed the plywood covering the window.

Grace shimmied through the opening and gave him a thumbs-up.

Henry dropped onto the recliner and put the plywood back in place. Unless someone came close enough to see that the screws were missing, they'd assume the window remained boarded shut.

Grace headed for the stairs but stopped. "The dishes are missing."

His heart pounding in his ears made it difficult to hear her, let alone understand her meaning. "Huh?"

Pointing to an empty spot on the metal shelves, she whispered, "The box of dishes we found the first day here. They're gone."

"Hope we're not too late." He hurried up the basement stairs and cracked the door. The bag was where they'd left it. "We're clear."

She nodded and followed him into the kitchen.

It took both of them using every ounce of muscle they had, but the twins managed to move an enormous china cabinet in front of the basement door. In the process, they left ruts in the Templetons' floor, but Henry doubted the couple would mind if they put an end to The Watcher.

Grace stuck close to the walls and crept to the stairs.

Henry followed her up to the master bedroom but hesitated outside the door. He'd gone over the plan enough times to memorize the details. One mistake could cost them more than a shot at capturing The Watcher. "I should check the attic door."

"I saw you lock it and test to make sure it worked." She turned the baby monitor on and sat on the floor with her back against the bed. "All we have to do now is wait."

An hour passed and nothing happened. No grappling-hook-using burglar came through the attic window. No calls from Davenport telling them to abort. No Tim Templeton showing up to ruin their trap. Nothing. Nada. Zip.

Henry stretched out on the floor and stared at the patterns on the ceiling. "If you squint, that swirl looks like a dragon."

Grace sighed. "I should have stashed my textbooks in here."

"I could sneak into the guest room and get my laptop."

She gave him a look that reminded him far too much of their mother, sighed, and motioned to the door. "Go, but hurry."

He rolled to his stomach and froze.

"Ouch. Dang it. Stupid kids." A female voice, thick with age, came from the first floor.

Wide-eyed, Grace mouthed, "What's *she* doing here?"

They'd painstakingly laid the trap in the attic, and Mrs. Grossman had strolled in through the front door?

Grace shot to her feet. "She must have a key. She's going to ruin everything."

I knew there was a reason I didn't like her! "Trophy keys, my foot. That board probably has a key to every house on the block. Listen."

The telltale sound of jingling and clanking told him the old woman had taken the bag, or worse, she was going through it. "She's going to know it's a trap."

Grace bounded for the door and flew down the stairs. "Hello? Who's there?"

Henry rounded the corner in time to see Mrs. Grossman standing in the kitchen holding the cloth sack.

The woman pressed her free hand to her chest. "My stars! What's wrong with the two of you? First, you leave your school bag in the middle of the floor, and then you come charging down here like a pack of wild elephants!"

"What are you doing here?" Grace set her hands on her hips.

The woman narrowed her eyes. "What are *you* doing here? I thought Sergeant Baker told you no one was to be in the house?"

"Mr. Templeton said it was okay." Henry motioned to the sack in her hand. "I'm going to ask you one more time. What are you doing here?"

"I came to retrieve Mrs. Anderson's pie plate. I asked to borrow it, but she said the two of you never returned it." She regarded them with disgust.

A thump sounded from overhead.

The twins glanced at the ceiling. The split second was all the little old lady needed to swing the bag like a weapon and nail Grace in the face. She spun and hot-footed it out the door.

Grace's hands flew to her bloody lip. "Ow. What the heck?"

Henry couldn't decide if he should chase Mrs. Grossman, help his sister, or stick to the plan and catch whoever was in the attic.

"Get the rope. There's no time to call Davenport." Grace shouted.

"I'm on it. Call 911." Henry ran out the front door and rounded the corner on the far side of the house.

As they'd guessed, a long rope hung from the attic window. All he had to do was make a wave pattern in the line to loosen the grappling hook. Unfortunately, he'd never done anything of the sort. Davenport had, which was why the military man was supposed to handle that part of the mission.

Grabbing the rope, Henry pulled down. Big mistake. The motion set the hook deeper. He moved his arms in wide arcs starting over his head and ending at his thighs. The rope moved like ripples on a pond, but the darned thing didn't release.

Grace ran to his side. "Why isn't it coming loose?"

"Don't know." He gritted his teeth and put more muscle into it. The line battered against the side of the house.

"Try smaller movements." Her voice came out thin and panicked.

Someone in a black ski mask stuck their head out the window and ducked back inside.

"I've called the police!" Grace shouted to The Watcher or burglar or whoever it was.

No reply.

"Go inside and make sure he doesn't escape the attic." Henry's arm burned, but he continued to fight to free the grappling hook.

"You go. I'll do this." She reached for the rope.

"Fine but be careful." He took his eyes off the window for a split second.

Grace screamed and pulled him to the side.

A box of old vinyl records crashed nearby.

Henry tugged her against the house. His brain seemed to have lost signal to his lungs. He gasped and wheezed but couldn't seem to get any air.

"Forget it—he must be trapped." She stared at the window. "We have to get the hook loose."

A voice shouted inside Grace's pocket.

She put her phone to her ear. "The burglar's trapped in the attic and is throwing boxes at us. Please hurry."

A torrent of hardcover books rained down on them. The twins covered their heads and crouched against the wall.

Taking advantage of the distraction, The Watcher tugged on the line hard enough it slipped through Henry's hands, taking a layer of skin with it.

Grace jumped forward, grabbed it, and ran toward the back corner of the house. The rope stretched taut, but it was too short to drag around the corner.

The burglar must have seen what she'd tried to do because he renewed his efforts to reel in the line.

Henry ran to his sister and wrapped the rope around his hand.

They pulled down, The Watcher yanked it back. The game of tug-o-war showed no sign of letting up. His wrist screamed in protest, but he refused to let go.

"We have to keep him up there," Grace shouted.

She was right. They had no way of knowing if they could apprehend the person on the ground, but he wasn't sure how much longer they could hold on.

CHAPTER TWELVE

The twins fought against The Watcher, but with each passing moment, they lost a few inches and the line grew tauter. They'd given up enough ground that their arms were stretched over their heads.

"He's tying it off." Henry gave one last heave. "I can't hold on much longer."

Sirens wailed in the background, along with what sounded like a small child.

"We have to try. The police are close." Grace's lip felt like hamburger, and her head was pounding.

Henry groaned, and the rope left his hand. "No!"

"Is that Abigail?" Grace split her attention between the window and the crying child. "What if The Watcher's armed? We have to warn Amy."

"He would have shot us by now."

Grace stared at the window, half-expecting more boxes to fall or the person to scramble down the rope. "Where is he?"

The color drained from Henry's face. "Other windows."

The twins ran to the back of the house in time to see a black-clad figure disappearing into the bushes along the back of the property. Henry darted after him.

I need to warn Amy. Grace's chest tightened.

She ran to the gate leading to the Andersons' backyard and found the toddler in her play yard. "Amy?"

Mr. Anderson came out of the house with a sippy cup in one hand and a water bottle in the other. "Amy stepped out for a bit."

Abigail stopped crying and turned toward Grace's voice. She reached her pudgy little hands over the top of the barrier as if asking to be held.

"Take her inside. There's a burglar on the loose. It's not safe."

The man stared for two heartbeats. "Carry her inside. I need to call my wife."

Grace scooped the girl into her arms. "It's okay, sweetie."

"What are you doing with my daughter?" Amy, dressed in black yoga pants and a black t-shirt covered by a powder-blue oxford button-up stood in the back corner of her yard.

Mr. Anderson dropped his cell phone. "Amy? Where..." He shook his head. "We need to get inside."

The sirens grew loud and red and blue lights flashed through the cracks in the wooden privacy fence.

Something was wrong and judging by the confused expression on the man's face and the rage in Amy's, the twins had solved one part of the puzzle.

But it created a new problem.

Grace had two choices: run which would alert Amy to the fact she'd figured it out, or play along and keep an eye on the woman until the police found them. She chose the latter. "There's a maniac on the loose. I came to warn you."

"Ain't you sweet?" The woman smiled, although it looked more like a snarl. "Put Abigail back in the playpen."

The man's eyes widened, and he glanced between his wife and Grace. "Honey, I don't know what's going on, but Abigail shouldn't be out here."

"Take her inside." Grace handed the child to him and took several steps toward the gate.

Amy turned toward her husband and daughter.

Any remaining doubt Grace had about the woman vanished when she noticed the hole in the back of Amy's shirt—a hole the exact size and shape as the piece of fabric Henry had found.

The beauty queen took her husband's hand. "Baby, please. I'm in serious trouble. If you love me, you'll take Grace to the basement and keep her quiet. We can't let her leave."

"What in Heaven's name has gotten into you?" Poor Mr. Anderson looked as if he'd have a stroke. He stood there gaping and stared at his wife.

Grace saw the moment the pieces snapped into place for him.

He staggered back. "Is this where the money—"

"Shut up," Amy snapped.

Grace ran. She pushed through the gate and crashed into Sergeant Baker.

He grabbed her arms to steady her. "Are you all right? We got a call—"

"It's her." She pointed behind her at Miss Georgia Peach 2010. "She broke into the house. She's The Watcher."

Walking through the gate, Amy laughed and rolled her eyes. "I stopped by to get my pie plate. Honestly, Grace."

Baker glanced from Grace to the blonde and frowned, but before he could form a sentence, a commotion next door stole his attention.

The officers drew their weapons and shouted, "Stop! Hands up!"

"I'm Henry Warner. Sergeant Baker knows me. My sister made the call."

"Don't move." Baker glanced between Grace and the couple, scowled, and jogged back toward the Templetons' house. "He's clear!"

Amy took advantage of the distraction and made a break for the backyard. She leapt into the air, grabbed the top of the fence, and vaulted over it like a gymnast on a high bar.

"She's getting away!"

Chaos ensued. Abigail screamed. Baker bellowed. The officers who'd stopped Henry gave chase. A woman shouted something in Spanish from behind the fence, and the sounds of an all-out brawl followed.

Grace hurried to Henry's side. "It's Amy. She's wearing the blue shirt. She's the parkour-ninja. She's The Watcher."

"Miss Georgia Peach?" His brows rose. "Who's with her? It sounds like a UFC fight."

"I don't know."

Davenport jogged across the lawn. "Sorry it took me so long. The police wouldn't let me back on my own property, let alone this one."

They turned as Baker hauled a bleeding and battered Amy out of the backyard in handcuffs. He stuffed her into the back of a patrol car.

Paulina Perez, looking a little battered herself, stood with her hands on her hips. The woman muttered what sounded like Spanish curse words.

Baker turned to her. "Assault and battery is a felony."

"Holy smokes," Henry whispered.

"Come on. We need to help her and tell him about the Grossmans."

"I saw her drop this when she was running through my yard." Ms. Perez handed Baker a black ski mask.

Henry said, "That's what the person we trapped in the attic was wearing."

Mr. Anderson's mouth moved, but no words came out.

Baker motioned to Grace's bloody lip. "Who did that to you?"

Grace touched her mouth and winced. "Mrs. Grossman. She also broke in. She stole a bag from the kitchen. She and her son Gary are involved in this too —201 Avenue E."

He scratched his head. "Anyone else?"

She sighed. "Not as far as I know."

He nodded to Mr. Anderson. "You're the husband?"

"Yes." He seemed to snap out of his shock and realize his situation. "I had nothing to do... I don't know what's..."

"Get him someplace quiet and determine what he knows." Baker motioned for an officer to take Mr. Anderson and turned to the twins. "I'll need you to add all of this to your official statement."

"We're looking forward to it." Henry grinned.

Baker frowned. "Right now, I need you two to stay out of the way. This is an official—"

A black sports car screeched to a halt in front of the house. Tim Templeton rolled down the window for half a second before slamming the car into Park and jogging to the twins. "My God. Are you two all right?"

Baker growled and gave Tim a once-over. "Do you have a reason to be on my crime scene?"

"I'm Tim Templeton. That's my house."

Sergeant Baker glanced at the twins. When they didn't dispute Tim's words, he said, "I'll need to speak to you once we have the suspects cleared out."

"Sure, whatever you need." He turned to the twins. "What happened?"

Baker stormed off, shouting orders at his men.

Henry motioned to the sidewalk. "We should stay out of Baker's way."

Tim cast a wary glance at the police sergeant as he followed the twins.

Henry and Grace told him everything, starting with the lost-and-found manila file and ending with the capture and arrest of the beauty queen.

He sagged against a police cruiser. "You're sure Sarah Staudinger wrote the letters?"

"Yes, and we need to report it to the police." Grace should have mentioned it when he'd asked about additional suspects, but she'd wanted to speak to Mr. Templeton first.

Tim drew a breath. "Would you give me an hour or two to speak to Trina?"

"Did you have something to do with the letters?" Henry folded his arms.

The man tensed. "No. I had no idea she'd take it that far."

"Take what that far?" Grace's stomach churned. Had he played some part in the scheme?

"We didn't know Trina was pregnant until after we bought the house. We could barely afford it with two incomes, but then Trina started talking about quitting her job to stay home with the kids." He sighed. "You have to understand, I'd do anything for her, so I contacted the Staudingers to see if they were still interested in the property."

"But you didn't tell your wife?" Her heart went out to him, but at the same time, she couldn't understand why he hadn't talked to his wife.

"I should have told her, but I didn't want to pressure her one way or the other. I thought I was hedging my bets while she decided what to do about her career."

Henry said, "And the Staudingers decided to push things along."

Tim hung his head. "Looks that way. Had I known they would do something like this, I never would have reached out to them."

"We won't mention it until we make our statements later today. That should give you time to speak to Trina." Grace glanced down the street and sighed. "Looks like they arrested Gary."

"Let's see if he's in a talkative mood." Henry strode toward the Grossmans' house with Grace and Tim on his heels.

Gary took one look at them and burst into tears. "I'm sorry. I didn't want to do it. My mother, she...she made me."

"Where is she now?" Grace wasn't exactly fond of the woman, but she didn't want to see her dragged out in handcuffs, either. Despite everything she'd done, it felt wrong to cuff someone who looked like a grandmother.

"She ran." Gary tried to wipe his nose on his shoulder but couldn't quite reach.

Henry scowled. "Are you responsible for the cameras?"

"It was my mother's idea, I swear. I didn't watch the video. I only listened."

His words sent a chill down Grace's spine. "You're a disgusting human being."

Henry wrapped his arm around her shoulders. "Come on. It's time we went home."

The twins emerged from the conference room and were immediately wrapped in their parents' arms.

Faith Warner squeezed Grace extra-tight. "Are you okay?"

She smiled through her exhaustion. "I am, actually. We helped the Templetons and stopped a neighborhood crime ring."

Henry laughed. "I still can't get over a pageant queen, an elderly woman, and Gary Grossman pulling off such an elaborate scheme."

Dad furrowed his brow. "There's more besides theft?"

Grace nodded. "Sergeant Baker said they've only begun to investigate, but they believe the three of them have been stealing from their neighbors and selling the goods for years."

Faith made a choking sound. "When I okayed you house-sitting, I thought you two would track down a teenager pulling a prank."

She kissed her mother's cheek. "There was no way any of us could have known about the robberies because no one reported anything."

"Tell me what it looked like?" Dad's voice went soft and dreamy.

"I almost fainted when I saw it." Henry beamed. "The pages were thinner than I would have thought, but it was a beauty. Near-mint condition."

Faith Warner raised a brow.

"They're talking about the comic book Henry found." Grace eased from her mother's embrace. "Can we go home now?"

"Sure, but don't you want to know about the surprise?" Ethan Warner grinned almost as broadly as his son had moments before.

The twins exchanged glances. Henry looked as tired as she felt.

"Not here. We'll tell them when they've had a chance to recover from their ordeal." Their mother herded them to the exit.

"We may be twins, but it's scary how much you're like Mom," Henry whispered.

Grace poked his side. "I take that as the highest of compliments."

The family piled into the pickup and headed back to the campground. The twins pretended to ignore their parents' backward glances and worried smiles. They had their own silent conversation going on. Henry's satisfied grin and wink told Grace she wasn't the only one happy to have life return to normal.

She met his gaze and slid her eyes toward the front seat.

He gave her a lopsided smile and asked, "Where are we heading next?"

"University of Pittsburgh. Dad and I are both lecturing. We're staying a little south of the city, and it's a bit remote. I'm not sure what mystery the two of you will find to solve there." Faith turned toward the backseat. "Whatever you choose, could you make it boring? Stick to urban legends and leave the criminals to the authorities?"

Henry snorted. "Hey, house-sitting for the Templetons was *your* idea. We were all set to investigate the sea serpent in Sandy Hook Bay."

"I agree with your mother. While I'm proud of both of you, a little less excitement would be nice." Dad glanced at them in the rearview. "We'll have plenty of adventure when the Warners go international for Halloween."

Grace sat up straighter. "What are these words you speak?"

Faith grinned. "Your father and I are teaching at a professional lecturers' retreat. We're spending two weeks on an island in the Bay of Naples."

Henry arched a brow. "You're getting paid to speak to a bunch of people who speak for a living?"

"That about sums it up." Dad chuckled.

"Sweet." Henry high-fived the hand his father stuck over the seat.

"That'll be fun, as long as we have some family time too." She pulled her phone from her pocket.

"We wouldn't drag you two across the Atlantic and leave you to your own devices." Faith winked. "Of course, you'll need to keep up with your studies while we're there. Grace, did you complete your English Lit paper?"

"I turned it in yesterday." She scrolled through listings of urban legends near Pittsburgh.

"Henry? Calculus?" Faith stared.

"I'm a chapter ahead of the class, thanks to Grace's tutelage."

"Good." She faced forward and took Ethan's hand. "We have great kids."

"Yes, we do." His smile crinkled his eyes.

Grace couldn't help but beam her joy as she handed Henry her phone with an article about Charlie No-Face, also known as The Green Man—a real person who allegedly suffered a horrific accident and became radioactive.

Henry read the story and nodded. "Charlie No-Face it is."

The fear and frustration of the previous days melted away in the warm glow of the afternoon sun. It was good to be home. Not the physical place most people thought of but the family.

CHARLIE NO-FACE

MONSTER CASE FILES BOOK 4

CHAPTER ONE

The girls climbed out of the car into a moonless Western Pennsylvania night. Piney Fork Tunnel, otherwise known as the Green Man Tunnel, waited at the end of the path.

Charlie No-Face—a man who'd melted his face and arm off in an electrical accident. Legend had it that Charlie prowled the old railroad tunnel waiting to electrocute his next victim.

You got this. Be brave. It'll be worth it. Kylie had repeated the mantra since she'd found out the last step to joining the cheerleading squad—fifteen minutes alone in Piney Fork Tunnel.

What choice did she have? Her parents had moved, and she had the displeasure of going to a new school. It was suffer through the hazing or have the worst senior year in history. Her only hope of survival was making the team. *You got this. Be brave. It'll be so worth it.*

"Sometime tonight, if you don't mind." Maddison, the cheer captain and queen of Southpointe High School, smacked her gum.

Kylie stiffened her upper lip and turned on her flashlight.

"That's cheating. No cell phone, either. Hand them over." She rolled her eyes and held out her hand.

"Sure." Kylie gave the girl her phone and flashlight. "See you in fifteen." *There's no such thing as ghosts or men who glow neon green. It's only fifteen minutes.*

"Give Charlie a big hug for me." Maddison tossed her golden curls over her shoulder.

Career death or fifteen minutes in the dark? Kylie saluted her soon-to-be leader and strolled boldly down the path for as long as she was able, her legs growing heavier with each step. Despite the dim light, the mouth of the tunnel gaped as if ready to swallow her. Kylie ignored her racing heart and sweating palms and forced herself into the darkness.

"This isn't so bad," she muttered and took a few more steps.

Her chem-lab partner had warned her to be careful. The county stored rock salt in the tunnel. He'd also given her a head's up about the concrete blocks and new gate they'd installed to keep unsuspecting kids from being buried in a salt avalanche.

Kylie moved forward until she reached the blocks. "Thank goodness for chem-lab."

About the time she settled in to wait, crunching sounds came from behind her. Chunks of rock salt pelted her head and shoulders. Squinting, Kylie spun, half-expecting to find Maddison or one of her minions, but it was no use. She couldn't *see* anything or anyone.

Moans and crackling noises echoed through the tunnel.

No freaking way am I letting whoever that is scare me off the team. Kylie stumble-shuffled to the wall and crouched. If she couldn't see the prankster, they couldn't see her. Surely her time was almost up. Soon, Maddison would come for her. "Very mature!" Her voice shook during her proclamation.

A scream tore through the darkness, and a few seconds later, someone beeped the car horn in one continuous screech.

Fearing it was a test, Kylie hunkered down.

"Is that Maddison?" a guy's voice said from somewhere above her.

"How the heck am I supposed to know?" a second boy's voice answered.

Kylie rolled her eyes. "Since I doubt either of you are named Charlie or glow in the dark, do I have to stay here?"

The horn continued to blast, but instead of a steady beep, it bleated like a dying sheep.

A guy she recognized from English class landed beside her in a shower of salt. "Where did Maddison park?"

The fear in his voice sent a cold shiver down her spine. "In the pull-off across the street."

Someone screamed again, and the horn went silent.

"Come on!" The second boy slid down the mountain of salt, stumbled, and made a break for the exit, running like his hair was on fire.

Kylie followed them up the path. The forest had grown quiet—too quiet. Not a squirrel scampered, or owl hooted. It was as if the living creatures had cleared out, including Maddison.

The driver's side door stood open, the car empty.

The contents of Maddison's purse stretched from the open driver's door to the tree line as if she'd left a trail of lip gloss and mini hand sanitizers instead of breadcrumbs.

"This way." The kid in her English class sprinted toward the forest.

Kylie stared after him.

"Are you coming?" The other boy had the most startling pale blue eyes she'd ever seen. They looked like they belonged on a wolf, not a dark-haired jock.

Chasing Maddison into the forest seemed like a dumb idea but staying behind didn't seem much better. She followed the boy into the woods, but after a few yards, the trail of cosmetics ended.

"What's that?" Blue-eyes pointed to what looked like a hairy creature hanging from a low branch.

Kylie's hands flew to her mouth. "It's Maddison's *hair!*"

"No way!"

Before he could get closer to the golden curls, a man stepped out from behind a nearby tree. Tall, broad, and surrounded by a green aura, he turned his featureless face toward them and groaned.

Living in a fifth wheel had its advantages. New cities, new neighbors, and new adventures—Grace had them all. Also cramped quarters, one bathroom, and listening to her brother snore in the bunk beside hers.

"Monster." Muttering, Henry rolled onto his back and continued to make a reverse sneezing sound, followed by a wheeze.

Grace threw a pillow at him.

He snorted once, batted the projectile away, and turned his unfocused gaze in her direction. "What time is it?"

"Twelve-thirty, and you haven't started your schoolwork." She motioned to the textbook in her lap.

"That's because I'm caught up in all my classes." Henry pushed himself upright and ran his hand through his hair, which only made it stick up more. "I'm starving."

"Give me ten minutes, and we'll go into town for lunch. I'm almost finished with this chapter." She'd done this to herself. Rather than hitting the books, she'd stayed up too late watching B-rated horror flicks with their dad.

"Coffee first, then shower." He shambled into the kitchen, poured himself a cup of coffee, and came back.

Another benefit of living on the road: the twins were homeschooled. In theory, as long as they kept up with their assignments, they could work at four in the morning or four in the afternoon. However, Grace had done neither for the previous two days.

"You can't be *that* far behind. Why are you so stressed?"

"I'm not stressed. I'm eager to finish and move on to more interesting things."

He took a sip of coffee and glanced around. The space hadn't changed, and it wasn't all that interesting, but Henry continued to sip and glance.

"You're dragging more than usual this morning."

"I didn't sleep well."

Grace hated to rush him, but she wanted to start their field research on Charlie No-Face, otherwise known as the Green Man. "Don't forget we have a mystery to solve."

Henry yawned and stretched his arms over his head. "I thought we'd start by interviewing some locals and then visit the tunnel."

Faith Warner, the twins' mom, knocked on the doorframe before entering Grace's and Henry's sleeping area. "Your father and I are heading out soon. We'll be home by six. Do you two need anything before we go?"

"We have our bikes and enough money for pizza. I think we're good," Henry said.

Faith arched a brow. "We have a fridge full of food. Healthy food."

"I'll make chicken stir-fry for dinner." Grace closed her history book. She could read later, but time with her parents was hit or miss, and lately, she'd done a lot of missing them. "What are you lecturing about this week?"

"The importance of systems modeling and simulation." Faith sat on Henry's bed. "It's critical that concepts are tested in controlled environments before they're released into the real world."

"The same could be said for most things in life."

"Ah, you're referring to college?" Her mother's mind worked like a super-computer.

"College is at the top of my list, but what an amazing world this would be if people could run their choices through a simulation to predict the outcomes *before* they did something foolish!"

"Technology hasn't developed enough to calculate the infinite variables of human deviations." Faith winked. "But we're working on it."

"If anyone can find a solution, you can." Henry sat next to his mother and slung his arm over her shoulder.

Faith's smiled and leaned into her son.

Watching them together made Grace's heart swell. It wasn't that long ago her brother fit under their mother's arm. They were growing up, and while some part of her said, "Bring it on," another part secretly wished she could slow it down.

"Am I permitted to ask which urban legend you've decided to research?" Faith redirected the twins.

"Permitted? Yes." Grace bit her lower lip to keep from giggling. "Will you like it? Probably not."

Faith arched a brow and twisted her lips to the side, which meant she likely agreed. Had she not done the lip-twist, it would have meant she wanted more information.

"We're planning to research Charlie No-Face." Henry yawned and pulled away. "It's a fascinating case of a real person morphing into a local urban legend."

"'Charlie No-Face?'" This time she arched a single brow.

"Some people call him 'the Green Man,'" Grace said. "But those who knew him called him Raymond Robinson."

"Knew? Is he dead?"

Henry nodded. "In 1985, from natural causes. He lived into his seventies, which was a miracle. He touched a live electrical line when he was nine. There are some discrepancies in reports, but it appears that the voltage burned off his nose, eyes, and part of his arm."

Faith ran her hands over her upper arms as if a chill had descended.

Grace frowned. "He became a local legend because he would walk along the local roads at night."

"Blind and wandering alone? That poor man." Faith shook her head. "But it sounds like the two of you have already solved the mystery."

Grace's stomach knotted. She and her brother had avoided telling their parents more than they needed to know about their projects for this specific reason—they wanted the autonomy to choose the topics and research methods.

Henry flashed a grin too bright for someone who'd been awake less than an hour. "We know what we read online. We don't know why the legend caught on, or which parts are true and which have been exaggerated, and why. Nor do we know anything about the man himself."

"I'm interested in studying Raymond Robinson's case in the context of history," Grace said, "For instance, was Robinson a product of the culture of the time, or could someone today suffer a tragic accident and become an urban legend?"

Faith nodded. "As much as we'd like to believe the human race has evolved—"

"Faith, Kenny and Kala want to meet the twins." It sounded like Ethan was calling from the front door.

"Good work, you two. I'm looking forward to reading your final report." Faith glanced at them. "Henry, put some jeans on and come meet Dr. and Mrs. Kaluza."

Dr. Kenneth Kaluza, an old colleague of her father's, taught at Pitt Law. He and his wife had offered their RV pad during the Warners' teaching gigs. As it turned out, Southpointe Township was less than an hour's drive from Pittsburgh and very close to the Green Man Tunnel. The location was perfect.

Grace followed her mother outside, and Henry joined them shortly after.

The middle-aged couple smiled at them.

Ethan Warner motioned to the twins. "This is Henry and Grace. Kids, this is Dr. and Mrs. Kaluza."

"I understand you two like to read?" The woman wore a plain tan pantsuit, plain tan shoes, and had pulled back her hair in a plain tan scrunchie. She looked over her horn-rimmed glasses and winked. Between her clothing and her glasses, Grace pegged her as a teacher.

"Everything from thrillers to the classics." Henry hitched his thumb toward his sister. "She prefers fantasy and horror over thrillers."

Mrs. Kaluza smiled. "Let me know if there's anything in particular you'd like to borrow while you're here. I work in the library."

Grace laughed. "If I wasn't set on becoming an engineer like my mom, I'd study library science and spend the rest of my life surrounded by books."

"A girl after my own heart."

Ethan glanced at his watch. "We have to go, or I'll be late for my first lecture."

Dr. Kaluza nudged him. "I'll ride with the two of you so we can catch up."

Faith turned back to the twins. "Are you sure you have everything you need?"

"We'll be okay," Henry and Grace chorused.

"Where have I heard that before?" Ethan chuckled. "Pick up some microwave popcorn while you're out. There's a *Night of the Living Dead* marathon on tonight."

Faith cringed. "I don't know how you guys can watch that stuff."

As if they'd choreographed it, Ethan and Henry held their arms out in front of them and groaned, "Brains..."

Two hours later, thanks to Henry insisting he needed breakfast before they left for lunch, the twins biked into town. Specifically, they rode to Smiley's Pizza, which was three miles from the Kaluzas' house. An early October chill had set in, and the leaves had begun to change from green to shades ranging from deep mahogany to yellow and everything in between.

"This is my favorite time of year." Grace turned her face toward the sky and breathed in the crisp air.

"Not me. I'll take a hot day at the beach over jackets and pumpkin spice." Henry blew past her.

Recognizing a challenge when she saw one, Grace picked up speed. They raced down a rolling hill and around a bend in the road, and the countryside gave way to suburbia. More houses, more businesses, and more traffic crowded into smaller spaces, but Southpointe hadn't lost its small-town vibe.

"There it is." Henry pointed to a green building with red trim. "I can smell the oregano from here."

Grace's stomach growled in response. She pulled up alongside the shop and removed her helmet. "Do you think it's okay to leave our bikes here?"

He shrugged. "As long as we're not blocking the sidewalk."

"You're better off parking in back." The woman wore a shirt with a smiley face made out of pepperoni on the front, but she looked like she hadn't smiled in a couple decades.

"Thanks. We're new here." Grace angled her bike toward the road.

"The lot's around the corner," the woman said over her shoulder before disappearing through a side entrance.

Henry gave Grace a what-the-heck look and pedaled toward the back of the building, which turned out to be more difficult than either had anticipated. They ended up biking around the block before finding the parking area.

"Let's hope the rest of the people here are friendlier." She tucked her helmet under her arm.

Henry could not have agreed more. They entered the restaurant through the back door.

Music, voices, and laughter spilled out the moment he opened the door. The aroma of Italian spices, fresh-baked bread, and tomato sauce beckoned the twins inside. The place was smaller than it had appeared on the outside, with an engaging, homey feel.

A younger woman wearing the same smiley-face pepperoni shirt glanced up from filling napkin dispensers and smiled. "Sit wherever you'd like."

Henry and Grace exchanged glances. The place was packed full of teenagers—not that the twins had anything against kids their own age, but they weren't up for small talk with strangers.

"Back corner?" Grace nodded to a table set away from the rowdy crowd.

"Sounds good."

Her skin prickled under the weight of their glances, but she pretended to ignore the stares and whispers.

The young waitress handed them each a menu. "Are you new in town? I don't remember seeing either of you in here before."

"We're passing through." Henry glanced at the menu and then at Grace. "Half your favorite, half mine?"

She tapped her lips. "Actually, how would you feel about splitting an extra-large calzone?"

"I could be persuaded if we throw in some sausage and pepperoni."

"Deal, and two Cokes. Please."

"Got it." The waitress jotted their order down on her notepad. "I'll bring you an order of garlic bread while you're waiting."

One of the boys in a green Southpointe High School letterman jacket shot to his feet and shouted, "Five hundred thousand hits and climbing!"

The group of kids cheered.

A girl with jet-black hair and matching lips scowled. She looked to be about the same age as the others but sat apart from the rambunctious group.

The apparent ringleader leaned over her table. "What's the matter, *Morticia?* You disapprove of YouTube?"

Grace had seen scenes like this played out in bad teen movies but never in real life. Her heart broke for the girl. It couldn't be easy sitting alone in a restaurant crowded with one's classmates, but to be called out like that? She couldn't imagine the humiliation.

The Goth girl picked a green pepper from her pizza and popped it in her mouth. "I have nothing against YouTube. It's not the website's fault that you and your idiot brigade use it to shame other people."

Grace dipped her head to hide her grin.

Henry leaned closer. "Wow."

The guy narrowed his eyes. "You're lucky you're Maddison's sister."

"Oh, yeah, Peter, I'm so lucky." The girl dismissed him with a wave of her hand.

CHAPTER TWO

Henry dug into the calzone while keeping a wary eye on the group of football players. One on one, guys like that weren't bad, but together they became a case study in mob mentality.

"I can't believe she stood up to them like that." Grace glanced at the girl, wearing black from her Victorian collar to her combat boots.

"It took guts." *It also takes guts to dress like that in a small town.* "It would be best if we don't interview anyone here until they leave."

Grace glanced at the group of athletes and nodded.

Thankfully, the guys left and took their frenzied energy with them. A hush fell over the restaurant as if the walls needed a moment to catch their breath.

Henry locked eyes with the Goth, and to his surprise, she grinned.

"Sorry about Peter and his lackeys. Someone must have put too much sugar in their Kool-Aid." She motioned to the door through which the boys had exited.

Grace laughed. "I was impressed by the way you stood up to them."

"They don't scare me." She hitched a shoulder. "But I hate what all of this is doing to my sister."

"All of what?" the twins asked in unison.

The waitress refilled Henry's glass. "They're not from around here, Morgan. They probably haven't seen it."

The girl in black frowned, stood, and moved to an adjoining table. "There's a video of my older sister running screaming through the woods."

Grace's eyes widened.

"She claims she was being chased by the Green Man." Morgan pressed her lips into a tight line.

The twins glanced at each other and back at her.

"You've heard of the Green Man, right?"

Henry sat back in his chair. "Oddly enough, we're researching him while we're here."

"Whatever Maddison saw, it wasn't the Green Man. Old Man Robinson died before any of us were born, and he didn't glow." The waitress sighed. "It was probably Peter or Jake or one of their teammates."

Morgan frowned. "No. Peter swears they were in the tunnel hazing a would-be cheerleader."

Henry's mind spun with possibilities. They had stumbled into their chosen mystery. "What exactly happened to your sister?"

The girl smirked. "Besides going blonde, joining the cheer squad, and becoming a narcissist?"

Whoa. "I take it you two don't have a close sisterly bond?"

"Nope." Morgan turned her head, but he'd seen the hurt in her expression. "Maddison took a cheerleader recruit to the old Piney Fork Tunnel. Peter and Jake were supposed to scare the budding pom-pom shaker. It's a lame rite of passage. They heard Maddison screaming, and found her hysterical and going on about Charlie No-Face chasing her."

Grace furrowed her brow. "Where does the YouTube video fit in?"

"The next day someone posted a video of the entire ordeal." Morgan stared at her hands. "It wouldn't have been a big deal, but her hair extensions caught on a tree branch and came off."

The twins shared a questioning look, and Henry struggled to make sense of what she'd said. Speaking to Morgan was like visiting Spain after a couple of years of high school Spanish classes. While he'd understood most of the words, he'd missed their meaning, and he didn't have the necessary skills to respond.

Grace, however, didn't seem to have the same problem. Her mouth fell open. "How awful. And the video has half a million views?"

"And counting." Morgan pulled up the webpage and handed them her phone.

The video was exactly as she'd described it, but that didn't make it easier to watch. The girl on camera was genuinely terrified.

The corner of Morgan's mouth curled up before she forced it down. "It's almost as amusing as it is wrong."

The waitress folded her arms. "I don't think it was funny at all, and neither does my grandfather. He knew Mr. Robinson. Considered him a friend. All this nonsense won't let a good man rest in peace."

That tidbit pulled Henry's attention from the video to the waitress. "Your grandfather knew Raymond Robinson?"

"Yes, and he had the pictures to prove it. He and his friends picked Mr. Robinson up one night off the side of the road, and the two of them struck up a friendship that lasted decades."

"Would it be possible for us to meet your grandfather?" Grace's voice came out uneven, a sure sign she was conflicted about asking.

The waitress squinted as she hesitated.

Henry said, "We're working on a year-long research project investigating different local urban legends. We aren't out to sensationalize the story. We want to know the truth behind the myth."

"I'll ask him if he'd be willing to speak to you." She smiled. "I'm Cailey Canter."

"Henry and Grace Warner. Our parents are lecturing at the University of Pittsburgh this week." He sipped his drink and tried to act nonchalant despite his racing pulse. "It'd be great if he could meet with us in the next day or so."

"Cailey, the dishes are piling up...that is, if you're finished chatting with the customers." The sour-faced waitress from outside folded her arms.

"I'll see what I can do," she whispered as she cleared their plates before heading to the kitchen.

Morgan cocked her head. "Are you two in online college or something?"

"We're seniors in high school, but yes, most of our classes are college level and we take them online." Henry braced himself for a million questions.

"That's freaking awesome. I would sell my teeth to never set foot in a high school."

"After what I saw today, I don't blame you." Grace nodded knowingly. "I thought that kind of thing only happened in 80s movies."

"There are days when I'd swear John Hughes got his inspiration from Southpointe High." Morgan grinned. "Seriously though, you should talk to my sister after you meet with Mr. Canter. Compare notes. It might help convince her that she didn't have a run-in with the Green Man's ghost."

"Sure, if you think she'll speak to us." Grace glanced at Henry.

"I'd like to interview the other people who were there that night." He paused. "But I'd prefer to interview them individually."

The Goth girl grinned again. "Unfortunately for you, you saw two of them today. The loudmouthed jocks."

He'd suspected as much, but that didn't stop him from cringing. "And the other one?"

"Kylie was only at SHS for a week. After the incident, her parents enrolled her in private school." She continued, "Peter's the loud quarterback, and Jake's a wilder version of Peter."

Tossing his napkin on the table, Henry muttered, "Of course he is."

"Don't let their public personas scare you. They're nice guys, or at least, they used to be." She frowned and shook her head. "I could take you to the scene of the crime if you want."

Although the twins had planned to visit the Green Man Tunnel after lunch, they had expected to do it alone. Henry weighed the pros and cons of Morgan joining them. As a local, she'd have an easier time finding it, and could possibly spot anything that'd changed in the last week or so—definitely pros. Cons, he and Grace wouldn't be able to speak as freely in front of her. Plus, they had no way of knowing if she'd keep their investigation quiet. The last thing they needed was for people to either stonewall them or tell them what they thought they wanted to hear.

"That'd be great." Grace focused on her phone for a moment. "According to Google Maps, it's about a thirty-minute bike ride."

Morgan's mouth fell open. "Bike?"

Henry hadn't spent much time with kids his age, but when he did, their aversion to physical activity always surprised him. "It's only five miles or so."

Morgan motioned to her layers of black clothing. "I'm not dressed for biking. Plus, do you see this lily-white skin? Do you think I achieved my graveyard tan by spending afternoons in the sun?"

Grace laughed, Henry didn't. He folded his arms and waited for her to agree or bow out.

The girl narrowed her eyes. "You'll never find it without me. GPS gets it wrong."

"We can leave the bikes here," Henry suggested.

Grace gave him a goofy grin. *No kidding we can leave them here.*

The sour-faced waitress appeared out of nowhere. "The lot is for customers only."

Morgan gave the woman what could only be described as sad-puppy-face. "Agnes, can't you bend the rules just this once? They *are* customers."

"*Were* customers. Now they're loitering." She made a shooing motion. "Time to go. We have to clean up this mess and set up for the dinner rush."

The twins exchanged glances and stood.

Snickering, Morgan whispered, "Don't mind her. She's all snarl and no teeth."

"Regardless, I don't think we should leave our bikes here." Henry left enough cash to cover lunch and a nice tip for Cailey on the table.

"They won't fit in my car."

Grace said, "Why don't you meet us at our place in a half-hour?"

While his sister and Morgan exchanged contact information, Henry walked toward the back of the restaurant to find Cailey.

The young waitress met him at the kitchen door. "I was just coming to check on you. Did you need anything else?"

"Pen and paper to write down our contact information in case your grandfather agrees to speak to us."

"Oh, I almost forgot." She glanced over her shoulder at Agnes before pulling him away from the door. "He said he'd meet you tomorrow morning at nine. Give me your phone."

He handed her his cell and watched as she typed an address and phone number into the contacts. "Thanks."

She lowered her voice. "Don't thank me yet. He's pretty upset about Maddison's video stirring up so much fuss."

"Reassure him that we'll do everything we can to respect his friend's memory."

Five minutes later, the twins were pedaling along the side of the road, with Morgan following a few feet behind in her car. Smiling and waving at the beeping and passing cars, the girl seemed to relish causing a traffic jam.

"She likes to draw attention to herself." Grace glanced over her shoulder at the black Mini-Cooper.

Henry refused to turn his head. "The wrong kind of attention. This was a bad idea."

"I disagree. She may be over the top, but she knows the area and the people involved."

Henry lowered his voice. "For all we know, she filmed the video herself."

As if she'd overheard him, Morgan beeped her horn.

By the time they'd reached the Kaluzas' driveway, he'd made up his mind to bow out of visiting the tunnel. Between the traffic and the incessant beeping, he wasn't in any frame of mind to have company, let alone solve a mystery.

"Wait, you live in that?" Morgan pointed to the fifth wheel. "It's like what rock stars take on tour."

"They usually have luxury bus conversions. This is a fifth wheel." Grace parked her bike.

"I'll take your word for it." She continued to stare at the rig. "I've never seen an RV with parts sticking out like that."

"They're called slides." Grace unlocked the door. "Want to see inside?"

Henry was torn between insisting the girls stay outside and showing off their awesome home. As a general rule, the Warners rarely let guests into their personal space. Not that they were antisocial or anything, but they liked their privacy. On the other hand, he couldn't remember when the last time a non-RVer his own age was so excited about taking the tour.

They didn't stay inside long despite Morgan's awe and wonder. They ended the short tour back where they started, in the living room.

"Aw, come on. One movie." Morgan gave him the same sad-eyed expression she'd given the waitress.

"Another time. I'd like to see the tunnel before we lose the sun."

"Afraid you'll run into Charlie?" She drew her index finger across her neck and dropped her head to the side with her tongue hanging out.

He took a step back. Never in his life had he met someone who simultaneously intrigued and irritated him as much as this girl. "Hardly. It's easier to get the full picture in the daytime."

She smirked. "*Au contraire!* You won't understand how dark and frightening it is unless you see it at night. Part of the reason the legend lives on is because of the place that birthed it."

Grace glanced at them. "Why not go now? Find what we can in the daytime and make plans to go again at night."

Morgan shrugged. "Or we could just hang there for a while."

"We can't. We have plans tonight with our parents." His declaration seemed to surprise their new friend.

A flash of emotion crossed her face, and her shoulders slumped before she stiffened her spine. "Sure. Whatever. Let's go."

CHAPTER THREE

The Green Man Tunnel turned out to be made of concrete, covered in graffiti, and filled with rock salt. Not exactly fear-inspiring unless the visitor was frightened by bad spelling and horrible paint jobs.

Morgan led the twins to the entrance and took a bow. "I give you...the scariest place in Southpointe Township."

"It's *interesting*." Underwhelmed, Grace smiled to hide her lack of enthusiasm.

Henry gave Morgan a you've-got-to-be-kidding glare.

"What? I didn't dig the tunnel or paint the walls."

He folded his arms. "Explain something to me. How is it three teenagers were inside? It's full of salt, and the entrance is blocked."

Morgan mimicked his posture and gruff voice. "I wasn't there, but it's not hard to climb rock salt. I assume the guys broke in through the other side or climbed over the fencing before Maddison and Kylie arrived."

Grace positioned herself between them. "What he means is, how could two boys hide in there?"

"Oh. Easy. Watch." Morgan walked to the opening, scaled the fence, and scurried to the top of the pile of salt.

Turning to her brother, Grace whispered, "What's gotten into you?"

He raised his brows and shoulders at the same time.

"You're being rude." She glanced back into the tunnel and frowned. The girl seemed to have vanished. "Where did she go?"

"She's showing you how two people could have hidden in there, remember?" He took two long strides toward the tunnel.

She grabbed his arm. "I'm serious. What's wrong?"

"Something about her bugs me," he whispered harshly, subconsciously playing with his hair.

"Because you think she had something to do with this?"

"Maybe, maybe not." He let his head fall back and closed his eyes. "But I'd rather do our sleuthing without company from now on."

"Okay." Smirking, she walked past him.

He'd been acting strange ever since they'd walked into the pizza parlor that afternoon, but she couldn't decide if it was the mystery or the people involved that'd caused his mood to sour. One thing was certain: she needed him to snap out of it.

Henry had great instincts, and she couldn't ignore them, but she had seen everything he had, and nothing had set her Spidey senses tingling.

The twins climbed over the concrete blocks at the mouth of the tunnel. Once inside, salt crunched and shifted beneath their feet loud enough to alert Morgan of their presence. However, the girl remained hidden.

"Morgan?" Grace pressed her hand to the mound. The sand-like texture surprised her. She'd expected it to be coarser.

Henry scowled. "Ten to one she jumps out and tries to scare us."

"Can the snark, will you?" She shot him a dirty look. In their seventeen years together, she couldn't remember him having a reaction like this to another human being. Sure, he'd met people he didn't like, but he'd either avoided them or gone quiet.

Henry ignored her comment and her glare. "Morgan? Are you up there?"

No reply.

"I'm getting worried. It's entirely possible, if not probable, for a person to suffocate under a rock-salt cave-in."

He climbed over the chain link fence and scrambled a few feet up the side of the mound before sliding down in a shower of salt.

"It wasn't a challenge to prove me right." Grace laughed, although she dearly wished he'd come back to the legal side of the barricade. "Nor did I want you to trespass or suffocate under a ton of rock salt."

"My foot slipped." Henry glanced from the top of the pile to the edges and adjusted course. Rather than scaling the salt head-on, he used the tunnel wall for support and went over at the shortest point.

"Where's Henry?" Morgan said from behind her.

Grace turned and stared. "He went to find you."

"Well, that was dumb. I'm right here." She brushed bits of salt and white powder from her clothing.

"Henry! She's here!" Grace balled her fists at her sides. Maybe Henry's gruffness toward her was justified after all.

He muttered something from deep inside the tunnel. The sounds of falling salt and sliding boy echoed against the concrete walls.

"No! Don't come back over! Walk to the other end!" Morgan's eyes widened. "He's going to hurt himself." She pushed past Grace.

Before Morgan could climb the mound, Henry slid down the side and crashed against the fencing. He grunted on impact but shot to his feet as if he did that sort of thing every day. "Okay, cool. We know how Peter and what's-his-name likely got in."

"Jake." Grace folded her arms.

Henry hopped over the fence and ran his hand through his hair. "Jake. Right."

Morgan dipped her chin to hide her smile.

She looked from one to the other, and the proverbial lightbulb came on over Grace's head. The Goth girl liked her brother. *That's interesting.*

"How does the hazing work, exactly?" He turned his back to them and studied the tunnel.

Morgan sighed. "Maddison brings the new recruits out here and has them spend fifteen minutes alone in the tunnel with no cell phone or flashlight."

"In front of the fence?" Grace pulled her phone from her pocket and took several photos from the mouth of the tunnel.

"I'm not sure. Probably. I mean, God forbid one of them chips a nail or gets their shoes dirty."

"The tunnel wasn't in the video." He turned in a full circle. They were surrounded by trees, and they all looked alike—thin, tall, and losing leaves. "There aren't any other landmarks. Do you know where it was filmed?"

"Not exactly, but Maddison usually parks in the same pull-off we did." She nodded to her car.

Grace took a couple of pics of the parking area on the other side of the two-lane road. "She wouldn't have run this way. The hill is too steep."

"There's a creek on the other side of the pull-off." Morgan frowned. "I don't remember if her shoes were wet that night, but that's the only way to go, really. Plus, they found her hair extensions in a tree."

Henry walked across the street to the parking area with the girls following. "The water isn't deep."

Grace turned and surveyed the lay of the land. The tunnel had a steep hill on one side and a road with a second tunnel on the other. Maddison likely wouldn't have run uphill, nor would she have followed the road back toward town. The one-lane tunnel was dangerous for cars, let alone pedestrians. However, she could have run north along the road in hopes of meeting a passing motorist. "Why would she have run into the forest instead of on the pavement?"

Morgan shrugged. "Fear will make people do crazy things." After a moment she added, "I guess."

Henry played through the most logical scenarios. The alleged Green Man had come at Maddison from one of two directions—the road, or from the vegetation surrounding the parking area. *That's it.* "Do a lot of people know Maddison brings new cheerleaders out here?"

The girl's shoulders tensed but she laughed. "Only the entire squad, the football team, and anyone who has overheard one of the pom-pom shakers talking about it. So, like, the whole school."

Grace met his gaze and grinned. "You're thinking they waited in the bushes for Kylie to leave."

"I am." He pointed north, away from the tunnels. "If it were me, I'd have come from that direction to force her to run into the forest or through the second tunnel."

Morgan stared at them with wide eyes. "You two are good at this."

"It's an educated guess. We won't know for sure until we speak to Maddison." Henry blushed and strode to the bushes.

Grace followed closely and lowered her voice. "What are you looking for?"

He grinned. "Heck if I know. Broken branches, footprints, maybe video equipment."

"Are you trying to impress her?"

He hitched a shoulder. "What's the point? We're leaving in a few days."

"In case you missed it, we have these fancy new tools called computers and cell phones and the internet. It's the age of technology."

Henry glanced back toward Morgan.

Leaning against the rear hatch of her Mini, she watched with an amused expression.

"I'm not discussing this now."

Grace lowered her voice. "She can't hear us."

"Regardless, subject closed." He took a few steps away from the parking area and stopped. "Hey, Grace?"

She sighed. "Yes, brother dear?"

"Does that look like a green handprint to you?"

"It's green, but I'm not sure if it's a handprint." Pulling her phone from her pocket, she moved closer and took several close-up shots of the smeared paint.

Henry wiped it with the tip of his finger, but it didn't budge. It did, however, come off the bark when he scratched it. "This is one of those times when it'd be nice to have a CSI lab."

"No kidding." She ran her thumbnail over the substance. "It could be makeup."

"Let's not mention this to Morgan. I'd rather hear what her sister has to say about the incident first."

"I agree." She made a show of wiping her hands on her jeans as she walked back to the car. "Tree sap."

"Um, yeah. It's pretty common on trees." The girl laughed. "Find anything else?"

"Nothing useful." Henry shoved his hands into his back pockets and rocked on the balls of his feet. "It's getting late. Would you like to have dinner with us?"

Grace did a double take.

"Oh, um." Morgan dipped her chin. "I don't think so."

"Why?" She knew she should stay out of it, but the girl's reply had shocked the common sense out of her.

"Parents." Morgan snorted and turned her head. "They take one look at me and freak out."

"Not our parents." She glanced at her brother for backup.

"Grace is right, but I understand if you'd rather not come."

What was I thinking? Henry had asked himself the same question a hundred times in the ten minutes it'd taken Morgan to drop them off at home. To make matters worse, Grace had given him a steady rotation of sad smiles, thumbs-ups, and playful nudges since his epic rejection.

"Dice the garlic a little finer." He leaned over his sister's shoulder and inspected her work.

"The recipe calls for a rough chop." She frowned and set the knife down. "It's my night to cook. You don't have to help me, unless..."

"For crying out loud, will you stop?" He slung an arm over her shoulder. "It's not like I asked her on a date."

Her eyes widened. "You didn't? Hmm. Then what do you call it when you invite a girl to dinner?"

"Manners." He smirked. "One, there's no sense in dating before college. Two, I don't even know if I like her. And three, I know enough about girls to not ask one to eat dinner with my family on our first date."

"What's this about a first date?" Faith stood in the doorway looking rather pale.

On the other hand, Ethan's grin put the Cheshire Cat to shame.

Henry groaned. "Nothing. It wasn't a date. Grace and I met a local girl, and I asked if she wanted to have dinner with us. I was being *polite*."

Their parents exchanged glances.

"Does this girl have a name?" Faith sounded as if she'd swallowed an insect.

"Her name's Morgan." Grace tossed the chicken into the wok and gave it a stir. "She's tied up in our latest mystery."

Ethan Warner put on his best courtroom face and used his lawyer voice. Too bad he couldn't take the twinkle out of his eyes since it ruined the effect. "Exactly how is a teenaged girl involved with a man who passed away twenty years ago?"

"That's privileged information." Henry folded his arms.

"There's no such thing in this house." Their mother turned to Grace, expecting an answer.

"It seems someone pranked Morgan's sister by pretending to be Charlie No-Face." She shrugged. "On a positive note, we have an appointment in the morning with a man who claims to have personally known Raymond Robinson."

Sighing, Henry slid onto a barstool. "So much for investigator confidentiality."

"Mothers are exempt from such rules and regulations." Faith Warner kissed his cheek and headed for her bedroom.

Ethan loosened his tie and sat beside Henry. "Son, if there's anything you'd like to discuss—"

"Nope. Nothing. Like I said, I was being polite." Most of the time, he loved his life. However, between the close-knit family and the closer living quarters, there were times when he longed for privacy.

"I know, Dad," Henry replied with a quick nod and a flash of a smile.

Seeming to pick up on his distress, Grace said, "Are we still on for the *Night of the Living Dead* marathon?"

"Marathon, no. One movie, yes." He stood and yawned. "I have back-to-back lectures tomorrow starting at seven in the much-too-early morning."

"One movie sounds great. I have reading to do before Friday." She turned and added veggies to the wok.

She nodded toward their parents' room. "Go change. It'll be ready in a just a few minutes."

As soon as their father disappeared down the hallway, Henry rested his head on the bar top. He would have banged it a couple times, but the noise would have drawn their mother's attention.

Grace tapped his arm. "What do we know?"

"Never to discuss dating anywhere within a hundred yards of Faith and Ethan Warner?"

She laughed and turned her attention back to the stir-fry. "Point taken, but what do we know about the case?"

He propped his chin in his hand. "The restless spirit of Ray Robinson could be haunting the woods near the tunnel, but it's far more likely a teenager's behind it."

"And the entire seven-hundred-plus students at Southpointe High School are suspects."

"Seven-hundred-plus, minus four. The two guys from the diner, Kylie, and Maddison have alibis." He stood and pulled four plates from the cupboard. "I'm adding Agnes the angry waitress to the list."

Grace giggled. "What was wrong with her? I've never seen such bad customer service."

"We weren't technically customers when she tossed us out." He waggled his brows and set the table.

"We should come up with a list of questions to ask Mr. Canter in the morning."

"Good idea. From what Cailey said, he seems protective of his friend's memory. We'll need to be careful not to upset him."

"I'd like to see the tunnel after dark." Grace placed the stir-fry on the table. "We should meet up with Morgan tomorrow night."

His mouth went dry at the thought. "I didn't get her number."

She shot him a triumphant smile. "I did."

CHAPTER FOUR

Carl Canter lived in a modest home on a not-so-modest piece of property near the Monongahela River. At first glance, the man appeared to be in his seventies. The droopy-eyed hound sleeping at his feet seemed just as old in dog years.

Henry took one look at the shotgun resting across the man's lap and stopped pedaling a few yards from the house. "Mr. Canter?"

"Who's asking?" He didn't stand as much as he pushed himself to his feet.

"Henry and Grace Warner, sir. Your granddaughter Cailey told us you agreed to speak to us this morning."

"I'm speaking, aren't I?" The man's back bent at such a sharp angle, he had to lift his chin to meet Henry's gaze.

Grace hopped off her bike. "Is it okay if we join you?"

Mr. Canter made a disgusted sound and fell back into his rocker.

"I'll take that as a yes," Henry muttered as he walked his bicycle up the drive.

The hound dog opened an eye, sniffed the air, and went back to sleep.

"What do you want with me?" He furrowed his bushy brows.

Grace opened her mouth to speak.

"I remember now. You're the kids wanting to interview me about old Ray Robinson?" Mr. Canter shook his head. "Such a shame you young people can't let him rest in peace."

"We hope to do just that, but we need your help. It'll only take a few minutes." She smiled, but her expression wilted when she looked at the gun.

The old man set the gun aside. "Don't let the weapon bother you. I ran out of shells ten years ago."

Henry sat on the top porch step and looked out over the rolling hills. "Beautiful property you have here."

"Twenty-seven acres bought and paid for by coal mining." A series of wet, shoulder-wracking coughs stole the man's breath. "Guess you could say my lungs were part of the payment."

Grace met her brother's gaze and frowned.

Henry had no reply. Somehow, he didn't think Mr. Canter would appreciate his sympathy. "How did you meet Raymond Robinson?"

"I was about your age the first time I laid eyes on old Ray." He stared off as if the memory had taken him to another place and time. "A bunch of us were determined to find Charlie No-Face. We spent every weekend night for over a month driving the country roads looking for him." He shrugged. "One night we found him."

"What happened?" Grace sat and ran her hand over the dog's orange coat.

"My friend stopped and offered Ray some beer. It took us a good ten minutes of coaxing to get him to talk to us, but when he did..." Mr. Canter grinned. "We couldn't get him to stop. He told us his story. How he'd touched a downed trolley line when he was a boy. How he earned a little money by making wallets and doormats from old tires. And how he liked to walk at night so he *wouldn't* scare people."

"Did he?" Henry paused but couldn't find a polite way to ask. "Did he scare you?"

"First time I laid eyes on old Ray, I screamed like a little girl caught in a spider web." Mr. Canter's laughter morphed into more coughing.

Grace said, "Can I get you a glass of water?"

"It won't help, but thank you for the offer." He cleared his throat and fell back into his memories. "All of us were nervous. You have to know we'd heard the rumors about Ray. Most of the stories about him weren't true, but they got it right about his face."

"What was he like?" Grace frowned. "Not physically. What was he like as a person?"

Mr. Canter stared at her for a long moment. "You can't separate the two and understand the whole man."

She couldn't have agreed more. "That's a good point."

He flashed her a toothless grin. "Ray's eyes were missing, and his eyelids were sealed shut. He had a hole where his nose would have been, and his mouth looked like it had too much skin hanging off it. Kind of like Bessie."

The dog lifted her head at the mention of her name, but the extra flesh hanging from her face still rested on the porch.

"By the time I met him, he'd suffered more than any man should have." Mr. Canter glanced down at his gnarled hands. "Times were different back when Ray was a boy. Families kept kids who were different out of sight. He never complained, but I imagine he was lonely. I think that was why he took to walking at night, but some folks were cruel to him."

"I understand he was struck by cars several times." Grace's voice came out strained.

"He blamed himself for the accidents. Said a man walking on the side of a dark road is bound to get run over now and then. But he never could understand why folks would beat him up or offer to give him a ride and dump him off in a strange place with no way to get home."

Henry dipped his chin. He'd read every article he could find on Charlie No-Face and he'd seen a handful of grainy photographs, but nothing had prepared him for the emotion in Mr. Canter's voice when he discussed his friend.

"I don't think I would have come through it at all, but old Ray never lost his spirit. He learned to read braille, worked as best he could, and made quite a few friends over the years." Canter shook his head the way people do when remembering better times. "What he lacked in looks, he more than made up for in heart."

Grace wiped her eyes. "Did you see him often?" Henry touched his sister's arm to share some of her empathy.

"Once a week for a few years, then I was sent to Vietnam. I looked him up when I came back stateside, and we talked or visited once or twice a month until he died."

Henry said, "Do you have any idea why the old Piney Fork Tunnel—"

"No. I asked him once. He claimed to have never been there." The old man's voice rose. "And this business with that cheerleader? It's nonsense."

"We agree with you one hundred percent and are determined to put an end to it." Henry's voice was firm, and he meant every word. Not only had the villain terrorized Morgan's sister, but the legend of Charlie No-Face had also taken on a new life. It was time people knew the truth about Raymond Robinson.

"It's definitely a hoax. All we have to do is prove it and expose the person or people behind it." Grace pulled out her phone. "We found what looks like green paint or makeup on a tree near the tunnel."

Canter squinted at the photo. "See that you do. The man suffered enough in life. He doesn't need his memory..." The old man's voice trailed off, and he bowed his head.

Grace rested her hand on his. "I'm sorry if we upset you."

"It wasn't you that upset me." He fought his way through another round of coughing.

"All right. That's enough questions. You two need to leave." The screen door opened and Agnes, the waitress from the diner, stepped onto the porch. "Carl, you need your oxygen."

The twins scrambled to their feet. Henry's heart leapt into his throat as if telling him to run away from the woman. Even the hound dog jumped off the porch and slunk under the stairs.

"I know what I need and when I need it." Mr. Canter caught Henry's gaze and winked, unseen by the woman behind him.

"Thank you for your time." Grace backed away from the house.

"Nonsense. We're just getting started. Sit down and let me tell you about the time old Ray and I went out for Halloween." He patted his thigh. "Bessie, come."

The old hound dog returned to her place at her master's feet.

The twins exchanged a glance.

Henry said, "We...um...don't want to take up too much of your day."

"I'll let you know when you've outstayed your welcome." He pointed to the porch. "Sit and let an old man talk."

Grace plopped down and gave Bessie a belly rub.

"We can stay as long as you'd like." His stomach growled in protest.

"Then I'm staying too." Agnes sat in a rocking chair and folded her arms.

"I'm hungry. Would you mind whipping up some sandwiches with the left-over ham?" Mr. Canter might have spoken to Agnes, but he winked at Henry again. "While you're at it, make enough for my new friends."

"Anything else *while I'm at it?*" Her words came out in a bark, but her smile softened the effect.

"Something to wash them down with."

"Would you like some help?" Grace moved as if to stand, but the woman shook her head.

"I can handle a half-dozen sandwiches and a few glasses of lemonade."

They say first impressions mean the most, but if the twins hadn't looked past the man's gruff exterior, they would have missed out. Mr. Canter had a mischievous streak, not to mention it was fun to see Agnes smile. Henry had the feeling it didn't happen often. The twins wanted to hear about his time with the real Charlie No-Face, and he was more than happy to share his memories. They spent the next three hours sitting on the porch eating the world's best ham sammies and listening to an old man reminisce about a dear friend.

"If you ask me, you need to look into where Morgan Monaghan was the night of the incident." Agnes had gone quiet after lunch, so quiet Henry had almost forgotten she was there. Unfortunately, she hadn't stayed that way. "The girl's as much of a menace as that sister of hers. If you ask me, the entire Monaghan family should have been run out of town years ago."

Mr. Canter eyed her for a long moment. "Just because the family has more money than God doesn't mean they're bad people."

"And how do you think they got all that money? Off the backs of the people in this town, that's how." Agnes turned to the twins. "Morgan's father's as tight as a camel's backside in a sandstorm except where Maddison is concerned."

Grace bit her lip to hold back a chortle.

Henry knew an opportunity when he saw one. The woman worked in a pizza place frequented by high schoolers and she was nosey, two facts he planned to use to his advantage. "Morgan did seem overly interested in helping us solve the mystery. I chalked it up to not having many friends."

His sister's eyes widened, but she remained quiet.

Agnes took the bait. "Don't let all that black clothing fool you. She has plenty of friends. You don't grow up in Southpointe with her last name without acquiring people."

He ignored Grace's frown and pressed on. "The football players didn't seem overly fond of her."

"Boy, for someone who's trying to solve a mystery, you miss a lot." The waitress smirked and folded her arms. "Morgan dated one of those football players for nearly two years before he threw her over for her sister."

"Peter." Grace sat up straighter. "Morgan dated Peter?"

Agnes nodded.

Henry tried to imagine the Goth girl with the jock but couldn't make the pieces fit. "I'm confused."

"That makes two of us." Mr. Canter barked a laugh.

"She's smart, too. Knows all about computers." Agnes's face twisted in disgust. "I bet her smarty-pants friends in the science club could have rigged something up to make one of them glow green."

The old man's mouth fell open. "They made a kid glow?"

Grace sighed. "We don't know if it was a teenager in the costume, but yes, the person had a green aura around them in the video."

"It's possible the glow was added to the footage later. We won't know until we interview Maddison Monaghan." Henry made a mental note to study the video again.

"Regardless, I'm listening to my gut, and it's telling me Morgan is the culprit. Who else could pull it off, and embarrass their arch rival at the same time?" The woman's face soured. "She had t-shirts made, for crying out loud."

The twins exchanged glances before turning back to Agnes.

"T-shirts?" Henry had no idea what she'd referred to, nor did he think he wanted to know.

"This morning, I saw one of Morgan's friends—short girl, glasses, always looks like she needs a shower—was wearing a Green Man t-shirt."

He scratched his jaw. "Are you sure it was Green Man and not Green Day?"

"Many cultures have a nature god called the Green Man," Grace added.

Mr. Canter chuckled. "And here I thought Ray and aliens were the only green men out there."

Agnes's frown deepened. "Listen, you two seem like nice kids. Be careful around those Monaghan girls. Maddie is as mean as a badger, and Morgan? Let's just say, she's just as mean but much smarter."

As if sensing the twins' discomfort with the topic, Mr. Canter yawned wide enough for Henry to see his tonsils. "If we're finished discussing the latest episode of *As the Pizza Burns*, it's time for my nap."

"I should get going. My shift starts in an hour." Agnes helped the man to his feet. She glanced at the twins. "Keep an eye on Morgan Monaghan. She's involved in this somehow."

Henry stood and offered Mr. Canter his hand. "It was nice meeting you, sir. I enjoyed hearing about Raymond Robinson."

The old man's grip was surprisingly strong. "Not many young folks look you in the eye, let alone know the value of a firm handshake."

"We aren't like most kids." Grace held out her hand. "We'll do your friend proud."

Canter pulled her in for a half-hug. "You two come back and visit any time."

"We're only in town for a few more days, but we'll visit again before we go." Henry walked toward his bike but turned back to Agnes. He had a hunch she'd do anything to help Carl Canter. "Will you let us know if you hear anything else about the video or the people who filmed it?"

"I will if it'll put an end to this nonsense, but your best bet is to be at the pizza parlor when school gets out at three."

He pressed his hand to his stomach. "Come to think of it, I could eat again."

"Sit in the corner booth closest to the kitchen. You can see the entire place from there." Agnes grinned. At least, he thought it was meant to be a grin. It looked more like a snarl.

"Thanks for your help." Henry hopped on his bike.

Grace made it to the end of the long driveway before she turned her head and stared.

"What?" Henry knew the conversation about Morgan had upset her, but he chose to play dumb.

"You can't believe that Morgan has anything to do with this just because that bitter old woman said so."

"It's too early to tell." He pushed ahead, trying to gain some momentum before climbing the next hill.

She huffed and picked up the pace.

"Come on, Gracie. We may not have been at this long, but we shouldn't rule anyone out just because we like them."

"*We.* True." She glanced in his direction. "It was smart to make an ally of Agnes, but she's so negative. I don't think we can take anything she says at face value."

"Everything is hearsay until corroborated by overlapping layers of proof." He winked and pedaled harder. "Hurry up. There's a large double-meat pizza with my name on it at the restaurant."

CHAPTER FIVE

The afterschool crowd was packed into the pizza place like anchovies in a can. The tables and booths had long since filled, but that didn't stop the steady stream of kids. As instructed, the twins had seated themselves at the corner table closest to the kitchen. It *did* have the best view of the busy dining area. However, Agnes had failed to mention the red vinyl booth sat two feet higher than the floor. It was like eating dinner on a stage.

Grace slumped her shoulders and tried to blend in, which shouldn't have been a problem, considering her cheeks were the same color as the booth.

Henry kept his gaze on the door as he wolfed down his sixth slice of pizza. "Agnes was right about the table. I can see everything from here."

"And every*one* can see us!" she whispered harshly as she tried to disappear into the sticky vinyl.

"Relax. It's not like we have to see any of these people again after Saturday —" His eyes bugged. "Holy smokes."

Grace followed his gaze to a group of girls standing by the entrance. "Please don't tell me you're turning into one of *those* guys."

He glanced at her with a yeah-right look. "While I do appreciate beauty, their shirts blew me away, not their legs."

She covertly stared. "Agnes wasn't kidding."

Each of the girls wore a t-shirt with a cartoon-like image of Ray Robinson. Two had I heart Charlie No-Face written across the front, while the other three read I Saw the Green Man - Ask Me Where.

Leaning closer, Henry whispered, "Where on earth did they get those?"

Grace went to the encyclopedia of all things—Google. The second entry on the search results page took her to a link to buy the t-shirts. "Someone's selling them online. There are a half-dozen different sayings to choose from."

He took the phone from her and scrolled through the website. "It's a print-on-demand service. They're also selling coffee mugs, phone cases, and—"

"Leggings." She wrinkled her nose. "It's one thing to pull a prank. It's another to make money off it."

"I agree. It's wrong, all kinds of wrong." Henry clicked around on the site. "The sellers call themselves 'I Bleed Green' but have no external website or contact info listed."

A loud cheer went up from Peter's crew. Most of the boys were staring at their phones. Some laughed, some shouted and slapped each other's shoulders, but all of them grinned like they'd found the golden ticket to the chocolate factory.

"What do you think that's about?" Grace cringed, blocking her face with her hand. She'd felt unsafe a handful of times while solving mysteries, but in those incidents, she'd come face to face with a monster or a gun or a monster with a gun. Never had she felt uneasy in a restaurant full of people, but the boys' frenzied energy made her skin crawl.

"No idea, but it can't be good."

Morgan Monaghan walked through the door in all her white-faced, flowy-black-dress glory. She took one look around the room, frowned, and strolled to the twins' booth. "Afternoon, Warners."

"Hi." Grace scooted over to make room for her to sit. "I love your dress. It'd be awesome for a Renaissance Fair."

"Why, thank you. I'm rather fond of it myself. I call it 'medieval vamp chic.'" Morgan didn't sit. She perched on the red vinyl like a giant raven waiting to swoop down on her prey. "I suppose you've heard."

"Heard what?" Henry sat back and folded his arms.

"There's another video." The girl inspected her chipped nail polish.

The twins glanced at each other and back to her.

Morgan pretended to ignore them and everyone else in the room, but judging by the tension in her shoulders and the tightness around her mouth, she was keenly aware of the tension and excitement.

Grace took her phone back from Henry and searched the internet for the latest video. The grainy images and camera angles looked the same as in Maddison's, but the person who'd posted the footage had added thought bubbles and graphics—*insulting* thought bubbles and graphics. "I wouldn't have thought it possible, but this is meaner than the first one."

Henry sucked in a breath. "Who's the girl?"

"A freshman cheerleader." Morgan hitched a shoulder and stole a piece of pepperoni from their pizza. "I don't know her."

Grace scrolled to the comments below the video and gasped. "They've set up a fundraising site."

"For what?" Henry looked as if he'd swallowed a garlic clove.

"They say they'll post a video for every two hundred and fifty dollars they raise." This time Morgan helped herself to an entire slice of the pie.

Henry watched in mild amusement. Despite what they'd heard, Grace still thought he liked the Goth. Usually, no one came between him and his food.

"Any idea who filmed it or who's selling those?" Grace nodded at the girls wearing the Charlie No-Face t-shirts.

"Not a clue." She scowled. "A girl in my physics class had on a pair of Green Man leggings. I've never seen anything as disturbing as dozens of face-less faces stretched across someone's butt."

"When did Maddison's video first go live?" Henry asked while typing furiously on his phone.

"Three days ago." Morgan grabbed his glass and finished his soda.

He arched a brow at her, shook his head, and continued typing. "The shirts take three to six business days to ship, plus the time it takes to receive the item. The seller must have set all of this up before the first video went viral."

"Maybe it's all related, maybe it's not." She glanced around the room and scowled. "Hey, Warners? Any reason you chose to sit at this table?"

Henry smirked. "Is there a problem?"

"Not yet, but there will be in five...four...three..."

Grace peeked around Morgan and caught sight of a band of angry-looking cheerleaders marching in their direction. The blonde at the apex of the V formation was the girl from the first video—Maddison Monaghan.

The queen bee flipped her perfect curls over her shoulder and folded her arms. "You're sitting in our spot."

Morgan made a show of searching the tabletop and the underside and shrugged. "I don't see your name or a reserved sign."

"Ha-ha, *Morticia*. I'd keep searching, though. You might find your sense of humor under there with the boogers and dried-out gum." Maddison flicked her hand in the twins' direction. "Take your new friends and move."

Grace's heart raced. Not only were the group of cheerleaders glaring, but the entire restaurant had gone silent.

The Goth girl scooted in farther, rested her back against Grace's side, and stretched her legs out. "The Warners were here first. It's their table. I just joined them. And why would you put your boogers and gum under the table? That's gross."

Henry watched the spectacle with an expression he'd learned from their father—stoic courtroom face. Anyone who didn't know him might think he was bored, but he was likely studying teenaged-girls' behavior in their natural habitat.

"I said move." Maddison shoved her sister's legs.

Grace opened her mouth to concede.

"Join us. I'd like to talk to you." Henry seemed to surprise them when he spoke.

The cheerleaders at the back of the bunch exchanged anxious glances, but Maddison didn't appear to have a nervous bone in her body. She looked him over from head to toe, glanced at Morgan, and a slow smile formed on her lips.

Grace didn't trust the smile or the girl wearing it. In fact, she wanted nothing to do with Maddison or her friends.

The blonde dismissed her posse with the same wrist-flick she'd tried to use on the twins. The other girls scattered like feathers in the wind, flitting and floating to various tables.

Morgan rolled her eyes and sat up straighter. "Maddie, this is Henry and Grace. Henry and Grace, this is Mad Maddie from Mean-girl-burgh. Don't let her blonde curls and long lashes fool you. They're both as fake as her smile."

Maddison ignored her sister and turned her full wattage on Henry. Twirling her hair around her finger, she dipped her chin and lowered her voice to a purr. "What did you want to talk to me about?"

To his credit, he didn't swoon or drool or trip over his words. Maintaining an interested but 'not interested' expression, Henry said, "The night the video was filmed."

She pushed out her lower lip. "Really? You have Maddison Monaghan's complete and undivided attention, and that's what you want to discuss?"

Rolling her eyes, Morgan whispered, "Referring to yourself in the third person? You can cut the crap. Henry's not going to ask you to homecoming. He's a good guy trying to find out who's making money off the videos."

Grace glanced around the room. The noise level hadn't returned to its previous volume. Most of the kids were either sneaking looks in their direction or openly staring, but none stared as hard as Peter.

"It's no use. I've asked everyone, and nobody's talking." Maddie slumped her shoulders and slid into the booth. "I don't care about the video anymore. I just want to talk to the person who filmed it. They had to have seen the same thing I did."

Peter motioned toward the table, and he and the boy with the icy blue eyes stared. The two stood and exchanged quick words.

Grace wasn't sure which was worse, Maddison believing she'd had a run-in with an actual monster or the actual monster about to have a run-in with Henry. She met his gaze and slid her eyes toward the angry football players. He nodded a fraction of an inch and turned his attention back to Maddison.

"Maybe you're asking the wrong people the wrong questions." Morgan smirked.

Henry said, "We've been to the tunnel. From what I can tell, the person came from the bushes along the north side of the parking area."

Maddison wrinkled her nose. "North?"

"The side farthest from the tunnel."

She nodded. "I was watching for Kylie to come back across the road. Charlie No-Face came up behind me making these awful moaning sounds."

He scrubbed his hand over the back of his neck. "Maddison, we found green paint on one of the trees near the pull-off. Whoever chased you into the woods wasn't Raymond Robinson."

"Who?" She glanced from her sister to Grace, and back to Henry.

Grace lowered her voice. "Raymond Robinson was a real person who suffered a tragic accident as a child. In the 60s, people would find him walking along the highways at night. That was how the legend of Charlie No-Face started."

Maddison twisted her lips to the side. "That can't be right, or they would have named him Ray No-Face."

Henry chuckled. "It doesn't have the same ring to it, but Grace is right. I can show you articles about Mr. Robinson and his part in the myth."

The color drained from her face. "No, you don't understand. That *thing* I saw—it *glowed*."

"Do you remember anything else about the...about what you saw? What was he wearing? Was he tall? Did you see where he went?"

Morgan sighed and opened her mouth to speak, but Grace poked her in the side. They needed information, and Maddison was their best source. She wouldn't let the Monaghans' sibling rivalry get in the way of solving the mystery.

"He was tall." Maddie furrowed her brow. "Kinda big. Not fat, but broad-shouldered. His face...looked like melted wax."

Henry nodded. "Anything else?"

"I was so scared." Maddison dipped her chin and sniffled.

Red-faced and tense, Peter strode to the booth and slammed his hands on the tabletop. "Are you upsetting my girlfriend?"

The guy with the blue eyes stood behind him snarling.

Grace startled, Morgan rolled her eyes, and Maddie gasped. Henry, on the other hand, didn't flinch.

"I asked you a question." The football player leaned across Maddison to put his face in Henry's line of vision.

"I heard you." He remained in place. "And no, I'm not upsetting anyone, but you are."

The guy glanced at the girls as if seeing them for the first time. Unfortunately, he didn't react well to being called out. "Look, I don't know who you are—"

Maddison laid her hand on Peter's arm. "Stop it. He's trying to help find the person who filmed the video."

The blue-eyed boy smirked. "What's he going to do that we can't?"

Morgan gave him a not-so-playful nudge. "Not everything can be solved with fists and shouting, Jake."

He opened his mouth to reply but snapped it shut and glanced away.

While neither of the football players could have been the one holding the camera, they'd certainly seemed to enjoy the videos. Grace wouldn't have been surprised to learn that Peter had put his teammates up to pranking the girls.

"Great. Then he should come out with us tonight." Peter stood upright and folded his arms. "The jerks with the fundraising page hit their goal today. They'll be looking for their next victim."

Henry glanced at Grace. They shared a silent conversation of "Should we go" before they said in unison, "What time?"

<hr>

"I don't like it." Grace pulled her black beanie over her ears and buttoned her jacket.

"I don't either, but it's our best shot at figuring out what's going on." Henry checked the time and frowned. "We have to hurry if we're going to get there before everyone else."

She grabbed her bike and walked it around the RV. "Think about it. The bad guys are going to want to get there early, too. They're going to see us and change their plans."

"Maybe, but it's a chance I'm willing to take." He tossed her a roll of duct tape. "Cover your reflectors."

Grace arched a brow. "No way. I'm not riding six miles at dusk on a country road with no reflectors on my bike. You know what happened to Ray Robinson. What makes you think we won't get mowed down?"

"Good point. Put the roll in your bag. We'll tape up when we're closer." Henry climbed onto his bike adjusted his drawstring backpack and pedaled away without a backward glance.

"Don't worry about me. I'll catch up," she muttered to herself.

The air had grown colder since they'd ridden home to change clothes and grab a few sleuthing supplies. Between the evening dew, the autumn chill, and Henry's ridiculous do-or-die speed, the wind cut straight through to Grace's bones. If they did manage to find the Charlie No-Face impersonator, they'd likely be too frozen to do anything about it.

Henry looked over his shoulder and grinned. "Perk up, Gracie. We're going to catch this guy."

"I'm too cold to be perky."

"I thought you loved the fall?" He swept his arm toward the trees. "Look at the leaves. I can practically smell the pumpkin spice lattes. It makes me want to sing *The Sound of Music!*"

And that was what he did, at the top of his lungs, off-key.

"You're a goofball." She laughed and came up beside him. "But a brave goofball. How did you stay so calm when Peter got in your face?"

"Who says I was calm?" He snickered. "I pulled a page from Dad's playbook and imagined myself in a courtroom interviewing a hostile witness."

"Ah, the old 'look 'em in the eye and pray you remembered your antiperspirant' routine," she managed to say between heavy breaths.

"You know it," Henry said casually, barely winded.

"How did you get in such good shape?" Grace panted.

"I greased my wheels. I think yours might have a little extra resistance." He chuckled with his tongue out as he pushed harder to go up a short but steep hill.

"We're switching bikes on the way back!" she insisted, standing as she pedaled faster and harder.

"Fine. I should have done yours, too," Henry admitted.

The sky darkened, and the scenery became more sinister. Nothing tangible, just a feeling. No wonder Morgan had insisted they should see the tunnel after nightfall. A car passed them from the opposite direction, forcing Grace to turn her head or go temporarily blind from the lights. Her front tire skidded off the shoulder, and she hit the brakes harder than she'd intended. A shot of adrenaline flooded her bloodstream a half-second before she lost control and spilled onto the ground. She rolled and slid to a stop. The bike fell over the embankment and wedged against a fence.

Sweating and gasping for breath, she lay there, trying to decide if she'd been hurt. She slowly stood and brushed herself off.

"Are you okay?" Henry circled back to her.

"I landed in the dirt." She reached over the embankment and dragged her bike up by the back tire until it was on level ground. "Nothing hurt but my wheel and pride." She tightened the drawstrings on her backpack and glanced around. "Are we close?"

"Yeah." He hopped off his bike. "And for the record, you were right about the duct tape. I didn't realize how dark it would be out here."

"What? Would you repeat that?" She cupped her ear. "I don't think I heard you."

"You. Were. Right." He laughed and checked his phone. "The tunnel is about a quarter of a mile away. We should ditch the bikes and walk the rest of the way."

"Good idea. I either messed up my bike, or I'm shaking too hard to ride. Maybe both." She squinted at her front tire but couldn't tell if she'd damaged it. They didn't have time to check. They needed to go.

The twins followed the path of the creek toward the parking area for what seemed like much farther than the GPS had suggested. Darkness had blanketed the sparse forest, and a hush had settled over the area. Grace desperately wanted to use the flashlight app, but it would have alerted anyone lurking in the trees.

Her foot sank in the mud and water rushed into her shoe. "Dang it!"

"*Shh,*" he whisper-shouted. "What's wrong?"

"Stepped too close to the creek." Something moved in her peripheral vision, and she turned in time to catch a glimpse of a faint green light and someone weaving their way through the forest. "Look!" She pointed at the ghostly figure.

"Let's go." Henry darted after the impersonator.

Grace heaved her foot from the mud but lost her shoe in the process. By the time she'd dug it out and put it back on, she'd lost sight of Henry. She didn't dare call his name, not if they had any hope of surprising the people behind the videos.

Scanning the area for signs of her brother, Grace angled in the direction of the parking area. If she didn't find him in the forest, he'd turn up at the tunnel sooner or later.

The sounds of a man groaning drifted through the trees.

Grace turned in a full circle but couldn't see more than a few feet in front of her. "Henry?"

The mournful sounds grew closer.

"Whoever you are, you can stop now. I'm not buying it." Her ears perked at the rustle of dead leaves. She swallowed past a lump of fear and hurried toward the noises.

A green light flared to life several feet in front of her. The person stood at least six feet in height, with shoulders half as broad, but his lower half was too skinny for the top. He looked as if someone had stretched his legs on a taffy puller.

Grace nearly fainted when she caught sight of the man's face. It looked identical to the images she'd seen on the website. If she didn't know beyond a shadow of a doubt the person in front of her was a fake, she'd have sworn Raymond Robinson had risen from the dead.

The man groaned again and held his arms out zombie-style.

"Oh no, you don't." Grace charged the guy.

CHAPTER SIX

Henry had assumed his sister would follow him when he took off after the shadowy figure, but he'd assumed wrong. Not only had he lost track of the person slinking around in the woods, but he'd also lost sight of Grace.

"Henry?" She sounded farther away than she should have. Then again, the blood whooshing behind his ear could have muffled her voice.

A dim green light glowed a dozen yards away, and this time he heard his sister loud and clear. She'd called the impersonator out, but what happened next had Henry waffling between laughter and panic.

Grace dipped her shoulder and barreled toward the guy like a defensive lineman. Adding to the bizarreness of the situation, the person in the Charlie No-Face costume stumbled back, turned, and sprinted away.

"Grace!" Praying no one was filming this, Henry darted after them.

He'd almost caught up with her when the person in the costume turned off the green glow. Though it wasn't that bright, the change in light left him blinking spots from his eyes. "Grace?"

"Hurry up. We're losing him," she called over her shoulder.

Following the sound of her footsteps, Henry reached into his pocket for his cell phone. He slowed long enough to open the flashlight app and shine it toward the retreating figure. "Gotcha."

Grace closed in on the guy, and Henry closed in on Grace. The twins were within several feet of the impersonator when the ground went out from beneath them.

One minute they ran on solid ground, the next they fell. The falling didn't bother Henry as much as the landing. He grunted from the impact, bounced, and grunted again.

"Ow," Grace complained.

"Are you okay?" He squinted in her direction, but it was no use. He doubted he could see his hand inches in front of his face.

"I think so. I landed on my bag. My back's a little sore, along with my dignity." She sucked air between her teeth and moved around. "Twice on my butt in twenty minutes. What the heck is it with Southpointe?"

Staring up at the sky through a hole in the ceiling, it took him a moment to realize he'd fallen on something soft and springy. "What did we land on?"

"That's what I'm trying to figure out."

He reached for his phone and groaned. "Dang it, I dropped my cell."

"You have a flashlight in your backpack, or did you drop that, too?"

A blinding white light illuminated the area. Henry hissed, shrank back, and shielded his eyes like a vampire from one of the cheesy horror movies she loved so much.

"Sorry." She didn't sound sorry. She sounded like she was fighting not to giggle. "Looks like we're in an old mine shaft on a disgusting old mattress."

He dug around in his supply bag for his flashlight. "A mattress?"

"And we didn't fall, we slid." She shined the light on a thick tarp anchored to the wall at an angle. "We're definitely in an old mine shaft."

"How can you tell?" He furrowed his brow. Nothing that had come out of his mouth since they'd fallen had made much sense. Thankfully, Grace understood Henry-ese.

"The rails are too close together, and the ceiling is too low for a train." She tapped her lips. "The question is, how do we get out?"

He pointed to the hole in the ceiling. "Same way we got in. We climb up the tarp."

"I don't think so. It's slick." She shined her light on the broken boards above their heads. "Plus, we'd likely fall through the boards again once we reached the top."

Some of the brain fog cleared and pieces of the puzzle snapped into place. "Someone put the tarp and mattress here to break their fall, which means they're using this as an escape hatch of sorts."

She nodded. "I had the same thought. It has to be the impersonator."

"Probably."

"That mattress wouldn't have fit through the hole, so there has to be a way out."

Henry stood and brushed himself off. "Yes, and all we have to do is find it."

"Which way?" She glanced in both directions and frowned.

"No clue. Does your compass app work?" He took several cautious steps to test the stability of the ground. Mines weren't like roads. They were often dug in interconnected layers and were notoriously unstable. Still, they hadn't fallen more than ten or eleven feet.

"Yes, surprisingly enough, but I'll probably lose reception when we move away from the hole. Remind me to add a real compass to my sleuthing bag for next time."

"I don't plan on falling through the ground again anytime soon."

"That was what you said last time," Grace deadpanned. "Expect the best, but plan for the worst. What if our phones are dead from no power?"

"Well, this time I mean it." He grinned, although he was sure his sister would never let him live down the incident on Star Island.

She shined the light on a cluster of timbers and followed them to the ceiling. "That way is almost due north, but unless I'm mistaken, the shaft slopes down."

Henry's foot splashed in shallow water—not a good sign. If the tracks did angle downward, the water would only get deeper as they went. "Let's try the other way."

She sighed and headed in the opposite direction.

The twins had walked approximately five minutes when the path became noticeably rockier. Grace illuminated the ceiling ahead of them and stopped. "I don't feel good about this. It's collapsed."

Henry agreed, but he hated the alternative. "Okay. I say we go back to where we fell through and call Mom and Dad. You had cell reception back there."

"Ugh. Not yet. Let's see if we can get out on our own first."

"We can try to climb the tarp like I suggested. Worst case scenario, we fall on the mattress."

"I hate it when you're right." She trudged toward the opening. "But if the impersonator's using the mine shaft as an escape route, there has to be another way out. We find that, and we may find more clues about the person behind this mess."

"I agree with all of the above, but this might be a part of the mystery better explored in the daylight with more gear."

They made it back to the opening and continued walking north. The farther they went, the more the ground sloped downward, and as he'd predicted, the higher the water rose. Worse, the tunnel had grown narrower and shorter. So much so, the twins had to crouch to get through.

Grace's teeth chattered. "My feet are frozen."

Ignoring the tension in his chest and the drumbeat of his pulse in his ears, Henry stopped and shined his flashlight over the area. "This can't be right. We must have missed something. Let's circle back."

"Okay."

He continued to use his flashlight to search the walls for passageways branching off the main shaft but found none large enough for them to squeeze through—not that squeezing through a potentially unstable tunnel was going to happen *ever*.

The trek back to the mattress seemed to take three times longer than it should have. Grace's teeth hadn't stopped chattering since the water had reached her ankles, and Henry's throat and eyes stung from the tainted air. Mr. Canter had spent his working life in a shaft like the one they were in and had developed lung problems as a result.

There has to be a way out of here. He kicked the mattress back in place, and one of the anchors holding the tarp came loose. "Oh, that's great."

Grace gasped and lunged for what looked like a plastic grocery bag stowed behind the tarp. "How did we miss this?"

"We were looking for a way out instead of searching the pitfall."

"There are dry clothes in here." She held up a pair of sweats that were far too long for either of them to wear without rolling up the cuffs. Considering Henry was an inch shy of six feet tall, that was saying something. "And several used tissues."

"We know we're looking for a giant with a runny nose."

"Here, drink this." She handed him a bottle of water.

He finished half the bottle and tucked the rest into his backpack.

Grace tugged on the other side. "This one isn't budging. I think we can climb it."

"Stand back." Henry gave it a heave, but whatever held the top corners in place appeared sturdy. "Here goes nothing."

Grabbing the taut edge, Henry managed to get halfway to the top before he lost his footing and slid back down. On his second attempt, he went up the middle and failed after making it about three feet up.

"Let me try." Grace cocked her head and studied the situation as if she were solving a calculus problem. She gripped the loose side of the tarp and went at it sideways, using a hand over hand maneuver. Not only did she fall, she rolled and face-planted on the mattress. "Ack. It smells like four-year-old gym socks and a wet dog had an odor baby."

Henry perked up. "Socks! That's it. Grace, you are a genius."

"Of course I am, but what are you talking about?"

He plopped down beside her. "We need more traction. Take off your shoes."

"Even wet socks are slippery."

He wiggled his freshly bared toes. "But skin isn't."

"Gross! Just when I thought it couldn't smell any worse in here."

Ignoring her comment, he started at the tighter side of the tarp and monkey-crawled up the first half without a problem. His left foot slid, but he managed to maintain his position by pivoting his weight onto the right.

"Grab the top seam." Grace shined her flashlight on the area.

Henry wrapped his fingers around the top of the tarp and reached for the ground above him, lost his grip, and slid back down. "Dang it."

"I have an idea." She eyed the tarp. "We leapfrog it. You climb onto my shoulders and grab the top. Then I'll climb up you to freedom."

He arched a brow. "And how do I get out?"

"I'll help you."

"No offense, but can you support my weight?" He glanced at the tarp. "Wait. You wouldn't have to hold all of it if you lay against the tarp."

"Correct." She grabbed their shoes, stepped back, and chucked them through the hole. "Ready?"

He frowned. "Don't have much of a choice unless I want to lose a toe or two to frostbite."

She rested the front of her body on the tarp. "Not cold enough, now go ahead."

Henry considered the best way to use his sister as a ladder. He put his hands on her shoulders and jumped while straightening his arms.

Grace crumbled. "Ow! What the heck are you doing?"

"I thought I could...never mind."

"Don't *vault* over me. Climb." She turned back to the tarp. This time she squatted with one knee to the side.

Henry planted his foot on her thigh, a hand on her shoulder, and tried to contort himself enough to get his other foot on her opposite shoulder. "Straighten your leg."

To his surprise, she lifted him the few inches he needed. With one foot on her shoulder, he had nothing to grab onto except her head. "Sorry."

"Just hurry."

"Right." He lifted the other foot and crouched before stretching to his full height and grabbing the top of the tarp. "I got it."

"I'm stepping back."

Henry pressed the balls of his feet into the slick fabric and held on for dear life. "I'm good."

Grace used his belt as a handhold and pulled herself high enough to wiggle her foot onto his thigh. She moved one hand to his shoulder and lifted her other leg.

Henry's arms screamed in protest. Holding his weight was one thing. Holding hers was like trying to do a pull up with a hundred-and-thirty-pound weight tied around his neck.

Speaking of necks, Grace grappled for anything and everything she could on her way up—hoodie, shoulder, neck, hair. At one point it felt as if she'd used his ear as a foothold, and then her weight lifted.

"I'm out!"

"Don't celebrate just yet. I've used up all of my upper body strength."

"Hang on. I need to make sure this will hold both of us."

Dirt fell into his face. "Stop whatever it is you're doing."

"I'm checking to see if there are boards beneath the topsoil on this side."

"You're killing me." He groaned. "Look at the side of the wall?"

Gauging from the nearness of her face, she'd stretched out on her stomach. "It looks safe. Grab my hand. I'll pull you up."

"Once again, you're killing me? Move back. I think I can do this."

"Oh, right. Sorry." Grace disappeared from the hole.

With one massive heave, Henry managed to get his head and shoulders out. "Little help here."

She took him by the upper arm, planted her feet, and leaned back into the pull.

Henry's feet slipped and slid on the tarp, but he scrambled to freedom. He looked back into the hole. "That sucked a lot more than it should have. Add rope to the list of stuff to carry."

"We should find your phone and get out of here."

Grace speed-dialed Henry's phone, and it rang not far away. He followed his ringtone until he was able to grab the phone. He thrust it over his head in victory.

Their bikes weren't so easy. The twins had found the road and wandered a half-mile or so in both directions with no sign of their bikes and no way to get home.

"This is ridiculous. I'm calling for backup." Grace shoved her flashlight in her bag and retrieved her cell.

"After all of that, you're going to call Mom and Dad?" He couldn't believe it. Their mother would take one look at them covered in mud and coal dust and have a meltdown.

"Nope. Better. This backup won't ground us until we're thirty." She smiled and walked a few feet away. "Hi, Morgan, this is Grace. I need your help."

Ten minutes later, a Mini-Cooper stopped on the side of the road and Morgan rolled down the window. "Seriously? You're going to get my upholstery dirty."

"I thought you loved black?" Henry chuckled despite his aches and pains and the fact he'd lost feeling in his feet an hour earlier.

The Goth girl smirked. "Get in before I change my mind."

"Thank you!" Grace slid into the backseat. "We'll pay to have your car cleaned."

She waved her hand much like Maddison had at the restaurant. "Don't worry about it, but I want details. What happened?"

Henry settled in beside his sister and listened to her replay the events of the evening, minus a few important facts like the mattress, tarp, and bag of clothes.

Morgan glanced over her shoulder. "I don't understand. How did you get out of the mine?"

"We climbed out," he said to save his sister from lying.

The Goth girl met his gaze in the rearview mirror. "I have to find my friend Nina before I take you home. She rode with me and will flip if I leave her here."

"No problem but crank up the heater. We're both wet and half-frozen."

Morgan pulled off the side of the road near the packed parking area. "I'll be right back."

The twins sat in the back of the car trying to warm themselves. A dozen or so flashlights flickered in the forest beyond the creek, and several more lit up the area in front of the tunnel.

Grace chewed her bottom lip. "What are we going to tell Mom? She's going to know something's up when she sees how dirty we are."

He shrugged. "We were out in the forest with a bunch of teenagers."

Giggling, she said, "Good idea. As long as we don't smell like cigarettes or beer, she'll be fine."

Henry couldn't believe his eyes. The same faint green glow they'd seen earlier in the evening moved along the edge of the creek. The impersonator was heading straight for them. "You've got to be kidding me."

Grace turned and gaped. "I figured he would have given up after we chased him."

Henry gripped the door handle. "This time he's not getting away. Wait for my signal."

CHAPTER SEVEN

Grace held her breath as the Charlie No-Face impersonator came closer to the car. The person in the mask had to know about the mine shaft. Had he led them there on purpose? Was this more than a prank?

"Wait for it." Henry white-knuckled the door handle. "We need him close. No chance he's getting away this time. Just a few more steps."

"Hey, Warners! I can't find Nina anywhere." Morgan knocked on the windshield.

Grace took her eyes off the impersonator for a split second, and when she glanced back, he was gone.

"He cut the light. Go." Henry flew out of the car and ran toward where they'd last seen the green glow.

"What the?" Morgan grabbed Grace's arm as she spilled from the car.

"No time. Come on." She pulled free and followed her brother, with Morgan on her heels.

Shining his light back and forth over the area, Henry shouted, "You may as well come out. There's nowhere to hide."

Grace moved farther north in hopes of spotting the guy, but he seemed to have vanished into thin air.

Morgan's head moved as if on a swivel. "Did you see him? Charlie No-Face? Was he here?"

"Yes, but he turned off the green light and we lost track of him." Grace knew she made no sense, but she didn't have the patience to stop and explain.

Henry shouted like a Viking warrior going into battle and darted toward the creek. There was a thud and a splash, and more shouting—from a girl.

"Uh-oh." Grace hurried toward where his flashlight had landed on the ground.

"Get off me!" The distinctly female voice rose loud enough to draw attention from other Charlie hunters.

"Sorry. I, um..." Henry scrambled to his feet.

Grace shined her light on a girl in a long black shirt and a blazer identical to the one the impersonator had been wearing. *It's too much of a coincidence.* "Where did you get that jacket?"

Henry frowned. "That's not the same person we saw earlier. She's short and is wearing glasses."

The girl glared.

Morgan cracked up laughing. "Wait, you guys thought Nina was Charlie No-Face?"

"I'm still not sure she isn't. Let me see that jacket." Grace held out her hand.

The girl, Nina, hissed like a feral cat.

The Goth girl burst into another round of uproarious laughter.

"I'm telling you, we saw a person with a green glow in a black jacket just like that walking toward the car." Grace stared at the strange hissing girl.

Still cackling, Morgan said, "She was with me all night until I went to rescue you. There's no way she's the person you chased through the woods."

Nina's eyes widened. "You chased Charlie No-Face?"

"We did." Henry offered the girl his hand. "I'm sorry I tackled you. Mistaken identity."

"I'll forgive you this once."

Morgan sighed. "Now that we've had our kumbaya moment, maybe we can get out of here? I hate nature."

When the girls headed to the car, Grace held back to speak to Henry.

"It wasn't her," he whispered.

"How do you know? There could be more than one."

"Her glasses were way too thick to be a prop, and there's no way she could have worn them under a mask."

"Good point." She sighed. "But I'm not convinced. Keep an eye on her legs. Dollars to doughnuts, she had pants on underneath."

"Warners! Moonlight's wasting," Morgan shouted from her car.

To say the ride home was awkward was the understatement of all understatements ever understated. Henry sat as close to the door as possible on his side of the backseat. Morgan continued to glance from the road to the rearview mirror, and Nina stared out the window and didn't say a word.

Agnes had said something about one of Morgan's friends wearing a Green Man t-shirt. She'd described the girl as short with glasses. She fit the physical description.

She leaned forward. "Nina, when did you order your Charlie No-Face t-shirt?"

The color drained from the girl's face, and she glanced at Morgan.

"She wouldn't be caught dead in one of those."

The leader of a clique answering for her underlings. Funny thing. Until that moment, Grace wouldn't have pictured Morgan as a queen bee. She'd seemed more of a loner.

"Another case of mistaken identity." She sat back.

Nina folded in on herself as if trying to melt into the seat.

Henry quirked a brow but remained quiet.

Morgan pulled alongside the fifth wheel and cut the engine. "I almost forgot. There's no school on Friday. The homecoming dance is Thursday night. You two should come."

Grace and Henry had remained stalwart after falling into an abandoned mine shaft, but the thought of a high school dance gave them both heart palpitations.

Henry cleared his throat. "Don't you have to be enrolled to attend a school function?"

Good point. Grace drew a breath in through her nose and sent it out through her mouth to calm her racing pulse.

"Psshhhtt." Morgan flicked her wrist. "Not if your dates are students."

"But we don't have dates." There. That would get her out of it.

"Henry can be my plus one, and Jake said he'd take you." She peered over her shoulder. "Relax. It's not a real date. It's a chance to see almost all of the students in one place. Jake and Peter are as eager to find the culprit as you are."

"I'm in," Henry blurted while opening the door to get out of the car. "What time should I pick you up?"

Grace's mouth fell open. *He agreed? Just like that? He hates these things as much as I do.*

Morgan looked at him the same way her sister had earlier in the day. "Eight o'clock. You'll need to dress up a little. No jeans or sneakers."

Oh, no. This can't be happening. Grace hadn't worn a dress since she'd attended her great-aunt's funeral. "I don't have a—"

"I have tons of dresses. I'm sure one of mine will fit." Morgan winked. "And they aren't all black."

"Okay." She forced a smile. "It was nice meeting you, Nina."

The girl lifted her hand in a half-hearted wave without looking at the twins.

Grace climbed out and took a minute to get her bearings before going inside. Of all the mysteries they'd solved, this one was perplexing her the most. Or maybe it wasn't the mystery at all. Maybe it was being thrown into the middle of high school drama complete with cliques and mean girls and dances.

Henry slung his arm over her shoulder. "We should get inside."

She pulled away. "How could you throw me to the wolves like that?"

"You heard Morgan. These aren't dates. It's a chance to see the students interacting and ask questions. The person we chased saw our faces. There's a good chance he or she will react when they see us again."

"You're not the one who has to go with Jake." She folded her arms, not ready to let her brother off the hook just yet.

"We're going as a group. We'll both be forced to hang out with Jake and Peter, and where Peter goes, Maddison goes. It's the trifecta of high school villains."

"Fine, but *you* don't have to wear a stinking dress."

A smile tugged at the corners of his lips. "I'll wear a dress if it makes you feel better."

She pinched the bridge of her nose.

"It's cold out here." Faith stood in the doorway wearing thick pajamas and a bathrobe. "Are you two going to come inside, or are you going to stand out there arguing all night?

Grace drew a deep breath and steadied her resolve.

The twins marched toward the RV. The second they stepped into the light, Faith Warner's eyes rounded. However, her surprise was short-lived. She pressed her lips into a thin line and motioned for them to enter.

Ethan glanced up from his novel and frowned. "Dare I ask?"

For the second time that night, Henry took the lead before Grace could respond. He ran his hand over his head and gave their parents a sheepish grin.

"We went to the Green Man Tunnel with a bunch of kids from the local high school. It turned into a scavenger hunt in the woods."

Faith's brows hadn't lowered since the twins had walked inside. "In the woods or in the mud? You two are filthy."

Ethan chuckled. "It looks like you had fun."

"It was a blast, but we'll need to borrow the truck tomorrow. It was too late to ride home on dark streets, so we left our bikes behind."

"We'll be back around four tomorrow. I'll take you then." Ethan Warner glanced at them as if he had more questions forming in his bear-trap mind.

Grace took a step back, and her soggy sneakers made a squishing sound.

"Off. Take them off and put them outside." Faith pointed to the door. "If it wasn't so chilly outside, I'd hose you both down from the spigot."

The twins removed their shoes and set them at the bottom of the steps. Henry met Grace's gaze and winked. She rolled her eyes and huffed.

When they came back inside, their mother nodded toward the bathroom. "Henry, shower first. I want to speak to my daughter alone."

He frowned and cast his sister a pleading look before walking down the hall.

Grace swallowed hard.

Ethan said, "Pull up a barstool. It's the only furniture we have that isn't upholstered."

"Wait." Her mom pulled a dishcloth from the drawer and spread it across the top of the stool. "Your father and I are concerned about the two of you."

Taking a seat, Grace ran through the most obvious reasons her parents would worry—bad grades, bad crowd, bad beverage choices. She came up blank. "Why?"

Her mother frowned at the floor, something she couldn't remember ever seeing the renowned engineer do. She didn't hang her head in defeat. *What in the heck is going on?*

Ethan cleared his throat. "When we chose to live on the road with two kids, our original plan was to settle in one place before you started high school. But you and Henry seemed to be doing well—"

"We didn't anticipate you'd start high school classes in the seventh grade, nor did we consider you'd enjoy being home-schooled as much as you do." Faith sighed. "Now we're questioning our decisions."

"What? *Why?* We love our lives." Grace had no clue what had sparked their concerns. She'd meant what she said. She wouldn't change a single thing about her childhood.

Her mother nodded. "I know you do, but you haven't had much of a chance to form friendships."

"But we have. Henry and I keep in touch with some of the kids from our online classes. I text with Miranda from Star Island a few times a week—"

Ethan nodded slowly. "Grace, we want to—"

"Wait. Let me finish." Once she'd gotten started, she found it almost impossible to stop. The mere thought that they would park the RV, buy a house, and put her and Henry in school made her blood run cold. "We get to see the country. Heck, we've been all over the world. We've seen more than most people do in their entire lives. We're closer to each other and you guys than other kids our age are with their families, and you really don't have to worry. Henry and I are going to the Southpointe High homecoming dance—"

Ethan choked on air or spit or whatever it was he'd planned to say.

"Together?" Faith used the voice she usually reserved for sad movies and abandoned puppies.

Grace let her head fall back and groaned. "No, not together. *Gross.* We're going with other people."

Faith Warner folded her arms. "I don't recall meeting any local kids."

"That's great, honey. This is exactly what we were worried about." Ethan stood and clamped a hand on her shoulder. "You two are amazing, but you haven't had much interaction with people your own age. We wondered if you would be able to adapt next year at college."

While Grace understood the sentiment, his words hit too close to her insecurities for comfort. Like an icepick in the eye instead of the temple hurt. "You thought kids our own age wouldn't like us?"

Henry walked into the room but froze mid-step. "Why do I get the feeling that I don't want in on this conversation?"

"Trust me, you don't." Grace turned away from her parents.

"You have it backward." Their father sighed. "We were concerned you wouldn't have much in common with your peers and would perhaps feel out of place."

"Ah, it's the old socialization-and-fitting-in lecture." Henry smirked. "Not sorry I missed it."

The elder Warners looked like they'd found half a cockroach in a sandwich they'd shared. Neither knew who'd actually eaten the insect, but both felt ill as a result.

Faith extended her arm as if to embrace Grace but stopped short. "I want to hug you, but…"

"I'm filthy. I know." She drew a breath and tried to take the bark out of her words. "Is it okay if I take a shower now?"

Henry met her gaze and one corner of his mouth turned down—a signal that he understood her frustration and they'd talk later. The simple gesture eased the sting of the conversation. She knew their parents wanted the best for her and her brother. Her reaction had more to do with the fact she'd worried about fitting in, too.

"Sure, go ahead." Faith's shoulders sagged.

Forget the dirt and the coal dust. Grace drew the woman into a bear hug. "I apologize for overreacting. I'm stressed out over the dance."

"You'll need a dress." Her mother pulled away and wrinkled her nose for a millisecond. She may have pretended not to notice the stains on her white robe, but Grace wasn't fooled.

"I'm going to borrow one from a friend." She turned for the bathroom.

Ethan Warner stepped into her path and flashed her a father-knows-best smile. "A girl's first date is a big deal. You should go shopping and have your nails done."

Grace hung her head. "I never said it was a date."

Faith grinned. "You're going to a dance with a human being who isn't your brother? Of course, it's a date."

Henry glanced at them like they'd all lost their minds. "No, really. I'm taking Morgan as a friend, and there's no way I'd let Grace go on a date-date with a guy like Jake."

Ethan responded to Henry's statement like a bull to a red cape. "Exactly what kind of guy *is* this Jake?"

"Nor would I let Henry date-date a girl like Morgan."

Faith's brows rose.

"I'm going to get cleaned up." Her back to her parents, Grace stuck her tongue out at her brother and mouthed, "Your turn."

CHAPTER EIGHT

Henry woke to the sounds of his parents preparing to leave for the day, but after the discussion they'd had the previous evening, he opted to stay in bed. They'd had a few hours to discuss his and Grace's social lives, the homecoming dance, and their not-date-dates. The next time the twins faced Ethan and Faith Warner would likely turn into a speed round of *Jeopardy*. "I'll take Awkward Questions for five hundred, Alex."

The front door closed and the pickup's hemi engine rumbled to life.

Grace sighed. "Are you awake?"

"Yep." He stared at the poster of the Declaration of Independence taped to the ceiling above his bunk.

"What do we know?" She sat upright and pulled her notebook from its hiding place.

"As I said before, never to discuss dating anywhere within a hundred yards of our parents? That is a minefield I don't want to ever walk through again."

"I second that statement, counselor, but what do we know about the case?" She tapped her pen on her lips.

"I need coffee before we get into this." Henry shoved to his feet and wandered into the kitchen.

Grace followed. "I've been thinking about the second encounter with the impersonator last night. I don't think it was the same person."

Dumping a mound of sugar into his mug, he said, "I noticed a height difference, but I chalked it up to the ground sloping down toward the creek."

"The guy I confronted in the woods was broad like Jake and Peter."

"But the face mask or makeup looked the same." He stirred in some milk and took a sip. "Have we checked to see if they sell Charlie No-Face masks online?"

Grace went back into the bedroom and returned with her phone.

Henry fixed her a cup of coffee and put a bagel in the toaster oven.

"That would be a 'no' on the masks, and I'd like to go on record as saying people have entirely too much time on their hands." She held up her cell and showed him image after image of weird masks.

"Someone local could have fabricated a mold and made several latex masks, but why go through the trouble to prank high schoolers?"

"Money." Grace scrolled through her phone. "The fundraising drive for those awful videos has hit a thousand dollars."

He put the bagel on a plate and added cream cheese before setting it in front of her. While he hadn't expected a standing ovation for making her breakfast, he certainly hadn't expected her to run from the room.

"Did you want eggs?" he called after her.

She slammed the bathroom door and turned on the faucet.

Henry knocked on the door. "What's wrong?"

"I'm a little angry...I need a minute."

"Okay." He walked back into the kitchen and grabbed his coffee. *I'll retrace her virtual steps and get to the bottom of this.*

Phone in hand, Henry sat at the barstool, took a bite of the bagel, and got to work. He typed in Charlie No-Face masks and several variations of the search terms before he came up with the same image results Grace had. He clicked on the All tab on the results page and scrolled down.

Several entries down, he found a link to the video fundraiser. He clicked it, and his mouth went dry. He started to get angry, too.

The impersonators had posted a new video all right, and it featured Grace. He lowered the volume on his phone and hit play. The same grainy images of the forest and the impersonator filled the screen. The screen went black for a split second before the camera focused on his sister's face. The shot panned out to include her upper body. She stood ramrod straight with her hands at her sides, eyes wide, mouth hanging open.

A speech bubble popped up beside her that read **You're cute!**

The video cut to the impersonator groaning and raising his arms toward her.

The next shot had Grace tilting her head and staring. The caption read **I wonder if he'll ask me to Homecoming?**

The final clip was of Grace chasing the impersonator, with a speech bubble of her begging Charlie to take her to the dance.

Henry's phone case made a cracking sound. He loosened his grip and let it fall to the counter. Running his hands over his head, he forced himself to take several deep breaths. He'd never been a violent person, but right then, he wanted to punch someone in the face.

Grace emerged from the bathroom and handed him her cell. "It's Morgan. She wants to talk to you."

He wanted to tell her she was better than the stupid video and the idiots who made it, but the determined look in her eyes stopped him. Instead, he took the phone and pressed it to his ear. "Hello."

"Have you seen it?" Morgan sounded as angry as he felt.

"Yes."

She sighed. "Grace is pretty upset. Is she going to be okay?"

He glanced at his sister. "She's stronger than any girl I know."

"It wasn't as awful as the last one. At least they didn't attack her appearance or call her names."

Henry thought back to the second video. *The beginnings. They were identical, but something was off.* "Thanks for calling, but I need to go."

"Will I see you after school? Same bat time, same bat channel?"

"I'm not sure. I'll let you know." He disconnected the call and turned to Grace. "I need to study all three videos. Would you rather not see it again?"

"I can't *not* see it." She tapped her head. "It's burned into my memory."

"Come on. I have an idea of what's going on, but I need your amazing research skills."

She stared at her brother.

"I know what you're thinking, and yes. One hundred percent. You're right up there with Wonder Woman and Mom on the females-who-kick-butt list. You're plenty tough. Don't let the buttwads get to you. The more they post, the more clues they give us."

"I'm worried that I'm too mad to see straight and I'll miss something." Grace's voice came across as questioning.

Henry gave her a playful shove. "Don't you know? Every superhero has a human side. They doubt themselves, and they want to give up. That's what makes it so great when they beat the villains and save the world."

She snorted. "I'm not giving up. Not by a long shot. Beating the villain. I like that idea."

"Good." He went to their room to get his laptop. "Find out what sort of extracurricular activities and clubs they have at the high school. I'm particularly interested in theater, shop, and anything related to video production."

"Got it." Grace retrieved her computer and sat at the dinette across from him.

Henry plugged in his headphones and got to work analyzing the videos. As he'd suspected, the first five seconds of all three Charlie No-Face clips were the same footage. However, the backgrounds of the segments with girls differed. Maddison's was shot from the parking area, but the second and third were filmed in the woods.

Henry removed his headphones. "You were right about the impersonator you confronted. He's NBA-basketball-player tall. They're using canned clips of Charlie's close-up, but the wide-angle shots could be different people."

Grace frowned and glanced over her notes. "SHS has a theater program, offers shop classes, and has an audiovisual club. The AV club's website has a section devoted to film production."

"Does the website list club members?"

"No, but interestingly enough, both the AV club and the theater program are running fundraisers."

Snap. Another piece of the puzzle. Henry glanced up from his computer. "We need to find out who's involved in the clubs. Once we have the names, we can start digging into the t-shirt sales and the video-crowd funding. Nothing online is completely anonymous."

"You're right about that." Grace clicked on something and turned her computer to face him. "This was on the theater website. It was taken during last year's production of *Arsenic and Old Lace.*"

Henry frowned at the photo of Morgan and Nina dressed in 1940s clothing. "We need to get our hands on a yearbook. Dad's old one listed everyone in each club. Unless they've changed over the last thirty years, it's our best shot at figuring out who participates in which activities."

"And the candid photos would give us a better idea of the cliques." Grace typed into her computer. "I'm accessing the catalog at the local library. Maybe they'll have the yearbooks."

They had too many suspects and too many unanswered questions. What they needed was to build a plan to narrow the list.

"Any luck?"

"Yes, they have them, but all of the volumes are at least ten years old. Nothing recent."

"Morgan will have one." He hated to ask and hated to force his sister into an uncomfortable situation. "Are you up for meeting her at the pizza place this afternoon?"

"Would you think I was a wimp if I said no?" She laughed, but it sounded hollow.

"Nope. It's your call."

"What's the worst thing that can happen? They'll all laugh at me. I'm sure they're doing it anyway." She shrugged. "Besides, it's not like I lost my hair extensions in a tree."

"There's that." He chuckled and clicked over to his online history class. "Blah. I'm in no mood to do actual schoolwork, but I think it's time we visited Southpointe High."

"This is what the inside of a high school is like?" Henry curled his lip. "It's so—"

Morgan covered her mouth to hide her grin.

"Showtime." Morgan walked through a set of double doors and marched to the long, narrow counter. "Hi. This is..." Her eyes twinkled. "Fred and Daphne. They're new. They have English Lit this period, but Mrs. Stallings is giving a test. She asked me to escort them here, but I need to get back. Time's a-ticking. Test and all."

Henry tightened his jaw, and Grace looked anywhere except at the librarian.

The elderly lady glanced from Morgan to the twins. "There are empty tables in the back."

Morgan flashed them a mischievous smile and headed for the door.

Henry lowered his voice. "Would it be possible to look at last year's yearbook? I'd like to see what kinds of activities the school offers."

"The yearbooks are in the reference section, second row." She turned to her computer.

The twins hurried to the back of the library, pulled yearbooks from the previous three years, and found a table.

"I'll start with the most recent." Henry took a notebook from his backpack.

Grace scanned the oldest of the three. Several pages in, she paused to take a closer look at a photo. "Look."

Henry glanced over. "Maddison and Peter during freshman year?"

"That's Morgan." She pointed to the smiling brunette in the green-and-white cheerleading uniform.

"Whoa! What a difference two years makes."

Grace flipped to the headshots of the freshman class and found both Monaghan sisters' photos. "They are in the same grade, both seniors now. Maddison must have repeated a year."

He checked the index and flipped to the theater department. Shoulders tensing, he scanned the page. "Morgan, Nina, and Jake are all in theater."

"Jake?" Grace couldn't wrap her head around the loud football player performing in a musical. "What about the AV club?"

He checked the index, turned to the correct page, and muttered. "You've got to be kidding."

Grace followed his gaze to a photo of Morgan and Peter in what looked like an editing booth. "This looks bad, but what possible motive could she have?"

"Money?"

"Agnes said the Monaghans are wealthy."

"She doesn't get along with Maddison. This could be a prank that snowballed into something much larger."

Grace tapped her lips. "Could be, but you heard her this morning. She was upset about my video."

"True. Maybe someone else stole her idea after the first video went viral."

A soft gasp came from behind them. Grace turned her head in time to see Nina backing away from their table. Whites showed all the way around the girl's eyes, and for good reason. She was wearing a Charlie No-Face t-shirt.

"I knew it." Grace pointed at her top. "Why did you lie?"

Nina took another step back. "I didn't, Morgan did."

Henry whispered, "She's right. Morgan answered for her."

"Same thing." Grace rolled her eyes. "Next you'll tell us that she made you buy it."

The girl gasped again.

"Did she?"

"Hey, aren't you the girl who chased Charlie No-Face?" A boy with red hair and ruddy cheeks and an incredible amount of hardware on his teeth pointed at Grace.

She froze.

"It's not her." Henry glared.

"It is." He turned and motioned for his friends to come over. "It's the girl from the video!"

Several people shushed him, but it was too late. The librarian stood behind the counter and scanned the area for the sign of the disruption, but not just any librarian. Mrs. Kaluza had replaced the elderly woman at the desk.

"We have to go. Now." Grace shoved her notebook into her backpack.

Three more boys joined the first, and all four laughed and pointed or snickered.

"It totally is her."

"No way, the girl in the video was hot." The dark-haired one looked Grace over as if she were on an auction block.

"That's enough." Henry stood and folded his arms. Her brother wasn't as big as Jake or Peter, but he had a commanding presence that quieted the jerks.

"*Now*, Henry." Grace tried to pull him out of view of their parents' friend.

Nina smiled like a shark scenting blood in the water. "What's wrong? *Henry and Grace Warner*, you *aren't* students here?"

Grace's heart thudded twice and started racing.

"I thought your names were Fred and Daphne?" The elderly woman emerged from the shelves containing old encyclopedias.

The boys burst out laughing, but the little old lady silenced them with one look. She glanced at the twins and her frown deepened. "You two come with me. We'll let the principal sort this out."

Despite spending most of his academic life learning from home, the thought of going to the principal's office sent a shock of panic through Henry.

"I'll take them, Mrs. Smith. The bell's going to ring in any minute. You don't want to get caught in the halls." Mrs. Kaluza spoke to the woman like she was a child asking for a second slice of cake.

"No, I don't." She pursed her lips. "Go ahead."

"This way." Mrs. Kaluza pointed to another set of double doors.

The bell rang, and chaos ensued. Students stood and rushed out while others rushed in.

Henry's knees threatened to give out. Head down, he strode toward the exit.

"You don't go here." It was a statement, not a question, and said loudly in the noisy hall.

"If we said no, would you still take us to the principal's office?" Henry stopped and tried to smile, but it was weak.

The woman shrugged. "I didn't plan to in the first place."

Grace heaved a sigh and leaned against the wall. "Thanks."

She showed the twins the least-monitored path off campus—the teachers' parking lot. Henry walked with his head held high. He'd long since learned that the key to not getting caught with your hand in the cookie jar was to look like the baker. Unfortunately, the trick hadn't worked in the library.

"How are we going to explain this to Mom and Dad?" Grace asked.

"Let's worry about that if and when we have to." He opened the rideshare app and ordered a car. "I'm formulating the beginnings of a plan. What do you say we set up some cameras of our own?"

"I'd say great. We should hide one near the mine shaft and one near the parking area, but we don't have any, nor do we have our bikes."

"That can be rectified." Henry nodded toward the intersection where they'd rendezvous with the driver. "What do you say we go spend some of our college funds?"

"Mom won't like it."

Henry smirked. "We may already be in trouble. Spending a couple hundred dollars on surveillance equipment we need to complete our research project is nothing compared to trespassing on school grounds."

"Go big or go home." She raised her hands over her head and did the victory dance from *Rocky*.

"Maybe go a little smaller next time."

In the four hours it took them to buy four battery-powered security cameras, hide said cameras near Piney Fork Tunnel, and find their bikes, which they had hidden too well the night before, Morgan had called eight times.

"Two in the trees, one outside the mineshaft looking at the entrance, and one attached under a board looking into the shaft. Is that enough?" Henry ran through the possible scenarios involving the impersonator. There were simply too many variables to cover every angle.

"It's too bad we don't have more time to test them. I'm going to be upset if the memory card is full of nothing but dragonflies and leaves."

"The box said the motion sensors required a significant amount of movement."

Grace's phone rang—again.

Glancing at the screen, she sighed. "It's her again."

"We'll be at Smiley Pizza in a half hour, less if we huff it." Henry had mixed feelings about the girl. On the one hand, he found her interesting, smart, and cute in a quirky vampire-meets-Audrey-Hepburn kind of way, but on the other, he'd seen and heard too much to trust her.

"Hi, Morgan. Sorry we missed your calls. We were shopping." Grace hung her head and turned her back to him. "Oh. I didn't know about a meeting—"

Henry shoved his hands in his back pockets and stared at the sky.

"We'll be there in a half-hour."

Henry motioned for her to hurry.

"Okay, bye." Grace bent to inspect her front tire for the third time. "Morgan's not happy."

"I'm not sure I care. Even if she's not behind the scam, she lied to us." He motioned to her bike. "If you're that nervous about the rim, we can head home."

"No, it'll be fine. I'm famished." She brushed imaginary dirt off her jeans. "Do you plan to talk to Morgan about what happened today?"

"Yes. Innocent until proven guilty."

She sighed. "Everyone deserves a chance to explain themselves."

"You're right. How does a half-pepperoni, half-pineapple and ham sound?" He nudged her shoulder. No matter how many times they'd dealt with horrible people while solving mysteries, she hadn't lost her faith in humanity. It would break her heart to learn Morgan had orchestrated the Charlie No-Face scam, even if she didn't necessarily like her.

***

The twins parked behind the restaurant. Her bike pulled to the left enough that she'd noticed, but not enough to cause serious trouble. However, Grace used the bent rim as an excuse to procrastinate about going inside. Between the mystery and Morgan and Mrs. Kaluza possibly ratting them out to their parents, she'd almost forgotten about the video of her. Almost.

"We can go home. You don't have to go in there," Henry told her.

"No way." Grace squared her shoulders and lifted her chin.

"Relax. Never let them know they got under your skin."

She opened the door, and a tidal wave of noise spilled out. The place was packed like the day before, but today it seemed as if the entire student body of SHS had shown up. Grace wanted to turn and run, but she forced herself to walk inside.

Several teens stared, a few pointed, and almost all of them whispered.

"OMG! It's her." A girl wearing a Green Man Rocks t-shirt shot to her feet.

Another kid shouted, "Is Charlie No-Face taking you to homecoming?"

Grace's feet felt like they weighed a metric ton each. She couldn't run, couldn't hide, and couldn't make it end. She could feel herself flush.

Some took pictures of her, and some rushed forward and asked questions ranging from her name to if she was dating the monster. Others made comments about everything from her clothing to her hair and weight.

The insults landed like gut punches but unglued her feet from the floor. Grace turned for the door, but the crowd had surrounded them. She met Henry's gaze and silently pleaded for him to do something.

An ear-splitting whistle cut through the din. Jake, the blue-eyed football player, stood and waved them toward Maddison's red booth. "Warners! Over here!"

The crowd fell eerily silent.

Grace took a step back. Henry stayed close by her, holding half the crowd at bay.

"We can go and never look back," Henry whispered into her ear.

It felt like everyone in the restaurant was staring, probably because they were. Her heart pounded and her palms sweated and her skull felt like a million bees had built a hive inside it. "We need answers."

She headed straight for the booth, brushing people out of her way. Maddison and Peter sat on one side, and Morgan and Jake on the other. The Goth girl didn't look thrilled to be there but judging by the dirty plate and half-full drink in front of her, she'd shared a meal with her sister and the two guys.

Peter and Maddison scooted over to make room.

Grace forced a smile, but before she could sit, Jake stepped in.

"Sit beside me." He set her backpack against the wall and tugged her to his and Morgan's side of the table.

Henry glared at Jake and took a seat beside Maddison.

"Sure. I guess."

Rather than sliding in, he waited for her to scoot across to the middle.

Morgan lowered her voice. "That was brutal. Are you okay?"

"Not really." She chewed her lower lip.

"Why didn't you wait for me or return my calls?"

Grace avoided answering the second question. "We didn't dare wait after our run-in with Mrs. Kaluza. That's her house we're parked next to. She knows our parents."

Morgan's eyes bugged out. "Why didn't you tell me you were squatting on Kaluza land?"

"I had no idea she worked at the high school."

Maddison made a sour face. "Ew. Please don't use the word 'squatting' in my presence."

"Sure, Princess, whatever." Morgan rolled her eyes.

Jake took Grace's hand and held it chest-high, an awkward angle that wasn't comfortable and allowed most of the crowd to see what he'd done. "We haven't officially been introduced. I'm Jake Johnson."

"Grace, and this is my brother Henry." She pulled free and rubbed her damp palms on her jeans.

"Will you go to homecoming with me?" He flashed her a toothpaste-commercial smile. "I know it's already set up, but I thought I should ask. You know, for appearances' sake."

She nodded. "Sure. I'll even dance. For appearances' sake."

Shooting to his feet, Jake shouted, "She said yes!"

Cheers went up from the same kids who'd committed the verbal equivalent of carrying torches and pitchforks minutes earlier.

"This is so weird." Grace slumped deeper in the booth and wondered if the kids had minds of their own buried somewhere deep within.

"Don't worry, he won't announce a play-by-play of the entire night. He's doing it to let people know to leave you alone or they'll have to deal with him," Morgan whispered.

Henry shook his head and turned his attention to the room.

Jake sat and downed his soda. "Tell me if anyone gives you a hard time."

"Thanks, that was nice of you." Overall, Grace found him obnoxious, but he was cute—not that cuteness made up for obnoxiousness, except with Labrador retrievers. Jake was exactly like a big goofy Lab who'd recently learned to bark.

"No problem." Stuffing half a slice of pizza into his mouth, he chewed and swallowed, then said, "So what's the deal with the video? Were you actually chasing Charlie No-Face?"

She struggled to focus on his icy blue eyes and not the half-chewed food in his mouth. The puppy analogy hit entirely too close to the truth.

"We were chasing someone dressed in a Charlie No-Face costume." Henry sat back and folded his arms.

Jake grinned and pointed at Henry. "Right. I like this guy."

Agnes stopped at the table, frowned at the local kids, and settled her gaze on Henry. "What can I get you?"

After he placed their order, he lowered his voice and asked, "How's Mr. Canter?"

Agnes's face softened. "He's been in better spirits since you two stopped by."

Grace said, "We'll visit again before we leave."

The waitress smiled at the twins, turned, and walked away.

Jake's mouth fell open—not a pretty sight considering it was full of pizza.

"Gross, Jake. Chew with your mouth shut." Maddie wrinkled her nose and glanced at Henry. "How in the world did you charm Angry Agnes?"

"For starters, we don't call her that. She's not so bad once you get to know her." Grace stretched the truth when it came to the waitress. "Besides, wouldn't you be angry if you had to deal with this every weekday afternoon? I bet they don't behave like this at home or in the school cafeteria."

Maddison glanced at the disaster area her fellow students had made of the restaurant. "I see what you mean, but isn't that, like, her job?"

Henry shook his head and looked away.

"That's it." Jake slammed his hands on the table, stood, and whistled again. "Attention! Your mother doesn't work here. You *will* clean up your mess. Don't leave it for the waitresses."

The other students stared as if waiting for the punchline.

"Now!" He plopped back down and rested his arm across the back of the booth.

The other teens shot into action, mopping up spills, picking up their garbage, and stacking dirty dishes.

Morgan widened her eyes and shook her head. "What was that about?"

"I did it for Grace." He grabbed the last slice of pizza. "She inspired me."

Henry did not seem impressed.

Morgan smirked. "Peter and Maddie have a plan to catch the people making the videos."

The twins exchanged a wary glance.

Peter rested his forearms on the table. "Thanks to Grace's contribution, they've raised enough money to post two more videos. Which means they'll be out tonight."

"Happy to help the cause," Grace deadpanned.

Morgan said, "Actually, there was a post on their fundraising page. They're taking a vacation until after homecoming."

Grace glanced at Henry and frowned. The more she thought about it, the more she could see Morgan masterminding the entire Charlie No-Face scam.

"That'll give us more time to plan. What exactly did you have in mind?" Henry hadn't so much as cracked a smile since they'd walked in, and judging by the tone of his voice, he wouldn't anytime soon.

Morgan snickered. "They want to dress the entire football team in black and have them lay in wait near the tunnel and in the forest."

"When she says the entire team, she means the varsity, JV, and freshman teams," Peter clarified.

Grace chewed her bottom lip, debating about pointing out the fatal flaw in his strategy.

"It won't work," Henry said.

The boys tensed.

"It won't work because they have hidden cameras in the trees. If they're being monitored, they'll see your teammates."

Jake flipped his hair back from his forehead. "Bro, that stinks. We *need* the element of surprise."

Henry cleared his throat. "You're on the right track, but the videos have all been of girls."

Peter chuckled. "You want us to use girls as bait?"

"No, I want your teammates dressed in normal clothes and listening for any screams." He scratched his jaw. "Have them spread out over the area, but not alone. Pair them off."

Jake frowned. "Like patrols?"

Grace picked up the thread. "Yes, but they can't be obvious about it. No pacing back and forth over the same place."

"Oh my God! I have an idea!" Maddison clapped her hands.

Morgan muttered, "Alert the Vatican. It's a miracle."

"Ha-ha." She glared at her sister. "Okay, so what if we assign each girl to one or two football players?"

Jake wiggled his brows. "I like the sound of that."

Henry hung his head.

"No, seriously. What if we have them watch their assigned girl from a distance? If Charlie or *whoever* shows up and scares their person, the players can tackle him." Maddie spat orange gum into a napkin and popped another piece into her mouth.

Grace liked the idea, but once again, there was a problem. "That could work, but we need to warn people not to wander too far. There's an old mine shaft a quarter mile or so from the tunnel. The boards are rotted. Someone could fall in."

The guys tensed.

Henry said, "She's right."

"They'll use flashlights." Peter shrugged.

"Easier said than done while running." Henry met Grace's gaze and half-frowned.

She gave him a quick nod. He hadn't mentioned they'd fallen through or that they suspected the impersonators used it as an escape tunnel, and neither would she.

Morgan narrowed her eyes at them.

Jake squeezed Grace's shoulder. "It's sweet you're worried people might get hurt. We'll warn them."

Henry leaned closer to the football player. "Dude. Could you stop manhandling my sister?"

CHAPTER TEN

Henry had been Grace's brother for seventeen years, but this was the first time he'd dealt with a suitor. Jake had found a reason to touch her on the average of once every three minutes like clockwork, and Henry didn't like it.

The larger guy sat back and held his hands up. "No offense."

Maddison made a whining sound. "I have practice in ten minutes."

"Same." Peter leaned forward to get Henry's attention. "I'll fill the players in on the plan. I wouldn't put it past them to lie in the post and be out there tonight."

"We'll only get one shot at this." Jake folded his arms. "And I don't want to waste it."

Henry took a moment to consider the situation. "Both valid points. Why not take tonight off and run the plan tomorrow after the dance?"

Jake stood, let out another wall-shaking laugh, and clamped his hand on Henry's shoulder. "I like this guy. He's wicked smart."

The bones in his shoulders screamed in protest, but he refused to let the other guy see him flinch.

Morgan smirked. "Dude. Could you stop manhandling my homecoming date?"

Jake smiled and shook his finger at her. "I see what you did there."

Maddison nudged Henry. "Move. We have to go."

"I'll see you tomorrow night." Jake winked at Grace and followed Peter and Maddie to the door.

Agnes appeared within seconds of the other's departure. The woman glanced around the restaurant, marched to the twins, and gave them each a bear hug. "I don't know how you did it, but I've been working in this place for thirty years, and this is the cleanest it's ever been after the high school crowd blows out."

Morgan grinned. "It was Grace's fault. She inspired Jake Johnson to be a better man."

"Man? *Psshhtt*. Two hundred pounds of little boy, that one." She laughed and covered her mouth as if she hadn't heard the sound in so long it'd surprised her. "Your pizza will be right out. It's on the house."

Morgan watched the waitress go before turning back to the twins. "Okay, spill it. You two are hiding something. I saw your weird silent conversation. Who knew two people could communicate with blinks, frowns, and grimaces?"

"It's a twin thing," they said in unison.

"I don't care if it's Morse code in pig-Latin. What aren't you sharing with the rest of us?"

"I could ask you the same question." He'd come off gruffer than he intended, but the football player had shredded his patience. "We saw Nina in the library today. Nice shirt she had on."

What little color she had drained from her face. "So?"

Grace sighed. "Nina said you have one too, but in the car—"

"I panicked, and I lied." She looked away.

"Why?" He glanced at the pizza. For the first time in his life, he couldn't bring himself to eat.

"Because I knew if you found out the truth, you'd think I was behind everything."

Henry had no reply because she was right.

Morgan turned to Grace. "The t-shirts were my idea. The theater program doesn't have the money to go to New York, and the other fundraisers weren't cutting it. Nina and I set it up weeks before someone started dressing up like Charlie No-Face and chasing girls through the forest."

"Are you keeping anything else from us?" He tilted his head.

The girl grinned and sighed. "I was once a pom-pom shaker, but I turned my life around and embraced the dark arts of Shakespearian Theater. My parents practically disowned me when I quit the team and dyed my hair black."

That he believed. His stomach growled, reminding him of the untouched pizza. He folded a slice in two, took a bite, and made a point of chewing with his mouth closed. "And film production?"

"Blah, no. Too manufactured. I prefer the stage—" She met Henry's gaze. "You saw the photo in the yearbook?"

The twins nodded.

"I've never been an official member of AV Club, but I taught Peter an editing program, and I help out sometimes." Her expression hardened. "Do you believe me?"

Henry wanted to, but a kernel of doubt remained. Thankfully, Grace spoke before he had the chance.

"Our turn for true confessions." She explained the tarp and mattress but left out the cameras they'd planted. Evidently, she had a kernel of doubt, too.

"I'd love to check out the mine shaft, but I'll be grounded if I'm not home by five."

Henry glanced at his phone. "We should get home too."

Ten minutes later, the twins pedaled down the Kaluzas' driveway, and much to Henry's horror, Mrs. Kaluza was waiting for them.

"Might I have a word with the two of you?"

"Sure." Grace plastered on a smile and parked her bike.

Henry cast a longing look toward their fifth wheel.

"Funny thing. I wonder why you two were at the high school today." The librarian peered at them over her glasses.

Grace's voice came out high and tight. "Oh, just research."

"I understand the Monaghan girl was involved?"

The twins hung their heads.

Henry said, "We needed to do some research."

"In high school yearbooks?" Her frown deepened.

Henry took a deep breath and explained the hows and whys of their visit to the school library. He would have preferred to leave Morgan's name out of it, but Nina had sent that ship to sea already.

"You realize you were trespassing?" Mrs. Kaluza glanced at them.

He said, "Yes, and wanting to find the person responsible for humiliating three girls including my sister is no excuse."

The librarian chuckled. "Oh, boy, that was expertly worded. I can tell your father is an attorney. Do you plan to follow in his footsteps?"

Henry's hand started for his neck, but he caught himself and stopped. "Unless I have a criminal trespass charge on my record, I intend to apply to Stanford."

She nodded and glanced at Grace. "Why didn't you come to me when you first saw the video?"

"I didn't know you worked there. If I had, we wouldn't have..."

"Trespassed?"

The twins nodded.

"I'm willing to keep this to myself on two conditions" She met each of their gazes. "Tell your parents what you've done, and don't set foot on school property again."

Henry said, "Done."

"We were invited to the homecoming dance. Does that count as setting foot on school property?"

Mrs. Kaluza tilted her head. "By whom?"

"Morgan Monaghan and Jake...I forgot his last name." Grace blushed.

"The dance isn't a problem. It's being held at the country club, thanks in no small part to Morgan's parents." She furrowed her brow. "Are you referring to Jake Johnson, the football player?"

Henry stiffened his spine. "Yes, Jake Johnson. Is he a troublemaker?"

"No, it's nothing like that." Kayla Kaluza sighed. "There's been a lot of talk about the videos in the teachers' lounge. The general consensus is that Morgan is the mastermind and Jake is the muscle."

Henry could dismiss circumstantial evidence and chalk Agnes's warning up to bitterness, but he couldn't deny the growing pattern of people who knew Morgan and assumed she was behind the videos.

He folded his arms. "Odd question, but do you know why the AV club is fundraising?"

"I believe one of the students wants to enter a filmmaker's contest, but there is a steep entry fee."

The rumble of their parents' pickup cut the conversation short.

"You *will* tell them what you were up to?" She narrowed her eyes.

"We will." The pizza he'd had for lunch felt like a double-cheese and pepperoni brick in his stomach.

To make matters worse, Ethan Warner reached into the backseat and retrieved a pink garment bag.

"They went shopping," Grace whispered.

Their mother raised two additional plastic bags in the air. "We couldn't let you go out in borrowed clothes."

Most kids would hate to have their parents choose their wardrobes, but Henry didn't mind. His Mom had great taste, and he hated shopping as much as he hated liver and onions.

Mrs. Kaluza waved to the elder Warners and walked inside.

Ethan's smile faltered. "If you hate what we picked out, you can exchange it tomorrow."

"We need to talk. Can we go inside?" Grace spoke loud and clear, but she shifted her weight from one foot to the other like a little girl.

Ethan and Faith Warner had taken the news of the twins' illegal activity better than Grace had expected. They were grounded, but Henry had negotiated concessions—namely, the homecoming dance. However, Faith and Ethan had refused to budge when it came to borrowing the truck.

"Remember, home by midnight." Ethan glanced over his shoulder.

Henry nodded.

"Thanks for the ride, Dad. And the dress." She smiled down at the ice-blue vintage number with matching shoes. The country club entrance called to them. High schoolers swarmed the area.

"You look beautiful." His eyes glistened, and his smile wobbled.

Henry opened the door. "We'll leave you before you make Grace cry and ruin her makeup."

"Makeup. My baby girl—"

He shut the door before her father finished the sentence.

"He's having some separation anxiety." Grace giggled.

"That's an understatement." Henry bounced on the balls of his feet. "Ready to attend our first high school dance?"

"I'm ready to get this mystery solved. Does that count?" She may have sounded indifferent, but her heart hadn't slowed since she'd slipped into the dress.

"Warners!" Morgan bounded toward them from the entryway. The girl stopped and looked Henry over from head to toe. "I love the black smoking jacket. You have this whole Ducky from *Pretty in Pink* thing going on."

Despite his dark Native American complexion, he blushed. "Thanks. You look nice yourself."

"This guy!" Jake pulled Henry in for a hug before turning to Grace. "Wow."

She'd never consider Jake Johnson her first date—that honor was saved for the real thing—but he would go down in her memories as the first boy to give her a "Wow."

He pressed his hand to his chest. "Did you match your dress to my eyes?"

"Complete coincidence."

Morgan laughed. "They just named Peter and Maddie Homecoming King and Queen. I say we make like the wind and blow."

Peter bounded outside. "That's done. Let's go."

Jake scrubbed his hand over his jaw. "Grace just got here. We haven't had a chance to dance."

"Dude. We have a plan."

Grace stepped back. "Peter's right. While it was fun to dress up, we have a villain to catch."

"A villain." Jake cracked up. "You sound like Velma."

Peter slapped Jake on the back. "And that would make you Scooby. Come on."

"Where do you think you're going?" Maddie stood behind them with her hands on her hips.

"To the Green Man Tunnel." Peter took his crown off and tossed it aside.

"No! You promised!" Maddison's shrieking drew attention. Too much attention. A few chaperones stared outside.

Henry pulled Grace to the side. "Are you sure you want to leave so soon?"

"This isn't my thing." She wrinkled her nose. "I'd rather chase monsters in the forest."

"Me, too. Let's go."

Morgan wiggled her brows. "Your spare clothes are in my car."

Jake glanced over his shoulder and winked. "See you there, Gracie!"

"Bye, Scoob."

"I thought you hated it when people called you that?" Henry gritted his teeth.

"He's not so bad." Grace grinned. She had to admit, it was fun watching him go into overprotective-brother mode.

"We're burning moonlight." Morgan grabbed Henry's arm and pulled him toward the parking lot. "You first."

He climbed into the back of the Mini-Cooper to change.

"Do you think we're going to catch the impersonator?" Morgan whispered.

"I think there's more than one, but yes, I do."

Groups of kids poured out of the building. It seemed like everyone had the same idea—leave early and head for the tunnel.

"Hurry up." Morgan knocked on the window. "We're going to need to install bleachers to handle the crowds."

Grace shivered. They hadn't seen any more escape hatches or caved-in mine shafts while installing the mini-cameras, but with so many people roaming around, she feared someone would get hurt.

CHAPTER ELEVEN

Cars lined both sides of Piney Fork Road. The area surrounded the tunnel was lit like midday, and countless kids with flashlights roamed the forest, some still in their dresses and suits. Henry leaned forward to get a better view. Their plan to slip away and check their camera feeds wouldn't work, not with so many people around.

"Morgan, make a U-turn and drop us off where you picked us up before." He drummed his fingers on the back of her seat.

"Do you honestly expect me to remember where that was?" She slammed on her brakes to avoid hitting a group of students crossing the street.

"I pulled the reflectors off my bike and duct-taped them to a tree. Look for the reflection."

"Of course, you did."

Grace turned and faced Henry. "Maybe we should come back tomorrow morning."

"No. I have a feeling something's going to happen tonight. This is a video-maker's dream." He rolled down the rear windows. Screams and laughter punctuated the otherwise quiet night.

"Good point. All someone would have to do is walk around with a body camera—" Her eyes widened. "What if that's how they're filming?"

"No, the footage was too steady. The cameras were stationary." He tapped Morgan's shoulder. "There, see it?"

She pulled onto the shoulder. "I'm coming with you."

Grace wasn't amused.

"You're not dressed for roaming the woods. Besides, you hate nature." Henry climbed out of the back seat. The last thing he wanted was for someone to slow them down, or worse, alert the impersonator of their presence.

Morgan got out and slammed the door, which was exactly what he was afraid of.

"We're going back into the mine shaft tonight. With so many people around, I think the impersonator will need to use it to get away, assuming that our bad guy isn't one of the high school kids." Grace slid her drawstring bag onto her shoulders.

The girl glared from one to the other. "You still don't trust me."

The twins exchanged glances.

Henry turned, paced away, and came back. "You're right. I'm not one-hundred-percent sure you've told us everything, but it doesn't matter. Every-one's entitled to their privacy."

Morgan hung her head.

"No, let me finish." He placed his hands on her shoulders. "Ever since we came here, people have told us to be wary of you, but I don't think they see past your hair or your clothes. Come with us if you want, but you're going to have to keep up."

She stared at him for a long moment. "I will."

Grace gave him a wide-eyed, close-lipped smile of approval. "And you have to be quiet."

"Now, *that* I may have a problem with." Morgan removed her skirt and ruffled top to reveal a pair of black skinny jeans and long-sleeved black shirt. "I borrowed some black grease paint in case I needed to camo my face."

Henry chuckled. "It's not necessary, but if it helps you get in character..."

"Maddie's a scream queen. I'm more of a method actor." She smeared twin streaks under her eyes and tossed the can on the driver's seat.

The trio crossed the creek and headed toward the tree line. A few flashlight beams shone to their left, but the other kids remained a respectable distance away. Henry navigated by way of the tiny scraps of reflective tape he'd used to mark the trees along the path. A branch snapped to his left, and he raised his fist to signal to the girls.

Grace eased closer. "What did you hear?" she whispered.

"Not sure." After a few moments of silence, he moved forward.

They reached the first of the hidden cameras and huddled together to block the light from the screen.

"You didn't tell me you had cameras out here," Morgan whispered.

"You didn't ask." He fast-forwarded through a handful of blips and images of squirrels. "Nothing."

Grace pointed to their left. "That's something."

Henry followed her gaze.

"I don't—" Morgan gasped. "Is that one of them?"

A large figure moved between the trees several yards away.

"Not sure."

"We can't jump a random person. We should follow him and wait until he turns on his green light," Grace said.

Henry hated to lose track of the guy, but video footage would be far better than a physical altercation. "We won't be able to find the path to the mine shaft again."

"I'll follow him. You guys go check the rest of the cameras." Morgan crouched and hurried to the next tree.

The guy stopped and glanced over his shoulder before continuing on.

"Why is my first thought that she's going to warn her friends we're filming them?" He sighed.

"You're not alone." Grace tugged his shirt. "Come on."

They made their way to the safe side of the mine shaft. However, the lights from the other kids were coming closer.

"We have to hurry." Henry crouched and reached inside to test the carabiner hooks holding the tarp. "Somebody's fixed the tarp."

Grace knotted a rope around the nearest tree and checked to make sure it was secure. "Ready for the line with the clip."

He pulled the longer rappelling line from his bag and snapped the end beside her knot. "It's a carabiner screw-lock."

"As long as it works, I don't care," she whispered.

Henry double-checked the rigging, grabbed the line, and slid down the tarp. Once inside the mine shaft, he turned on his flashlight.

Grace came down faster than he had and ended up skidding onto the mattress. "Gah, it still stinks."

"I don't think anyone came through and Febreezed it." He shined his light behind her. "Check for the bag."

She lifted the loose side of the tarp. "Three bags."

"We were right. There's more than one of them." He ran his hands over his head. "And they're planning to come back here tonight."

"Check the camera while I go through the bags." She gasped. "Holy orange Bubblicious! There are at least four or five wadded-up napkins with Maddison's gum inside."

"That's disgusting but check the clothes before we jump to the wrong conclusions."

Grace held up a green SHS Cheer sweatshirt. "It says Captain. I think we have a winner."

"Why would she humiliate herself?"

"Morgan called her a scream queen, and the video went viral." She shoved the shirt back into the bag. "Why is it that all roads point to Morgan?"

"I wish I knew." Henry pressed Play, but before he could watch the recording, someone slid down the tarp.

Grace gasped and shined her light in Nina's face. "You!"

The girl wore the same black jacket she had the night they'd met, only this time she held a latex Charlie-No-Face mask in her hand. Nina shoved Grace out of the way and dove behind the tarp.

"What the heck?" Henry lifted the loose corner and shined his light on the wall. "There's a horizontal shaft waist-high. It's big enough to drag a mattress through."

Grace scrubbed her hands over her face. "How did we miss it?"

"We would have had to stand under the tarp with a flashlight to notice it."

"Get the camera. I'm going after her!"

The ground shook over their heads, and bits of debris rained down. It sounded as if a freight train was barreling through the forest straight toward them. Scrambling to his feet, Henry lunged for Grace and pulled her against the wall farthest away from the hole.

Boards snapped, the earth fell, and people screamed.

Grace eased from behind Henry and sucked in a breath. Big mistake. The fresh collapse had thickened the air to the point it felt like she'd breathed in the gaseous equivalent of mud. Coughing, she covered her mouth and nose with her arm.

Light flooded in from above, creating an almost ethereal feel to the gruesome scene. Jake lay sprawled on the floor of the mineshaft. his leg twisted at an odd angle beside him.

"He's hurt! Get help!" Grace shouted. Although she couldn't see them, she knew there were people above them.

"Calling 911," a male voice yelled back.

Henry crouched beside Jake. "Can you hear me?"

He moved as if to sit upright.

"No, don't. It's best if you stay still." Henry met Grace's gaze and frowned. "Get the clothes from the bags and cover him."

Thankfully, all except the bag she'd pulled out were still beneath the tarp and not buried in debris. Her stomach lurched each time she glanced at his twisted leg, but she managed to spread sweats and thick hoodies over him. "We should do something."

"Hang in there." Henry took off his jacket and eased it under the guy's head.

"Who's there?" He groaned. "I can't see right."

Her chest tightened. Jake had fallen through a few feet from the mattress. From the looks of it, his leg had taken the brunt of the damage, but he'd likely hit his head on one of the tracks.

"Henry. Grace is here too." Her brother's frown deepened. "You fell through the roof of an old mine shaft. It's probably dirt in your eyes, but try not to move.

Grace pulled a water bottle from one of the plastic bags and showed it to her brother. While it probably wasn't a good idea to move Jake enough to give him water, they could wipe some of the grime from his face.

Henry nodded. "We're going to clean your face, okay?"

"Thanks." Jake swallowed hard. "How bad is it?"

She removed her jacket and pulled her relatively clean sweatshirt over her head. It was the most sanitary thing they had on hand. She knelt beside Jake and poured a little water onto the upper sleeve.

"Your leg is broken. Close your eyes." Henry wiped the guy's face, folded the shirt over, wet it, and repeated the process. "Better?"

Jake blinked several times and stared at the ceiling. "Much."

Sirens wailed in the distance, and the ground above their heads creaked and groaned.

"Stop!" Grace shot to her feet. The threat of another collapse had sent her into panic mode. "Back up! It's going to collapse again!"

Their voices grew fainter and the unstable earth stilled for the time being, but they'd taken the light source with them.

"Where are the flashlights?" Henry managed to keep his voice calm, but she'd known him since before they were born. He wasn't fooling her. He was scared.

"They have to be buried near the mattress." She picked her way through the fallen debris until her hands stung but couldn't locate either flashlight. Her throat tightened, and tears burned in her eyes. "They were on when the ceiling collapsed. Why can't I find either of them?"

"Gracie, breathe. It's okay. The sirens stopped, so help is close by," Henry comforted her.

Help should have been a good thing, but all she could think about was a horde of emergency responders walking across the unstable ground. "We should use the mattress for protection."

"There's no room to flip it over. We'll have to get the debris off and drag it." This time Henry's voice came out thin and unsteady.

Jake murmured something she couldn't make out.

Henry said, "No. We're not going to leave you here. They'll make the hole bigger and pull you out in a basket like they do with water rescues."

"Grace?"

She knelt beside Jake and took his outstretched hand.

"There's a passage." He closed his eyes and took several short breaths. "Under the tarp. Waist-high."

Blood whooshed behind her ears. Jake was part of this. How else would he know? "We know. Nina came down the tarp before you fell."

He turned his head. "It wasn't supposed to be like this."

"Forget about all of that. Right now, we need a safe way in and out." Henry asked, "Is the passage a straight shot?"

"Mostly."

She clung to her anger, but Jake was in pain. There'd be time enough for answers once the rescuers freed him. "Where does it come out?"

"Twenty yards west. There's an old building." His eyelids drifted shut.

"Jake, you have to stay awake. You could have a concussion." Henry pressed the damp shirt against the guy's face.

"Climb out and talk to the first responders." Her voice came out louder than she'd intended. Between the shock of her not-date breaking his leg and the realization he'd played a part in the scam, her nerves were frazzled. "See how they want to move him."

More debris fell into the shaft, and the twins moved to protect Jake. Chunks of rotted wood, rocks, and earth pelted their backs and shoulders. When it stopped, Grace met Henry's eyes. One of them needed to go explain the situation to the people trying to help them.

"Go." He shoved her toward the rope.

"You're stronger. It makes more sense for you to go." She turned back to Jake and brushed the dirt from his face.

"If anything happens to you—" Henry let out a guttural cry and bolted for the tarp.

"I'm sorry, Grace." Jake squeezed her hand. "I never meant..."

"I don't understand why you'd do something like this and still go along with Peter's plan tonight as if you knew nothing about it."

"Maddie set up the first video. Some of the guys from the AV Club filmed it." He sucked in a breath. "Peter and I did the second two. She wanted fame, and we wanted to win the film competition."

"What was Morgan's part in this?"

"Maddie set her up. If things went bad, people would blame Morgan." He grimaced, either from pain or guilt.

"It almost worked." The larger picture formed in her mind, but it didn't help her to understand how things had gotten so incredibly out of hand. "Why on earth did you film *me*?"

"I didn't know who you were. Then you chased me, and I wanted to know you."

"That was you? In the costume?" She grinned despite herself.

"Yes, but I had nothing to do with the editing." He winced and tried to adjust his position. "Peter has more video. From Smiley's and from the dance."

"Wait, he filmed the five of us planning to capture the imposter...to capture you?"

"Not me, Nina. She got spooked and bailed down here."

"I can't say I blame her. It sounded like a herd of rhinos chasing her."

"Just the football team." He trembled as if he were resting on a block of ice. "I'm sorry. I tried to make it up to you."

"Shhh. Quiet for now. We'll have plenty of time to talk once we're out of here."

CHAPTER TWELVE

The twins huddled together and watched the paramedics load Jake into the back of an ambulance. Most of the kids had vanished when the fire department and police arrived. Of those Henry knew, only Morgan had stuck around.

A paramedic who'd assisted in getting Jake out of the mine shaft offered the twins a broad smile. "What you kids did back there was brave."

"Is he going to be okay?" Grace's voice cracked.

"He's going to need time and physical therapy, but he'll recover. He might even play ball again." The man shook his head. "He's lucky you two were there."

The events of the day finally caught up to him, and Henry blew out a sigh. "We were happy to help."

Morgan sidled up next to Grace. "Have you watched the recording from the mineshaft camera?"

"Not yet." Henry glanced down at his dirt-crusted clothes. "Any chance you can give us a ride home? We have a ginormous television and microwave popcorn."

"I told you, parents hate me."

"And we told you our parents are different." He shrugged. "Besides, I told them you were coming when I called to say we were going to be late."

Grace slung her arm over the girl's shoulder. "I hope you like thrillers because you're going to be shocked when you see the stars of the film."

"I'll give you a ride and eat your popcorn, but the suspense is killing me. Who was it?"

"And ruin the ending?" Henry took Morgan's hand and pulled her toward her car.

Saturday morning, the sun shone brightly in the clear autumn sky. Students, teachers, and guests gathered in the school courtyard to attend the Raymond Robinson Memorial Garden groundbreaking ceremony. The Monaghans had agreed to sponsor the tribute to the original Green Man after an anonymous person had sent the principal a video starring their elder daughter.

"I still can't believe she did it." Grace had a difficult time understanding Morgan's and Maddie's relationship, let alone how their parents could so blatantly choose favorites.

"She lives for attention." Morgan nodded to the golden shovel in the principal's hand. "Even now, people will associate this garden with Maddison Monaghan."

Henry squeezed the girl's shoulder. "In ten years, no one will remember her, but you'll be receiving your third Tony award and starring on Broadway."

"Are you sure you can't stick around and remind me of that every time I flub a line or miss a cue?"

His cheeks heated. "As Grace likes to remind me, this is the age of technology. I'm an email, text, Skype, SnapChat, Facebook message, or phone call away."

Behind them, Ethan and Faith Warner whispered.

Henry glanced over his shoulder and his dad gave him two thumbs-up.

"I wonder what will happen to Peter, Jake, and Nina." Morgan turned to Grace. "Did Mrs. Kaluza say anything?"

"They agreed to hand over the footage they shot and donate the money they raised to the memorial garden." She'd thought they'd gotten off too easy until she learned that all three had planned to attend film school after graduation.

Morgan's face paled. "What about the t-shirt sales?"

Henry said, "Your fundraiser might have been in bad taste, but it didn't break school policy. Looks like the theater kids are New York-bound in April."

"If there's any left over, we'll donate it to the garden."

Grace's hands flew to her mouth. "Look."

Agnes pushed Mr. Canter's wheelchair down the sidewalk. The old man wore a black suit and a fedora, a far cry from the worn-out jeans and flannel he'd worn the first time they'd met.

The twins had stopped by his house to tell him they'd solved the mystery and invite him to the groundbreaking ceremony, but he'd declined. However, he'd treated them to two hours of stories from his days in the coal mines.

Grinning like he'd won the lottery, Henry strode to Mr. Canter and took over for Agnes.

"Who is that gentleman?" Faith leaned closer and whispered.

"He was a friend of Raymond Robinson's for many years." She hurried to the old devil and gave him a hug. "You look so nice that my mom referred to you as a gentleman."

"Agnes made me wear the tie." He flashed her a toothless grin.

The once-cranky waitress straightened said tie. "It suits you."

The principal clapped her hands three times. "If I could have everyone's attention, we'll start with a few words from a man who had the honor of knowing Mr. Raymond Robinson for over fifty years, Mr. Carl Canter."

The retired coal miner pushed to his feet.

Henry moved to his side and offered him an arm. Together, they walked to the front of the gathering.

Mr. Canter lifted his head as much as his bent spine would allow. "Raymond Robinson was a man who never gave up. He never let his differences hold him back. He would have been tickled to know the kids in this town finally found out his real name. May his story inspire others to be better people. Now, let me tell you about the time old Ray and I..."

As she listened to another of Mr. Canter's tales, Grace's heart filled with a bittersweet emotion she couldn't quite name. It felt like sunshine through rain and laughter through tears and old memories.

Her parents wrapped their arms around her and beamed at Henry, who was proudly helping an elderly man stand to address a crowd.

Morgan whispered, "Forget you guys staying here. Please adopt me."

"I always wanted a sister." Grace embraced her friend. "Promise to email me once a week?"

"I will and call at least once a month." She sniffled, pulled away, and laughed. "Southpointe Township's going to be dull without you and Henry."

Grace turned in time to see her mother tilt her head and smile. "What is it?"

Faith said, "You were right. We have nothing to worry about. You and your brother are okay."

Later that afternoon, the Warners packed up their fifth wheel and said their goodbyes to Dr. and Mrs. Kaluza, only this time they planned to take a plane to their next destination.

"Do you have your passports?" Their mother dug through her carry-on bag for the third time in ten minutes.

Grace held up the navy-blue booklets where she could see them. "I have mine and Henry's in the front pocket of my backpack, along with some Euros, an English-Italian dictionary, and my cell phone."

She nodded and turned to her husband. "Ethan, do you have the plug adaptors for the laptops?"

"Yes, dear." He set his hands on her shoulders and pressed his forehead to hers. "What has you so frazzled? We travel for a living."

"We travel with our house. This is different." She laughed and rubbed her nose against his. "Have I told you how much I love you?"

Henry groaned and stared at the sky. "Please tell me the rideshare will be here soon. You guys are so sweet, I'm getting cavities watching you."

Their parents separated. Ethan ran his hand over the back of his neck, and Faith blushed like a teenager.

He motioned at them. "Even now my teeth are decaying."

Faith Warner quirked a brow. "Do you two have a mystery to solve in Italy?"

"Not yet," Grace said. "There isn't a lot of information online about Ischia."

"She's right. Other than it sits in the Bay of Naples and is a sister island to Capri, we don't have much to go on."

Ethan hitched his bag higher on his shoulder. "There's Aragonese Castle. It was built by Hiero I of Syracuse in 474 BC. I'm sure there's a ghost or two haunting the halls."

Grace pulled out her phone and searched for the castle. The first entry drew her attention. She clicked on the link and read about the Poor Clares and the nuns' bizarre burial practices. "This is...disturbing."

Henry peeked over her shoulder. "Those are some fancy toilets."

"They're not toilets, they're death chairs. When a nun died, they would sit the corpse upright and let the decomposition juices—"

Their mother held up her hand. "Please. We get the idea."

"I think you may be onto something, Grace." Henry pursed his lips and nodded. "If the death chairs don't *pan out*—"

"Nice pun." Ethan chuckled.

"I'm a *punny* guy." Henry waggled his brows. "I say we investigate if the rumors are true about Naples being the birthplace of pizza. We can eat our way through the city for research purposes."

Faith motioned in their general direction. "We haven't forgotten about the trespassing incident. You two are still grounded. Find an urban legend on Ischia or write a paper on its history."

"Death chairs and haunted castles it is." Henry glanced at Grace.

"Sounds wonderful." She bit her lip to keep from laughing.

Ethan said, "If that's not gruesome enough for you, we're planning to visit Herculaneum. There are three hundred skeletons from the 79 AD Mount Vesuvius eruption on display."

Faith Warner pinched the bridge of her nose. "Is a week with no monsters, ghosts, or burial mounds too much to ask for?"

"Yes," the other three said in unison.

CASTLE OF GHOSTS

MONSTER CASE FILES BOOK 5

CHAPTER ONE

Brianna Bennet turned her face toward the setting sun and breathed in the salty air. The Tyrrhenian Sea glittered in the fading light like a kaleidoscope of blues, greens, purples, and other colors she couldn't possibly name. "You're not in London anymore."

"No, you're in Ischia, where *normal* people come inside when it's cold." Alessio, a fellow archeology intern and her research partner, kissed her temple.

"You shouldn't do that where people can see us."

Alessio spread his arms wide. "This is Italia. Hugging in public is as normal as breathing."

Bri glanced over her shoulder to make sure they were alone. "I'm not kidding. What we uncovered today is huge. We can't risk anyone finding out about our relationship. Until this assignment is over, we are *colleagues*."

He shoved his hands in his pockets. "Are you sure you want to write the report tonight?"

"You know the rules. We have to send our findings to the university." She would have loved more time to investigate the ruins to be certain. Unless she was mistaken, they'd discovered artifacts from the ancient Roman city of Aenaria.

He tapped his watch. "How long have you been daydreaming?"

A quick check of the time sent her heart into a gallop. She shot to her feet and glanced around for her tablet. "Too long, and I seem to have misplaced my iPad. You know—the one with our photos and notes?"

"I saw it downstairs. I would have brought it up, but I thought you were planning to return to the dig site."

"Please tell me you're joking." Blood whooshed behind her eardrums. "I would swear I had it with me."

"Afraid not." Alessio said, "You're frightened. I will go with you."

No one, not even the owners, willingly went into the bowels of the castle at night.

Every fiber of her being shouted, "Yes, please," but she said, "Don't be silly. It's a long walk."

"I'll happily brave the castle's angry spirits for more time with you." Alessio gave her a crooked smile.

"Go. I'll be fine. I don't believe in ghosts."

"But do they believe in you?" He chuckled. "*Ciao, bella.*"

"*Ciao.*" She watched him walk away and sighed.

Brianna hurried through the eighteenth-century church and down a level to the medieval chapel. The final flight of stairs ended in a musty hallway.

Though the castle's owners had installed some modern lighting, the lower levels remained dim. The air seemed thicker, making it harder to breathe. Worse still, the lingering scent of decay clung to the walls.

She reached the excavation site and turned on the shop light. Her tablet was there, but she could have sworn she'd brought it upstairs with her.

Footsteps echoed from down the hall.

"Tourists." She grabbed her things.

At least once per week, visitors found their way into restricted areas. Some were lost, but others snuck inside and hid until after closing to hunt ghosts and ghouls.

"Hello? Who's there?" Brianna stilled to hear the reply.

Muffled voices came from inside the *putridarium.*

A ball of ice formed in her stomach. "*Buongiorno?*"

A scampering sound, too loud to have come from a rat, echoed through the space.

"This area is employees only, and the castle is closed to visitors. You're going to have to leave." She used her phone as a flashlight and took three steps into the T-shaped room.

No one was there.

"And I'm officially hearing things." She shined the light around in the adjacent chamber and turned to go.

The door slammed shut—quite the feat, considering the hinges had rusted in place centuries earlier.

She rushed forward and tried to open it. "Hello? Please, the door is stuck."

No reply.

She knocked until her hand ached. "This isn't funny. Open up!"

Silence.

Don't panic, she told herself but the emotion train had already been sent down the tracks.

Brianna panicked. Pushing and shoving and slamming her body against the heavy wood, she screamed until her throat became raw. "Help! I'm trapped inside!"

She glanced over her shoulder at the throne-like chairs and shivered.

A voice, soft as a baby's sigh, drew her attention.

She squinted into the darkness. "Is someone there?"

A woman whispered in a language that sounded like Neapolitan Italian mixed with Latin.

Brianna understood just enough to realize the woman was reciting a prayer. "Please. Help me with the door."

A translucent image of a kneeling woman appeared in the center of the room. The apparition kissed the floor and continued to chant the prayer.

Gasping for breath, Bri huddled against the door. *This can't be happening.*

She watched in horror as ghostly figures appeared in the death chairs. As they had in centuries long past, Poor Clare nuns sat in the stone thrones staring with unseeing eyes as their bodies slowly but inexorably decomposed.

The journey from Pittsburgh to Naples took twenty hours—three flights with stops and layovers, including the inevitable delays. Exhausted and hungry, Grace wanted nothing more than a shower and a bed.

Henry had other ideas. "Do we have time to see some of the city before we board the ferry?"

Normally, Grace would have enjoyed sightseeing, but she was ready to collapse. Plus, the wheel on her suitcase had blown out somewhere between New York and Munich. "Please, no. We have to catch a taxi and a ferry and another taxi."

Ethan Warner, the twins' father, took her bag. "You look like you need a break."

"Thanks." She rolled her shoulder to relieve the tension.

"Hang in there. The ferry ride takes about an hour. That'll give you time to relax before we get to Ischia." Her mother smiled, but Grace suspected the double espresso she'd downed before landing was the only thing keeping her upright.

"You two should have slept on the plane." Henry veered toward a pastry shop. "Mmm, breakfast."

Neither of the Warner women could sleep in a moving vehicle, including cars. However, Grace had used the extra hours to get ahead on her schoolwork. In theory, giving her more time to enjoy Italy once she caught up on sleep.

"Coffee and croissants. Just what the doctor ordered." Faith yawned and followed Ethan in.

Grace scarfed down her pastry and finished her demitasse of espresso in one small gulp. Within minutes of the rich black liquid hitting her bloodstream, she found her second wind. "Are we ready or are we ready?"

Her parents exchanged quick glances.

"I was born ready." Henry cleared their table and took her broken suitcase. "We have ninety minutes before the ferry leaves Molo Beverello. I bet the cab driver will take us on a quick tour if we pay extra."

"That's a thought." Grace reached into her purse for her phone. "I'll map a route."

Ethan placed a hand on each of their shoulders. "We have ten days after the conference to explore Italy, but your mother has about an hour before the caffeine wears off."

Grace laughed and walked through the double doors into the Italian sunshine. The sky seemed bluer and the trees greener and the flowers brighter than in the States. A smile spread slowly across her face. She loved the allure of the exotic mixed with the history.

Henry motioned to the line of people waiting for cabs. "Holy smokes, it's as bad as Space Mountain at Disney World."

"Rule one: no complaining." Faith Warner, a brilliant mechanical engineer turned guest lecturer, narrowed her eyes. "Rule two: see Rule One."

Forty-five minutes later, they piled into a cab and headed for the port. The driver wove through traffic with one hand while using the other to punctuate his words, none of which Grace understood. Even when he spoke English, she found it impossible to focus on the conversation while hurtling toward certain death on the busy highway.

Faith white-knuckled the handhold above the window. "We aren't in a rush."

The driver smiled and hit the gas. "I get you there faster."

She glanced at her husband for assistance.

"Not faster. *Slower.* Slower please." He enunciated each syllable as if that would help the guy understand English.

"*Sí*, we are almost there."

Laughing, Henry recorded a video of the adventure. "Holy bumper cars, did you see how close we came to that semi?"

"Not helping," Ethan remarked through gritted teeth.

The driver took a corner sharply and came to a stop. "Molo Beverello."

Grace climbed out of the cab and gasped at the enormous castle on the other side of the street. Horns blared, mopeds raced in every direction, and machinery wailed, but there it sat, like a sleeping giant in the middle of a crowded city.

"Whoa." Henry snapped a few photos. "That's incredible."

Their mother frowned at a sign listing the ferry schedules. "You two stay here while we get the tickets."

The twins found seats in the shade and took to Google.

"It's Castel Nuovo, built in the thirteenth century." Henry studied the imposing structure.

"It's open for tours."

He nodded without taking his eyes off the castle. "I'll add it to the to-do list."

Grace lowered her voice in case their parents returned. "Speaking of the list, I'm a little concerned we won't find a mystery in Ischia. I searched the entire internet and came up with nothing."

"If the island is anything like Naples, we'll find something. History suggests there has to be a mystery. And would it be so bad if we didn't have to run from someone?"

One look at the island and Grace knew Ischia was nothing like Naples. The air had a salty but fresh quality instead of the exhaust fumes and dust of the larger city. Coffee shops and boutiques lined the street, and row after row of colorful buildings spiraled up the mountainside.

"It's like we've arrived on another *planet* instead of another country." Henry gawked at the scenery. "Do you smell that?"

"Sea and sunshine?"

"Garlic and oregano and, oh man, I don't know, but I'm looking forward to finding out." His tongue lolled out of his mouth, much like a hungry dog's. He took her broken bag and headed down to the pier.

Grace turned to check on her parents.

Ethan and Faith Warner strolled hand in hand, both wearing smiles as large as the sun.

"If I didn't know you, I'd think you were a couple of honeymooners."

"I like to think we've had a twenty-year honeymoon." Her father pulled her mother in for a quick kiss.

"We've lost Henry to the siren's call of Italian food." She motioned toward her brother.

"Go with him, or we may never get to the hotel," Faith ordered.

After a quick slice of pizza, the Warners hailed another taxi. Like the first, the driver navigated the roads while talking over his shoulder. He pointed out restaurants, swanky stores, and a handful of churches along their route.

"Holy smokes." Henry craned his neck as they turned a corner. "Did you see it?"

"You'll have to be more specific." She'd done nothing but take it all in since they'd stepped off the ferry.

"There." He pointed.

She followed his gaze to an islet off the main island. A castle perched on the highest point and draped down the rocky hillside as if carved from the land. Her heart leapt into her throat. "It's beautiful."

Henry dipped his head to get a better view. "The *Castello Aragonese d'Ischia.*"

Grace had seen pictures of it on the internet, but they'd failed to properly portray its size. Her eyes misted. "I-I don't think I've ever been hit this hard in the feels by looking at a building."

Faith reached back and patted her hand. "It's not just a building. You're looking at over two thousand years of history. It's a lot to take in."

"I thought the fortress beside the port was impressive, but this... It's..."

Henry swiveled his head back toward the castle each time they rounded a corner. "When can we visit?"

Ethan and Faith Warner exchanged knowing glances.

Faith said, "I would suggest you nap first, but—"

"We'll have the driver stop at the castle's causeway." Ethan winked. "That is, if you're up for it now."

"Yes!" the twins said in unison.

CHAPTER TWO

Henry had visited a lot of places, but there was something special about Ischia. Standing in the center of a long stone bridge, he glanced behind him at the sleepy fishing village and turned back to the massive castle before him.

"It doesn't seem real," Grace said over the sound of the waves crashing against the rocks.

"You're right. It doesn't."

"Can you imagine what this was like when it was new?" Grace snapped several pictures. "It's like meeting an elderly woman and seeing the echo of her former self in her features. She's still beautiful, but different."

"You've been in Italy three hours, and already you're a poet." Henry slung his arm around her shoulder. "I have a good feeling about this place. I bet we'll find a dozen or so mysteries to solve."

"I'll settle for one. Let's go inside while we're still hopped up on espresso and sugar."

Small groups of people walked back toward the main island. A few muttered in unhappy tones, but Henry couldn't understand the different languages. A man dressed in safari shorts and a plaid shirt met his gaze, said a few words in German, and pointed at the entrance.

Henry furrowed his brow. "It's closed?"

"Ja." The man nodded.

"Now what?" Grace glanced up at the castle like a kid with empty pockets staring at a candy display.

"We go ask about their hours."

The young man behind the ticket window took one look at Grace and sat straighter. "We are closed for the day."

"When will you reopen?" Henry asked.

The guy shrugged.

Thinking the strange reaction had to do with a language difference, Henry pulled his phone from his pocket to use a translation app.

Grace stepped closer to the booth and read the Italian's name tag. "Hi, Matteo. I'm Grace. Do you speak English?"

"Of course. As well as German and Spanish." He winked. "Grace from America, yes?"

"Yes, my *brother* and I are from Florida. Do you know when the castle will reopen?"

"I do not know. We are closed for the day, possibly tomorrow." Matteo glanced away. In fact, he seemed to look anywhere except at the twins.

Henry's newly honed detective senses kicked in. *He's hiding something.*

"That's disappointing. We're only in Ischia for a few days. It'll break my heart if we can't see the inside of the castle," Grace said, smiling.

The guy turned and stared as if contemplating giving her a private tour. "Perhaps you will come back tomorrow?"

Henry did *not* appreciate the way the Italian looked at his sister. He needed to get the conversation back on track. "Why are you closed? Was it planned, or did something happen?"

Matteo's frown deepened.

Henry leaned closer and lowered his voice. "Is it unsafe? In a place this old, I can imagine people have accidents..."

The guy's eyes rounded before he could smooth his expression and stiffen his spine. "No, nothing like that. The castle will open tomorrow or the next day."

"Thanks, Matteo. It was nice meeting you." Grace tugged Henry's arm.

"You're welcome." He motioned for the group of tourists behind them to move forward.

Henry took a guidebook from the counter and walked back outside. "That was odd."

"To say the least." Grace laughed. "You were intense in there."

"He was hiding something."

"Yes, but like our grandmother always says, you catch more flies with honey than vinegar." She squinted in the midday sun.

"And you know what Grandpa always said in reply. You catch the most flies with...you know."

Grace ignored his jibe. "What now?"

"Let's grab some lunch before we head back to the hotel."

She pressed her hand to her belly. "My stomach feels like I've been snacking on sulfuric acid."

"Pasta will help. It's a miracle cure." He wiggled his brows.

"If you say so."

The twins ducked into a little seafood restaurant at the end of the bridge. The dining room consisted of a long row of tables adjacent to the kitchen, but the host led them to a waterfront patio in the back.

The waiter brought a basket of bread and waited to take their orders.

Grace skimmed the menu. "Spaghetti Bolognese sounds good."

Spaghetti Bolognese is a foreign invention," Henry told his sister. He glanced around at the other patrons' food and spotted a seafood concoction that looked amazing. "I'll have that."

"Would you like wine?"

"Water, please." Grace smiled.

The server retrieved a tall bottle and two glasses from the bar inside and placed them on the table.

Henry waited for the server to leave before speaking. "You saw Matteo's reaction. There must have been an accident for them to close the castle. It's the top attraction on the island. It's not like there's much else to do here."

"Besides the thermal spas, beaches, gardens, and shopping?" She gave him a patient smile, enjoying their different definitions of interesting things to do.

"Right, but it's off-season. Too cold to swim." Henry downed half a glass of water.

"The Aragonese Castle is still closed to the public, then?" The young woman at an adjacent table spoke with a heavy British accent. "Forgive me, I didn't mean to eavesdrop."

"Not a problem, it's a small space. I'm Henry, and this is my sister Grace."

"Bethany." She smiled, but it seemed empty. "Nice to meet you."

"You too. To answer your question, yes, it's closed. Do you know why?"

"Unfortunately, I do. One of the interns working in the new excavation site was trapped in a *room* for a bit." She glanced at her hands.

Grace said, "I don't understand."

That makes two of us. Henry reached for a piece of bread but hesitated. It seemed rude to eat given the current topic.

Bethany lowered her voice. "It wasn't just any room. Brianna was locked in the Nuns' Cemetery. She broke a small bone in each hand banging on the door. Plus, she was in a hurry to flee and hit her head on the way out. She has a concussion."

"Why?" Grace's eyes widened. "What happened to her in there?"

"No one knows. She refuses to talk about it." Bethany dipped her chin and fidgeted with her napkin.

Her reaction surprised Henry. It seemed far more personal than someone repeating a rumor. "Is Brianna a friend of yours?"

"My sister, actually." She cleared her throat and squared her shoulders. "I came straight away from London when I learned she needed surgery on her hands. They're transferring her to Naples later today."

Henry's chest tightened. He and Grace had found themselves in a few dangerous situations while solving mysteries, but so far they'd come through relatively unscathed. Had his sister been hurt, he doubted he'd have had the wherewithal to calmly discuss it with strangers.

Grace motioned to the empty chair at their table. "Would you like to join us?"

"I would, thank you." She dabbed her eyes with her napkin.

Henry cleared a space for her. "You mentioned that Brianna is an intern?"

Teacup in hand, Bethany settled into the chair. "She's brilliant. Studying for her Ph.D. in Archaeology at Cambridge. She was so excited when she won the internship on Ischia."

"I can imagine. It's absolutely gorgeous here, and the castle...the history is fascinating." Grace gazed at the islet and sighed.

"I prefer technology to the archaic, but yes, it was an incredible opportunity for her." Her expression fell. "I just wish she would tell me what happened. Brianna hated that part of the castle. I can't imagine why she would have gone in there."

"You mean into the Nuns' Cemetery?" Henry had read a little about the weird burial practices at the convent.

"Yes. She said it freaked her out, and she wasn't the only one. From what I understand, none of the people who work in the castle willingly visit the lower levels at night."

"You said she was working on an excavation?" Grace asked.

"Brianna and her research partner found something 'astonishing.' Her words, not mine." Bethany's eyes lit as she spoke. "It's all very top secret. I couldn't pry the details from her, but I suspect the discovery is Roman in nature."

"Wow." Had he not decided to follow in his father's footsteps and study law, Henry could see himself as an archaeologist digging for lost civilizations in an ancient land.

Grace said, "If it's as old as you think, it stands to reason the site would be under the castle. Do you know where it is in relation to the putridaria?"

"Nearby, I think. Brianna loved her work, but she complained about having to walk past the chambers several times per day. Plus, she grumbled about the superstitious security staff. They insisted she stop working before sunset."

Henry asked, "Have you spoken to her research partner?"

"The only person I've been permitted to see is the head of Security. I phoned the private owners directly but couldn't get past their secretaries." Bethany lifted her chin. "I'm certain they're afraid bad publicity will hurt tourism, but I can't help but think there's more to it."

While the woman was looking away, Grace gave Henry a slight smile and hint of a nod. The game was afoot.

"Oddly enough, we're working on a year-long research project involving urban legends. We may be able to help you find out what happened to your sister." He broke off a chunk of bread and slathered it with butter.

Bethany gave him a dubious look. "While I appreciate the thought, I'm not sure what you could do."

Grace sat straighter and used a more professional tone. "Because few people see two teenagers as a threat, we've been able to investigate all sorts of mysteries. Something must have happened there for your sister to have had such an intense reaction—"

"Ghosts." Her cheeks turned pink. She'd likely not meant to say the word out loud. "I mean, if I had to guess, I'd say she saw ghosts."

A shiver of fear slid down Henry's spine like a spider on a strand of silk. Despite his sister's skepticism, he firmly believed he'd seen the Lady in White on the Cursed Isle.

A nervous laugh escaped Bethany's lips. "It sounds foolish, I know, but I believe there's more to this world than what we can physically see and touch."

"I don't rule anything out, but I tend to think most cases of unexplained phenomenon can be solved by looking deeper into the motives of the people involved," Grace replied.

The woman paused for a moment and nodded. "I'm in no position to refuse help. You have my blessing to investigate what happened to Brianna, but I'm afraid you'll need more than that."

Henry remembered the guy in the ticket booth's reaction when he'd pushed for more information. "You're probably right, but we'll do our best."

Grace pulled her phone from her purse and exchanged numbers with

Bethany. "We're staying at the Hotel Delfini until Friday. Please call if anything changes with your sister's condition or if you learn anything new from the castle staff."

"I will." Bethany stood and smoothed her jacket. "I have to catch a ferry to Naples in thirty minutes. Thank you both for...everything."

"You're welcome," the twins said in unison.

She gave them a curious expression. He'd seen it before on countless people when he and Grace did that, finished each other's sentences, or communicated in secret twin language.

Grace waited until the woman had left the restaurant. "What do you think?"

"I *know* I didn't want to get involved with another ghost mystery." He smirked. "Besides that, I don't know what to think. You were right, though. Something must have happened to Brianna while she was locked inside the cemetery room."

"Still not over your encounter with the Lady in White?" She laughed.

"I'll get over it when we find a logical explanation for what I saw."

She opened her mouth but snapped it shut. "I'm still researching it."

The waiter returned with their food, but the conversation had ruined Henry's appetite.

"*Grazie.*" Grace put her napkin on her lap and rearranged her silverware.

The server glanced at their drinks and the bread basket, nodded once, and walked back the way he'd come.

He whispered, "I can't decide if it's a language barrier or if people here are aloof."

"The island depends on tourism. I'm sure it's probably cultural differences more than unfriendliness." Picking at her pasta, Grace eyed his seafood arrabbiata. "That looks good. Are those clams and mussels?"

"Both. It also has fish, shrimp, and scallops." He grinned. "Would you like to trade?"

"Yes, please!" she lifted her plate from the table.

He pulled his plate closer to his chest. "First you have to admit that there is no *logical* explanation for what we *both* saw on Star Island."

She groaned. "Okay, I admit it. I have yet to find a *scientific* explanation for the Lady in White."

"Close enough." He swapped plates with her and dug into the pasta.

Halfway through their lunch, the guy from the ticket booth walked onto the patio. He took one look at the twins and hesitated.

Grace waved. "*Buongiorno*, Matteo."

The Italian grinned and held his arms out to his sides. "The castle, she's still closed, *bella*."

"I figured." She flipped her hair over her shoulder and smiled. "Come join us?"

Henry's jaw hit the table. Sure, he'd seen girls flirt before—heck, he'd been on the receiving end of it—but he'd never seen his sister do it.

"After I break your heart, you give mine flight." Matteo pressed his hand to his chest. "I would love to."

Henry gave her a what-are-you-doing look.

Grace pressed her lips together and shook her head a fraction of an inch before turning her attention back to Matteo. "Are you on your lunch break?"

"*Sì*, I am picking up food for my co-workers." He sat in the chair Bethany had abandoned. "You will be happy to hear, the castle, she is open for business tomorrow."

"That's very good news." Grace sipped her water.

Sitting back, Henry said, "Did they discover who locked Brianna the intern in the putridarium?"

The whites showed all the way around Matteo's dark-brown irises, and in his haste to retreat, the guy knocked Grace's glass over. "*Scusa, mi dispiace.* Eh. So sorry."

"It's okay." She mopped the spilled water from the table. "But why are you so nervous?"

"Beautiful girls make me this way."

Henry wanted to puke.

"Gee, thanks." Grace bit her lip as if to hold back laughter.

Matteo glanced between the twins. "I could lose my job for speaking of this."

"We don't want to get you into trouble." She lowered her voice. "We just want to know what happened. Brianna's sister is worried about her."

"Matteo, there you are. Where is the food?" Another young Italian man stood at the patio entrance with his hands on his hips. He gave Grace a once-over and smiled. "Ah, you were distracted by America the Beautiful. No?"

Henry gritted his teeth. *It's going to be a long five days.*

CHAPTER THREE

Grace walked onto the balcony and soaked in the first few rays of the morning sun. Although it was late October, the scent of flowers mixed with the salt of the sea air. If a perfumer could capture the fragrance in a bottle, it'd sell like crazy.

"Good morning, sunshine." Ethan joined his daughter with a cup of American coffee in his hand.

"No espresso?"

"I prefer the watered-down variety." He nodded toward the castle. "How was it?"

"Closed, but we're going back today." She rested her elbows on the railing and continued to stare off into the distance. "Ready for your first day of lectures?"

"As I ever will be. Who would have thought your mom and I would be teaching classes on how to become professional guest-lecturers."

"Me, for one. I've sat in on enough of your classes to know you guys are awesome."

"Yes, I suppose we are, but I'm not sure I can compete with this view." He sipped his coffee and smiled. "To tell you the truth, I'm not sure I want to."

Grace glanced over her shoulder. "You aren't considering playing hooky, are you?"

"Your mother would never allow that. She did, however, agree to cut out early and soak in the thermal baths with me."

Grace couldn't help but grin. "You two should get mud treatments. I hear the volcanic soil is good for you."

"Can you see your mom covered in mud?" He pressed his lips together to suppress a grin.

Grace gave him a nudge. "If you talk her into it, take pictures."

Henry shambled past the French doors without as much as a glance in their direction. From the looks of it, he hadn't quite left the weird place between sleeping and waking.

Ethan chuckled. "You two have fun today but stay out of trouble."

"And don't forget to put a little time in on your studies." Smiling from the balcony beside the twins, Faith Warner wore linen pants and a flowing top. Even more perplexing, she'd left her dark hair down.

"Who are you, and what have you done with my mother?" Grace had never seen her dress casually for work, nor had her mom ever used the "little time" and "studies" in the same sentence.

"It's this place. It's magical. I feel like a girl again." She opened her arms wide as if to embrace the island.

Ethan stared at his wife with the goofiest of goofy smiles.

"If we hurry, we can have breakfast on the terrace before our classes begin." Her mother turned and went inside.

"You heard the woman. Let's head downstairs." Ethan took one look at Henry, who had zonked back out on the bed, and sighed. "Breakfast for three it is."

Grace rolled her eyes. "You go ahead. I'm not hungry yet. Plus, someone needs to light a fire under him, or we'll never make it to the castle."

An hour later, Henry had showered, dressed, and eaten enough carbs to fuel him for a couple of hours. "What's the plan?"

"Buy tickets and scope it out. The Nuns' Cemetery is open to the public." She slid her feet into her sneakers and tied a hoodie around her waist.

"Let's hope Matteo isn't working today."

"And what if he is?" She slung her bag over her shoulder and headed for the door.

"No hair-flipping or lash-batting today, okay?" He lowered his voice in the hall. "This isn't the States. Italians are different."

"Oh, how I noticed." Grace laughed.

Henry didn't.

"I promise, today is all about solving the mystery." She picked up her pace until they reached the street. "One of us should navigate and use the language-translator app, and the other should conserve their battery for any unforeseen circumstances."

"There will be no emergencies. This time we're going to work smarter, not harder, and avoid falling through the floor or the ground or off the terraces." He pulled his phone from his pocket. "This way."

The walk started off like any other, but once they passed the first hairpin turn, the road narrowed. Complicating matters further, a line of parked cars blocked one of the traffic lanes. The sidewalk, half as wide as any in the United States, provided some safety, but not enough for Grace's liking

She peeked over the side of the cliff, and her stomach fell. "Wow, that's a lot farther down than I would have thought."

Henry glanced from the steep drop to the stone wall on the opposite side of the street. "GPS says it's a twenty-five-minute walk. We'll be fine if we go single file."

She had her doubts, but Henry was proven right.

The twins made it to the castle's ticket window at precisely nine. Unfortunately, the person scheduled to work the morning shift did not.

Grace chewed her lower lip. "The website says they open at nine. What if they're closed again today?"

"Then we hang out on the causeway until Matteo goes into town to get lunch."

"Ha ha." She rolled her eyes. "What do you have against him?"

"I know he's hiding something."

"Uh-huh. Is that all there is to it?"

"*Buongiorno.*" A woman who looked old enough to have witnessed the construction of the place tottered from a door behind the ticket counter.

"Two, please." Grace grinned and decided to try out her limited Italian. "*Due, per favore.*"

Henry snickered. "Holding up two fingers works, too."

"When in Ischia." She shrugged and paid the woman.

Armed with the guidebook Henry had marked up the previous night, the twins strolled toward the entrance.

"A tunnel." Grace stared up at the stone archway. "I'm not sure I've fully recovered from the Green Man Tunnel and the abandoned mine shaft."

He looped his arm with hers. "Me either, but we made a pact not to fall into or off anything, and I intend to keep it."

Grace pointed at the square holes in the ceiling. "Medieval skylights?"

"Sort of. Soldiers on the upper levels dumped molten pitch and hot oil on anyone foolish enough to attempt to invade the castle."

"Nice." She quickened her pace up the old donkey path along the outer edge of the castle.

Henry stopped walking to gawk at the ruins of a fourteenth-century cathedral.

"It's breathtaking." Grace stared as well, placing it forever into her memory.

"Time and war have taken their toll, but it's still beautiful. Maybe more so now than before."

She gave him an odd look. "The ceiling and most of the walls are missing."

"There's a romantic tragedy to it." He motioned to the exit. "Would you like to see the crypts of the noble families, or head straight to the Cemetery?"

"Let's follow the designated route for now." She took another look around the Cathedral of Our Lady of the Assumption, then followed him down a flight of stairs into the crypts. "Why is there Plexiglas on the floor?"

"Good question." Henry looked through the transparent covering and found a set of stairs carved into the stone.

Grace frowned at the graffiti scratched into the frescoes.

"Too bad all the art isn't protected." She sighed. "Let's keep moving. The putridaria are down these stairs."

Once below ground, the air grew stale, and it had a humid-but-dusty quality to it that made Henry's nose twitch. Dim lights set into the stone near the ceiling illuminated the dust, giving it a ghostly feel.

"Which way?" Grace whispered.

"I suspect we keep going down." He descended a half-flight of stairs and came to another hall. The ceilings were arched, yet low enough that he fought the urge to hunch his shoulders.

"Whoa." Grace stopped in a doorway. "I found it."

Henry peered past her into a room lined on three sides with stone thrones seemingly carved from the walls. Each seat had a circular hole cut out of the middle of the seat. "It looks like a medieval bathroom."

Grace gave him side-eye. "Not funny."

"It kind of is." He walked to the center of the space. "All they need are dividers and pots beneath the holes."

"They *did* have basins under each chair to catch the juices as the bodies decomposed."

"You're right. It's not funny." He frowned and glanced around for the second time. "I'm confused. Bethany said her sister was locked inside. Where's the door?"

Grace stepped into the hall. "There are more rooms this way."

The twins continued down the hall and found two additional putridaria, neither of which had the means to lock someone inside. However, a modern door, complete with a stainless-steel handle, lock, and keypad blocked their path.

"My guess is they removed the individual doors when they opened the rooms to the public." He backtracked to the first chamber and inspected the arched entryways. "There aren't any holes or indentations where hinges would have been."

"Hang on. The lighting's pretty bad." She opened the flashlight app on her phone and shined the beam around the edge of the archway.

Henry moved back and forth to view the plaster from different angles. "Take a look and tell me what you think."

Grace changed the angle of the light several times. "There's a slight difference in the paint color where I'd expect to see hinges."

"They could have removed the door after what happened to Brianna, but my gut tells me this isn't the right place. If I had to guess, I'd say there's another room like these in an area closed to the public."

"Right. How do we get behind that door? I haven't seen any staff members since we bought our tickets." She slipped back into the room. "No security cameras in here. Have you noticed any outside?"

"None, but that doesn't mean they aren't there. They could be hidden."

"True." She shuddered. "Let's get out of here. This place gives me the creeps."

"There's a café near the cathedral. We can grab some food and caffeine while we scope out the staff."

"It's a start." Grace took one last lingering look around and marched up the stairs.

The twins made their way to a terrace containing a small restaurant, a gift shop, and restrooms. Other than a half-dozen cats enjoying bowls of kibble, the place was empty.

"It's my turn to pay for our food." Grace handed him twenty Euros. "I'd love an American coffee and a croissant."

Henry chuckled and took her money. "Don't think I haven't noticed that it's only your turn when the meals are cheap?"

"I'd planned on springing for lunch too, but if you'd rather go Dutch..."

"Kidding." He backed away.

"I'm going to wash the grave dust from my hands and check out the gift shop while you speak to the café's employees."

"Divide and conquer. I like it." Henry turned and stared at the menu board. While he felt confident in his ability to order coffee and pastries, he worried that he'd ask for chicken and end up with tripe.

"*Buongiorno.*" A green-eyed young woman smiled from behind the counter.

"*Parli Inglese?*"

"Yes, a little." She cocked her head to the side. "What would you like?"

"Two American coffees, a croissant, and a sandwich." He pointed to the meat and cheese hoagie in the display case.

The woman set the food on the counter. "The coffee will be some time. Would you like water now?"

"Yes, thank you. My name's Henry."

"I am Rosa." She reached into the cooler and set two bottles on the counter. "You're visiting Ischia for the day?"

"My family is here until Friday." He ran his hand over the back of his neck. "I'm a friend of Brianna Bennet's sister."

"I see." The woman busied herself with wiping down the already clean counter.

"Do you have any idea what happened to her?"

"My English, it's not so good." Rosa glanced at the door as if expecting someone.

"Your English is better than some Americans I know." He remembered what Grace had said about honey and vinegar and smiled to sweeten the conversation. "My sister and I visited the Nuns' Cemetery and were wondering if there were more chambers in the Employees-Only area."

Rosa opened her mouth as if to speak but was cut short by a booming voice.

"Ah! America the Beautiful. Did you come in search of Matteo?" The dark-haired guy from the restaurant stood in the entryway staring at someone in the courtyard—most likely Grace.

"*Ciao,* Alessio!" Rosa's smile lit her entire being. Gone was the café employee who pretended she didn't speak a language to avoid a conversation; in her place stood a woman clearly smitten.

Alessio glanced at her and sighed. "Hi, Rosa."

If she'd picked up on the fact he wasn't interested, she didn't let it show in her expression. "This is Henry, a friend of Brianna's sister. You will stay and speak to him, yes?"

Emotions crossed Alessio's face like windows on a slot machine—surprise, fear, frustration, anger, and settled on indifference. "Brianna is my research partner. I've called her several times but haven't heard back. How is she?"

CHAPTER FOUR

The shop beside the café turned out to be more of an art gallery than a place to buy cheap postcards and trinkets. Paintings covered the walls, handwoven scarves hung from ornate racks, and jewelry glistened in glass cases.

"Buongiorno." An older woman stood behind the counter wearing layers of shimmering fabric that made Grace think of tents in the desert and exotic spices.

"Good morning." A skeleton-key pendant drew Grace's attention, and she met the shopkeeper's gaze and motioned to the necklace. "May I?"

"Yes, of course. Let me help you." The older woman lifted the heavy key and chain from the case. "Where are you visiting from?"

"The United States. I was born in Florida, but my family travels a lot." She tilted her head. "Your accent has me stumped. It's Eastern European but a little Italian, and maybe British?"

"A woman never tells her age or her history." The shopkeeper smiled.

"Ah! America the Beautiful. Did you come in search of Matteo?" a man called from outside.

Grace recognized both the voice and the nickname instantly. However, knowing who'd spoken and knowing how to respond were two entirely different animals.

The shopkeeper whispered, "Watch out for that one. He is trouble on two legs."

"I can tell," Grace replied conspiratorially.

"Now, our Matteo—he's the one you should know."

Blushing, Grace glanced at the price tag, and her stomach fluttered. "Is this right?"

"Yes, twenty Euros."

"I expected it to be much more. I'll take it. Could you gift wrap it for me?" She caught movement in the corner of her eye and turned to see Henry and *Signore* Trouble sit at a table together. "On second thought, I'll wrap it when I get home."

The woman pursed her lips. "Are you sure? It will only take a moment. Why don't you go speak to the boys while I take care of this for you?"

"Thank you. I'll be right back." Grace paid for the gift and headed outside.

The Italian stood and took her hand. "We haven't been introduced. I'm Alessio Alfani."

"Grace Warner."

"He's Brianna Bennet's research partner." That fact should have thrilled Henry, but he frowned and sipped his coffee.

She stared at the Italian, but try as she might, she couldn't picture him in a doctoral program at Cambridge. Before she judged too much, she corrected herself. She didn't know any doctoral students at Cambridge, but thanks to her parents, she had met a vast number of students in advanced degree programs. "Do you know what happened to her in the Nuns' Cemetery?"

"Straight to the point." Alessio motioned to an empty chair. "So very American. I love it."

Grace sat and stared, waiting for an answer.

"I don't know why the door stuck. I only know that I heard her screams and came to help. When I arrived, Brianna was sitting on the ground with a bump on her head." Alessio sank into the chair, rested his elbows on his knees, and clasped his hands. "I understand you are a friend of her sister. Do you know how Bri is doing?"

"We spoke to Bethany yesterday. Brianna was transferred to a hospital in Naples. Besides the concussion, she broke a couple of bones in her hands."

Alessio looked away, pressed his lips together, and squinted as if struggling to hold back his emotions. "She was afraid of that place. I never should have sent her there alone."

Henry sat up straighter. "What do you mean, you sent her there?"

The Italian held up his hands. "She forgot her iPad in the excavation area. I offered to accompany her, but she refused. I should have gone with her."

"Your work site is close to the putridaria?" Grace had suffered a case of dislike at first sight with Alessio, but her heart broke for him then. Deserving or not, guilt was a difficult emotion to live with.

"Yes. We must pass the rooms each time we come or go." He sat back and dragged his hands down his face. "Is Bri accepting visitors? I would like to see her. I may be able to help."

Henry shrugged. "I don't know, but I'll ask the next time I speak to Bethany."

"There's something I don't understand. We were in the Nuns' Cemetery earlier, but there were no doors." Grace softened her voice. "How did Brianna get locked in? Are there burial chambers that aren't open to the public?"

He nodded. "Tourists are only permitted in about twenty percent of the buildings. Much of the interior has not been renovated and isn't safe."

"Only twenty percent?" That tidbit intrigued her. *It would be amazing to explore the islet unhindered.*

"The place is like a lasagna—layer upon layer of buildings and ruins. Few areas are stable enough for visitors."

Henry sipped his coffee, set the cup down, and leaned closer as if preparing to strike a deal. "Any chance you can get us into the crypt where Brianna was trapped? She refuses to talk about it, but I'd like to understand exactly what she went through."

Alessio made a sound of disgust and threw up his hands. "This is why I should go to see her. I know this rock as well as she does...and I *know* her. She will tell me what happened."

"I agree, but we have no idea when she will be able to have visitors. In the meantime, we need to find out what happened down there." Having pled his case, Henry sat back and folded his arms.

"No. I cannot. I would lose my internship. Brianna and I...our work is too important."

Grace sighed and glanced back toward the horizon. The skies had darkened. A storm was coming.

A petite woman came out of the café with two American coffees and an espresso. "I thought you may want another?"

"Thank you," the twins said.

Normally, when they spoke in unison, the people around them commented. However, both Alessio and the woman seemed distracted, him with his thoughts, and her with *him*.

"Is everything okay?" The pretty Italian leaned into Alessio's line of vision.

He waved her off like one would a gnat. "*Sí*, Rosa. Go, please."

And just like that, whatever compassion Grace felt for the guy vanished.

"Who would we need to speak to in order to gain access to the room where Brianna was held?" Not only had he threatened to go over Alessio's head, Grace doubted he'd used the word "held" by accident.

"A local theater company is performing a historic reenactment here tonight. Security will be busy." The man stood, combed his hand through his hair, and sighed. "I will *try* to take you to the lower levels, but I make no promises."

Grinning, Matteo stepped out of the café. "Since when do you not make promises to beautiful girls?"

Grace did a double take. The young man wore tattered pants, a tunic, and stage makeup. He looked like an extra on the set of a pirate movie.

"We are filming a commercial for the evening castle tours." The young man motioned to his clothing. "I would have preferred to play King Alfonso of Aragon, but alas, I am too young and handsome."

She giggled. "You make an *interesting* pirate."

He pressed his hand to his chest. "Pirate? No, I am a *guest* in the Bourbon prison."

"Excuse me. I have work to do." Alessio quickly made himself scarce. Grace and Henry glanced after the retreating young man.

Henry muttered something under his breath and took a huge bite of his sandwich.

Matteo watched Alessio go before looking from one twin to the other. "Did I interrupt something?"

"No, we were talking about Brianna. He wants to visit her in the hospital." Grace had chosen her words carefully. She didn't know Matteo well enough to guess how he'd react to Alessio sneaking them into a restricted area.

"I was here when the ambulance came. She was...how do you say?" He frowned at his hands. "Whiter than usual?"

"Pale," Grace supplied.

"Yes. Pale, and very frightened."

She leaned closer and rested her hand on his arm. "Did Brianna say anything?"

"Only that she didn't want to discuss it." He sighed. "You will come tonight for my performance?"

"I'm looking forward to it." Grace smiled to cover her half-truth, ignoring the fact that Alessio had invited them.

Henry tilted his head. "Will it be crowded tonight?"

"It is off-season, but the evening performances are new." Matteo glanced at the storm clouds in the distance. "If the rain is finished, we will have guests. People love to visit the ghosts of the past."

"Maybe not everyone." She winked at her brother.

"I suspect you are right, *bella*." The Italian stood, his expression turning somber. "I must go."

"See you tonight." She watched him leave and shook her head.

Henry scratched his jaw. "Is it me, or is everyone who works here melodramatic?"

"It's not just you. Those were two of the oddest conversations I've ever had." She tore a piece from her croissant and wrinkled her nose. "I bet this was awesome when it was warm."

"Ask Rosa to heat it up." He took another bite and rolled his eyes back. "Better yet, order one of these."

"You're a genius."

He chuckled and pointed to his empty plate. "No, whoever came up with that combo of meat and cheese was a genius."

She tossed her napkin at him. "I was wracking my brain for an excuse to speak to her."

"About what?"

"Brianna Bennet. Rosa obviously has a crush on Alessio. I could be wrong, but I think he has a thing for Bri. You know what they say about scorned women."

He gave her a crooked grin. "I'll be right here enjoying the view and avoiding the drama."

Grace took her pastry into the café and found the tiny woman crying behind the counter. "Oh, excuse me."

Wiping her eyes, Rosa said, "More *caffé Americano*?"

"I was hoping you could warm this for me." Grace motioned to the croissant.

"I will get a fresh one." She took the plate.

"Are you okay? Alessio was rude to you outside."

"Eh, he does not mean to act that way. He was away from home too long and forgot himself." Rosa hitched a shoulder and handed Grace a fresh pastry.

"You're old friends?"

"Since we were this small." She curled her hand and left a three-inch space between her thumb and her forefinger. "He lived next door."

Grace hated to cause Rosa anymore pain, but the sooner they solved the mystery, the sooner they could help Brianna. "He seemed very upset about his research partner."

"Everyone here is upset. A storm is coming. You should leave soon. The waves cross the causeway in bad winds." The woman walked into the kitchen.

She wanted to ask more questions, but Rosa was right. The breeze had picked up considerably in the time Grace had been inside the café. She wrapped her snack in a napkin and headed outside.

Henry met her gaze and frowned. "No luck?"

"A little, but not enough. We should get going before the weather gets any worse."

"You realize nasty weather is a bad omen in every mystery novel I've ever read?" He stood and took his garbage to a trashcan on the side of the courtyard.

"And you realize that the story is always darkest just before the heroes triumph over the bad guys." Grace laughed despite her frustration.

"*Signorina!*" The woman from the gift shop waved. "Your necklace."

"*Grazie.* I almost forgot." Hurrying to the store, Grace hunched her shoulders to ward off the blast of chilly air racing across the terrace.

The shopkeeper pulled her inside and whispered, "You be careful. Bad intentions hide behind innocent faces."

How do I respond to that? She stared into the woman's dark, soulful eyes and nodded. "Thank you. We have to go before the storm comes."

"Take care, *Signorina.*"

By the time the twins reached the bus stop on the main island, the skies had opened. Being born in Florida, Henry and Grace were no strangers to torrential downpours and strong winds. However, Orlando had a warm subtropical climate, while Ischia sat at almost the same latitude as Boston. Getting drenched was one thing. Getting drenched in frigid air was miserable.

"Holy Tyrrhenian typhoon!" Henry wrapped his arms around himself and tucked his chin.

"Why isn't the bus stop covered?" Shivering in her soaked hoodie, Grace prayed the bus would arrive before hypothermia set in. "So cold."

A car horn blared, which was nothing out of the ordinary. Italians used their horns like they used their hands to punctuate vocal communication. It blared again—louder.

"America! Get in." Alessio sat in the driver's seat of a rather expensive-looking sports car.

Grace locked eyes with Henry.

He frowned and turned his back on the Italian.

"The bus. It doesn't come in storms," Alessio shouted.

"Stay here if you want. I'm getting a ride." She hurried to the cherry-red beauty.

Groaning, Henry followed.

"Thank you." She folded herself into the smallest backseat she'd ever seen. "They really should put up a warning sign if the bus isn't coming."

The Italian grinned. "I will mention it to my father."

"Is he a bus driver?" Henry slid into the front and buckled his seatbelt.

"He was for many years, and now he is a manager. Where to?"

"The Hotel Delfini." Grace shifted sideways to make room for her knees.

Alessio hit the gas, turned up the music, and sang along.

"What are you listening to? It sounds a lot like The Rolling Stones." She'd loved their music since she was a little girl.

"You have a good ear. It is from their 1967 album, *Between the Buttons*."

Henry grumbled, "Maybe you could turn it down?"

Alessio sang louder and sped down Ischia Ponte's main road—past the turn for the hotel. When the song ended, he said, "I thought perhaps you could give me Bethany's cell phone number."

"I should make sure she's comfortable with that before—" Grace grappled the seat to keep from sliding.

"You missed the turn." Henry pointed back toward the intersection. "And I'd appreciate it if you would slow down."

The Italian's brows rose, but he eased his foot from the accelerator. "You don't like me much, but I was born here. I know the roads. That way is not safe in the rain. I would rather not risk plummeting to my death from the cliffs."

Ignoring them, she typed a quick text to Bethany regarding Alessio's request.

"Right. Makes sense." Henry sounded as if he'd guzzled soured milk.

Grace's phone rang. "It's Bethany."

She pressed the Answer button and covertly lowered the volume to keep Alessio from overhearing.

"This is Bethany Bennet. I'm so glad you texted. There's no need to give him my number. My sister is doing much better."

"That's great news." She caught Alessio staring in the rearview mirror and looked away. "Is she up for visitors?"

"Not yet." The woman lowered her voice. "Tell him Bri will reach out when she's ready. She's said some things...disturbing things."

Grace had a million questions, but they would have to wait. Right then, she needed to reassure the Italian so he could focus on the road. "One moment. I'm with him now."

The line went quiet.

Grace met his gaze in the rearview mirror. "Brianna is doing much better but isn't able to receive visitors. She will call you as soon as she feels up to it."

"Send her my...regards." His brow wrinkled and his words came out strained, as if they had pained him.

"I'll call you back later. The doctors are here." Bethany sighed and disconnected the call.

Alessio parked in front of the hotel. "You will let me know if you hear more about her progress?"

Grace eased toward the door. "I will. And if you learn anything about what happened to her in that room..."

He tightened his grip on the steering wheel. "Tonight you may see it for yourselves."

CHAPTER FIVE

Before traveling to Italy, most people planned which cities to visit and sites to see. Henry wasn't most people. He believed the best way to experience a culture was to taste it. His pre-trip research had consisted of internet searches for reviews of the island's many restaurants. Ristorante Vittoria lived up to its reputation.

"I don't understand how Italians stay so thin." Grace tossed her napkin on the table.

"They walk everywhere. Besides, I don't think they eat like this every night." He motioned to her plate. "Are you going to finish that?"

"How can you possibly have room for more food?" She pushed the remainder of her fish toward him.

"It's all about pacing myself."

Grace rested her hands on her stomach. "I know, I know. It's a marathon, not a sprint, but don't forget, we have to climb to the top of the castle soon."

"I thought about that, and have it covered. Espresso with dessert will negate my food coma." He eyed a tray of sugary masterpieces.

"I'm sure they'll have coffee and sweets after the performance." She searched through her bag for her buzzing phone. "It's Bethany. Do you want to speak to her this time?"

"Track down the waiter. I'll be outside." He took the cell and headed for the door. "Hello? It's Henry."

"How are things coming along?" Bethany's words melted together as if she'd just woken.

"We're heading to the castle tonight to see the room where Brianna was trapped—"

"That may not be the best idea. My sister...she's...well, she's going on about ghostly nuns. She is convinced that what she saw in there was real. What if she's right?"

He drew a deep breath. "It's a possibility, but what if she's wrong? If there's even a slim chance we can find a logical explanation for what happened to her, we have to try."

"I suppose you're right," Bethany said. "I should tell you, Alessio has called several times. Brianna needs to focus on her recovery. Work can wait."

"I doubt he's calling about the excavation site. He seems to care about—"

"Brianna isn't involved with Alessio or anyone else. She's one hundred percent on her research." She paused as if to collect herself before issuing a warning and disconnecting. "Be careful."

Henry looked at the phone hoping to see Bethany was still on.

Grace emerged from the restaurant, took one look at Henry, and frowned. "Bad news?"

"Brianna is convinced she saw the spirits of the Poor Clares. Bethany's worried we're going to experience the same thing." He'd said the right thing on the phone, but now doubt began to creep in. One unexplained encounter with a ghost was enough. He didn't want another one.

"We won't know what we're dealing with until we see the room."

"There's more." Henry relayed the part of the conversation concerning Alessio.

"Unrequited love is a motive far too often. Chalk that up as a tentative maybe on a definite possibility." She looped her arm with his and half-dragged him toward the castle.

The twins purchased their tickets and took the elevator to the top of the islet. Only a handful of people milled about, and Henry preferred it that way. While the lack of crowds would make sneaking into the restricted area more difficult, having the place mostly to themselves was amazing.

When Alessio mentioned a performance, Henry had assumed he meant a play of some sort. He certainly hadn't expected Alfonso of Aragon to greet him on a terrace.

Dressed from head to pointed boots in period clothing, the king pressed a hand to his chest and launched into a speech.

Henry's grasp of the Italian language consisted mostly of phrases useful when ordering food. However, the actor's body language more than made up for the language barrier.

"Where is everyone?" Grace glanced around the empty courtyard.

"Maybe the bad weather scared people away."

She lowered her voice. "Or rumors of what happened to Brianna got out. Bethany mentioned the staff here were superstitious, and Matteo said he'd lose his job for discussing it with us."

"Something tells me we'll have a prime clue when we learn why they are so intent on keeping the incident a secret."

The twins walked into the ruins of the cathedral and stopped to watch the performance of an actress dressed in a wedding gown. Although she spoke, her voice rose and fell like an aria in an opera.

She laughed, she wept, she knelt at the altar and pantomimed taking communion. The actress curtseyed low to the ground. When she stood, her dress turned from pale blue to black.

Henry took several steps back. "Whoa."

Holding a flashlight under her chin, the actress cackled and pointed toward the crypts.

Grace laughed and pulled him out of the cathedral. "Come on."

"How did she do that?" He stared at the woman over his shoulder.

"I've seen the trick before. The gown had blue fabric between the black layers. She released the Velcro at the shoulders to hide the lighter color when she stood." Grace bypassed the crypts and headed straight for the café. "Why didn't we think to get Alessio's contact info or arrange a meeting place and time?"

"Because we were both drenched and afraid for our lives in that car of his." Catching up to her, he lowered his voice. "And I for one can't stand the guy."

Grace glanced away. "I've tried to give him the benefit of the doubt, but I agree with you."

"I say we find him, see the room, and have a good night despite our arrogant Italian friend."

She flashed him a grin. "That sounds like a plan. I bet Rosa will know where he is."

"I think that's a good bet." Henry opened the door, and the aromas of coffee and fresh-baked bread eased the growing knot in his gut.

A middle-aged woman with salt-and-pepper hair and a warm smile stood behind the counter. "*Buonasera.*"

"*Buonasera.*" Grace bit the inside of her lip as if trying to find her words. "We are looking for Alessio."

The lady spoke slowly, but Henry had no clue what she'd said.

He pulled his phone from his pocket and opened the translator app. After a couple attempts, he managed to learn Alessio's whereabouts while ordering two espressos in the process.

The lady chuckled and set two miniature white mugs on the counter.

Grace finished her drink in one gulp. "The Bourbon Prison is on the way. We can check two items off our to-do lists in one trip around the castle."

"Since when is visiting the Bourbon Prison on your list?"

She gave him a less-than-patient look. "Since we told Matteo we would watch his performance."

"One, you told him *you'd* watch his performance. I'm not sure I care for him any more than I do Alessio. Two, it isn't even a performance. It's a speech." He folded his arms and waited for her to argue.

"I prefer to call them mini-one-man shows spread throughout the castle." Grace winked, turned on her heel, and headed for the door, leaving her grumbling brother to catch up.

The twins followed a labyrinthine path of narrow walls and arched doorways past a beautiful building known as the House of the Sun. They continued walking through a less dense portion of the castle.

Dressed in his prisoner costume, Matteo leaned against a fountain in the center of a stone courtyard. He glanced at the twins, or more specifically, he stared at Grace and smiled. "You made it."

"Of course we did." She stopped a few feet from the guy, but Henry hung back near the door.

"Shall I begin?" Matteo shifted his weight from one foot to the other.

"Please do." Grace cast a quick glare over her shoulder.

Henry raised his hands and walked closer.

The young Italian tilted his head as if waiting for permission to begin.

Grace nodded.

Matteo launched into a dramatic soliloquy. The guy begged and pleaded and fell to his knees. The next moment, he railed, shaking his fists at the night sky. The one-man show ended with him pantomiming hanging in the stocks.

Grace applauded. "Bravo."

Henry couldn't quite tell if the character had died or fallen asleep. Either way, Matteo had performed with gusto.

The guy took a bow. "How was I?"

"Enthusiastic." Henry grinned. "I don't feel like I missed anything, despite not understanding the language."

"I could do it again. In English."

Grace pinched the back of her brother's arm. Hard. "No...I mean, you were wonderful. Like Henry said, you told the story with your entire being. The words weren't necessary. Do you plan to study acting?"

Her brother gritted his teeth and resisted the urge to rub his bruised triceps.

"I have dreamed of being nothing else since I was a boy. The theater company, we are auditioning in Roma tomorrow morning." Matteo's smile dimmed. "My father is not happy. He wants me to work in the family restaurant like my uncles and brothers."

"You'll do fabulous at the audition," she said. "And I understand about the pressure to work in the family business. We've chosen to follow in our parents' footsteps. Henry will be an attorney one day, and I'm planning to be an engineer."

The guy furrowed his brow after she said "engineer." He opened his mouth, probably to ask for clarification.

Henry cut him off before he had the chance. "Do you know where Alessio is?"

Matteo glanced between them as if trying to decide who to address first. "He's working."

Grace turned to the confused Italian. "Where? We need to speak to him. It's important."

"You have missed him by two minutes." Matteo pointed toward the fortress on the north side of the islet. "He is with Giuseppe restoring a fresco, but you cannot follow. It is not open to the public."

"*Grazie.*" She gave him a quick hug and strode past Henry to the courtyard's exit.

Matteo called after her, "Wait. Please. I would like to ask you to dinner tomorrow."

"I can't tomorrow. I have plans with my parents." Grace replied over her shoulder.

Henry waved and followed his sister.

The twins took the path along the outer wall of the dilapidated stronghold.

Grace sighed and hung her head.

"What's wrong?"

"I hope I didn't hurt Matteo's feelings. Should I find him later and apologize?"

"You weren't rude." Henry leaned close to her. "There's nothing wrong with turning down an invitation. Forget about Matteo."

The look she gave him suggested she wasn't about to follow his advice.

Henry opened a map program on his phone and studied the aerial photos. "Our best bet is the guard tower adjacent to the Terrace of Olive Trees."

She stared at the screen for a long moment. "I agree but, there's no guarantee we'll find Alessio."

"If he's not there, I say we head back to the café and wait."

They reached the triangular-shaped terrace and made their way to a gatehouse attached to the tower. Pieces of what looked like scaffolding rested against the side of the building, but light shone from inside.

Ducking under the debris, Henry entered a cavernous space. Shop lights illuminated an enormous fresco of a map of Naples. Judging by the brushes, chemicals, and equipment scattered about, they'd found the restoration project Matteo mentioned.

"Wow." Turning in a circle, Grace took in her surroundings.

A large man with a larger mustache rounded the corner. He wore blue overalls splattered in paint and reminded Henry of one of the Mario Brothers. The guy shouted in Italian, or at least he thought it was Italian.

The twins took several steps back.

"*Dov'è Alessio?*" Henry tried to ask where to find the intern, but he feared he'd somehow insulted the painter.

Mario Brothers pointed to the entrance and shouted again.

"*Alfini!*" The man narrowed his eyes and bellowed more words Henry couldn't understand in the odd dialect.

"*Sì, Giuseppe?*" a voice replied from down the hall.

"That's him." Grace walked toward the sound of the young man's voice, but the big guy stepped in her path.

"No." The man folded his arms. "You stay."

Rolling his eyes and muttering under his breath, Alessio came into the room. "Why are you here?"

Grace said, "You told us to meet you tonight."

"Yes, I know this. Why are you *here* in this place *now*?"

Henry drew a deep breath and reminded himself they needed Alessio's help. "Looking for you. We realized too late that we forgot to set a meeting place and time."

"Fine." He turned to the big guy and muttered something in Italian, then motioned to the hall. "Come with me."

They trailed him down three flights of stairs to a tunnel so narrow, Henry had to hunch his shoulders to squeeze through.

Alessio pulled a flashlight from his back pocket. At Grace's questioning look, he explained, "It is a shortcut. Stay close."

The deeper they walked, the darker it became, until their only light source rested in Alessio's hand.

She whispered, "Is it much farther?"

Henry clamped a hand on his sister's shoulder for reassurance—hers *and* his.

"Almost there. This is why only a few areas are open to the public." The Italian turned down a hall marked with a yellow arrow.

A few yards later, they came to a steel door. Alessio punched in the key code to an underground office. Two desks sat against one wall, and a file cabinet occupied the other.

Grace stopped and stared.

A framed picture of Bethany and a young woman caught Henry's attention. "This is Brianna's desk?"

"Yes, one of them. The internet doesn't work here. We use this area only to document our findings while they are fresh in our minds. We also have office space in the castle hotel during the off-season." Alessio seemed to look everywhere except at the photograph. "Which reminds me, I have to finish our report."

Henry scratched his jaw. "I'm confused. You said before she went to the excavation site to get her iPad. Why would she have it there and not in here?"

"We are required to take photos of the findings." He took the iPad from Brianna's desk and sank into his chair.

"You're not coming with us?" Grace assumed he would insist on accompanying them. In fact, she found it odd that he would allow them to go alone.

He motioned to the door on the opposite side of the room. "The putridarium is twenty-five meters on the left. Come back to the office when you are finished."

The twins exchanged quick glances before walking into another passageway. Thankfully, regularly-spaced shop lights hung from the ceiling every few yards and provided more than enough light.

"This is it." Grace gulped loud enough for Henry to hear her over the pulse beating against his eardrums.

The door to the burial chamber stood open, the apex of its arch mere inches from the hall ceiling. Henry pushed it to test its weight, but it didn't budge. "Help me with this."

Grace joined him, and together, they pulled the heavy wood a few inches from the wall. "I can't tell if it's the weight or the hinges causing it to stick."

Henry opened the flashlight app on his phone and shined the beam at the rusted metal securing the door to the wall. "My guess is both."

She frowned. "How many people would it take to close it?"

"Two or three." He searched along the perimeter of the ancient door.

Grace recalled a physics lecture on the impacts of gravitational force on simple machines. "Let's try again, only this time, we need to lift up enough to take the pressure off the hinges."

Although heavy, it didn't take much to relieve the pressure. The door soundlessly swung inward.

"That could explain how she got trapped in here. It confirms that it was no accident. Now let's see if we can find an explanation for the ghosts." Henry entered the putridarium and gagged. Covering his nose and mouth, he asked, "How long has it been since these were used?"

"Centuries." Grace made a sour face. "What is that stench? It smells like rotten potatoes."

"I stand by my original assessment. These are more like death toilets than chairs."

"Still not funny."

A single light illuminated the first burial chamber, but Henry had to use his phone in the second room. He swept the beam over the floor and gagged again. "Dead rat."

Grace made a yelping sound and turned for the exit.

The rusty hinges groaned, and a split-second later, the door slammed closed.

Henry's heart skipped a beat, then another, and another. "Grace?"

CHAPTER SIX

"Stay calm. This is probably Alessio's idea of a joke." She tried to appear brave on the outside, but inside, her heart hammered out an S.O.S.

"I *am* calm." His jaw tightened, and he narrowed his eyes. However, his ashen skin betrayed his fear.

She banged on the door. "We got the point. Let us out."

No one replied.

Henry moved past her and pounded hard enough to rattle the hinges. "Joke's over."

Silence.

"Maybe we can lift it again?"

The twins pushed up, but it didn't budge.

"There isn't enough clearance between the top of the door and the wall." Henry kicked the heavy wood and winced. "Perfect."

She frowned at the lack of bars on her phone. "Do you have cell reception?"

"Nope."

Grace tied her hoodie around her mouth and nose to hold back the stench of decaying rodent. She started to examine the room in detail.

He followed her lead and covered the lower half of his face with his flannel shirt. As if administering a test, Henry asked, "What are *you* looking for?"

"If Brianna saw ghosts, as she claims, we're looking for a projector or evidence that someone mounted one." She turned on her flashlight app.

"The convent was founded in the 1600s. From the looks of it, the tufa stone hasn't been repaired since the putridaria were built," Henry offered. Pieces had chipped off the stone in places, and deep gouges marred others. Henry set his foot on the seat of a death chair and hoisted himself up. "I hate to say it, but this would be the perfect room to hide a mini-projector."

Grace's chest tightened. "What are you doing? Get down."

"It's made of solid rock. It'll hold."

"I know it will hold your weight, but it's wrong." While she didn't believe in spirits, she couldn't help but feel they were desecrating graves.

Henry sighed. "Gracie, we're not in here to destroy the place. We're here to help a living, breathing young woman. I think the ghosts of long-dead nuns will approve."

She motioned for him to continue, before turning her back and searching the lower portions of the room.

Henry said, "A projector would need a straight shot at a flat surface or corner for the images to seem real."

The sounds of his feet moving across rock set her teeth on edge. "We need more details on exactly what Brianna saw and where."

"Agreed, but she was traumatized. How reliable will her memories be?"

"True." Shining her light around the room at waist height, Grace searched for any fresh damage. "It's too dusty to tell if anyone drilled into the walls recently."

Henry grunted and scrambled on the rough stone.

Grace turned in time to witness her brother standing on the arm of a death chair, his enormous sneaker millimeters from a mound of melted candle wax. "Henry, please be careful. This is a sacred space."

He glanced down and curled his lip. "Don't tell me that's sixteenth-century wax."

"It could be, or it could be something else. They collected the juices and wet bits in basins below the chairs, but the women's arms rested there. What's to say that isn't left over—"

"Nope. Stop. Don't finish that train of thought to Creepy-time Station." Henry shuddered.

"Then don't step on anything that isn't rock." She resumed her search and found a small chunk of light-blue material hanging from the back of the chair closest to the adjoining room. Grace took a photo of it before gently pulling it from the stone. One side appeared to be painted the same color as the rest of the rock.

Her mouth went dry. She had no idea what it was but knew it didn't belong. "I found something."

"So did I." Henry hopped down and pulled the shirt from his face. "See the hole up there?"

Grace followed the beam of his flashlight. "I think so."

"Unlike the others, the edges are clean."

"Like it was recently drilled?"

"Correct." He grinned. "You can't tell from down here, but there's a two-inch, perfectly circular, indentation around the hole."

"What could have caused it?" She adjusted her makeshift facemask.

"No idea, but I think there's another one on the opposite wall."

She opened her palm and revealed the block of blue material. "This was glued to the back of a chair."

He held it to the light. "Now, *this* is interesting."

"What do you think it is?" She tilted her head to get a better look.

"Foamboard."

"Why would anyone paint foamboard..." A piece of the puzzle snapped into place, and Grace grinned. "To look like stone. To blend in and hide a small projector."

Henry nodded. "They have apps that will turn cell phones into projectors now. It's hard to tell from this small piece, but the depth is the same as a phone."

"Let's get some photos of the room and mark the locations of the holes and the chair with the foam board. We may have found our logical explanation for what Brianna saw."

The shop lamps flickered once and died.

"You have got to be kidding me," Henry shouted.

"We have no idea how long we're going to be stuck in here." Holding her phone, Grace flashed the light toward her brother. "Turn your cell off to save the battery."

He moved closer and did as she asked. "I'd like to dangle Alessio over the cliff until he cries like a toddler."

"You'll need to take a number." Grace eased toward the blocked exit. "This has gone from childish to ridiculous."

Henry sat on the ground with his back against the door. "What do we know?"

She crouched beside him. "While we need to do more research, it looks like the ghosts Brianna saw were created by a projector."

"Yes, but we're missing something. The chair where you found the foamboard faces another wall. If the images were simply projected, they would have appeared flat. Not to mention, there would have been a beam of light."

"True, but the holes near the ceiling tell me they might have hung something, like a screen. When we were researching the Lady in White, I read about a thing called a scrim, made of a gauze-like material, which is then backlit to show the projections."

Henry said, "A tension rod would explain the weird circular indentations. Between the foam board and a hanging screen, my money is on the theater company. But why?"

"I'd say money, but then why would everyone be so tight-lipped about Brianna seeing ghosts?"

"I don't know." He sighed. "Before we go farther down this line of reasoning, there's a problem. The screen theory only works if she was standing in the back corner, but what was the first thing we did when the lights went out?"

"Ran for the door." She closed her eyes, conjured up a floorplan of the space, and considered the lines of sight. "You're right. The angles are off."

"We'll figure it out."

"We're talking in circles." Grace scooted closer. "It's unbelievably creepy in here."

"I can see why Brianna would have panicked."

A scurrying sound sent Grace's heart racing. She shot to her feet and shined her light over the floor. "Did you hear that?"

Henry stood. "What the heck was that?"

The sound grew louder.

His eyes rounded. "Holy smokes. Is that a rat?"

"Or a small dog." Scrambling onto the closest chair, Grace's previous concerns about desecrating the sacred space disappeared in a flash of gray.

Henry climbed up beside her. "Where is it?"

Her hands shook, along with the light from the phone. "I don't know."

Another sound prickled her ears—a feminine whisper.

"Do you hear that?" Henry put his arm in front of her like a parent would do before slamming on the brakes.

"Uh-huh." Grace focused on the facts as she understood them. *Painted foam. New holes in the walls. Possible projector and scrim. Fake. Fake. Fake.* "It's not real. Alessio said we'd see for ourselves what Brianna went through."

"Right. It's all part of the plan to scare us." Henry didn't sound convinced.

The ghostly woman's voice grew louder but no less alluring. The chanted syllables had a lullaby-like quality to them that Grace would have found soothing in any other situation.

"It's not real," Henry repeated her words.

"I want out of here." She gripped his arm as if it were the only thing keeping her upright, and maybe it was.

"Alessio will come once he's done messing with us." Henry drew her into an embrace. "I bet he's filming us right now and having a good laugh." He might have said the right things, but he couldn't hide his trembling.

The chanting went on for what felt like hours. After a while, Grace began to pick up on a few of the words, thanks to the repetitive pattern.

"It's a recording of a prayer," she whispered.

Henry nodded. "Have you checked the time since we've been in here?"

"I only thought to look a few minutes ago."

He stiffened his spine. "We may need to mentally prepare ourselves in case we are stuck here until morning."

"I'm not sleeping if that's what you think."

"No, but we should sit." He helped her down from the death chair.

She searched the floor for signs of the rat they'd heard earlier. "I'd rather stand."

Henry sighed and seated himself with his back against the door. "Suit yourself, but it may be a long night."

"Fine." She plopped down beside him and pulled her knees to her chest.

"Mom and Dad are probably freaking out."

Grace sent up a silent prayer. "I hope so. I hope they are so worried they storm the castle and demand to know where we are."

"Barbarian hordes, the French, and Faith Warner—the only ones who could breach the castle's defenses in its long history." Henry chuckled.

Bang. Bang. Bang.

The twins startled and scurried away from the door as if expecting the Italian version of Dracula to waltz in and relieve them of their blood.

"Grace! Are you there?" a female voice called from the hall.

"Yes!" they shouted in unison.

"I will free you. One moment."

Henry asked, "Was that Rosa?"

"Maybe?" She pressed her ear to the door but couldn't hear over the recording of the chanting nun.

Another loud bang echoed off the stone walls.

"Step back," the woman shouted.

Henry said, "It opens out—"

The massive door pushed in and over before it swung out. Whoever had moved it knew exactly how to open it.

"Are you two okay?" The lady from the gift shop shined a light into the dark room. Beside her stood the large guy in the painters' overalls, and another man Grace didn't recognize.

"Yes. Where's Alessio?" Henry motioned for his sister to go first.

She walked from the putridarium and choked out a sob.

The gift shop woman wrapped her arms around Grace. "Alessio was called away for a family emergency. He was understandably upset and left without telling us you were here."

"Then how?" Henry ground his teeth. "How did you find us?"

"Alessio remembered you were here and called Rosa from the mainland. And Rosa called me." She released Grace and touched the young man's arm. "Alessio's father. He is in the hospital."

Grace wanted to argue. To tell them Alessio had locked them inside and turned off the lights, but she couldn't find the words. "I want to go to the hotel."

Henry met her gaze and nodded once. "I agree."

The woman looked him over from head to toe and smiled. "My name is Vadoma, and this is Giuseppe. I will drive you."

He glanced at Grace.

"She works in the gift shop. I trust her to get us to the hotel safely."

"I'm Henry Warner." He gave her a firm handshake. "We would appreciate a ride. It's been a long night."

"Yes, for all of us." Vadoma and the large man led the twins to the elevator.

Grace found the woman's response more than a little odd. "Has something else happened?"

The shopkeeper fluffed her layered skirt. "It's nothing to worry yourselves with. The people didn't come as we'd hoped."

Henry said, "Is the castle struggling financially?"

"Most things in Italy are struggling financially, and we are no exception." She pressed her lips together. "I work for the love of this place, but others rely on the income."

"What about Matteo?" Grace had seen the sadness in his eyes when he'd mentioned working at his family's restaurant.

Giuseppe perked up a bit, likely recognizing the name of a fellow employee.

"Ah, young Matteo. He is too handsome to ever be poor." Vadoma gave her a knowing grin. "He and the other actors left for Rome hours ago. They are auditioning for a new play."

Henry sucked in a breath. "Besides you two, who is left on the islet tonight?"

She cocked her head. "It's only us. The owner and his family are not here, and the hotels closed to tourists last week."

Grace turned and met the woman's gaze. "How long ago did Alessio leave?"

"Hours." She asked the man something in Italian. "Giuseppe says Alessio received the call shortly after he met you in the guard tower."

Henry's frown deepened. "Someone locked us in the putridarium tonight. If it wasn't Alessio, then who?"

Vadoma's hand flew to her throat. "You did not close the door?"

"No," they said in unison.

Grace stared out the window at the gray clouds hanging over the darker gray sea. While dreary, the weather suited her mood. Besides, a bright Italian sunrise after four hours of sleep would have been the perfect recipe for a headache.

The ferry to Naples bounced and bobbed in the rough water, causing her stomach to churn. She rummaged through her bag for the container of motion sickness pills and reread the label—one dose an hour before traveling, another every four to six hours. *Great, three hours to go.*

Henry smacked his lips together and stretched his arms over his head. "Did you get any sleep?"

Grace shook her head.

"The Dramamine should have made you drowsy."

"Trust me, between my nightmares, getting up at zero-dark-thirty, and the medication, I'm beyond tired."

He eased back from her as if he thought she may bite. "Did you bring the foamboard?"

"It's in my bag." She pressed her fingers to the chilly window. "I'm worried Brianna isn't going to take the news well."

"Bethany knows her sister. She wouldn't have asked us to visit if she thought it would cause her more harm than good." He ducked his head to get a better view outside. "I see the port. Let's grab a spot by the door."

After disembarking, the twins made their way to the bus station.

"I wouldn't mind a little shopping. Morgan's birthday is coming up." He grinned and dipped his chin.

They'd met Morgan Monaghan while investigating Charlie No-Face. In less than a week, the twins had developed sound friendships, although judging from Henry's blush, one of them may have been more.

"I picked up an awesome skeleton-key necklace in the castle gift shop for her," Grace said.

He stopped and stared. "You bought her jewelry? Way to put on the pressure."

"We could make it from both of us. It was only twenty Euros."

"Deal, but I'd like to look for a little something else, too." He motioned to the oncoming bus. "This is our ride."

While the weather hadn't improved, the scenery had. Each building they passed seemed more elaborate than the last. Unlike in New York or Chicago, people had built *out* instead of *up*. The massive structures took up entire city blocks.

"Call me crazy, but I prefer Ischia. This is controlled chaos." Henry glanced from one side of the bus to the other. "It's too much to take in."

"I agree." Grace checked her GPS. "The next stop is the hospital. I'll text Bethany and let her know we're close."

The exterior of the *ospedale* looked like a smaller, pinker version of Versailles. The twins entered the lobby and stopped to take in the enormous space. Several sets of double doors led to arched halls that were better suited to a palace than a hospital.

Bethany Bennet stormed into the lobby with an older Italian man on her heels. His voice spilled into the room, but she stared straight ahead as if he weren't following.

"What's that all about?" Grace took a step forward but stopped. A cluster of nuns in the back corner sent a chill through her veins. She doubted she'd ever look at a woman in a habit the same way again.

Henry gave her a knowing look and took her hand. "Let's find out."

The Italian stepped in front of Bethany. "Where else would he be?"

With Grace on his heels, Henry hurried to the woman's side. "Is there a problem?"

Bethany motioned to the shouting man. "This is Mr. Alfini, Alessio's father. He seems to believe his son came to Naples to see Brianna." She smirked. "If he did, he never made it to her room."

Mr. Alfini ran his hand through his thinning hair. "My son, he is missing."

"Missing?" the twins asked.

"*Sì.* He did not come to dinner last—"

"Wait. You're Alessio's *father*?" Grace's brain spun like a roulette wheel.

"*Sì.*"

She shook her head. "We were told Alessio left the castle last night because you were in the hospital."

The man widened his arms. "I am in *ospedale.*"

"*Un momento.*" Bethany held her hand up and turned to Grace. "Who told you Mr. Alfini was ill?"

"An employee at the castle." Grace hadn't gone into detail when she'd spoken to Bethany the previous evening. Fearing the woman would take them off the case, she'd only explained what they'd found in the crypts and why they needed to speak to Brianna.

Bethany turned to Mr. Alfini and said something in broken Italian.

The man's eyes widened. "No. No emergency. Who said this?"

"Rosa told Vadoma." Henry glanced at Grace and frowned.

"No. Rosa is like a daughter, and Vadoma, she is a good woman." He dragged his hand over his face and muttered words Grace couldn't understand.

Bethany offered the man a tired smile that wasn't much of a smile at all. "As I said, Alessio hasn't been here. My sister is not receiving visitors."

Mr. Alfini motioned to the twins. "Except these?"

"They are here to see me." Her voice held an edge that hadn't been there a moment before. "Now, if you will excuse us? We have matters to discuss."

The older gentleman glanced from one to the other as if they were his last hope. "You will call if you see him?"

"Yes, of course." Bethany turned and walked away.

Grace's heart went out to him, but there was nothing they could do to help—not in a foreign country where they didn't speak the language. "You'll find him."

"*Sì.*" Shoulders sagging, Mr. Alfini headed for the exit.

Henry whispered, "I'm not sure I like the new side of Miss Bennet."

"Me either, but we need her if we want to have any hope of speaking to Brianna."

"True." Henry hurried after the mercurial woman.

"Well, *that* was interesting." Bethany drew a deep breath. "If I had to guess, I'd say Alessio made up the story about the call to get out of work early."

He nodded. "It's possible."

Grace had her doubts but chose to keep them to herself. "How's Brianna today?"

"Better." The woman's face lit up at the mention of her sister. "She had surgery on her hands yesterday. The doctors expect a complete recovery."

"And her mood?" Henry asked.

"About that...she didn't want to tell anyone about the ghosts because she's afraid she'll lose her internship." Bethany glanced between the twins. "Which is why it's so important you tell her what you told me."

"You're probably right." Again, Grace had her doubts. What she'd gone through in the putridarium paled in comparison to Brianna's experience, but it had affected her more deeply than she cared to admit.

Henry nodded to the hall. "Shall we?"

On the third floor, the scents of cleaning supplies and antiseptics stung Grace's nose. For the most part, the third floor looked like a typical hospital, only older, louder, and more crowded.

Bethany led them into the room and bent to whisper something to her sister.

The pretty blonde nodded and forced a smile. "Hello."

"Hi. I'm Henry Warner, and this is my sister Grace." He stepped toward the bed to shake Brianna's hand, stopped short, and blushed.

Brianna grinned and raised her bandaged hands. "If you don't mind, we can skip the formalities. Beth tells me you found something in the putridarium?"

Henry cleared his throat. "Yes. A piece of foam board glued to the back of one of the stone chairs. It was painted to blend into the rock."

Standing at the foot of the bed, Grace pulled the chunk of foam from her bag and handed it to Bethany. "It's the sort of material that is used to create stage props."

She turned it over a few times and handed it to her sister.

Brianna frowned. "I'm familiar with foam core. I've used it for presentations, but I don't understand what this has to do with the...with what I saw."

Henry seated himself in a plastic chair beside the bed. "We found two holes near the ceiling. They appeared to be freshly drilled, and both had a circular indentation around them—what you'd expect a tension rod to leave behind."

The woman's eyes widened. "You think someone created Pepper's ghost in the putridarium?"

"Pepper's ghost?" Henry glanced between the women.

"Or phantasmagoria." Bethany said, "It's an old theater trick. It involves placing a large piece of glass or Plexiglas at an angle between the stage and a room out of view of the audience. They manipulate the lighting, so the reflection of the actors in the secret room is refracted and appear on stage. It's where the term 'smoke and mirrors' comes from."

Grace knew the science behind the trick but had never heard the expression. "Right. It's the same principle as a teleprompter. They also use it at Disney to create the spirits in the Haunted Mansion."

Henry nodded. "Then, yes. We think someone used a variation of Pepper's ghost to scare you."

Brianna winced. "Why?"

"That's what we're trying to find out." Grace took a sketch she'd drawn of the chambers from her bag. "But before we discuss possible motives, would you mind showing me where you were in the room?"

"Sure." Unable to use her hands, the young woman struggled to sit upright.

Bethany moved in to help, but Bri waved her away.

Grace rested the paper on Brianna's lap. "Where were you when you first saw the images."

"By the door."

Henry asked, "Had you gone farther into the room at any point?"

"I heard noises from the hall and took a few steps inside."

He pointed to the center of the space. "About here?"

"Not quite that far." She glanced between the twins. "Oh, and I walked around this corner to check the other room."

"The Xs are where we found the screw holes at ceiling height." Grace said, "The blue square is where the foamboard was glued to the chair, about four feet from the ground."

Bethany stared at the drawing, tilted her head to the side, and frowned. "It's off."

Grace's cheeks heated. She'd make a horrible mechanical engineer if she couldn't manage a simple sketch. "I had to guess at the dimensions—"

"No. I mean the angle is off. If the projector was where you found the foam core, the images would have appeared at the side of the room. The corpses were along the back, and the *living* one was in the center." Brianna's voice cracked.

Henry leaned closer to get a better look at the paper. "It would work if the projector was hidden in the second chamber."

"I would have noticed a giant piece of Plexiglas." She sniffled and turned her head. "I'm sorry, but this...it's a stretch. I-I know what I saw and heard."

Grace whispered, "A woman praying in Italian."

Brianna locked eyes with her. "Yes! An old Neapolitan dialect."

"We heard it too. It completely creeped me out. Thankfully, we didn't see anything." She wrapped her arms around herself. "But then it repeated, and I figured out it was a recording."

"Recording?" Brianna tilted her head. "You're sure?"

"Absolutely. There was static at the beginning."

Bethany motioned to Grace and Henry. "Why do I get the feeling there's more to your story? What really happened?"

Henry relayed the entire ordeal, starting with Alessio leading them through the underbelly of the castle and ending with Vadoma and Giuseppe rescuing them.

Bethany took a deep breath in through her nose and exhaled through her mouth. "Alessio is the common factor in both incidents."

"I've already told you. He would never lock me in the putridarium." Brianna shook her head. "I feel like even more of an idiot. How did I not realize it was all staged?"

"I knew it was fake, and I was still scared." Grace held off on telling the sisters she'd had nightmares the previous evening. "Whoever did this was a master. And the smell! The dead rat in the next chamber added to the scary factor."

"Rat? There was no rat when I was there."

Henry sat up straighter. "Are you sure?"

"Quite."

"The state of decay was too far progressed for it to have only been dead two days." He glanced at Grace as if waiting for her to come up with an explanation.

She didn't know anything about the decomposition process of a rat the size of a housecat, nor did she intend to study it.

Bethany gasped. "Yuck. What if someone put it there?"

"Please." Brianna smirked. "Next you'll tell me Alessio is a serial rodent-killer responsible for the murders of hundreds of innocents."

Between the woman's tone and her words, Grace realized Brianna liked the guy. She glanced at Bethany and couldn't help but wonder if she'd told her sister about Alessio's disappearance.

Bethany looked as if she had more to say, but Brianna silenced her with a glare.

"Grace and I have to go." Henry stood. "But we plan to keep working on this. We would like to know who's behind it, and why."

"Call us if there's anything else we can do." Grace pulled her purse to her shoulder.

Brianna said, "There is something rather urgent. Would it be too much trouble to get my iPad to Bethany? Alessio and I made a significant discovery and are required to report it to our professors. I'd ask him to bring it, but I'm not permitted to make phone calls—"

"I'm quite sure your research partner took care of the legalities." Bethany locked eyes with Grace. "He is still working on the excavation."

Grace struggled to keep her shock from showing on her face. Not only had Bethany kept secrets from her sister, but she'd also flat-out lied.

"We'd be happy to bring you the iPad. Where exactly is it?" Henry asked in his no-nonsense-future-attorney voice.

"How do you feel about a little minor trespassing?" Brianna bit her lip and wrinkled her nose.

"You can't be serious." Bethany's face reddened to the point where Grace wouldn't have been surprised to see smoke coming from her ears like in a cartoon.

Henry wiggled his brows. "What do you have in mind?"

CHAPTER EIGHT

Grace had thought of nothing except Bethany Bennet since they'd left the hospital. The woman had lied and manipulated her sister when Brianna needed her the most, but why? What did she hope to gain by keeping Brianna isolated from the world?

"Bethany might not be responsible for what happened to Brianna, but she's victimizing her now."

Henry paid for two tickets into the Aragonese castle and turned to Grace. "That's between them. We shouldn't get involved."

"I know, but I don't like it. Brianna has a right to make phone calls and have visitors. Not to mention, someone should break the news her research partner is missing," Grace countered.

"Bethany's heart is in the right place. She wants her sister to focus on her recovery. *Again*, this isn't any of our business."

She stabbed the elevator call button several times in rapid succession. "Maybe we should try to find Alessio while we're working on uncovering the people behind the so-called hauntings. His disappearance could be related."

"It's possible, but we only have two days left in Ischia. If we split our attention, we might not solve either mystery."

"I'm not saying we change the focus, but it won't hurt to keep our eyes open. We've all but proven it was someone who knows about stage props and tricks."

Henry followed her into the waiting elevator. "About that... The actors left the castle last night, but Vadoma didn't mention anything about a production team."

"Do they even have one?" Grace folded her arms. She hadn't shaken her foul mood since leaving the hospital, but her new focus had cleared her mind of their experience from the night before.

"I would assume they have people taking care of lighting."

She pinched the bridge of her nose. *Why didn't we think of this sooner?* "Actors wouldn't know how to set up a projector and scrim or Plexiglas or whatever they used—"

"They might if they worked their way onto the stage, but the lighting and sound engineers definitely would."

"Maybe I should reconsider Matteo's invitation." She let her head fall back and stared at the ceiling. Dinner would be a means to obtain information on the actors and stage crew and nothing more. It wasn't like the handsome Italian had won her over, or not completely, anyway.

"Maybe not." Henry pressed his lips together and stepped out into a crowd. "Whoa."

"No kidding. Where did everyone come from?"

"I don't know, but we need to get to the guard tower without anyone we know seeing us." He walked in the opposite direction of the café and cathedral.

They'd planned to get in, grab Brianna's iPad, and get out, preferably without anyone seeing them. Only time would tell if the herds of tourists would help or hinder their mission.

Taking the long way around the main buildings to avoid the employees, they speed-walked past the ruins of the main fortress. By the time they reached the triangular terrace, sweat ran down Henry's face and Grace bent at the waist to catch her breath.

She grinned. "I bet you regret that enormous dinner you scarfed down."

"I'll never admit to such nonsense." He pressed his hand to his gut and winced. "Ready?"

"As I'll ever be." Grace ducked beneath the pieces of scaffolding partially blocking the entrance to the guard tower and stilled to listen for signs of life. When she didn't hear anything, she peeked into the large room with the fresco. "Coast is clear."

They made their way down the hall and into the tunnel that Alessio had taken them through the night before. After about five minutes, Grace stopped and glanced behind her.

"What's wrong?"

"Weren't we supposed to turn left before now?"

"The passage had a sign with an arrow. We haven't come to it yet." He squeezed past her and continued walking.

A woman's scream seemed to surround them. Grace's heart skipped a beat.

"Keep going until we find the sign. If we take a different hall, we may never find our way out." Henry tugged her forward.

A second scream tore through the dark tunnels.

"We can't ignore her. What if she's hurt?"

He turned, and the color drained from his face. Mouth moving in silent words, he pointed past her.

Grace's world slowed and constricted until nothing mattered except whatever stood behind her. She glanced over her shoulder, and her knees turned to jelly.

The spectral image of a woman floated near the ceiling. She looked into Grace's eyes and shrieked in a pitch no human voice could reach.

Henry yanked her arm. "Run!"

They ran as fast as the tight space would allow.

"There's the arrow!" Grace had never been so happy to see a sign. She followed him around the corner. "There!" The office was close.

Eyes wide and shoulders heaving, he stopped. "Go first. I'll watch our backs."

The ghost screamed again, only this time the sound faded rather than surrounding them.

Grace stopped and stared into the intersection of the two hallways. "She hasn't passed us."

"Good. Let's get out of here before she does." He nudged her forward, but she stood her ground.

Now that the initial shock had worn off, the synapses in her brain began to fire again. "Henry, think about it logically. She's probably not real—"

"Says the girl who took one look at her and ran like her feet were on fire." He chuckled, but it came out more like a nervous giggle.

Grace eased to the end of the hall and peeked around the corner. "It's gone."

"Until it isn't." He shook his head. "Fake or not, that was a rush, but not in a good way."

She pulled her phone from her pocket and shined the light at the ceiling.

"What are you doing?" Henry whisper-shouted behind her. "We need to find the iPad and get the heck out of here before we're arrested for trespassing."

"Give me a minute." Retracing her steps, Grace gauged where she'd last seen the apparition and flashed the beam along the top of the arched passageway.

Muttering beneath his breath, he followed close behind.

A glint of metal caught her eye. Grace focused her light on the spot, and her stomach did a somersault. However, her relief was quickly replaced by anger. "It's a *track*."

"What the..." Henry stared at the thin strip of metal attached to the ceiling and groaned. "When I find these people..."

"I'm with you." Grace wasn't happy with their tormentor for frightening years off her life—twice. "I'm thinking the projector slides down the hall on either a mechanized pulley or by gravity."

"I'm leaning toward an electrical mechanism. If it were gravity, it would still be here." Henry took a few more steps. "There aren't any scrims or Plexiglas. What was it reflecting off?"

"Are you sure?" She squinted at the apex of the arch. "It's so high, the cell phone flashlight isn't doing a great job, and the hallway lights are aimed down."

He smirked. "You could stand on my shoulders and feel around."

"No, thank you." She stuffed her phone back into her pocket. "At this point, the hows don't matter to me as much as the whys."

"And ultimately, the whos."

The twins made their way to Brianna's and Alessio's office. Grace entered the code Brianna had given them, opened the door, and caught Rosa riffling through one of the desk drawers.

The woman jumped back and pressed her hand to her chest. "You scared me."

Henry folded his arms. "What are you doing in here?"

"Ah...I thought I could... Alessio is gone." She hung her head, and a microsecond later her shoulders shook and her wails rivaled the volume of the fake ghost's screams.

"You thought you could what?"

Giving him an odd look, Grace wrapped her arms around the hysterical woman. When all of this ended, she'd have a conversation with him about witness-badgering. "We heard he was missing. Do you have any idea who would have told Alessio his father was ill?"

Rosa choked back a sob. "No. Everyone loves him. *Everyone*."

Grace took the opportunity to scan Brianna's desk. The iPad sat beside a gigantic black purse that hadn't been there when Alessio had shown them the office.

"Has he done this sort of thing before?" Henry said, "Disappeared for a while and returned?"

The tiny Italian recovered enough to glare at him. "You think he is off having a party?"

He held up his hands. "I didn't say that."

Grace bugged her eyes out at him from behind Rosa's back. "Has anyone called the police? They could check the ferry records to see if he purchased a ticket or check the security footage at the port."

The woman's mouth hung open.

"It's worth a shot, right?" This time when Grace looked at Henry, she pleaded for assistance.

"No police. I don't think it is a good idea." She gripped her throat, seemed to realize what she'd done, and dropped her hand. "Signore Alfini...he is a quiet man."

Henry's brows climbed into his hairline. "You're saying he won't ask the authorities to find his son because he's a private man?"

"My English is not so good." Rosa dried her cheeks on the back of her hand. However, halfway through the gesture, she stopped and narrowed her eyes. "How did you get in here?"

Grace chewed her lower lip. She had a huge problem. She couldn't lie to save her life. If she started to answer the question, she wouldn't know when to stop.

Seeming to read her mind, Henry went for a preemptive strike. "I don't think any of us are supposed to be here, but you're trying to help find Alessio, and we're trying to find an explanation for the ghosts Brianna saw—"

"Ghosts. Bah." Rosa lifted her chin.

He lowered his voice. "Why don't we all leave and forget we ran into each other?"

"Yes." She sighed. "But you leave the ghosts alone. They are good for business."

Henry glanced at Grace and the strange woman. "Is that why so many people are here?"

Rosa made a sour face. "Everyone is asking where to see them. No good Catholic would search for such things."

Grace resisted the urge to grin. While researching places to visit in Italy, she'd come across several churches with rooms decorated solely with human bones. Italians seemed to have an ongoing fascination with death.

"You don't approve of ghost-hunting, but you want it to continue?" Henry scratched his head.

Rosa blew out a breath and rolled her eyes. "Yes. It is not...complicated."

Rock music blared from the desk. *Satisfaction* by the Rolling Stones.

Rosa started and darted to her purse. She fished the phone out and pressed the screen and the buttons on the side and bottom before it stopped ringing.

The twins exchanged a quick glance.

"It's new." She slung her enormous bag over her shoulder and marched to the door. "We never saw each other here."

"Right." Henry widened his eyes and nodded toward Brianna's desk.

It was Grace's turn to take the hint. They'd come for Brianna's iPad, but it was gone.

Henry followed the woman out of the office. "Rosa, does the theater company have a production staff?"

"What is a production staff?" Her hand trembled to the point it took her three attempts to lock the office door.

"Someone who does the lighting and sound?"

"Ah. No. Nothing like that." She led them down the hall past the putridarium.

Grace was focused on the woman's purse, so much so, it took her a moment to realize what Rosa had said. When Matteo had joined them on the terrace, he'd mentioned something about filming a commercial. Either Rosa had misunderstood the question, or she'd lied. She'd bet on the latter.

Hanging back, Henry whispered, "Got it?"

"No, she beat me to it."

He narrowed his eyes.

"Would it be okay if we took some photos in there?" Grace forced a smile. She had to stall long enough to think of a way to separate the woman from her bag.

"No." She motioned for them to go ahead of her.

That was blunt.

They walked through the door separating the restricted and tourist areas and into a line of people waiting to access the Nuns' Cemetery. Some of the visitors spoke Italian, but the majority conversed in either German or English.

"Oh, no." Grace tugged Henry's sleeve. "I recognize several of them from the hotel. I bet they're attending Mom's and Dad's classes."

"Kids!" Their father's voice boomed over the din of the crowd. "Fancy meeting you here."

Grace froze. "Double oh-no."

Henry rose to the balls of his feet, waved at his parents, and pointed to the ceiling. "We'll see you upstairs."

"Your parents?" Rosa seemed to enjoy their discomfort. She smirked and took her sweet time weaving through the tourists. "They will take you to your hotel now?"

"I hope so." Grace saw the opportunity and took it. Pretending to stumble, she grabbed the leather strap on Rosa's purse and dragged it and the petite Italian to the ground.

Rosa shouted a slew of words that, judging by the shocked expressions on the tourists' faces, were probably not those a good Catholic girl would normally say.

Never one to miss the action, Henry turned and fake-stumbled over Rosa.

The contents of the woman's purse flew through the air like confetti, only confetti didn't hurt when it landed.

Red-faced, Rosa shouted and scampered to collect her things, but there were too many people in the tight space. A lipstick case broke beneath a man's heel. Papers scattered. A wallet burst open. Cash and credit cards spilled. Gold coins rolled in every direction.

Henry tugged on Grace's arm. "I have it."

Crouching, she made her way to the edge of the startled crowd and followed Henry upstairs. "Where?"

He patted the small of his back. "Safe and sound."

"Why would she steal it?" Grace whispered.

"No clue." He glanced over his shoulder and pulled her into an alcove. "What do you think she was doing down there?"

"Besides stealing, I think she was looking for clues to Alessio's whereabouts. She cares about him. I believe she's upset, but I think she either knows or suspects who's behind the fake hauntings."

"Grace! You have returned." Matteo walked toward them with his arms wide. "Should I tell my father to reserve our best table for two?"

Faith Warner cleared her throat. "Would one of you mind explaining what *that* was about?"

Henry shrugged. "Grace tripped, and chaos ensued."

"Uh huh." Their mother arched a brow.

"Who is this?" Ethan nodded toward the Italian standing entirely too close to Grace.

She plastered on a smile. "Matteo, these are my parents, Ethan and Faith Warner. Mom and Dad, this is Matteo. He works in the castle."

The young man didn't miss a beat. He shook their father's hand and kissed their mother's. "You will all join me for dinner, yes?"

Grace winced.

"Or you could join us?" Ethan glanced at the twins, likely trying to read the situation.

"No, I insist. You must come to my family's restaurant. My *Nona*, she makes the best sauce in all of *Italia*." Matteo tugged Grace to his side. "Two beautiful American women at my table. I would be honored."

Ethan pressed his lips into a tight line.

Henry tried to hold his laughter in, but it was like kinking a garden hose. The effort only made it come out in a sudden burst.

The Warner women were not amused. Grace glared, and Faith pursed her lips.

"Sorry." Henry held his hands out at his sides and took a step back.

Faith turned to Matteo and smiled. "We would love to join you."

Rosa emerged from the lower levels and narrowed her eyes.

Grace broke out in a cold sweat. *She knows we have the iPad.* "I'd like to clean up before dinner. Can we go back to the hotel, now?"

Her mother glanced between Rosa and the twins and nodded. "I think that would be wise."

CHAPTER NINE

"It wasn't what it looked like." Henry hung his head and sighed like a fourth-grader with a bad report card.

Faith tapped her foot on the tile floor. "I saw you come out of the employees only door with that woman. Next thing I know, you two are on the floor, along with the contents of her purse."

"I tripped and grabbed her strap on the way down." Grace white-knuckled the edge of the bed.

Ethan clasped his hands behind his back and paced the hotel room. "That doesn't explain what you were doing in a restricted area or why the woman you were with was visibly upset. She looked as though she'd been crying."

For the first time since the twins had started their senior-year research project, Ethan and Faith Warner had stumbled into the middle of an investigation. To say Henry didn't care for it was like saying Marie Antoinette had a slight kink in her neck.

Grace met his gaze and nodded once.

She's cracked under the pressure. Henry braced himself for what would happen next.

"There is a portion of the Nuns' Cemetery that's not open to the public. An archeology intern experienced some alleged paranormal activity in the chamber. Her research partner allowed us access to it yesterday." Grace squared her shoulders.

Although she'd shocked him, Henry worked hard to keep his expression neutral. She'd managed to give them just enough information and hadn't stretched or bent the truth.

"Rumors of the hauntings are all over the island. Our students staged a coup and demanded a field trip to the castle this afternoon." Ethan grinned. "What did you find?"

"Ethan..." Faith shook her head. "They haven't explained why the woman was upset."

"She doesn't approve of people seeking out ghosts," Henry said at the exact moment Grace blurted out, "She's in love with one of the interns, and he doesn't return her feelings."

Faith arched a brow. "Which is it?"

"Both," the twins chorused.

Their mother gave them the same look she'd given them since they were old enough to get into mischief. "Very well. I'm going to get dressed for dinner. I suggest you do the same."

Once inside their room, Henry removed Brianna's iPad from the back of his pants. "Get a shower. I'll let Bethany know we have this."

"Try calling the hospital directly and speaking to Brianna." Grace headed for the bathroom.

Unfortunately, Bethany answered the phone.

"Hi, it's Henry. We have the iPad."

"Perfect. Could you leave it with the front desk? I'll come first thing in the morning to pick it up." She sounded downright cheerful.

Henry didn't trust her. No one was that happy about spending two hours round trip on a ferry.

On the cab ride to the restaurant, Henry explained the concept of Pepper's ghost and went over the material evidence they'd found that suggested the hauntings were indeed fake.

Ethan clapped his son on the shoulder. "I have to say I'm impressed and intrigued."

"As am I." Faith smiled. "Is this typical of the mysteries you've solved so far?"

"Each one is different, but we use a similar process to solve them." Grace tugged at the black wrap dress she'd borrowed from their mother.

"I have to admit, I had my doubts about this project, but you two have done some amazing things." Faith rested her hand on Grace's arm. "Stop fidgeting. The dress is very flattering on you."

The cab stopped in front of a bustling restaurant, and Ethan paid the driver.

Henry climbed out and stretched. He loved Italy but missed the legroom in the family pickup truck.

Fussing with the dress again, Grace whispered, "I have a bad feeling about this."

"Why'd you wear it?" He grinned, knowing good and well she wasn't talking about her choice of clothing. "Relax. We'll get the information we need."

"Yes, but what if he mentions Alessio or the—"

"You look great." Her father slung his arm around her shoulder. "Now, about this boy."

"Dad!" She jabbed her finger into his side.

In addition to asking about the mystery, her parents had given her a thorough interrogation about Matteo at the hotel. Henry didn't blame her for wanting to avoid another round of questions from the prosecution.

"I know, I know." Their father chuckled. "But Italian boys—"

"Are different." Henry smirked. "I warned her the first day we arrived."

"I hate this conversation more than papercuts and road rash."

Sensing her daughter's distress, their mom pulled Grace away from the Warner men and led her toward the entrance.

Matteo greeted them at the door with a wide smile and a kiss for each cheek. He met Faith Warner's gaze and winked. "We made the special arrangements as you requested."

"What arrangements?" Henry glanced at Grace and his mother.

Ethan clamped a hand on his shoulder. "Mom and I will be dining at a private table while you kids eat *al fresco*."

Matteo's brows climbed into his hairline. "In *Italia*, we say *all'aperto* for eating outdoors. Here, *al fresco* means to spend time in jail."

"We wouldn't want that, now, would we?" Ethan gave a deep, rich, belly laugh.

The twins followed Matteo to a table on the patio. The lights from the harbor and colorful lanterns illuminated the space. The table was a sight to behold—candles, platters of antipasti, and enough silverware for six people for six courses. Matteo had gone all out.

"It is very pretty out here." She seated herself in the chair he'd pulled out for her.

"*Grazie.*" He sat beside her and filled her glass with red wine.

"Thanks, but I don't drink."

Matteo shrugged and took a sip from the glass.

Sitting across the table, Henry watched the exchange with a grin. "How did your audition go?"

"Very well. I am hoping to hear good news." Matteo frowned. "I am sorry to say our evening will be short. I must work tonight. The castle, she is very busy."

"I understand." Grace sighed, but Henry suspected it had more to do with the mystery than losing her dinner companion.

Henry filled his plate with meats and cheeses. "Does your theater company have light and sound technicians?"

"The company, no, but the owners of the castle provided us with such people for performances and to film the commercials. Why do you ask?"

He debated playing it cool or getting straight to the point. They only had two days before they left for Rome, not to mention a missing person.

Grace beat him to the punch. "We know how the ghosts were created, but we don't know who's behind it."

Matteo dropped his knife, and in his haste to stop the clattering, he spilled his wine. He muttered something under his breath and mopped up the mess. "Forgive me. I am...surprised. How do you know the spirits are not real?"

She shook her head. "The culprits are using stage tricks to make them appear."

Henry didn't particularly care for the guy, but he couldn't help but feel sorry for him. She'd put Matteo on the spot before they'd finished their first course. "We aren't planning to run to the press with the story. We only want to understand what happened to Brianna."

Grace added, "She had surgery on her hands to repair the bones she broke trying to get out of the room, and she's suffering from nightmares. I'd hate to see her give up her work because she's afraid to return to the castle."

Matteo looked everywhere except at her. "I am sorry for what happened to Brianna, but it was an isolated incident."

"It wasn't. Someone locked Henry and me in the same room." She leaned closer and forced him to meet her gaze. "I had nightmares, too, and I knew what was happening around me wasn't real. Can you imagine how Brianna must have felt?"

His eyes widened. "Last night? After you watched me perform?"

"Yes."

Henry found himself waffling between confidence and doubt. Matteo knew something, but he didn't seem the type to mastermind a scheme. "Alessio let us into the restricted area, then supposedly received a call and left the islet, but *someone* closed the door and locked us inside."

Matteo snapped his head in Henry's direction. "You were with Alessio? What time was this?"

"Right after we left you."

The Italian stood, strode away, muttered something, and paced back. "I will tell you what I know after you help me find Alessio."

Grace's mouth fell open, although she should have seen it coming. "Are you part of the scheme to create fake ghosts to bring in more tourists?"

He let his head fall back and uttered a prayer. "I am not responsible for anyone being tormented in the putridarium, but I played a small role in the plan to save the castle."

"How small a role?" Henry folded his arms.

"Find Alessio, and I will explain everything."

Grace stood. "Thank you for everything, but I've lost my appetite."

"Hang on a minute." Henry turned to Matteo. "What makes you think we can find him? We don't know the area or the language."

The guy offered Grace a sad smile before turning back to Henry. "Because you are smart and have gone out of your way to help a woman you don't know. Alessio is like a brother to me. He's in trouble and deserves the same consideration, does he not?"

A woman carrying a tray piled high with food stepped onto the patio and hesitated.

Grace glanced from the mountains of pasta to her brother.

Henry gave her a tight-lipped smile meant to convey he'd go along with whatever she decided.

She sighed. "Fine. We'll do what we can to help—on one condition."

Matteo pressed his hands together as if praying. "Anything."

"You tell us the truth about what's going on now."

The guy's shoulders slumped much like Mr. Alfini's had at the hospital. "You must swear you will not tell anyone I told you."

Henry said, "The way I see it, we learn to trust each other, or this will never work."

"You are right. I will tell you." Matteo turned to Grace. "But I don't know much."

"And we'll help you find Alessio." She sat and put her napkin back in her lap.

"Prego. We have a second mystery." Henry clapped his hands together. "Bring on the pasta."

Grace lacked Henry's enthusiasm. She'd hoped against hope that Matteo wasn't involved in the ghost scheme. Not only had he played a role, but he'd also successfully strong-armed them into helping find Alessio.

Matteo waited until the twins had served themselves before speaking, "Do you remember the commercial we filmed for the evening tours?"

"Yes." She braced herself for the worst.

He lowered his gaze. "Months before, we filmed other...*things*."

Henry's fork froze mid-bite. "Such as?"

"I hung in stocks. Others were strapped to harnesses and pretended to fly. A few dressed as deceased nuns." He made the sign of the cross.

"The actors filmed the footage used to fake the hauntings." Grace's heart rattled against her sternum. "Who set up the equipment?"

Matteo looked her square in the eye. "I don't know for certain."

"Someone must come to mind." Henry sat back.

"Giuseppe has done many amazing things with the lighting in the castle." His voice rose. "You must understand. Many people rely on the income from the castle. Not just the employees, but many local businesses as well."

Grace glanced through the window at the people working in the kitchen. "Vadoma mentioned that the castle was having financial issues."

The Italian grinned. "Yes, but with Alessio's and Brianna's work—"

The twins exchanged glances.

Matteo leaned in and lowered his voice. "I should not mention this, but they discovered the lost city of Aenaria. The coins alone would pay to restore the entire castle."

Stunned, Grace ran through the facts as she knew them. Aenaria was an ancient Roman city on the coast of Ischia, but the experts believed that changes caused by volcanic eruptions and rising tides had buried the city under the sea. If he was right, the interns' discovery would rival that of Herculaneum.

Henry pushed his plate to the side. "What are the Treasure Trove laws in Italy?"

"I do not understand?" Matteo glanced between them.

"In the United States, when someone finds a treasure, they keep a portion, and the landowners keep a portion." He pulled his phone from his pocket and frowned. "Weak signal."

"I know who to ask." She stood.

"No, please. You cannot repeat—"

"I won't share the details." She walked into the main part of the restaurant and found her parents sitting side by side sharing a bowl of gelato.

The couple seemed so happy, she hated to disturb them. However, a young man had gone missing, and if her hunch was correct, she had discovered a motive.

Ethan glanced up and smiled. "Gracie. Have you finished your dinner already?"

She chewed her lower lip as she approached.

"Uh-oh. That doesn't look good." Her mother motioned to the chair beside her. "Dessert makes everything better."

Grace blinked. Her mother never advocated sweets. In Faith Warner's mind, bananas were too much sugar. "Actually, I need Dad's expertise for a few minutes."

Her father lowered his brows. "Is it a quick question, or shall I join you?"

She frowned at the crowded tables surrounding her parents. "Maybe it's best if you come with me."

He took one last bite of the frozen chocolate cream and stood. "Lead the way."

"I'm coming too." Faith grabbed her purse.

Matteo turned an odd shade of pale green when he noticed her parents approaching. Grace understood. It likely had nothing to do with the company and everything to do with spilling a secret that could cause a boat-load of trouble—if it hadn't already.

Ethan held a chair out for his wife before seating himself. "What can I do for you?"

"Sorry to interrupt your dinner. I don't have cell reception, or I would have looked it up." Henry said, "What do you know about the Treasure Trove laws in Italy?"

He nodded once. "Strangely enough, they are very straightforward. Because the country has lost millions of priceless objects to theft, they changed the laws in 1939. The state owns any artifacts and items they deem to have historical or artistic value."

"I thought I read that somewhere." Grace sighed. *I bet that was why Brianna was so concerned about reporting the discovery.*

Matteo frowned. "They give rewards, no?"

"In some cases, but from what I understand, it's up to the discretion of the authorities." Ethan chuckled. "A history professor in my seminar this morning is a metal-detector enthusiast. He researched it before he came. It made for a fascinating debate."

Her mother cocked her head. "Why do you ask?"

Henry sat up straighter. "A friend of Matteo's thinks he hit the lottery because he found some old relics."

Ethan Warner gave the Italian his best judicial smile. "I wish your friend luck, but I wouldn't advise him to quit his day job."

"I'm sure there's still a huge black market for old coins and artifacts." The words fell out of Grace's mouth before she thought them through.

Her mother arched a brow.

"As with most things, criminals will find a way." Ethan's voice deepened. "However, I wouldn't advise going that route."

Henry's laugh was too loud and too high-pitched. "Well, look at the time. We have a castle to storm and a mystery to solve."

It took Matteo a few seconds to catch on, but he stood and tossed his napkin on the table. "Yes, we must go breach defenses."

"Young man, I would rather not think of you breaching any defenses with my daughter along." Ethan deadpanned.

CHAPTER TEN

"I do not understand. Why are you going to the castle? I have to work and cannot visit." Matteo still wore the shell-shocked expression he had at the restaurant twenty minutes before.

"We're looking for clues." Henry couldn't tell if the thought of them accompanying him to the castle or if Ethan Warner's not-so-veiled-threats had freaked the guy out.

"For Alessio?"

"And the people behind the fake hauntings." Grace sighed for the hundredth time since her father had brought up everything from the legal definition of assault to medieval torture techniques—all in the course of a short and seemingly polite conversation.

Matteo watched her from the corner of his eye. "Your father...he is knowledgeable about removing fingernails. Has he visited the torture museum?"

Grace sighed for the hundred and first time. "He was pulling your leg."

The Italian gave her a dubious look. "Not yet, but I think he will if I touch you."

"She means he was joking, but I wouldn't test him." Henry set his hands on his hips and stared up at the imposing structure. "Is there an employee entrance?"

"Yes, but I still do not understand. How are you to catch the villains?" Matteo shoved his hands in his pockets, shifted his weight from one foot to the other, and then folded his arms. For an actor, he fidgeted a lot.

"It's simple. You know what was filmed and where the supposed ghosts will appear, right?"

"Not exactly."

Grace folded her arms and gave her brother a death stare. She knew him well enough to know he was making the plan up as he went along. Not to mention, he hadn't consulted her.

He would apologize after they'd caught the schemers. "But you can make an educated guess based on the scenes the actors filmed and find us a place to hide."

"*Sì.*" He looked away as if considering the options. "King Alfonso will visit the crypts of the noble families. It is a small area with places to wait out of sight."

"You're suggesting we hide in the vaults, aren't you?" Her voice cracked.

"Yes, *bella*, but do not fear. The only ghosts are on film." Matteo squeezed her hand. "It is safe."

"Where have I heard that before?" She shot Henry another dirty look and followed the Italian through the employees' entrance.

They wove through several tunnels and ascended five flights of stairs without sighs, complaints, or snarky comments, which suited Henry just fine. It gave him time to think through his plan.

Matteo pressed his finger to his lips and eased past a set of glass doors.

Henry couldn't help but peek inside.

Vadoma, Giuseppe, and a handful of costumed people sat at a table eating dinner. For a bunch of people sharing a meal, they didn't seem happy.

Grace tugged Henry away from the door and shook her head.

He crossed his eyes and stuck out his tongue.

She was not amused. Rather than the smile he'd hoped for, she pointed down the hall.

He sighed and trudged on.

Unlocking a metal door, Matteo whispered, "I must go change into my costume. Follow this hall for twenty meters and turn left. You will see the crypts straight ahead. Avoid the Plexiglas in the ceiling or someone may see you."

Grace chewed her lip. "When does the castle open to the public?"

"In forty-five minutes." He gave her a resigned smile. *"Ciao, bella."*

The twins found the crypts without incident and settled into a corner that allowed them to observe the lower level as well as portions of the top.

Henry wiggled around to get comfy on the stone slab. "This isn't so bad."

"You're sitting on a grave."

Before he could think of anything clever to say, the all-too-familiar scent of decaying rodent wafted through the tomb.

Covering her mouth and nose, Grace pressed against the wall.

A man wearing dark pants walked across the Plexiglas window above their tomb. A few seconds later, a woman wearing layers of multi-colored clothes followed.

Pointing at the ceiling, Grace mouthed, "Vadoma and Giuseppe."

Henry fumbled for his phone. Video footage of the couple setting the scene for the fake hauntings would close the case once and for all.

Scraping like stone against stone came from entirely too nearby for comfort. Grace motioned him closer.

Crouching behind the sarcophagus, Henry pressed Record on his phone.

"I hope the bad weather holds off until we close for the evening." Vadoma spoke with a British accent—a far cry from the vaguely Eastern European one she'd used before.

"It could be comin' down in buckets, and they'd still come." Giuseppe sounded like a man born and raised in East Central Texas.

"Holy cowboys," Henry whispered. The second he opened his mouth, the dead rat smell entered and clung to the back of his throat. His hand shot to his mouth to keep him from coughing.

Grace pressed her finger to her lips.

The Texan chuckled. "Wait till they get a load of the wailing woman tonight. Once word gets out, the hotel will be booked solid year-round."

"I hope you're right." She spoke like a woman wearing a bright smile. "The motion sensors worked?"

"Like a charm, darlin'. Like a charm. She flies down the hall like a banshee."

Holy smokes, that was how the screaming ghost appeared at exactly the right time.

A scampering sound much like the one the twins had heard in the Nuns' Cemetery made it impossible to hear the rest of the conversation.

"What is that?" Grace whispered.

"No clue." He gagged. "Oh, man. I can taste dead rat."

The tomb went silent.

Vadoma asked, "Did you hear someone?"

"Didn't hear a thing besides the sound of cold hard cash rollin' in." The man laughed again. He must have done something to his accomplice because she squealed and giggled.

"Stop fooling around and finish setting up."

"Yes, ma'am."

Henry did his best to remain quiet—easier said than done with the stench growing thicker by the second.

The couple finished whatever it was they were doing and left the tombs the same way they'd come.

Henry counted to twenty after the scraping noise stopped and stood. "We can't stay here. I'm going to be sick."

"Cover your face with your hoodie. I'm going to see what Vadoma and Cowboy Joe set up down here." Grace walked farther into the crypt.

Following, he waved his phone like a madman. "We have them on video admitting to the scheme."

"I know, but aren't you the slightest bit curious?"

Henry closed his eyes and pinched the bridge of his nose. "Nope, not at all. What I am is suffocating on the foulest odor known to man."

"Wow." Grace pointed to something in the next chamber.

"Whoa." Henry moved closer to the contraption.

Giuseppe or Joe or whatever his real name was had used a rectangular recess in the wall to mount a small projector aimed at a sheet of mirrored plastic. Unlike Plexiglas, which had the same shape and feel as real glass, the foil-like material was thin. So thin, the guy had used it in a portable projection screen stand instead of the traditional white matte fabric.

"Call me crazy, but I think the scampering sound we heard was the screen unrolling." Grace positioned herself in front of the projector, raised her arm, and squinted at her upturned thumb.

He followed her line of vision to the mirrored screen. Based on the forty-five-degree angle of the reflective surface, Henry gauged the image would project through an opening in the ceiling—or the floor of the room above.

"Any clue what's above that hole?" Grace stretched above the sarcophagus, directly beneath the gap in the stones.

"If I had to guess, I'd say we found the real reason only one of the mourners' alcoves was enclosed with glass."

Her eyes widened. "This is exactly what Brianna referred to as Pepper's Ghost. If you're right, which I believe you are, whatever is projected on the screen will appear in the room above."

"Safely out of reach of the hordes of tourists who will be arriving any minute." He shot a quick video of the contraption. "I think we have enough evidence."

"I disagree. The set-up in the putridarium was completely different. There was no hidden chamber or foil screen. I'd like to know how they pulled it off."

"It had to be a similar setup or something like the screaming ghost in the hall." He shook his head. "I'm not going back in there. Ten to one, Vadoma and Giuseppe put another rat carcass in the chamber."

"So? Since when do we let minor obstacles prevent us from finishing a case?"

"When they stink, that's when."

"Then I'll go alone."

Henry groaned, let his head fall back, and found himself staring into King Alfonso of Aragon's angry eyes.

The costumed man on the other side of the Plexiglas snarled. Had Henry been able to hear, he'd have bet his front teeth the guy had growled.

"We've been spotted. Time to go." He grabbed his sister's arm and tugged her toward the door.

Grace dug her heels in. "Look"

He glanced at the Plexiglas in the ceiling. This time all he saw was feet. "They must have opened the doors."

"Which means we'll have an easier time getting to the putridaria." She turned toward the exit.

"I know you're down here." A man's voice boomed through the crypts. "Come out now, or I'm calling the police."

Henry's heart leapt into his throat. "King Alfonso."

She froze in place as if trying to blend in with the fresco on the wall behind her.

The projector came on, flashing bright light directly into Henry's eyes. He shielded his face and ducked to the side.

Above them, chaos ensued. Men shouted and women screamed, or maybe women shouted and men screamed. Henry couldn't tell over the shoes pounding on the Plexiglas and the roar of voices.

"Someone's going to get hurt." Grace lurched for the projector.

Though the ghostly image above had vanished, the stampede continued. Worse still, King Alfonso of Aragon rounded the corner.

The man glanced from the projector in her hand to the foil screen to the bedlam in the room above. "What have you done?"

"Us?" Grace shouted. "We haven't done anything. You and your theater company caused this!"

Wide-eyed, he sputtered, "What? We did no such thing. What are you talking about?"

Henry motioned to a slab at the top of stone stairs beside the sarcophagus. "Vadoma and Giuseppe were here, but they didn't come through the regular door. Is that how they got in?"

The actor hesitated a half-second too long before he shook his head.

"He's lying. Let's go." Grace climbed the steps and pushed up on the slab. The stone moved a few inches at best.

King Alfonso shouted, "Wait. You can't go that way—"

"Watch us." Henry joined his sister, and together, they managed to move the covering. He poked his head through the opening and immediately regretted his decision.

A woman standing near the sheet of glass fainted. The man beside her didn't seem to notice. He stared in horror as Henry appeared to climb from the grave.

"Everyone, please calm down." He held his hands at his sides, palms open.

Grace made her way from the coffin-shaped stone square. "This was a bad idea," Grace reiterated the king's caution.

The man who'd looked at Henry as if he were a medieval zombie narrowed his eyes. "She's holding a mini-projector! It's all a scam!"

People shouted in different languages, and some pounded on the glass barricade separating the twins from the angry mob.

Henry stepped in front of her and widened his stance. "Get below."

"We'll be arrested." Her voice rose over the din.

Using the word "arrested" around a bunch of ticked off tourists was the worst idea in the history of bad ideas. The sheet of glass strained to hold back the pitchfork-carrying villagers.

Henry took her by the shoulders and forced her to meet his gaze. "Go!"

She went.

He scrambled after his sister and didn't bother to replace the stone slab.

King Alfonso had lost his crown and cloak and most of the color from his face. "I tried to warn you."

Above them, the plexiglass cracked.

"We have to get out of here." Grace moved past the actor and sprinted for the door.

Henry followed. The guy could stay for all he cared. The actors might not have planned the scheme, but they'd gone along with it.

The twins reached the end of the hall before King Alfonso caught up.

"What's going on? And before you accuse me of causing this, I have no bloody idea what any of that was back there." He spoke perfect English, although he had the coloring of someone from the Mediterranean.

Grace pressed her back to the wall and hung her head. "This scheme may have brought traffic into the castle, but people are getting hurt."

"Scheme?" The actor shook his head. "Before you answer, I'm Rudy, and you are?"

"Henry and Grace Warner. We're friends of Brianna Bennet." He folded his arms.

Grace gave him the CliffsNotes version of the situation, starting with Brianna in the putridarium and ending with Vadoma's and Giuseppe's conversation.

Rudy stared at her as if she'd sprouted horns. "Are you sure?"

"One hundred percent," they said in unison.

"Does this have anything to do with Alessio's disappearance?"

"We don't know." Henry motioned down the hall. "We should get out of here."

"It's not safe for you two above-ground." Rudy ran his hands over his head. "I could get you to the exit, but there's no guarantee some of the people from the crypts won't recognize you."

"That could get ugly." Grace's eyes rounded. "You should warn the other actors. I have a feeling more fake ghosts will appear tonight."

Henry hadn't thought about that. Once word got out, the entire place could turn into a battle of tourists versus actors. "Do you guys have radios or a means to communicate with each other?"

"Only cell phones, and most of the actors don't carry them while in character." He motioned to his pantaloons. "Puffy legs, but no pockets."

"Great." Henry hated standing around wasting time. "What about the halls? Can we travel underground to reach the areas where people are performing?"

"We need to warn Matteo." Grace's voice thinned.

Rudy gave her an odd look. "You say you're friends with Bri?"

They nodded.

"I'll let you into her room, but you must swear to stay put."

"No way. We need to find Vadoma and Giuseppe. They know where the other ghost sightings will be. They're the only ones who can stop this." Henry would rather face an angry mob than allow Rudy to lock him and his sister away.

"I'll handle Vadoma and Giuseppe." The actor's expression darkened. "You'll wait in Bri's room, or you'll explain yourselves to the *polizia*. Your call."

CHAPTER ELEVEN

Grace counted to one hundred after Rudy left and turned the doorknob.

It didn't budge.

"He's locked us in." She couldn't believe it. "How is that even possible? This is a hotel. How can the doors lock from the outside?"

"You're probably right, but there's always the balcony." Henry rushed through the French doors and groaned. "Scratch that, unless Brianna has a parachute lying around."

Grace joined him on the private terrace. "Nice view. Not bad for an intern." Grace studied the area systematically, looking at the area beyond the balcony, the hotel above them, and the terrace itself looking for something that would give her an idea.

"Rosa said the hotel was closed during the off-season." He stared toward the ruins of the cathedral and frowned. "How do you think it's going back there?"

"Nothing's on fire. It can't be too bad." She leaned against the railing, trying to open her mind to possibilities that she couldn't see. The cold breeze felt good. The air smelled of ozone and salt water. "It's going to rain soon."

He took her by the shoulders and moved her away from the edge. "We promised not to fall through or off anything."

Grace smiled despite her mood. Not only did she worry about Matteo's safety, she couldn't help but wonder if they'd been duped. "I'm not so sure Rudy isn't in on the scheme."

"I've had the same thought about Matteo. They are actors, after all."

She smirked. "Until now, I would have said not very good ones."

The song, *Satisfaction* by the Rolling Stones, played from a room or two away.

"That's Rosa's ringtone." Henry leaned over the balcony to get a better view.

"She probably stays here too." Grace sank onto a lounge chair. "It's funny. I never would have pegged her for a classic rock fan."

As soon as the words left her mouth, she tensed.

Henry turned and stared. "Say that again."

"Rosa doesn't seem like a Rolling Stones fan." Grace's pulse raced.

"But Alessio does." A grin spread across his face.

"It was *his* phone she had in the office. No wonder she acted so weird." She tapped her lips. "Why does she have his phone? He allegedly called to tell her we were in the putridarium, which may or may not be true."

"There's only one way to find out." Henry cupped his mouth and shouted at the top of his lungs. "Rosa!"

"Cut it out. Even if she hears you, she's not going to tell us the truth."

He wiggled his brows. "No, but we might be able to trick her into unlocking the door."

"Good point." Grace stuck her fingers in her mouth and whistled loud enough to shatter crystal.

"A little warning next time." Henry winced and covered his ears with his hands. "Rosa! We know you're there!"

After five or ten minutes, the twins gave up calling for the woman and went inside.

"I'm starved." Henry plopped down on the bed.

"Me, too. We did more talking than eating tonight." She heard knocking and stilled. "What is that?"

"Last time you asked that question, we ended up playing the Frankenstein Monster to a crowd of angry villagers."

The banging grew louder.

Henry went to the door. "No one's there."

Grace crouched and pressed her ear to the wall. "It's coming from the adjacent room."

"Weird."

"Knock once if you can hear me." She spoke in a loud, clear voice.

The person knocked one time, paused, and knocked in an irregular pattern.

"Holy smokes. I think that's Morse code." Henry grabbed a pad and pen from the nightstand.

"Are you using Morse code?" Grace felt like an idiot talking through the wall. If this turned out to be another fake ghost situation, she would bring a new meaning to the word "medieval."

The person knocked once, paused, and repeated the pattern of soft and harder taps.

Henry shot to his feet. "It's Alessio!"

The person knocked several times in rapid succession.

Before Grace could make sense of what was happening, Henry bounded to the terrace.

"A little help here," he called from outside.

She stepped out, and her knees threatened to buckle. Her twin brother—the person by her side since before birth—stood on the railing of a balcony high enough to make the cars below look like toys.

He gripped the drainpipe running down the side of the building and glanced over his shoulder. "Come over here."

Grace swallowed past the lump in her throat. "What? No. Get down."

"I'd love to, Gracie, but I can't. My shoe is untied, and I'm standing on the lace."

She wanted to scream or cry or shut her eyes, but she couldn't just stand there and watch him fall to his death. "Only you."

He waited until she'd tied his shoe and stepped onto the neighboring balcony. "I'll be right back."

<hr />

Henry handed Alessio his third water bottle since they'd brought the guy across the balcony. For the most part, the Italian seemed uninjured. He had dark circles under his eyes and rope burns on his wrists and ankles, but no visible bruises.

Grace put some of the cheese and salami they'd found in Brianna's mini-fridge onto a paper plate and handed it to the young man. "I don't understand. How did you end up bound in your own room?"

"Rosa—she called and said my father was gravely ill in Naples. I came to my room for my jacket and wallet, and her brother was waiting." Rubbing the back of his head, Alessio winced. "I dropped like a sack of grain. When I awoke, I was tied up."

"Didn't anyone think to check for you there?" Henry asked.

He dipped his chin. "It's not technically my room. I live with my family on the main island. Vadoma owns the hotel, and she lets me stay here sometimes."

"Why did Rosa do it?"

"To stop me from reporting my and Bri's discoveries to the authorities." The young man coughed and took a swig of water. "She has been stealing artifacts and coins."

Grace's hand flew to her mouth.

Henry knew finding the missing intern had shaken his sister, but her reaction seemed off. "What is it?"

"There were coins in her purse when we tripped her. I assumed they were Euros, but they were bright gold."

"They were not Euros. If Bri and I are correct, they are Roman from 300-200 BCE." Alessio sighed. "Is she still in the hospital?"

He shifted gears so quickly that it took Henry's brain a moment to understand the question. "Brianna had surgery on her hands, but Bethany said she's expected to make a full recovery."

Alessio closed his eye and murmured a prayer.

Grace softened her tone. "I hate to ask, but are you aware of the scheme to create ghosts in the castle?"

"Yes." The Italian hung his head. "But I never meant for Bri to get hurt. It was a joke."

Henry looked at him in disbelief.

"Bri, she is a skeptic. I thought if we could fool her..." He choked back a sob." I hid her tablet so she'd return downstairs, but the door stuck. I could hear her screaming. I reached her as fast as I could."

"I'm sure she'll understand once you explain it to her." As much as Henry hated to admit it, he understood practical jokes gone wrong. He'd walked in Alessio's shoes a few times before, and probably would again. "Why lock us in the putridarium?"

"I didn't." He shook his head.

"Then who?"

"We have bigger problems." Grace stood and wiped her hands on her jeans as if she'd touched something filthy. "We should call the police."

"Things work differently here than in America. The police will want details before they proceed. There is no time." Alessio pushed himself to his feet. "Rosa is leaving the country tonight. We must catch her before she boards the boat."

"The door is locked." The twins said together.

The Italian cracked his first smile. "The key is above on the frame. Bri put it there after locking herself *in* four or five times."

"Why does it lock from the outside?" Grace retrieved the key.

"Old buildings." He shrugged. "I must use your phone."

Henry pulled the red-cased cell with the Stones' ringtone from his pocket. "This wouldn't be yours, by any chance?"

Alessio grabbed the phone, said something in Italian, and kissed it. "Thank you. I will have my father meet us downstairs."

Lightning lit the night sky, and thunder rolled across the sea. A second later, the skies opened, and rain fell in sheets. The storm had come.

Huddling in an alcove near the employee parking lot, the twins caught him up on the goings-on in the castle since his abduction. For his part, Alessio seemed genuinely distressed. Perhaps getting clocked in the head and tied up for a couple of days had toned down his bravado.

The cherry-red sports car screamed to a stop, and Mr. Alfini jumped out. He took one look at his son and burst into tears. The men hugged and laughed and hugged again, all the while speaking in Italian.

"I will drive." Alessio strode toward the car, but halfway there he wobbled.

Grace rushed to his side. "You may have a concussion."

"*I* will drive." Mr. Alfini took the keys.

They piled into the tiny car and headed for the main island. Unfortunately, the tourists in the castle clogged the causeway. Mr. Alfini, in traditional Italian style, laid on the horn. With no care for the rain pelting his face, he hung his head out the window and shouted at the pedestrians.

"We aren't going to make it." Alessio drummed his fingers on the armrest. "I should call the police."

"No *polizia.*" Mr. Alfini hit the accelerator. "Rosa is a daughter to me. We talk first."

Henry's heart skipped a beat when Mr. Alfini turned onto the narrow road leading to the hotel. "I thought you said this way wasn't safe in the rain?"

"It's not." Alessio grabbed the handle above his door. "*Babbo,* slow down!"

The older man increased the speed of the wipers *and* the car. "Barano?"

"*Sí.* She has a boat from Barano." Alessio gritted his teeth.

Mr. Alfini white-knuckled the wheel and aligned the car with the white line in the center of the road.

Headlights from an oncoming car flashed, and the crazy old man swerved back into his lane. This continued until he encountered another vehicle traveling in the same direction. Mr. Alfini laid on the horn again.

Alessio leaned forward and placed his hand on his father's arm. "That's Rosa's car."

He beeped, steered, and managed to lower the window at the same time. One arm hanging from the car, Mr. Alfini shouted at the vehicle in front of them.

Rosa sped up.

Both Alfini men shouted words that if spoken in English would likely have sent the twins' grandmother in search of soap to wash their mouths out.

The twins slid from one side of the miniscule backseat to the other on the tight corners, which, oddly enough, Henry considered a blessing. He was too busy defending himself from Grace's boney elbows and knees to notice the cliffs.

"I can't look." Grace buried her face in his shoulder.

Rosa took a sharp right turn without slowing.

Time seemed to crawl.

The passenger's side wheel caught the curb and sent the car spinning toward the cliff. The woman overcorrected, fishtailed, and hydroplaned toward the stone wall on the opposite side of the road.

Slamming on the brakes, Mr. Alfini narrowly missed clipping Rosa's front bumper.

Metal crunched against stone and tires squealed, but the car didn't stop moving. The momentum of the crash coupled with the lack of friction on the wet roads caused her to careen back toward the steep drop-off. The car squealed and skidded. The brake lights turned the rain red. The twins held their breath, watching as if it were happening in slow motion. The tires finally gripped, and the vehicle stopped. The back axle rested too close to the edge.

"*Dio mio!*" Alessio climbed out and stumbled toward the wreckage.

Grabbing his chest, Mr. Alfini followed his son. "Rosa!"

Henry peeled Grace off him and stared until she met his gaze. "Are you okay?"

"I think so." She peeked out the window.

Henry followed her gaze and watched as they pulled Rosa kicking and screaming from the car.

"She could have died." Grace shook her head.

"She doesn't seem to have cared about that part."

CHAPTER TWELVE

As he had the previous evening, Matteo met the twins at the door of his family's restaurant. He offered them a quick smile, though not as bright as the night before. "*Buonasera.*

"Hi." Grace turned her head. Her nerves had gotten the better of her since Alessio had called and asked them to join the castle employees for an after-hours meeting.

Matteo grinned and held out his hands. "No need to look so sad, *bella*. You are welcome here."

Henry scratched his jaw. "What's this all about?"

"We are to discuss plans to save the castle, of course." He pulled Grace into an embrace, kissed her cheeks, and turned to Henry.

He arched a brow but couldn't fight him off. Henry suffered through the traditional Italian greeting.

"Come. There are food and Coca-Cola especially for you."

Laughter, clanking silverware, and lively chatter greeted them inside the restaurant. It seemed like a typical family dinner—if family dinners involved makeup and medieval costumes.

Grace let out a breath and tried to relax.

Vadoma spotted them and walked over. Lowering her voice, she said, "I must apologize for locking you in the putridarium. I thought I could scare you away."

Grace's brain stuttered.

Henry laughed and looked away. "That was you?"

"Yes, and I'm so glad my plan didn't work. If it wasn't for the two of you, we might not have found Alessio before he wasted away to skin and bones." She met Grace's gaze. "Please forgive me."

"You're forgiven, and it's forgotten. I'm not one to hold a grudge."

"Forgive me too, while you're at it." Cowboy Joe grabbed Henry's hand. "I'm Joe. Nice to finally be able to talk to you. I would have said more sooner, but the accent gives me away every time."

"Why hide it?" Grace furrowed her brow.

"Discrimination. I came to this country to restore art, but not many take me seriously once they hear me talk."

"Restore art? I thought you were the technical wizard who created the ghosts?" Henry asked.

The big guy dipped his chin. "That's just a hobby."

"You're awfully good at it." Grace tapped her lips. "There's one thing we couldn't figure out. How did you make the ghosts appear in the putridarium?"

Henry nodded. "We found the screw holes and indentations where you hung the scrim and a chunk of foam board, but the angles were off."

"It was a challenge. It took me the better part of a week to find the right angles." Joe grinned. "The piece you found must have broken off the projector mount when I was still in the testing phase."

"Let them sit before you descend on them like hungry birds." Alessio motioned for the twins to join the table.

Grace sat between Alessio and Matteo, taking it upon himself to fill her plate with pizza.

Henry squeezed between Rudy, aka King Alfonso, and the actress who played Vittoria Colonna. "How is Rosa?"

The table exhaled a collective sigh.

Alessio shook his head. "We were forced to hand her over to the authorities."

Grace wasn't sure how she felt about the news. On the one hand, she hated the idea of someone going to prison. On the other, Rosa deserved it.

King Alfonso raised his glass. "To the Warners, without whom we never would have decided to open the Castello Aragonese Phantasmagoria!"

The others at the table toasted, but Henry and Grace exchanged confused glances.

Matteo said, "The ghosts were popular, but it was wrong of us to trick people. We've decided to use Joe's devices to, uh…"

"What he means is, the actors will do their regular monologues as ghosts." Vadoma squeezed Joe's hand. "Thanks to my husband's brilliant designs."

"Husband?" Henry chuckled. "Yep, I can see it now."

The front door opened, and the Bennet sisters walked in. Bethany wore her usual business suit, but Brianna wore jeans and a wrap that hid her hands. She looked years younger than she had in the hospital. Until that moment, Grace hadn't noticed the age difference between the women.

Alessio sucked in a breath and stumbled to his feet.

Bri gave him a wobbly smile and nodded toward the far side of the room.

Bethany plopped down in the chair he'd abandoned. "Well done, Henry and Grace. Well done."

Cheers and applause rose from the table.

Grace's cheeks heated. This was the last thing she'd expected when Alessio had called. They'd exposed the scheme, so she'd assumed the employees would blame her and Henry for sending the castle into bankruptcy, not treat them like heroes returning from battle.

Henry said, "Did you pick up the iPad from the hotel?"

"No, but we will when we leave here." Bethany lowered her voice. "I hope you don't think I'm an ogre. Bri's my kid sister. I may have overreacted to her injuries a smidge, but I did what I thought best."

Grace glanced at Henry, who was laughing it up with the actors. "I can't imagine how I would react if my little brother was hurt."

"Little? I thought you were twins."

"I'm two minutes older."

"And she never lets me forget it." Henry's eyes rounded and he pointed to something behind her.

Grace and Bethany turned and gasped.

Alessio had dropped to one knee, and Brianna was nodding. Both had tears streaming down their faces.

"Did you know?" Grace whispered.

"She told me this afternoon." Bethany watched her sister with a wistful smile. "Had I known sooner, he might not have—"

"Don't. You had no way of knowing what would happen to him. Besides, everything turned out okay."

The room quieted as everyone watched the couple.

King Alfonso said, "What is it to be, a celebration or a wake?"

Alessio shouted, "She said yes!"

Henry would never admit it out loud, but he enjoyed the spa. Specifically, he enjoyed soaking in a thermal mud bath. It reminded him of playing in the sprinklers and making dirt pies in his grandparents' backyard.

Grace snapped a few more pictures of the Warner clan covered in the gray volcanic soil.

Faith threw a towel at her daughter. "No more photos, and I don't want to see these on social media."

"Your mother's right. She has a professional image to uphold." Ethan scooped up a handful of mud and tossed it at Grace.

Faith arched a brow. "You have a reputation to uphold too, dear."

Ethan leaned in and kissed his wife. "Yes, but I'm not wearing a bikini."

"Thank goodness for small miracles," Henry muttered.

Faith sunk her hands into the goo and turned her face toward the sun. "How did the mystery turn out?"

"Really well. The theater company did such a great job scaring people; they decided to use the technology in their evening performances from now on. The extra revenue will help keep local businesses afloat during the off-season," Grace said.

Henry yawned and rubbed his stomach. "Anyone else hungry?"

"I could eat. We should grab something before we catch the ferry." Ethan pulled himself from the mud bath. "What did Matteo's friend do with the relics he found?"

Grace shot Henry a quick glance. "You should tell them."

"Tell us what?" Their mother's secret-detecting radar went on high alert.

"Alessio and Brianna are interns working in the castle. They think they found portions of the lost Roman city of Aenaria." Henry told them about how the discovery would challenge modern archaeological theories about the early Roman settlement and about the layers of history beneath the castle.

His parents listened intently, but Ethan seemed more troubled with each word.

Henry shrugged. "It's all fascinating."

Ethan turned to him. "You know, Stanford has an outstanding archeology program..."

"Henry has wanted to study law since he could talk." Faith glanced at the Warner men.

"She's right. I may take an archeology elective or two, but the law is in my blood." He gave his father a muddy bear hug.

"Now that we've settled that, are you two excited about visiting Pompeii and Herculaneum?" Ethan rubbed his hands together. "With so much death and destruction, I bet there are tons of mysteries to solve."

The twins said, "We're on vacation."

"Come on, what do you say about a family mystery? I'm eager to learn from the masters." Ethan glanced at them.

Grace pretended to look at her watch. "Look at the time. We'd better get cleaned up if we want to eat before we catch the ferry."

"They obviously don't want our help." Faith climbed out of the mud bath.

Not one to be deterred, Ethan continued, "Once we're back stateside, we're heading to Buckhannon, West Virginia. I've done some research on the Trans-Allegheny Asylum, and they say it's haunted—"

Henry groaned. "No more ghosts."

"I agree. I'm ghosted out." Grace laughed.

"How about the Mothman? Who doesn't love a winged humanoid creature with glowing red eyes?" Ethan wiggled his brows.

Thankfully, Faith stepped in and rested her hand on her husband's shoulder. "Darling, this is the twins' senior-year independent study project. It wouldn't be right for the two of us to get involved."

"Then you and I will find our own mystery."

Desperate to change the topic, Henry said, "I need to stop in one of the shops before we board the ferry."

"Our friend Morgan's birthday is next week. We want to bring her a piece of Italia." Grace picked up on his train of thought.

"She's a lovely girl. I'm sure you'll find something beautiful for her, Henry." Faith gave them a knowing look and walked toward the showers.

Grace and Henry leaned back, letting the warm mud embrace them as they cleared their minds, at least for the moment.

MOTHMAN

MONSTER CASE FILES BOOK 6

CHAPTER ONE

"Ollie!"

Gravel crunched under the front tire, and the car lurched. Snapping awake, Professor Oliver Orion guided the vehicle back onto the road. "Sorry, Darling."

"I don't know which is foggier, your brain or the road." His wife's voice came out in a nervous croak.

"We're almost home." He lowered the window. The blast of cool night air perked him up better than three cups of coffee. "I have too much to do to fall asleep at the wheel."

Professor Orion had a lot on his mind —robots, robots, and bagels. As the chairperson of the Eastern Conference of the Future Applications of Robotic Sciences & Technology competition, his duties included everything from appointing judges to signing off on breakfast menus.

"I bet we could create a machine to spread the cream cheese." Professor Orion yawned and gripped the steering wheel tighter.

"Cream cheese?" His wife was lost.

"For the bagels." He waved his hand. "Never mind."

"Ollie, I understand the FARST competition means the world to you, but you're only one man. There's nothing wrong with asking for help."

"I've delegated as much as I dare. This isn't about my ego. It's a chance to put our engineering program on the map."

No one was more surprised than him when West Virginia Wesleyan College won the bid to host the competition. After all, Buckhannon wasn't exactly Orlando or Vegas. The town in the foothills of the Allegheny Mountains had a population of less than six thousand and only a handful of hotels.

"I know, dear." She patted his thigh. "Have the judges arrived in town?"

"Everyone except Faith Warner." He yawned again, widened his eyes, and focused on the road. "She should be here tomorrow."

"It's Sunday, and she's your keynote speaker. That's cutting it a bit close. Isn't it?"

"Dr. Faith Warner is one of the most sought-after guest lecturers in mechanical engineering." He rolled his head from side to side. "We're lucky to have her."

The old woman smiled. "I'm proud of you for sticking with it after your star students were disqualified."

"What in the world?" Professor Orion leaned forward to get a better view of the strange red lights hovering above the road.

"I only meant to say—"

"Not that, dear." He pointed at the windshield. "What do you make of those?"

She squinted at the glowing orbs. "Is it a motorcycle?"

The words had no sooner left her mouth when the lights shot into the sky. *It was unnatural.*

Mrs. Orion gasped. "What was that?"

"I don't know, but I intend to find out." Heart racing, Oliver eased the vehicle onto the side of the road and opened his door.

"What are you doing? It's not safe to park here." She tugged his sleeve. "Get back in the car."

"You saw that, right? It traveled vertically!" He searched the sky, but the strange lights had vanished.

"Ollie, please. Let's go home."

A whoosh of air and a gentle flapping came from above his head. He instinctively ducked and twisted to see what it was. It hadn't sounded like feathers, more like sheets blowing on a clothesline.

A winged creature landed gracefully on the road a few feet in front of the headlights.

Mrs. Orion screamed.

Oliver stood rooted in place, battling between an urge to flee and a need to find a scientific explanation for what he was seeing.

The creature stood six, maybe seven-feet tall and had a wingspan twice as wide. It was humanoid, probably male. With the exception of its insect-like glowing red eyes, it was an indistinguishable shade between brown and gray.

"What are you?" Professor Orion took a tentative step forward.

The creature pointed at the man and shrieked in a voice reminiscent of a needle scratching across a vinyl record.

He pressed his hands against his ears and stumbled backward.

The monster drew a line across its throat—the universal symbol for death—and screeched again.

"Get in the car, Ollie. Get in the car right now!" His wife's voice tinged with fear.

Professor Orion no longer cared about the monster's origin. He dove into the driver's seat, slammed the door, and hit the locks. Fumbling with the keys, he started the car.

The creature folded its arms as if challenging the human to try something foolish.

Oliver acceded to its wishes. He slammed the car into drive and hit the gas.

———

Grace Warner loved mountains and small towns and robots, so what more could she ask for than a robotics competition in Buckhannon, West Virginia?

The girl hummed an old John Denver tune about mountains and mamas while she worked to set up the fifth wheel her family called home.

Henry, Grace's twin brother, seemed less impressed with their surroundings. "Call me crazy, but two weeks in Italy wasn't enough to see the country."

"Of course, it wasn't. That's like saying you can do everything in California in half a month." She motioned to the flashlight in his hand. "Could you point that this way?"

He shined it in her eyes before lowering the beam onto the hose. "Cali may be close to the same size, but it doesn't have a tenth the history. I could have spent an entire month in Rome alone."

"Me too, but I'm glad to be home." Grace stood and patted the side of the fifth wheel. "There's nothing like sleeping in your own bed."

Henry made a sound in the back of his throat. "I already miss the food."

She resisted the urge to demand he stop complaining and help her set up the RV. It wouldn't do any good. He hadn't stopped whining since they'd boarded the plane in Venice. "We could save up and go back next summer before we start college."

"Or we could take a gap year and backpack across Europe." He wiggled his eyebrows.

"What's this about a gap year?" Faith Warner, the twins' mother, set her hands on her hips. Judging by her expression, she hated the idea.

Henry held up his hands. "Just a thought."

"Mmmhmm." She tapped her foot. "Is this *thought* the reason you missed the early application deadline to Stanford?"

Grace had wondered the same thing. In fact, she suspected her brother might have delayed sending in his application to buy himself a couple of extra months to research other universities. Of course, he'd denied it when she'd asked. Henry had always planned to follow in their father's footsteps and go to law school, but his love for history had become an obsession while they were in Italy.

"Not at all." He laughed higher and louder than usual. "I wanted more time to work on the urban legends research project so I could include it in my packet."

Faith frowned, but thankfully, let the subject drop. "Speaking of the project, have you two found a new urban legend to explore?"

Traveling from town to town while their parents worked the college lecture circuit had many unexpected benefits. So far, the best part of their senior year was a year-long research project on urban legends and local lore, aka solving mysteries.

"We have a few ideas." Grace kept her voice low. Ethan Warner, her father, hadn't stopped dropping hints that he wanted to give it a go since he'd inadvertently stumbled into the middle of their last mystery.

"The Trans-Allegheny Lunatic Asylum." Ethan's voice came around the corner before he did. "Otherwise known as the Weston State Hospital. It's said to be haunted by former patients, civil war soldiers, and a little girl named Lily."

The twins exchanged quick glances.

Ethan clamped his hand on Henry's shoulder. "They have private ghost tours in the evenings. Do you think we can handle eight hours alone in the building?"

"We?" the twins asked.

"Well, yes. You need an adult chaperone to attend private tours. Insurance purposes and all." His smile broadened. "I thought we could go tomorrow night after your mother's keynote address."

Grace had researched the facility during the long flight home. At 242,000 square feet, the imposing Gothic structure was said to be one of the most haunted places in the state. Between the barbaric mental health treatments and severe overcrowding, the hospital had seen more than its fair share of death.

"After the Aragonese Castle, I'm not sure I'm up for another haunted building." Grace avoided meeting either of her parents' gazes.

Ethan tilted his head. "I understand, but it's no different than charging admission to see a concentration camp. It's a part of paying to maintain history."

"I guess." She nodded at the fifth wheel. "Water and electricity are hooked up. I'll open the slides when you're ready."

"Go ahead. The stabilizers are down, and the rig's level." Mom winked and turned to her husband. "Let the kids choose their mystery. This is their project, and we shouldn't get involved."

"I agree, but they need an adult to accompany them to the asylum. And then there's the matter of purchasing liability insurance." He followed their mother around the back of the rig.

"They don't need to be involved with anything that requires liability insurance." Faith's voice rose.

Henry hitched a thumb in their parents' direction. "He's not going to let this go. He's caught the mystery-solving bug."

"I know, and I don't like it. We have yet to solve a mystery without engaging in questionable behavior. I for one don't want to spend the next year grounded." She climbed into the RV and pressed the kitchen's slider button. The familiar grating mechanical sound made her smile despite her concerns. If only life were so simple—press a button and presto change-o, everything fell into place.

Once the slider stopped moving, Henry said, "I think the three of us should go on the private ghost-hunting tour. Once he sits in an abandoned building overnight, he'll change his mind."

"Maybe, but what if he sees a ghost or something bizarre happens?" She activated the living room slider and watched as the couch and dinette moved into place.

"What are the chances?" Henry yawned and stretched his arms over his head. "Slide out our bedroom. I'm ready to crash."

Grace opened her mouth to argue, but her parents stepped inside.

Holding a cell phone to her ear, Faith frowned. Ethan, on the other hand, grinned like an eight-year-old who'd received a pony for Christmas.

"I see." Faith pointed at the twins and then the phone. "Yes, I can imagine it would be alarming for one to believe they'd encountered a monster on a country road late at night."

"It can't be this easy," Henry whispered.

Grace folded her arms. "Or this hard."

"There's no need. I would be happy to make the opening remarks in addition to my keynote address." Still frowning, Faith said, "Thank you for calling. I'll see you in the morning."

The second she disconnected the call, Ethan Warner, Esquire, lifted his hands to shoulder height and spread them wide as if reading a movie marquee. "Monster causes car accident. We have a mystery."

His wife and children stared with varying degrees of concern.

"I would tell you your enthusiasm is inappropriate, but I don't think it would make a difference." Faith sank into a chair and glanced at the twins. "The chairman of the robotics competition was involved in an accident last night."

While Grace hated the idea of someone getting hurt, she couldn't get past the word *monster*. "Dare I ask what happened?"

"I'll explain what I know, but first I need my laptop." Faith sighed. "And someone put on a pot of coffee. It's going to be a long night."

Henry headed for the door, presumably to retrieve his computer bag. Ethan went into the kitchen and pulled the coffee maker from the cabinet, and Grace sat beside her mom. Ten minutes later, the Warners regrouped around the table, each with a steaming mug and a copy of Faith's speech.

"We're all here." Ethan nudged Faith's shoulder. "Making us wait to hear the details is a form of cruel and unusual punishment."

"As I said, Dr. Orion and his wife were in an accident on the way home from Wesleyan College last night. Both claim to have seen some sort of creature on the road. Evidently, the professor attempted to hit it with his car." She sipped her coffee.

The twins exchanged glances.

Henry cocked his head. "Any idea why he'd do that?"

"Not a clue, but the animal escaped unharmed, while the Orions sustained minor physical injuries. They're at home, but he's unable to attend the opening ceremonies."

Grace suspected the couples' physical injuries paled in comparison to their mental distress. "Dr. Orion is the chairperson. Whatever happened must have rattled him pretty badly for him to miss the festivities."

Faith nodded. "Precisely."

"I'm glad to hear they weren't hurt." Ethan tried for a solemn expression, but the twinkle in his eyes ruined it. "Did you get a physical description of the creature?"

"Dad!" The twins scowled.

Faith pressed her lips into a tight line. "Dr. Orion's assistant didn't go into detail except to say the *thing* flew."

Henry pulled out his phone and typed. "The Mothman legend originated about three hours from here in Point Pleasant. It could be the same monster."

Much to Grace's chagrin, she found herself intrigued. "Or more likely, someone imitating the Mothman."

Ethan cleared his throat. "I'll completely understand if the two of you would rather solve the mystery without a third wheel…"

Between the hopeful hitch in his voice and his please-say-yes expression, Grace couldn't help but laugh. She met Henry's gaze and lifted a brow.

Her brother chuckled. "You're not a third wheel, but there are rules. Think of Grace and me as partners at a law firm and yourself as our intern."

He smirked. "You mean I'll do all the work while you two take all the credit?"

Faith choked on her coffee. "What they're trying to say is, you can accompany them, but they call the shots."

"Exactly." Grace motioned to the papers on the table. "And the first shot I'm going to call is no more talk about this tonight. Mom needs our help."

"I second that." Henry picked up a copy of the speech. "What do you need us to do?"

Faith squeezed his shoulder. "I need to split this into a welcome speech and a keynote address without being redundant. I go onstage in less than eight hours."

"Which means we'll start monster hunting in seven." Ethan rubbed his hands together.

Faith narrowed her eyes.

"Make that ten. We wouldn't dream of missing your keynote address." He lowered his head and dug in.

Grace met Henry's gaze and shook her head a fraction of an inch. The entire situation reminded her of a movie where the parents and kids swapped bodies. *How in the world are we going to solve a mystery while keeping Dad out of trouble with Mom?*

CHAPTER TWO

As a general rule, Henry hated mornings. However, hate didn't come close to explaining his feelings for waking up after only three hours of sleep. "There isn't enough coffee in the world."

"I definitely see a nap in my future." Grace pulled her hair into a ponytail.

Ethan emerged into the hall with a blazer slung over his arm. Nothing out of the ordinary there, but his jeans and boots were another story. "Good morning."

Henry scratched his jaw. "Have you seen Mom since you got dressed?"

"She took a rideshare to the college an hour ago." He glanced down at himself and frowned. "It's a little casual, but I'm not presenting."

"And you thought it best to skip the tie while assisting us?" Grace wore the same expression she'd had the night before—amusement mixed with fear.

Ethan held up his hands. "Let the record reflect that I heard your concerns and will change clothes *ex abundenti cautela*."

"Out of an abundance of caution is right." Henry would have chuckled if he were more awake.

Grace rested her hand on their father's back. "Henry and I have learned the hard way to keep a bag with a change of clothes, flashlights, and other essentials handy."

"Always be prepared. I should know these things. I was an Eagle Scout back when dinosaurs roamed the Earth." He disappeared down the hall.

She walked to Henry's side and lowered her voice. "I can't help but feel like I've woken up in the Twilight Zone."

"Relax, it'll be fun. Besides, Dad is one of the most brilliant people we know." He poured himself a travel mug of coffee and grabbed his jacket.

"Of course he is, but we're smart too. Think of all the trouble we've gotten ourselves into," she whispered. "People pointing guns at us, attempting to kidnap us, falling into mineshafts, locking us in creepy places..."

"Let's not forget reporting us to the police and smoke-bombing the house we were staying at." He slung his arm over her shoulder.

"We have done some questionable things that turned out well. What if Dad stops us mid-stride? We can't expect Dad to keep secrets from Mom."

She had a point, but Henry chose to look at the glass as half-full instead of broken. "Think of it this way: Dad may find alternative ways to do things that we don't know about."

Ethan Warner returned to the room wearing a dark suit and a smile. "Better?"

"Much," the twins said.

West Virginia Wesleyan College was one of the most beautiful campuses Henry had visited. With its sprawling green lawns and red-brick buildings, it gave off a serene aura, or at least it did until they walked into the bustling exhibition hall.

Every square inch was filled with booths, people, and gadgets. Machines rattled, hummed, or beeped. Adding to the chaos, the occasional cheer or chorus of groans rose over the mechanical din. It made Comic-Con look like a garden club meeting.

"Where do we go?" Grace glanced around the enormous hall.

"Better question, why aren't any of the teams seated for the opening ceremony?"

"They're taking advantage of every available second to work on their robots." Dad pulled out his phone. "Mom's text said to meet her by the stage."

As if on cue, the overhead lights flashed on and off three times. The flow of people started slow and ended in a raging river of bodies.

"Stay close." Ethan wrapped his arm around Grace's shoulder to protect her from the rush. Thankfully, the crowd thinned near the stage.

Faith waved from the front row. "I was beginning to think you weren't going to make it."

"And miss seeing you in action? Never." Ethan kissed her cheek. "Break a leg."

A woman in a bright red suit moved behind the podium and adjusted the microphone. "Ladies and gentleman, it's my honor to introduce Dr. Faith Warner. In addition to championing initiatives to encourage girls to study science, technology, engineering, and math, her early work in additive manufacturing led to the creation of 3D printers and numerous other technological advances..."

Henry found himself sitting up straighter as the introduction continued. Of course, he'd heard his mother's bio many times before, but it always amazed him that so many people admired her.

Grace grabbed his hand when their mother walked onto the stage to a round of applause. "I always get a little misty-eyed at these things," she whispered toward Henry's ear.

Faith took a moment to look over the crowd before she adjusted her glasses and launched into the speech they'd cobbled together the night before. As with the introduction, Henry knew every word, but knowing what she would say hadn't prepared him for hearing her say it out loud. His mother loved what she did, and it showed in her delivery.

The crowd laughed. They listened. They gasped. And did it over and over, as if sharing one brain.

Dr. Faith Warner knew machines, but she also knew people. By the time she'd finished, Henry wanted to join a robotics team. He loved the law and he loved history, but neither field offered the chance to make something new from nothing but spare parts and sweat.

The red-suited woman retook the stage and shushed the crowd. "Now for some housekeeping. You've all been given a schedule. Teams that are tardy for an event will be disqualified..."

Seating herself in the chair beside Henry, Faith whispered, "How did I do?"

"Amazing." He hugged her tight.

After the robotics teams were released to continue their work, a middle-aged man with a bandage on his forehead approached the family. He wore the expression of someone who'd survived a battle but disagreed with the war.

Henry didn't need an introduction to know he was Dr. Orion.

"Dr. Warner, might I have a moment of your time?"

Mom turned, recognizing the man who had contracted with her for the event. "Of course."

He glanced at the floor and sighed as if rethinking his request.

"I'm Ethan Warner, Faith's husband." Ethan shook the man's hand.

"Oliver Orion." He spoke his name as if it were a question.

"Perhaps we should sit. I understand you were involved in an accident." Faith motioned to the empty chairs.

"I can't stay. I'm needed at home. I just came to thank you for this morning." Dr. Orion's voice wobbled. "This competition...it's important to the college and to me."

"It was my pleasure."

Ethan lowered his voice. "Forgive me if this is out of line, but would you mind telling us what you saw last night?"

Grace went wide-eyed, and Henry cringed. They'd learned a thing or two about interviewing people. Sometimes the direct method worked, but more often than not, a subtler approach was best.

Dr. Orion took a step back. "What...do you mean?"

Faith placed her hand on her husband's arm. "When your assistant called last night, he mentioned that you and your wife had seen some sort of creature. My twins are working on a research project concerning unexplained phenomena and urban legends. They've solved several cases, and even found a missing child."

The professor glanced at the twins. "I see."

Henry resisted the urge to groan. This was why he preferred to work with Grace and only Grace. "This isn't the time or place for this sort of conversation, but we'd like to talk to you about what happened last night when you're up for it."

Grace nodded. "We maintain strict confidentiality."

The man snorted. "My dear, while I appreciate the thought. I'm afraid that ship has sunk. If my assistant told your mother what happened, I'm quite certain he's told others."

"We might be able to help. We've been able to get to the bottom of a handful of unexplained events. One need only find the right curtain to look behind," Henry assured him.

Dr. Orion drew a deep breath. "Are you familiar with the Mothman?"

Henry glanced at his father before turning back to the professor. "I did a little research on the creature before we arrived."

Orion nodded. "The monster my wife and I encountered fits the description to a T. Humanoid. Large red eyes. Six and a half to seven feet tall, with a wingspan twice that."

Ethan leaned in. "Wingspan? Did it fly?"

"Yes, but not like a bird or even an insect. He shot straight into the sky without using his wings." The man's gaze became unfocused.

Grace tapped her lips. "Your assistant said you attempted to hit it with your car?"

The professor snapped his attention back to the twins and drew a breath as if to speak but dipped his chin and exhaled. Several heartbeats later, he said, "Only after it threatened me."

"It tried to attack you?" Faith glanced between Orion and the twins.

"No, he pulled his finger across his throat." The professor demonstrated the gesture, complete with sound effects. "Now that I think about it, maybe he was trying to warn me about something."

A handful of students loitered nearby, whispering. Although Henry couldn't make out their words, their smirks and laughter were hard to miss. "Dr. Orion, would it be all right with you if we continued this conversation somewhere private?"

Picking up on the situation, Grace added, "I'd like to speak with Mrs. Orion too if she's up for it."

The woman in the red suit marched over with a young man on her heels. She took one look at the shell-shocked professor and frowned. "Oliver, I didn't expect to see you here so soon after..."

Judging by her sour expression, Henry suspected she was more concerned about his sanity than his physical injuries. Stiffening his spine, he said, "I apologize, but I didn't catch your name earlier."

She gave him a once-over, curled her upper lip, and turned back to the professor. "Rumors are circulating around campus—"

Faith Warner's jaw tensed. "Allow me to introduce my twins, Henry and Grace."

"I-I didn't realize." The woman's cheeks turned the same color as her suit, and she shook their hands. "I'm Dr. Hester Hargrave. It's a pleasure to meet you both."

Henry folded his arms to keep from wiping his palms on his pants. The woman was his least favorite type of human being—phony.

The young man who'd shadowed the obnoxious professor leaned closer to Dr. Orion. "I've fielded several phone calls this morning. There's a concern that alcohol was involved in the accident."

Who are these people? Can't they see the man is suffering? Henry glanced at his father and widened his eyes. Surely, his dad would do something to stop the conversation.

Ethan Warner cleared his throat. "I'm sure all of this can wait until Dr. and Mrs. Orion have had a chance to recover from their injuries—"

"Actually, it can't. We have the national spotlight on us right now. We simply cannot afford a scandal." Hargrave narrowed her eyes as if daring him to argue.

"She's right. I should go." Shoving his hands in his pockets, Dr. Orion headed for the door.

"I would strongly suggest you hire an attorney," Hargrave called after him.

Orion flinched and turned back. "You can't be serious."

"Maybe, maybe not, but the staff and faculty sign morality contracts. I believe driving while intoxicated constitutes a breach." The woman smiled like a cat with a lizard under its paw.

Grace glanced over her shoulder and frowned.

The students who'd gathered nearby gawked. Soon enough, word of the conversation would spread. Someone needed to do damage control, and fast. Henry might be young, but Dr. Hargrave had already declared Dr. Orion guilty as a broadside in the court of public opinion. The older man seemed ill-equipped to respond. In that vein, he had already lost.

Grace and Henry shared a horrified look.

Ethan smiled at Dr. Orion gesturing with his hands for calm. "I'll be happy to take a look at your contract and advise you as necessary. I'm sure there's nothing to worry about." The smooth constitutional lawyer turned to the onlookers and assumed center stage. "Perpetrating and perpetuating slanderous claims makes everyone equally liable. It can get real expensive real fast."

The professor squared his shoulders. "Thank you. We can discuss it, and the *other* matter, this afternoon."

Grace moved to Dr. Orion's side and took out her cell.

The young man who'd accompanied Hargrave scoffed. "And you are?"

An image of his father saying, "Your worst nightmare," in a Clint Eastwood voice flashed through Henry's mind.

"Ethan Warner." He offered his hand, throwing down the gauntlet as lawyers did.

Go, Dad! Henry did a mental fist pump.

Hargrave gave her minion a less-than-patient look before turning to Faith. "I apologize for the—" She waved her hand. "Drama. I assure you, I have only the best intentions for the engineering program."

Mom arched a single brow and gave the woman her cut-the-bull expression.

Dr. Hargrave patted her hair and offered a strained smile. "Yes, well, I have much to do. I'll see you this afternoon for the keynote address."

Oliver Orion watched the horrible woman and her minion go. "I should have known better than to trust either of them."

Grace asked, "Who are they?"

"David is my assistant, and Hester is a colleague. She and I are both being considered for dean."

A slow smile spread across Ethan's face. "Competing for the same position is a strong motive."

The professor's eyes widened. "Motive? You think she had something to do with the monster?" He took several steps back. "I know what I saw. I'm telling you, it was real."

Grace stepped beside her father. "We have no doubt it was real." She could feel it in her bones that it was indeed real, but just as confidently, she knew there was a human behind it.

Henry watched in silence, studying the body language of the players as he added names to a growing list of suspects.

CHAPTER THREE

Interstate 79 was the quickest way to Point Pleasant. Trees, foothills, and some dead spots with low-speed data reception made for a challenging two-and-a-half-hour trip. Under normal circumstances, the twins would have spent the time discussing the case, but these were far from normal circumstances.

Ethan Warner gripped the steering wheel tighter. "Let the record reflect that I'm aware I shouldn't have discussed motive with Professor Orion."

Grace thought back to the mysteries she and Henry had solved. They hadn't known what they were doing when they first started out. Most of the time, they still didn't. "It's okay, Dad. Henry and I made plenty of mistakes in the beginning. We didn't have a clue."

"You must have had a few clues, or you wouldn't have solved the cases."

"No dad jokes." Henry snorted. "We might as well ban him from speaking lawyer-ese while you're at it."

"I'll attempt to withhold my awesome humor while working." Ethan relaxed his shoulders. "How do you suggest we approach Dr. Orion?"

"I'm not sure. He seemed pretty adamant that he didn't want to speak to us when I called him earlier." Grace chose not to directly quote the professor for fear of hurting her father's feelings.

"He'll loosen up once we prove the monster he saw was real, but that it wasn't a real monster," Henry said.

Confident in their ability to get to the bottom of the mystery, Grace nodded. "He's right. People are usually embarrassed that they fell for a scam—"

"—and then they get angry." Henry finished.

Ethan glanced at his son in the rearview mirror. "That sounds like it came from personal experience. Have you two had physical altercations because of your project?"

Grace cringed before she could stop herself.

"Once or twice, but nothing we couldn't handle." Henry leaned forward as far as his seatbelt would allow. "The trick is to follow their lead. You can usually tell when a person is ready to hear the truth."

"I know what you mean." Ethan turned off the highway onto a country road. "My experience with criminal law is limited. The innocent ones went through the same series of emotions— denial, anger, bargaining, depression, and acceptance."

"Those are the five stages of grief." Grace relaxed as the realization hit her. "Why didn't I see it before? They aren't mourning the death of a person. They're grieving the change in their perception of reality."

"Bingo." Ethan winked. "What's the plan when we reach Point Pleasant?"

"We visit the Mothman Museum and learn everything we can about the original creature." Henry fiddled with his phone. "I'll give you the address once I have cell reception."

"I thought we were proceeding under the assumption that the monster was a fake?"

Grace said, "Chances are, the people who are behind this conducted the same research. Knowing what they know might help us predict their next move."

Ethan chewed on the idea for a moment. "How can we be sure Dr. Orion was targeted and not just in the wrong place at the wrong time?"

"We can't, but we have to start somewhere." Henry let out a whoop. "I have the address."

Like almost every other American small town, Main Street Point Pleasant consisted of parallel rows of square brick buildings separated by a road. It hardly resembled the type of place one would expect to find a monster—with one exception. The citizens had replaced the usual monument to a fallen war hero on a rearing horse with a metal sculpture of the Mothman.

"Would you look at that...*monstrosity*?" Ethan wiggled his brows. The twins didn't bite. They had their game faces on.

Grace hopped out of the truck and made a beeline for the statue.

Catching up to her, Henry grinned up at the Mothman's face. "I'm...speechless."

The sculpture had large almond-shaped eyes that reminded Grace of

1950s aliens, only the little green men didn't have a beaked nose or twin fangs or six-pack abs.

"Why do you suppose the artist put hair on his chest?" Henry chuckled and walked to the back of the statue. "Ugh, and didn't include pants?"

Grace giggled as she snapped several pictures. "Let's hope the sculptor took liberal creative license when he made it. I'd hate to think of Professor Orion running into the real-life version of this."

"The museum is on the corner." Ethan nodded toward a tan brick building.

Henry pressed his hand to his stomach. "I say we grab some food first. I'm starved."

She'd expected him to complain of hunger on the trip over, but there hadn't been many fast food places along the stretch of highway. "No way. The museum closes at five. We don't have time to eat first."

Ethan held out his hands. "Relax. I have a plan. There's a pizza place nearby that has hundreds of good reviews. We'll go there after the museum. In the meantime, the coffee shop next door has Mothman cookies and Mothman poop candy."

Grace's mouth fell open.

"Coffee, cookies, and poop candy sounds great." Henry started in the opposite direction of the museum.

She shook her head. "Meet me inside after you've had your snacks."

Ethan glanced at the twins as if trying to decide which child to follow. In the end, he went to the coffee shop. Grace wasn't surprised.

Like the statue, the museum turned out to be a little bit of weird in the middle of the quaint town. Grace bypassed the gift shop and headed straight for the exhibits. She perused the collection of props from the Richard Gere movie *The Mothman Prophecies* and moved on to a display of press clippings from 1966 and 1967.

She couldn't help but imagine the voice of an old-fashioned radio announcer when she read the headlines: *Giant Fuzzy Bird Chases Auto in Storm, Night Rider in the Sky Afraid of Lights, Four More Say They Saw Red-Eyed 'Whatever.'*

For the most part, the articles said the same thing. Dozens of people had come forward claiming to have seen the creature in or around the area. The eye-witness descriptions included red eyes, gray or brown body, and wings. Some of the articles mentioned the creature's strange flight pattern. However, there was something that permeated beyond in the words and yellowing paper.

Fear.

The headlines sounded like those found in modern tabloids, but the articles had come from local newspapers. The reporters had painted a vivid image of what it was like for the people living in Point Pleasant. The creature had terrorized the town and the surrounding area for almost a year.

What the heck was the Mothman? The technology of the time didn't support the sort of flight described in the articles. *Could it have been a lie that spread because of mass hysteria and rumors? Or was it something more?*

A woman wearing a shirt with the museum logo smiled. "Let me know if you have any questions."

"What do you think the creature was?"

"Alien, demon, mutant from the munitions stores... or a bunch of kids who saw a bird and caused a panic." She shrugged. "No one knows for sure."

"It's one thing to read blogs or watch documentaries, but it's different seeing it in print like this."

"A lot of folks have that reaction." The woman's expression hardened. "I didn't live here then, but I've spoken to people who did. It was a dark time."

"I can't begin to imagine." Grace motioned to the display. "Do you allow pictures?"

"We're not supposed to, but pretty much everything you see has been photographed and put online."

"That's okay. I'd hate to get you into trouble." Grace pulled a notebook from her bag.

The woman waved her hand. "Go ahead and take your pictures. I've worked here too long for them to fire me now."

"Thanks." She zoomed in on each article and snapped a photo. "Are any of the eye-witnesses still in town?"

"A couple, but they rarely do interviews. Those who do will charge you for it."

Grace nodded and moved on to the handwritten police reports. She'd read them online but seeing them scrawled in the witnesses' own handwriting made them seem more authentic.

"You seem awfully interested. Are you a paranormal investigator?"

"Not exactly. I'm doing a research project on urban legends." She eyed the woman's name tag. "I'm Grace."

Betty had the sort of smile normally reserved for grandmothers, and it set Grace at ease.

"Do you get a lot of visitors?"

"More in the summer months, but three or four stop in most days during the off-season."

Grace debated about telling Betty about the latest Mothman sighting, but she'd learned to play it safe when it came to sharing facts. As it turned out, most villains didn't look like villains at all. Some even looked like grandmothers. "Have you had anyone in recently who seemed overly interested in the memorabilia? Maybe college age?"

Betty pursed her lips. "How recently?"

Good question. If Dr. Orion had been targeted, the perpetrators were most likely students. "Between last spring and now."

"We did have a couple of college boys pretty much set up shop here for a week last April. They claimed they were making a documentary. Promised to send me a copy, but I never heard from them again."

Grace's stomach did a somersault. "Did you happen to get their names or the university they attended?"

"They wrote a nice review on TripAdvisor and signed the guest book. I'll see if I can find it." She walked into another room.

Ethan's booming laughter, followed by Henry's, announced their arrival. Her brother may have inherited their mother's Native American coloring, but he'd gotten his voice from their father.

She met them near a replica of the Mothman, this one draped in black fabric.

Henry looked at it while asking, "Did you find anything interesting?"

"Possibly. Look around. I'm waiting for the proprietor. She's looking something up for me." She met Ethan's gaze. "Don't spook her."

He held his hands out as if to show they were empty. "How could I possibly spook someone who works alongside such horrors?"

"Go." She smirked and pushed him toward the main exhibits.

Betty returned a few minutes later with a Post-It note. "I was wrong. Only one of the boys signed, and he only used his first name."

"It's a start." Grace took the paper. "Quinn's an unusual name. Maybe I can track him down."

"Oh, I didn't realize that's what you intended. I guess I should have asked." The woman tilted her head. "You don't look like the stalker type, but if you are, don't tell the police where you got the name."

"It's for research purposes. Comparing notes. Um, my dad and brother are here now. I should..." She motioned toward the other room.

"Of course." Betty laughed. "Let me know if there's anything else you need."

The Warners spent another half-hour in the museum before Grace's stomach demanded attention. They drove to Village Pizza at the other end of Point Pleasant and piled out of the truck. Despite the fact father and son had snacked less than an hour earlier, they insisted on ordering an extra-large pizza.

"We'll have the Mothman." Ethan grinned and rocked back on his heels.

Grace groaned. "Do you even know what's on it?"

"Red-cherry pepper and green-olive eyes, pepperoni body, mushroom wings, and green-pepper feet," the guy behind the counter deadpanned. "Would you like some pepperoni rolls with that?"

"Sure, and three sodas." Ethan pulled out his wallet.

Henry motioned to a table near the window. "The best part about Dad helping to solve mysteries is that he pays for the food."

"I heard that. But, he and Mom pay for everything anyway. We haven't exactly been earning our own keep."

Laughing, Grace sank into a chair. "I have the first name of a college-age guy who spent a lot of time in the museum last April. Betty remembered him and his friend because they claimed to be making a documentary."

Ethan joined them with their drinks. "Is it too soon to be identifying suspects?"

"They're more persons of interest than suspects." Henry leaned forward and set his elbows on the table. "We have no idea who's behind this, so we follow what we have. It may be a dead end—"

"—or it could lead us to a suspect or point us in a new direction," Grace finished.

"After seventeen years, you'd think I'd get used to the two of you finishing each other's sentences."

Grace pulled out her notebook. "What do we know?"

"Hargrave and Orion's assistant want to take him down." Henry scratched his jaw. "And some guy named Quinn has, or had, an unhealthy obsession with the Mothman."

Grace blew the paper wrapper from her straw at him. "'Unhealthy' is too subjective a term. If he was making a documentary, he'd want as much information as possible."

Ethan frowned. "A documentary or a robot?"

The twins exchanged glances.

"That's a good point," Grace said.

"We're getting ahead of ourselves." Henry drummed his fingers on the table. "We aren't sure this is directly related to Dr. Orion or the college."

The server set the pizza in the middle of the table. The guy behind the counter's description didn't do the pie justice. The toppings were, in fact, arranged to resemble the monster right down to his skinny little green-pepper legs.

Grace snapped a picture.

"Your pepperoni rolls will be right out." The server smiled. "Are you in town to visit the museum?"

"We just came from there." Henry peeled a mushroom from the pizza and popped it into his mouth.

The girl leaned in close, as if sharing trade secrets. "This was where the first people to see the monster, the Scarberrys and the Mallettes, stopped after they saw the Mothman."

"Wait, *this* is Tiny's Drive-In?" Goosebumps broke out on her arms.

"It used to be."

Grace shook her head. "I assumed it was a drive-in movie theater, but a diner makes much more sense."

The girl winked. "Let me know if you need refills."

Ethan waited until she left and lowered his voice. "The urban legend is big business for this little town."

"A boost to tourism is the most obvious motive." Henry helped himself to two slices of pizza, folded them over into a makeshift sandwich, and dug in.

"If that's the case, then why have the creature make an appearance two and a half hours away?" She took a slice. "Unless it was a trial run..."

"Have either of you checked the internet today for other sightings?" Ethan glanced at them.

"I'm on it." Henry typed with one hand and held his pizza with the other.

CHAPTER FOUR

"Have you all lost your minds?" Faith Warner stood in the center of the living room simultaneously giving three people in different areas a Mom look. "What do you intend to do, drive up and down the road until the boogeyman flies overhead?"

"When you put it like that..." Henry knew better than to laugh, but he couldn't hide the grin tugging the corners of his mouth. After spending the entire day doing schoolwork and scouring the internet for any recent sightings, he needed to get out of the fifth wheel. What better way to spend an evening than a

monster stake-out?

"There won't be any driving back and forth. We're accompanying Dr. Orion to the scene of the crime." Ethan avoided her gaze by tying his boots.

"There haven't been any other reported sightings. This is a chance to find more clues, especially if Dr. Orion was only a trial run." Grace put half a dozen peanut butter and jelly sandwiches into a bag and reached for the chips. "Besides, it's the only way the professor would agree to meet with us."

Mom stared at the ceiling as if she'd find the answers to the universe, or a little patience. "Has it occurred to any of you that Dr. Orion might not be the victim in this scenario? What if Hargrave was justified in her accusations? We don't know Oliver Orion's history."

That hadn't occurred to Henry until she tossed out the possibility. He rolled the thought around in his mind and came up with more questions than answers.

"Personally, I believe in the presumption of innocence, but the only way to prove guilt is to gather facts. We can't do that by researching monster sightings from fifty years ago. We have to spend time with the parties involved. Also, the admission of seeing a creature can only damage a reputation. I believe Oliver's too smart to think it would improve any facet of his life." Ethan stood and pulled on his jacket.

"Well said, Dad. You're getting the hang of this." Henry chuckled.

Setting the bag near the door, Grace said, "You saw how freaked out he was today in the exhibition hall. Hargrave and what's-his-name were horrible. They were playing to the crowd to ruin a man's reputation."

"I agree with Grace. Hargrave and David definitely had an agenda, and Dr. Orion did seem shaken up. Speculating if his mental state was caused by seeing a monster or fear of losing his job won't get us anywhere, though. We need facts."

"I'll search police records tomorrow. Chances are, if he has a history of drinking while driving, I'll find something." Grace hugged herself as if the idea caused her pain.

"Don't look so glum." Ethan tugged on her ponytail. "We'll discover the truth, and hopefully, help the world embrace his innocence."

Faith slid onto a barstool. "I like Dr. Orion too. I was merely presenting an alternate theory."

"It's an aspect of the investigation that needs to be confirmed or discounted. It's easier to fight lies with truth." Grace squared her shoulders. "Are we ready to hunt the Mothman?"

For a man who'd spent the majority of his adult life in a courtroom or lecture hall, Ethan Warner failed to hide his excitement. He hooted, did a little jig, and bounded for the door. "Let's get this show on the road."

"Be safe tonight." Faith chuckled.

Ethan turned back and kissed her cheek. "Always."

Henry slung his bag over his shoulder, hugged his mom, and headed for the truck.

Ten minutes later, the Warners parked in front of a farmhouse on the outskirts of town. Cows grazed in an adjacent pasture, chickens roamed the yard, and a yellow Labrador retriever sat on the front porch. In short, the white-washed two-story looked like it belonged on a postcard from the 1800s.

The hairs on the back of Henry's neck stood at attention, and he had the feeling someone was watching them. "Are you sure this is the right address?"

Grace checked her phone. "Positive. What's wrong?"

Ethan waved to a woman standing in a second-floor window. "I don't think Mrs. Orion is happy to see us."

The woman frowned as she looked down at the trio, shook her head, and let the curtains fall back into place.

Professor Orion stepped onto the porch with a bag in one hand and a shotgun in the other.

"Whoa." Ethan held up his hands. "We won't need firearms tonight."

"You didn't see that...*thing*." Orion's expression hardened. "I'm not going out there unarmed."

"That's fine." Ethan's tone said it was anything but fine. "But I feel just as strongly about my kids potentially getting caught in the crossfire."

Grace glanced at Henry, surprise on her face.

He nodded a fraction of an inch and pressed his lips together. He understood his father's concern.

Ethan turned to the twins. "If the gun comes out, I expect you two to hit the ground. No arguments."

"Yes, sir," the twins said in unison. They tried to look innocent but the only thing they could think about was the times guns had been pointed at them. They secretly and silently vowed to never let their parents on another investigation.

With Dr. Orion secured in the front seat, they headed west. The farther out of Buckhannon they traveled, the fewer lights they passed and the darker the road became. Henry gazed up at the night sky and sucked in a breath. The number of visible stars quadrupled.

"Take a left and follow the signs toward Stonecoal Lake Wildlife Management Area." Professor Orion also scanned the sky, but likely for a very different reason. "My wife and I were on our way home from dinner with friends. It was around midnight when the creature appeared."

Grace softened her voice. "That must have been traumatic. Is Mrs. Orion all right?"

A ghost of a smile crossed his features. "She's still quite unnerved about the entire ordeal. The assaults on my character haven't helped."

Ethan glanced at the professor. "How did she find out?"

"It's all over social media, but she probably heard it from David. He and my wife have worked together closely to keep me on track since Wesleyan won the bid to host the FARST competition."

"How does Mrs. Orion feel about David sucking up to Dr. Hargrave?" Grace asked.

"Honestly, I've been so busy I haven't thought to ask her." Professor Orion laughed. "I've been so harried, I'd scratch my watch and wind my backside without someone to keep me straight."

Henry marveled at the change in the professor's posture. Not only had his shoulders relaxed, but his expression softened, and his eyes twinkled.

Grace cleared her throat. "Dr. Orion—"

"Please, call me Oliver."

She nodded. "Oliver, there's something I don't understand. David is your assistant, but he seemed more interested in helping Professor Hargrave ruin your reputation than in defending you."

The man glanced over his shoulder. "David is almost as brilliant as he is ambitious. His loyalties lie with himself first, and whoever he thinks will benefit him the most second."

"That's horrible." She sat back.

"That's life." Oliver sighed and waved a hand dismissively.

Ethan said, "Did you go to the hospital after the accident?"

The professor nodded. "And to answer your next question, they tested my blood-alcohol level."

"Why didn't you mention that when Hargrave accused you of driving under the influence?" Henry's head spun. "If a simple blood test can clear your name, why bother searching for the monster?"

"Because the truth doesn't always matter in the court of public opinion." Ethan flipped on his turn signal even though they hadn't passed another car for miles. "Nor does it always prevail in courts of law."

While Henry understood the concept, the reality of his father's words hit him like a gut punch. How could a member of the legal system have such a cynical view?

"I couldn't have said it better myself." Orion motioned to a scenic overlook. "Park there."

Ethan pulled into a parking spot, and everyone climbed out.

Professor Orion surveyed the lay of the land. "Let's climb to the top of the hill. It'll give us a good vantage point over the reservoir."

They hiked several yards up the incline. The adults set their chairs at one end of the summit, and the twins at the other. The distance gave Henry and Grace some much-needed time to discuss the case without parental input.

She pulled a sandwich from the cooler and tossed it to him. "What do we know?"

"Not much."

"The shotgun and the fear in Professor Orion's eyes didn't convince you he's telling the truth?" Grace opened a water bottle and took a sip.

He hitched a shoulder. "This is our seventh mystery. If there's one thing I've learned, it's that no one is completely innocent, and there are some things that can't be explained."

She rolled her eyes. "Other than the ghost we may or may not have seen on Star Island, every case of paranormal activity has been man-made."

The mention of the Lady in White sent a shiver down his spine.

"I'm ninety-nine-point-nine percent sure that Oliver Orion didn't play a role in creating whatever it was that he encountered on this road."

"Agreed." Henry took a bite of the PB&J. "I'm not ready to rule anything out, including the slim chance this thing is real. You read the articles from the first Mothman sightings. Over a hundred people claimed to have seen either the creature or UFOs over a nine-month period. It's hard to dismiss that many eye-witness reports."

It was Grace's turn to shiver. "I agree. It's incredibly odd. We're talking about a tiny country town in the 60s. Times were different then. Simpler. There was no internet or YouTube. I doubt people pulled stunts to get their fifteen minutes of fame like they do now."

"Different, yes. Simpler? I'm not so sure. Remember, the country was in its second year of the Vietnam War, we were in the Space Race, and *Star Trek* came out. Everyone was hunting little green men."

"Possibly." She tugged her scarf tighter around her neck and huddled in her chair. "I can't figure it out, though. If the original was a hoax, how could someone have pulled it off? The technology of the time wouldn't have allowed—"

"What is that?" Ethan pointed out over the reservoir.

Scrambling to his feet, Henry searched the sky.

Grace gasped. "Do you see it? Red lights at your two o'clock."

Once Henry spotted it, he couldn't look away. The object or creature or whatever it was flew over the water at a fast clip—heading straight for them.

Professor Orion shouted something and ran for the shotgun he'd left in the truck.

"Get down!" Ethan ran toward them, waving his arms.

Henry dropped to the ground.

"Now!" Ethan's voice left no room for argument. Henry tugged on Grace's leg. She dropped prone, where she could still see.

"Look at its wings! It looks just like the statue in Point Pleasant."

Circling the scenic overlook, the creature screeched in a frequency pushing the boundaries between human and canine hearing.

The Mothman hovered and stared back with creepy red eyes, pointed his finger, and dove toward the twins.

Ethan darted toward them, only to drop to one knee and cover his head when the monster flew too close.

Cocking his gun, Professor Orion aimed for the Mothman a second too late.

As if recognizing the threat, the creature changed course and headed back into the sky.

Grace twisted around as she looked for it. "Where did it go?"

"I don't know." Henry craned his neck looking for the Mothman.

"It's coming back!" Orion pointed the shotgun toward the sky directly above them.

"No!" Ethan lunged for the professor.

The Mothman flew close enough for Henry to make out swirling patterns in its wings.

Letting loose a slew of curse words, the professor stumbled forward, caught his balance, and sprinted into the woods. "It's getting away."

"Stay put." Ethan pointed at the twins before turning and running after the professor.

The color drained from Grace's face. "Did you see the claws on its hands and feet?"

Henry ran a trembling hand over his head. "Yeah. I don't like this. Dad shouldn't be out there with that *thing*. Safety in numbers, right?"

Grace drew a deep breath, but the whites of her eyes glowed with her fear.

A shout and the heart-stopping shotgun blast cut through the night air.

"That sounded like Dad." Henry didn't wait. He was up and running without looking back.

CHAPTER FIVE

"No!" Grace jumped up and sprinted, adrenaline driving her legs faster than should have been possible. She dove and caught her brother behind the knees, taking him to the ground. "Are you crazy? You can't run into an area where someone's shooting!"

"But Dad!" He pushed herself upright and struggled to break free of entangled bodies. He was every bit as protective as their father.

"Will walk out of there with the professor," she said evenly. "He has to."

When Henry had protested her father joining their mystery-solving team, he'd been worried he would disapprove of their methods or interfere or drive them crazy with dad jokes. Never, not once, had he considered he might get hurt.

Grace reiterated her point. "This is why we stay together. He shouldn't have left us behind."

"We learned that lesson the hard way. Remember when I left you outside and went into the taxidermy shop? Or when I ran ahead and fell through the rocks?"

"How could I forget? But this is different. He's genetically programmed to be a dad first. He's never going to allow us to run toward danger, with or without him."

Henry leaned into her line of vision. "Would you want him to?"

"No." She grinned despite the gnawing concern that her father wouldn't walk out of the woods. "We could call to him. See if he answers."

He counted down from three on his fingers, and they shouted, "Dad!"

No reply.

The twins repeated the count and yelled several more times, without so much as a peep in response.

Grace sighed and pushed to her feet. "This is crazy. I'm going to call him." She checked her phone. No reception. "We're going after him."

She'd taken four, maybe five steps when something large and heavy trudged through the underbrush nearby.

"Get down," Henry whispered.

"What *is* that?"

He pressed his finger to his lips.

A shadowy figure shambled a few yards to their right. The creature didn't have wings, or at least none she could see. It was large. Grace hadn't thought to research West Virginia wildlife to know what could be around.

Henry remained stock-still until the animal had passed. "I'm pretty sure that was a bear. We need to get back to the truck."

"We can't leave Dad out here with who-knows-what prowling around."

"You stopped me, now I'm stopping you. There's no benefit of us getting lost in the woods, too. He's liable to come out from a different direction. He'll look for us in the parking area, which is where we would look if we'd been lost. The Mothman is gone, isn't it? I don't hear anything." Henry looked to the sky.

She hated it, but he was right. "Fine. I think it's gone, too, both of the nasties."

The trees looked the same in the dark. Thankfully, they hadn't gone too far into the forest. If they had, they might never have found their way out again, driving home the point that they were ill-suited for a night exploration of the heavy wood.

The thought stopped Grace in her tracks. "Dad didn't have a flashlight."

"He'll be okay. He's with Dr. Orion."

"Dad wouldn't ignore us calling for him, so they must be pretty far away by now." She gave her brother a dubious look. "Do you honestly believe that Oliver Orion spends enough time in the woods to find his way back here? In the middle of the night?"

Henry hung his head.

"I have an idea." Grace pushed past him and hurried to the truck. The keys were missing. Not only had their father gone into the forest without a flashlight, he'd gone with the keys in his pocket. "Dang it. I thought we could at least turn the headlights on, but without the keys, the battery will go dead."

"We should be okay if we only leave them on for a little while."

"I'd hate to get stuck out here because we mistimed it." She rummaged through her emergency sleuthing bag for her flashlight.

"Good point." Henry pulled an old blanket from behind the back seat, spread it in the truck bed, and sat.

Shining the light in a wide arc over the tree line, Grace settled beside him. "Did you get a good look at the Mothman?"

"Not as good as I would have liked." He pulled the edge of the blanket over his legs.

"Is it possible it was a drone?"

"I didn't see any rotors."

She sighed and rested her head on his shoulder. "Me either, but there's a robotics competition happening. It's too much of a coincidence to ignore."

"Agreed." Henry checked the time on his phone. "How long do you think it's been?"

"Half-hour, maybe?" She chewed her lower lip. At some point they would need to call the authorities, but when? "Do you have reception? You know, in case we need to call the police?"

"Last time I checked, I didn't. I'll take a turn holding the light." His voice quivered, whether from the cold or worry, Grace couldn't tell.

She handed him the flashlight and drew her knees to her chest. "Do you find it odd the Mothman showed up so soon after we arrived?"

"Since I don't believe in coincidences, one of two things is going on. Either whoever's behind this lives around here, or they're following Professor Orion." He jabbed an elbow in her side. "Or the Mothman has a nest nearby."

"Ha-ha. Despite its weird history, I refuse to consider any theory that's based on the Mothman being real."

"Oh, it's real. A real creature, or a real hoax? That's the question."

Ignoring his comment, Grace pressed on. "Why would someone target Professor Orion? Besides Hargrave, who has a motive?"

"Good question."

"A student didn't like his grade? Someone wasn't accepted into the engineering program? An innocent prank gone awry?" She spoke more to herself than to her brother. Without her notebook to write down her thoughts, she found that brainstorming out loud helped her to remember.

Henry shook his head. "I realize these are rhetorical questions, but my money's on Hargrave and/or David. She teaches engineering and has a motive."

"Right, but if it's a drone-type robot, someone has to be nearby to fly it." Grace's eyes widened.

"Holy remote control, you're right. I wonder if Dr. Hargrave and David have alibis for tonight and Sunday?"

"I'm sure she has an assistant who keeps her calendar." Grace looked toward the trees and sighed. "Dad should have been back by now."

Henry glanced at his phone. "I'm five minutes away from calling the police."

"Call now. I can't stand any more of this waiting." Her father and the professor should have returned to the parking area, so either they were lost or injured. Neither option sat well with Grace.

Henry dialed, held the phone to his ear, and frowned. After repeating the process three more times, he said, "It's not going through."

Her chest tightened. "I'm scared."

"Me, too."

Sometime later, the sounds of engines and squealing tires snapped Grace to attention. She shot to her feet as two pickup trucks pulled into the scenic overlook. "Henry, wake up. This can't be good."

Five, maybe six, armed men dressed in camouflage piled out. The largest of them, and apparent ringleader, turned to her. "You Grace Warner?"

"Yeah?" Henry stood beside her in the bed of the truck.

The man spat from the corner of his mouth and hiked up his pants. "I'm Bugs. Got a call from some buddies staying up the mountain. They got a call from Mrs. Orion, who got a call from your mama. Seems she got a call from your daddy."

Grace blinked. "What?"

The guy laughed. "Your dad's lost up there, right?"

"Yes. Do you know where he is? Are you here to find him?"

"Not exactly, but there's a darn good chance we will." He spat again.

Henry stiffened his spine. "If you're not here to look for our father, why are you here?"

"My buddies seen the Mothman flyin' around earlier tonight. Seen some strange yellow glow on the hill. They're heading down and asked us to head up. We're plannin' to trap the alien between us."

"There is no alien. The Mothman is probably a drone or robot, and any glow is more than likely the person controlling it."

"Monster or trespasser, it's all the same to us. This here's private land." Bugs grinned, but Grace couldn't tell which part he found amusing—the creature or the possibility of catching trespassers.

Henry asked, "I thought it was part of the wildlife management area?"

"About two miles short of it." He pulled off his ski cap and scratched his shaggy head. "You say you think there's a cyborg runnin' around up there?"

"Drone. Like a remote-controlled plane with a human holding the controls." Grace reached behind her for Henry's hand. "It's dark. How will you know what you're shooting?"

"Relax, missy. We've been hunting these woods since we could walk. We ain't never shot one of our own." He nodded to the tall, thin guy on his right. "Ain't that right, Skinny Jimmy?"

"Not by accident, anyway." Skinny Jimmy flashed the twins a gap-toothed smile.

"We're coming with you." Grace grabbed the discarded flashlight.

"No can do, ma'am. Your mama and Mrs. Orion are on their way. If we found you, she said to tell you to stay put until they got here. We're going in to find us a monster, I mean, your pa and Oliver." He motioned overhead, and the group fell in behind him. "Let's rock and roll."

Grace watched in grim fascination as the men headed into the forest in a V-formation. "I don't like this."

"There's nothing we can do to stop them." Henry nodded to a car turning into the parking area. "Besides, we have different problems."

Faith Warner leapt from the car the second it stopped. She caught a glimpse of the hunters and gripped the door to keep upright.

The twins jumped down from the truck bed and hurried to their mother. Grace had been worried before but seeing her normally strong mom so distraught undid her.

Henry drew his mother into an embrace. "They're going to find him."

Pale-faced and wide-eyed, Faith held her arm out to Grace.

The family, minus one, huddled together, trying to take whatever comfort they could from one another.

"Bugs grew up on this land. He'll find Oliver and Ethan." The delicate woman in an oversized coat and boots offered a quivering smile.

Grace eased out of the group hug. "You must be Mrs. Orion. I'm Grace, and this is my brother Henry. Thank you for sending help."

The woman nodded. "You're welcome."

"If this is a search party, why are they armed?" Faith wondered, her voice quavering.

Mrs. Orion turned toward the hills surrounding them. "It's bear season."

"Ethan! No..."

Just when Grace thought her mom would wither, she lifted her chin and folded her arms. "Exactly what happened before your father ran into the forest?"

Henry told her everything, starting from setting up the lookout to the moment she stepped out of the car.

"You two did the right thing by staying near the truck." She glanced at the twins, nodded once, and turned her head—likely to hide her worried expression.

Mrs. Orion pulled her coat tighter. "We should wait in the car where it's warm."

Once settled in the backseat, Henry asked, "What did Dad say when he called?"

"The connection was terrible, but basically he was worried about the two of you." Faith drew a deep breath. "He lost sight of Oliver while looking for the... *creature* and couldn't find his way back here."

Seconds dragged into minutes, which dragged into hours. Somewhere in her research, Grace had read that the chance of finding a missing person decreased exponentially with each passing hour. The thought made it hard for her to breathe.

They say a person's life flashes before their eyes at the end, but Grace experienced a similar sensation in the safety of the back seat. Memories of her father flooded her mind like a parade of happiness. Dad had been there for every milestone, every success, every failure. The thought that he might not be around...

Henry fumbled for the window. "Did you hear that?"

Faith opened her mouth to speak, but the words died on her tongue.

A faint yellow glow bounced along the tree line.

Grace grabbed the back of Mrs. Orion's seat. "Turn on the high beams!"

Light flooded the edge of the forest, blinding Ethan Warner and making him stumble.

Faith cried out, and the twins flew from the car.

Ethan shielded his eyes with his arm and squinted. And in the light, they saw him grinning.

Faith threw her arms around her husband.

Henry and Grace joined the fray.

Shouting men poured out of the woods, only to come to a grinding halt a few feet from the family.

"I'll be darned." Bugs eyed the faint yellow glowstick in Ethan's hand. "You must be Mr. Warner?"

"I tried to tell you." Dad's voice sounded as if he'd swallowed sandpaper.

"Sorry 'bout that. We thought you were the *cyborg*. That glowstick of yours didn't do diddly."

"The cold temperatures affect the brightness—" He closed his eyes and sighed. "Thanks for not shooting me."

"Psshh. No need to thank me for that."

Grace could only imagine what had transpired between the hunters and her father.

"Cyborg?" Faith raised a brow.

Henry muttered, "That was our fault. We tried to explain the Mothman—"

"Don't worry about it. All's well that ends well." Ethan hugged them again.

"What happened to you? We heard a gunshot." Grace asked. With newfound energy and the relief from the reappearance of her missing father, her mind cleared and seemed supercharged.

"Oliver shot the creature, and it dove toward the ground. We tried to find it, but lost sight of each other." Ethan glanced around. "Did he make it back?"

"Not yet." Mom glanced toward the thin woman in the oversized coat. "His wife gave me a ride here. Would you speak to her?"

"Sure." He pulled away from the twins and walked to Mrs. Orion and Bugs.

Grace refused to leave her father's side. He was dirty, smelled like mud, and had a slight limp, but he was okay.

Mrs. Orion smiled, but her concern belied it. "Thank heavens you made it out."

"I saw the headlights from your car." He held her gaze but hesitated as if searching for the right thing to say. "Oliver—"

"He's not much of an outdoorsman now, but he spent a lot of time in these parts as a boy." Her words came out in a rush.

"He seemed to know what he was doing up there."

The woman glanced away. "You should take your family home, Mr. Warner. It's been a long night, and the kids shouldn't be out in the cold."

"We can stay until they find Professor Orion." Grace met her father's eyes for confirmation but found none.

"I'll have Jimmy sit with her when we head back up." Bugs squeezed Mrs. Orion's hand. "If that's okay with you?"

"That'd be fine." She turned to Grace. "Thank you for your offer, young lady, but I'll be okay. I've known Jimmy and Bugs their entire lives."

For a fleeting moment, Grace wondered what it would be like to grow up and grow old in the same place. Besides her immediate family and her grandparents in Florida, she couldn't say she'd known anyone her entire life.

Ethan slung his arm around her shoulder. "Let's go home."

And just like that, she realized she didn't need to live in one place to have roots. The Warners were like air plants; they didn't need soil binding them in place to thrive, only sunshine, rain, and love.

Once en route to Buckhannon, Faith turned in her seat and said, "No more sleuthing. This case is officially closed."

Henry sighed and stared out the window. His silence bothered Grace more than their mother's proclamation. Normally, he would have at least tried to plead their case, but nothing was normal.

She met her father's gaze in the rearview mirror and tried to convey her despair.

He winked and turned his attention back to the road.

Grace smiled. *Maybe he'll plead our case after all.*

CHAPTER SIX

West Virginia Wesleyan College had suffered an invasion of the robotic variety. Machines in every shape and size imaginable filled the greens, flew overhead, and walked the halls. Making matters worse, each robot came with a team of excitable humans.

Henry ducked to avoid a collision with a rogue drone. "That's it. I'm ready to go back to the fifth wheel and work on my English homework."

Grace tugged him out of the way of a battle-bot. "What's wrong? You were super quiet yesterday and have been in a bad mood since you woke up this morning."

"Besides a missing professor? I don't know. How about our father getting lost in the bear-infested wilderness?" He hadn't slept much the previous two nights. The Mothman, and what would have happened if his father hadn't walked out of the woods, had haunted his dreams.

"Dad getting lost freaked me out, too." She stared at a drone overhead. "I was thinking about what you said. It's too much of a coincidence that the robotics competition is going on at the same time there's a monster flying around."

"You heard Mom. The case is closed. No more sleuthing." The situation bugged him. They hadn't run off into the forest, but their senior project hung in the balance just the same.

"I also saw the twinkle in Dad's eye." Grace sat with her back against a tree and pulled out her phone. "We may have been forced to take a day off, but I'm not giving up. Dr. Orion is out there, and so are the people responsible for this mess."

He hated it when she pushed his buttons. She knew darned well that if she appealed to his sense of justice, he'd fall back in line.

"Are you with me, or are you with me?"

"Not this time." Henry turned to go.

"No way! Henry, wait." Grace's fingers flew over her cell phone. "There was another sighting last night."

Henry hung his head. "Where?"

"Point Pleasant."

"That's over a hundred and sixty miles away." He was no expert, but it didn't take a robot scientist to know that the average non-military drone didn't have that kind of range. "How is that possible?"

She shook her head. "It's not, unless there are two of them."

"What time was the creature spotted in Point Pleasant?"

"Two in the morning." She focused on the screen. "A woman named Mary Mason claims to have seen the Mothman in her chicken coop."

"Something fishy is going on." He held out his hand. "Come on."

"Where are we going?" She stood and grabbed her backpack.

"To talk to Dad. I suddenly have a craving for a Mothman cookie."

Inside the building, people milled around the judges' booth, but unlike the first day, no one smiled. The nervous excitement had morphed into concern with an undercurrent of fear-fueled-anger. For their part, the experts, dignitaries, and faculty worked hard to answer questions and calm the students' concerns—except Hargrave.

Professor Obnoxious stood in the eye of the storm glaring at anyone who dared to approach.

Faith Warner spoke to a girl wearing a University of Florida sweatshirt. "I understand there are rumors, but we have every intention of concluding the competition on time."

The Florida Gator said something Henry couldn't make out.

His mother's frown deepened. "The second round of judging has been postponed until this evening. Dr. Orion is still missing, and one of the teams is assisting with the search."

"It's in the official rules. They should be disqualified. Everyone else is sticking to the schedule." The girl raised her chin.

"I understand your concern. However, you might take this opportunity to work on your people skills. We are engineers and scientists by trade, but we are human beings first." Faith caught sight of the twins and left the girl with her mouth hanging open.

"Wow." Henry didn't know what else to say.

Mom lowered her voice. "I wish that was an isolated incident."

"Was it a local team who decided to join the search for Orion?" Grace asked with a hopeful lift to her voice.

Faith ran her finger down her clipboard. "Here it is. The group from Ohio University. They seemed to know some of the Wesleyan students."

Henry motioned to the paper attached to the board. "Is that your official scoring sheet?"

"Yes, as well as their names and the locations of their workstations. I'd be lost without it." She glanced back toward Hargrave and ushered the twins out of earshot. "The Wesleyan team was disqualified, but I haven't been able to get to the bottom of why."

Grace met Henry's gaze and bit her lip, a sign she wanted him to speak for both of them.

Henry took the opening. "We could ask some questions. The students are more likely to talk to a couple of high school kids than a guest judge."

Faith pursed her lips. "Promise me you'll stay out of trouble *and* the woods."

"I'll keep an eye on them." Emerging from the crowd, Ethan Warner held up three fingers in the Boy Scout sign. "Scouts honor."

"And who's going to keep an eye on you?" Faith went for a smirk-double-brow-raise but ended up frowning.

Slipping his arm around her waist, Ethan whispered, "We'll be fine."

"I was asked not to repeat this, but the three of you should know." Once again, she glanced back toward Hargrave and the others. "Another professor is missing in action. He's one of the judges."

Grace lowered her voice. "What does this mean for the second round of the competition?"

"Thankfully, Dr. Callen completed his evaluation forms, but he hasn't been in this morning or attended any of his regular classes. Without him, we can't finish the final round."

Henry pressed his hand to his churning stomach. "Do you know any of the details?"

"No. Hargrave isn't volunteering any additional information. If he's not located, we are one judge short and will have to cancel the competition."

David, Professor Orion's assistant, cleared his throat. "Dr. Warner, you're late for your breakout session."

Faith glanced from her husband to her children and finally to David. "I'll be right there."

He tapped his clipboard. "I must insist you follow me. Your tardiness reflects poorly on the college."

Henry couldn't stand the guy, but he understood his type. What's more, he knew how to use David's ambition to find answers they desperately needed. "Mom, before you go. What time did you want to interview the guy about the mentorship?"

Faith Warner picked up on the ruse without batting a lash. "Have him send his resume. His flexibility and willingness to help out impressed me."

"I agree. He seems like a strong candidate for the position." Grace sighed deep and loud. "But between the excellent starting pay and the chance to work alongside you, you'll have your pick of new engineers. Why rush to a decision?"

Ethan glanced between them as if they were speaking in Mandarin.

David took a step forward. "I wasn't aware you were hiring someone? Is this a new project?"

"It is." Mom made a show of looking at her watch. "I should get to the breakout session."

"I'll escort you." The guy stumbled over his feet to get to her side.

"No need. I know where it is." Faith turned and cut through the crowd.

The assistant glanced at the remaining Warners as if trying to decide who to suck up to. He settled on Henry. "We haven't officially met. I'm David Dillinger, and I'm a senior here. Second in my class."

Ethan set his hand on Grace's shoulder and turned to go. "If you'll excuse us, we were just leaving."

She paused. "Who's first?"

David's eyes widened. "Excuse me?"

"You said you were second in your class. Who's first?"

Not the line of questioning Henry would have chosen. He would have gone with the missing professor or Hargrave's whereabouts on the nights of the creature sightings, but Grace had obviously hit a nerve.

"I'm second by a fraction of a point. The grades won't be officially calculated until after finals next semester." He hesitated as if to see if she'd accept his answer. When Grace didn't reply, he said, "Quinn Quaglieri, a local. Managed to get the Wesleyan team disqualified from the FARST competition."

"*Quinn* Quaglieri?" Her voice came out as breathy and strained as if she'd taken a hit to the solar plexus.

"You've heard the name?" David narrowed his eyes. "That's your candidate? The one who's applying for the position?"

"If you'll excuse us, we are late for an appointment." Ethan used his no-nonsense courtroom voice.

"Of course." He snarled, although he'd probably meant to smile. "When can I speak to Dr. Warner about the position?"

"After the awards ceremony. She's booked solid until then." Henry followed his family out of the building.

Grace held her tongue until she felt she would burst from the effort. She climbed into the truck and waited until her father had started the engine. "Forget going to Point Pleasant to talk to the chicken lady. We have to find Quinn Quaglieri."

Ethan Warner made a timeout sign. "Dare I ask who or what the chicken lady is?"

Henry snickered. "A woman in Point Pleasant claims to have seen the Mothman in her chicken coop last night."

"But that's a two-and-a-half-hour drive." He glanced at them.

Grace held up a hand. "The story is obviously fake or a copycat. We find Quinn, we find the person controlling the Mothman."

Dad arched a brow. "Counselor, do you have evidence to support that statement?"

She wanted to groan or pound the dashboard or scream they were wasting time. "Betty at the museum remembered two college-age men hanging around last spring. She found where one of them had signed the guestbook with the first name 'Quinn.'"

"Go on." Judging by his expression, he planned to shoot down her theory.

"Quinn is an engineering student. A good one, to be at the top of the class. And he's into robotics."

Henry whistled. "You were on the right track, but the last statement assumes facts not in evidence."

This time Grace did groan and slap the dashboard. "Enough with the legal talk."

"Easy there, slugger. I agree with you. Based on what we know, Quinn is the most obvious suspect, but you're forgetting something." Ethan turned to Henry. "Do you see the flaw in her logic?"

He hesitated for a couple of seconds. "We're presuming guilt?"

"There's that, but no." He put the truck in reverse and pulled out of the lot. "Betty said there were *two* people researching the Mothman. Quinn isn't working alone. If we find him before we build a solid foundation, we risk losing the other person involved, not to mention the element of surprise."

Henry pinched the bridge of his nose. "I think we've already given up the tactical advantage."

"David." Grace stunk at lying, even by omission. She should have put an end to Dillinger's speculation rather than allowing him to believe a lie. "The jerk will probably confront Quinn and blow our cover."

"Maybe, maybe not." Ethan tossed her his cell phone. "Text your mother and tell her what we know. She's great at running interference."

"Good idea. She could tell David everything's highly confidential."

"Where are we going?" Henry asked from the back seat.

"To check on the search for Oliver, speak to Mrs. Orion, and if there's still time, to see the chicken lady."

The mere mention of the missing professor changed the mood in the truck. Grace hated to think of the family hanging in limbo wondering if they'd ever see their loved one again. The few hours her father had been missing had nearly broken her. She couldn't imagine the agony of hours stretching into days.

Seeing the area in the daytime gave Grace a new understanding of the land and how easily someone could get lost in the thick trees. She had no idea how far out of Buckhannon they'd traveled, but a police roadblock told her the scenic overlook was close.

Ethan rolled down his window and spoke to an approaching officer. "Good morning. I'm Ethan Warner. I was here Tuesday night with Dr. Orion."

"Go on through." The officer repeated her father's name into the radio.

He nodded and eased the truck through the barricade. Vehicles lined both sides of the road, but the police continued to motion them forward. A large man in a different uniform than the others pointed to an empty spot at the edge of the parking area.

"Looks like I'm going to need to speak to the authorities. Again." He pulled the keys from the ignition and tossed them to Grace.

Henry leaned forward and peered through the windshield. "When did you talk to them the first time?"

"Yesterday, on campus." He pointed at the twins. "You two stay in the parking area. No wandering off."

Pulling on his jacket, Ethan walked to the waiting sheriff.

Henry clamped his hand on her shoulder. "Looks like we're going to be here for a while. What do you say we walk around and eavesdrop?"

"Sure."

At first glance, the goings-on seemed like controlled chaos, but Grace soon realized the police had organized the volunteers into groups. Some came, others went, but they all had the same routine—grab a cup of coffee and check in with the officers inside the tent-turned-command post.

"Henry! Grace!" Mrs. Orion waved from the refreshment table. Although she'd shucked off the oversized coat, the woman wore the same clothing she had two nights before.

Grace steeled her nerves and forced a smile. "Our dad wanted to check on you. Any word?"

"Nothing yet, but there are reports of chimney smoke from a cabin on the next ridge. The forest rangers should get there soon." She patted Grace's arm. "How are things on campus? The competition...it means the world to Oliver."

A lump formed in Grace's throat, making it impossible to breathe, let alone talk.

Seeming to sense her distress, Henry said, "Everyone is concerned about Dr. Orion. One of the judges, Dr. Callen, seems to be missing, too, but they're doing their best to stick to the schedule."

"If you'll excuse me, I'd like to be near the radio when the rangers call in." Mrs. Orion walked into the tent.

Henry stared after her. "That was odd. She didn't so much as flinch at the mention of another Wesleyan professor coming up missing."

"I doubt she's slept much in the last two days. She may not have caught everything you said."

"Good point."

"Didn't expect to see you two back here today." Skinny Jimmy yawned widely enough for Grace to see his tonsils and filled a Styrofoam cup with cream, sugar, and a dash of coffee.

"Have you been here all night?" Grace looked around for food or wrappers or anything that would lead her to believe they'd fed the volunteers. Between her mental state and the lack of light the first time they'd met, she hadn't realized Jimmy was in his early twenties. She'd pegged him and the others as older.

"Family don't leave family." His words came out strong, but his shoulders slumped.

"Are you related to Dr. Orion?"

Jimmy glanced back toward the tent. "He's my uncle by marriage."

She thought back to the conversation she'd had with Bugs and Mrs. Orion. Neither had mentioned the relationship. Then again, everything had been nuts that night. "Have you eaten anything?"

"Coffee, and we found a cooler of peanut-butter sandwiches up on the hill."

Grace blanched. In all the chaos, she'd forgotten about the picnic she'd packed.

As if the mention of food had woken his stomach, it growled. "The others are working in shifts, but us guys won't go until we find my uncle."

Henry nodded toward Ethan. "We were on our way to Point Pleasant, but we can bring some food when my dad's finished talking to the sheriff."

"Whatcha planning to do there?" He cocked his head. For a man who likely hadn't slept or eaten since the previous evening, he seemed to have his priorities mixed up.

Grace said, "There was a Mothman sighting there last night. We thought we'd go try to speak to the eye-witness."

Jimmy's shoulders tensed. "Sounds like a waste of time to me. If you're lookin' for something to do, we could use some help here."

"I don't think my dad would go for it, but you're right. I'll ask." She softened her voice. "In the meantime, how many of you stayed last night? The least we can do is feed you."

"There's me, and Quinn—"

"Quaglieri?" Henry spoke loud enough that several people turned and stared. "Quinn Quaglieri. He's here?"

"That's right." His spine went rigid, and the color drained from his face. From the looks of it, he'd said something he shouldn't have.

"Where's Quinn now? We'd like to speak to him." She caught movement from the corner of her eye and turned to face Mrs. Orion.

The woman folded her arms across her chest. "Quinn's searching for Oliver. Why?"

Dang it. Grace didn't want to add to Mrs. Orion's stress, but she saw no way to backtrack out of the situation.

"We inadvertently led someone to believe Quinn was in the running for a job with our mom. We'd really like the chance to explain what happened before David Dillinger ambushes him." Henry either came to the rescue or threw them under the bus. Only time would tell.

"Dillinger." Jimmy spat on the ground near Grace's feet. "I'd like to see him try to ambush a bag of kittens."

"In other words, you lied and want to cover your backsides." Mrs. Orion narrowed her eyes. Sleep-deprived or not, she had a firm grasp of the situation —at least the partial truth Henry had shared.

Ethan Warner chose that moment to interject himself into the conversation. "What they are too polite to tell you is we have reason to believe Quinn may have played a part in creating the Mothman."

The woman's face turned a shade of red usually reserved for Muppets and stop signs. "You can't think Quinn had anything to do with this! Who do you think you are? And what gives you the right to say such things?"

An officer emerged from the command center with a walkie-talkie in his hand. "Mrs. Orion, we've located your husband."

CHAPTER SEVEN

Henry considered himself to be of above-average intelligence, but he doubted he would ever understand people. Sure, human behavior made sense when studied in large groups or civilizations, but individuals never ceased to amaze him. Mrs. Orion should have been overjoyed by the news that the rangers had found her husband, but instead, she insisted that the Warners leave the area.

"Don't let what happened back there upset you." Ethan Warner met his son's gaze in the rearview mirror. "She had a rough night, and I'm afraid I didn't help matters."

Grace glanced up from her phone. "Dad's right. Mrs. Orion wasn't upset with us. She was upset with the situation. Once she knew Oliver was safe, the anger set in, and we were easy targets."

"I don't understand what he was doing in an old hunting cabin. To take shelter at night is one thing, but why hang out there so long?" He couldn't shake the feeling that they were missing something obvious. A clue that, when found, would cause the other pieces to fall like a tower of dominos.

"Good question." She tapped her lips. "Didn't Bugs mention a friend of his was staying in a cabin nearby?"

"Hang on." Ethan waited until he had their attention to speak. "We can't assume Professor Orion stayed in the same cabin. I'm sure there are dozens in the area."

"True, but the thing about sleuthing is that you have to learn to trust your gut. Mine tells me there are too many coincidences involving Professor Orion to ignore."

"I'm more of a facts man myself." He grew quiet for a moment. "But I do see your point."

Staring at her phone, Grace sucked in a breath. "There were three more Mothman sightings in the Point Pleasant area. Strangely enough, all of the witnesses reported seeing the creature on the ground. There's no mention of flying."

"Interesting. Very interesting." Ethan spoke in a ridiculous German accent.

Henry raised a brow. "Shouldn't you use a Victorian-London accent?"

"I would, but it would end up sounding more like Scar from *The Lion King*." To prove his point, he did his best Jeremy Irons imitation. "I do find it curious that the creature in Point Pleasant hasn't been spotted in the air, yet we were unable to find it on the ground here."

"I would say the good people of Point Pleasant are worried they'll lose tourism dollars if their town monster moves east, but none of the Buckhannon sightings have made the internet." Henry turned to Grace for confirmation.

"Nothing yet." She tossed her phone on the seat beside her. "And I've lost reception."

"We'll be there in a half-hour." Ethan drummed on the steering wheel. "What's the plan when we arrive?"

"We may catch Betty before the museum closes. If not, I found Mary Mason's address online. I'd like to get a better idea of what she saw and when," Grace said.

"Solid plan." He concentrated on the road, holding the steering wheel tightly as if his life depended on it.

Despite arriving fifteen minutes after closing time, the Warners walked into a stream of people when they entered the still-open World Famous Mothman Museum. Betty and a teen boy moved like shepherds, ushering visitors toward the door.

The boy waved at the Warners. "Sorry, we're closed. You'll have to come back tomorrow."

Grace stood on tiptoes. "I'm here to see Betty."

"Wait in the gift shop."

"Sure, okay."

He leaned down to speak to a little girl. Standing, he yelled, "Did anyone misplace their kid?"

The twins perused the collection of Mothman hoodies and t-shirts while Ethan checked his emails. Ten minutes later, the last of the tourists left the building.

Betty turned the lock and rested her back against the door. "What a day!"

"Seems like the sightings were good for business." Ethan slid his cell into his pocket.

"About that." She nodded toward Grace. "I don't suppose you know why the Mothman has returned after forty years?"

She glanced at Henry.

He nodded and folded his arms across his chest. "The first sighting we know of was outside Buckhannon. A professor from Wesleyan and his wife encountered the creature while driving home around midnight. It flew over their car."

"And we saw it the night before last. It was terrifying. I don't think I can rest until I know what it was." Grace laid it on thick.

Betty's eyes widened. "What did it look like?"

"Almost exactly like the statue outside, but it was black and wearing flowing robes."

"My stars." Betty hurried behind the cash register and pulled out a notebook. "Would you mind documenting everything you saw?"

"Sure." She walked to the counter, grabbed a pen, and started writing.

"It's just like back in 1966." The woman rubbed her upper arms. "I've had two dozen people in here today claiming to have seen the creature."

Grace asked, "Have any of them seen the creature flying?"

"Now that you mention it, no."

"Wesleyan College is hosting a robotics competition this week. Because of the technology needed to make something that large fly, we have a theory that students created the monster near Buckhannon." Henry motioned to a rack of costumes. "Have you sold any of these lately?"

"I don't think I like where this is going." The woman stared as if he'd sprouted horns and a tail. "Some of the folks who saw the creature are my friends. We may be small-town, but we know the difference between the Mothman and some yahoo dressed in a cheap costume."

Grace glanced up from the notebook. "You may be right, but we'd like to look into it further. If it's a fake, we'll put a stop to it quietly."

"Quietly, my Aunt Fanny." She glared. "I know how this will turn out. Bad for business."

"Grace is right. We likely can't prove the creature is real, but if the unbelievers get wind of a hoax, it could negatively impact the museum," Ethan said. "Either way, we have no desire to go to the media with our findings."

The woman glanced from one Warner to the next and sighed. "I sold a costume yesterday."

Yes! Henry kept his expression neutral. "Do you remember what the person looked like?"

"Middle-aged man, short, balding, glasses."

Ethan dragged his hand over his face. "That sounds like Professor Orion. What time was he in?"

"First thing in the morning." Her frown deepened.

So much for that idea. Henry met Grace's gaze and shook his head. "It wasn't the professor. He was at the college after the opening ceremonies."

"Which started at ten and ended around eleven thirty. He could have made it in time." Grinning, Grace set the pen on the paper. "Did he pay with cash or a credit card?"

"Cash, and before you ask, I didn't get a name."

"Is there anything else you can tell us? Any detail, no matter how small or insignificant, might help."

The woman shrugged. "He wasn't planning to wear it. He would have taken a large, but he insisted he needed a size small."

Once again, the information seemed important, but Henry couldn't make sense of it. "Do you have the names and addresses of the people who claimed to have seen the Mothman?"

Betty raised her chin. "I do, but I can't share them with you. Confidentiality and all."

Grace said, "It's okay. I found her address online. She lives on a farm on the Ohio side of the river, right?"

"That she does, but you won't have any luck getting past the gate on the old Callen farm. It's done up tighter than Fort Knox."

Snap. One of the missing pieces of the puzzle dropped onto the board. "Callen? Any relation to Professor Callen at Wesleyan?"

"I'm not going to confirm or deny other people's personal business." Betty set her jaw. "I've known her since I moved to these parts, and she's not the type to make up stories."

"We came all this way. Couldn't you call her or one of the others and ask if they're willing to speak to us?" Grace dipped her chin and widened her eyes.

Henry followed her lead. "It's important that someone look into these new sightings. We'd be happy to share our findings with you."

Betty looked around the gift shop as if considering her options. "I had everyone who claimed to have seen the Mothman write anonymous accounts."

Grace's face lit up. "In this notebook?"

"It's not leaving the museum, but you can snap pictures of their entries."

Grace thanked Betty profusely before pulling out her phone and going to work.

"And I don't suppose it'd hurt to give Mary a call."

Henry's mouth fell open. Too bad his parents didn't fall for Grace's sad-puppy face that easily.

"Thank you. Please tell her we will use the utmost discretion and respect her privacy." Ethan folded his arms.

"Are you a lawyer or something?" Betty eyed him while she dialed an old-fashioned wired telephone.

"Or something." He walked to Grace's side and read over her shoulder, likely to avoid any additional questions.

Mary Mason could have been a model in her youth. The willowy woman stood a solid six feet tall and carried herself like someone who'd spent years at a ballet barre. Her beauty, however, was ruined by the deep-set frown on her otherwise lovely face.

Ethan stepped forward and offered his hand. "I'm Ethan Warner, and these are my kids Henry and Grace."

She turned her nose up. "I understand you have some questions for me about my encounter with the Mothman?"

Henry met Grace's gaze and rolled his eyes toward Mary.

His sister squared her shoulders. "Did the creature fly?"

"Betty said you read my statement. Did I mention it flying?"

Ethan quirked a brow. "I take it that's a no?"

"It was standing on the roof of my chicken coop. I didn't see how it got there, nor did I see how it got down. I would assume it flew." She raised her chin. "Is there anything else?"

Fearing the interview would end before her she actually answered any questions, Henry went for a softer approach. "Ms. Mason, have we done something to offend you?"

The woman snapped her head in his direction, narrowed her eyes, drew a breath, and exhaled slowly. "I wrote everything in the notebook. There's nothing else I can tell you. I only came here as a favor to Betty."

"We appreciate your time." Grace tilted her head. "I do have one more question. Is Professor Callen from Wesleyan College related to you?"

"Yes." Mary's expression went from shocked to scared to angry in the time it took Henry to blink.

Ethan stepped toward her. "When was the last time you saw him? He's missing from campus. I don't know if anyone from the college has alerted the authorities."

The woman's hand flew to her throat. "There's no need to call the police. Casper's at the farm. He was visiting and came down with the flu. He must have forgotten to call into work."

"That's a relief." Ethan flashed her a smile. "The faculty have been quite worried. Would you mind asking him to contact Dr. Orion?"

"I should get home and check on him." Mary Mason all but ran from the building.

Groaning, Grace said, "Add Callen to our list of suspects."

***

The next morning, the twins accompanied their parents to Wesleyan College. Their plan was simple: attend the second round of judging while scoping out the competitors and the machines. However, even simple plans had a way of going awry. Well over half the team workstations in the exhibition hall were empty.

Grace had a sinking feeling. "Where is everyone?"

"I'm not sure. The Wesleyan students work in their labs, but the others should be here." Faith Warner frowned. "Why don't you two go get something to eat? Dad and I will catch up when we find out what's going on."

She nodded and watched her parents hurry away.

"This is bad." Henry made a sour face. "And for once, I'm not hungry."

"Me either but come on." She tugged his arm. "I bet everyone's in the cafeteria. We might be able to eavesdrop and find out why so many teams have dropped out."

The twins entered the cafeteria. As Grace had predicted, the place was packed. She spotted David Dillinger and debated the wisdom of speaking to him. If anyone knew what had happened, he would. However, he likely wouldn't care to share if he'd confronted Quinn about the fictitious position with her mother.

"Give me a second. I can't shake the feeling David's involved in this. I'm going to sneak a pic of him and send it to Betty." Grace used her brother for cover and snapped several photos.

"Good idea." Staring toward the far corner, Henry grunted. "Whoa."

She followed his line of vision to the last two people she'd expect to find in a college cafeteria—Bugs and Skinny Jimmy. Adding to the bizarre factor, both men wore Wesleyan sweatshirts. "Now, *that's* interesting. What do you want to bet one of the guys at the table is Quinn?"

"I'm not in the habit of taking losing bets." He shoved his hands in his pockets and slumped his shoulders. "Blend in. I don't want them to see us."

"I hate to tell you, but slouching like Quasimodo is the opposite of blending in." Grace nodded toward a condiment and drink station a few rows over. "Let's head that way. It'll provide some cover."

A guy wearing a red and gold sweatshirt spoke over the noise. "I'm telling you, with Wesleyan's team disqualified and so many teams leaving, we've got it in the bag."

His teammate didn't look convinced. "No one will win if they cancel the competition."

"I'll sue for emotional distress and expenses." Mr. Red and Gold Sweatshirt smirked.

His teammate noticed the twins listening and whispered something Grace couldn't hear.

A few tables away, the girl from the University of Florida glared. "Hey, I know you two. You're Dr. Warner's kids."

Henry nodded. "Guilty as charged."

"I'm Cassie." She smiled like a shark that'd identified its next meal. "Have a seat."

"We're a little busy." Grace glanced at Bugs' and Jimmy's table. Although they showed no signs of leaving, she didn't want to take a chance on missing them.

"It'll only take a sec. We have questions." She motioned to her teammates.

Henry took a chair, turned it backward, and sat. "Are you an all-female team?"

Cassie nodded. "The only one in the competition. What's the deal? Are they going to cancel the entire thing because they lost another judge?"

His eyes widened before he could smooth his expression. "Another judge besides Professor Callen?"

One of the girls at the table huffed. "You don't know what's going on either, do you?"

Grace said, "Callen has the flu. Did another judge quit?"

"Yep." Cassie leaned closer and lowered her voice. "Word is, the other teams left because some of the faculty advisors and judges saw the Mothman last night. It's the same creature that almost killed Professor Orion."

Dipping his chin, Henry grinned. "Professor Orion was lost in the forest, not attacked by the Mothman."

"If you ask me, the whole thing is ridiculous. It's probably the Wesleyan team getting revenge because they were disqualified." Cassie met Grace's gaze as if expecting her to confirm or deny the theory.

When she didn't respond, another member of the Florida team said, "It's kind of gross. I mean, the entire team is related to Professor Orion. The college should have picked another chairperson if they wanted their team to compete, but now they're ruining it for the rest of us."

While Grace didn't trust the girls to have their facts straight, part of what she'd said rang true. She would never have pegged Jimmy and Bugs as academic types, let alone engineers, but there they were in Wesleyan colors.

Cassie reached over and knocked on Grace's head. "Hello? Anyone home?"

Jerking back and glaring, Grace said, "Is the home team that good? I mean, my mom said the monster flew, but there were no visible rotors. It's also capable of interacting with its environment. That would suggest whoever's controlling it has a visual on its surroundings. Not to mention, it can make hand gestures."

The girls at the table stared with varying degrees of shock.

Cassie smirked. "As if. That's like Department of Defense-level tech."

"My mother was quite impressed." She knew it was wrong to gloat, but it felt darned good.

Henry stood. "Sorry to cut this short, but there's an empty table in the back corner. We should grab it."

Grace turned in time to see Bugs and his crew exiting the building. *Darn it!*

CHAPTER EIGHT

Henry rewrote the conclusion to his English paper for the fourth time. On the fifth attempt, he gave up and stormed into the kitchen.

Grace closed her laptop. "What's wrong? Besides the fact you are a weirdo who doesn't like Jane Austen."

"I'm a guy. Do the math." He smirked and pulled a tub of ice cream from the freezer.

"Don't you mean assess the literature?"

He gave her a don't-test-me look and turned to the fridge.

She joined him and grabbed a spoon. "Relax. I'm only teasing."

"This mood of yours wouldn't have anything to do with the case, would it?" Ethan set aside his notes for an upcoming lecture. "Is that Rocky Road?"

"Yes on both counts." Henry filled three bowls to obscene levels. "It's Friday night. The competition ends on Sunday, and we're no closer to solving the mystery than when we started."

Grace threw the empty carton in the trash. "That's not true. We're farther away than when we started, and suspects keep crawling out of the motherboards."

Ethan folded his arms. "Have you thought about how you'll write this chapter of your research project if you don't solve—"

"No," the twins said in unison.

Grace pushed the ice cream around in her bowl. "I'm on a mission to get pictures of Quinn, Bugs, and Jimmy, I could send them to Betty for a positive ID."

"Good idea. Anything to help narrow the field." Henry shoveled a huge bite into his mouth, then pressed his fingers to his temples, likely to stave off brain freeze. "I'm still in a state of shock that Bugs and Skinny Jimmy are students."

Ethan rubbed the back of his neck. "I hate to admit it, but I agree."

"I can't figure out Mary Mason. She came into town to meet with us, then all but refused to answer our questions." Grace picked at her ice cream.

"It's not the first time we've interviewed a hostile witness." Henry laughed.

She gave him a warning look. They did not need to discuss former mysteries in mixed company. "Dad, did you get the name of the second judge who quit the competition from Mom?"

"Dr. Baxter from Georgia Institute of Technology, and he didn't quit. He was called away but will be back in time to finish the competition." Ethan's phone rang, and he stepped into the master bedroom to answer it.

"That's one less person we have to question." Henry smirked.

Grace lowered her voice. "What does your gut say about the case?"

"Everyone we've met is guilty."

"Same here."

Ethan walked back into the room. "There's been another sighting. The Mothman was outside when Dr. Hargrave and the judges left the restaurant."

Henry's heart sped. "Judges? Was Mom with them?"

"Yes, and she's pretty upset." Ethan waved his phone. "How would you two feel about a fourth Warner working on the mystery?"

Henry froze, unsure how to answer the question. His dad was bad enough, but Mom? She'd never follow instructions. *Ugh. We can't exactly say no.* "Sure, why not? Maybe she can make sense of this."

"I was hoping you'd say that." He grabbed his melted ice cream and walked to the door. "She's on her way home. It might be best if I speak to her alone first."

"Is she that freaked out?" Grace opened her laptop.

"It scared her," he said over his shoulder as he walked outside.

The twins spent the next twenty minutes in their bunks googling the Mothman, the competition, and the judges.

"Anything new?" Henry asked.

Grace shook her head. "Nothing, except a text from Betty. She didn't recognize David from the photo I sent her."

"It was worth a shot. Regardless, I'm not ready to cross him off the list."

"Me either."

Headlights flashed, and the truck's engine growled outside for a few seconds before dying abruptly.

Henry cut his light and peered out the window.

Faith Warner did not suffer fools lightly, nor was she the type of woman who believed in ghosts, ghouls, or monsters—two facts Henry reminded himself of when he saw the frightened expression on his mother's face.

Ethan stood and went to his wife. The couple spoke in hushed tones, embraced, and continued to whisper.

"She looks more than a little upset." Henry motioned for Grace to join him.

She peeked outside. "And angry."

Faith's voice rose. "Why would anyone do this?"

"We don't know, but we're going to find out." Ethan slid his arm around her shoulder and guided her into the fifth wheel.

"She's too busy with the competition to get involved in the mystery." The lift in Grace's voice turned the statement into a question.

"Absolutely. Much too busy." Henry wasn't so sure. Between Dad getting lost in the woods and having a first-hand encounter with the Mothman, their mother might make time.

Keeping their heads down and eyes low, the twins walked into the living room.

Faith set her hands on her hips. "I want to know everything you know about this so-called Mothman and the people behind it."

Despite his apprehension about having another parent involved in the case, Henry smiled. His mom looked like a wild-eyed, power-suit-wearing superhero.

Ethan and the twins spent the next two hours relaying everything from the history of the creature to their latest conversation with Betty at the museum. For her part, Faith read the newspaper articles from the 60s, blog posts, and the handwritten accounts Grace had photographed.

When she'd consumed all of the information, Mom sat back in her chair and frowned. "There is no logic to this."

The twins exchanged glances.

Ethan chuckled. "Of course not. That's why it's a mystery."

She narrowed her eyes at him. "Who are your suspects?"

"The list is long." Henry understood her frustration. The situation was especially aggravating, but he'd felt the same way at one point or another on every case. Each mystery presented different challenges, and the culprits were never who he expected.

"Quinn Quaglieri." Grace set her elbows on the table. "We know he spent a considerable amount of time researching the Mothman. We also know he's a—"

"She." Faith pressed her lips into a line. "Quinn is a she."

"That's not possible. The woman at the museum said two college-age men were researching the monster. One signed their name Quinn." Grace motioned for him to back her up.

Henry thought back to their conversations with people who knew Quinn—Dillinger, Skinny Jimmy, and Mrs. Orion.

Losing her patience, Grace said, "I'm absolutely positive Mrs. Orion referred to Quaglieri as him or he."

Henry groaned. "She did, but she gave us a weird look."

"You're right, and we missed it." Grace dropped her head to the table. "This case is like an infinite loop of frustration."

"You'll solve this one like you did the others." Faith squeezed her hand. "And if it will help, I'd be happy to introduce you to Quinn."

This time Faith's phone rang. She glanced at the number on the screen and frowned. "Hello?"

"This is Oliver Orion. Are you with Ethan?" The professor spoke loud enough for everyone in the room to hear.

"Yes, one moment." Faith set the phone in Ethan's waiting hand.

"Oliver, what can I do for you?"

"There was another sighting—"

"At the restaurant. Faith told me."

"No. At my place."

Ethan glanced at the twins. "Hang on a minute while I put you on speaker."

Henry bit back laughter. Being on speakerphone was redundant. The man hadn't stopped shouting since Faith answered the call.

"Okay, we're all here." Ethan took Faith's hand.

"My wife and I were outside having dinner when we spotted the Mothman. He circled the house several times, then seemed to have a malfunction. We thought he would crash into the barn."

Grace leaned closer to the phone. "Where is he now?"

"From the sound of it, he crashed in the back of my property. We could use some help searching for him."

Faith sat back in her chair and stared at the cell as if it had exploded.

The twins nodded.

Ethan said, "We're on our way."

"You realize this could be a ruse?" The color drained from Faith's face. "Or a trap to lure us to the middle of nowhere."

One look at his mom and Henry knew two things for certain. One, the last few days had worn heavily on her. And two, if they didn't wrap the mystery up in a nice, safe red bow, she'd put an end to their sleuthing once and for all.

Ethan said exactly the wrong thing at the wrong time. "If anything, it's a ruse. If Professor Orion wanted to hurt us, he had the perfect opportunity."

<hr>

Grace followed her mother's gaze over the expanse of the Orions' land. "It'll be okay."

Faith turned her head and studied her daughter for a long moment. "Were you scared when you saw the Mothman?"

"Scared doesn't cover it. Once I got past the shock, the scientist part of my brain and the need to know more kicked in."

Faith lowered her voice to prevent Ethan and Henry from overhearing her. "I don't care what that *thing* is. I'm here to protect my family and find the people responsible for scaring ten years off my life."

"Hopefully, we won't need protecting." She motioned to Professor Orion, who was waiting for them at the side of the house. "We should get started."

"Thank you for coming." He pulled a hankie from his back pocket and dotted his brow, but a fresh layer of sweat returned before he'd lowered his hand. "The others are already in the back pastures."

"Others?" Faith frowned.

"My niece was having dinner with my wife and me. She called a couple of friends to help."

Henry hiked his emergency sleuthing bag onto his shoulder. "This is a big place. Do you have a way to contact one another should someone find the creature?"

This time the professor wiped his forehead on his sleeve. "We didn't think of that."

Grace exchanged glances with her mother. The idea of Dr. Orion luring them here under false pretenses made more sense by the minute.

Ethan pulled a referee's whistle from his knapsack. "We'll signal with this and flashlights."

"I'll have my folks do the same." The professor shoved his hands into his pockets and turned for the barn. "Follow me."

The Warners followed the man through a cow pasture to a split-rail fence on the eastern side of his property. Trees, growing as thick as those surrounding the scenic overlook, loomed several yards past the barrier. Making matters worse, storm clouds covered the moon—their only light source.

"You've got to be kidding." The words fell out of Grace's mouth before she could stop them.

"Is there any reason you have us searching the woods while people who know the area are in the pastures?" Ethan didn't sound any happier than his daughter.

Keeping his gaze low, Orion shifted his weight from one foot to the other. "I believe the creature fell just beyond the tree line, but my niece insisted he went down elsewhere."

Henry said, "You're coming with us, right?"

"I...uh..." He wiped his face again. "I should stay near the phone in case I'm wrong and they find something."

The Warners stared, unconvinced and unmoving.

Dr. Orion motioned toward the house. "The floodlights are on. You can see them from a distance. Plus, the road borders the land on two sides, this fence on the third, and a creek along the back."

"One second." Grace pulled out her phone.

"You won't have reception out here," the professor said.

"I don't need it. I took screenshots of a map of the area after you called." She enlarged an image of the eastern side of his farm. "He's right. The only way we can get lost is if we wander in circles."

"And my compass app works offline." Henry pressed a few buttons on his cell. "All set."

Orion pointed toward his barn. "The creature appeared to go down beyond the back corner. It was difficult to gauge the distance, but I don't believe it was too deep in the forest."

"Are we doing this?" Ethan glanced at Faith.

She nodded and removed a flashlight from her back pocket.

"Before you go..." The professor lowered his voice. "I wasn't one-hundred-percent honest with you before."

Mom narrowed her eyes. "About?"

"I sent my niece and her friends in the wrong direction on purpose." He glanced at Faith and Ethan. "I don't know who's behind it."

His words hit Grace between the eyes. "Wait, you think your niece and her friends created the Mothman?"

He shook his head too quickly to provide any reassurance. "I didn't say that."

Henry took a few steps toward the professor. "Then what exactly *are* you trying to tell us?"

"I trust you all to do the right thing." He sucked in a breath. "What I mean is, if there's something out there, I'd rather you found it. I trust you."

"We'll do our best." Faith pointed with her chin toward the fence, and the others followed.

Flashlights in hand, the Warners made their way across the strip of cleared land. Silence hung between them as thick as the gathering storm clouds.

Henry glanced back toward the barn and stopped walking. "It's a straight line between me, the corner of the barn, and the house."

Ethan said, "Let's fan out six feet apart."

"That's too close. We should stay just beyond each other's flashlight beams." Grace shined her light in an arc in front of her. "Ten is better."

"Six feet is plenty far enough." Faith's tone left no room for argument. "And we stay together, no working ahead or falling behind."

"Yes, ma'am," the twins replied.

Keeping her eyes on the ground, Grace entered the woods. She focused her light a couple feet in front of her and worked in sweeping motions.

"Are we going to talk about the elephant in the forest?" Henry stopped walking.

"Keep up." Ethan aimed his light at his son's face. "And we should wait to discuss the situation until we're certain we're alone."

"Agreed." Faith stopped and glanced back the way they had come. "We'll go a little farther, but we head back the second we lose sight of the house lights."

They worked in a straight line, turned, and covered the same ground. When they reached the clearing, they fanned out and started the process again twenty-four feet from where they'd started.

The search continued for what felt like an eternity. Grace used the time to go over the facts as she understood them and came up with more questions than answers.

She sighed and rolled her head from side to side. In a tree not five feet from where she stood, something metallic caught her eye. "Hold up!"

Henry reached her first. "What is that?"

Inching closer, Grace trained her flashlight on the object. "I'm not sure. It looks like some sort of net."

"Check the ground around the tree. You don't want to step on any evidence." Ethan walked a wide perimeter around the discovery.

Faith squinted up at the object. "How on Earth are we going to reach it?"

Henry chuckled. "Grace and I have it covered."

She wiggled her brows. "Mineshaft maneuver?"

"You know it." He moved to the edge of the tree and dropped to one knee.

"Kids?" Ethan held up his hand.

Before Dad could tell them to stop, Grace planted one foot on Henry's thigh. Using the tree trunk for balance, she put the other on his opposite shoulder. He gripped her calf, and she brought her other foot to his shoulder.

"Steady." Henry stood slowly.

Grace reached her hand above her head and snatched the netting from the branch. "Got it."

"Impressive, but how do you get down?" Faith sounded more worried than impressed.

"The same way I got up." Grace dropped the strange object. "Catch."

Ethan let it fall to the ground in favor of holding his arms like a human safety net.

Henry slowly dropped to one knee, and she descended one foot at a time.

Mom blew out a breath. "New rule—no standing on each other's shoulders. Ever again."

"Not even in the pool?" Henry chuckled.

"Never again." Faith picked up the netting. "This is...amazing."

The family huddled, everyone staring at the delicate metallic mesh.

"I've seen that pattern before." Henry's eyes widened. "It's a piece of the Mothman's wings."

CHAPTER NINE

"Who are you?" The short female with a tall gun raised the barrel. "And what are you doing here?"

Henry held his hands up. "The Warners. Dr. Orion asked us to come."

"Dr. Warner?" The young woman shined her light over the family.

"Yes, it's me," Faith said. "Quinn, would you mind pointing that thing away from my family?"

That's her? Henry eyed the mysterious Quinn Quaglieri. She was pretty in a girl-next-door kind of way—that is, if the girl next door was decked out in camo and holding a gun the size of a cannon.

"Sorry about that." The young woman pointed the barrel at the ground. "Oliver asked you here?"

Faith said, "He wanted extra boots on the ground to help search for the creature."

"And did you?" She pointed to the netting. "Find something?"

Grace sucked in a breath, and Henry held his. Dr. Orion's confession flashed through his mind. If the professor didn't know if he could trust his own family, how could they?

"We did." Faith motioned for the woman to come closer. "It appears to be a piece of the creature's wing."

Folding his arms, Ethan watched Quinn as if daring her to try something.

"If it's missing part of its wing, it has to be around here somewhere." The young woman glanced toward the barn. "Where have you looked?"

"We started perpendicular to the barn and worked our way toward the front of the property," Ethan said.

"The creature may not be here." Grace took the mesh from Faith and held it to the light. "This is too porous to be used for flight. It's more than likely for show..."

"You mean it doesn't use its wings to fly?" Ethan cocked his head.

"No." Her eyes widened. "Unless I'm mistaken, this is used to hide rotors while still allowing airflow."

Henry ran his hand over his head. "So that's how they did it."

Quinn looked the twins over from head to toe. "You figured that out from a scrap of material?"

"We assumed it was some sort of drone hybrid because of the way it flew," Grace said.

He shrugged. "And I recognized the pattern in the netting."

"In theory, it could be a drone, but the creature is able to move its arms and make hand gestures. The materials required to make a humanoid robot that size would add a considerable amount of weight," Faith said.

"Hand gestures?" Quinn's voice quivered. "What sort of hand gestures?"

"It pointed at me. Orion said it slid its finger across its throat." Henry turned to his mother. "Did it do anything to you and the other judges?"

"Yes. Much the same, and it waved."

Quinn swayed. "That can't be."

Grace started to speak, but Faith shook her head while the young woman wasn't looking.

Ethan glanced between them. "Should we continue the search?"

"Yes," Quinn said.

"No." Faith took the netting from Grace. "It's late. I'll contact the local authorities and the national FARST representative in the morning. Whoever is doing this has broken several laws."

Even in the dim light, Henry saw the color drain from Quinn's face.

"The FAA rarely enforces their commercial drone regulations." The woman seemed to realize she'd said the wrong thing and waved her hand. "I mean, definitely contact the FARST people, but the local police won't know what to do about it. They'll probably blow it off as a prank."

Faith narrowed her eyes. "Your uncle was missing for over forty-eight hours. Do you have any idea how much that sort of search costs? I'm quite sure the town would like to know where to send the bill."

Henry almost felt sorry for Quinn. He'd been on the receiving end of his mother's anger once or twice in his life and swore never to end up there again.

However, much of the young woman's reaction made him suspect she'd master-minded the entire ordeal.

"I understand...but the college... This will be a black-eye on the engineering program." Quinn's voice cracked.

Ethan Warner rarely frowned, and he had never frowned at his wife—until then. "She's right. We should find those who perpetrated this hoax before we decide how to proceed."

"If this hasn't been resolved by Sunday, I'm going to the authorities." Faith glanced at each of them as if to make sure they understood she meant business. "We are going home."

Quinn and the Warners trudged back toward the Orion farm.

Henry motioned for Grace to hold back. Once the others were out of earshot, he whispered, "We need to corner Dr. Orion."

"Agreed, but Mom seems determined to get home."

"Distract her with engineering talk when we get to the house."

Faith glanced over her shoulder. "Stop dawdling."

"Sorry." Grace smiled.

Bugs, Skinny Jimmy, and a handful of other camo-wearing guys met the Warners on their way across the field. Bugs lifted a brow, but Quinn shook her head. He frowned and motioned for the others to follow.

Dr. Orion stood when they approached. He'd stopped sweating but looked no less nervous. "Did you find anything?"

"A piece of material we believe came from the creature's wing." Faith made no move to show the man the mesh.

"But not the creature?"

She shook her head. "You'll have to excuse us. It's late."

"Mom, the professors would recognize their team's work, right?" Grace blurted out the question as if it'd just occurred to her, but Henry knew better.

Faith seemed to consider the possibility. "Yes, if the students responsible for this had received approval for the project, but that's highly unlikely."

Henry leaned closer to Dr. Orion. "May I use your bathroom?"

The professor glanced between him and Faith. "Of course. It's the third—"

"Show me." Henry smiled to soften his words. "Please. I have a thing about other people's homes."

Ethan gave him a knowing smile and walked to his wife.

Oliver nodded. "Right this way."

Henry waited until they reached a long hall before turning to the man. "I'd like to know why you stayed in the hunting cabin instead of finding your way back to the parking area once the sun rose."

The professor winced. "I was lost. There were bears."

"Bears? You've got to be kidding me." Quinn stood at the far end of the hall with her arms folded. "Try again, and this time, I want the truth."

Henry took a step back.

"Quinn..."

"You've been to the cabin a million times. You could have found your way back, but you let Auntie O suffer." She closed the distance, stopping when she was toe to toe with the professor.

Staring at the family photos, Henry attempted to blend into the wall. One picture in particular caught his eye. Quinn as a little girl, a man who looked vaguely familiar, and Mary-freaking-Mason. *What the heck?*

"It was a different cabin," the professor said.

"Bull. I know it was you. I was staying there for a couple of days to avoid the craziness of the competition. After you were found, I went back to get my things. Imagine my surprise when I found your jacket." She pressed her index finger against his chest. "Tell me why."

His voice cracked. "I needed time to think. I figured it out."

"You figured what out?" Quinn balled her hands into fists.

The professor sighed. "The creature. The way it moved its hands. I recognized your tech."

The young woman froze. "Me?"

"I'm going to fix this." He ran his hand over his balding head.

"Fix what? You honestly believe I'd risk a full scholarship to Johns Hopkins by terrorizing a bunch of FARST judges?" She covered her mouth with both hands. "The accident. You actually think I'd do that to you and Auntie O? I'd never put you two in danger!"

"Everything all right in here?" Bugs called into the hall.

"No. It's not." Quinn looked at Henry as if she'd forgotten he was there. "I didn't do this."

He nodded, and he meant it. Unless she'd studied drama in her spare time, there was no way she could have faked her reaction.

Quinn ran from the house with Bugs on her heels.

Professor Orion slumped against the wall. "If not her, then who?"

The representative from Future Applied Robotic Sciences and Technology called an emergency meeting Saturday morning to discuss the problems plaguing the competition. While Ethan Warner had joined his wife in the closed-door session, the twins opted to do some problem-solving of their own.

"I still don't understand who's related to who." Grace sketched a stick-figure-tree. "Mom referred to Professor Orion as Quinn's uncle."

"Right." Henry rubbed his forehead. "And I saw a photo of a man Professor Orion's age, Quinn, and Mary Mason. My guess is the guy in the photo is Orion's brother."

"The last names are different. If you're right, he's related to Mrs. Orion." She tapped her lips. "We need to figure out who he is and why he looked familiar to you."

"It could be my imagination." He sighed. "There was a lot going on in that hallway last night."

"We aren't going to figure this out now, and we have a more important mission to accomplish."

"Agreed."

Grace chewed her lip. "Hargrave is in the conference room, but I haven't seen David. He wasn't in the exhibition hall."

"He has to be on campus." Henry's stomach growled. "Let's check the cafeteria."

"Forget it. You ate a half-dozen pancakes and a pound of bacon before we left this morning." She stuffed her notebook into her bag. "Come on, he's Orion's assistant. He has to have a desk near the professor's office."

"Unless he's moved in with Hargrave."

"That'll be our next stop." She forced her shoulders to relax and walked down the hall toward the faculty offices.

Henry pointed to a tidy desk outside Orion's door. A photo of David holding a huge fish sat next to the monitor. "This has to be it."

"Are you sure? What kind of person displays a photo of themselves in their workspace?"

"People like David Dillinger." He motioned to the end of the hall. "Stand guard while I search the drawers."

"No one keeps paper calendars anymore." She nodded at the computer. "Look for a Post-It with his password."

"I'm on it. Go."

Grace hurried to the end of the hall. It was Saturday morning. Other than a couple of students in visiting university sweatshirts, the faculty area of the building was empty. Though, they had no idea when the FARST meeting would end and the faculty would return to their offices.

She glanced over her shoulder, and her heart skipped a beat. Evidently, Henry found the computer password because he had his phone out taking pictures of whatever was on the screen. Movement in the corner of her eye caught her attention.

Quinn Quaglieri took one look at Grace and frowned.

Oh no. Hurry up, Henry. Hurry, the heck, up!

"Hi." Grace walked toward Quinn in hopes of keeping her from glancing down the hall and catching him in the act. "All of the professors are in an emergency meeting."

"Then what are you doing here?"

"Waiting for Henry to get out of the bathroom." She forced a smile.

David Dillinger came around the corner and narrowed his eyes. "Well, well, well. What do we have here? Discussing a fictitious job with a fictitious candidate?"

Grace's brain screeched to a halt. She couldn't form a thought, let alone a word.

The jerk took her silence as a win. "That's right. I know you made the entire thing up, but what I can't figure out is why."

"Don't you have some puppies to kick or something?" Quinn deadpanned.

"Whatever." He glared between them. "I've accepted a position with Dr. Hargrave at UCLA, so you," He pointed at Quinn, "can tell your uncle he didn't lose the position as dean to a better candidate. He lost because he's a..." David hesitated as if searching for the right word.

"Loser?" Quinn folded her arms.

David made a checkmark with his finger and turned to Grace. "And you're a waste of my time. I have work to do. The competition must go on."

Resting his hand on Grace's shoulder, Henry said, "Or must it? The FARST rep is deciding that as we speak."

David's mouth moved, but no words came out.

Quinn smirked. "You didn't know about the meeting?"

"Of course, I knew." He turned on his heel and marched away.

Quinn shook her head. "Don't let him get to you. He and Hargrave deserve each other."

"I've met her only once. I have met David at least twice now. I'm not sure I disagree," Grace said.

"Try having her as a faculty advisor." The young woman cracked a smile. "She made my life miserable for the last four years, and my dad is a tenured professor in the engineering department."

The twins exchanged glances.

"That was why I recognized him. He was at the opening ceremonies." Henry hung his head.

Grace felt as if she'd only caught half the conversation. "Who?"

"Dr. Callen is my stepfather." Quinn stared at Henry.

Although she now had the missing information, Grace still felt as though she'd missed something. "That would make Mary Mason your great-aunt?"

Quinn furrowed her brow. "How do you know Mary?"

Henry motioned to a table and chairs. "We should sit. This is going to take a few minutes."

The twins explained everything from their year-long research project to the clues they'd uncovered about the Mothman drone.

When they were finished, Quinn sat back in her chair and laughed. "First off, that is the coolest project ever. Second, what did you find in David's calendar?"

Henry pulled out his phone and showed them the photo of the schedule. Big black Xs filled Sunday, Tuesday, and Friday nights. "It's circumstantial evidence, but he marked off each time the creature made an appearance."

"He's not smart enough to pull something like this off." She started to say more but hesitated.

"What is it?" Grace touched Quinn's arm. "You can trust us. We've told you everything."

"The creature...as you heard from my uncle, it *is* my technology."

Henry sat up straighter. "But you're not the one doing this?"

"No. I made it my senior year of high school. Granted, the exoskeleton and wings are completely different, but I designed the Mothman drone."

"Why?" The twins asked.

"Every year Point Pleasant has a Mothman Festival. It's great for the local economy. I made it to be a crowd pleaser, but I never used it. My great aunt was ill. I was too busy taking care of her to finish it. And then I went to college and mothballed the project."

"You designed that in high school?" Grace felt faint. She'd never doubted her academic talents, but then again, she'd never compared herself to a prodigy. "The technology is incredible."

Quinn shrugged. "It earned me a scholarship to Johns Hopkins Biomedical Engineering program, but I had to pass it up to take care of Auntie Mary."

Henry said, "I don't understand. It's your tech, but—"

"Someone stole my work, and I need to find out who before I'm blamed for the entire fiasco."

CHAPTER TEN

Henry turned at the sound of footsteps. Wesleyan faculty, along with robotics team members filled the hall, but he ignored them all except his parents and Dr. Orion. The trio marched toward the twins like harbingers of doom. Evidently, the meeting hadn't gone well.

"This looks bad." Henry sat straighter.

"Very." Grace glanced at Quinn, who swallowed hard.

Dr. Orion spoke without slowing his stride. "It's good you are all together. Please follow me into my office."

The twins hurried to repack their bags, but Quinn didn't move.

Grace turned to the young woman. "Are you coming?"

"Yes, sorry." She pushed to her feet and followed them into the professor's office.

Ethan Warner closed the door and motioned to an empty chair in front of the desk. "Miss Quaglieri, please sit."

"I'll stand."

Henry leaned against the doorjamb and folded his arms. Whatever happened in the meeting had to do with Quinn, which likely meant she'd run out of time to find out who'd stolen her drone.

Professor Orion leveled his gaze on the young woman. "Hargrave presented proof that you developed the technology used to create the Mothman."

She sank into the chair. "That's correct, but I'm not responsible for what's happened since. Someone stole my drone, finished the exoskeleton, and added new wings."

Faith set her hand on Quinn's shoulder. "Do you have any idea who?"

She glanced between the adults in the room. "If I had to guess, I'd say Hargrave or David Dillinger. As my faculty advisor, she knew about the project."

Orion sat back and steepled his fingers beneath his chin. "And Dillinger?"

Quinn turned and met Henry's gaze.

He froze. She hadn't outed him for breaking into David's computer, but she could any second.

"Henry, is there something you'd like to add?" Ethan asked.

Grace said, "David doesn't have an alibi for any of the nights the creature appeared in Buckhannon."

"And you know this how?" Faith raised a single brow.

All moisture left his mouth. *So long, freedom. Hello, grounded until college.* "I have photos of his calendar."

His mother continued to stare. She wouldn't let the subject end without further explanation.

"His computer password was in his desk drawer."

The elder Warners exchanged wide-eyed glances.

The professor chuckled. "I don't suppose you checked Hargrave's schedule while you were at it?"

"No." Henry lowered his gaze.

Grace cleared her throat. "What happens now?"

"I believe grounding is in order," Ethan sputtered.

"I understand, but I meant, what happens with Quinn?"

The amusement drained from Dr. Orion's face. "Dr. Hargrave plans to start disciplinary procedures. She claims this was an unauthorized project conducted with college resources."

"Because the so-called project disrupted the FARST competition, I'm afraid the college will have no choice but to pursue expulsion to save their reputation." Faith's voice thinned. "In addition, the matter will be turned over to the police."

Quinn slumped. "Why is Hargrave doing this? I'm supposed to graduate in May."

None of the adults replied.

Henry stared at his father unable to comprehend how a man who'd dedicated his life to the justice system would stand there and do nothing. "This is unacceptable. We have to do something."

Ethan's jaw tensed. "I completely agree. However, I'm not sure what we *can* do. We're leaving tomorrow evening after the competition."

"If there *is* a competition," Faith said.

"What do you mean?" Grace's knee bobbed, a sure sign she was as impatient to get back to work as Henry.

Continuing to watch Quinn, Dr. Orion said, "We are still one judge short. Your stepdad hasn't returned."

"I don't care about the competition." Henry pushed off the wall and squared his shoulders. "I refuse to give up. We have twenty-four hours to prove Quinn didn't do this."

Grace nodded. "That's more than enough time to sort this out with the six of us working on it."

Faith sighed, which was not exactly the reaction Henry had hoped for.

"Kids, I admire your determination, but like it or not, Mom's working to save the competition, and I—"

"Your father volunteered to stand in as a guest judge. The FARST rep is contacting the powers that be to see if it's allowed since he isn't in the field." Faith turned to Henry. "I believe things will go easier for Quinn if the college is able to finish the competition."

He knew she was right, but an innocent woman's future hung in the balance. "Grace and I will do this on our own if we have to."

Quinn raised her hand. "And me. I'm not going down without a fight."

"I understand we're grounded, but could you possibly postpone it until tomorrow night?" Grace pressed her hands together. "Please."

"You have our permission to do what you must to resolve this." Faith motioned between them. "As long as it's legal."

"Thank you," the twins said.

Faith turned back to Quinn. "I owe you an apology. I showed the piece of mesh we found at the farm to the committee members, including Professor Hargrave."

Keeping her gaze on the ground, Quinn nodded. "It's not your fault. I keep thinking I should have come forward the moment I realized what was going on."

"We should get back to the meeting." Orion stood, walked around the desk and pulled Quinn into an embrace. "You've already given up so much to take care of Mary. I promise you, I'll do everything in my power to set this right."

The young woman tensed for two heartbeats before collapsing against her uncle. "I'm sorry for the things I said to you."

Sighing, he closed his eyes. "And I'm sorry for making a bad situation worse."

Henry wanted to ask for clarification from the professor, but he needed to tread lightly in front of his parents. Unfortunately, the adults hurried from the room before he found the right words.

Waiting until the door closed, Grace asked, "What did he mean about making it worse?"

"I don't know, but it doesn't matter right now." Quinn wiped her eyes on the back of her hand. "How do we go about proving Hargrave stole my tech?"

"First thing, check her calendar." Henry motioned to the door.

Quinn stood and moved to the other side of the desk. Without a word, she booted up Orion's computer and logged in.

"Faculty members have shared calendars?" Grace grinned.

"Yep." Leaning closer to the screen, she frowned. "Sunday, Tuesday, and last night?"

"Yes." He stared over her shoulder.

"If this is correct, she was either in meetings, out to dinner with the judges, or getting her hair done when the monster appeared."

Grace snapped a picture of the screen. "We knew about the dinner, but we need to verify the other two appointments. Besides, it only takes one person to fly the drone. She could have arranged to be in a crowd on those nights to cover her backside."

"This is true." Quinn's expression brightened. "Have either of you considered the fact that all of the current judges are in the building right now?"

A slow smile spread across Henry's face. He liked the way the woman thought. "This would be the perfect time for the Mothman to make an appearance."

Grace shook her head. "Why bother? Hargrave already pinned it on Quinn."

"Yes, but in case you haven't noticed, David is a megalomaniac. It'd be hard for him to resist one more shot at the spotlight." She rubbed her hands together. "Meet me at the northern exit. I may be able to override the drone's control system."

Grace surveyed the area outside the exit closest to the meeting room. Buildings lined three sides of the courtyard, and the fourth side opened to the manicured green in front of the massive chapel. Other than a handful of trees, the area didn't have much cover.

Henry pointed to the structure on the left. "My guess is the person controlling the drone will have it circle a few times and disappear."

"I agree. There's no sense in trying to cover the green." She nodded toward the bookstore. "Cebe Ross Field is behind that building, along with the closest parking lot. My guess is, it'll come from that way."

"We should split up. You take the corner closest to the bookstore. I'll take the one nearest the science building."

Grace hesitated. Every time they'd split up on other cases, terrible things had happened. "Or we could stay together in the center."

"I know what you're thinking, but this isn't like the other mysteries. We're on a college campus, not in the middle of nowhere. We'll be able to keep a visual on each other."

"Fine, but I reserve the right to say I told you so. And I want to stay closest to the exit in case Quinn comes out."

He held up his hands. "As you wish, Buttercup."

She grinned at the reference to her favorite fantasy movie, *The Princess Bride.* "Go. The meeting could end any time now."

An hour passed, and the faculty still hadn't emerged from the building—and neither had Quinn. Grace scanned the sky for signs of the Mothman drone for the millionth time. She doubted David or whoever was flying it would be stupid enough to bring it out again. Then again, David didn't seem like the reddest apple in the bushel.

Ethan Warner stepped out the door.

Grace remained in place and typed a quick text to Henry. **Dad's out.**

I see him.

She held her breath, waiting for the rest of the FARST people to emerge from the building.

No one came out.

"Dad." She waved to him from her hiding spot.

He looked past her once before he caught sight of her. "What are you doing outside? It's freezing."

"Come over here, please."

Glancing over his shoulder every few steps, Ethan walked toward her. "Is there a reason you're slinking around in the shadows?"

"With all of the judges in one place, we thought this would be the perfect time—"

"For the Mothman?" He tilted his head back and scanned the sky. "I doubt it will show. Dr. Hargrave already let the cat out of the bag, so to speak."

She resisted the urge to agree with him and blame Henry and Quinn for her standing outside in the cold. "How much longer is the meeting going to last?"

"They should be out any second now. The committee was voting on appointing me as an interim judge, but it doesn't look good." His voice softened. "Gracie, you know Mom and I want to help Quinn. We believe in her innocence, but the circumstances—"

An ear-piercing whistle split the night air.

"That's Henry." Grace searched overhead for the creature.

Her brother waved his cell and pointed skyward.

"I don't see it," Ethan said.

"Me either. It must be behind us."

The door to the science building opened, and Quinn ran to the center of the courtyard. She had a dark object about the size of a shoebox in her hands.

"What's she doing?" Shouting, Ethan split his attention between Quinn and the door.

"I think it's an alternate controller for the drone."

"If the others see her..." He darted toward the young woman.

Everything happened at once, yet time seemed to slow. The door to the building opened, people poured out, and the Mothman flew overhead. Dad reached Quinn, but not before a couple of the judges spotted her with the controller.

"Oh, no." Grace's pulse raced.

"We've caught her red-handed!" Dr. Hargrave turned to the others.

They descended into a chorus of demands for immediate disciplinary action. If someone didn't do something, they'd likely hang Quinn from the nearest tree.

Faith Warner waved her arms over her head. "Everyone calm down! I'm sure there's a logical explanation for this."

No sooner than the words came out of her mouth than the Mothman buzzed the crowd. Upstanding members of academia hit the ground in a flurry of screams, grunts, and curse words.

"I'm trying to override the other controller!" Quinn continued to press buttons and wiggle joysticks.

The creature circled high overhead and dove again. This time the bottom of its filmy robes grazed the angry judges.

"What did I tell you?" Dusting herself off, Professor Hargrave emerged from the ball of confusion. "The girl clearly has psychological issues."

"Quaglieri, I order you to stop this nonsense right this minute!" A middle-aged man wearing a University of Florida sweatshirt stamped his foot like a toddler.

The Mothman, or more specifically, the person controlling it, dove for the Florida Gator. The poor man shrieked and ran for the trees.

"Look!" Running into the fray, Henry blew his whistle, pointed, and blew it again. "Up there!"

Grace scanned the top of the building and gasped. The Mothman stood on the rooftop staring down at the crowd.

"That's impossible! It flew in the other direction!" The professor from UF gawked like a fish in an oxygen tank.

Everyone stared at the creature on the roof.

Grace could practically smell the synapses in their brains frying. Sure, a few of hers had short-circuited too, but there had to be a logical explanation.

Dr. Hargrave smirked. "It circled back. Now, will someone take the controls from Miss Quaglieri before one of us is injured?"

The Mothman on top of the building turned and *ran*.

Quinn gasped. "The legs aren't robotic!"

Dr. Orion inserted himself between his niece and the others. "She's right. It's never used its legs, only its hands and arms."

"Come on." Henry grabbed Grace's wrist and pulled her toward the building.

"Where are you two going?" Ethan called after them.

"After it," Henry said as if that explained anything.

Grace followed, although she thought her brother had likely lost his mind. The building was three stories high. Surely, by the time they reached the roof, whatever that thing was would be gone.

The twins hit the stairwell at a dead run with a parade of parents, judges, and faculty following. As they reached the landing on the second floor, something crashed in the hall on the other side of the door.

Grace peered through the rectangular glass window and caught a glimpse of a wing disappearing into one of the empty classrooms. "There it is."

Henry put his hand on the handle, but Ethan stopped him.

"Stay here." Ethan pushed past them and ran down the hall.

The twins looked at each other, frowned, and followed. They reached the classroom in time to see their father drop a shoulder and tackle the Mothman.

A distinctly feminine wail came from the creature, but it fought back valiantly—kicking, punching, and screaming in an all-too-human voice.

Grace's heart leapt into her throat. "It's a woman."

Henry watched the scene before him with wide eyes.

A handful of adults crowded into the doorway and froze. Like the twins, they stared, awestruck, watching Ethan Warner wrestle with the winged creature.

Dad took a punch to the gut and eased off. "A little help here!"

The Florida Gator pushed his way into the room.

The costumed woman showed no signs of giving up. She moved with the grace of a ballet dancer and the efficiency of a ninja. Hands, feet, and wings struck the men. When that failed, she turned to a shelf and lobbed textbooks at the men.

Grace had the distinct impression her father could have taken the woman in the Mothman costume down, but he seemed to be holding back, as if trying to subdue her without hurting her.

"Easy." Ethan locked eyes with the Florida Gator and nodded to the left, and the other man faked left and lunged to the right. The woman hesitated for a split second—enough time for Ethan to slip behind her.

He reached between the wings and grabbed the back of the helmet-like mask.

One, two, three tugs later it separated from the rest of the costume but didn't come off. Likely sensing defeat, she sank to her knees. "Enough."

The Gator stepped in front of the person and ripped the mask free.

Mary Mason hung her head.

Henry's mouth fell open. "No freaking way!"

Certain her legs would go out from under her, Grace clutched a desk to stay upright.

Somewhere in the hall, Quinn cried out, "Auntie Mary?"

The older woman turned her head. "I'm sorry, sweetheart."

"Why?" Quinn raised a trembling hand to her throat. "Why would you do this?"

"Don't blame her. This is my fault." Professor Orion made his way into the room and offered Mary his hand.

The people whispered, but one voice came through loud and clear—Dr.

Hargrave. "They're trying to cover for Quinn. This is a ruse to throw us off-track."

"You have it half-right. When I recognized the creature as Quinn's work, I assumed she was behind this. I enlisted Mrs. Mason and my brother-in-law to dress as the Mothman to create a distraction."

"Why didn't you come to me?" Quinn stared between her uncle and great-aunt.

Orion slipped his arm around Mary's waist and helped her to her feet. "I'd planned to when I invited you to the house for dinner, but before I had the chance, I was convinced it wasn't you. I told them to stop the ruse, but—"

Mary Mason elbowed him in the ribs. "But nothing. I had to try one last time to clear your name."

"By playing dress-up?" Quinn's voice cracked.

"Why should we believe any of this is true? The entire family has tried to deceive us," Professor Hargrave shouted.

"Okay, everyone out." Holding her arms wide, Faith walked into the hall. "We've heard enough. We need to give them a few moments alone."

Dr. Hargrave opened her mouth as if to argue, but snapped it shut and followed the herd of professors back to the courtyard.

Grace caught Henry's gaze, bugged out her eyes, and nodded to a quiet corner.

He'd taken one step when his father clamped a hand on his shoulder and pointed toward the sky.

Silhouetted against the light of the moon, the Mothman circled overhead.

CHAPTER ELEVEN

"Quinn is inside with her family. Who's flying the drone?" Henry spoke loud enough for the crowd to hear.

As if on cue, the creature flew toward the athletic field.

Hargrave rolled her eyes and scoffed. "She still has the controller."

"It wasn't in her hand when she walked into the classroom, and it's too large to fit in her pocket." The professor from the University of Florida scratched his jaw. "I don't know what's going on around here, but I'm not sure we're pinning this on the right person."

Three or four others nodded.

"Grace and I have work to do," Henry whispered to his father.

"Do you have money for a rideshare home?" Ethan asked without taking his eyes off the debate being waged in the center of the courtyard.

"We do, but it looks like you guys are going to be here for a while."

"You may be right." He sighed and stepped into the crowd.

Shaking her head at the adults, Grace turned to Henry. "I have a plan. Let's get inside before they lock the building for the night."

"Good idea." Henry stuck to the shadows, slipping away without Hargrave or anyone else noticing where they were going.

Once inside, Grace led him through the exhibition hall.

"Where are we going?"

She grinned. "Remember what Mom said? The visiting robotics teams have workspaces here, but the Wesleyan students work in labs. I'm thinking we should investigate David's."

"Right, but how do we know which one is his?" As soon as he'd said the words, he remembered his mother's clipboard. "The scoring sheets."

Grace bit her lip. "I'm sure they lock them up. Plus, is it legal to break into the judges' booth?"

"We aren't competing, nor are we looking at the scores." Henry was convinced he stood on firm ground.

The twins hurried to the cordoned-off area reserved for officials. Someone had tidied the booth since the last time he'd seen it. Other than a few random pens, the tables were empty.

Henry slipped under the yellow caution tape to get a better look. "This is disappointing."

"Hurry."

"Relax. No one's in here." He found a box of files beneath the skirted table at the front of the booth and crouched to get a better look.

She looked from side to side as if her head were on a swivel.

Henry heard her gasp and footsteps, but he didn't dare move.

"Grace? When I didn't see you outside, I thought you'd gone home for the night." Quinn stood beside Dr. Orion and Mary Mason.

"We're heading out in a few minutes." She spoke loud enough that her voice echoed through the cavernous room. "Henry had to use the restroom."

He crawled halfway under the table and prayed they couldn't see him.

"Thanks for everything you've done, but I'm calling it a night." Quinn sighed.

"I'm sorry about the scuffle with my dad. Are you okay?" Grace said, presumably to Mary.

"I'll be fine. I'd like to think I gave him a good fight, but I think he was going easy on me."

"You're very agile."

Come on, Grace. Now isn't the time for chit-chat. Henry's neck cramped. He rolled his head from side to side and grinned. A list of participants and their workstations rested on top of the box.

"Good night, Grace. Thank you again for your assistance," Dr. Orion said.

He waited until the hugs stopped and their footsteps faded before he scurried from beneath the table.

"It's clear. Did you find anything?" Grace continued to glance around.

"Room 203. Let's go."

David Dillinger's workspace looked like a machine had exploded. Pieces and parts of metal littered every available space, including the floor. Wires and screws and circuit boards filled the smaller spaces. In short, it was a disaster zone.

Henry pinched the bridge of his nose. "I hope you know what we're looking for."

"I'll know it when I see it." She didn't sound convinced. In fact, she sounded exhausted. "It'd be a lot easier if we could turn on the light."

He used the glow from his cell to keep from tripping over the debris. "Tell me about it."

Grace worked methodically, searching the tables along the perimeter. Every now and then she'd pick up a gizmo or gadget and hold it closer to her phone.

"Can I help?" He knew how most machines and electronics worked but had no idea how to put them together.

"Keep an eye out for netting like we found at the Orions'. Otherwise, probably not." She moved to a small filing cabinet and eased the top drawer open. "Actually, there is something you can do. Go through these schematics. You're looking for anything—"

"—that looks like a humanoid drone." He laughed and walked to her side. "Give me some credit. I live with you and Mom. I know a little about how this stuff works."

Voices echoed from down the hall—two males. Neither sounded like David Dillinger, but the guy worked with a team. Not to mention, Henry had no desire to explain what they were doing in the lab.

Grace's eyes shot wide. She glanced around quickly and darted behind a large piece of equipment.

Henry slid between the filing cabinet and the wall. Not exactly the best cover, but it was better than nothing.

Light flooded the room, leaving Henry seeing spots.

"Did you hear the professor from Florida scream like a little girl?" The guy laughed.

The voice sounded vaguely familiar, but he couldn't place it.

A second male said, "It's hard to miss a man that size in a bright orange sweatshirt. Help me find the spare rotors. It's time the Mothman retired."

The door flew open. "What the heck happened out there? It came too close to the ground! You could have damaged the drone. Again."

David Dillinger. Henry would have recognized that nasally whine anywhere.

"What does it matter? We're done. The competition is going to be canceled."

Henry had lost track of the speakers, but he understood the context. David and the other two men were responsible for everything that had happened. All that was left was to confront them. He drew a breath and gathered his courage.

"What was Quinn doing? She wasn't supposed to be here."

Henry froze. *Did she have something to do with this after all?*

"Trying to override the control, but she couldn't get through the safety measures I added."

"What safety measures? Did you document the changes?" David sounded like he'd moved closer.

"Why should I? Like I said. It's done. The drone goes back in the barn where it belongs."

"No, it doesn't." David barked a laugh. "We're going to take it apart. It's coming with me to UCLA this summer."

"That wasn't part of the deal." The guy's West Virginia accent bled through.

Skinny Jimmy. Henry finally placed the voice.

Henry unfurled himself from his hiding spot. "That's not happening."

"It's absolutely not happening." Grace stepped out from behind what looked like a piece of a fuselage and blinked. "Jimmy? Bugs? Why would you do this to Quinn?"

David turned as white as the walls. "What are you doing in my lab?"

"*Our* lab." Bugs folded his arms and met Grace's gaze. "I did this *for* Quinn."

Keeping an eye on the men, Henry moved to his sister's side. "Are you aware that she's facing expulsion?"

"They have no idea what they're talking about." David waved his hand. "But they know too much. We can't just let them walk out of here."

Jimmy's eyes widened. "They're just kids, and I never signed up to hurt anyone."

Ignoring his teammates, Bugs focused on Grace. "What do you mean, expulsion?"

She lifted her chin. "Dr. Hargrave went to the FARST committee this morning and accused Quinn of engineering the Mothman drone. They were in a closed-door session all day. They decided to turn her over to the college for disciplinary action, but David already knows this."

Dillinger took several backward steps.

Henry nodded. "The college has a huge black eye because of the fiasco with the competition. Expulsion is the least of her concerns. She'll be arrested for FAA violations to start with, but there will more than likely be other charges."

Jimmy glanced at the twins and Bugs. "You said it wasn't illegal?"

"I said they never prosecuted people flying hobby drones." He scratched the stubble on his jawline. "David, did you know about this?"

Dillinger stopped a few feet from the door. "I had no idea."

"He's Hargrave's lapdog. He knew." Skinny Jimmy shook his head. "We can't let this happen, Bugs. We can't. Not to Quinn. It ain't right."

"What about your *Aunty O*?" David said the name as if it were something foul. "Are you going to come clean and send her to jail along with you?"

Grace gasped. "Mrs. Orion is involved in this?"

Bugs sat on the edge of a table and glanced out the window. "Shut up, David."

He didn't shut up. If anything he took Bugs' reluctance to answer her question as a sign of weakness. "Think about it. The only ones who can implicate us are standing right here. We can fix this. Everything will be fine. We just have to shut them up."

"I'm not going to hurt a couple of kids." Jimmy moved to stand between the twins and his teammates.

"Do you really want to spend the rest of your life here?" David softened his tone. "I thought the plan was for you to make something of yourself. Impress Quinn. Buy the white picket fence in some swanky New England town and live happily ever after."

Bugs scowled. "What do you suggest we do with them?"

David turned his back on the twins. "I'm not saying we have to hurt them ourselves. You know the mountains. I'm sure there's somewhere we can leave them that they'll never be found."

Henry glanced at his sister, not sure if it was to reassure her or himself. He couldn't believe it. She'd used the skinniest guy in history to block David's and Bugs' view and had her cell phone in her hand.

Bugs sighed and pushed to his feet. "Have the professors left campus?"

Dillinger moved to the window. "Lot's empty except for a truck, but I believe it belongs to these two."

"We do this and find a way to pin it on someone else. Quinn doesn't get hurt by this." He glanced at Henry, winked, and shook his head while David wasn't looking.

What the heck? He's bluffing? Henry hoped he'd read the signals right.

Bugs turned back to Dillinger. "You hear me? I'll send the three of us to prison for life before I let anything happen to Quinn."

The weasel of a man paled. "It won't come to that."

"What are you saying?" Jimmy's voice thinned. "You can't mean you're going to leave them to die somewhere!"

"What choice do we have?" Bugs sighed.

Wide-eyed, David pointed at Grace. "What is she doing?"

"We aren't the only ones who know the truth." Grace lifted her cell phone so the others could see it. "I recorded this entire conversation and texted it to my parents. They were waiting for us downstairs the entire time."

Henry swallowed past the lump of ice-cold fear in his throat. *She's bluffing too.*

CHAPTER TWELVE

Grace couldn't lie to save her life—until she had to do just that. The lie was easy since all she had to do was say the words. Making sure they believed her presented the real challenge.

Keep it together. Her body revolted. Still waving the phone like an idiot, she fought to keep herself upright. A line of sweat ran down her back, although she trembled as if she stood on a block of ice. Her mouth went dry, and her head spun.

"She's lying. Check her cell." David took another step toward the door, although Grace couldn't tell if he planned to lock it or run.

Skinny Jimmy twisted enough to hold his hand out to her, but not enough to turn his back on David. "Give it to me."

Glancing at Henry, she pressed her lips together, dipped her chin, and hoped he picked up her meaning. She'd bluffed. There was no text to their parents. No help would come. They were on their own.

He winked. "Her passcode is Nikola Tesla's birthday, 0-7-1-0."

"Now." David's voice rose in pitch and volume.

Skinny Jimmy took the phone from her, punched in the numbers, and frowned.

Time slowed. Grace held her breath waiting for him to say the words that would lead to Bugs and David dumping them in a ravine somewhere.

"She's telling the truth." He held the power button down until the screen went dark and slid the phone into his back pocket.

David Dillinger turned and ran.

Bugs stared at the open door for several seconds before turning his attention back to the twins. "You two can go."

Grace blew out a breath and headed for the exit.

However, Henry remained in place.

"Don't forget your phone." Skinny Jimmy held it out to her.

Snatching the phone from the man's hand, she gave her brother a what-the-heck look. "What are you doing? Let's get out of here."

Henry stared at Bugs. "Why'd you do it?"

"Which part?" The guy's hollow laughter sent a chill down Grace's spine. He'd lost all hope, given up, and resigned himself to his future—but that could change, and the twins could find themselves stranded in the wilderness.

"Henry, I'm not kidding. Let's go." She put herself in his line of vision. "He was going to kill us."

"No, he wasn't." He offered her a weak smile before turning his attention back to Bugs. "Were you?"

"Nope."

Skinny Jimmy sighed. "I don't know how the kid figured it out, but you had me going there."

"He signaled when David wasn't looking," Henry said without taking his eyes off Bugs. "Why'd you steal Quinn's tech?"

"Long story short..." He shoved his hands in his hoodie pockets. "I had a point to prove. Quinn was devastated when the FARST committee disqualified the team from the competition. I wanted to show the judges her creation."

Grace believed him but knew there was more. Much more. "You wanted to make them pay for hurting her. Otherwise, you would have had the Mothman dance into the award ceremony tossing rose petals."

Jimmy grinned.

"That's correct."

She nodded, feeling vindicated that their previous theories about the person's motive weren't entirely off-base. "What happened to your West Virginia accents?"

"When you and your daddy turned up with Orion, I figured you were fixin' to start puttin' the pieces together. We thought we'd throw you off our trail by talkin' like a couple of hillbillies." Bugs laid on the accent thicker than he had the night they'd first met.

Jimmy frowned. "No one pays attention to a couple o' hicks."

Grace had met all sorts of people while traveling with her parents. She believed all humans were equal and inherently good, at least until they gave her a reason to believe otherwise. "That's not true."

Bugs grinned. "Isn't it? Did you for one second imagine we were engineering students?"

Ashamed, she looked away.

"I didn't think so." He motioned to the door. "You two should go. I'd appreciate the chance to speak to Quinn and my family before they hear about this from someone else."

"Actually, I'd rather stay." As if to prove his point, Henry moved several circuit boards out of his way and sat on the table. "What was the purpose of flying the drone over Professor Orion's farm?"

"We were trying to hide the darned thing in the barn, but it malfunctioned and the eye-lights came on. Oliver spotted it and lost his marbles," Jimmy explained.

Their story rang true, but Grace still had questions. "How does Hargrave fit into this?"

"She doesn't." Bugs smirked. "If anything, she threw a wrench into our plans when she recognized Quinn's technology."

"And Mrs. Orion?"

Jimmy and Bugs exchanged glances.

"You'll need to tell us the entire story so we can figure out a way to help." She glanced at Henry to confirm he was on board with finding a way to save the guys from themselves.

He nodded.

Bugs narrowed his eyes. "Why would you help us?"

"Because no one deserves to have their future ruined over one bad decision."

"Agreed." Henry motioned for Bugs to answer the question.

Jimmy caved first. "Unveiling the Mothman was her idea. She thought it would force the judges to acknowledge Quinn's talent. Her mistake was enlisting Dillinger to give her information on the events."

Grace said, "You can't let him claim Quinn's technology as his own."

Bugs stood and paced the room. "I don't intend to. I'll turn myself in and take full responsibility for this mess."

"No." Henry grinned. "I have an idea. Grace, get Betty on the phone. We need Dr. Callen's phone number."

"Betty?" Jimmy furrowed his brow. "You know Betty from the Mothman Museum? Is that why you thought Quinn was a he?"

"Yes." She glanced at them and laughed. "Let me guess, you two were the ones claiming to make a documentary about the creature."

Bugs held up his hands. "I'd ask how you knew that, but won't bother."

"This is it. The final day of the FARST competition, and we're still one judge short." Faith Warner turned her face to the sky and closed her eyes. "We need a miracle."

Nudging his sister, Henry whispered, "Tell her."

"It's a surprise." She winked and walked ahead of the rest of the Warners.

"This better work," Henry muttered under his breath.

"Did you say something?" Ethan Warner narrowed his eyes.

"Nope."

"Uh-huh. What do you and your sister have up your sleeves?"

"Who, us?" He held his hands out, laughed, and jogged to catch up with Grace.

The twins entered the exhibition hall and stopped in their tracks.

Dr. Casper Callen stood inside the judges' booth wearing a suit and a tie and a huge grin.

Mom gasped from behind them. "He's back."

"It looks like you received your miracle." Ethan glanced at the twins. "Do you two know anything about this?"

Before they could answer, Faith sighed. "It's great, but there's not enough time for Callen to complete his evaluations."

Henry couldn't hold it in any longer. "Actually, he finished them last night after we called and explained the situation."

Her lips moved, but nothing came out. It wasn't everyday Faith Warner was rendered speechless.

Ethan chuckled. "Are you all right, dear?"

"I'm stunned by what amazing kids we have." She hurried to the judges' booth.

Two hours later, Hargrave stood on stage in another red power suit announcing the winners, but Henry didn't hear a word she said. His attention was split between David Dillinger, who was glaring from three seats down, and

Quinn Quaglieri. The young woman sat ramrod straight, with her hands folded in her lap. Occasionally, Dr. Orion leaned over and whispered something to her, but Quinn only nodded and stared straight ahead.

"She's miserable. We should have told her the plan." Grace chewed her lip.

"We agreed to keep quiet for a reason."

"I know, but I hate it."

"Imagine how she'd feel if the plan backfired and she still faced disciplinary action." Henry stood along with the crowd and applauded the winners of the competition, the University of Florida team. The women weren't his favorite people, but they'd presented a solid project.

Grace nodded to the stage. "It's showtime."

Dr. Orion walked up the stairs and took the microphone. "That concludes the official portion of the Eastern Conference Future Applications of Robotic Sciences & Technology competition. I'd like to thank the participants, judges, and faculty for your participation. Now, if everyone will step outside to the courtyard, we have a special surprise."

Professor Hargrave's brows climbed into her hairline and she reached for the mic, but Dr. Orion clutched it to his chest. The two exchanged words, but they were lost in the noise of people exiting the building.

Quinn made eye contact with Henry and mouthed, "What's going on?"

He shrugged and nodded toward the exit.

Outside, laughter filled the air, along with boisterous conversation. The energy of the crowd reminded Henry of the first day of the competition. They were probably relieved the insane week had ended with an award ceremony instead of a cancellation.

The screech of feedback from the microphone drew everyone's attention, and Professor Orion tapped it a few times to stop the noise. "As many of you have heard, the FARST competition was haunted by a local urban legend."

Hargrave stormed to a group of older gentlemen in dark suits. Judging by the way they held themselves and their stoic expressions, Henry guessed they were high up on the Wesleyan administration food chain.

"Ladies and gentlemen, I give you...the Mothman." Orion waved his hand at the sky like a ringmaster introducing a flying trapeze act.

The creature flew overhead in large figure eights.

A hushed silence fell over the crowd. Some pointed and others gawked, but everyone watched Quinn's drone complete barrel rolls, loop-de-loops, and other aerial aerobatics Henry couldn't name. It wasn't dancing and rose petals, but the moves were impressive.

When they were finished showing off, Bugs and Jimmy brought the drone level with a balcony on the far side of the courtyard. It hovered in place for several seconds before descending to reveal the men.

The crowd cheered. Even Professor Hargrave and David gave the performance half-hearted applause.

Henry leaned closer to Grace. "Now for the hard part."

Dr. Orion wiped his brow and raised the mic to his mouth. "The Wesleyan robotics team was unable to compete in this year's competition, but they couldn't resist showing off their tech."

Hargrave continued to speak to the officials, but the men glanced between the drone and Dr. Orion.

"As some of you may have heard, the Mothman drone was spotted several times over the previous week. My personal encounter with the monster raised my insurance premiums." Oliver chuckled. "David Dillinger has asked to apologize and explain how the creature escaped to terrorize the competitors and judges."

David glanced from side to side without moving his head, swallowed, and robotically put one foot in front of the other.

"He's a little shy. How about a round of applause for the West Virginia Wesleyan College Robotics team member David Dillinger?" Dr. Orion had missed his calling. The man clearly belonged on a stage. Not only did the crowd cheer, but the college officials called encouragement along with them.

David took the microphone. "The team ran several trials this week in remote areas. Unfortunately, they weren't remote enough, and people saw the creature."

"He's getting off easy," Grace said.

Henry nodded. "Too easy, but once this is over, we will sit down and tell our parents he threatened to leave us in the mountains. I have a feeling Dad will call our uncle at UCLA and have a long chat about David Dillinger's integrity."

"He should go to jail."

"I agree, but people like him always find their way to prison sooner or later."

David cleared his throat. "I'd like to apologize to the FARST committee for last night. We intended to test the drone over the athletic field but suffered another malfunction."

Henry hoped the speech would be enough to put an end to any talk of disciplinary action or expulsion. If not, Bugs and Jimmy swore they would take responsibility for their actions.

Quinn wove her way through the crowd. "How did you do this?"

Grace nodded to Bugs and Jimmy on the balcony. "We'll let them tell you the whole story."

"Just don't be too mad at them. Their hearts were in the right place." Henry grinned.

"Thank you." Quinn pulled the twins into a group hug.

"You're welcome." Henry caught sight of his parents and shoved his hands in his pockets.

"That's some amazing work, Quinn. Johns Hopkins will be lucky to have you." Faith embraced the young woman.

Ethan pulled the twins to the side. "I want to know everything."

"We'll fill you and Mom in on the details when we get back to the fifth wheel." Grace glanced at the men on the balcony. "Did you suspect them?"

"Not for a second." Ethan laughed. "Faith, we need to go if we're going to make it to Loveland tonight."

"One moment. I'm trying to convince Miss Quaglieri to share her secret recipe for integrating the small motor movements into the drone's control system."

"Ohio?" Henry groaned. "When are we heading south? It's almost winter."

"We'll be in a warmer climate before the snow gets too deep, but first, I'm giving a lecture series at the University of Cincinnati College of Law."

Grace pulled out her phone. "Why does Loveland, Ohio sound so familiar?"

Ethan wiggled his brows. "There's a haunted castle there. They host overnight paranormal investigations."

Faith looped her arm with her husband's. "After all this, I thought you'd give up sleuthing and focus on something simpler like constitutional law."

"I think I'll leave the mysteries to the experts." He kissed her cheek. "But you should give sleuthing a try. I feel much closer to our kids after working on this case."

"The Loveland Frog!" Grace turned her phone so they could see the screen. "It's been around since the 50s. In 2016, two teens claimed to have seen it while playing Pokémon Go, but there have been a rash of recent sightings."

Faith wrinkled her nose. "You're going to hunt a four-foot-tall frog?"

"Sounds like my kind of mystery." Henry rubbed his hands together. "Loveland, Ohio, ready or not, here we come."

THE LOVELAND FROG

MONSTER CASE FILES BOOK 7

CHAPTER ONE

The first snowfall of the season fell on the banks of the Little Miami River, but Barney Buell refused to give up the hunt. Armed with a video camera and a frog gig, he slogged through the mud. The creatures lurked nearby; he could feel their slimy eyes staring from the darkness.

"We're back to where we started. I'm tired, and my toes are numb. I'm out of here." Lyda Lawrence, his best and only friend, headed for drier ground.

"Ten more minutes. The frogmen are out there. I can feel them." He couldn't continue the hunt without her, and she knew it. "If you leave, it'll be three cryptids against one human."

"You said ten minutes an hour ago." Lyda continued walking. "I'm sorry, Barn. I have biology homework, and I have to open the coffee shop before school."

"Promise we'll try again tomorrow night?"

Lyda was the only human being on the planet, besides his parents, he trusted to keep her word. If she said she'd come back for the fifth night in a row, she would—only she didn't promise. She clamped her mouth shut and looked everywhere except at him.

"Fine." Barney rested his frog gig on his shoulder. "But I'm telling you, we capture a frogman and even the popular kids will stop picking on us."

"Trust me. They won't care." Lyda pulled her keys from her pocket. "They've pushed us around since seventh grade."

Something large splashed downriver. A split second later, a sound like a baby crying echoed through the trees.

Barney shined his flashlight in the direction of the sound and caught a fox scurrying around a tree.

Lyda raised her hand and pointed behind him. Her face a mask of terror.

Great, now she's trying to prank me. "You should try out for the leading role in a horror movie."

She continued to point, and Lyda's lips moved, but no sound came out.

Barney smirked. "You're not fooling me. Foxes make all sorts of creepy noises."

A shriek stabbed his eardrums. At first, he thought it'd come from his friend, but Lyda's scream was silent and before him.

Afraid he'd find a wild animal crouched and ready to attack, Barney turned in triple-slow motion.

Five feet behind him stood a trio of frogmen. Yellow eyes, leathery skin, webbed feet and hands—the creatures were hideous and headed in his direction.

Lyda slipped in the mud and scrambled on all fours until she reached drier ground. "Run!"

Barney dropped his tiny frog gig and ran as if his life depended on it.

Loveland called itself the Sweetheart of Ohio, and Grace agreed. Brick sidewalks, park benches, and tree-lined streets set the historic area apart from other places the Warners had traveled. Between the downtown area, amazing bike trails, and an honest-to-goodness castle, Grace fell in love at first visit.

"I can't wait to explore Loveland." She pressed her hand against the window as if trying to touch the passing scenery.

Her twin brother Henry glanced up from his e-reader and shivered. "It looks cold. I'll be spending my time indoors, thank you very much."

"It's late November. Of course, it's cold. That's why man created jackets."

She laughed, refusing to let his aversion to winter spoil their fun. "How are we going to investigate the Loveland Frog from inside the trailer?"

He wiggled his brows. "That's why man created the Internet."

Faith Warner, the twins' mother, twisted in her seat. "Since we'll be here for two weeks, I want the two of you to do some volunteer work."

"That'll be fun." Grace nudged her brother's side. "Right, Henry?"

"Sure. As long as it's not cleaning the river or anything outdoors." He traded his e-reader for his phone.

Grace enjoyed helping others no matter what the location, but some places were more gratifying. "Next week is Thanksgiving. Maybe we could work at a food pantry or soup kitchen."

The Warners had a long-standing family tradition of volunteering four times per year: Thanksgiving, Spring Break, and twice over the summer. Besides Christmas, and the time they spent helping local communities, their parents rarely took a break from the college lecture circuit.

"Hmm. How about this?" Henry turned his cell so she could see the image of a senior center on the screen.

"That's perfect. Do they list volunteer opportunities on the website?" Grace took her phone from her backpack. "What's the name? I'll look it up."

Ethan Warner, aka "Dad," glanced in the rearview mirror. "What did you find?"

"A senior center and nursing home not too far from the campground." Henry grinned. "I'm homesick for Gram and Pops."

Faith sighed. "I miss them, too, but we'll see them over Christmas."

Henry's face softened into a goofy contented expression. "I'm looking forward to Gram's cooking and the Florida sun. Until then, I'll spend some time with other people's grandparents."

Grace loved living the life of a gypsy, traveling from place to place. She'd seen and done more in her seventeen years than most people would in a lifetime, but she cherished her time with her maternal grandparents. Not only did they live near the beach in Florida, but their favorite hobbies were visiting theme parks and spoiling their grandkids—two things both Grace and Henry whole-heartedly supported.

Waving his phone in Faith's direction, Henry said, "The senior center has an urgent call for volunteers. Should I sign us up?"

"Go ahead and register the four of us. Dad and I can help out over Thanksgiving weekend."

"We don't have any assignments due until the following week, but we do have the Loveland Frog mystery to work on. How many hours do you want us to volunteer?" Grace bit her lip, half-expecting her mother to put the kibosh on a new case.

They'd run into a few interesting situations while investigating their last mystery, including Ethan getting lost in the woods. In the end, they'd solved the case, but Faith Warner disagreed with Niccolò Machiavelli. The end did *not* always justify the means.

Faith furrowed her brow and took her sweet time replying to the question.

Henry poked Grace's arm and nodded toward the front seat. He obviously wanted her to ask again.

She pressed her lips together and shook her head a fraction of an inch. In twin-speak, this meant for him to be quiet because Grace wasn't going to do it.

Without turning her head, Faith said, "Since you're both still grounded, I think twenty-five hours each week is fair. In addition, I want you to work ahead on your assignments. The semester will be over before you know it."

Ethan raised a brow. Even by Mom's standards, it was a heavy workload.

The twins exchanged glances. While they had anticipated some parental resistance to their sleuthing activities, neither had expected quite so much.

Faith folded her hands in her lap and stared straight ahead.

An awkward silence choked off the air in the truck like a five-alarm fire, only quieter. Thankfully, Ethan turned into the campground before the mood grew grimmer.

Grace waited until her parents had walked into the office to check in before turning to Henry. "Dad seemed as surprised by the number of volunteer hours as we are. I'm sure Mom will reduce it once he talks to her."

"Twenty-five hours isn't so bad. It's like a part-time job. We'll manage."

"How? There's only so much time in a day."

Henry hitched a shoulder. "She'll stop worrying when we stop giving her reasons to worry. Until then, we'll either give up sleep or not get as deeply involved in the mystery."

"We never set out to fall down the sleuthing rabbit hole."

"Not this time. We investigate the history of the Loveland Frog, talk to a couple of people about the recent sightings, and get out. Nothing dangerous." He nodded to their parents, who were exiting the camp office.

"And we follow all applicable rules and laws." She dipped her chin and fiddled with her phone.

"Agreed."

Ethan climbed in and started the engine. "There was a miscommunication with our reservation, but we're all set now."

Grace glanced between her father's hard-set jaw and her mother's stiff spine. "You weren't inside very long. What sort of mix-up?"

"They have us in a smaller site than we reserved." Ethan glanced in the rearview and winked. "It'll be tight, but we'll manage."

Faith gave her husband a dubious look and turned to the twins. "Your dad is more optimistic than I am. This set up is going to take some world-famous Warner teamwork."

Grace smiled and nodded. Fear made people do strange things. Faith Warner had been afraid during the Mothman debacle, and she most assuredly did not like it. Grace looked to Henry and with a simple head shrug, they agreed not to push their mother any farther into the danger zone.

To say the campsite was small was an understatement. The Warners lived in a forty-nine-foot fifth wheel. Even if they could manage to park the rig, the trees surrounding the front of the pad would make it next to impossible to extend the slides.

Ethan said, "Kids, hop out and guide me in."

"Should I go back to the office and ask for a site with fewer trees?" Faith opened her door.

"The manager said this was our best bet. Worst-case scenario, we park the truck in the vacant spot behind us." Ethan squeezed her hand. "We'll make it work. We always do."

"I reserve the right to say I told you so." Faith kissed his cheek before climbing out of the truck.

With their mother taking up a position at the front, the twins marched to the back of the fifth wheel. Grace guesstimated the distance of the trees to the landing pad and frowned.

Henry rocked back on his heels and whistled. "This is going to be interesting."

On his first attempt, Ethan managed to back the rig a third of the way in before Faith signaled for him to try again.

"This is going to take a while. We might as well discuss the case," Grace said. "The Loveland Frog hadn't been seen since 1972—"

"Until 2015, when a couple of kids claim to have seen it near Lake Sybella." Henry motioned for their father to continue backing in. "But then it disappeared until two months ago."

"Right, but since then, there have been sightings every few days. There has to be a reason why it has returned." Grace tapped her lips. "Why now? And why are there three? The early reports only mentioned one frogman."

"Excellent questions." He held his hand up for a high five.

She slapped his hand. "Practice makes perfect."

"Stop. You're too close on the right." Faith's voice boomed through the otherwise peaceful campground. "Pay attention back there! I can't see past the first axle."

The twins snapped to attention. "Yes, ma'am."

Henry muttered, "Even if he manages to back in, the site isn't deep enough for the truck."

Grace turned and studied the vacant spot behind them. It was half as deep as the site they had been assigned, but the trees sat farther apart.

"Okay, back it in." Henry waved his arms like a member of a ground crew guiding a jet to the terminal. Fitting, considering the fifth wheel was larger than some planes.

Grace put her fingers in her mouth and whistled. "Wait!"

The rig stopped moving.

Careful to stay within the view of the side mirrors, she jogged to the driver's side window.

Ethan, red-faced and sweating, lifted a brow. "Please tell me that brilliant mind of yours has come up with a solution."

"Maybe." She pointed to the left. "Go around the loop and pull in from the site behind us. You'll have more clearance."

"Are you sure the ground isn't too wet? I'd hate to get stuck."

Faith came from the opposite side of the truck. "She's right. You'll have a straight shot, and it's not too muddy back there. Put the front axle on our pad and the back on the other."

Ethan nodded, although he didn't appear convinced. "I'll go around. You two watch the tires."

Grace slung her arm around her mother's shoulder and lowered her voice. "What are the chances he's going to get stuck?"

"I'd say fifty-fifty, but we have less than a ten percent chance of backing the rig in with enough clearance to set up." Their dad took the rig around the circle and lurched up a path that was little more than two wheel tracks in the dirt and grass. Ethan swung wide and carefully lined up to pull through their site.

The roar of the truck's diesel ended the conversation. Tires spun, and mud flew.

Holding her breath, Grace attempted to use the Jedi mind trick to force the vehicle forward. "Come on..."

The truck lurched forward, and the front tires reached the back of the concrete pad.

Henry pumped his fist. "Yes!"

Ethan grinned like a man who'd just planted his flag at the summit of Mount Everest.

Faith took her jacket off and rolled up her sleeves. "We have twenty minutes to unhook the rig from the truck or Dad and I will be late to our meeting."

"What are you teaching this time?" Henry grabbed the tape measure from the glove compartment.

Ethan stepped out of the truck and eyed his parking job. "A lecture series on judicial biases in law at the Ohio Innocence Project. We're dissecting a fairly recent conviction."

"Wow. That's awesome." Grace had heard about the program at Cincinnati Law. Their mission was to free every innocent person in Ohio who had been convicted of a crime they didn't commit. To date, the program had seen the release of twenty-eight people.

Henry stared at his father like a little boy meeting a superhero. "I'd love to sit in on your lectures."

"You know I'd love that." Ethan clamped a hand on his son's shoulder.

Grace did some quick mental math and working ahead on school assignments plus volunteer work plus attending Dad's lectures equaled no time for a mystery.

CHAPTER TWO

"Brain freeze." Henry pressed his tongue to the roof of his mouth, but it didn't help alleviate the pain.

"It's not a brain freeze when you breathe through your mouth." Grace laughed.

"*Brainstem* freeze." The technical name for the ache in the back of his throat didn't matter. The only thing that would help was to get off the bike and into a warm building. "Let's grab a cup of hot chocolate before we go to the senior center."

"Now you're speaking my language. We'll stop in the historic district." Grace pedaled past him.

Henry groaned and picked up his pace. Normally, he loved biking, but "normal" usually involved temperatures above forty degrees Fahrenheit. "I'm getting frostbite on my face."

"At least the snow melted." Grace slowed to let Henry catch up to her. "What I was saying yesterday about the recent sightings of the frogmen..." Grace glanced over her shoulder. "On the surface, it reminds me of the situation we encountered with the Mothman."

"How so?" He followed her to an intersection and hopped off his bike.

"The physical descriptions from the latest witnesses match the early reports. Assuming the frogmen aren't real, that would mean—"

"—whoever's behind the hoax did their research." Henry followed his sister across the street.

"Exactly. Only there isn't a Loveland Frog Museum or any other central place to learn about the myth. There were only three sightings between 1955 and 1972, a traveling salesman and two police officers, one of whom later claimed he mistook a mangy coyote with a four-foot-tall frog walking on its hind legs."

"Right. The people behind the prank must have read the same half-dozen internet articles we did."

"Exactly."

"Unless they spoke to the kids who saw the frogman in 2015." Henry held up his hand. "Scratch that. The so-called video evidence from that encounter is sketchy at best."

"And fake at worst." She parked against a bike rack and unraveled the chain and lock.

Henry glanced around. "This doesn't look like the kind of place people lie in wait to steal bicycles."

"I'm not taking any chances."

Not that long ago, Grace wouldn't have bothered with the lock. They'd experienced the worst in people, but they'd also seen the best. Henry didn't know what to make of the new, overly-cautious, side of his sister.

"What?" She set her hands on her hips.

"Nothing. Just thinking." He chained his bike, too. "There may be no agreed-upon mythology for the frogmen, but the recent encounters have taken place in a relatively small area."

"Which makes our job easier." She grinned. "For once."

The coffee shop smelled like what Henry imagined heaven would smell like if heaven had freshly ground dark-roast fumes wafting through the air. He took a deep breath and rethought his beverage choices. "It's your turn to buy. I'll have a mocha."

"Anything to eat? It's about time for your mid-afternoon snack." Her voice sounded as sticky sweet as the flavored syrups behind the counter.

"Surprise me." Henry plopped into an oversized leather chair and checked the alerts on his phone. A red dot appeared next to the Loveland Frog channel. He made sure the volume was fairly low and hit Play on a new video.

Much like the previous dozen posts, the grainy footage showed three frog-like creatures walking on their hind legs. The latest victim was a teen girl who appeared sufficiently freaked-out as she ran past the camera.

Henry scratched his jaw and replayed the video. The film quality and angles reminded him of another case he and Grace had solved, with one major difference. In the Charlie No-Face mystery, a handful of teens had mounted video cameras in the forest to capture their classmates fleeing in terror from the so-called monster.

Grace sat in the chair beside him. "Our order will be out soon. What are you doing?"

"Watch this and tell me the first thing that pops into your mind." He handed her the phone.

She focused on the screen, tilted her head, and frowned. "Who's shooting the video?"

"My question exactly." Holding the cell so they both could see, he replayed the footage.

"It's bouncing too much to be a stationary camera. How did the alleged victim not see someone filming her?"

"What if the people in the videos are in on the hoax?" Henry loved this part of sleuthing—putting the first pieces of the puzzle together with absolutely no idea if the final picture would be a landscape or a bowl of fruit.

"That *is* the most likely explanation." She seemed unconvinced.

The server, a girl who looked to be about the same age as the twins and vaguely familiar, brought out their coffee and cookies. She peered down at Henry's phone. Her mouth fell open in disbelief. "Please tell me that's not a new frogman video."

The twins stared. People snooped. It was human nature, but most didn't ask questions during the act.

She seemed to realize what she'd done and took a step back. "Sorry. I didn't mean to be so nosey. It's just..."

Henry took another look at her face, glanced at his phone, and back at her. "Whoa. Are you the girl in the video?"

"I haven't seen it, but there's a good chance it's my friend Barney and me. Did you notice if one of the people had on bright orange sneakers?"

"There's only one person in the video, and she looks a lot like you."

"I hate my life." She set their coffee on the table and turned to go.

"Wait. Please." He handed her the phone. "Take a look to be sure."

Her expression went from skeptical to horrified in the space of a millisecond. She gave the cell back and hung her head. "It's me."

"We'd like to talk to you about what happened that night." Grace stood, nearly knocking over the steaming-hot coffee.

The server chewed her lip. "I don't recognize the two of you. Do you go to Loveland High?"

"No, we're passing through. Our parents are guest-lecturing at the University of Cincinnati." Henry motioned to the empty chair beside him. "Do you have a few minutes to answer some questions?"

She glanced back toward the empty counter.

Grace said, "We're working on a project about urban legends. A huge part of our research is getting to the bottom of unexplained phenomenon."

"You mean solving mysteries." The girl had a way of looking at them without meeting their eyes.

"Exactly." He smiled in hopes of settling her nerves. "I'm Henry Warner, and this is my twin sister Grace."

"Lyda Lawrence."

Between her dark hair and eyes and the name, a little bell rang in the back of his mind. "How do you spell that?"

"L-Y-D-A."

"As in Lyda Conley, the first Native American woman admitted to argue a case before the Supreme Court?" Henry lifted a brow.

Lyda's mouth fell open. "You're the first person I've met who's known that."

Grace laughed and sipped her coffee. "We should have mentioned that our father is lecturing at Cincy Law."

"And we're one-eighth Seminole," Henry added.

"One-half Cherokee, one-half Wyandot." She sank into the chair beside the twins. "What do you want to know about that night?"

Everything. Henry sat back. "Anything you can remember, starting with the exact location."

"We were off of Cones Road, between the Little Miami River and O'Bannonville Creek. Barney had the brilliant idea of capturing one of the frogmen. After a couple of hours, I was ready to go home. That's when they appeared." She dipped her chin. "When this whole thing started, I thought it was some kind of prank, but after seeing them, I'm not so sure."

Grace turned her phone so Lyda could see the map on the screen. "Is this the right area?"

"Yes." She glanced at the twins. "You aren't going after the frogmen, are you?"

"It's what we do." Henry popped half a cookie into his mouth.

Grace rolled her eyes. "We're pretty good at solving mysteries."

The girl glanced toward the counter. "I should get back to work. I'm the only one here until my mom gets back from picking up my little brother."

"One more question." Henry lowered his voice. "Did you notice anyone else out there with you?"

"No, why?" Her voice cracked as if the question frightened her, but what could have caused that?

"The video is shaky like someone was holding it rather than it being set up on a tripod or mounted in a tree."

Lyda stared for three heartbeats before laughing. "Now that you mention it, so were the others that showed up on YouTube. I can't believe Barney and I fell for it. Of course, it's fake. Cryptids don't post videos on the internet."

Henry held up his hands. "No judgment here. Knowing something is a hoax is one thing but coming face to face with a creature in the forest late at night is another."

"We've fallen for a few hoaxes ourselves. I'm not sure we would have noticed the video shaking, except we've worked on a case like this before." Grace pulled a pen from her bag and wrote her number on a napkin. "Please call us if you think of anything else."

Lyda stuffed the paper into her apron pocket. "Thanks."

Henry finished his coffee. "We'd like to talk to your friend Barney. Do you think you could arrange a meeting?"

"I'll ask, but he's wary of people he doesn't know." She lowered her voice. "And most of the ones he knows."

The bells on the door chimed, announcing the arrival of a customer.

"I'll let you know what he says." Lyda offered them a quick smile and hurried behind the counter.

Grace watched the girl for a moment before turning to Henry. "What do you think?"

"It's too early to say for certain, but I doubt she's involved. Even if she did seem overly cautious."

"I agree, but I'm baffled by her and her friend failing to notice the person with the camera." Grace stood. "Where to next, the scene of the crime or the senior center?"

"The senior center is open until six. I'm thinking we explore the area of the last sighting while the sun's still up." Henry slid into his jacket and zipped it to his chin. "I, for one, am not looking forward to frog-hunting in the dark."

"Agreed." Grace headed for the door. "What about Dad's lecture? Are you going?"

"I'll catch the next one."

Outside, a group of high school kids walked past the twins—three tiny girls and four bulky guys, each displaying designer logos from their ski caps to their boots and sneakers. All seven had an air of superiority as impenetrable as the forcefield around the Death Star.

Henry had never attended a brick-and-mortar high school, but he knew the popular crowd when he saw them.

Two girls gave Grace a once-over, sniffed, and turned their heads. The rest of the teens barely spared a glance in the twins' direction.

"Ready?" Grace's voice came out strained.

He nodded but took his time unlocking his bike.

Snickering and pointing, the teens peered through the coffee shop's front window.

"OMG. She's in there." A dark-haired girl with cherry-red lips sneered. "How can she show her face after that ridiculous video?"

"I know, right?" One of the blondes imitated Lyda by pressing her hands to her face and screaming in a pitch high enough to make dogs bark.

A guy in a Loveland High jacket took a step toward the door. "I'm going in. I need a caramel macchiato double-shot to get through my science homework."

"As if I'd touch anything she made. She'd probably spit in it." The pixie-like ringleader of the mean-girl squad stamped her foot.

Her blonde ponytailed minions nodded.

"Stay out here if you want. I'm going in. If anyone knows where that loser Barney Buell is, she will." The guy cracked his knuckles, puffed out his chest, and walked inside.

Two of his sidekicks followed.

Henry bit his lip to keep from laughing. The kid reminded him of Foghorn Leghorn from the old Bugs Bunny cartoons, an overinflated bag of wind with more muscles than common sense.

Grace gave him a warning look and motioned across the street.

Ignoring the situation seemed wise, but sometimes good people did dumb things for the right reasons. Henry took out his phone and covertly snapped a few pictures of the teens.

"What are you doing?" Grace whisper-shouted.

"What does it look like I'm doing?" He slid his cell into his pocket. "They may as well be holding a flashing neon sign that says, **Suspect**."

"And you're asking for trouble. Come on, let's go before they notice you staring." She pulled her bike from the rack but hesitated.

"People like that want to be stared at. Why else would they go through so much trouble with their clothes and hair products?"

"Poor Lyda." Grace sighed. "She doesn't seem like the type to handle teasing well."

"She did seem rather nervous." He ran his hand over his face. "You know, I think I'll have a second cup of coffee, after all."

A slow grin spread across his sister's face. "I could go for a slice of pound cake."

Henry cut through the group of popular kids. "Excuse me."

One of the girls muttered something under her breath he didn't catch.

Weaving between them, Grace somehow managed to glare and smile at the same time.

The girls seemed unsure of what to make of her. They waited until she reached the door before they huffed and puffed and mumbled among themselves.

Henry followed Grace inside and drew a breath. The shop no longer smelled like heaven. Instead, a thick layer of teenage bull-crap hung in the air.

Leaning across the counter, Foghorn Leghorn spoke to Lyda through gritted teeth. "Tell me now."

As if that wasn't bad enough, his sidekicks had fanned out—one at the end of the counter and the other behind Lyda, clearly blocking her means of escape.

"Hey, Lyda. Is everything all right?" Henry folded his arms.

All three guys turned and stared. Foghorn said, "We're closed."

Wide-eyed, Lyda glanced between the twins and the bullies.

Grace surprised the heck out of everyone when she marched behind the counter and pulled an apron from the hook. "Perfect, then you three won't mind leaving."

Much like the girls outside had done, the guys stared as if unsure of how to respond. They'd likely never had someone stand up to them.

Foghorn stiffened his spine and glared.

Henry turned the sign to Closed and motioned to the door. "We'll reopen at three."

The jerk turned back to Lyda. "I know you know where the twerp is. Tell me now, and I'll go easy on him."

"I told you. He's at home." The girl's voice quivered.

Grace reached under the counter and retrieved a cordless phone. "You have to the count of three to leave, or I'm calling the police."

The sidekick behind the counter smirked. "Go ahead. My dad is on the force."

"Good, then he can explain the legal definition of trespassing to you." She tilted her head to the side. "One...Two..."

"You had your chance." Foghorn knocked a container of biscotti from the counter, smirked at the mess, and strode to the door.

The guy closest to Grace raised his hand as if to send a rack of mugs flying, but she stepped between him and the counter.

"Think very hard about the penalties for vandalizing property before you make your next move."

He pointed at her, shook his head, and followed the others out.

Henry locked the door behind them.

Lyda covered her face with both hands and burst into tears.

"It's okay. We'll stay here until your mom gets back." He joined the girls behind the counter.

"You don't understand what you've done." She met his gaze. "Kirk and his friends will take this out on Barney. The flyers will take it out on me."

"Flyers?" Henry couldn't wait to hear the reason behind the nickname.

"They're the cheerleaders who get tossed into the air. You know, the girls at the top of the pyramid?"

"Gotcha. No wonder they're so petite."

Grace nodded to the group of angry teens glaring through the window. "We have an audience."

Henry guided Lyda to the backroom. "Where is Barney now? Can you warn him to lay low?"

"He's looking for the frogmen. His phone is off or on silent. I've been trying to reach him for over an hour."

"I don't understand. What did he do to make them so mad?" Grace peeked around the corner to confirm the mob was still there.

"Nothing. They've picked on us since seventh grade."

Henry hated the injustice, but most of all, he hated the fact that there was nothing he could do to change the situation. People like Foghorn and his friends lived to make other people miserable.

Grace gasped. "Holy smokes, they're messing with our bikes."

"We forgot to relock them." Heart-pounding, Henry pulled out his phone, crouched, and slipped behind the counter. He might not be able to save Lyda and her friend from the injustices of high school life, but he could cause the bullies some trouble.

"What are you doing?" Lyda whispered.

"Filming them."

CHAPTER THREE

"Tell me again why we let them destroy and then steal our front tires and didn't call the police?" Grace huddled inside her coat and speed-walked down the bike trail.

"We'll call later tonight if we have to, but I have a better idea of how to use the video." He pointed at the creek running alongside the path. "Is this O'Bannonville Creek?"

"I think so. According to the map Lyda drew, it ends up ahead. We should be able to backtrack to the woods between the stream and the river." She glanced over her shoulder for the sixth time in half as many minutes.

"Relax. We'd hear them if they were following us."

"I hope so." Inside the coffee shop, she'd acted without considering the consequences. In doing so, she'd potentially made things worse for Lyda and her friend. "What are the chances we're going to find Barney?"

"I don't know. Either way, we have ammunition to slow Kirk and the others down."

"The video? You're going to give it to Barney to use as leverage?"

Henry grinned. "If he wants it. If not, we'll present the evidence to the local authorities."

"Good plan. It probably won't stop their bullying, but it will cause them a little pain."

"My thoughts exactly."

The twins followed Lyda's directions to a wooded area at the head of the creek. While Grace couldn't see the river, the unmistakable sound of rolling water told her it was there. The scenery might have been beautiful, but the frigid wind ruined it for her. Adding to the misery, the downward slope, coupled with the soggy ground, made walking a challenge.

"Okay. I admit it. It's freezing," Grace said.

Henry slipped and slid his way to the flat strip of land between the creek and river. "I thought you loved winter?"

Grace's foot sank deep enough that mud seeped into her sneaker. "This is the pits, but it's the perfect environment for frogs."

"True, except in this weather, the aquatic varieties would be at the bottom of the water and the terrestrial species would be buried under the leaf litter with the excess glucose in their organs keeping them from turning into toad-sicles."

"Frog antifreeze. Gotta love it." Grace wrinkled her nose. "It's a good thing the Loveland Frogs are of the human variety."

"Or are they?" Henry wiggled his fingers and made ghost sounds.

She smirked. "Okay, we're here. Any idea how to find Barney without calling his name and possibly alerting Kirk and the goon squad to our whereabouts?"

"Other than keeping an eye out, no." No sooner than the words had left his mouth than something large and vaguely human darted toward a heavily wooded area half a football field ahead of them.

"What the heck was that?" Grace pressed her hand to her chest.

"My guess is Barney Buell." He sprinted after him or tried to. Halfway to where the guy had disappeared, Henry fell face-first into the mud.

Laughing at other people's misfortune was not only rude, but a sure-fire way to ruin one's karma. Unfortunately for Grace's spiritual peace, knowing the rules and following them were two different things.

The giggle started as little more than a snort and ended up as a full-blown belly-buster. Poor Henry looked like a milk-chocolate-covered banana with eyes and a mouth.

"Laugh it up." He wiped a glob of mud from his face.

"Sorry." She bit her lip, but it did no good. The more she tried to silence her giggles, the more they spilled out.

"As Gram always says, what comes around goes around." He flashed her a grin.

The combination of white teeth and mud mask sent her into another fit of laughter.

"It's all fun and games until we have to explain to Mom why we didn't make it to the senior center today." Henry scooped up a ball of mud and flung it at her.

The freezing-cold blob hit her in the chest and splattered onto her face. Pretending to be angry, Grace snarled, "I can't believe you did that. I was going to suggest I go in and get the volunteer applications. You know, since I *was* clean."

"It's a good thing you carry wet-wipes in your bag." Henry tried to scrape his face clean before wandering toward the trees where the person or animal or who-knew-what disappeared. "Let's hope he left tracks."

"Did you get a look at him? Are we sure it's Barney and not Kirk?" Half-expecting her brother to hurl more mud, Grace followed at a safe distance.

"Not really. Whoever it was moved fast and was covered in a dark material, but if it were Foghorn, he would have run at us, not away."

"Foghorn?" Images of old cartoons danced through her head. "The rooster! It's a perfect description."

"I thought so." Henry ducked under a low branch.

"This is ridiculous. If it was Barney, he's probably long gone."

"I'm afraid you may be right." Grace kept her eyes on the ground to avoid tempting fate. One slip in the mud or stumble over a fallen branch, and she'd end up looking like Henry.

"What do we have here?" He crouched beside a hollow tree trunk. Bits of brightly colored paper stood out in sharp contrast to the brown leaf litter. "Candy wrappers."

"They could be unrelated to the frogman mystery, but they seem too new to have been here for long."

Henry inspected a bright yellow wrapper. "Weird. This one has red lipstick smears on it."

She folded her arms. "Like the girl outside the coffee shop?"

"Maybe." He handed it to her.

"I can't say for certain, but the shade is close." Grace unzipped her backpack and dropped the wrapper inside.

"As much as I hate to say it, we're going to need to stake out this area after dark." He shivered as if saying the words made him colder.

"I agree." Grace glanced at the time on her phone and frowned. "It's getting late."

"We can't go back to the fifth wheel without volunteer applications." Henry sighed. "Call Lyda and tell her we couldn't find Barney."

"You know Lyda?" A boy stepped out from behind a tree. At first glance, he looked thirteen, but upon closer inspection, Grace noticed a hint of dark hair on his upper lip suggesting he might be older.

"We met her in the coffee shop today. Are you Barney?" She took a step forward but stopped when the guy backed away.

"Who's asking?"

"I'm Henry, and this is my sister Grace. Lyda sent us to warn you that Kirk's looking for you. That is if you're Barney Buell."

"I am." The color drained from his face. "Did they harass her?"

Grace frowned and nodded.

"We stood up to them, but Lyda's afraid we made things worse." Henry took out his phone. "I have a video of Kirk and the others vandalizing our bikes and stealing the tires."

Barney grinned, but the expression seemed off somehow, like his facial muscles weren't used to moving up instead of down. "What are you going to do with it?"

"Could you use it to keep them off your back?" Henry asked.

The guy stared at the phone for several seconds. "Why would you help me? What's in it for you?"

Grace had encountered all sorts of people, but she'd never met someone her age so full of fear and distrust. "Besides the fact we can't stand people like Kirk, we're interested in solving the mystery of the Loveland Frogs."

He folded his arms as if waiting for her to say more.

Henry scratched the dried mud on his cheek. "Lyda has Grace's number. Think it over and let us know if you want the video. We have to go."

She glanced at her phone and frowned. "Dang it. We're never going to make it to the senior center."

"It's not far. Clean up a little." Henry turned his back to Barney. Though it seemed rude at first, he'd likely done it to give the guy time and space to think.

Grace pulled a pack of wet-wipes from her bag and dabbed at the mud on her jacket and face. "I'll run in and get the applications. We can return them tomorrow."

"You want to volunteer at the Golden Years?" Barney glanced at them.

"Yes. We're only in town for two weeks, but we thought it would be fun to help out while we're here." She stuffed the dirty wipe in a plastic bag and checked her face in a handheld mirror.

"It's a nice place. My grandpa goes there every weekday." He smiled, and this time, it seemed real. "There's a shortcut. I can show you if you want."

"That would be great. We told our mom we were going to apply today but were side-tracked at the coffee shop." Henry took the wipes and attempted to make himself presentable. After the fifth one, he gave up.

With Barney's help, the twins reached the senior center in five minutes. Granted, they had to cut through the woods, someone's backyard, and a playground, but they made it in time.

"Thank you." Grace smoothed her hair and squared her shoulders. "Let's hope my dirty jacket doesn't put them off from letting us help out."

"Are you kidding? They all but beg for volunteers from my school, but no one ever signs up." Barney sighed.

"Why?" She furrowed her brow. "Even if you're not into community service, it looks great on a college application."

"Most everyone has a grandparent or great-grandparent at the Golden Years. It's the happening place to be for the over-seventy crowd." Barney laughed. "I might as well say hi to Gramps while I'm here."

Henry motioned to himself. "I'll wait outside."

"That's probably best. You look like you lost a fight with a mud golem." Barney blushed. "It's a creature from *Dungeons and Dragons*."

"Who doesn't love a cryptid whose hugs count as a melee attack with a plus-six to hit?" Henry laughed.

Once again, Barney stared as if trying to determine if Henry was a real boy or a figment of his imagination.

Grace motioned to them. "I'll leave you two to discuss role-playing games."

The Golden Years Senior Center consisted of a room the size of a gymnasium attached to the large nursing home. Long tables filled the center of the space, and shelves containing everything from books and board games to arts and crafts supplies lined the walls. A gigantic gameshow-style bingo board sat on a stage at one end of the room. All in all, it looked like a fun place to volunteer.

"Hello, may I help you?" The woman who asked stood an inch or two short of five feet and wore a smile almost as wide as she was tall.

Grace fell in instant like with her. "I'm Grace Warner. I'd like four volunteer applications, please."

"I'm Inez Ingram." She motioned to the nearest table. "Sit and tell me why a young girl like yourself wants to work with a bunch of old farts. And why you need four applications to do it."

Biting her lip to keep from laughing, Grace sat. "My family is interested, too. Henry, my brother, will be available for an interview tomorrow."

"That answers one question. How about the other?" She perched on the edge of the table. "And don't give me any bull about how you just love spending time with senior citizens."

"But I do." She'd never had an interview quite like this one. It made her nervous. "I only see my grandparents twice a year—"

"Ah. You're looking for a surrogate granny? I see."

Grace shook her head. "No. I mean, sort of. I guess. But it's more than that. I like helping, and this seems like a great place. I'm available any time and can work twenty-five hours this week and next."

Inez lifted a sparse grey eyebrow. "You're not in school? How old are you?"

"Seventeen. My brother and I are homeschooled."

The tiny lady leaned closer and narrowed her eyes.

"Inez? Who is your friend?" A middle-aged woman in a light-blue pantsuit and no-nonsense shoes hurried across the room. "

"This is Stacie Warninski. She's looking for work for her family. A bunch of hippies who don't believe in a good old American education."

Her mouth fell open. "I'm Grace Warner, and I never said any of that."

Inez winked.

"I'm Ms. Simon, the volunteer coordinator. Are you the girl who called this morning?" She gave the elderly woman the side-eye but managed a smile for Grace.

"Yes." She glanced at them.

"Wonderful. We're thrilled your family is interested in spending some time with us, but I thought you said your brother was coming with you?"

"Henry had a slight accident and isn't...presentable. If your schedule allows, he can come back in the morning for an interview."

Inez snickered. "If her schedule allows. She's single, no kids, and no life. She'll be here."

Ms. Simon's cheeks flushed. "You'll have to excuse Inez. She's one of our more colorful residents."

"Pssh." The old woman waved her hand. "That's a nice way of saying I'm a pain in the—"

"And that will be enough, Inez." Ms. Simon's left eye twitched. "Grace, follow me to my office, and I'll get those applications for you. Have each family member fill out a separate one. You can return them tomorrow morning at nine and attend a brief orientation."

"Brief." Inez trailed them to the volunteer coordinator's office. "That's like saying it'll take a little extra time to trim the lawn with a pair of manicure scissors instead of a mower."

Grace found herself drawn to the cantankerous old woman.

Ms. Simon pressed two fingers to each temple. "The orientation lasts two hours and is mandatory for minors who wish to volunteer. Your parents will go through a thirty-minute overview before their first shift."

"Henry and I will be here before nine."

"Remember, each person has to fill out their own application." Ms. Simon handed her a stack of papers. "And I'll need copies of everyone's driver's license."

"Thank you. I'll make sure you have everything you need."

Inez hooted out a laugh. "Be careful what you promise. Unless you have a single man tucked away somewhere—"

"Mrs. Ingram, it's after six. Shouldn't you be in the dining room?" The volunteer coordinator's voice rose on the last few words.

"It was very nice to meet you, Maisie." The elderly woman turned and shuffled down the hall.

Grace stared after her.

"Rest assured, most of the seniors here aren't like her. Many don't have family nearby and enjoy working with volunteers."

"Does she have many visitors?" Grace met Ms. Simon's gaze.

"I'm afraid not, but she's befriended several of the residents and day-program participants."

"I'd like to spend more time with her."

"Oh, I'm sure we can pair you off with another more amenable resident, or even one of our seniors who come for the day program."

Grace glanced back down the hall and shook her head. "She needs visitors, and I like a challenge. Inez and I will get along great."

Four cups of coffee, two hours of orientation, and a stale bagel later... not exactly a morning Henry planned to memorialize in his journal. However, now that he had the classroom portion of training under his belt, he looked forward to a game of chess or perhaps backgammon with a surrogate grandfather.

Standing outside the senior center's door, Henry rubbed his hands together. "Do I go in and pick my senior, or is there an introduction period?"

Grace elbowed his side. "This isn't like the pound, where you walk up and down the aisle staring into cages until you find the dog of your dreams."

"I suspected as much, but two hours of training later, I have no idea what to do." He turned to Ms. Simon for clarification.

She smiled, or tried to, but it looked as if she worked too hard to make it happen. "Since your sister insisted on working with Inez, I thought I'd pair you with Gladys. They are best friends."

"Sounds good." Henry mentally cringed. Grace had told him about her encounter with the elderly woman the night before. While he appreciated a sense of humor and fiery spirit, he hoped Gladys was a bit more mellow.

Ms. Simon led the twins to a table in the back of the room. "Ladies, this is Henry and—"

"Lacie Waterloo!" The tiniest woman Henry had ever met stood and held her arms wide. "I thought I'd seen the last of you last night."

Grace laughed. "I don't scare that easily, even if you do keep butchering my name."

Ms. Simon sighed and pointed at each of the ladies in turn. "This is Gladys and Inez."

Henry held his hand out to Gladys. "Nice to meet you."

The woman gave him a dubious look and a firm shake. "Henry was my husband's name. Do you live up to it?"

Wide-eyed, Henry stammered, "I...uh..."

Inez pressed her lips together and rolled her eyes. "Don't mind her. She's been in a snit since Kennedy was president."

"Where's Pearl today?" Ms. Simon folded her arms. "And Herman? And the rest of our posse?"

Inez hitched a shoulder. "Darned if I know, but I don't blame them for skipping day-prison."

"Pearl is the third Musketeer. She lives with her family but comes for our day programs. Herman is a sidekick, his word, not mine, and quite the character. The rest of the posse? One never knows who is in or out with these vagrants." Ms. Simon spoke to the twins, but she kept her eyes on the ladies. "I'll come back to check on you two before lunch. If you need anything in the meantime—"

"We'll show them where the toilets and vending machines are." Inez turned to Henry. "Trust me, you'll want to pack a lunch tomorrow. The food here makes military rations look like gourmet fare."

Ms. Simon smoothed her jacket. "As I was saying. I'll be back to check on you before lunch."

The ladies waited until the volunteer coordinator had walked a few feet away and cackled.

The twins exchanged quick glances.

"Are you two going to stand there all day?" Gladys motioned to the empty chairs. "Sit."

Inez cracked her knuckles. "Looks like we have a full table. You kids bring your cash?"

"Cash? Why would we?" Grace lowered her voice. "Ms. Simon had us put our things in her office. Should we go get—"

"Something tells me these two are card sharks about to take our allowance in a game of five-card stud." Henry chuckled.

"We prefer Texas Hold 'Em." Gladys shifted her dentures around. "You play?"

"A few times with our grandparents, but we use chips instead of the real thing." He glanced around the room for something that he could substitute for poker chips.

Inez looked over both shoulders, leaned close, and whispered, "How about candy? You have any sweets?"

"Not here, but we can get some." Grace's eyes twinkled.

"Well, what good are you?" Inez dismissed them with a wave and turned to Gladys. "Did you see YouTube?"

Henry choked on his surprise. Coughing, he said, "You watch YouTube?"

Gladys patted his hand. "Yep, and we know all about the internet, too."

"That's really cool." Grace pulled her phone from her pocket.

Inez narrowed her eyes. "I thought you said Simon made you lock up your things? That's contraband."

Grace said, "It's on silent, but one of us has to keep a cell on us in case our parents call."

"Your parents or your boyfriend?"

"Parents. I don't have a boyfriend."

Inez scoffed. "That's right, you don't go to school. So what? You'll grow up to be a sister-wife?"

Grace's mouth moved, but nothing intelligible came out.

Whoa. She did not say that. Henry thought. People from three tables away were already staring. "I'll have you know she had a perfect score on her SAT and is going to MIT next year."

Ignoring the conversation, Gladys asked, "Do you have PayPal? That'd work for poker."

"Oh. I don't think..." Grace met Henry's gaze and bugged her eyes.

He held up his hands. "We're still in high school. We don't have PayPal accounts, but we can play with chips and sneak in some candy tomorrow."

"Unless you're diabetic." Grace forced a smile.

"Diabetic, my Aunt Fanny." Once again, Inez waved her hand in the twins' direction and turned to her friend. "That last video was a doozy."

"They keep getting better and better." Gladys giggled. The sound so unexpected, Henry checked his ears to make sure it had come from her.

Grace drew a deep breath and squared her shoulders. "Which videos? I'd like to see."

The ladies turned their heads, stared, and returned to their conversation without a word.

"Or not." She dipped her head and stared at her hands.

Faith and Ethan Warner had raised the twins to respect their elders, but they'd never encountered the likes of these two. Not only were they rude, but they'd also hurt Grace's feelings. Though many decades older, they were behaving like the mean girls outside the coffee shop.

Henry figured they might as well get some work done while they sat unwelcomed and unwanted. He stood, walked to the shelves, and returned with several sheets of paper and two pens. "What do we know?"

"Now?" Grace glanced at the ladies and sighed.

"Why not? We have nothing *else* to do." He slid a pen in her direction. "What do we know?"

"Okay." She drummed her fingers on the table. "The location of the sightings."

"That's a start. What does your gut say about Foghorn?"

"He's a bully."

"Must be something in the water here." Henry directed his comment toward the cackling women. Though they pretended not to hear, Gladys's shoulders tensed, and Inez frowned.

Grace said, "I don't think he's smart enough to pull it off. The costumes are impressive."

"I agree, but we don't know enough about him. His mother could be a master seamstress."

"True." Her eyes widened, and she typed into her phone. "In the third video, they came out of the water."

Henry caught the women staring but focused on his sister. "Right?"

"It's cold. The costumes have to be made from some sort of wetsuit material."

Inez cleared her throat. "Warnerooskis? Are you talking about the frogman videos?"

Seeing an in with the ladies, Grace flashed them a smile. "Yes. Henry and I are working on a year-long research project investigating urban legends in each of the places we visit."

"What do you mean, you're investigating?" Gladys's expression softened, but Henry didn't trust it.

He leaned forward and lowered his voice. "That's top secret intel. I'm not sure we should share it."

"Why not?" Inez moved her dentures around again.

"How do we know we can trust you?" Grace picked up where he'd left off.

"We'll tell you what we know." Inez glanced at her friend as if to confirm she'd cooperate.

Gladys's frown deepened.

"It's just basic sleuthing," Grace said. "Looking for clues, suspects, and motives. There's no way the frogmen are real, so—"

Inez narrowed her eyes. "And what makes you think that?"

"Tell us what you know first." Henry tilted his head. The ladies were acting strange, and that was saying something, considering their behavior up until that point.

"There's a woman, Dapylil, who lives out on O'Bannonville Road. She knows about the frogmen. Claims to have raised one from a tadpole." Once again, Inez glanced at Gladys, who frowned. Again.

Grace's brows climbed to her hairline. "Wow. That's..."

"She doesn't believe us," Gladys said.

"I believe you, but I'm not sure I believe Dap...what did you say her name was?"

Henry scribbled something on a piece of paper and held it up. "Dapylil? As in lily pad spelled backward?"

Inez threw her hands up. "She can't help the name her parents gave her."

"Give them the address. Let 'em go see for themselves." Gladys smirked.

The glint in the woman's eye made Henry nervous. She knew something they didn't, and he doubted they'd enjoy the surprise.

"We're volunteering until two." Grace sounded unsure of herself, or perhaps it was the situation.

"We'd love the address." He waved the pen as if to prove his point.

Grace had a bad feeling. Not only had Henry faked a headache to get out of volunteering, but they'd also spent the last of their cash on a rideshare to get to a bridge on the outskirts of town. Climbing out of the car, she set her hands on her hips and frowned.

Henry turned back to the driver. "This can't be right."

"My GPS says this is 1000 O'Bannonville Road. There's a house at 996 and 1050, but as you can see, nothing in between."

"Thank you." Grace forced herself to be calm. "They did say we'd probably find her where the creek met the road. This may be it."

"Why do I get the feeling the ladies sent us on a wild goose chase to get rid of us?" Henry watched the driver pull away.

"Because they probably did. Those are two of the meanest little old ladies I've ever met." She hated to admit it, but she'd made a huge mistake when she'd asked to work with Inez. "I'm going to ask Ms. Simon to pair me with someone else tomorrow."

"Same here. Three hours is a long time to be ignored. At least we had the exciting two hours of training to lighten the day." Henry peered over the bridge. "We're here. We might as well go check it out."

"Do you think this Dapylil person exists?"

He shrugged. "Probably not, but we've come all this way. I say we enjoy a little nature before we have to pay for our ride back out of our college funds."

She let her head fall back and groaned. "Fine. Let's get it over with. If we hurry, we can call the driver back before he gets too far. Which way?"

"This side has the bigger bank." He walked to the end of the guardrail.

"Okie-dokie." She followed Henry down.

Thankfully, the incline leading to the water wasn't too steep. However, the vegetation made it difficult to navigate. From the looks of it, no one had come that way in quite some time—if ever.

Henry skidded to a stop at the bottom. "Holy lily pads!"

Grace didn't see any lily pads, but she found it impossible to take her eyes off the woman sitting beneath the bridge.

Not only was she dressed in layers of fabric in every color green known to man, but she'd also painted her face in a bright camouflage pattern and topped off her ensemble with a hat made from a giant yellow paper flower. There was little doubt they'd found the right person, but Grace had to say something. "Are you Dapylil?

The woman turned her head and slowly curled her lips back from her teeth in a crazy-eyed, Jack-Nicholson-in-*The-Shining* smile. "What is the password?"

The twins exchanged glances.

Henry stammered. "Inez told us where to find you. She didn't give us the password."

"What do you think, my lovelies? Should we speak to them without the password?" Dapylil moved her arm as if petting something in her hand.

Grace's knees turned to rubber. The woman was covered in frogs. Now that she'd noticed, she couldn't stop seeing them. Large bullfrogs, toads of various sizes, tiny tree frogs... Dapylil was a walking, breathing amphibian habitat.

"Uh." Henry took a step back. "We should be going."

"You don't want to learn about the frogmen?" The creepy woman smiled. "Don't be afraid of my children. They are harmless." She lifted her hand as if offering one of her slimy babies to them.

Grace swallowed past the lump in her throat. "Did Inez call and tell you we were coming?"

"I don't know anyone by that name." She stared off into space.

Henry mouthed, "What the heck?"

"The trees told me you were coming." She motioned to several large rocks. "Sit. We will tell you what you wish to know."

Grace didn't want to sit. She wanted to get out of there before Dapylil ordered her frog children to attack.

Unfortunately, Henry took a seat on a rock. "What can you tell us about the frogmen?"

Staring straight ahead, Dapylil spoke in a low, seemingly detached tone. "They are confused by all the attention they've received. They merely wish to be left alone, but the teenagers have made a game of hunting them in their home."

Grace waited for several heartbeats for her to continue before giving up and asking, "Near where the Little Miami River meets O'Bannonville Creek?"

Dapylil started as if waking from a trance. "That is where they were born, but they've moved to a quieter place."

"Where?" Henry somehow managed to keep a straight face, but Grace didn't know whether to laugh or cry out for help.

Dapylil's voice turned spooky again. "You will find them between a moose and a railway."

"Can you be a little more specific?" Grace snapped before she could stop herself. "Please?"

"I've already said too much." The strange woman stood up and walked into a darker recess under the bridge.

Henry sucked in a breath and shook his head. "That was...terrifying."

"To say the least." She pulled out her phone and opened a map of the Loveland area. On a whim, she typed in the word "moose."

"What are you searching for?" Henry stood and moved to her side. "None of that made any sense."

Grace closed the browser and ordered a rideshare. "On the contrary. I'm pretty sure I know where the frogmen will make their next appearance."

CHAPTER FIVE

Old-fashioned idea or not, brothers had certain responsibilities when it came to their sisters: protect them on the playground, threaten their dates, and irritate them as much as humanly possible. Henry excelled at all three, especially the last one. He popped a slice of potato into his mouth, leaned close to Grace, and crunched extra-hard.

"That is so gross!" She pushed him away. "Besides the taste, Gram says eating raw potatoes gives you worms."

"I'll take worms over frogs any day." He chomped down on another one.

Grace pointed the kitchen knife at him. "Something's bugging me about Dapylil."

"Just one thing? I can think of a hundred or so reasons the crazy frog lady will give me nightmares."

"Obviously Inez and Gladys tipped her off." She sliced into the next potato as if it'd personally offended her. "But who was she really?"

Henry backed away. "My guess is the missing third Musketeer, Pearl."

"I'm calling Ms. Simon." She dried her hands and grabbed her phone. "We need intel on Inez and her friends."

"While you're at it, ask her how often the residents are allowed to leave." He reached for another slice, but between his sister's glare and the huge knife, he changed his mind.

"I'll put her on speaker." She dialed the number.

"Golden Years, this is Samantha Simon." The volunteer coordinator sounded downright chipper—a far cry from the stressed-out woman he'd met that morning.

"Hi, Ms. Simon. This is Grace Warner. Do you have time to answer a couple of questions?"

"I sure do. How's Henry feeling?"

Grace rolled her eyes. "Better. The migraine didn't last long."

Henry gave her a thumbs-up. Since they'd starting sleuthing, her ability to bend the truth into a pretzel had improved.

She stuck her tongue out at him. "Inez said something that has me a little worried. She referred to the program as 'day-prison.' How often do the residents leave the facility?"

"We schedule two or three outings for our residents each week. We also offer a wide variety of activities in-house for those who *aren't healthy enough to leave.*" Ms. Simon emphasized the last few words.

Grace met his gaze and frowned. "How...how long has it been since Inez and Gladys have gone on an outing?"

"Gladys isn't a resident, she comes for the day program. I'd have to review the signup sheets to give you an exact time, but it's been a couple of years since Inez has gone out." The woman's voice lowered. "Please be honest. Did Henry's headache have anything to do with Inez and Gladys? They can be quite the handful."

"No." Grace looked away and cleared her throat. "They aren't easy, but like I told you before, Henry and I enjoy a challenge."

"I'm glad to hear it."

"Inez's friend Pearl...is she more independent?"

Henry nodded to encourage his sister. She walked a tightrope between innocent questions and asking Ms. Simon to break patient confidentiality laws.

"Pearl is one of the lucky ones. Her family is able to take care of her, but no. She could never live on her own, drive a car, or any of the other indicators we use to determine independence."

"For instance, you wouldn't expect to find her on a nature hike?"

Ms. Simon laughed. "Absolutely not. On her bad days, she's in a wheelchair. On her good days, she gets around with a walker."

"Thank you." Grace turned to Henry and frowned. "I have one more question. Are residents allowed to use the phone?"

"Of course. There are landlines in the rooms, and some residents have personal cell phones."

"Thank you. We'll see you in the morning."

"Have a good night, and Grace?" She paused as if searching for the right words. "It's refreshing to meet a young person with such a big heart, but please believe me when I tell you, Inez is well cared for here."

She smiled and nodded. "I know she is. I'm just trying to understand how everything works."

"See you tomorrow."

Grace disconnected the call. "She was trying to tell me Inez is too sick to leave the nursing home."

"I got the same message." Henry gave her shoulder a playful shake. "On a positive note, we can rule Pearl out as a suspect."

"Maybe so, but I'm still convinced Inez called Dapylil, or whatever her real name is." She marched back into the kitchen and took her frustration out on more innocent veggies.

"Me too, but I'm beginning to wonder if the crazy frog lady routine was for real."

Grace stopped mid-chop and stared. "You can't be serious."

"Why not? We've met some strange characters since we started this project."

"Yes, but a woman in green makeup and clothes, wearing a huge flower on her head and frogs for accessories is by far the most bizarre to date." She sprinkled seasoning on the potatoes and put them into the oven. "Mom and Dad will be home soon. How are we going to convince them to let us hang out at the Moose Lodge tonight? We're still grounded."

"About that." Henry had replayed the conversation with Dapylil over and over, and each time he'd come to the same conclusion. "It's a trap."

"Which is why we need a reason to leave the campground after dark." She slapped three steaks on a plate and shoved it in his direction. Put these on the grill."

"Let's not forget we need a ride. We're still without our bikes." He walked outside, with Grace on his heels.

"I haven't heard anything from Barney or Lyda." She blew out a breath as if sucker-punched by her thoughts. "With the volunteering and schoolwork. I've lost track of time."

Henry set the meat on the grill and closed the lid. "Call her, but don't mention the new location or our meeting with Dapylil."

Grace dialed a number she found on the internet and pressed the phone to her ear. "Hi, Lyda."

The disembodied voice reminded Henry of the parents from Charlie Brown. He heard her making noise but had no idea if she'd spoken actual words.

"Oh, that's great news. We'll pick our bikes up in the morning on the way to the Golden Years. Please tell Barney we're grateful." Grace gave him a thumbs-up. "Sure. I'll have Henry send the video to you as soon as we hang up."

The color drained from her face. "When and where?"

Henry didn't like the sound of that. He inched closer to eavesdrop, but his sister turned her back to him.

"He has to know the frogmen are people in costumes." Grace's voice rose. "He can't be out there with weapons. Someone's going to get hurt."

The unmistakable roar of their parents' truck echoed through the quiet campground. A few seconds later, headlights flashed through the trees.

Henry motioned for her to hurry.

"We'll try. Tell me where he is." Grace nodded and ducked around the side of the fifth wheel.

"Where's she going?" Ethan Warner shut the truck door, scented the air, and grinned. "And when is dinner? I'm starved."

"Grace is on the phone." Henry opened the grill to check the steaks. "Dinner in five."

Adjusting the computer bag on her shoulder, Faith stared after her daughter.

Henry knew his mom had questions but avoided making direct eye contact. Instead, he hyper-focused on flipping the meat. *No sudden movements. No volunteering information.*

"I'm going in to change." Faith tilted her head. "Anything interesting happen today?"

"Nope." He looked up in time to see his mother narrow her eyes. *Dang it. I have to give her something.* "Actually, yes. Grace and I were paired with two rather difficult seniors today."

"Oh?" She set her bag in a deck chair. "Difficult as in ill? Because your sister has a tender heart. She won't do well with—"

"No, not ill." Henry waved the grill fork. "More like the Golden Girls meet the Mean Girls."

"Changes in personality and anger are symptoms of dementia."

"Trust me, these two don't have any cognitive problems. They were just... rude. They ignored us when they realized we didn't have any intention of playing poker for actual money."

Ethan burst out laughing. "Ah, you were assigned to a couple of gambling grannies. I know the type. One time when I was in Vegas—"

"What happens in Vegas stays in Vegas." Faith folded her arms. "Give them a little more time. If they aren't engaging with you by the end of the day tomorrow, perhaps you should ask to bring your volunteer joy into someone else's life."

"That's the plan." Henry pulled the steaks off the grill. "By the way, Grace and I would like to check out the place where the frogmen were spotted."

She raised a brow. "Tonight?"

"Yes, but it's easily accessible and visible from the Loveland Bike Trail." He dipped his chin and grinned. "We won't be late. We have to be at the senior center at nine."

"Since you're still grounded from the incident in West Virginia, your curfew is eleven-thirty." She glanced around the rig. "Where are your bikes?"

"We'll get them tomorrow. We took a rideshare home." Henry chose his next words carefully. Too much truth and they wouldn't be allowed to go out. Too little, and his mom would smell a lie. "I had a headache. The women were quite the handful."

"Learning to deal with difficult people is a good lesson to master while you're young." Faith gave him a knowing look and a half-hug.

You have no idea.

"I'll take these inside. Go find your sister and tell her to end her call. It's family time."

Ethan parked the truck in front of the coffee shop. "I'll pick you up here at eleven-thirty."

"You have an early day. We can call a rideshare." Grace reached for the door handle. She needed to get out, meet Lyda, and find Barney before he did something he couldn't take back.

"I'll be up. I have a mountain of student essays they handed me that need feedback and notes for tomorrow's case study."

"Okay. We'll call if we finish early." She climbed out before he could ask any questions.

"Have fun." Ethan waved and pulled away.

Henry tugged her out of view of the coffee shop's windows. "What exactly did you mean when you said Barney was armed?"

She'd given him a quick rundown before dinner but hadn't had time to get into the gory details. "Lyda said he's carrying a large spear like they use for fishing."

"You mean a harpoon?" His eyes widened. "We're going after someone carrying a freaking harpoon?"

"I don't know what it is. It could be a really big frog gig."

"That would be a trident. Not much better." He shook his head. "I'm not a fan of anything with pointy ends that isn't kept in a kitchen drawer."

She turned for the door. "Me either, but we need to get moving. Dinner and family time took forever."

Lyda met them on the sidewalk wearing jeans and a worried expression. "Barney is still not answering his phone."

Despite the cold lump of fear sitting next to the steak and potatoes she'd eaten for dinner, Grace managed to smile. "We'll find him."

"The bikes are around back." She locked the shop door and led them down a narrow alley.

This time Grace smiled for real. Barney had not only found their tires, but he'd also straightened the bent spokes and rims and put the bikes back together.

Henry whistled. "I thought for sure the wheels were goners. Where did he learn to do that?"

"His grandpa started the first bike shop in Loveland ages ago. Barney's dad runs it now." Lyda hopped on her ten-speed. "Follow me. I know a shortcut."

The twins were in good shape, but Lyda made them look like slouches. The girl sped down the service road in a blur. When she reached the end, she turned right, crossed the street, and slowed to allow them to catch up.

By the time they'd reached the end of O'Bannonville Creek, Grace had to bend at the waist to catch her breath.

"Sorry. Loveland is a huge cyclist town. I spend more time on two wheels than two feet." Lyda stashed her bike in a copse of trees near the path leading to the river.

Henry wiped sweat from his brow. "I'm officially impressed. Do you race?"

"I used to, but..." She shrugged and looked away. "We should find Barney."

Grace's Spidey sense told her Kirk and his goons had something to do with her giving up competitive cycling, but it wasn't the time to ask.

The trio trudged through the wooded area. Thankfully, it hadn't rained or snowed in a couple of days, so the ground had dried out—mostly.

"Shouldn't we call his name?" Henry shoved his hands in his pockets.

"I'm not sure we're alone out here. Kirk's backed off since Barn threatened to go public with the video you shot, but it's only a matter of time before he gets tired of playing nice."

Henry scowled.

Grace lowered her voice just in case Lyda was right. "Why doesn't someone report him? Most schools have anti-bullying policies."

"Loveland High has a zero-tolerance policy, but when the biggest bully is the superintendent's son, not even the principal is willing to enforce it." She pressed her finger to her lips and crouched.

Grace peeked around a tree and froze. The girls from outside the coffee shop stood huddled together a few yards away.

"This is bad," Lyda whispered. "Kirk is out here somewhere. They wouldn't have come out here alone."

One of the flyers tossed a candy wrapper on the ground. "If they aren't back by the time I finish this, I am so out of here."

"You'll leave when I say you can leave." The head mean girl snarled. "There's water on three sides. Kirk has the little twerp trapped. All he has to do is find him and *convince* him to delete the video."

Grace's heart leapt into her throat. She didn't know Barney, but statistically speaking, he had a better chance of Kirk hurting *him* with the weapon than the other way around. "We have to do something."

"I have a plan. Stay here, and call 9-1-1 if anything goes wrong." Henry pulled his phone from his pocket, hit the flashlight, and shined it at the girls. "Any of you seen three four-feet tall frogs walking on their hind legs?"

CHAPTER SIX

Despite countless research studies to the contrary, Grace believed in twin telepathy. She'd finished her brother's sentences since they could talk. As for mind-reading, no one could deny the Warner twins knew what the other was thinking. That was, until Henry stood up and shouted at the group of girls.

"What's he doing?" Lyda curled in on herself as if trying to disappear.

"I have no freaking idea." Grace's chest tightened to the point she struggled to catch her breath. She hated hiding in the shadows waiting for the worst to happen. While she doubted the girls would do more than verbally assault Henry, Kirk and his friends lurked nearby.

"I was told I could find the Loveland frog out here." Henry continued to shine the light in the flyers' faces. "Is this the right place?"

Shielding her eyes, the queen bee shouted, "OMG! Seriously? Put the phone away."

"Then how would I see?" Henry's voice rose. "I've been searching for the darned frog all night. I thought I saw Bigfoot, but it turned out to be some jock."

Grace cringed. *What is he doing?*

Two of the ponytailed girls giggled, but their leader cut them off with a glare. "That big jock is my boyfriend."

"How unfortunate." He kept the flashlight app pointed in their direction, likely to prevent them from recognizing him. "Strange night. Besides the big guy, I passed a scrawny kid running toward the bike trail. I figured he'd seen the frogmen."

One of the flyers gasped. "That has to be Barney. Text Kirk."

The head mean girl's thumbs flew over her phone. "Duh. I'm already doing it. And we are so out of here."

Henry cut the light and ducked behind a large tree.

Sinking lower to the ground, Lyda whispered, "He's smart."

"That's not how I would describe it." Grace inched farther into the shrubbery.

Illuminated by the light of their phone screens, the flyers glanced around.

Blonde ponytail number one asked, "Where did he go?"

"He seriously just vanished." Blonde number two pulled her coat tighter around her body.

"You two are idiots." The queen bee huffed. "Who cares where the weirdo went? Let's go. Kirk said he'd meet us at the bike path."

Grace held her breath until they'd walked past her. "Thank goodness."

"Stay down. We have no idea where Kirk is." Lyda rested her hand on Grace's shoulder.

Henry hadn't come out from his hiding place, but she thought she could see his outline a few feet away.

Male voices and laughter intruded upon the otherwise-quiet forest. Shortly after, Kirk and his goons stepped into the clearing. The big guy shined the brightest flashlight Grace had ever seen over the area.

Lyda gasped and dropped to her belly.

Kirk pointed the light in their direction. "Check over there. I heard something."

"Dude, Tiffany said Barney ran back to his mommy."

Grace had no idea which one of the boys had spoken, nor did she care to raise her head and find out.

"No, she said some guy told her he saw a kid running away." He moved the beam in a wider arc, then whipped it back in her and Lyda's direction. "Check around those trees."

Oh no. No. No. No. Grace ran through her options. She could sit tight, but that would risk Lyda being discovered too. The poor girl had started crying the second Kirk had glanced in their direction. Henry would probably do something to protect them, but he didn't stand a chance against the four muscle-bound jocks.

It's up to me.

She eased to her feet, squared her shoulders, and walked toward the river.

"Stop! Put your hands up!"

Grace didn't know his name, but she assumed he was the son of a police officer. Pretending to start, she turned toward the guys and raised her hands.

"It's the chick from the coffee shop." The dark-haired boy narrowed his eyes.

Kirk ran his hand over his jaw. "Where's the guy that was with you the other day?"

"You mean my brother?" Still holding her hands up, she shrugged. "He's probably with Lyda at the coffee shop."

"What are you doing out here?"

"Besides feeling stupid?" She lowered her hands to her hands to her hips. "I let Barney talk me into searching for the frogmen. Next thing I know, he's gone, and I'm lost trying to find my way back to the bike trail."

The dark-haired boy snickered.

Kirk, on the other hand, looked her over as if trying to figure her out. "You don't go to Loveland High."

"My dad just started working at the University of Cincinnati." It wasn't a complete lie. She hoped she'd convinced him she was an innocent damsel in distress.

"We'll show you the way out." Raising the light to her face, Kirk stood in place.

"Thank you." She flashed them her brightest smile and channeled her inner teen diva. "Like for real. I was beginning to think I'd be stuck here all night. I did the thing where you walk in a straight line until you find a road or something, but all I found was water. I must have been walking in circles."

The dark-haired boy frowned. "We should leave you here after that crap you pulled in the coffee shop."

Kirk nodded. "That video is causing me problems."

Grace fought the urge to panic and run away. "I'm really sorry about that. Like I said, I'm new here. I didn't know who you were. I can make sure all the copies disappear...if you help me out of here."

The guys whispered among themselves, but she caught the gist of their conversation. Two wanted to leave her behind, one believed she could help them delete the video, and Kirk remained quiet.

Lyda or Henry or someone made a noise to her left and Grace's heart went into overdrive.

She pretended to cough and tightened her scarf. "I'm going to die of pneumonia before you decide what to do." Waving her hand, she said. "Never mind. I'll find my own way out."

"What's your name?" Kirk strode to Grace's side and took her by the arm.

"Grace." She forced herself to stay calm. He was a bully, but she doubted he'd hurt her. She was, after all, *just a girl.*

"You're coming with us." Half-dragging her, Kirk walked toward the bike path. "If your brother or that twerp Barney are out here, they'll come looking for you."

She cast a quick glance in Henry's and Lyda's direction. *Please stay where you are. Please. Please. Please.* "What time is it?"

The dark-haired boy checked his phone. "Wouldn't you like to know?"

"How mature of you." Grace had no clue how long they'd spent in the woods, but her father would be waiting at the coffee shop at eleven-thirty. As long as they didn't lock her in a trunk or something equally awful, she had a means of escape. "I was just wondering if you guys are planning to hold me prisoner past eleven-thirty."

Kirk jerked her to a stop. "Why eleven-thirty?"

"I turn into a pumpkin a little ahead of schedule."

"Uh-huh. Let's go." He pulled harder on her arm.

She smirked. "You can let go of me. We've already established I don't know my way out of here."

He released her with a shove. "Keep walking."

Crouched and ready to spring into action, Henry watched and waited for Grace and the others to walk past him. It'd taken every ounce of his willpower to stay hidden when she'd stood and walked into the open. She'd trusted him when he'd acted on a hairbrained idea, so he owed her the chance to do the same, but that did *not* include allowing Kirk to drag her out of the forest.

Henry inched from his hiding spot.

Feathers, leaves, and who-knew-what rained down. He thought an animal had disturbed a flock of birds until something heavy and covered in vegetation landed a few inches from him.

Henry yelped and leapt back to get a good look at the person.

Dressed in a ghillie suit and bright orange sneakers and wielding a harpoon, Barney Buell let out what could only be described as a battle cry. He hoisted the weapon over his head and charged toward Grace and Kirk.

"No!" Grace threw herself in front of the bully.

Images of his sister taking a harpoon to the gut flashed through his mind. Henry sprang to his feet and rushed into the fray.

The dark-haired kid shouted, "What the—"

At the last minute, Barney spun the harpoon and slammed the blunt end into the guy's stomach.

"Ooomph." The jerk sank like cement in water.

Kirk shoved Grace out of the way, or tried to, anyway. She put every second of the time she'd spent in self-defense classes to good use. Moving with the momentum, she whirled and delivered an uppercut to Foghorn Leghorn's nose.

The big guy blinked, cupped his face, and dropped to his knees—not surprising, since he'd taken a heck of a hit. Like the proverbial playground bully, Kirk wailed and let loose a series of words that would have sent Henry's grandmother running for the Ivory Soap.

Taking advantage of the situation, Barney spun the harpoon again and pointed the business end at Kirk. Once he had the guy at his mercy, he pulled off the hood of the ghillie suit and exposed his face.

"No! Drop it." Grace split her attention between the two. "Barney, you need to go. Now."

"I'm not finished, and I'm not going anywhere until I put an end to his torture once and for all."

Henry widened his stance and his arms in preparation to tackle Barney if necessary.

His voice rose. "Lyda? You there?"

"I'm here." Lyda emerged from her hiding place with her phone pointed at Kirk.

Henry moved closer to Grace and whispered, "Are you okay?"

"I'd be better if he'd put that thing down."

The other two of Kirk's goons flanked Barney and the twins.

The big guy signaled to his friends and pushed to his feet. Judging by the look in his eye, he planned to beat the harpoon-wielder from a solid to a liquid.

Henry pulled Grace to the side. She could hold her own, but it'd be a cold day on Mercury before he didn't at least try to get her to safety.

Lyda smirked at Kirk. "Uh-uh. Don't even *think* about doing anything foolish."

Barney grinned. "Did you get all that?"

She nodded. "You mean did I record Kirk getting his butt kicked by a girl and you taking down Jeremy? Why, yes. Yes, I did."

Kirk looked like he was counting the ways to make Barney, Lyda, and the twins pay their pounds of flesh.

Jeremy, the dark-haired guy, groaned. "Again? What is it with you people and videos?"

Henry's head spun. "Wait a second. You two planned this?"

"Somewhat." Lyda slid her phone into her pocket. "We thought we'd catch him beating you up, but this…" She laughed. "This is better than we ever could have imagined."

"You were pretending this entire time?" Grace's hands flew to her mouth. "You would have let Kirk hurt Henry so you could blackmail him?"

Barney frowned. "It wouldn't have been any worse than what you did to Kirk."

"Or what Henry did with the video of them breaking your bikes," Lyda said.

Grace glanced at the big guy and winced.

Henry refused to buy into the claim that the twins had done it so it was okay. While they had a point, they'd taken the seed of an idea and turned it into a redwood tree.

"Delete it." Kirk folded his arms.

"Sorry. No can do." Lyda fiddled with her phone. "There. Sent it to the cloud. Anything happens to us, and I'll make sure it's sent to the entire student body."

Barney jabbed the harpoon in Kirk's direction. "Don't try anything. We're leaving."

"I'm going to make you pay for this." The big guy spoke through gritted teeth.

"Has it ever occurred to you that you brought this on yourself by behaving like a Neanderthal?" Grace glanced from one guy to the next and settled on Kirk. "You need to get a life or a hug or something, but stop threatening people."

Lyda giggled.

"And you!" She shook her head. "You two are as bad as he is. How dare you set us up? We were trying to help you."

Barney tightened his grip on the harpoon. "The end justifies the means."

"Then I'll end it." Be it his sanity or his patience, something inside Henry snapped. He lurched forward, grabbed the shaft of the weapon, and jerked it away from the kid.

His sister and the rest of the teens stared.

"Come on, Grace. We're going to be late." Henry settled the harpoon on his shoulder.

She blinked, nodded, and walked past him.

"That's mine. You can't take it!" Barney rushed forward but stopped when Henry turned and glared.

"Watch me." He motioned between the traitors. "Unless you two want to be out here alone with them, I suggest you come with us."

Lyda and Barney followed Grace, casting glances over their shoulders at the bully and his friends.

The group made their way to the scenic trail in silence. Thankfully, their bikes were where they'd left them, and in one piece.

Grace turned to Barney and nodded back toward the clearing. "This isn't over, you know. Kirk was here tonight to force you to delete the first video."

He shrugged. "I had to do something. You don't know what it's like. He's made our lives miserable."

"Going after him with a harpoon isn't the way to handle it."

Lyda rolled her eyes. "That thing is from his grandfather's antique collection. It couldn't cut butter on a warm day."

Barney nodded. "It's part of my Davy Jones costume for Megacon."

Henry took a closer look at the harpoon. Sure enough, someone had dulled the blade and duct-taped parts of the shaft to hold it together. "It's a wonder it didn't break in half when you hit Jeremy with it."

"Can I have it back?"

Henry handed Barney his prop. "You got lucky tonight. I wouldn't suggest trying something like this again."

Barney and Lyda glanced at each other before hanging their heads. Neither had anything to say in their own defense, which suited Henry just fine. He doubted anything they produced would change his mind about unwittingly being used as bait.

"Well, this has been...enlightening." Grace checked the time on her phone. "It's eleven twenty-five. Dad will be at the coffee shop in five minutes."

He pinched the bridge of his nose. "Great. We wasted the entire night."

"Sorry." Lyda dipped her chin. "I swear, we wouldn't have let him... It's just, your dad's an attorney. We thought he would press charges."

"Save it." Grace hopped on her bike, and Henry followed.

Once out of earshot of the two, Henry said, "I can't believe they set us up."

"Me either. I understand they're desperate to put an end to Kirk's bullying. I feel sorry for them that they've been driven to this extreme."

"Yeah." He couldn't shake the guilt. "They were sort of following our lead, though."

She winced again. "Yes, but I wouldn't have punched Kirk in the nose if I hadn't been trying to prevent Barney from ruining his future."

"True, but I gave them the idea for the video."

"From now on, we stick to solving mysteries. No getting personally involved."

"Easier said than done. Besides, think of all the good we've done on other cases. Would you really want to miss out on the chance to help someone?" He batted his lashes at her.

She chuckled. "No, but we need to find a balance between the two."

"I have an idea. A crazy one, but it just might save the night. Do you trust me?"

"That depends on what you're planning to do." Her grin told him she'd have his back no matter what.

He stopped and dialed their father's number.

"Henry, I'm almost to the coffee shop. Are you two ready to go?" Ethan's words came out faster than usual. He'd likely polished off a pot of coffee while working.

"Not quite. How would you like to get in on our latest mystery?" He glanced at his sister and wiggled his brows.

Shaking her head, she mouthed, "Bad idea."

"Is this about needing my help or needing to stay out past curfew?"

"Maybe a little of both. I'll explain when we see you."

"I can't wait to hear all about it." Ethan disconnected the call.

Grace covered her mouth as if to keep her words from tumbling out. It didn't work. "What have you done? Didn't we learn this lesson in West Virginia?"

"Remember, you said you trusted me." He pedaled away.

"No, I said it depended on your plan."

CHAPTER SEVEN

All things considered, Ethan Warner took the news of the twins' escapade with Dapylil well. He didn't yell or ask a million questions or ground them for life. He simply listened and nodded. When they'd finished, he closed his eyes, drew a deep breath, and remained uncharacteristically quiet.

"Dad?" Grace touched his arm.

She'd never seen him react in such a way. Normally, he behaved like an attorney. He took in the information, asked for clarification, and presented his arguments on the good, bad, and ugly of the situation. His utter silence worried her.

Ethan cleared his throat. "When exactly did you meet this woman?"

"We left the senior center a little early," Henry said from the backseat. "The residents we were assigned to sent us to meet her."

"Let me make sure I understand. Did you actually have a headache, or did you lie to the volunteer coordinator, your mother, and me?"

"No, sir."

"I'm disappointed in you both."

Grace's stomach felt like a mop in a wringer bucket. "You're right. There's no excuse for our behavior. We should have told the truth, the whole truth, and nothing but."

He scrubbed his jaw. "We're going to tell your mother about this in the morning."

"Yes, sir," the twins said in unison.

Ethan started the truck.

Grace glanced over her shoulder at her brother and sighed.

"Shouldn't we tell her tonight?" Henry squared his shoulders.

"No. She'll be asleep by the time we get back from the Moose Lodge." Ethan grinned and hit the gas.

Grace's mouth fell open.

Henry chuckled. "You're the best dad ever."

"You're still grounded," Ethan said. "In fact, I'm tacking on an extra week for the lying. I'm sure your mother will agree."

From the outside, the Lodge looked like a typical two-story house—if a typical house had a huge meeting hall attached to the back of it, a handful of cars in the parking lot, and music seeping from the building.

Grace zoomed in on the map of the area. "There's a baseball field in back. The creek is on the other side, past some trees."

Ethan slowed the truck to a crawl. "Moose Lodges are members only. I'm going to park near the other vehicles. Otherwise, it'll look suspicious."

"Whatever happens, we stick together." Grace nudged her father's side. "And no running off alone to chase the monsters."

"These are alleged frogs, not crazy flying robots dressed as the Mothman." Ethan smirked. "Did this Daffydill woman say what time to be here?"

"Dapylil..." Henry climbed out of the truck. "Nope, but everyone knows midnight is when the creepy-crawlies come out to play."

"Of course, it is." Ethan zipped his jacket and put on a brave face. "Did she really have dozens of frogs crawling on her?"

"Do I detect a note of fear in your voice?" Grace grinned. Her father had a spider phobia, but otherwise, she'd never seen him get squirrely about nature.

"I'm not a fan of toads."

"Good thing it's cold. The only amphibians we have to worry about are the human variety...or the supernatural..." She imitated Rod Serling from the Twilight Zone.

Ethan muttered, "Thanks, but I'm not sure that's better."

Laughing, Henry led them across the ballfield. "How are your lectures going?"

"The students have turned the tables on the professor. Rather than spending the entire class listening to me talk, we're diving into an actual case."

"Whoa, you're actively working to free a convict?" Henry's eyes lit up.

"I'm not convinced he's innocent, but yes, we're looking into the evidence," Ethan said. "We have access to DNA from both the perpetrator and the victim, but it wasn't presented in the original trial."

"Does it match the man who was convicted?"

"Don't know yet. We're waiting on court orders to run the analyses."

Grace glanced between her father and her brother. "I'm beginning to understand what you two must feel like when Mom and I talk engineering."

Ethan shook his head. "I doubt that. The law might not be your cup of tea, but you can follow our conversations."

"True." She moved her flashlight over the tree line and nodded to a footpath. "This way."

Henry lowered his voice. "Will the judge rule before we leave for Wisconsin?"

"It's not likely, and I definitely won't be around when everything is settled."

Grace compared her father's situation to the current mystery. Even if they did prove Kirk and his friends were behind the hoax, they wouldn't be around to see if anything changed for Barney and Lyda. "Why go through all the trouble if you don't believe he was wrongfully convicted?"

"Some do, some don't. He was the obvious choice. He had a motive, and circumstantial evidence places him at the scene," Ethan said.

"But?"

"But when you look deeper, there were two others who had even better means and reasons to commit the crime." He turned to her and smiled. "Human behavior is almost never obvious or as cut and dried as it is on detective shows. It's messy, although usually, the most obvious perpetrator *is* the one who did it. Those cases represent the vast majority, and they almost never go to trial."

Once again, Grace filtered their mystery through his words. They had one bunch of suspects: Kirk and his crew. The twins had pretty much decided their guilt based on the red lipstick, the mean girls' height, and finding them in the right place at the right time. She turned to Henry. "We need to widen the net."

He stopped and stared. "I was thinking the exact same thing. We're basing our assumptions solely on circumstantial evidence."

"It's difficult being the parent of two individuals who share the same brain." Ethan chuckled.

Henry smirked. "It's not always easy having someone inside your head."

She elbowed him in the side. "Okay, back to the matter at hand. The railroad tracks are on the other side of the creek."

Ethan eyed the water, the trees beyond, and finally, his kids. "You're not suggesting we cross it? It's freezing out here."

"Dapylil said we'd find them between a moose and a railway." Grace moved closer to the creek and shined her light over the water. "We might be able to walk across those rocks."

Henry followed her gaze. "I'm with Dad on this one. The water isn't deep, but it's cold."

"Even if our feet get wet, we won't die of hypothermia. The truck isn't *that* far away." She set her hands on her hips and tilted her head. "Afraid you can't make it across without face-planting?"

Henry narrowed his eyes. He might have tried to look menacing, but he couldn't hide his grin. "Is that a challenge?"

Ethan cleared his throat. "Kids?"

"Heck, yes. Last one across cooks dinner for a month." She made clucking sounds. "Or are you chicken?"

Henry rubbed his hands together. "You're on."

"Kids!" Ethan pointed across the creek. "We have company."

Grace caught a glimpse of her dad's freaked-out expression and followed his line of vision. "Oh!"

On the far side of the creek stood three creatures with large mouths, yellow eyes, and dark green skin. Grace didn't know if they were more humanoid or frogoid or just downright bizarre. What she did know was they'd found the Loveland Frogs.

Henry ran toward the rocks.

One of the frogmen shrieked, and the other two ribbited. However, they remained standing near the tree line.

Ethan hesitated for a heartbeat, shook his head, and followed.

"Don't let them out of our sight!" Rather than hopscotching across the rocks, Grace plowed straight through the water.

The shrieking frog twirled a staff, pounded it on the ground, and pointed it at Grace.

Before she could puzzle out what was happening, a loud boom filled her ears and a blast of light left her seeing spots. Only they weren't just spots. Several balls of sparks shot in her direction. She had no time to scream or think or do anything except hit the water.

"Grace!" Ethan called to her.

The light had left her vision blurry, but she made out the silhouette of her dad slogging toward her. "I'm okay. Go after them."

"I don't care about them. I'm worried about you." He hoisted her to her feet and looked her over.

The reality of what had happened left her colder than the water. "They tried to incinerate me."

"Take deep breaths. You're okay."

"Stop!" Henry's voice broke through the haze of her fear.

She turned in time to see her brother disappearing into the trees on the far side of the creek. "We have to help him."

"Go back to the truck and turn on the heater." He wrapped his jacket around her shoulders and shoved the keys into her hand. "I'll go after him."

"No. We said we weren't going to split up." She clamped her mouth closed to stop her teeth from chattering.

Ethan made a sound in the back of his throat. "Right. Let's go but stay close."

Grace reached for her phone, only to realize she'd lost it in the creek. "I don't have a light. My cell drowned, and my bag is in the truck."

"My cell is there, too. I left it behind in case your mom called." He winced at the admission.

"We'll manage."

A flashlight beam bounced through the forest like the ball in a sing-a-long video. Unfortunately, it grew farther away by the second.

"I see Henry. Let's hurry." She trudged through the creek and hit the tree line at full speed.

"Be careful," Ethan called from behind her.

Henry let out a strangled scream from somewhere to her left. "Whoa! Easy. I mean no harm."

Heart thundering, Grace glanced back at Ethan.

He pushed past her and ran in the direction of his son's voice.

So much for sticking together. Grace followed a little slower than before. She'd never admit it out loud, but it felt like her blood was the consistency of a slushie.

"Trespassers!"

Grace didn't recognize the voice, but whoever it belonged to sounded ancient.

"We're leaving right now." Ethan raised his hands. "Right, Henry?"

"Right, but did you happen to see three giant frogs?"

She eased behind her father and peeked around his broad shoulders. As she'd suspected, the wildman made dirt look young. He had wild hair, wore wild-animal pelts, and had a wild look in his eyes. "Forget them, Henry. Let's get out of here."

The crazy guy shook his walking stick at them. "Get off my land before I sic my hounds on you!"

As if said hounds had heard their master, barking echoed off the surrounding trees.

"Sorry we disturbed you and your dogs." Henry swallowed hard and took several steps back.

"Go!" The wild-man shouted.

Ethan nearly tripped over Grace in his haste to retreat. Once out of arm's reach, he set one hand on each of the twins' shoulders and guided them away from the strange man.

"Is that guy for real?" Henry glanced over his shoulder.

Ethan moved his hand to the back of Henry's neck. "Keep moving."

"Dad, it's okay." Grace bit her lip. While the situation seemed serious, she couldn't shake the feeling they'd been played. "I think this was all staged."

Gritting his teeth, Ethan said, "They fired a roman candle at you."

"Not a very big one." Henry grinned. "Plus, they were well out of range. The firework hit the water a good five feet in front of her."

"Out of range or not, your sister could have been burned." Ethan stopped when they reached the creek. "As it is, she's half-frozen."

Grace hung her head. She couldn't argue with the truth.

Henry, ever the debater, refused to give up. "I understand if you want us to stop trying to solve the mystery, but there's something you should know."

"I'm listening but keep moving." He led them to the rocks.

"Grace and I believe the town bully is mixed up in all of this. He's been harassing two teens for years, and no one can do anything about it." Henry went across first.

Ethan motioned for Grace to go. "Why not?"

She took the rocks extra slow to avoid falling in again. "His dad is the superintendent of schools, and his best friend's father is a police officer."

"That certainly complicates matters." He crossed the creek and motioned toward the path. "I've been involved for, what? Two hours now?"

The twins nodded.

"I'm surprised you don't see it." Ethan grinned.

"See what?" Grace blew on her hands to warm up.

He chuckled. "You two are falling into the trap of focusing on the obvious perpetrator."

Henry face-palmed. "Unless Kirk knows a Hollywood-quality makeup artist, there's no way that man-beast back there was one of his goons."

Grace groaned. "Which means we're way off-base."

"Or there are more people involved than we thought." Henry shook his head. "I think we need to have a word with Inez."

CHAPTER EIGHT

People packed every available chair in the rec room at the Golden Years Senior Center. The tables were filled with cards, daubers, and trinkets. It seemed as though every oldster within a thirty-mile radius had turned out for Bingo Day.

"Be quiet and stay near the wall. Only cross in front of a table when someone calls bingo or needs a new dauber." Ms. Simon spoke in a tone far too serious for the occasion. "After some unfortunate incidents, we were forced to purchase special markers that don't stain the skin. They are expensive. Each player may have *one* dauber at a time. Understand?"

Henry glanced from the basket of markers in his hand to the volunteer coordinator. "Piece of cake."

She leaned into his personal space. "Trust me, you do *not* want to block their view of the board. They take their bingo very seriously."

Grace chewed her lip. "What do we do if we find the person marked their card incorrectly?"

"Ask for a recall, and I'll do a second review."

The twins exchanged glances.

The man on the stage, who was wearing a bright purple suit, tapped the microphone. "New round in five...four...three..."

A silence fell over the room as the seniors readied their daubers. Henry experienced the same sense of nervous anticipation he had felt when taking the SAT. Pencil poised, waiting for the proctor to instruct them to open their test packets, it had felt like his entire future hung in the balance.

"This is insane," he whispered.

"Shhhh!" Several seniors glared.

"Two...one!" Purple suit guy pressed a button on the machine, and a ball flew into the tube. "B-3. B-3." He checked the flashboard and called the next number.

"Ms. Simon wasn't kidding." Grace glanced around the room.

"This can't be good for their blood pressure."

"There's Inez."

Henry squinted. "Where? It's hard to tell who's who when they all have their heads down."

"I'm pretty sure that was an ageist comment."

He gave her a dubious look. "Intent is nine-tenths of the law."

"That's possession, not intent." She nodded toward the front left corner of the room. "Yellow t-shirt, third row."

"I'm going over there." He slid his arm through his basket handle and stepped between two tables.

The lady sitting in the second seat stood and swatted him with a doll dressed like Mariah Carey. "Get out of the way!"

Rubbing his arm, he said, "Sorry."

More seniors shushed him.

Holy bingo, these people are intense. Henry had walked around the perimeter of the room, halfway to Inez, when a gentleman with long silver hair raised his hand. Henry ducked to avoid another doll incident and made his way between the tables.

"Green, please." The man held out his hand.

Henry checked his basket. "I don't have green. How about blue?"

"And mess up my system?" His voice rose in pitch and volume. "I need green and make it snappy. I'm missing numbers. You're costing me money!"

"Shhhhh!" The seniors surrounding them glared.

Henry nodded and duck-walked his way out of the row.

Grace's face had turned red, likely from holding back laughter. She signaled to herself and pointed at Inez.

Rolling his eyes, Henry hurried to the back of the room, where the supplies were kept. There must have been a hundred bingo daubers, but not a single green one. *Dang it.*

The silver-haired gentleman waved both arms as if imitating windshield wipers. This, of course, started a mini-riot behind him.

Ms. Simon shot into action.

Seeing his opportunity to bail on the hunt for a green dauber, Henry hurried to Grace.

"What was that about?" She stared at the commotion on the other side of the room.

"He wanted green. I didn't have it."

"Of course, you didn't have it. They banned green daubers when the players began fighting over the color. But you would know that if you'd paid attention to the bingo orientation."

Henry dragged his hand over his face. "Since when is green everyone's favorite color?"

"Since it looks like money."

Inez glanced in their direction, narrowed her eyes, and yelled, "Bingo! Warinskis! I have Bingo!"

"Oh, boy." He ran his hand over the back of his neck.

Grace plastered a smile on her face and hurried to Inez.

Inez presented her card with the same triumphant expression she'd worn when she sent the twins to meet the crazy frog lady. Henry didn't need psychic abilities to know she had something up her sleeve.

Grace glanced from the card to the flashboard and back several times before scanning the crowd for Ms. Simon.

The volunteer coordinator had her hands full with the silver-haired gentleman and the angry seniors around him. From the looks of it, things were about to get ugly. Very ugly.

Inez narrowed her eyes. "Well?"

"I need a second opinion." The bingo card trembled in Grace's hand.

"This isn't a surgery consultation, honey." Gladys smirked. "Did she win or not?

"I'll do the recall." Henry stepped forward and took the card from his sister.

Ignoring him, Inez turned to Gladys. "I wonder if there will be a new video today? I heard Mary Margaret tell Edward her grandson had a run-in with the frogmen last night over by Lake Sybella."

Grace whispered, "That's funny, because I heard they were behind the Moose Lodge last night."

"You know frogs. They get around." Inez shrugged. "I'd be happy to introduce you to Mary Margaret. Her grandson visits every day after school."

"No, thank you." Grace leaned closer. "But I'd like a word with you after the game."

"Make me a happy woman, and you can have all the words you want."

Henry compared the woman's card to the flashboard. She had three of the five letter-number combinations, a far cry from bingo.

"Well, son. What's the verdict?" The guy in the purple suit called from the stage.

"She's mistaken. Go ahead and call the next number." Smiling, Henry handed the card back to Inez.

"You'll be sorry you did that."

"Maybe, but I don't like cheaters any more than I like wild goose chases."

"He's got spirit. I'll give him that." The lady beside Gladys laughed and applied bright red lipstick.

Before Henry could ask her name, the game resumed.

Inez furrowed her brow and glanced around. "Susan? Where's my little girl? Oh, Susan! Where can she be?"

Henry blanched. While he had a hard time believing Inez's cognitive functioning had changed that quickly, he was no expert on dementia.

The bingo caller leaned closer to the microphone. "Is she all right?"

"I'm not sure," Henry said.

By this point, Inez had gone into full-blown hysteria. She climbed onto the table and shouted, "Susan! Be a good girl and come back to Mommy."

Grace whisper-shouted, "We have to do something."

"What do you suggest?" Henry held his arms wide in case Inez stumbled on the bingo cards and good luck charms. "Please come down from the table."

Giggling, Gladys scooped hers and Inez's cards from the table.

"This isn't funny! She could get hurt." Henry split his attention between the ladies.

"She warned you." Gladys winked and popped a candy into her mouth.

She winked!

Any doubt Inez was faking the entire episode evaporated when he caught the gleam in her eye.

"Uh-oh." Grace tensed beside him.

Inez pointed a bony finger at the twins. "They took her! The Warners took my baby! Someone arrest them!"

"*Now* she gets our names right?" Henry muttered.

Four staff members in putrid-yellow scrubs struggled to make their way to Inez, but the seniors at the surrounding tables blocked their path. Some seemed confused by the commotion, some angry, and others grinned like they were in on the joke.

Grace held her hand out to Inez. "Mrs. Ingram, please come down off the table before you—"

"Fall and break a hip?" The woman beside Gladys cackled.

Henry met her gaze and tilted his head. She seemed familiar. Very familiar. "Have we met?"

"No, I don't think so." She patted her hair, grabbed her walker, and headed for the other end of the table. "Excuse me."

Moving her dentures around, Inez watched her friend go. She turned back to the twins, winked, and threw her arm over her face.

"Miss Inez, you need to come down from there." A male staff member about the same size as Kirk offered his hand.

Inez Ingram could have been a soap opera actress in her younger years. She drew a breath, sighed dramatically, and fake-fainted into the man's arms.

"Oh, brother." Grace shook her head.

Gladys leaned close and lowered her voice. "Don't mess with us. We might be old, but we aren't afraid to play dirty."

"You're telling me?" Grace sighed.

"Warners. A word, please." Ms. Simon tapped her foot.

Henry had seen his mother wear the same exasperated expression when he'd made some bone-head move, but it was different coming from someone other than a parent. Scarier, somehow. The twins followed the volunteer coordinator into the hall.

"What happened back there?" The woman's voice rose to the point Henry wondered why she had bothered to take them from the main room.

"The gentleman asked for a green dauber—"

"Herman and several others claim he asked for a blue marker, but you refused to give him one."

Henry's mouth fell open. "That's not—"

"What happened with Inez?"

Grace said, "She thought she had Bingo, but she'd mismarked her card. She had some sort of breakdown—"

"It wasn't a breakdown. She has Alzheimer's." Ms. Simon sighed. "Perhaps it's better if the two of you find another place to volunteer."

Grace gasped.

"Ms. Simon, these two went above and beyond to assist Inez during her episode. I, for one, would hate to see them go." Pearl had evidently eavesdropped on the entire conversation. She made her way toward them with the help of her walker, one slow step at a time.

The volunteer coordinator glanced at them.

"And Herman is a horse's patootie. It wouldn't be the first time he tried to scam a new volunteer out of a green dauber." Pearl smiled the first genuine smile Henry had seen since setting foot in the place. "Let them stay."

Ms. Simon sighed and motioned to the rec room. "You can stay, but please give Inez some space. For some reason, you two seem to set her off."

The twins resumed their position by the wall and did their best to ignore Gladys's evil eye.

Grace whispered, "I can't figure it out. They seem to know a lot about the frogmen, but there's no way Inez and the others are behind the hoax. Is there?"

He'd asked himself the same question too many times to count. "Remember what Dad said about motive and means? They don't have either."

"Right, but she definitely sent us to Dapylil."

Henry snickered. "That name."

"Focus." Grace nudged his shoulder. "The frog lady sent us to the trap at the Moose Lodge. Who was the hermit? And who are the people in the frog costumes?"

"Better question is, why did they send us there in the first place?"

"Probably to scare us off the case."

"That makes sense, but what do these oldsters have to do with frogs?" The entire situation made his head spin, but it also gave him an idea. "We're going about this backward. Besides Kirk, we have no suspects—"

"—but we have victims. And more are showing up on YouTube every few days."

"Bingo." Henry laughed.

Rather than tempting fate, or Kirk, the twins left their bikes at the senior center and walked to the coffee shop. If anyone could identify the people in the videos, Barney Buell could. Plus, he owed them big time after the stunt he and Lyda had pulled the night before.

Henry peered into the window. "Empty except for a couple at a table and Lyda behind the counter."

"That's good. I guess." Grace swiveled her head to check the sidewalks.

Henry understood her apprehension. He'd met some horrible people since starting the research project, but Kirk was a triple threat—muscle, no brain, and minions to help with the dirty work. "I'm not looking forward to running into Kirk either. Let's get in and get out."

"Deal." She gave him a ghost of a smile. "I want a pumpkin spice latte. It's your turn to buy."

Lyda glanced up and sighed. "I didn't expect to see you two in here again."

"You have the best coffee in town," Henry said. "I'll have a mocha, and she wants a pumpkin spice *blah*-tte."

"Cute." Lyda reached for the mugs.

"To go." Grace glanced over her shoulder.

Lyda gave them a knowing look. "Anything else?"

"A little help identifying the other people in the frogmen videos."

"We thought Barney could help us track them down." Grace eyed the pastries in the display case.

Lyda rubbed her forehead. "I've been thinking about what happened last night, and I'm sorry. We should never have used you as bait."

While he appreciated the apology, her terminology left much to be desired.

"You can make it up to us by helping us solve this mystery," Grace told her.

Lyda coated the bottom of a to-go cup with chocolate syrup. "Done. And I'll throw in free coffee for life."

"Add two slices of that pound cake, and you have a deal." Henry wiggled his brows.

"It's the least I can do." Lyda worked her coffee magic behind the counter. "Barney wasn't at school today. He says he's coming down with something, but I know it's because he's afraid of Kirk."

Grace's shoulders slumped. "There has to be something or someone who can stop Kirk from terrorizing the two of you."

"I wish." Lyda opened the case and pulled out two slices. "See that couple over there? They're the stars of the video before mine and Barney's. I'll introduce you."

Coffee and treats in hand, the twins followed Lyda to a table in the back corner. The couple stared—not smiling, not frowning, just stared—as if unsure what to make of the interruption.

"Wayne and Jen, this is Grace and Henry Warner." Lyda motioned to the twins. "They're trying to figure out who's filming and posting the frogmen videos."

The couple glanced at each other before they lowered their gazes to their mugs.

"We don't want to talk about it." Wayne spoke in a low but forceful tone.

Jen took his hand.

Lyda knelt beside the table. "I know you're scared, but—"

"I'm not scared." Wayne snapped.

Jen said, "Since that stupid video was posted, we can't walk down the halls at school without someone laughing at us."

Henry had watched all the recent frogmen footage numerous times. Wayne's and Jen's video was particularly embarrassing because he'd run away and left his girlfriend behind to fend for herself.

Grace sat at the adjacent table. "Did you happen to see anyone else in the woods that night?"

"Barney Buell." Wayne stared at Lyda as if expecting an explanation.

"He's been hunting the frogs since this started." Lyda folded her arms. "But he couldn't have been the one holding the camera. He was with me the night I saw the frogmen."

Jen furrowed her brow. "So? He could have had a hidden camera."

"The footage was too shaky to have come from a mounted camera." Henry sat beside his sister. "We think someone else was out there. It stands to reason the same person is recording all the videos."

"Yeah, I guess that makes sense. Barney doesn't seem like the type to do something like this anyway." Jen sighed.

Grace nodded. "Besides the obvious, did you notice anything strange that night?"

The couple exchanged glances.

"We passed Tiffany and the Tinkerbell twins on the bike path. I thought it was strange they were so close to nature." Jen's tone and the curl of her lip told Henry she didn't care for the flyers.

"Tiffany?" Grace glanced at Lyda.

"Kirk's arm candy."

"Ah. Right." Laughing, she rolled her eyes. "I should have guessed when you said the Tinkerbell twins."

Wayne pressed his lips together. "Look. We don't want any trouble with

Kirk. The flyers were probably walking home from a movie or something. We're not saying they had anything to do with this."

"I'm sorry, but I can't take it anymore." Jen squeezed his forearm before turning to the twins. "I'm one-hundred percent sure Kirk is behind this.

"Jen." Wayne shook his head.

She continued speaking, "He knew about the video before it posted."

Henry fought to keep his expression neutral, but they were finally getting somewhere. "How do you know?"

The girl shrugged. "He teased me in third-period Math, but the time stamp on the video was four-fifteen."

Wayne motioned to the twins. "You can't repeat that to anyone."

"We've had a couple of run-ins with Kirk. We wouldn't do or say anything to cause someone else the same fate." Grace pushed her pound cake away. "But we're going to do everything in our power to put an end to the frogmen fiasco."

"And the bullying." Henry broke off a piece of her dessert and popped it in his mouth.

CHAPTER NINE

All the talk of bullies left Grace with a stomachache and a worsening case of paranoia. She speed-walked down the bike path and ducked into the forest as soon as they'd reached the head of O'Bannonville Creek. Skulking around at night was one thing, but doing it in broad daylight was asking for trouble.

"Try to relax. You're making me nervous." Henry chuckled. Loud.

She gave him the side-eye. "I'll relax when you quiet down and tell me why we're invading Kirk's hunting ground."

He arched a brow. "Which is it? Do you want me to be quiet or explain?"

"You're too young for dad jokes." Grace drew a deep breath to calm her nerves and to keep her from socking her brother in the arm.

"We're here to get a better lay of the land."

"And why do we need that?" She had a feeling she knew his answer, but she wanted to hear him say it.

"Because we're going to set a trap, and I'd like to find a couple of hiding places before we're running for our lives from firework-shooting frogs, or bullies, or both."

"That's what I was afraid you were going to say. Are you crazy?"

"Probably." He laughed and walked farther into the woods.

Grace followed close behind.

He stopped in the clearing where the altercation with Kirk had taken place. "There's basically one way back here that doesn't involve swimming. We'll set the cameras near the bike path. We need to find someplace we can lay low, and while we're at it, we might as well look for clues."

Grace checked the time and frowned. She'd been grounded a grand total of five times in her life, three of which had been since they'd started solving mysteries. "We don't have much time before Mom and Dad get home."

"That reminds me. What's on the menu tonight?" Turning a full circle, Henry studied the area as he went.

"It's your turn to cook." She walked to the trees on the Little Miami River side of the clearing.

"You have dinner duty for a month. I made it across the creek first." He snatched a decent-sized stick from the ground and rooted through the leaf litter where the girls had stood the previous night.

"Because a frog shot a bottle rocket at me."

"Excuses won't save you." Henry knelt and picked something up. "Gotcha."

"What did you find?"

"I saw one of the mean girls drop a candy wrapper last night." He held it up to the fading afternoon sun.

"While I applaud your concern for the environment, we already have one of those." She swept the stick over the ground as she walked the tree line.

"This one is a different brand of chocolate." He stood and moved to her side. "Is the other one still in your bag?"

Grace fished the lipstick smeared one out of her bag and compared it to the other. "It's possible she likes to mix it up when it comes to sweets, but you have my attention."

He pointed to the wrapper in her hand. "Pearl—Inez's friend?—was eating this brand today at bingo."

"And she was wearing red lipstick." Her pulse sped for a half-second before she remembered the woman used a walker, and even then, she seemed to struggle. "But this can't belong to her. She could barely make it up the hall, let alone all the way out here."

"I hate to say this out loud, but what if she's faking her condition like Inez did today?"

Grace stared. "Why on earth would someone pretend to need a walker?"

He frowned and kicked the dirt. "I have no idea."

She thought back to what Barney said about the Golden Years' being the hot hangout for the senior crowd. They'd had quite the crowd for bingo, but not everyone there used a walker or seemed ill. "Does a person need a medical diagnosis to come to the day program?"

Henry said, "I zoned out for most of the orientation, but I remember Ms. Simon saying some of the activities were open to anyone over sixty-five."

"Like bingo."

"Exactly, but Pearl and Gladys attend on other days, too." He let his head fall back and groaned. "We're right back where we started. No real suspects. Kirk's too tall for the frog costumes."

"The mean girls are pretty short, and Jen said they were in the area the night they saw the frogmen."

Henry pressed his lips together. "Do you really believe those three would mess up their hair wearing a giant frog mask?"

Grace giggled. "Not a chance."

"We should head home." He rested his stick against a tree and froze in place.

She stilled and listened for Kirk's loud voice. "Did you hear something?"

"No, but I may have found something." Henry crouched, reached into the hollow trunk, and retrieved a white plastic bag.

She recognized it instantly. Ms. Simon had given the twins the same type of bag to store their belongings on their first day. "What's inside?"

Henry pulled two women's blouses, two pairs of slacks, and a sweater. The shirts were both pullovers, each in a pastel flower pattern, and the polyester pants had an elastic waistband. "These aren't something a teen would wear."

"I'm not sure what to make of this." Grace struggled to wrap her brain around the find. "Okay. Let's say these belong to one of the frogmen. Wouldn't we find the costume instead of the street clothes?"

"That would make more sense."

"Check to see if there's a name written on the inside."

Henry riffled through the clothing. "G. Gibson."

"Should we take them to Ms. Simon? She may know who they belong to." As soon as she'd said the words, she regretted it. "On second thought, never mind. We can't ask her without telling her why we want to know."

"No, but there are a couple of others we can ask." He put the bag back where he'd found it.

Arts and crafts class at the Golden Years didn't have the same draw as bingo. Only a few dozen seniors gathered to paint watercolor landscapes. Fortunately for the twins, Inez and crew had decided to channel their inner Bob Ross today.

"What do we do if this doesn't work?" Henry peered around the gigantic bouquet of flowers the twins had purchased on the way to the senior center.

"It'll work. No woman can resist pink roses and white lilies." Grace winked. "We have to hurry. Ms. Simon will be back from lunch soon."

"I still can't believe we were almost fired."

"Can you imagine having to tell Mom we were canned from a volunteer position?"

"That's the stuff of nightmares." Henry shuddered.

Waving a small red envelope, Grace called out, "Excuse me. Is there a G. Gibson in the room?"

His sister wasn't kidding. Every lady in the room stared at the flowers. Some sighed, some smiled, some frowned, but they all watched with hopeful expressions. It broke his heart that only one of them would receive the gift.

"G. Gibson?" Grace searched the room.

Inez raised her hand.

Henry chuckled. "Nice try Mrs. Ingram, but I doubt you have an alias."

"Not me, Warneroofus. Her." She pointed to the woman sitting next to her.

Gladys smiled. "I'm the only G. Gibson here."

Smiling back, Grace spoke without moving her lips. "How is it possible the clothes belong to her?"

"I don't know, but I intend to find out," Henry whispered.

The twins made their way through the maze of tables and art supplies to the ladies. Pearl and Gladys stared at the flowers as if they were made of gold, but Inez hadn't stopped glaring since they'd walked into the rec room.

"Are you sure you're the only G. Gibson? This is a big place." Henry glanced over the room.

"Well, there *is* George, but I don't think anyone would send that old geezer roses." Gladys cleared a spot for the vase. "Give me the card."

Grace cupped it in her hand. "Not yet. I have some questions first."

The ladies exchanged glances.

Inez pressed her hand to her chest and moaned.

"Nice try, Inez." Henry would never be able to look at himself in the mirror if he was wrong, but he highly doubted the ornery old woman's heart had given out.

"He's got your number." Pearl laughed, high and melodious. She reminded him of his grandmother. *Except Gram keeps better friends.*

Gladys said, "Pearl, didn't you say Ms. Simon told these two to stay away from us?"

She bit back her smile. "Only Inez, but I think it was more for *their* good than the drama mama's."

Inez dropped her hand. "Who are you calling a drama mama?"

Pearl turned to Grace. "Go ahead and ask your questions. None of us are getting any younger."

"Why do you have a bag of clothes stashed near O'Bannonville Creek?" Grace smiled like she'd thrown down the winning hand.

The twins hadn't won yet, not by a long shot. All it would take was for one of them to fake an attack of lumbago or something, and the twins would be out on their backsides.

Folding his arms, Henry watched the ladies' reactions.

Gladys sniffed and turned her head. "I don't know what you're talking about."

"Someone must have stolen her things and dumped them in the old tree trunk." Inez lifted her chin.

A slow smile spread across Grace's face. "I never mentioned they were in the tree trunk."

Pearl stared at the ceiling, but she couldn't seem to tame her smile. In fact, she looked downright amused.

Inez narrowed her eyes, pressed her hand to her chest again, and groaned even louder than the first time.

Several nearby seniors turned and stared, but none seemed concerned. They'd likely spent enough time around the woman to know her tricks. Thankfully, the staff in the room didn't seem any more concerned than the others.

Henry sighed. "All right. We thought we'd do this the easy way, but since none of you will tell us the truth, we'll take the clothes to Ms. Simon."

"No," Gladys snapped. "Don't do that. We'll cooperate."

The twins seated themselves across from the ladies.

Pearl opened her mouth as if to speak, but Gladys elbowed her.

Inez said, "Some of us grew up in Loveland. That little bit of land between the creek and the river is special to us."

"My Henry took me on a picnic there for our first date." Gladys sighed.

"I used to go down there and sketch the trees." Pearl lifted her watercolor painting so the twins could see it. "Sometimes I still do."

"It's beautiful." Grace smiled. "You captured the mystique of the place."

"Thank you." She leaned closer and lowered her voice. "You realize it's very close to here..."

The twins nodded.

Henry held his breath, waiting for her to continue.

Pearl sat back and gazed at her painting as if it were a photograph of a long-lost love.

"Are you trying to tell us that some of you still visit the forest?" He couldn't keep the surprise out of his voice.

"We did…" Inez hesitated as if deciding how to continue. "Until the teenagers ran us off."

Henry could picture how Kirk and the others would react to finding a bunch of senior citizens in his hangout. "Did they harass you?"

"You could say that." Inez sat back and folded her arms like a spoiled child.

Grace's mouth fell open.

"I don't mean to be rude, but how long ago was that? Are we talking recently or years ago?" Henry asked.

Glancing at the others, Pearl said, "About three months back."

"How?" Grace shook her head. "I mean, how do you manage the walk? The banks are pretty steep."

The ladies shrugged in unison.

"We have our ways." Inez snickered.

Gladys added, "We'd tell you, but we'd have to cut your tongues out to keep you silent."

Pearl, the apparent voice of reason, shook her head. "One of the nurses' aides likes to nap on her overnight shift. It's pretty easy to break Inez and some of the others out of here. The part-timers don't know which of us live here and which come for the day program."

Grace wore a horrified expression.

The women cackled.

The puzzle pieces began to click together to form a picture in his mind, but the center remained a giant hole. "What, if anything, does this have to do with the frogmen?"

"The kids dressed like giant frogs and scared the dickens out of us." Gladys narrowed her eyes. "And before you say it, we know they aren't real."

He scratched his head. None of the videos on YouTube showed the frogmen chasing senior citizens. "Did they film it?"

Inez said, "Nope. We figure they came up with the idea to document scaring people after they saw how we reacted."

"You may be right." Henry could see it, but something didn't fit. "If you know they aren't real, why send us to Dapylil—"

"—and the Moose Lodge?" Grace added.

"What I wouldn't have given to see the two of you talking to Pearl under that bridge!" Inez threw her head back and laughed, and the others joined in.

"That was you?" Grace laughed along with the ladies. "How could you stand to let those frogs crawl all over you?"

"The one in my hand is my great-grandson's pet. The rest were fake." Pearl sat up straighter, clearly pleased with herself. "Did you like my costume?"

Grace nodded. "It was...interesting."

"I've worn it to pass out candy for Halloween going on ten years now." She winked. "With the same frog! Did you know they can live for twelve years? Sometimes longer."

Grace made a face. "I had no idea."

Henry sat back in his chair. "I'm impressed, but you still haven't told us why you sent us out there."

Gladys shrugged. "We figured you would tell the other kids. Thought we'd give you all a taste of your own medicine."

While her explanation made sense, it didn't clear up one vital detail. Henry glanced at Grace to read her reaction. After all, the frogmen behind the Moose Lodge had attacked her.

She looked from Inez to Gladys to Pearl. "If you three aren't the frogmen, how is it they were behind the Moose Lodge the night you sent us there?"

The ladies had similar reactions to the question—wide eyes, open mouths, gasps. They'd done a good job fooling him up until then, but he doubted they could have faked their surprise. Someone would have broken ranks with a smirk or a glare.

"I'm confused, and it's not dementia this time." Inez said, "If you had a run-in with the frogs, why isn't there a video of the two of you on YouTube?"

"We don't know." Henry scratched his jaw. "It could be the person didn't have a good place to hide."

"Thank goodness, there isn't," Grace said. "One of them shot a firework at me. I had to dive into the creek to avoid getting burned."

Henry nodded, although she'd stretched the truth a wee bit.

The ladies stared.

"You poor dear. I wasn't aware..." Gladys pushed to her feet and glanced around the room. "Herman, might I have a word with you?"

The silver-haired gentleman who'd caused the ruckus over the green dauber stood. He took one look at the twins and headed for the door.

"You have got to be kidding me." Just when Henry thought the ladies couldn't surprise him any further, they proved him wrong.

Inez shouted, "The jig is up, you old fart. They know."

Herman stopped and flashed them a smile. "About which, the woods or the game?"

Grace pressed her fingers against her temples. "Just when I think we've heard the worst. I realize we've only scratched the surface of their shenanigans."

Reaching across the table, Pearl took her hand and whispered, "We didn't mean to get you into trouble. Inez has never won a single round of bingo. She was desperate for bragging rights."

"But that's cheating! Plus, someone could have been hurt in all the hullabaloo."

"Can you forgive us?" Pearl dipped her chin. "While you're at it, I should put an end to—"

"What can I do for you?" The silver-haired gentleman frowned.

At first glance, Herman didn't resemble the hermit in the woods and looked like Dapylil more than Pearl. Henry squinted, imagining the man with his hair teased to rival Einstein's. Add in some dirt smears, and he could see it. In fact, he wondered how he'd missed it the first time.

"Were the frogs in the forest the other night to scare the Warnipsees?" Inez moved her dentures around.

"Not that I saw. I hid between the creek and the railroad tracks like you said." He flashed them a toothless grin. "I scared you both, didn't I? Your dad, too."

"You could say that." Henry ran a hand over his head, but nothing could relieve the tension.

Grace asked, "Didn't you hear the loud boom? The frogs shot a roman candle at me."

Herman's expression fell. "No, miss. I left my hearing aids out so I'd be sure to yell. I couldn't hear a darned word any of you said."

"Any idea how the people in frog costumes knew where we'd be?" Grace glanced at them.

"You didn't tell anyone?" Inez cocked her head.

"No," the twins said in unison.

"What are you going to do now?" Gladys cocked her head to the side.

"The flowers are from us. Enjoy them." Grace slid the red envelope toward her. "As far as I'm concerned, this mystery is solved. We know which teens are pretending to be the Loveland Frogs. We know who Dapylil and the hermit are. There's nothing else for us to do."

There she went, bending the truth again. Not that the ladies hadn't twisted and bent the truth into a balloon animal of their own. Henry trusted her instincts. She had her reasons for leading the ladies to believe they were stopping their investigation—even if he still couldn't see the puzzle finally assembled.

"Please be careful if you go back to the creek. The kids behind this aren't good people. They're bullies who hurt their classmates and destroy other people's property." Grace stood.

"That's it?" Inez frowned. "You're not going to stop the bad guys and give us back our land?"

"I'm afraid not. Some things are beyond our abilities." She forced a smile.

"Henry and Grace Warner, a word, please." Ms. Simon tapped her foot.

"This keeps getting better and better." He resisted the urge to pound his head on the table.

CHAPTER TEN

"I can't believe they fired you." Faith Warner pushed her plate away and tossed her napkin on the table.

"We shouldn't have gone near Inez after Ms. Simon told us to avoid her, but it's hard to say no to someone her age." Grace had pulled out all the stops. She'd added peas and carrots to the chicken and dumplings. Gross, but her mother loved it that way. She'd set a vase of fresh flowers on the table. Heck, she'd coaxed her brother into helping clean the entire fifth wheel—but nothing could soften the blow.

"You're right. You should have followed your supervisor's instructions, but firing a volunteer seems rather extreme." Faith sighed. "Why did she tell you to avoid this woman?"

Henry cracked a grin. "There was an incident at bingo. Inez tried to cheat. When we refused to play along, she pretended to have dementia."

Faith's eyes rounded. "It sounds as if this was quite the learning experience."

"It absolutely was." Grace smiled. "It's not all bad, though. We were invited to visit our friends at the Golden Years any time we wish."

Ethan dipped himself a second helping of dinner. "My guess is the facility was worried about liability more than your behavior. I wouldn't take this personally."

"That makes sense. We aren't trained to tell the difference between a medical emergency and a temper tantrum," Grace said.

Their parents laughed.

Henry detected a high note in the conversation and took his shot. "Mom, we need to go out tonight after we clean the kitchen. It has to do with our research project."

"You're grounded." All things considered, she spoke in a surprisingly soft tone.

"I know, and we wouldn't ask if it wasn't important," Grace said.

Pausing mid-bite, Ethan said, "I'm willing to hear your case."

"Very well." Faith glanced at the twins.

Grace looked at Henry, but he motioned for her to speak. "Remember the bullies we were telling you about?"

Ethan nodded.

"They've stooped as low as picking on senior citizens." Grace stood and took her dishes to the sink. "We have a plan to catch them in the act, but we can't do that if we aren't allowed out after dark."

Faith drummed her fingers on the table. "Why can't the seniors report it?"

"They aren't supposed to leave...to be out at night. Reporting the bullies would backfire and keep them from visiting the creek." Henry sighed. "You should have heard this sweet old lady, Gladys, talking about having her first date with her husband on the banks."

Grace choked on her own spit. Using the words "Gladys" and "sweet" had been challenging. "One of the women painted a picture of the trees. They're all heartbroken they can't go to their favorite place."

Faith glanced between the twins. "These are residents of the nursing home. They shouldn't be out at night unaccompanied."

"Pearl and Gladys aren't residents. They come for the day program but live with their families." Grace took a page from Inez's book and went for sympathy. "I'm sorry. These women—they have so little to look forward to. It's awful. A bunch of jerks is keeping them from enjoying a place that means so much to them."

Henry coughed, likely to keep from laughing.

Faith turned to her husband. "Are you buying any of this?"

He chuckled. "I believe what they're saying is true. The dramatics are questionable."

Grace rolled her eyes. "Okay. I may have overplayed it, but it makes me angry that one over-inflated..." She struggled to find a word to describe Kirk that wouldn't get her into more trouble.

"Calling this guy a jerk is an insult to jerks." Henry joined her at the kitchen sink. "He had some of his friends dress up as giant frogs to scare the oldsters. He enjoyed it so much that they started filming their victims."

"Whoa." Ethan made a T with his hands. "Time out. Are you saying these kids are the ones who fired a roman candle at Grace?"

"A what?" Faith rarely raised her voice, but when she did, she meant business.

"Uh-oh," Grace whispered.

Ethan seemed to realize his mistake and offered his wife a sheepish grin. "It wasn't as bad as it sounds. The kids were too far from her for it to... It never would have reached her."

"Ethan Joseph Warner, you should thank your lucky stars you're too old to be grounded." She laughed, surprising them all.

He chuckled. "I'd be game for a week with my family with nowhere to go and nothing to do."

"Hang in there. Winter break will be here soon." Faith turned to the twins. "As for going out tonight. What are the chances you can catch this kid and his friends without getting hurt?"

Grace's brain screeched to a halt. *Is she considering letting us go?*

"I'd say better than ninety-nine-point-nine percent. We've done this sort of thing before to catch the people pretending to be Charlie No-Face," Henry said.

"What sort of thing? I want details."

Their mother teetered on the edge of giving them permission. All she needed was a push. Something that would appeal to her engineering mind.

Grace grabbed a piece of paper from the drawer and sketched out a rough drawing of the area between the river and the creek. "The existing frogmen videos are shot from around here." She made an X between the trees and the slope leading to the bike trail.

Henry took the pen and drew a series of circles. "This area is heavily wooded and provides excellent cover. We believe they're hiding here because none of the victims have seen the person with the camera."

Faith arched a brow. "Then how are you sure this bully is behind it?"

Henry sat beside their mom. "The frogs are between four and five feet tall. Three cheerleaders who hang around Kirk fit the description."

Grace smiled. She had this in the bag. "For this age group, those heights are in the third percentile on the growth chart. There are about fourteen hundred students at Loveland High. If half are girls, that would mean approximately twenty-one are less than five feet tall. Assuming our suspects are juniors or seniors—"

"Okay." Faith held up her hands. "Good work. Now tell me the rest of the plan."

"I can't believe Mom let us go out." Grace's face hurt from smiling. Not only had their mother given them permission to stake out the forest, but she'd also packed them a snack bag.

"You dazzled her with statistics." Henry pedaled past her. "Hurry up. We have to get there in time to set up the cameras."

"About that." She pushed hard to catch up. "I didn't want to interrupt you once you started talking logistics, but what do you think about wearing the cameras instead of mounting them in a tree?"

"I like it. We have four. I say we put two in trees leading to the bike path and strap the other two to ourselves."

Grace pulled off the trail and went to stash her bike in the place Lyda had shown them and stopped. In the distance, a person was moving through the brush. "We have a problem."

Henry walked over and frowned. "What's Lyda doing out here?"

"Probably looking for Barney. This is going to complicate things. We should do this another night." She should have thought to call and check in with Lyda before they begged permission to come out. While her parents had surprised her once, the chances of them allowing the twins out a second time were slim to none.

"I'd rather not. We're here now. Hopefully, we can set up the cameras before we run into her." Henry hid his bike beside the others and hurried to the spot most likely to catch Kirk in action.

Pulling a roll of duct tape from her bag, Grace stepped back and used her flashlight to get a better look at the trees lining the escape route. Three large oaks sat in a triangle with several feet between them. The underbrush provided enough cover for a bully to hide but was sparse enough to allow movement.

"Perfect." Grace chose the one farthest from the path to attach the small camera. After double-checking the tape and triple-checking the angle, she hurried to Henry's side. "What's the holdup?"

He motioned between two trees. "These are the only ones with a clean shot of the ground, but neither has branches low enough to disguise the camera."

She frowned and circled the trunks. "What if you mount it low? The shrubs will hide it."

"For one, that's a holly bush, so I'd rather not stick my hand in it. For two, even if I get a clean shot now, it's windy. There's no guarantee the leaves won't obscure the lens." Henry fiddled with the camera hidden in his jacket. "At least we have these."

"I'd rather not get close enough to the big jerk to use the body cams." Grace tapped her lips. "It's dark. Cover everything but the lens with tape and affix it to the tree. It'll blend in with the bark."

"I hope so. These babies weren't cheap." Henry knelt and got to work.

"Grace?" Lyda stepped onto the path. "What are you doing out here? I thought you were grounded?"

Not exactly the warmest greeting, but she chalked it up to Lyda's concern for her friend. "We are, but we have a get-out-of-jail-free card for the night."

"Looking for Barney?" Henry popped out of the bushes.

Lyda started and pressed her hand to her chest. "Jeez! A little warning next time?"

"Sorry. I thought you saw me when you walked by." Chuckling, Henry said, "Did you lose Barney again?"

"Yes, even though I swore I wouldn't come back here." She sighed. "I need to warn him to get back to his house. He thinks Kirk and the flyers will be at the football game until ten, but it was canceled."

The news sent a shiver down Grace's spine. She'd focused on getting everything set up and hardly spared a thought to Kirk's whereabouts. "In that case, we should all be more careful. Let's get off the path."

Henry walked deeper into the forest.

Lowering her voice, Lyda followed. "After what happened last time, Barney promised to check his text messages while hunting the frogs, but he must have forgotten."

"Get off my land!" Herman, hair wild and dressed in animal pelts, stood on a boulder waving his walking stick. The costume was the same as the night behind the Moose Lodge, with one notable difference—he'd painted himself green.

Lyda yelped and backed up. "What the heck?"

"And *that* solves the mystery of the green bingo-daubers," Henry deadpanned.

Grace groaned. The last thing they needed was a bunch of oldsters running around with Kirk lurking nearby. "Get down from there before you hurt yourself."

"I said, get off my land!" He tried again, this time with more growl in his voice.

Henry grinned. "I bet he took out his hearing aids."

"This is a disaster. Help me get him down from there before Kirk hears him." Grace climbed up the rocks. "Herman, it's me, Grace Warner, Inez's friend. We need you to go home. It isn't safe here tonight."

"Did you say 'Herman?'" Lyda shined a light on the silver-haired gentleman and gasped. "Why is Barney's grandpa dressed like Shrek?"

CHAPTER ELEVEN

"Well, well, well. What do we have here?" Kirk smirked and folded his arms. Dark shadows ringed his eyes, and his nose was still swollen from Grace's fist.

The goon squad fanned out around him like a muscle-bound dance troop.

Henry had to get them away from the rocks before Grace or Herman made a sound. Although he doubted Kirk would stoop low enough to hurt an old man or a girl, he wouldn't risk it. "What do you want, Kirk?"

"Who says I want anything?"

"Come on, Lyda. I'll walk you back to the coffee shop." Henry moved as if to walk around the guys.

Jeremy, the kid Barney had taken down with a harpoon shot to the gut, growled.

While he understood the guy's frustration, Henry had no intention of becoming an outlet for Jeremy's misplaced aggression. "We're leaving."

"I don't think so." Kirk stepped forward and shoved Henry hard enough that he stumbled back. "You and your sister have been nothing but a pain in my neck since you got here."

Lyda stared between them.

"Fine. Whatever. Just let the girl go." He met her gaze and nodded.

Jeremy grabbed Lyda's arm. "No can do. She filmed us. Besides, where she goes, Barney is sure to follow."

"What do those muscle-heads want with Barney?" Herman's voice skittered down the boulder, along with a mini-landslide of pebbles and sand.

Kirk glanced up, glared, and punched Henry in the stomach. "Who's up there?"

The sudden burst of pain left him wheezing and gasping for breath. There was one silver lining, though. The camera remained in place and filming.

"Hey, dum-dum. You're supposed to let the prisoner answer before you hit them." Herman threw a rock at the bully, but it landed a few feet away.

"Go bring whoever that is to me." Kirk waited until his friends shot into action before punching Henry again. Thankfully, he was distracted and didn't hit quite as hard as the first time.

Henry bit back a groan. He refused to give Kirk the satisfaction, or not so soon, anyway. A couple more blows and his pride would be the last thing he had to worry about.

Struggling to break free, Lyda shouted. "Herman's an old man from the senior center. Leave him alone."

As if on cue, Herman let out a battle cry. A heartbeat later, a series of larger rocks sailed down from the boulder. The goons had no choice but to scramble out of the way.

"Get him!" Kirk wailed.

I have to help Grace. Drawing a breath made Henry see stars, but he took advantage of the momentary distraction. In one move, he righted himself, swung, and caught Kirk in his still-bruised nose.

Much to Henry's chagrin, the big guy remained upright.

Kirk yowled like a police siren and staggered back. "You're dead! Get him, Jeremy."

The guy released Lyda and smiled the sort of smile that promised pain and suffering.

Henry widened his stance and brought his fists up to protect his face. He weighed half as much as his opponent, but he had proper self-defense training and speed on his side. "Lyda, run!"

She ran. Not toward the bike path as he'd expected, but around the boulder to help Grace and Herman.

Three things happened at once. Kirk rushed forward, someone or something shrieked nearby, and a rock the size of a softball bounced off the bully's head.

The big guy blinked and raised his hand to his scalp. Kirk collapsed like a harpooned Macy's Parade balloon.

Jeremy and the other two stared at Henry, the boulder, and their fallen leader.

"If any of you have a phone, now is a good time to call 9-1-1." Henry backed away.

"I'll help Kirk, you two take care of the twerp." Jeremy knelt beside the jock.

"I'm not kidding. His head is bleeding. He could have a concussion or—"

The shrieking came closer.

"What the heck is that?" Jeremy widened his eyes. The other two seemed almost as confused.

At the end of his patience, Henry snapped. "Tell them to give it a rest. We know Tiffany and the flyers are the Loveland Frogs."

The guys continued to glance around for the source of the noise, but Jeremy turned to Henry. "What are you talking about?"

Their reaction made no sense. They had to recognize the screeching... unless the girls weren't the ones in the frog costumes. Once again, Henry had the distinct impression he and Grace had made a huge mistake.

Rather than answer and lose precious seconds arguing, he jogged around the boulder to find his sister and the others.

Holding the walking stick like a weapon, Grace stood in front of Herman. "What's going on over there?"

"Kirk fainted or has a concussion, I'm not sure. The others are confused without him calling the shots."

Lyda grinned. "I think it was the sight of blood that did him in."

Grace widened her eyes. "What are we waiting for? This is the perfect time to escape."

"I haven't had this much excitement since I left the service." Herman was quite a sight to behold in his pelts and bingo-dauber-green skin. "She's got quite an arm on her. Should have played for the Cincinnati Reds."

"She sure does." Any other time Henry would have at least cracked a smile, but they didn't have time to chat. They had monsters to catch. "Get him to safety. I'm going to take down a frog or three."

"No. We stay together. Bad things happen when we split up."

Grace turned to Herman. "I need you to be very quiet and stay between Henry and me. Okay?"

He squared his shoulders and nodded. "I was in the war, you know. Army. I know how to march."

Lyda looped her arm through his. "Shhh. We're sneaking across enemy lines."

Grace led them along the riverbank, with Henry watching their backs. Every now and then the trees thinned, giving them a view of Kirk and the others. Thankfully, the guys seemed more concerned about the shrieking frog noises than the escapees.

"What's that noise, and what the heck happened?" Kirk shouted over the racket.

Grace's heart stuttered, stopped, and exploded into action. As soon as the big jerk realized someone had clocked him with a rock, he'd order his friends to murder Henry—and her, too.

"Move." Henry whispered, "I'll keep them distracted. Call for help as soon as you can."

"We are staying together. End of story." She glanced over her shoulder at her brother and froze.

The Loveland Frogs stood not ten yards behind them. Worse still, the one in the middle held the firework shooting stick in her hand.

Pointing, she whispered, "Behind you."

Herman turned and grinned. "There you are! I was wondering when you'd stop making all that noise and show yourselves!"

The frogs ribbited in reply.

The twins froze. Lyda covered her mouth and reached for Herman's to quiet him, but the man fended her off.

On the other side of the trees, Kirk shouted. "They're by the river! I want those Warner punks taken down."

Grace's mouth went dry. They had nowhere to run. Crossing a creek was one thing, but crossing a river without knowing its depth was another. Not to mention, they'd have to drag Herman into the freezing-cold water with them. *We're doomed.*

Henry grabbed her shoulders. "Run, Grace. Take Lyda and go."

"No." She couldn't leave him behind. It'd taken every ounce of her courage not to shout when Kirk had punched him in the stomach. Twice. "I have my body camera."

"So do—" Henry pressed his hand to his chest. "Dang it."

Jeremy and the goon squad broke through the tree line, and Grace's world erupted into chaos. Henry turned and ran toward them instead of away. Lyda screamed and hurried toward the water, but Herman moved just as fast toward the frogs.

Grace couldn't save them all. Heck, she doubted she could save herself, but she tightened her grip on the walking stick and followed her brother.

Henry managed to get one or two swings in before Jeremy tackled him. The other bullies formed a ring around the brawl, making it impossible for Grace to tell who was winning, although if she had to guess, she'd say Jeremy had the upper hand. Otherwise, the rest of Kirk's minions would have jumped in.

"Let him go!" She whacked the first guy across his back.

Hardly flinching, he turned and grinned. "You shouldn't have done that."

She held the stick in front of her and prayed. Unless a miracle happened, she didn't stand a chance in a fight against any of them, but she would go down swinging. "I hate bullies!"

"Is that so, buttercup?" Kirk joined the others.

A familiar thump and boom filled her ears, followed by a flash of light. Fireballs erupted from the frogman's staff.

Kirk and his goons turned their heads toward the sound. Even Henry and Jeremy stopped swinging. The fireworks landed within inches of the guys.

One boy screamed in a pitch usually reserved for little girls and guinea pigs, and the other broke and ran. Jeremy was so busy staring at the frogmen, Henry managed to scramble away.

Kirk, on the other hand, pointed at the frogs. "I don't know who you are, but if you do that again, you're dead meat."

Grace rolled her eyes. He really needed to expand his vocabulary.

The middle frog aimed her staff at Kirk, and the big jerk hit the ground.

Holding his gut, Henry said, "I take it that isn't Tiffany and the Tinkerbell twins?"

Her stomach fell into her sneakers. He'd already taken a beating. Why on earth would he egg Kirk on?

Kirk growled and shot to his feet.

"Kirkland Eugene Kimber! Stop this instant." A woman's voice rang out over the sounds of the river.

The big guy whipped his head in the direction of the frogmen—or women. Who knew anymore?

The middle frog dropped her staff and removed the head of the costume. Gladys Gibson glared at her grandson.

"Nana?" He swayed and took several steps back.

"What do you think you're doing, young man?" She marched upriver toward the teens.

"Me? I wasn't... These boys were..."

Gladys reached Kirk, grabbed his earlobe, and pulled. Hard. "Don't you lie to me. I saw what was going on here with my own eyes."

The other guys backed away.

"And you three. Do your parents know what you've been up to?" The woman turned to Grace. "These are the bullies you were talking about?"

She nodded. "I'm afraid so."

"You're responsible for the videos on YouTube?" Her voice dropped to a low growl.

Grace could *hear* the family resemblance.

"No. It wasn't me. I swear." Kirk hung like a wet mop head from his nana's fingers.

"Oh, boy." Herman ran his hands over his head. "It wasn't him. This was my doing. I put Barney up to it—"

"I knew it!" Lyda groaned. "I'm going to strangle him."

The twins exchanged glances.

Herman lowered his brows. "Don't be too hard on Barney. I saw how much fun the ladies were having and asked him to put the videos on YouTube for posterity."

Grace gasped. "Barney filmed the videos?"

"He thought he could catch the bullies that way." Herman nodded before giving Gladys a sheepish smile. "I had no idea one of them was your grandson."

"Neither did I." She turned the full weight of her stare on Kirk. "But I intend to see he changes his ways."

Grace plopped down beside Henry. "Are you hurt?"

"Nothing some Advil and three days of taking it easy won't fix." He nodded toward the other two frogs. "Any guesses?"

"I'd say the other two Musketeers, but we've been so wrong up until now, who knows? It could be the Easter Bunny and Santa in those suits."

Pearl and Inez removed their giant frog-heads and waved to the twins.

Henry chuckled, winced, and pressed his hand to his stomach.

"Wow." Grace had figured out the identities of the others, but seeing them in the suits shocked her.

Inez cackled. "Close your mouth, dear. You might catch a fly."

Grace didn't know whether to laugh or cry.

CHAPTER TWELVE

Grace loaded the last of the boxes into the bed of the pickup truck. "Hurry up! We're going to be late."

Ethan Warner emerged from the fifth wheel wearing jeans, a blazer, and a huge smile. "Relax. We don't have to be there early to set up since we were fired."

"I still don't understand how your father and I were terminated along with the two of you." Faith laughed. "It hardly seems fair."

Henry closed and locked the door behind him. "I'm not going to cry over spilled gravy. We still get to join the seniors at the Golden Years, only now we get to share the meal instead of serving it."

Rolling her eyes, Grace climbed into the backseat. They hadn't spoken to the ladies since the night at the river, but Ms. Simon had called to invite the Warners to the pre-Thanksgiving meal. She claimed Inez had insisted they attend.

Grace couldn't wait to see them again. She had about a million questions for the Loveland Frogs.

Faith glanced at the twins. "You both look nice."

Henry loosened his tie. "Thanks, but if Dad isn't wearing a neck-noose, neither am I."

"I think Inez and the ladies will love it." Grace smiled and batted her lashes.

He dropped his hand. "Do you have the list?"

"Yes, but I don't think we'll have time to get through all of it." She patted her purse.

"What list?" Ethan glanced at her in the rearview mirror.

"Questions. We have tons of questions."

He chuckled. "I have a few myself."

Henry said, "How did your case turn out?"

"The DNA evidence came back negative. While it doesn't automatically exonerate our guy, the attorneys at the Innocence Project have requested a new trial."

"I'm sorry I didn't make it to any of the lectures," Henry said.

"The classes were tedious. We spent most of the time poring over case notes and arguing about the evidence. The real fun starts with the retrial." Ethan turned into the senior center parking lot. "You kids did good work here. I'm proud of you."

Faith glanced over her shoulder. "So am I."

The twins hopped out and hurried to the back of the truck. They might have missed their father's lecture, but they'd put their time to good use securing donations to surprise the seniors. Each Warner carried a box of precious cargo into the building.

Ms. Simon's eyes widened the moment she caught sight of the gifts. "My goodness. What is this?"

Grace felt as if she'd explode if she kept the secret another minute. "Henry and I used the remainder of our volunteer time to solicit businesses around Cincinnati. Expect deliveries of arts and crafts supplies, healthy treats, clothes, and other supplies between now and the first of the year."

Ms. Simon sighed. Not exactly the reaction Grace had hoped for. "I can't thank you enough. That you would do this after I let you go..." She turned to the elder Warners. "You have some amazing kids."

Faith smiled. "Yes, we do."

Henry nodded to the box in his arms. "Is it all right to hand these out?"

"Yes. Please! The seniors will love them." She opened the door.

The crowd gathered rivaled the one on Bingo Day. It seemed like all eyes turned to the family when they walked in carrying two boxes filled to the brim with roses, lilies, and a myriad of other flowers fashioned into corsages and boutonnieres.

Several staff members came forward to hand out the flowers, but the twins kept four special ones back.

Henry grinned. "Looks like Inez saved us some seats."

The tiny lady waved her hands over her head. "Yoo-hoo! Warners!"

Grace couldn't believe her eyes. While the rest of the seniors had dressed up, Inez and the other musketeers wore their frog suits, minus the enormous heads.

Faith arched a brow. "That's Inez? The woman who ran you two through the wringer while you were here?"

Smiling, Grace spoke without moving her lips. "Don't let her size fool you. She's an evil genius who sometimes chooses to use her powers for good."

"I'll keep an eye on her." Ethan chuckled. "Those costumes don't look as scary under fluorescent lights."

Faith muttered, "Nothing ever does except wrinkles and cellulite."

The twins shook their heads.

After introductions and a round of hugs, the family settled into their seats. Pearl, Gladys, Inez, and Herman were on one side of the table, the Warners on the other. An awkward silence hung in the air as if the two opposing teams were waiting for the other to flinch.

"Well, are you going to hand out those beauties or what?" Inez shifted her dentures around.

"Of course." Henry wiggled his brows. "Or should we keep them until you've answered all of our questions?"

Inez and Gladys tilted their heads and pursed their lips.

Pearl laughed. "We'll tell all, as long as it stays at this table."

Grace said, "We promise."

"Then, give me those gorgeous flowers." Inez rubbed her hands together.

Henry and Ethan helped to pin the corsages to the ladies' frog suits. Each contained yellow roses and miniature white lilies on a silk lily pad with a tiny bejeweled frog.

Grace fastened a matching boutonniere on Herman's furry lapel. "Okay, first question. Were there really dogs behind the Moose Lodge?"

"Those came from my remote-control boom box." The silver-haired devil laughed. "Fooled you, didn't I?"

Ethan grinned. "I thought we were surrounded."

Herman's voice grew serious. "I don't mess around when it comes to my tunes."

"How did you pull off the fireball-throwing staff?" Faith took a sip of her water. "I didn't see it, but I understand it was remarkable."

"That was my design." Gladys sat straighter, clearly proud of her invention. "I used silver fulminate to create a small explosion, which ignited the fuse to my homemade roman candle."

Grace sat back. "You made a bang-snap powerful enough to light a fuse and carried it in a stick?"

"Sure did."

Henry's mouth fell open. "Where did you learn to do that?"

"I worked in a munitions factory in my teens, and I taught high school chemistry for almost forty years." She turned to Grace. "I'm sorry about the night behind the Moose Lodge. I never dreamed you'd cross the creek. A few more steps and I would have had to shoot it into the air."

Ethan sucked in a breath and turned to Pearl. "May I ask why you three pretend to be..."

"Sick?" She smiled.

He nodded.

"We've been best friends since we were in grade school. Once Inez came to stay here, Gladys and I convinced our families this was the best place for us. Nine to five on weekdays, anyway."

Inez, never one to be outshone, leaned forward and waved. "I'm no invalid, nor am I a slouch. I'm the brains behind the entire operation. I wanted those kids off our land."

Herman snickered. "That's my line."

Gladys rolled her eyes. "It's true. Inez convinced Pearl to sew the costumes, and me to make the fire-throwing staff and drive the getaway car—"

"You drive?" Henry gasped.

Gladys glared.

The hint of normalcy helped Grace come back down to Earth. She didn't know what to make of these women chatting away. They hardly seemed like the same grouchy ladies she'd come to know. "I'm still not sure I understand how Barney became involved in all of this."

Inez nodded to a group of teens serving the meals. "You can ask him yourself when he brings the turkey."

Grace did a double take. Not only were Barney and Lyda waiting tables at the senior center, but Kirk, his goons, and the flyers also carried trays of food, drinks, and dirty dishes to and from the kitchen. Hairnets and aprons were a far cry from the designer clothes they normally wore, but Grace couldn't find an ounce of sympathy for them.

Henry gawked. "How did *that* happen?"

"Penance." Gladys pressed her lips into a thin line. "I spoke to a lot of parents over the last few days. Needless to say, someone isn't going to be riding his high horse anytime soon."

While she appreciated justice being served along with the stuffing and cranberries, Grace thanked her lucky stars that her grandmother was nothing like Gladys. "Why is Lyda here?"

Herman shrugged. "She volunteered."

Barney made his way to the table between dinner and the pumpkin pie. He glanced at the adults, then motioned to the twins. "Can I talk to you?"

"Excuse us." Grace and Henry stood and followed him to a quiet corner.

He rubbed the back of his neck. "I'm sorry I didn't tell you I was the one making the videos. My gramps? It was his idea, but I took it too far. I thought I could get Kirk off my back."

Henry folded his arms. "Why film Lyda?"

Barney hung his head. "To take the pressure off me. Jen and Wayne saw me in the forest. They didn't realize I was wearing a body cam, but it was only a matter of time before someone figured it out."

Grace's lunch sat heavy in her stomach. While she couldn't excuse his actions, she understood his motives. "Jen said Kirk knew about the video before it went live. How is that possible?"

"I'd posted it in the morning but deleted it after I heard Kirk teasing her." He sighed. "I thought if I could pin the videos on him..."

"You could hurt his reputation." Henry shook his head. "But everyone already knew he was a jerk. It only made them more afraid of him."

"I'm sorry so many people were hurt because of me." His voice cracked. "I was trying so hard to take Kirk down that I became as bad as him."

"What you did was wrong, but you have a good heart." Grace pulled the boy into a hug. "Just remember, the end doesn't always justify the means."

Barney sniffled. "I should get back to work."

The twins returned to the table

Resting her hand on Grace's arm, Faith whispered, "Are you all right?"

"Yes, but I'd like to say my goodbyes now and skip dessert."

She cleared her throat and turned to the others. "I hate to cut this short, but we need to get on the road. We're expected in Wisconsin on Monday."

Inez shot to her feet. "You can't go yet. We have a surprise for you."

Pearl and Gladys grinned, reached under the table, and put on their frog heads.

Herman stood and did a little jig. "Showtime."

Faith openly stared. "Those costumes are amazing. Pearl, you made them?"

"Inez and I worked in the theater together. She was an actress. I was the costume designer and seamstress."

Herman set a boombox on the table and hit play. The old 70s song, *Jeremiah was a Bullfrog,* blasted through the room.

The ladies moved far slower than they had outside the facility, and Pearl used her walker, but they climbed onto the stage and danced in their frog suits. Before the second chorus, the seniors and staff of the Golden Years had joined in—and so had the Warners.

Ethan watched the ladies groove. "You weren't kidding. Those three are a handful. Add in Herman, and you have yourself a quartet of trouble."

"You're awfully quiet." Faith bumped hips with Henry. "Have you two decided on a mystery to solve in Wisconsin?"

"We've been busy soliciting donations and haven't had much time to think about it." He walked like an Egyptian over to Grace. "Any ideas?"

"No, but I'd love to take a break from creatures for the next one." She danced a circle around her parents.

Ethan, who had two left feet, did something along the lines of the Carlton. "A friend of mine owns a haunted restaurant."

The twins groaned and stopped dancing.

Faith draped her arm around his shoulder. "It's time to go."

"Perfect timing, Mom." Grace headed for the exit, with Henry on her heels.

Laughing, Ethan caught up with them at the door. "It was a gangster hangout in the 1920s and 30s. Vince offered to give you two a job for a week if you can solve the mystery."

Henry gave his father his full attention. "You're saying we'd get paid?"

Grace grinned. "Real money?"

Ethan deadpanned, "I don't think he intends to pay you in lily pads."

"Done." The twins high-fived each other on the way to the truck.

THE ROARING 20S

MONSTER CASE FILES BOOK 8

CHAPTER ONE

Vince Villenti squinted at the numbers on the computer screen. After three hours of paperwork, inventory, and food orders, his eyes stung, but Vince never complained. After all, how many poor kids from the wrong side of the Brooklyn Bridge grew up to run their own restaurants?

He was one of the lucky ones, and he knew it.

Like most things in their nineties, the building creaked and sighed. After five years of running The Wonder Bar, Vince had grown used to the structure's noises—or so he thought.

A door slammed on the first floor.

Vince glanced at the clock. He'd shown the last of the employees out around midnight, nearly three hours earlier. Grabbing his Louisville slugger from behind the office door, he eased into the hall.

He rounded the corner with the baseball bat held to his shoulder as if he were standing at home plate in Yankees Stadium waiting for a fastball.

Not a living soul occupied the first floor. More troubling, the doors to the restrooms, storeroom, and wine cellar stood open.

How can that be? Vince stilled and listened. "Hello?"

The lilting dirge of a woman crying drifted from the second floor.

Thinking one of his employees had returned, he lowered the bat and walked to the center of the room to get a look at the upstairs dining area. "Who's up there?"

The sobs quieted.

He headed for the stairs.

"Stop beating your gums. I'm leaving." The redhead stood at the second-floor railing in a 1920s flapper dress, complete with a beaded headband and a feather boa.

"How did you get in here?"

"What do you mean, how did I get in here?" The redhead huffed in a distinct Brooklyn accent. "Forget about it. You must be new here."

"Look, lady. I don't know what game you're playing, but I'm calling the police if you don't leave by the count of three."

"Threatening to call the coppers?" She threw her head back and laughed. "Your mother must have dropped you on your head as a baby."

"One...two..."

"You don't know who I am?" She motioned to the portrait hanging above the fireplace.

The skin on the back of Vince's neck prickled. Many of his employees had reported seeing ghosts in the building, and a handful had quit after their so-called encounters. He'd chalked the incidents up to tall tales, convenient excuses, and gossip. Yet, there he stood gawking at the woman who was a dead ringer for the person in the painting.

"Where's Eddie?" She glanced around and sniffled ready to return to the tears. "And why does the juice joint look so different?"

Vince shook his head to clear his thoughts. He hadn't gotten to where he was by playing the fool. There was no such thing as ghosts, especially not tall redheaded ones who spoke in 1920s slang. He hit the stairs at a full run and, taking them two at a time, he reached the second floor within seconds.

The Lady in Red was gone.

Pulse racing, he searched and came up with nothing. He froze and stared at the portrait of a young woman with flowing red hair. The painting had come with the building. No one knew who she was, but Vince was convinced of one thing: the girl immortalized on the canvas had paid him a visit.

"I still don't understand how you met someone like Vince Villenti." Henry met his father's gaze in the rearview mirror. He'd asked the same question several times on the drive from Ohio to Madison, Wisconsin, and planned to keep asking until he received a straight answer.

Grace, his twin sister, grinned without glancing up from her phone.

Ethan Warner turned his attention back to the highway. "Early in my career, I worked as a public defender."

"Yeah?" Henry had found some interesting information about Villenti on the internet. While none of the articles accused him directly of breaking the law, they implied that he enjoyed tap dancing on the line between the law-abiding and a stay in the gray-bar motel.

"Vince and I struck up a friendship when I represented his brother." Ethan hitched a shoulder as if to say it was no big deal.

Grace glanced from Henry to their father. "What was his brother accused of?"

Faith Warner turned and arched a brow. "Final exams are this week. I've arranged for proctors at the university. You should be spending your time studying instead of digging up dirt on our host."

The University of Wisconsin in Madison had hired the twins' parents as guest lecturers. Ethan was scheduled to present a series on constitutional law, while Faith hosted discussions on career opportunities in mechanical engineering with a small group of new grad students. Needless to say, Ethan and Faith Warner had a busy week ahead of them.

"I'm ready." Grace smiled and turned to Henry.

Way to put the pressure on. Henry needed to spend some time cramming for his English Lit exam, but he decided to keep that little tidbit to himself. "Piece of cake."

Faith narrowed her eyes. "Are you sure? You aren't required to work at The Wonder Bar this week or take on another mystery. School comes first."

"I'm sure." He tapped his skull. "It's all up here."

He enjoyed the thrill of the investigations and he wasn't worried about the finals. He needed to focus on them, but that didn't mean he couldn't relax with another good mystery. This case piqued his interest on multiple levels. The infamous Touhy brothers had opened The Wonder Bar at the height of the Roaring Twenties. Between the bootlegging and a rivalry with Al Capone, Henry found the brothers' stories fascinating.

Likely picking up on his distress, Grace skillfully changed the subject. "Are we really going to stay in Mr. Villenti's house?"

"We are." Ethan chuckled. "And before you two super-sleuths dream up a conspiracy theory, it's time for the fifth wheel's annual maintenance. New tires, system checks, the works."

The twins exchanged glances.

Henry cocked his head. "Why here and not in Florida like always?"

Faith said, "Our regular place is booked through mid-January."

"Plus, it's shaping up to be an early winter. I'd rather be safe than break down in a snowdrift," Ethan said as he turned onto a long driveway.

Henry leaned forward to get a better view of the house. The combination of straight lines, sharp angles, and tons of windows gave the place a Frank Lloyd Wright feel—modern, spacious, and expensive.

"What lake is that?" Grace pointed to the water at the back of the property.

"Lake Monona. There are plenty of watersports around here in the summer." Ethan climbed out of the truck. "I believe there's an ice rink and sled hills nearby—"

"You're in luck. We're expecting snow." The man held his arms out wide. "Ethan Warner. What's it been? Ten years?"

Between his accent and the slicked-back dark hair, Vincent Villenti could have played a walk-on part in an Al Pacino movie. Henry liked him instantly, and not because he looked and spoke like the stereotypical wise guy. He seemed like the kind of person who didn't mince words.

"Vince." Ethan gave him a half-hug-shoulder-slap.

"Good to see your ugly mug again." Vince pulled his chin back and pressed his lips together. "Faith, you haven't changed a bit."

"Thank you for inviting us to stay in your beautiful home...and the compliment." She gestured to the twins. "This is Henry and Grace."

"Ah, my undercover paranormal investigators." He shook their hands. "We have much to talk about, but first, let's get you settled in."

Henry hoped settling in included lunch. He hadn't seen food since the burger he'd eaten on the road.

"Faith and I can't stay long. We have to drop the rig at the shop and head to the university." Ethan retrieved their bags from the fifth wheel.

Grace reached for her suitcase.

"Let me help with that." Vince took it from her, grabbed Faith's, and headed toward the front door.

"Thanks," the Warner women said in unison.

The interior of the house blew Henry away. Floor-to-ceiling windows, buttery-soft leather couches, abstract art on the walls—the ultimate bachelor pad. "Holy smokes, look at the size of that television!"

Vince chuckled. "How else would a homesick New Yorker watch the Yankees?"

"How long have you lived in Madison?" Grace surveyed the room.

"Five years this spring." He motioned to a spiral staircase. "Guest rooms are on the second floor. The second master suite is on the third. Make yourselves at home."

Faith glanced at her watch and frowned. "I hate to cut this short, but Ethan and I should get going."

Henry said, "I'll take your bags up."

Vince grinned and hitched his thumb in Henry's direction. "Good kid you got there."

"We couldn't agree more." Ethan gave the twins a quick hug. "Call us if you need us and try to stay out of trouble."

Faith pointed at Mr. Villenti. "That goes for you, too."

"Like I said, you haven't changed a bit." He laughed. "Relax. I'm good with kids, even the teenage variety."

Grace kissed Faith's cheek. "We'll be fine. Go knock 'em dead."

Henry couldn't help but wonder if Vince or his brother had ever knocked someone dead for real. Then again, he doubted his parents would leave him and his sister with a real live mobster.

With the elder Warners out of the house, Vince clapped once and rubbed his hands together. "All right, what'll it be? Grinders or pasta?"

"Yes, please." Henry placed the bags at the bottom of the stairs.

Grace rolled her eyes. "Whatever is easiest. I'm interested in learning more about The Wonder Bar, our jobs, and the ghosts."

Vince's shoulders tensed. "In my line of work, it's better to get to know a person before you get down to business."

"The restaurant business?" Henry regretted the question the second the words came out of his mouth. *What other business would he refer to?*

"Hospitality, finance, law... It all works the same when you're dealing with people." Vince pulled a package of sausages from the fridge. "Have a seat."

"Thanks, but we've been sitting for seven hours straight." Mentioning the drive made Henry's back tighten.

"Suit yourselves." Vince eyed them. "Either of you vegetarian, vegan, avoiding gluten or dairy or allergic to anything?"

Grace laughed. "Unless you're cooking lima beans or liver, I'm good."

Henry nodded. "Same here, but I also have an aversion to fruit on pizza."

Vince shuddered. "You and me both, kid."

"We will agree to disagree on Hawaiian pizza." Grace smirked. "I know what you mean about dealing with people. The hardest part of solving mysteries isn't finding clues, it's getting others to trust us."

Henry nodded. "No one enjoys telling complete strangers about having the daylights scared out of them."

Vince ran his hand over the back of his neck. "You can say that again."

He'd hit a nerve. *We should ease him into the ghost conversation.* "Did our dad tell you anything about us?"

"You're both wicked smart, on your way to fancy colleges next year, and the mystery-solving bit is a senior project." Vince tossed the sausage into a pan and went to work slicing onions and peppers. "That was nice work, saving that little girl out on Star Island."

"Thanks." Grace grinned. "Of course, he told you about *that* mystery, but did he happen to mention he worked with us on the Mothman case?"

"You mean, your dad getting lost in the woods?" Snickering, Vince pulled a container of sauce from the freezer. "Your dad and I have emailed back and forth for years."

Henry took a minute to chew on the new information. His parents had colleagues and former classmates all over the world, but they seemed distant somehow. Learning that his father stayed in close contact with Vince felt like hearing someone call a teacher by their first name.

"You grew up in New York?" Grace pulled up a stool and sat at the kitchen island.

"Was it the accent that gave it away?"

"That and I googled you."

Vince's eyes widened. "Find anything juicy?"

She raised a brow. "Is there anything juicy to find?"

"You *are* your mother's daughter." The man laughed and turned his attention to the frying pan. "Yes, I was born and raised in Brooklyn. My grandparents emigrated from Sicily."

"Dad mentioned you have a brother."

"Several, actually." Vince laughed again. "I'm the second-youngest of eight kids. Six boys and two girls. Dad was a cop. Mom taught third grade, but she died in a fire shortly after my sister was born."

"I'm sorry. That must have been awful." She glanced at Henry.

He pressed his lips together and shook his head. Vince's story was identical to the original founder of The Wonder Bar, Roger "The Terrible" Touhy. Henry didn't believe in coincidences, but why would Vince lie? "What do your siblings do?"

"My sisters are teachers. Two of my brothers are cops, two are criminals, and one writes screenplays in California." He added the vegetables to the pan. "I've done all sorts of jobs, mostly in the restaurant business. Everything from delivering pizza to owning my own place."

"You must be doing well." Grace motioned toward the living room. "Your house is gorgeous, and from what I read, The Wonder Bar is successful."

Waving a spatula, Vince said, "I've busted my butt to get where I am. I'm not about to let some ghost get in my way."

Henry rested his hip against the counter and folded his arms. "Do you think the ghost, or the people pretending to be ghosts, want to hurt your business?"

"I've had a handful of employees quit because of the so-called hauntings." He turned his back to the twins while assembling the sandwiches. "Training new people costs money."

Grace held up her index finger. "Hold that thought. I need my notebook."

"Eat first. Write later." Vince set the grinders on the island and grabbed two bottles of water from the fridge.

"But I..." She looked longingly at her bags.

"We'll have plenty of time to get into details later, but the food won't stay hot forever."

While Henry appreciated the sentiment, he couldn't shake the feeling that the guy had fed them a load of bull. Before they started working on solving the mystery of the haunted restaurant, he intended to call Vince Villenti out on his fictitious history. "Have you heard of Roger Touhy?"

"I own the business he started, and his face is on my wall." Vince glanced at his ringing phone and frowned. "Excuse me, will ya? I need to take this call."

CHAPTER TWO

Grace waited until Vince had closed the door behind him before turning to her brother. "What's gotten into you?"

"Unless he's somehow Roger "The Terrible" Touhy's cosmic twin, his story is bogus." He bit into his sub, closed his eyes, and grinned. "But he sure can cook."

She remembered reading about the Prohibition-era gangster. While the stories were eerily similar, she refused to believe their father would befriend an outright liar. "So what? He comes from a large family and lost his mom at a young age. It's not uncommon for first-generation immigrants to have a lot of children."

"Maybe, but it's not common for a person's mother to die in a house fire."

"No, it's not, but I'm not going to accuse the guy of lying because that's irrelevant to the ghost sighting. We should talk to Dad about it later tonight." She sighed and took a bite of her grinder. The flavor explosion of sausage, peppers, cheese, and just enough sauce made her smile, even if the conversation didn't.

The twins finished their meal in silence, although Grace couldn't say if her brother was lost in thought or too busy enjoying the grinder to talk. Probably both.

"I'd love to speak to the former employees. They had to have seen something terrifying to quit their jobs." Grace took their plates to the sink.

Henry whispered, "Or maybe they didn't want to work there anymore, and the ghosts provided an excuse to quit."

"Or that." She sighed. "I understand you're suspicious, but it's too early to jump to any conclusions."

Vince returned to the kitchen with his keys in hand. His hair stood up in odd directions as if he'd tried to pull it out. "I'm needed at the restaurant. Do you two want to come along, or would you rather have the house to yourselves for a few hours?"

While a shower and some downtime sounded good, Grace suspected something bad had happened at The Wonder Bar. "We'll go with you."

Henry tilted his head. "Everything all right?"

Vince hesitated a moment. "Another waitress quit, and someone vandalized the men's room."

"Are the two related?" Henry asked.

"Seems that way. Come on, I'll explain in the car." He strode to the door.

Grace climbed into the front seat of Vince's dark-windowed, luxury SUV and caught herself running her fingers over the soft leather. The man certainly seemed to enjoy the finer things in life.

Vince waited until the twins had buckled in before starting the vehicle. "Averi, the waitress who quit, claims she checked the restrooms at the beginning of her shift. About an hour later, she heard a racket. When she checked it out, she found two of the four toilets busted up."

"Did she see anyone going in or out?" Henry leaned forward.

"No. We don't open until five, and the employees have their own restroom in back." He gripped the steering wheel tighter. "Depending on my plumber's schedule, we may not open for business tonight."

"Because the men's room is out of service." Grace frowned and glanced out the window.

"Exactly."

On the surface, damaging toilets seemed like a juvenile prank. However, Grace couldn't think of a better way to hurt a man like Vince Villenti than to hit him in the wallet.

Henry asked, "Is this typical of the hauntings the other employees reported?"

"Mostly they talked about bottles falling off shelves. Things being moved. Hearing footsteps or doors opening and closing." Vince turned into the restaurant's parking lot and cut the engine.

Grace peered out the windshield at the building. It would have been boring if not for the twin turrets at either side of the square structure, which gave it a stubby castle-y feel. She imagined the random gray stones around the doors and windows were once openings for Tommy guns, but on closer inspection, they appeared to be nothing more than decoration. "This is the most serious incident to date?"

"From the alleged ghosts, yes." Vince opened his door. "We had someone try to break through the back door with an ax about a month ago. The police never caught the guy."

"Have there been any other break-ins or vandalism in the past six months to a year?"

"We get people trying to come through the old bootlegger tunnels sometimes. Other than that, no." Vince sighed. "Let's go inside and get this over with."

Grace met Henry's gaze and cocked an eyebrow. *Bootlegger tunnels,* he mouthed.

He nodded once and climbed out of the SUV.

After stepping through the back door, Grace gave her eyes time to the adjust to the light. A storeroom was on the left, and a table and chairs sat on the right. Judging by the posters on the wall, the employees used the space during their breaks.

"Are you coming?" Henry tugged her arm.

The twins walked past a gigantic freezer and into the kitchen. Two men in chef's coats gave them curious expressions but returned to work without a word. Likewise, a young man in black pants and a black button-down shirt looked them over from head to toe before hurrying away.

Henry whispered, "They don't seem happy to be here."

"I'm beginning to see why so many people have quit."

"Warners?" Mr. Villenti called from the front of the building.

They found him at the entrance to the men's room, staring blankly.

Grace peeked around his shoulder and gasped. The perpetrator had pulverized two toilets and portions of the wall.

"Whoa." Henry gawked. "That happened with people in the building, and no one saw who did it?"

"Seems unlikely, eh?" Vince stepped back and motioned to the bartender. "Noah, what time did you clock in?"

The guy looked like he belonged on the cover of a magazine rather than behind a bar. Then again, Grace wasn't old enough to drink. For all she knew, all bartenders looked like movie stars.

"Right after this happened." Noah tossed his towel on the counter and walked toward them.

"You didn't see or hear anything out of the ordinary?" Henry eyed the bartender.

The guy stopped, gave him a once over, and smiled. "We haven't met. I'm Noah."

"I'm Henry. This is my sister Grace."

Villenti said, "They're the kids I told you about. Their parents are working at the university this week."

"Ah, right. Encyclopedia Brown and Nancy Drew." He chuckled. "Must have slipped my mind. Welcome to The Wonder Bar."

Grace rethought her first impression of the guy. He might have been easy on the eyes, but good looks couldn't make up for an unsavory personality.

Vince either didn't notice or ignored the patronizing insult. "Noah is my right-hand man. If you need anything, he's the one to go to."

"Great," Henry deadpanned.

Noah clasped his hands behind his back and turned his attention to Villenti. "Averi's waiting for you in your office."

"Is she still upset?"

"You could say that."

"You two wait for me in the employee area near the back door. I shouldn't be long." Vince walked away.

The twins made their way through the kitchen and seated themselves at the table in the break room.

Leaning forward, Grace whispered, "How many swings of a sledgehammer would it take to demolish two toilets?"

"Several. Anyone in the building would have heard it long before the perpetrator finished."

"Unless the damage was done before anyone arrived." She shook her head. "That doesn't work. Vince said the waitress checked the men's room at the beginning of her shift."

A slow grin spread across Henry's face. "They could have used some sort of explosive."

"Ghosts blowing up toilets." Grace dropped her head to the table with a thud.

Vince's voice echoed down the hall. "You're quitting without notice?"

She strained to hear the other person's reply, but it was no use. "Come on."

"Where are we going?" He followed her.

"Into the kitchen to eavesdrop."

"Go, but don't expect a reference!" Mr. Villenti shouted.

A pretty woman not much older than the twins emerged from the office.

Wiping her cheeks on the back of her hand, she hurried into the kitchen but stopped when she noticed the twins. "If you're here to apply for a job, do yourselves a favor and don't. The place is haunted, and the boss is a jerk."

The chefs kept their heads down and chopped faster.

Grace lowered her voice. "We saw the toilets in the men's room. What happened?"

The waitress glanced over her shoulder, leaned closer, and whispered, "Ghosts. A guy in a trench coat and fedora. He's always hanging around the men's bathroom or with a tall redhead at the top of the stairs."

Henry ran his hands over his arms. "Did you see him this morning?"

She nodded. "He was in there, but he vanished before anyone else saw him."

"You think he damaged the toilets?" Grace glanced between the woman and her brother.

"'Damaged.'" She smirked. "Destroyed is more like it."

"Has this sort of thing happened before?" Henry folded his arms.

The waitress shrugged. "Nothing this violent, just doors opening and closing, things moving on their own. Typical haunted house-type stuff."

"I see." Grace bit her lip to keep from speaking her mind. Despite Henry's vehement claims to the contrary, she didn't believe in ghosts. Manifestations of spirits were nothing more than plays of light, tricks of the mind, and/or human creations. However, now was not the time or the place to discuss her views.

The waitress frowned. "I don't care if you think I'm crazy. I know what I saw. Spend any time here, and you'll see them for yourself."

"Hate to see you go, Averi." One of the chefs moved from behind the prep counter and drew her into an embrace.

"I hate it too. You know I need this job." She sniffled. "But the toilets were the last straw."

"Give Allyssa a big hug and kiss from Uncle Jack, will you?"

Averi burst into a fresh round of tears.

The situation broke Grace's heart. "Wait. It's Averi, right?"

"Yes."

"Don't quit. I'm sure Mr. Villenti would agree to work with you on another solution."

The woman set her hand on her hip. "Like what, exactly?"

Henry frowned. "We're new. One of us could shadow you or something."

"That could work." Grace had never had a paying job, but she'd seen servers training new people at other restaurants. Why not here? "You wouldn't have to face the ghosts alone. One of us would be with you."

"What makes you think Vince would go for that?" Averi sounded doubtful, but at least she'd stopped crying.

Grace lowered her voice. "Because he can't afford to lose a good server."

The chef nudged Averi's side. "She has a point."

As if on cue, Vince Villenti marched into the kitchen. He took one look at the four of them and stopped. "What's going on?"

Henry said, "How would you feel about Averi sticking around long enough to train us?"

The man arched a brow. "I'd planned on making you the dishwasher and your sister the hostess."

"Oh." The twins frowned.

"But I'd be willing to bring one of you on as an assistant server if Averi agrees to stay." He folded his arms.

Grace wanted to be the one to shadow the woman, but she would take one for the team if it meant Henry wouldn't spend the next week elbow-deep in dirty dishwater. "I'm good with seating people."

Vince glanced between Henry and Averi.

The woman nodded. "I'll stick around long enough to train him."

"Then it's settled." He motioned to the twins. "You two, come with me."

Averi made a sound in the back of her throat. "I should run him through opening duties."

"There will be time for that after I'm finished with them."

The waitress nodded but remained rooted in place.

Grace's heart thudded against her ribcage. They'd prevented the woman from quitting, but she had no doubt Averi would walk at the first sign of trouble. "She's freaked out about what happened earlier. You know how upsetting it is to have a run-in with a spirit."

Averi winced. The chef sucked in a breath. Henry closed his eyes. Grace had said too much.

Villenti pinched the bridge of his nose. "Right. Everyone, go ahead and take the day off...with pay. The plumbers can't get out here until late this afternoon. We can't open without an operational men's room."

The employees stared as if Vince had sprouted wings and a halo.

"Warners, come with me."

The twins followed Villenti to his office.

"I'm sorry about that." Grace's voice trembled. "It's just...she has a daughter to take care of, and you need the help."

"Daughter?" Vince glanced between them.

Henry said, "Allyssa."

Vince threw his head back and laughed. "Allyssa is a spoiled-rotten French Bulldog."

Some detective I'm turning out to be. Grace wanted to curl up in a little ball and roll away. "I assumed..."

"Don't worry about it. You saved me a world of stress by convincing her to stay." He waved his hand. "I saw your faces when Noah mentioned your detective work. Is there a problem?"

"People are more prone to talk when they don't know what we're up to," Henry said. "Especially the guilty parties."

"You don't need to worry about Noah. He's been with me since New York. I trust him with my life."

Famous last words. Grace nodded.

"Now, about your jobs. You'll start tomorrow. I'd planned to have one of you in the back and one in the dining room. Will you be able to keep an eye on things if you're both up front?"

"That would have made things easier." Grace sank into a chair. She'd made a mess of things by getting involved with the Averi situation.

Henry squeezed her shoulder. "We'll manage, and if not, Grace will make an excellent dishwasher."

CHAPTER THREE

After a trip to the mall to purchase black clothing suitable for their new positions, the twins reported to The Wonder Bar for their first day of work. The place didn't open for business until five, but the busy staff more than made up for the lack of patrons.

Henry adjusted his tie. "I didn't realize it took so many people to run a steakhouse."

"Me either, but we don't usually eat at places this expensive." Grace turned to him and smiled. "You look good with your hair slicked back. Did you get into Vince's beauty products?"

He raised his hand but dropped it before touching his head. "He insisted I update my image. Which isn't fair. He didn't force you to wear makeup."

She fidgeted with her black knee-length dress. "I'd rather wear makeup than heels."

He winced at her shoes. Twins sympathy pains shot through his ankles.

Noah came out from behind the bar and smiled at Grace. "Vince asked me to show you the ropes. There's a bit more to hosting than putting people at the first available table."

"Will I be alone up here tonight?" The pitch of her voice betrayed her nerves.

"Our regular maître d' quit last week, but Averi's agreed to take fewer tables tonight so she can help cover the door."

Grace rolled her lips in and nodded.

The bartender glanced at Henry. "Averi's waiting for you in the kitchen. I heard what the two of you did for her. Saving her job. Stay close to her tonight. We can't afford to lose another employee."

"Will do." Henry walked through the dining room. Despite Vince's reassurances about the guy, something about Noah bugged him. Then again, he wasn't sure he could trust Villenti either.

"There's my new assistant." Averi's smile lit the room and took years off her face. Giving him a half-hug, she whispered, "Thanks again for agreeing to do this."

"Are you kidding? I'd much rather help you then sweat it out over the dishwasher."

She laughed. "You may change your mind before the end of the night. It's Monday. The older crowd comes in early for the senior special."

"I'm not scared of a little gray hair." After spending two weeks in Loveland, Ohio volunteering with a mischievous bunch of septuagenarians, he felt he could handle anything the oldsters threw his way.

"Don't say I didn't warn you."

He glanced over his shoulder to make sure no one was listening. "Any more alleged paranormal activity?"

"So far, so good." Averi led him to a table in the back of the dining room and went over the menu, the specials, and the process for entering orders into the computer.

Henry sat back and stared. He'd understood everything she'd said but putting it into practice concerned him.

Averi gave him a knowing look. "Relax. It's like anything else: it gets easier the more you do it. For tonight, focus on keeping their glasses full—except the booze. You're not old enough to do that yet."

Henry glanced back toward the bar, where Grace and Noah sat presumably discussing her job duties.

"Any questions?"

"A few hundred." He lowered his voice. "But there's one I keep asking myself. The staff turnover... Is it really because of the ghosts, or is there another reason so many people have quit?"

She blinked, opened her mouth, and snapped it shut.

Dang it, I upset her. "Sorry if that was too blunt."

Averi shook her head. "Vince can be demanding, but he always apologizes and does right by the employees."

"Like giving you last night off with pay?"

"Exactly like that. Vince never asks one of us to do something he isn't willing to do himself. Lately, he's been stressed out, but it's because he loves this place." She sighed. "Whatever is going on around here, ghosts or human nonsense, is taking a toll on all of us."

Henry wanted to reassure her, tell her he and his sister would figure out who or what was causing the problems, but before he could find the words, the first patrons arrived.

The night passed in a flash of hungry faces, endless customer demands, and aching feet. Grace locked the front door, turned off the neon sign, and collapsed into a chair. The shoes she'd borrowed from her mom had a two-inch heel, and after standing for six hours straight, she was incapable of remaining on her feet.

"You did great tonight." Noah set a tall glass of Coke on the table in front of her.

While Grace appreciated the compliment, she disagreed with his assessment. "Thanks, but you don't have to sugar-coat it for me. I know I messed up more than I got right."

He gave her a whatever-you-say look. "Listen, you managed to get everyone seated without tears or hysterics. That's better than most newbies accomplish on their first night."

She rolled her head from side to side. "That party of two waited for over an hour. Thank goodness you comped their meals and gave them a voucher for a second meal on the house."

"There's truth to the old saying that a happy customer tells five people about their experience, but an unhappy one tells anyone who will listen." He shrugged. "Comping meals is the cost of doing business."

"I get that, but I also forgot to rotate the sections and irritated every server here."

He chuckled. "Not all of them. Mike made out like a bandit."

"Ha ha."

"I'm serious, kid. You did good."

"Thanks. This was my first day on my first-ever paying job."

Noah widened his eyes. "No kidding. I never would have guessed... and they say your generation has no work ethic."

"I blame my work ethic on my parents." She downed the soda and stood. "What are the closing procedures?"

Once again, Noah looked at her in surprise. "You're done for the night. Go home and put your feet up."

The idea of soaking in a hot bath made her smile, but pampering wasn't in her cards. "I have to wait for my brother. Plus, Vince is my ride home. I'd rather keep busy than sit here watching the hands move on the clock."

"All right." He stood and scratched his jaw. "Why don't you help the servers set up for tomorrow? Fold napkins, set tables, that sort of thing."

"You got it." She left her shoes off and stood in bare feet.

He tilted his head. "Vince prefers the female hostesses to wear dresses and heels, but the employee handbook says you can opt for flats and pants."

"There's a handbook?" Grace made a mental note to speak to Mr. Villenti about his new employee orientation.

"This can't be right." Averi's voice rose over the clatter of dishes and silverware. "Mondays aren't big money nights, but I usually make at least two-hundred or so."

Grace cringed. Between Averi helping her seat people and having fewer patrons in her section—thanks to her mistakes—she'd cost the woman money.

Henry frowned at a pile of cash on the table. "I gave you all of our tips."

The woman counted the money and shook her head. "We're over a hundred and fifty dollars short."

"How? Most of the tables paid with credit cards."

"Bar tabs and a couple of cash customers." Averi stood and emptied her apron. "This isn't on you. I handled the register tonight. I must have counted the change wrong."

The color drained from Henry's face. "I rang up a bill while you were at the bar."

Grace stood and hobbled to her brother. "Everything okay?"

He avoided her gaze. "We're short."

"How is this sort of thing usually handled?" She glanced at Henry and Averi.

The server sighed. "We'll have to pay it out of our tips."

"Hang on a sec." Noah typed something into the computerized register and waited as a strip of paper, too long to be a receipt, printed. "What's your total?"

"One hundred eighty dollars and thirty-seven cents," Henry said.

Averi nodded.

Noah skimmed the paper and whistled. "You owe one-fifty-three-twenty-nine."

The bartender grabbed a calculator. "The difference between your tips and the shortage is—"

"Twenty-seven dollars and eight cents," Grace said.

The adults stared.

She shrugged. "I'm good at math."

Henry pulled a pad from his apron and flipped through the pages. "Is it possible I messed up when I rang up the cash order? It was a few cents short of ninety-five dollars, and they paid with a hundred."

"I see it." Noah pressed more buttons on the register. "Everything looks correct."

Averi slumped her shoulders. "This is on me. You would have given them change back from the till, not our tips. I must have miscounted."

They checked and double-checked the numbers, but each time Averi and Henry came up exactly one hundred eighty dollars and thirty-seven cents short.

Averi handed Henry his share of the remaining tip money.

He shook his head. "No way. You keep it."

"Keep my five percent, too," Grace added.

Noah sighed. "I'm not about to be shown up by a couple of teenagers. You're welcome to my share."

"Thank you." She pressed her lips into a thin line. "I'll go tell Vince what happened."

"I'll come with you." Henry stood.

"Trust me, you don't want to do that." Averi offered him a soft smile. "He's never happy on Mondays."

"But I'm not supposed to leave you alone."

"She'll be fine between here and the boss's office. Come have a soda on me." Noah nodded toward the bar.

Henry slid onto a barstool and turned to Grace. "How'd you do tonight?"

"She did outstanding," Noah said. "And don't let the discrepancy with the money ruin your night. You worked hard, and the patrons seemed to love you."

Henry glanced away. "I feel bad for Averi."

Noah set two colas on the counter. "I do too, but it's the nature of the business. Some nights the cash rolls in, other nights you're lucky to make enough to afford a cup of coffee."

The twins sat in comfortable silence, sipping their sodas and waiting for Mr. Villenti to emerge and drive them home. Employee after employee left the building until only Noah, Averi, Vince, and the twins remained.

"You'll be here until the wee hours waiting for Vince." Noah tossed his bar rag into a basket. "I'd be happy to give you a ride home."

Grace yawned. "We don't mind."

"Nonsense, it's two miles from here."

"I'm exhausted." Her brother sat with his chin propped in his hand and eyes half-closed.

She motioned down the hall. "Should I tell Vince we're leaving?"

"Henry?" Averi's voice rose in pitch and volume.

He snapped to attention. "Yeah?"

The waitress stood in the back of the dining room, staring at a table—or more specifically, something on the table. "Would you care to explain this?"

Grace's mouth went dry. She had no clue what he'd done, but Averi didn't sound happy. *Looks like we won't be leaving after all.*

"What?" He stood and shambled his way to the woman but stopped a few feet from the table. *The missing money.*

"Where did you find it?" Averi narrowed her eyes. "Or did you have it all along?"

Henry took a step back. "I didn't put it there."

Noah jogged over and whistled. "Would you look at that!"

"My guess is it's exactly one hundred eighty dollars and thirty-seven cents." Grace pressed her hand to her chest.

"Uh-uh. Nice try." Averi planted her hands on her hips. "Which one of you is responsible for this?"

Noah raised his hands. "He's not lying. They were with me at the bar from the time you went to see Vince until you returned."

The twins nodded.

"Then who?" The waitress glanced around the empty room.

"It had to be one of the other employees." Henry spoke as if trying to convince himself. "No one else was here."

"The kid's right." Noah motioned to the money. "My guess is, someone caught a case of the guilty conscience and returned what didn't belong to them."

"The exact amount she was short?" Grace tapped her lips. "That doesn't make sense. The cash, I can see, but how could someone have stolen the change?"

"And if they did, why leave it all fanned out like that?" Henry added.

Feminine laughter drifted down from the second-floor dining room. "So what? Someone got caught glomming some cabbage. Big Deal."

"Glomming some cabbage?" Grace arched a brow.

"Stealing cash," Henry whispered. "I think."

Frowning, Noah backtracked into the center of the room and peered up at the railing. "In case you didn't notice, we closed hours ago. You'll need to vacate the premises."

"Woohoo, listen to Mr. Hoity-Toity. Eddie pay you extra to use such big words?" The woman purred. "No, that ain't it. I bet it's that cake-eating smile of yours he pays for. What's your name, handsome?"

"Look, lady, I don't know who you are, but you have to leave." Noah's voice rose.

Goosebumps broke out across Grace's arms. "The way she talks—"

"—is like an old gangster movie." Henry knocked over a chair on his way to Noah.

Grace ran to the far side of the room and gawked at the redhead.

The woman was beautiful, decked out in 1920s clothes, not the tacky beaded flapper dresses sold in costume shops. The straight-cut chemise hit right below the woman's knees and was decorated with embroidery and delicate beading. It belonged in a fashion museum.

The redhead rolled her eyes. "Now we have us a bunch of lookie-loos? Why don't one of you be a doll and go find Eddie for me."

No one moved.

Vince trudged down the hall, took one look at the four of them staring at the railing, and blanched. "She's back, isn't she?"

Grace nodded.

Henry ducked back under the overhang and ran toward the back of the building, likely to take the employees' staircase to the second floor.

Noah seemed to catch on and took the dining room stairs two at a time.

The woman huffed, tossed her boa over her shoulder, and disappeared from view.

A split second later, Noah shouted, "She's gone."

Vince threw up his hands. "It's the same M.O. as the other night. She shows up, asks for Eddie, and vanishes before anyone gets near her."

Averi wrapped her arms around herself. "She seemed so real."

"Too real." Grace marched up the stairs determined to get to the bottom of the situation and found Noah and Henry staring at a portrait above the fireplace.

"Gracie, come and take a look at this." Her brother pointed to the painting.

"She looks..."

"Exactly like the woman in red." Noah finished her thought.

"Maybe so, but I don't buy it." Heart pounding, she turned from the hearth and dropped to her hands and knees where the woman had stood.

"What are you looking for?" Vince called from below.

"A feather or a bead or something to prove she's real." *She was a human in a nice dress. There's a perfectly good explanation for the likeness. There are no such things as ghosts.* Grace chanted the words over and over but couldn't convince herself they were true.

"How's that working out for you?" Villenti grinned, but the color hadn't returned to his face.

"It's not. Not at all." Grace sat back on her heels. *Did we just have a conversation with a dead woman?*

CHAPTER FOUR

Henry woke to his sister clickety-clacking on her laptop in his room. He threw his arm over his face to block the midday sun and groaned. "We finally have our own rooms, and you insist on working in mine?"

Grace threw a wadded-up piece of paper at him and continued typing. "It's one in the afternoon. We have to be at work in four hours. I need that brilliant brain of yours to help me solve the mystery."

Staring at the ceiling, he counted backward from ten. When that didn't ease his irritation, he tried again—this time from fifty.

"Come on, Henry, I'm serious. I don't want to go back there without a plan."

He lifted his head from the pillow. "Do I detect a note of fear in your voice?"

"Nope." She banged harder on the keyboard.

"Hmm... Could it be a little crow I smell on your breath?"

Grace glared. "To eat crow, one would have to be humiliated as a result of admitting one's mistakes or defeat. Since I'm neither humiliated nor defeated, that would be a no."

Pushing himself upright, Henry muttered under his breath, "It's way too early in the morning for this."

"It's after one."

"Exactly. We're keeping bar hours now. One is the same as four A.M. to day-walkers."

Ignoring him, she pressed on. "I can't find any information about the woman in the painting. The artist died decades ago, and no one who still has a pulse can tell me who she is. Was. Her identity."

Henry scratched his head. "I need carbs and caffeine."

Without turning from the computer screen, Grace pointed to the night-stand. She'd brought him a cup of steaming hot coffee and an egg sandwich.

"Bless you." He took a sip and sighed happily. "What do we know?"

"Quite a bit." She faced him. "We know Vince is hard on his employees, but most are loyal to him anyway. Noah isn't as horrid as I originally thought—"

"The jury is still out on that one."

"We will agree to disagree where Noah Nelson is concerned. He was a huge help last night." She smirked. "Okay, back to the matter at hand. We know losing employees is costing Vince money. Blowing up toilets and forcing him to close for the night also hit him in the wallet."

"Whoever is doing this does seem to be economically motivated." He took a huge bite of the sandwich to give him time to think. "The Wonder Bar is doing well. Maybe someone wants to run Vince out of business so they can buy it?"

"I'll add that to my list of questions for Villenti." She furrowed her brow, never a good sign. "But what does the Lady in Red have to do with it?"

He hitched a shoulder. "Besides potentially scaring off his employees?"

"She wasn't particularly scary." Grace drummed her fingers on the desk. "She just shows up, insults people, and vanishes."

"About that. I read an article about the original owners, Roger and Eddie Touhy, that claimed Eddie was buried in the second-floor fireplace."

Grace shivered. "Did you ever ask Dad about Vince's family?"

"Nope, but now is as good a time as any." He stood, stretched, and wandered to the door.

"Mom and Dad left for the university hours ago." Grace shook her head. "Speaking of which, you realize Mom arranged proctors for our finals at nine in the morning tomorrow and the day after."

"Add getting off early to the list of questions for Vince." He rummaged through the pants he'd worn the night before and retrieved his phone. "I'll call Dad."

Ethan Warner answered on the third ring. "Henry, everything all right?"

"Yes and no." He ran his hand over the top of his head. "Weird question. What do you know about Vince's childhood?"

The line went quiet. So quiet, Henry thought the call had dropped. "Dad?"

"I'm here." He cleared his throat. "He had a rough start. Two of his brothers ended up on the wrong side of the law because of it."

Henry lowered his voice. "Vince told us his mother passed away when he was young."

"Vince was two. His brother Vaughn was four. Their father was a police officer at the time. He left the older children in charge of the little ones while he worked. Needless to say, they received very little guidance."

Henry sighed. "Thanks for the intel."

"Why do you ask?"

"Oddly enough, his story is almost identical to the original owners of The Wonder Bar." He felt like a jerk for questioning the guy's life history.

Ethan chuckled. "I hate to point out the obvious, but why do you think he bought the place?"

"To make tons of money and live the American dream?"

"There's that, but Vince has a fascination with Capone-era organized crime."

He glanced at Grace and frowned. "I enjoy a good gangster movie as much as the next guy, but that doesn't mean I'm going to go out and buy Baby-Face Nelson's summer home."

Ethan said, "I have to get to class. My advice? Talk to Vince."

"Thanks." Henry disconnected the call. "How much of that did you hear?"

"Most of it. Dad learned to whisper in a chainsaw factory." She scribbled down some notes. "I'm adding asking Vince about his fascination with gangsters to my to-do list."

"You do that. I'm going to take a shower and get some studying in before work." He eyed his English Lit text like it was a viper coiled and ready to strike.

Grace followed his gaze. "Need me to quiz you?"

"Sure, but I'm not worried about it." Henry pulled a pair of jeans and a sweatshirt from his suitcase. "I did the math. The final is worth twenty percent of my grade. Even if I get a seventy on it, I'll still finish the class with a low A or high B."

"B?" Grace's mouth fell open as if he'd suggested they go on a five-state puppy-kicking campaign.

"Yes, a B. Somehow I don't think the world will come to an end if I screw up my perfect GPA."

Grace shook her head. "Have you *met* our mother?"

Armed with her growing list of questions, Grace joined Vince in the kitchen at four o'clock. At three minutes past the hour, the man's phone rang.

"Excuse me." He glanced at the screen, muttered something under his breath, and took the call. "Villenti here. Password is four-eight-seven-six-seven-nine. What's going on?"

The longer he listened, the redder his face grew until he resembled one of the beefsteak tomatoes sitting on the counter. "I'm on my way."

Grace hopped off the bar stool. "I'll get Henry and my purse."

Vince set the phone on the island and walked away, then turned and came back. "You two should stay put. There was an attempted break-in."

A million or so reasons why they should come along crossed her mind, but she managed to squeak out, "Please. Criminals often return to the scene of the crime when the police arrive. Henry and I can keep a lookout while you're dealing with the responding officers."

He folded his arms. "Make it quick and bring your laptops. Your mother made me promise to make you study."

Grace made a beeline for the guest bedrooms. She burst through the door and shoved her computer into her backpack. "We have to go. Now."

"What's wrong?" Thankfully, Henry started moving without further prompting.

"There was a break-in. We have to hurry, or Vince is likely to leave us behind."

The twins made it downstairs in under five minutes. Mr. Villenti opened his mouth as if to speak but shook his head and motioned to the door.

The five-minute drive to The Wonder Bar seemed to take an hour. By the time they arrived, four police cruisers and two unmarked sedans sat in the parking lot.

"Man, that's a big turnout. Did they say what was stolen?" Henry gawked.

"They did not. Keep your eyes open. We'll talk when the cops leave." Vince zipped his jacket and strode toward two uniformed officers standing near the front door.

Grace motioned to a small crowd of people gathered in the adjacent parking lot. "See anyone you recognize?"

"It's hard to say from here." Henry pulled his phone out and opened the camera app. "Let's get a closer look."

"Careful not to let anyone see you snapping their picture." She climbed out of the SUV with Henry on her heels.

For the most part, the people gathered seemed like typical office staff. Men in ties and dress pants, women in power suits. One or two individuals in jeans stood out, but they seemed more interested in their phones than the flashing lights in front of the restaurant.

Grace squared her shoulders. "Did anyone see what happened?"

The adults exchanged glances.

An older woman with thick glasses and a Midwest accent said, "I was on my way to my car when the police arrived."

Several others nodded.

A man in a dark pinstriped suit cocked his head. "Wasn't that Vince Villenti you came here with?"

"Yes, do you know him?" She smiled. "He's our honorary uncle. He and my dad go way back."

"Do *you* know what happened?" His stare unnerved her.

"Someone broke into the restaurant." She glanced over the crowd. "Which is why it's really important to come forward if you saw something. Every detail can help the police find the person responsible."

Mr. Pinstripe continued to stare as if waiting for her to say more.

Grace sent up a prayer that Henry had taken the guy's photo.

A second woman raised her hand. "Miss, I may have some information for the police."

Henry slid his phone into his pocket. "Come with us."

"Thank you." She chewed her lower lip and stepped forward.

Grace did a double take. The woman seemed familiar, but she couldn't place her. "Have we met?"

"You seated my husband last night. I'm Mrs. Connors. You probably don't remember me. You were so busy."

"I don't think I will ever forget you, Mrs. Connors. It was my first night." Her cheeks heated. She'd forgotten to seat the elderly couple for over an hour. It wasn't until the woman asked that she remembered to add their name to the list.

"It's all right, dear. The bartender gave us coupons for a free steak dinner." The woman offered a smile that reminded Grace of handmade quilts and homemade cookies.

The officers at the front of the building stood straighter when the trio approached.

Henry said, "This is Mrs. Connors. She thinks she has some information about the break-in."

"My daughter works next door. I stopped by to drop off some mail that came to my house." She glanced around as if expecting someone to jump out of the bushes. "I saw a man leaving the back of the building with a duffle bag."

The larger of the two officers said, "Can you describe him?"

"I didn't see his face. He had the collar on his overcoat turned up and his fedora pulled down."

Fedora? Grace glanced at her brother.

Henry winked.

While the hat had made a comeback in recent times, the likelihood of a burglar wearing the same outfit as one of the alleged ghosts Averi had seen was slim.

"Would you mind giving a statement?" The second officer motioned to the door. "It will only take a moment."

"I suppose it's my civic duty." The woman raised her chin and walked inside like she owned the place.

Grace shook her head and followed Mrs. Connors and the officers inside. The dining room looked like a miniature tornado had blown through. Tables and chairs were in disarray. Silverware littered the floor, along with pieces of shattered stemware. Whoever had broken in had trashed the place as part of their misadventure.

Vince gestured for the twins to join him and the detective. "Who's that?"

Henry said, "We found her in the crowd from the building next door. She saw a man in an overcoat and fedora leaving the area with a duffle bag."

The blue-eyed detective grinned. "Nice work. Is she giving a statement?"

Henry nodded.

"These two related to you?" He motioned between Villenti and the twins.

Grace smiled. "He's our honorary uncle."

Vince winked, seemingly pleased by her description.

"This is still an official crime scene. I should insist that you wait outside, but it's colder than a..."

Vince arched a brow.

The detective grinned. "The second floor is clear. You two can wait up there."

The twins marched up the stairs. Unlike the main dining room, the area looked the same as it had the night before—except for a red envelope resting on the table nearest the hearth.

"What's that?" Henry reached for the note but hesitated. "Should we tell the police?"

Grace leaned closer to read the scrolling handwriting. "It's addressed to us."

He clasped his hands behind his head and walked in a wide circle. "It's like the Watcher all over again."

"Not necessarily." She lifted the corner of the envelope. "We really should tell the detective about this."

"They'll put it into evidence, and we might or might not ever see it again."

"Good point. I'll tell them after we read it." She opened the wax seal on the back and pulled an old-fashioned card from the envelope and read aloud, "Dear Henry and Grace, I've watched you over the last two days. You seem like good kids. The kind who help people in need."

"That doesn't sound good." He sank into a chair.

"You see, I took something that didn't belong to me years ago, and now I must return it. My soul can't rest until I find what was lost. Please help." Grace sighed. "It's signed, The Lady in Red."

He glanced at the portrait hanging over the mantle and frowned. "Oh, boy."

"This has scam written all over it." Grace studied the green-eyed beauty in the painting and shivered. "Whoever wrote this must be close. They knew our names and that we helped Averi."

"I know you don't want to consider a non-scientific explanation for all of this, but it is possible—"

"Nope. I refuse to believe a ghost wrote us a letter asking for our help." She shoved the note back into the envelope and slid it into her pocket.

Henry chuckled. "Then why aren't we handing that over to the police?"

"I want to run it by Vince first." She turned to him and smiled. "If he agrees, I think we should help her find whatever it is she's searching for."

CHAPTER FIVE

Funny thing about restaurants; when closed, they made great places to study, between the plethora of tables and chairs, the peace and quiet, and the access to unlimited amounts of food. Empty restaurants were like anti-libraries. The people running it expected their guests to talk, laugh, and eat while working.

Henry glanced from his English Lit book to Vince Villenti. The man wore a ten o'clock shadow, wrinkled clothes, and a frown. All of which was to be expected after spending the previous six hours going over insurance paperwork, inventories, and police reports.

"I come bearing gifts." He raised a tray of food to his shoulder and performed a balancing act that would make a circus performer jealous. Within seconds, he'd placed salads, bread, entrees, and various side dishes on an empty table.

"That smells awesome." Henry had spent the previous evening serving food, but he hadn't sampled the fare.

"Thank you, but you really didn't have to feed us." Grace's stomach punctuated her words with loud growls.

"I cook when I'm stressed. It calms me." He sat between them.

"Did it work this time?" Henry skipped the salad and went straight for the steak.

Vince popped a cherry tomato into his mouth. "Not at all. I owe you two a huge debt for sticking around today and finding that witness. We can leave once I let the emergency cleaning crew in."

"We were happy to help." Grace sipped her iced tea. "Was anything missing?"

"Nothing." The frown he'd worn since receiving the call from the alarm company deepened. "I can't figure it out."

Henry lowered his voice. "Are all of the police gone?"

"I fed them and locked the door behind the last one just before I came up." He motioned to the food. "Eat while it's hot."

Grace filled her plate. "We found something when we came upstairs. A note."

Mouth open and fork hovering, Vince stopped mid-bite.

"From the Lady in Red." She nodded toward the painting.

He gave her a quizzical look. "Up here? After the cops were finished scouring the room?"

"A bright red envelope sitting in the middle of a table is hard to miss," Henry said.

Vince chewed his steak, nodded, and washed it down with red wine. "Any reason you two didn't hand the note over to the detectives?"

Henry glanced at his sister. After all, it was her idea to run the plan by Villenti.

"I wasn't sure if they'd take it as evidence or tear this dining room apart again looking for clues." Grace pulled the note from her pocket and handed it to Vince. "Read it."

He opened the envelope and scanned the words, once, twice, three times, before turning and staring at the portrait of the redhead. "You think she wrote this?"

The twins exchanged glances.

Henry wiped his mouth and tossed the napkin on the table. "Grace and I disagree about the existence of ghosts, but we do agree on one thing. We need to figure out who wrote this and whatever it is they believe is in this building."

Holding the note, he pointed from one twin to the other. "You guys are right about that, and about not turning this over to the police."

Grace said, "We plan to play along. Do whatever it is the *alleged* Lady in Red asks us to do. Sooner or later, we'll find what she's looking for and the person's true identity."

"That is, if you agree," Henry added.

Sitting back, Vince split his attention between the portrait and the twins. "I'll agree on two conditions."

Grace dipped her chin and grinned. "Which are?"

"Nothing dangerous or illegal." He took another bite of steak. "And you keep me in the loop. No sneaking off to Timbuktu in the middle of the night without telling me where you're going."

"Deal," the twins said in unison.

Vince glanced at them and chuckled. "My brother and I used to do that when we were kids. Say the same thing, finish each other's sentences. I used to swear I'd feel pain if he was hurt."

"Are you two still close?" Grace took a bite of the chicken and sighed. "This is so good."

"Thanks. I was a chef before I was an entrepreneur." Villenti finished his wine. "To answer your question, Vaughn and I had a falling out shortly after we met your father. We've talked a handful of times in the last twenty years, but no, I'm not close to any of my siblings."

Henry detected a note of remorse in the man's voice and couldn't help but think there was far more to the story. "By the way, your childhood is amazingly similar to Roger "The Terrible" Touhy's."

Grace's eyes widened.

Vince chuckled again. "More than you know, kid. More than you know."

What is that supposed to mean? Henry waited, hoping the man would elaborate.

"Do you have any idea what the Lady in Red is looking for?" Grace continued devouring her dinner.

"Not a clue, but at this point, nothing would surprise me." Vince motioned to the fireplace. "Some say Eddie Touhy is buried behind those bricks."

"We read that on the internet." Henry frowned and gestured to the windows. "Are there still secret compartments where the gangsters hid their Tommy guns?"

Vince nodded. "Yep. A previous owner covered them with drywall, but the ones in the back of the building are still intact."

"And the gun slits in the turrets?" Grace pushed her plate back and rested her hands on her belly.

"They weren't that obvious. Some of those gray rocks around the windows and door weren't mortared in place." He wiggled his brows. "If the place was raided, the wise guys could push the stones out and shove the barrels of their guns through. It was genius."

"I *knew* those rocks seemed out of place." Grace laughed. "But with so many modifications to the building, the treasure could be hidden anywhere."

Vince glanced at the portrait again. "Do me a favor and don't tear out any drywall without checking with me first."

A crash from the downstairs dining room brought them to their feet.

A loud thump, followed by the tell-tale sound of breaking glass sent Vince and the twins running for the first floor.

"Marone!" Vince stopped at the bottom of the stairs.

One of the glass shelves behind the bar had come loose and sent bottles of liquor to the stone floor. The resulting mess of booze and shattered glass covered the one portion of the dining room the burglar left intact.

Grace gasped and pointed to a table near the door.

A red envelope like the one the twins had found upstairs rested against a candle.

Henry wanted nothing more than to tear into the note, but someone needed to clean up the boozy mess. "I'll get the broom and garbage can."

Vince scrubbed both hands over his head. "Leave it. The cleaning crew will be here soon."

Grace glanced around before opening the envelope. "Dearest Henry and Grace, I last saw the goods on Skid Road. Search for the skull and crossbones. The Lady in Red. P.S. Don't forget to bring a shovel."

Henry bit back a grown. "Skid Row?" Isn't that slang for a place where the homeless and criminals—"

"Skid *road*, with a D." Grace pulled her phone from her pocket.

"In the 20s, Skid Road was a place where bootleggers met." Vince frowned.

"Does she mean the tunnels?" Henry grinned. He'd wanted to explore the old smugglers' route since they arrived.

Villenti folded his arms and shook his head. "No way. Uh-uh. You two aren't going down there at night, or ever. It's not safe."

"If whoever wrote this wanted to hurt us, they would have done it by now. It's obvious they can get in and out of the building without being heard." Grace waved the note. "But there's something down there they want us to find."

Vince's expression hardened.

"We aren't made of paper." Henry grinned to lighten the mood. "We'll be okay."

"I'm coming with you."

Grace's brows rose. "You can't. You have to wait for the cleaning crew. Besides, the person sent the letter to Henry and me. We don't want to spook them so soon."

He seemed to consider his options. "You have fifteen minutes. If you're not back, I'm coming after you."

Shovel in hand, Henry made his way down the rickety metal staircase. "Shine the light below my feet. I don't want to fall because I didn't see a rusted-out step."

Grace aimed the flashlight down. "I can't believe this is still here. Why didn't Vince tear it out?"

"Because it's cool, and he's obsessed with Prohibition-era gangsters." Henry reached the bottom stair and tested the ground before stepping off. "I think the tunnel is carved out of the rock."

She shined the light over the floor and walls. "Seems that way, but we still need to be careful."

"I seriously wish the Lady in Red had given us more to go on than a vague comment about a skull and crossbones." He pulled his phone from his pocket and opened the flashlight app.

"Me too." Walking a few feet ahead, she shined the light in wide arcs.

"How do you think Red is getting into the restaurant?" Henry stopped to examine some graffiti carved into the wall.

"I'm not sure, but we should scour the upstairs dining room for a hidden staircase or room." Grace doubled back. "Find anything?"

Running his fingertips over the stone, he said, "Someone carved a bunch of numbers and symbols into the rock."

She leaned close as if to get a better look. "Can you take a picture of it? I'd like to research what all of that means."

"I suspect they're coordinates or a tally of some sort." He handed her the shovel and snapped several photos. "The pics are dark, but we can lighten them once we download them to the computer."

Grace whipped her head in the direction of the lake.

Henry's throat tightened, making it difficult to speak. "What did you—"

She put her hand over his mouth and shook her head. A split-second later, she turned off the flashlight.

Henry pressed his cell against his jeans to block the light.

Standing in complete darkness, he strained to listen for whatever it was that Grace had heard. Several heartbeats later, he gave up. "There's nothing—"

"Shhh." Grace grabbed his free hand and pulled him farther into the tunnel.

Sure enough, male voices filtered their way to Henry's ears, along with the first flickers of light.

Holding the shovel like a weapon, Grace eased closer to the wall and crouched.

Henry pressed his still-lit cell phone harder against his leg. In hindsight, he should have turned it off, but at the time, he was more concerned with tripping over loose rocks than discovering a clandestine meeting.

A tall man wearing a fedora and trench coat glanced over his shoulder before whispering, "Did you find it?"

The guy had the same build as Noah Nelson, but his voice sounded different. Squinting, Henry tried to make out his features. It was no use. Like Mrs. Connors had said earlier in the day, the man wore his collar up and the brim of his hat low.

"Yeah, but it took some doing. Villenti must have changed the alarm code. I wasn't in the building two minutes before it went off." The second guy chuckled. "Good thing the cops took their time getting here."

"Where is it now?" Mr. Fedora's voice hardened. He either didn't care for his partner in crime or he didn't want to stand around chatting, or maybe both.

"You'll get it when I get paid."

Mr. Fedora pulled a fat envelope from his pocket but held it out of the other man's reach. "I have the cash. Give me the drive."

"It's all here." He handed the man something.

"Time's up! Where the heck are you two?" Vince Villenti called from somewhere behind them.

Henry's heart leapt into his throat as if to escape his body. Beside him, Grace sucked in a breath.

The man in the fedora turned and shined a flashlight in the twins' direction, but by some miracle, it went over their heads. "What's he doing down here?"

"I...I..don't know."

"Did you tip him off? Is this a setup?" Mr. Fedora grabbed the other man by the collar. In the process, he illuminated their faces.

Henry recognized the second man as one of Vince's busboys, the same jerk who'd given him the once-over in the kitchen.

"Warners? Don't think for a second I won't call your parents!" Vince may have shouted, but he sounded as uncertain as he did angry. "Henry? Grace?"

Gripping the guy in the fedora's hands, the busboy said, "He's looking for those kids he hired."

Mr. Fedora released him and hurried toward the mouth of the tunnel.

The busboy blew out a breath and bent at the waist. The encounter seemed to have freaked him out almost as much as it had Henry.

"Don't move!" Grace lurched forward.

Henry suffered a moment of blind fear. The guy in the fedora could have heard her. He could have a gun. Heck, the busboy could be armed. In his panic, he forgot about the phone in his hand. The all-too-bright-light of the flashlight app flared to life like a beacon.

Grace froze in place, holding the shovel over her shoulder as if she intended to use the busboy's neck as a tee-ball stand.

The guy yelped and covered his head.

Shooting to his feet, Henry rushed forward before the guy got any funny ideas about hurting Grace. "Vince! Down here!"

"Who was that, and what were you selling him?" She tightened her grip on the shovel.

"I don't know what you're talking about!" The guy glanced left and right so quickly he should have sprained an eye muscle.

Henry didn't trust anyone who looked like a caged animal. "Vince! We need help!"

Villenti replied, but his words were lost in the busboy's battle cry. The wiry young man sprang forward in a blur of movement. Grace swung, but she'd reacted a split second too late, and the shovel missed him completely. The guy caught her around the waist and they headed for the stone floor. Grace let the shovel go.

Henry reached for the back of the busboy's shirt. Before he could get a grip, Grace put her years of self-defense training to use. She twisted and sent the man around her and upside down. He slammed into the hard rock and she rode him down, sitting across his chest while securing her grip on both his ears.

The busboy swung his fists like a third-grader pinned down by the playground bully. He managed to catch her once in the jaw before Grace bounced his head off the floor, just hard enough to show him the errors of his ways.

"Marone!" Red-faced and winded, Vince Villenti pulled Grace off the wheezing busboy. "What's going on here?"

CHAPTER SIX

Grace pressed the icepack to her jaw and winced. For something that would reduce the pain, the cold hurt. She glared at the guy sitting next to her.

Paul, the busboy, avoided making eye contact.

Vince sat back in his office chair and steepled his fingers beneath his chin. "For the last time, who did you meet with, and what did you give him?"

"I didn't catch the guy's name." Paul squirmed in his chair, likely still sore from Grace's knee.

"What was on the flash drive?" Henry leaned against the wall and folded his arms.

The busboy turned to Vince. "You have to believe me. I'd never betray your trust."

Grace resisted the urge to roll her eyes. They'd questioned the guy for thirty minutes and gotten nowhere. "Mr. Villenti, who has access to your computer files?"

"Just me and my accountant." He frowned. "Noah has access to the inventory and my contacts, but not much else."

"Do you keep your passwords written down somewhere? A desk drawer? Taped to the monitor?"

Vince narrowed his eyes. "No."

Henry motioned to the busboy. "We should check his phone. My guess is, he spoke to the guy in the fedora recently."

Every muscle in Paul's body tensed.

Villenti's computer wasn't booted up. Considering the police were combing the building from the time he'd arrived until shortly before Vince had cooked dinner for the twins, the likelihood he'd turned it on since the previous evening was slim.

Grace asked, "Have you touched your keyboard since last night?"

Vince stared at her for a beat before a slow smile spread across his face. "I have not."

"Call the detective and ask if they dusted it for prints."

"The CSI folks left black dust everywhere they checked." Villenti made a show of wrapping a tissue around his fingers before flipping the keyboard over. "There's no dust."

"Have the detective come back and do it now." She turned to Paul. "He can get your prints while he's at it."

Beads of sweat formed on the busboy's upper lip and brow. "Mr. Villenti, you gotta believe me. I wouldn't have done it if I wasn't desperate. I lost my second job, and the rent's two months past due. My girl, she's expecting a baby..."

Vince closed his eyes and let his head fall back. "What was on the flash drive?"

"Nothing important. The guy. He said to copy a folder named Villenti TWB Menu." Paul shrugged.

If it were possible to witness someone's blood pressure rise, Grace did just that. Vince's eyes widened, his face reddened, and the veins in his neck and forehead bulged.

Henry met her gaze and mouthed, "Noah."

She swallowed past the lump in her throat. "I take it the folder didn't really contain menus?"

"No." Vince held his hand out to Paul. "Your phone."

"I didn't know, Vince. I wouldn't have..." The busboy handed over his cell so fast Grace almost felt sorry for him. Almost.

Villenti scrolled through the cell, jotted down some notes, and made a call.

Grace held her breath. If he'd done what she thought he'd done, the guy in the fedora would answer the phone.

Paul mumbled, "He probably thinks I'm calling about the money."

Vince disconnected the call and nodded to Grace. "You sure this nitwit didn't get paid?"

"The envelope didn't change hands."

"You two should go back to the house. Take my SUV. I'll call a cab once I'm done here." Vince stood and took his keys from his pocket.

"What are you gonna do, Vince? What are you gonna do to me?" Paul's voice went up an octave or two. "Call the detective like she said. I'll cooperate with the police."

Henry glanced from the keys to the busboy and finally to Vince. "We'll wait for the detective to show up. He'll probably want us to give a statement."

"No. I got this." Vince's eyes never left Paul. "It's late. You two have exams in the morning."

Grace's knees wobbled when she stood. Not from the pain in her jaw, but from the sense she'd walked into a scene from *The Godfather*. She couldn't leave the busboy here, not if Vince intended to hurt him—and judging by Paul's reaction, he expected a couple of broken kneecaps.

Henry said, "Vince, can we speak to you alone?"

"Sure, kid. But then you're leaving." Villenti motioned to the hall.

They stayed close enough to the office to keep a visual on the door but far enough away that Paul wouldn't overhear.

"You should call the police. They can track the guy in the fedora with his cell phone number." Grace tried to keep her voice calm, but her words came out in a rush.

Vince clamped a hand on her shoulder. "How's your jaw?"

"It's sore, that's all." She didn't care for him changing the subject or what it might mean.

"You two did good tonight." He sighed. "Things are starting to make sense, but I still can't figure out how the redhead plays into all this."

"We'll keep digging until we find out." Henry frowned. "There's something you should know. The other man in the tunnel? He had the same build as Noah."

Villenti's expression went from concerned to annoyed to amused. "Be that as it may, it wasn't him."

"I know he's your right-hand man, but how can you be sure?" Grace asked.

"Because he's been here since shortly after you two went into the tunnel." Vince nodded toward the main dining room. "I needed him to tally up the losses in the bar."

Henry sighed. "What was in that file?"

Vince rubbed his forehead. "My personal and The Wonder Bar's financials, documents from the sale, and some miscellaneous files I'd rather not have fall into the wrong hands."

Grace didn't want to imagine what sort of information he'd lost. If the size of the envelope was any indication, someone was willing to pay a lot of money to get their hands on it. "Are you going to call the police?"

"Nah." He glanced back toward his office. "You heard Paul. He's in a jam. It won't do his woman or his unborn kid any good to put him away."

Her brain stuttered. "You can't seriously be considering letting him keep his job?"

"I'm not *that* stupid." Vince chuckled. "He's fired, but I'll cut him a break and leave the cops out of it for now."

Grace disagreed, but she had no grounds to argue.

"Go home and get some sleep. I don't want your mother to blame me if you bomb your exams."

"It's probably best to stay on her good side." Henry grinned. "Speaking of which, it's not a great idea to tell her Grace was assaulted by a busboy."

Her jaw felt better, but once he mentioned it, the dull ache turned into a throb.

Vince shook his head. "I'm not above bending the law now and then, but I draw the line at lying to mothers."

Grace's opinion of the man climbed a few steps.

"Conversation's over. It's past your bedtimes." He nodded toward the exit.

"Just let me grab my backpack and we'll go." Henry grinned again, only this time he looked like he had something up his sleeve.

Henry eased the trap door to the metal stairs open. They had to be quiet, or they'd risk Vince catching them sneaking back into the tunnel.

"I don't feel right about this." Gripping the shovel, Grace glanced above their heads to the basement ceiling. "What if he notices the SUV is still in the parking lot?"

"He won't if we hurry." Henry waited until his sister descended the stairs and turned on her flashlight before closing the door.

"We had to be near the entrance when we ran into Paul, and we didn't find a skull and crossbones. What makes you think we'll find one now? In the dark? Why not come back in the daylight?"

"It doesn't matter when we search. It's always dark underground." Henry drew a breath through his nose and exhaled through his mouth. Her nervous energy was contagious. "And I don't want to wait. Think about it. The Lady in Red may not give us another clue until we've found the markings."

Grace mumbled something about pigs and stubborn and trouble, but she followed him deeper into the old bootleggers' tunnel.

"What do you make of Noah's alibi?" He shined the light from his phone over the walls and floor as they went.

"Unless Vince had the timing wrong, it's airtight." She stopped to get a better look at some graffiti. "The guy in the fedora was roughly the same height and build, but so are a lot of men."

"True. I still don't trust the guy."

"I didn't like him at first either, but he was really helpful the other night." She stopped again. This time she pointed the beam of light at the ceiling. "Do you think this goes all the way to the lake?"

"Hard to say. There's a highway and a park between the bar and the shoreline. I suspect it was all woods back in the 20s." Henry found more of the strange numbers and symbols etched into the stone. Some were deep, some were little more than a scratch. "We may have a problem."

"Just one?" She laughed then groaned. "Oww. Don't make me laugh until I've taken some ibuprofen."

"I'll do my best. Hang in there. We have to be close to the lake." He motioned her over.

"What's the problem?"

"Some of the symbols may no longer be visible."

"They're almost a hundred years old. Even down here, there would be some erosion." Grace ran her fingers over a series of numbers. "I wonder if this was some sort of inventory."

"It was." Noah Nelson called from a couple of yards away. "The lower level guys didn't keep books. They would have marked what they brought in and out of the bar on the walls to cover their backsides."

Henry's stomach did a triple backflip and landed in his shoes.

Pressing her hand over her heart, Grace said, "A little warning next time you sneak up on us."

"Sorry, I figured you heard me coming." Noah laughed—a good sign considering he'd caught them skulking around. "Vince sent me down here to tell you to go home."

The twins exchanged glances.

Villenti was no fool. He'd probably expected them to pull a fast one on him, but Henry still felt like a dog caught rooting through the trashcan.

"Did you find anything?" Noah tilted his head.

"Not yet." Grace shined her light toward the tunnel exit. "How much farther is the lake?"

"Not far. I'll help you search, but then you have to go home before Vince has a meltdown."

Henry didn't love the idea of the bartender joining them, but he didn't have much choice. "We're searching for a—"

"Skull and crossbones. Vince told me about the letters from our resident ghost." Noah walked ahead of them.

"Do you have any idea what she's looking for?" Grace searched one wall while Henry searched the other.

"Nope, but if I had to guess, I'd say cash, gold, or jewels." Noah stopped and leaned closer to a seemingly random stone on the ground. "Take a look at this."

Grace shined her flashlight on the rock and grinned. "Not exactly what I imagined, but that could be it."

Two long narrow rocks made an X in front of a rounded stone with two indentations roughly where eye sockets would be. Henry never would have noticed it. In fact, he found it odd that Noah had found it so easily.

"Where do we dig?" The bartender glanced at the twins.

Henry said, "Look for sand. If something is buried here, it wouldn't be beneath the bedrock."

Grace gave Henry an odd look and handed the shovel to Noah. "Try between the skull and the wall."

Noah dug a hole three feet wide and two feet deep before he hit rock.

"Try under the skull and crossbones." Henry might not have wanted the bartender along for the search, but he rather enjoyed watching someone else do the dirty work for a change.

Grace whispered, "Try not to look so smug."

He rolled his eyes and stepped forward. "I'll take a turn."

Noah glanced up and wiped his brow. "Sure, but I think it may be a lost cause."

Henry stepped into the hole and took the shovel. Rather than following the same wide circle the bartender started, he dug a line from the rock formation to the hard-packed dirt near the path. Once he had a trench, he widened from there.

Thunk.

"What was that?" Grace's flashlight left him seeing spots.

Henry poked around with the shovel until he heard the same hollow thud. Careful not to damage the object, Henry used the edge of the shovel to remove enough dirt to reveal a wooden box about the size of a loaf of bread. "It's not heavy enough to be gold."

Grace took the box and struggled to pry the lid open.

"Let me try." Noah pulled a pocket knife from his jeans.

Minutes later, the top came free. Inside the rough wood sat an ornate jewelry box wrapped in decaying fabric.

"What's inside?" Henry's words came out breathy. *This is it. The clue that will tell us the identity of the Lady in Red.*

Noah opened the art deco container and frowned. "It's empty."

"What do you mean, it's empty?" Grace took it from him and felt around inside. "There must be a hidden compartment or something."

"Why would someone bury an empty box?" Henry climbed out of the hole and rested the shovel against the wall.

The bartender shrugged. "It could be a decoy, or maybe whoever buried it stole what was inside?"

Grace groaned. "Dang it."

Henry had no idea of the time, and he wasn't sure he wanted to know. With final exams starting in a matter of hours, they needed to get home, shower, and crash. "Bring the darned box, and let's go."

"What are you going to do with it?" Grace eyed him.

"I'm going to hide it in my bag and smuggle it out of the bar. Let's put the redhead to the test. If she's a ghost, she'll know it was empty. If she's human, she either won't know we have it or will think we stole whatever was supposed to be inside."

Grace frowned. "That makes no sense. If she's human, she could walk down here and see the hole in the ground."

Noah scratched his head. "I don't think ghosts are omnipotent. How would she know the box was empty?"

Henry grabbed the shovel. "It's late. I'm exhausted. I don't have a clue what to do with the box, so I'm taking it with me and forgetting I was ever here."

Grace rested her hand on his shoulder. "Whatever you do, don't use that logic while taking your English Lit exam."

CHAPTER SEVEN

Grace couldn't name a teen in the history of teenagers who enjoyed getting up early. However, Henry took his loathing of mornings to an entirely different level. He groaned and scratched and yawned like a twenty-year-old hound dog with an unreachable itch.

"Here. Drink this." Grace shoved a cup of coffee under his nose.

He sniffed, opened one eye, and grunted something close to appreciation.

"Why are you wearing a scarf inside?" Faith Warner eyed her daughter.

Grace's hand flew to the thick wool wound around her neck. "I was cold."

"Uh huh. Come here, please."

Dipping her chin to hide the bruise on her jaw, Grace walked to her mother.

Faith put her hand on her daughter's forehead and frowned. "You do feel warm. What time did the two of you come in last night?"

"Around midnight." She turned her attention back to her calculus text.

They'd made it home at 12:55 and to bed an hour later, but midnight sounded a lot earlier than one.

"Do we need to reschedule the exams?"

She would have loved more sleep but getting stuck in bed all day because she'd bailed on her exams would cost them valuable time. "No."

"Text me if you feel worse after your first exam."

Grace nodded with as little movement as possible.

Henry glanced up from his breakfast and coughed. "How many tests are we taking today?"

"Three today. Two tomorrow." Faith arched a brow. "Don't tell me you're coming down with something, too?"

"Possibly." He curled his lips and downed the way-too-hot-to-drink coffee. "I'll text..." He coughed again. "If I need to come home." And again.

Grace rolled her eyes. Their mother gave them a perfectly reasonable out, but Henry was going to mess it up by overplaying his hand.

Ethan Warner walked into the kitchen wearing a suit and a bright smile. "Wow. That's one heck of a bruise."

Grace froze on the outside, but inside her fight-or-flight response waged war.

Henry coughed again, but she suspected he'd choked on his eggs.

"Remind me to never use my arm to hold an elevator open again." Faith chuckled and tugged her sleeves over her forearms. "Eat. We have to leave in less than five minutes."

Grace forced herself to breathe normally.

Ethan grabbed a bagel from the counter and turned to the twins. "How's the mystery coming along?"

"It's coming." Henry stood and rinsed his plate.

Keeping her head down, Grace pretended to study.

"We can discuss the mystery after they've finished their exams." Faith tapped her watch. "Everyone ready?"

"Yes, ma'am." She shoved her textbook into her backpack.

The elder Warners gasped.

The thick scarf Grace had used to camouflage her jaw had loosened enough to reveal the ugly black and blue mark.

"Wow. Now *that's* one heck of a bruise." Ethan pulled the fabric away from her face.

"You caught a chill, huh?" Faith motioned to the door. "We have to go, but you will explain yourself on the way."

On the short commute to the University of Wisconsin, the twins gave their parents a watered-down version of the events of the previous days. To Grace's surprise, neither parent interrupted or asked questions. They simply listened, nodded, and made appropriate sounds to let the twins know they were listening.

"Vince fired the busboy. He won't bother Grace again," Henry finished.

Ethan turned into the faculty parking lot.

Faith turned toward the backseat. "My first instinct is to ground you and insist you stop working with Vince. However, this is about a man's livelihood."

The twins stared at their mother with the same open-mouthed, shocked expressions.

"You may continue working on solving the mystery, but..." She lifted her index finger. "No more chasing the bad guys."

The twins held their hands up. "It's kind of what we do," Henry said.

Faith held up a second finger. "And you will tell us if you get injured."

"We can do that," Grace said.

Henry nodded, although he continued to stare at their mother as if he suspected aliens had inhabited her body.

The twins spent the next three hours elbow-deep in final exams, but Grace struggled to focus on the questions. Her mind drifted from the Lady in Red to her parents' uncharacteristically calm reactions to the files Paul had handed off to the guy in the fedora. They were missing something, and she had a feeling it was obvious.

Henry closed his computer and rolled his head from side to side. "How did you do?"

"I'm not sure."

He gave her a "Yeah, right" look.

"I'm serious. I couldn't concentrate." She powered down her laptop. "We have to find the connection between the Lady in Red and the files Paul stole."

"What if there *is* no connection?" Henry wiggled his brows. "What if the woman showing up is a coincidence?"

They had solved eight mysteries together, each one unique, but one thing had been constant. "You don't believe in coincidences."

He shrugged, the physical equivalent of a non-answer.

Annoyed with him, herself, the mystery, and her exams, Grace pressed her lips together and stood.

Henry chuckled and reached for her arm. "Don't go away mad. Let's take a few minutes to figure out what we know."

"Fine." She snatched her backpack from the floor. "But we'll do it in the cafeteria."

"Now there's an idea I fully support." Henry waved to the grad student who'd served as their test proctor and followed his sister to the door.

Campus map in hand, Grace made her way to Rheta's Market, a cafeteria-style restaurant with a wide variety of food stations. While Henry opted for Mexican, she needed comfort food. A warm blanket and a good book sounded perfect, but for the time being, she made do with chicken tenders and mac and cheese.

"Is that Averi?" Henry took a huge bite of his burrito.

Glancing over her shoulder, Grace smiled and waved.

"Hey, what are you two doing here?" The server plopped into a chair.

"Taking our finals." He wiped salsa from his chin. "Our parents pulled some strings to arrange a proctor."

"Are you a student?" Grace hadn't spent much time with Averi, but she seemed nice enough.

"Guilty as charged." Her eyes widened. "Your father is Ethan Warner?"

The twins nodded.

"*The* Ethan Warner?" She sat back in her chair.

"The one and, hopefully, the only." Grace picked at her food.

Averi laughed. "I'm attending his lecture series. He's terrific. Just the right amount of serious and funny."

"We're immune to his humor." Henry smirked. "Have you heard from Vince today? Is the restaurant open tonight?"

"Yes, knock on wood." She banged on the Formica table top. "He's re-keying the place and changing the alarm codes after the Paul thing."

Grace perked up and rapid fired her questions. "Do you know Paul well? How long has he worked there? Does he have a criminal background?"

"He's only been there about six months. He mostly kept to himself." Averi lowered her voice. "As for his record, it wouldn't surprise me. Vince has a soft spot for ex-cons."

Henry set his burrito down. "How so?"

She glanced away. "I shouldn't gossip."

In Grace's experience, the phrase "I shouldn't gossip," came before a whole lot of gossiping. "Someone's going out of their way to cause Vince a lot of financial trouble. Anything you can tell us will help us put a stop to it."

"Vince told me you were trying to solve the mystery of the Lady in Red. I don't know much..." She sighed. "But several of the staff have criminal records, everything from white collar stuff to armed robbery."

The information shocked Grace, although, knowing what she did about Vince's upbringing, it shouldn't have surprised her. "I think that's great.

One of the leading reasons people return to jail is a lack of job opportunities."

"Yes, but it's not just the wait staff and busboys. Even Noah—" Averi covered her mouth. "Forget I said that."

Henry furrowed his brow. "Noah has a record?"

"It sounds much worse than it is." She stood. "Please don't tell Vince I told you. I really shouldn't have mentioned it."

Grace had a million questions, but she settled on one. "What did he do?"

"I'm not entirely sure. Racketeering, if you believe the gossip." Averi sighed again. "I have to get to class."

Henry waited for the waitress to leave before leaning forward. "For someone to be convicted of racketeering, the prosecutors must prove the person was involved in organized crime and had a pattern of criminal activity. Usually, things like gambling, murder, kidnapping, arson, drug dealing, and bribery."

Dressed in their head-to-toe black uniforms, the twins arrived at The Wonder Bar an hour and a half before their shift. They might have looked like funeral attendees, but Averi's information renewed their determination to solve the mystery. Vince deserved to know the truth, even if he chose not to believe it.

Henry opened his locker and a red envelope fell to the floor. "Hey, Grace?"

"Yep?" She checked to make sure her lock was secure.

"We have mail."

Stone-faced, Grace motioned to the supply closet.

"No one's here except Vince, and he's locked in his office doing paperwork."

"I'd rather not chance someone overhearing." She stepped inside and gave him a hard look.

Henry rolled his eyes. "Like it matters. Everyone here knows we're trying to solve a mystery."

Ignoring his comment, Grace pointed at the letter. "What does it say?"

"Henry and Grace, You're the duck's quacks. Thanks a million for finding my box. It seems I got bamboozled. Search the cellar next. Look for the loose brick near the old brew kettles. The Lady in Red." A sliver of fear ran down his spine like melting ice. The woman or ghost or whatever she was knew they'd found the box. She even knew it was empty, but how?

Grace took the card, looked it over, and sighed. "The cellar is better than the tunnels, but we need to start looking now, or we'll have to wait until after our shift."

Normally, Henry appreciated his sister's pragmatic side. At that moment, it irritated him. "How could she have known we found an empty box?"

"Noah must have mentioned it to someone. Probably Vince. We both know he can't keep a secret."

Henry pinched the bridge of his nose. "And you *still* don't think Noah is involved in any of this?"

"We have to keep open minds. Unless Noah has perfected cloning, he wasn't the guy in the fedora. Besides, we don't know if the robbery is related to the redhead."

He stared, blank-faced. "There's too much to unpack in what you just said. We need to start searching the cellar."

"Okay, but don't put all our eggs in Noah's basket. We need to keep our eyes open."

"You're right." He cracked a grin and opened the door. "I'll poke a hole in the Noah basket and follow the breadcrumbs, because we have a great track record of our first impression of the perpetrator being wrong. We should assume we're wrong and operate from that premise."

"Say that again? You lost me with the mixed metaphor." Grace glanced toward the stairs leading to the main dining hall before hurrying to the unfinished portion of the basement.

"Ha-ha. The note said 'cellar,' which could mean anywhere down here." Henry hated to nag, but they didn't have time to spare. They needed to find the brew pot, locate the loose brick, and retrieve the treasure or whatever it was the Lady in Red needed them to find.

"You're right, and oh so wrong. I saw a bunch of old pots near the wine cellar. Now that I think about it, they were too big to cook soup in. Unless they were feeding an army."

He knew next to nothing about brewing beer, but he'd seen plenty of pictures of moonshine stills. "That sounds promising."

Grace led him to the enormous climate-controlled wine cellar.

Henry did a double take at the stacks of furniture, boxes, pots, and other alcohol-making paraphernalia. "It's like we rounded the corner and stepped back in time."

"I'd love to take an afternoon and go through some of this stuff." She typed into her phone and furrowed her brow. After a few moments of searching and scrolling, she turned the screen toward him. "We're looking for something like this."

He took one look at the large metal pot and bit the inside of his cheek to keep from laughing. "We're surrounded by things that look like that."

She rolled her eyes. "Fine, then start looking for a loose brick. Quietly. We don't need anyone to know we're down here."

Grace, the future engineer, started on one side of the space and methodically searched one wall. Henry didn't have the patience to inspect every square inch. Instead, he went from pot to pot and checked for loose bricks.

Footsteps echoed through the room.

The twins froze.

Henry hurried behind a heavy cast iron cauldron and motioned for his sister to join him.

A man wearing a trench coat and fedora stepped into the storage area. He leaned against the wall farthest from the wine cellar and removed his hat. Other than his tall, muscular build, the guy looked nothing like Noah. What was left of Mr. Fedora's hair was as dark as his eyes. He had a Roman nose, a squared-off jaw, and an expression that promised violence.

A few heartbeats later, Noah Nelson walked around the wine cellar. "You can't be here."

The guy held his arms out at his sides. "Yet, here I am."

Henry placed his accent as New England, but unlike Vince, who sounded like the stereotypical New Yorker.

"I told you I'd do it, but I need time." Noah shoved his hands in his pockets. "Things are messy. We do this wrong, and it's over for both of us."

"My patience has limits." The guy set the fedora back on his head. "As does my bank account."

"I'll talk to Vince, but you have to know he isn't going to like it."

"Let me worry about what he likes and dislikes. Your job is to get me the meeting."

Noah sighed. "You sure you want this? It didn't end so well for you the first time."

Henry met his sister's gaze and frowned. He wouldn't say, "I told you so." He didn't have to. She'd heard the conversation.

They waited until the footsteps had faded before coming out of their hiding spot.

Grace shook her head. "I can't believe it."

"I wish I could say I'm surprised." He turned back to the wall. "We need to find out what's going on more than we need to continue this scavenger hunt for the Lady in Red."

"I disagree. We have to be getting close to finding whatever it is she's looking for. What if this is all connected somehow? The ghost may be our best shot to figure this out." She pushed past him, knelt beside the cauldron, and fiddled with a brick.

Henry's head pounded, his stomach growled, and his nerves were frazzled. "I can tell you exactly what the ghost has to do with Noah and the guy in the fedora. It's a distraction to throw Vince, us, and anyone else who's paying attention off the real trail."

Standing, Grace smiled. "Are you finished?"

He paced the room. "Nope. I'm just getting started. We need to tell Vince what we saw and heard. We have to make him see Noah is up to no good."

"Henry?"

"What?" He turned and stared.

Grace dangled a diamond bracelet from her fingertips. "Still think the Lady in Red is a distraction?"

CHAPTER EIGHT

The evening dragged on and on. Unlike their first night on the job, only a trickle of customers flowed through the front door. The lack of work, coupled with his lack of sleep, made Henry grumpy. He and Grace needed to have a long chat with Vince about Noah, not to mention they had to set a trap for a certain redheaded ghost. A trap using diamonds for bait.

Averi pulled him aside. "Are you okay?"

He hitched a shoulder. "Vince shouldn't have to pay both of us when there's barely enough work for one."

"I thought you were upset about what I told you earlier."

"Not really." Henry yawned. "I'm not feeling—"

"I'm going to tell Vince I'm clocking out. You're more than ready to fly solo, and I have an exam at seven in the morning."

His mouth fell open. She had to know he was about to bail. Plus, while he'd never admit it out loud, the thought of waiting tables without Averi's supervision freaked him out. "I have two finals tomorrow. Besides, I've only had one real night of training and three tables tonight."

"It's dead in here. We haven't even opened the upstairs dining room. You'll be fine." She winked and hurried away.

Henry started to go after her when Grace sat an older couple in his section. *Dang it.*

She flashed him a smile as if she'd done him a favor.

Grabbing the water pitcher, he made his way to the couple. "Good evening, and welcome to The Wonder Bar. Have you dined with us before?"

The elderly gentleman muttered something under his breath.

The woman tilted her head. "We met on Tuesday. I gave the police my statement. Don't you remember?"

Henry looked at her face for the first time since he'd approached the table. "Mrs. Connors. Of course, I remember you. Sorry about that. You look different tonight. Did you change your hair?"

He'd laid it on thick, but he'd likely insulted the woman and her husband.

"I had it done this morning." She patted her teased and shellacked hair. "Did the police find the person who broke in?"

"Afraid not." Henry filled their water glasses. "Do you know what you'd like to order, or do you need a few minutes?"

Mr. Connors dropped a complimentary meal voucher on the table and raised his chin. "We'll have seafood trios, and I want a ribeye. The big one."

"I'll have a filet mignon with my seafood trio, and bring us a bottle of the Château Cos D' Estournel." Mrs. Connors scanned the menu. "And be sure to save me a crème brûlée. You were out last time we were here."

Henry blinked. They'd ordered the most expensive items on the menu. "You're aware that is a six-hundred-dollar bottle of wine?"

Mr. Connors tapped the voucher. "Our meal is on the house."

Oh, no. Of course, this would happen after Averi abandoned me. He cleared his throat. "That is a complimentary meal voucher, not a gift certificate. It doesn't include alcohol and is good for one entrée per guest."

The elderly woman slammed her menu on the table. "This is unacceptable. I want to speak to the owner at once."

Noah crossed the distance from the bar to the table in four strides. "How can I help you?"

Mrs. Connors narrowed her eyes. "You aren't the owner."

The bartender flashed her a smile. "No, but Mr. Villenti isn't available. How may I help you?"

The woman glanced around the dining room and turned back to Noah. "You didn't tell us any of this when you gave us the phony gift certificate. I want to speak to Eddie."

"Dear..." Mr. Connors rested his hand on his wife's arm.

"Don't you 'dear' me. I'm not going to let these two hooligans get away with this." She glared. "You obviously don't know who I am. I demand to speak to Eddie Touhy this minute!"

Eddie? Henry's heart went out to the lady. She appeared to suffer from dementia, or perhaps Alzheimer's.

"Ma'am, as I said, the owner isn't available." Noah spoke in an even tone.

She waved the voucher. "This isn't worth the paper it's printed on. If we'd known, we would never have set foot in this dump again!"

"Quite right!" Mr. Connors shouted.

The man's reaction took Henry by surprise. He couldn't understand why Mr. Connors was playing along. Then again, Henry had no clue how best to de-escalate the situation.

"The food is overpriced, and with the health code violations, I'm surprised you're still open!" The woman's ranting drew the attention of other customers.

"The what?" Henry felt faint.

Noah, on the other hand, continued to smile. "You're confusing us with one of the previous owners. We haven't had a violation since Mr. Villenti bought the restaurant. However, if you're concerned about the quality of our food, you're welcome to leave."

Mrs. Connors lowered her voice to a hissed whisper. "Villenti is a crook and a charlatan. My uncle's associates should have finished him like he did—"

"We aren't leaving without the value of our meals in cash." Mr. Connors spoke over his wife's rantings. "We ordered the seafood trios."

Noah nodded to Henry. "Give them a cash refund for the amount of their meals, and be sure to get a signature on the voucher."

Henry glanced between the bartender and the couple and thanked his lucky stars he'd chosen to go into law instead of the hospitality business. A few more days and he'd never have to wait tables again.

Grace met him at the cash register. "What was that about?"

"They ordered the two most expensive meals each, along with a ridiculously expensive bottle of wine, and expected the complimentary voucher to cover it." He pulled one hundred and twenty-four dollars from the drawer.

"Unbelievable. She seemed so nice Monday night, and again in the parking lot." Grace peered over her shoulder at the couple. "I wonder what set her off?"

"I don't think she's well. She asked for Eddie Touhy and said her uncle's associates should have finished Vince off.

Grace sighed. "That poor woman."

"Her husband doesn't seem to know what do to. He went from trying to calm her to playing along."

"I wouldn't know how to handle it either. It's a difficult situation." She glanced at the couple again. "Tragic, really. They were so sweet with one another Monday night."

"Thank you."

"What for?"

"Helping me to see the situation from another perspective. But do me a favor." Henry leaned closer. "Averi left early. Don't seat anyone else in my section unless the place is full."

"You got it." She hurried back to the hostess stand.

Drawing his courage, Henry crossed the room and offered Mr. Connors a pen. "I need your signature on the voucher, please."

The man smirked. "I'm not signing that."

Henry glanced around the nearly empty restaurant and knelt beside them. "Mr. and Mrs. Connors, I can understand your frustration, but I need your signature to prove I gave you the money. Without it, I may have to take it out of my tips. I'm just a high school student. I don't have an extra hundred and twenty dollars."

Mrs. Connors snatched the pen from his hand. "That's one hundred and twenty-four dollars, plus tax, and the cost of two iced teas."

Henry pulled what little he'd earned that night from his apron. "Sales tax is five and a half percent, and non-alcoholic beverages are roughly three dollars each. That comes to a difference of thirteen dollars and fifteen cents." He handed them an extra twenty. "This more than covers it."

The Connors stared, but the elderly woman scribbled her name on the voucher.

"Have a nice night." Henry forced a smile.

The elderly couple sauntered to the door.

Once they'd gone, he pulled the voucher from his pocket and read the darned thing. The terms and conditions were spelled out in plain English, including it not being redeemable for cash. They probably hadn't bothered to read it. Henry flipped it over and gasped.

Mrs. Connors had signed the voucher, *Celia Capone*.

"Something wrong?" Noah asked from behind the bar.

"I'm not sure."

Before he could show the bartender the voucher, a woman to his left gasped and pointed to the second-floor dining room.

"What a sad group of wet blankets you all turned out to be! Where's the music? Where's the hooch?" Frowning, the Lady in Red leaned her hip against the railing.

The customers stared. Some smiled and laughed, while others shifted in their chairs as if unsure of what to make of the situation.

Henry moved closer to Grace without taking his eyes off the so-called ghost.

"Well? What do you have to say for yourselves?" The redhead made a sweeping motion and narrowed her eyes.

"What is she doing?" Grace whispered.

"I have no idea, but she seems angry."

Coming out from behind the bar, Noah folded his arms and glared, but remained quiet.

"It's a show!" A man in the corner booth laughed. "Brilliant."

"A show?" The Lady in Red pointed a small handgun at the misguided customer. "I'll give you a show!"

The man laughed louder.

"We have to do something." Henry took a step forward at the same time the gun went off.

Grace grabbed his arm and pulled him behind the hostess stand.

"Everyone out!" The redhead aimed the gun at a party of four.

Chaos ensued. Women screamed. Men shouted. Some scrambled beneath the overhang out of view, while others ran toward the door.

"What's changed? Why is she so angry?" Grace's voice came out too high, too loud, and too frightened.

"Maybe she knows about the bracelet." He peeked around the podium but couldn't see the redhead.

Vince ran into the room, assessed the situation, and bounded for the stairs.

"Warners, make sure no one is hurt and get them out of here!" Shouting over the noise, Noah followed.

"What are they doing? They can't go up there." Grace lurched forward as if to follow.

"Neither can you." Henry blocked her path. "Not until we know she's gone."

"It's clear," Vince called from the second floor.

She squared her shoulders and surveyed the remaining customers. "Is everyone all right?"

Despite a couple of nods and assurances, they didn't look all right.

"Help me get everyone to the kitchen." Henry motioned to the rear exit. "Quietly, just in case she's still in the building."

Grace nodded and hurried to a group of people hiding in a booth.

Working from the opposite side of the room, Henry moved to the nearest customers. "I need you to go into the kitchen."

The woman who first spotted the Lady in Red clung to her friend beneath her table. "Is it safe?"

"I think so, but just to be sure, we'll go out the delivery door." Henry offered his trembling hand.

The women scurried out of their hiding place and ran toward the kitchen. The few remaining customers followed. Within three minutes, the twins had cleared the restaurant, and police cruisers filled the parking lot.

An hour later, Vince and Noah spoke with the officers outside the building. Given the circumstances, their grim faces made sense. However, their constant movement and quick glances made them look more guilty of a crime than traumatized by a crazy woman with a gun.

Henry whispered, "Is it me, or do they seem—"

"—off." Grace walked out of earshot of the others. "Is it possible that Vince knows more about the situation than he's letting on?"

"Maybe, but you saw how he reacted when we caught the busboy. He fired him on the spot."

"Yes, but Villenti never called Paul his right-hand man." She glanced at the men and frowned. "We have to tell him about Noah and the man in the fedora tonight."

"I agree, but he's not going to like it." Henry folded his arms.

The detective who had investigated the break-in joined the twins. "I understand the two of you witnessed the shooting. Would you mind giving statements?"

"We're happy to help." Henry turned and caught Vince staring. The expression on the other man's face sent a chill down his spine. Once again, it struck Henry as odd that Villenti seemed more nervous than concerned. "Did you find any bullet holes inside?"

The detective's eyes widened a fraction before he smoothed his expression. "No. No shell casings, either."

Grace said, "There won't be any shells. She was using a revolver. It looked like an antique. Like something you'd see in an old movie."

This time the detective didn't bother to try to hide his surprise. "Can you be more specific?"

"It was bright silver, and I think it had pearl inlays on the handle."

Henry blinked. He had been too busy worrying about getting shot to notice the details of the gun.

"Everything about her is authentic to the 1920s, including the slang she uses." Grace frowned. "Whoever she is, she's gone to a lot of trouble to maintain the illusion."

"Of a ghost, you mean?" The detective smirked.

"Yes," the twins said.

"I take it you don't believe we're dealing with a spirit?"

"No."

The detective motioned between them. "Do you always answer as a unit?"

"It's a twin thing." Grace smiled. "Is it possible the woman was using blanks?"

"That's the best-case scenario." He clasped his hands behind his back. "Worst case, we haven't found the points of impact. Did you see where she went after she fired the gun? Mr. Villenti and Mr. Nelson both said she was gone when they reached the second floor."

Grace shook her head.

"I was more interested in making sure everyone was all right." Henry hesitated to say more until he and Grace had had a chance to speak to Vince. The man seemed to know more than he was letting on. "It's been a long night. Can we write down what we saw and go home?"

"Of course." The detective waved a uniformed officer over. "Take their statements and turn them loose."

CHAPTER NINE

Grace sat on the guestroom floor, surrounded by Post-It notes. No matter how many times she rearranged the paper squares, she couldn't see the big picture. The break-ins, the toilets, the guy in the fedora, the Lady in Red, Noah—the pieces were related somehow. They had to be.

"What time is it?" Henry rubbed his eyes.

"It's two in the morning. Go back to sleep. I'll wake you when Vince comes home." She tapped her lips. *What am I missing?* "Do you mind if I look through the pictures you took the day of the break-in?"

"Sure." He handed her his cell. "What are you looking for?"

"I honestly don't know." She scrolled through the photos.

"I keep thinking about Mrs. Connors, aka Celia Capone. It seems weird she asked for Eddie Touhy, and mentioned her uncle *taking care* of people on the same night the Lady in Red showed up with a gun."

"Are you saying you think the uncle she referred to was Al Capone, the gangster?"

"Unless I'm completely off-base, that's what *she* believes." He walked to the window.

Grace zoomed in on a picture of Mrs. Connors taken on the day of the break-in and gasped. "Take a look at this."

Henry studied the screen. "Holy fedora, the man in the pinstripe suits looks a lot like the guy in the cellar."

"I thought the same thing." She pulled her computer from her backpack. "Let's upload it and take a look on a bigger screen."

A few moments later, the twins studied the grainy image on the laptop. Henry opened Photoshop and adjusted the brightness and resolution. Each tweak brought the man's face farther into focus until they had a fairly clear picture.

Goosebumps rose on Grace's arms. "That's him."

"I think you're right." Henry hurried to the window. "Vince is home. We should see if he recognizes the guy."

"Good idea." She saved the image and closed the laptop.

"I'm not looking forward to telling him about Noah."

"Me either, but it has to be done. I wrote down all the information we found and a list of questions in my notebook." She reached into her backpack, and a bright red envelope caught her attention.

"Is that a new one?" Henry's voice rose.

"Yeah. I put the others under the mattress with the diamond bracelet." She met his gaze. "The bag was in my locker or in my possession all night."

Henry furrowed his brow. "Then how..."

"Either someone has my locker combination, or..." She mentally retraced her steps from the time she'd retrieved the backpack from the employee lockers to when they'd hitched a ride with another employee. "No, wait. I left it on the counter when I went into a stall in the ladies' room."

"I was outside the door. No one went in or out."

"Or did they?" Grace sighed. "The Wonder Bar was built by a bunch of gangsters. It wouldn't surprise me if they included a few secret passages in their designs."

"That would explain how the Lady in Red vanishes into thin air every time she makes an appearance," Henry said. "But wouldn't the police have found it?"

"Maybe, maybe not. Who knows if they even thought to look for one?"

His pulse raced. "We need to visit the restaurant when no one else is around."

"Add that to the list of things to talk to Vince about." Grace opened the envelope and read the note aloud. "Henry and Grace, You must think me a featherhead. Look in the window boxes next. The lost items are in the building. I just know it. The Lady in Red."

Henry tilted his head. "That doesn't sound like it came from a woman on the verge of pulling a gun on unsuspecting customers."

"No, it doesn't." Grace sighed. "She could have written it before she decided to scare the heck out of us and everyone else."

"Maybe." He grinned. "But I'd bet my right arm she doesn't know we found the bracelet."

"You're right. She had to have seen us downstairs. If she knew, she would have demanded the bracelet while she was armed." Grace pumped her fist. "She's not omniscient. She's clueless, because we didn't tell anyone. We can use this to our advantage."

"We tell one person at a time and wait to see how she responds."

A slow smile spread across Grace's face. "Exactly. If that doesn't work, then we take a page from her book and write a note to set the trap."

"I don't like the idea of using the real diamonds as bait."

"Me either. Nor do I love setting a trap for someone we know is armed."

"I agree." He nodded to the door. "Before we do anything, we need to talk to Vince."

The twins found Mr. Villenti sitting in his home office, staring at the wall. Shoulders sagging, the man had a half-full glass of whiskey in one hand and a framed photograph in the other.

Grace knocked on the open door.

Vince glanced up, sighed, and set the picture on his desk. "Why aren't you two asleep?"

Henry said, "We have some things to tell you. Mind if we come in?"

"Sure." He sat back and sighed like a man ready to collapse under a heavy weight. "The police think she fired blanks."

"Do they have any ideas about how she escaped?" Henry asked.

"Nope." He motioned to the chairs on the other side of the desk. "Have a seat."

Grace glanced at the photo and missed a step. The man with Vince looked *very* familiar.

Catching her before she fell, Henry furrowed his brow. "Are you okay?"

She held his gaze and hoped against hope he'd take the hint. "I'm more tired than I thought. Maybe we should have this conversation in the morning."

Villenti studied the twins. "You're here. Tell me what's going on. What *else* is going on."

Henry sat on the edge of his chair. "This afternoon before our shift, we—"

"—we found a diamond bracelet. I think it's what the Lady in Red has been searching for." Grace spoke louder and faster than she intended, but she couldn't let her brother tell Vince about the guy in the fedora—not yet.

Henry gave her a side-eye.

Vince exhaled loudly as if he'd expected other news. "Where was it?"

"In the cellar behind a loose brick. Exactly where she said it would be." Grace forced a smile. "We received another letter from the alleged ghost after we came back here tonight. With your permission, we'd like to set a trap for the Lady in Red."

"No." He offered no explanation. No sigh or facial expression to soften the word. He simply shut them down. "Absolutely not."

Grace sucked in a breath. "We're too close to solving the mystery to stop now."

"Everything changed when she pulled a gun." His voice rose.

"For all we know, it was a stage prop." Henry purposely lowered his voice in hopes Vince would do the same. The last thing any of them needed was to wake the twins' parents. The second Faith Warner heard the word "gun," she'd put an end to their sleuthing.

Grace nodded. "She ratcheted up the anxiety tonight, but if she wanted to hurt someone, she could have. I think she's getting desperate, and desperate people make mistakes."

Villenti sat back and folded his arms. "What sort of trap?"

She glanced at her brother and sent up a silent prayer he'd caught on when she'd avoided mentioning Noah's involvement. Telling Vince what they'd seen could jeopardize their plan to flush out the Lady in Red's accomplice.

"We'll leave her a note telling her what we found and arrange a meeting." Henry shrugged. "Or we could leave a look-a-like bracelet on the table in the upstairs dining room and hide until she appears."

Grace thanked her lucky stars he'd said the right thing.

Villenti arched a brow. "Where would you hide? It's one large room."

She said, "About that. There must be a hidden room or passageway. That's the only logical explanation we can come up with for her disappearing act."

"I haven't found any secret passages, but it makes sense." Vince shook his head.

Henry said, "We need access to the building before any of the other employees arrive."

"Let me know when you want to go, but I'm going with you." He rolled his head from side to side to relieve the tension.

"If we're right, it's best if Grace and I go alone. We don't want to spook her."

"This isn't a democracy. My restaurant. My rules."

"As long as you don't mind adding a few hours to your already-long day." Grace grinned.

"If it meant keeping you two safe, I'd sleep there." He rubbed his eyes. "Where exactly do you plan to find a decoy necklace?"

"The accessory shop in the mall has tons of costume jewelry. I'm sure we can find something passable," she said.

"You intend to replace a diamond bracelet with a cheap piece of costume jewelry?" Villenti waved his hand. "I know a guy who can make a fake. Where's the bracelet now?"

The twins exchanged glances.

"Upstairs," Henry said.

"Give it to me, and I'll take care of it in the morning."

Grace wanted to ask about the photo, but she couldn't decide how to bring it up. Instead, she stalled. "Did Noah tell you about the incident with Mr. and Mrs. Connors tonight?"

"Yeah, he told me," Vince said. "I understand why he gave them cash, but I don't like it."

"Weird thing." Henry shrugged. "Mrs. Connors signed the voucher 'Celia Capone.'"

Villenti scratched his jaw. "Now, that *is* interesting. She's the same woman who claimed to have seen someone leaving the restaurant with a duffle bag?"

Henry nodded. "I believe she has dementia. She asked to speak to Eddie Touhy and mentioned something about health code violations."

"That's unfortunate, but I'd like to be notified if they return." Vince stood. "Unless there's anything else, I'm going to bed."

Henry opened his mouth to speak, but Grace cut him off.

"Who's that with you in the photo?" She picked the picture up and turned it toward her twin.

"Whoa," Henry said under his breath.

Vince's entire body tensed. He snatched it from her hand and tossed it into a desk drawer. "No one. Didn't your parents teach you it's rude to touch other people's things?"

She'd heard the man shouting at his employees but never experienced his temper firsthand. "I'm sorry. I saw you looking at it when we came in…"

Henry glanced at them and settled on Vince. He didn't say anything. He didn't have to. His what-the-heck expression said it all.

"I didn't mean to snap at you." Villenti sighed. "He's my brother, Vaughn. It was taken shortly before he went away."

Grace wanted to ask where he'd gone. Away as in moved to another state, or away as in prison? However, she had no intention of tipping her hand any more than she had. Unless she was mistaken, Vince's brother was the man in the fedora.

"When's the last time you saw him?" Henry's words came out clipped.

"I don't remember the exact date, but it's been a while. A long while." Vince motioned to the door. "It's been a heck of a day. I'm going to bed."

The twins said their goodnights and headed back to their rooms.

Grace followed Henry in and packed up her laptop. "It wasn't just me. You saw the resemblance between the guy in the fedora and Vaughn Villenti, right?"

"The man in the photo was younger, thinner, and had more hair, but yeah. I'm ninety-nine percent sure it's the same person."

"This puts a kink in our plans." She took a moment to jot down a few notes about their latest conversation with Vince. "You saw how he reacted when I asked about the photo. We have to be absolutely sure about what's going on before we tell Vince about his brother and Noah."

"I hate to say it, but maybe we should let this one go. For the first time since we started solving mysteries, learning the truth might do more harm than good."

She couldn't disagree more. In fact, she couldn't believe he'd said that. "It's like Mom said: this is about a man's livelihood. It's going to hurt when he finds out his brother is out to get him, but learning the truth after he's financially ruined would be worse."

"You're right." Henry sighed. "Maybe it's the exhaustion talking."

"I understand, but I refuse to give up." She stood and pulled her backpack to her shoulder. "We should try to get some sleep before we take our final exams."

"Good luck with that." Henry flopped onto the bed. "I can't figure it or him out."

"Which? The case or Vince?"

"Both." He stared at the ceiling. "Villenti seems to lose his temper anytime he's put on the spot, which tells me he's hiding something."

"I had the same thought." She tapped her lips. "But what?"

"That's the million-dollar question."

CHAPTER TEN

Henry's brain hurt, and not from his last two final exams. He'd gone over every possible way to tell Vince that his brother and his right-hand man Noah were plotting against him. Short of writing a note on the way out of town, Henry had come up blank.

Grace climbed into the back of the rideshare after finishing the last of their exams and sighed long and deep. "Today is going to stink."

"I agree." Running on precious little sleep, their tests, and stressing out about a mystery was nothing new. While experience told him they'd figure it out, he still had to get from Point A to Point Mystery Solved. "Is Vince at The Wonder Bar?"

Grace yawned. "Yes, but he doesn't have the fake bracelet yet."

"We don't need it. The redhead most likely doesn't know we have it. All we have to do is share our discovery with Noah. If the next note mentions the diamonds, then we know he's involved with the woman as well as with Vaughn."

"That could work, but only if we tell him somewhere other than the restaurant. She could be lurking about."

"That's easier said than done." He needed coffee and food and more coffee to make it through the rest of the day. "How do we go about searching for a hidden passageway?"

"If it works like in the movies, all we have to do is press the correct brick or pull the right candlestick."

He gave her a dubious look. "Somehow I don't think it'll be that easy."

It wasn't that easy.

After checking in with a grumpy Mr. Villenti, the twins searched every square inch of the upstairs dining room. The walls didn't move. The hearth didn't spin. The floor didn't open.

"We need a better strategy." Henry plopped into a chair. "The secret passage can't be on the exterior wall, or there wouldn't be windows."

Grace said, "Anything along the railing is out."

He turned and surveyed the other two walls. "We're looking for something that doesn't line up. An unexplained difference in the walls or unaccounted-for space."

"I know that." She frowned at the painting of the redhead above the fireplace. "The stones."

Henry followed her gaze. "We've already checked. Besides, Vince has a roaring fire when the place is open."

"This area was closed last night. Before then, the Lady in Red only showed up after hours." Grace stood and ran her hands over the stones again. "The coals would still be hot, but I'm not sure about the rest."

"Now that you mention it, the hearth is very wide in comparison to the actual firebox." He crouched, opened the screen, and peered inside. "It's thin all the way up."

Grace grinned. "The part that sticks out the roof is narrow, too."

Being born in Florida and spending most of his life in a fifth wheel, Henry knew next to nothing about fireplaces. "There's a lever in here."

"It's to open and close the flue." She continued to poke and prod the side of the hearth.

"What's a flue?" He pulled the handle down.

Shooting to his feet, he bumped his head on the mantel. At least, he thought it was the mantel until he saw what had caused the ruckus. The stones along the side of the hearth had split to reveal a small crawlspace and a worn-out rope ladder. "Can that thing hold someone's weight?"

"Let's find out." Grace ducked inside.

"Be careful." He stilled and listened for signs of distress. Amazingly enough, he couldn't hear her moving around inside the passageway.

"You have to see this." Her voice sounded far away, too far for the short distance she'd traveled.

"I doubt it will hold both of us."

"I'm not on the ladder. Come on."

He stuck his head into the opening and squinted into the darkness, then sucked in a breath and climbed down. When he reached eye level with the space between the first story and second, Grace waved from inside a wooden tunnel running between the two floors. "Holy smokes."

"You have to crawl," Grace told him.

Henry wiggled his way inside and followed the sound of her voice. "We're between the stories, but this is bigger than in a typical building. My guess is this was another Touhy modification."

"It's genius. They build this place to be a fortress but included escape routes in case the defenses failed." Grace crawled faster. "Now that we know how she pulled the disappearing act, let's see where this goes."

Feeling a bit like a gerbil in one of those tube contraptions, he trailed behind her. "They thought of everything. The wood is as smooth as a tabletop."

"Which would explain how the Lady in Red managed to pass through here without ruining her dress." She stopped moving. "There's a ladder."

He tapped on a large cylinder. "I'm no expert, but these look like water pipes. My guess is they run from the second-floor bar through the restrooms and connect with the pipes in the kitchen before meeting up with the city lines outside."

"Stay here. I'll check." Grace disappeared through an opening as small as the one on the fireplace. "There's a false wall in the handicap stall."

"In which restroom?"

"Both. It opens into both." Grace climbed back up and made a sour face.

"Besides the gross factor, that explains how someone blew up the toilets in the men's room—"

"—and slipped a note into my backpack."

Henry shined his light around the space. "Go that way. It looks like the escape route branches out toward the front of the building."

Grace made it a few feet before sneezing. "Dust. I don't think anyone has been through here in a long time."

"Good to know." He backed up to allow her room. "This is pretty cool."

"I feel like a rodent scurrying around in an attic." She giggled.

"Speaking of rats, I wonder if you can hear what's going on in the dining rooms from here?" Henry shined his light through a gap in the wooden tunnel and guesstimated their location as being near Vince's office. "Or to spy on Villenti."

"That's a sobering thought. We'll talk to him about it as soon as possible."

"Let's test the theory now." He counted the rafters to the side wall. "His office should be about twenty feet that way."

Staying on the smooth boards, Grace crawled in the direction he'd indicated. "There's another trap door."

Henry whispered, "It has to be the office. Can you hear anything?"

She shook her head. "Should I open it?"

"This is Vince Villenti. I'm calling to check on the status of the sale of my business." The man's voice came through loud and clear.

He cut the light.

Grace put her finger to her lips.

Below, Vince said, "I see. Is there someone else I can speak to about speeding things up?"

Henry's stomach clenched. They'd overheard more than they'd bargained for. While Villenti had mentioned that the closures and repairs had cost the restaurant money, he'd had no idea the situation was so dire.

Frowning, Grace pointed in front of her.

He motioned for her to go.

Near the side wall, she stopped again. "Found another ladder, but it must be longer. I can't see the bottom."

"Hang on, and I'll give you some light." He reactivated the flashlight app on his cell. "Is there a lever?"

"Not that I can see. I'm going down."

Inching closer to the opening, Henry pointed the phone down to illuminate as much of the area as possible.

A thud, followed by metal creaking, echoed from below.

"I'm on the stairs leading to the bootleggers' tunnel," Grace called up to him.

How long is that ladder? Henry did some quick calculations. The crawl space was between the second and first floors, and add in the basement. "That's at least two stories down."

"Two and a half. Come see for yourself."

As he climbed down, the walls changed from wood to brick to the dark stone of the bootleggers' tunnel. Henry set his foot on the platform midway up the metal staircase and shined his flashlight around the space. "Like you said, this is genius. We've been here before but didn't notice the ladder."

"That's because of this." She tugged a thin cord, and the ladder rolled up like a window shade. "There's a groove and a metal hook to hide the pull cord."

"Too bad the Touhys went into a life of crime. They could have made a killing as architects." Henry motioned above his head. "Come on, we need to be aboveground when Noah arrives."

Grace grabbed his arm and motioned for him to be quiet.

The jingling sound of keys echoed off the stone walls.

They needed to get out of there and fast. Henry met her gaze and widened his eyes.

"Up or down?" Grace mouthed.

He eased down three stairs, the metal creaking and groaning with every step.

Grace tugged his shirt, slipped under the railing, and dropped to the ground. Had he not been scared out of his wits, he would have laughed.

The twins huddled in the shadows beneath the metal platform for what seemed like an eternity before they heard heavy footsteps. Grace tensed, and Henry held his breath.

The man stopped walking several yards from the twins. Light from his cell phone illuminated his profile and the brim of his fedora as he typed something into his phone.

Vaughn Villenti glanced toward the metal stairs and back the way he'd come as if trying to decide which way to go.

Breathing entirely too loud, Grace pressed closer to the wall.

Henry squeezed her hand and willed her to be quiet. They didn't know the guy or what he was capable of, but he doubted Vaughn would be happy to discover they were on to him.

The click, click, click of high heels announced the woman's presence long before her silhouette came into view.

In the dim light from the phone screen, Henry saw the man's lips curl into a smile. *What the heck?* He had no way of knowing for sure if the woman was the Lady in Red, but who else would be slinking around in the old bootleggers' tunnel with Vaughn Villenti?

"Carrie." He drew her into an embrace. "Any news?"

"Nothing yet. We can't go inside today. Vince is upstairs with those kids."

"This early?" He chuckled. "That could mean—"

"Or he could be catching up on work. Until I hear otherwise, I'm going to assume they haven't found it." Her voice trailed off and she sniffled.

Vaughn whispered something to her.

"I hope you're right. I'm running out of options. I need those diamonds."

"We'll find them with or without the kids' help." He pulled back and took her hand. "Come on. Let's get out of here."

"We can't be seen together."

He sighed. "Soon, nothing will stand in our way."

The couple walked farther into the tunnel hand-in-hand.

Grace gasped. "What did we just witness?"

"Vaughn Villenti and the redhead are—"

"A couple?" She shook her head. "That's the missing thread that ties the Lady in Red to the break-ins and vandalism."

"No, it can't be that simple. Vaughn mentioned wanting a meeting with Vince." As soon as the words came out of his mouth, the pieces clicked together in Henry's brain. "A meeting that probably already took place."

Grace's mouth fell open. "What?"

He didn't know if he should laugh or punch something. "Vince's reaction last night when we asked about his brother makes so much more sense now. He knows what's going on and is trying to protect Vaughn."

"From what? Us?" Grace gave him a dubious look. "I don't think so. Besides, how does Noah fit into all this?"

"Maybe he's a pawn in their scheme. Think about it. The conversation we overheard wasn't *that* incriminating. Vaughn was pressing him to set up a meeting with Vince."

She held up her hands. "You're on Team Noah now?"

"No, I'm on Team Solve This Dang Mystery." He pointed to the stairs. "And there's only one way to do that. It's time we had a long chat with Vince."

Grace's phone vibrated. She glanced at the screen and frowned. "The chat will have to wait. Vince texted. The restaurant is closed tonight. He said to call Dad when we're ready to go home."

"Yes!" Henry couldn't believe their luck.

"You're happy about this, why?"

"Because this is our chance to set a trap."

Grace shook her head. "We need bait before we can catch a crook."

He motioned to her cell. "Text him back and ask if he has the fake bracelet."

Her fingers flew over her phone.

A few seconds later, her cell pinged.

Grace smiled. "He left the bait in his desk drawer."

CHAPTER ELEVEN

Grace glanced up from the novel she was pretending to read. "Good afternoon."

Keys in hand, Noah Nelson froze just inside the back door. "How did you get in here?"

"Vince let us in early to search for clues." Grace tilted her head. "Why are *you* here?"

"To catch up on paperwork." He rubbed his jaw. "So, did you find anything?"

Henry walked around the corner, waving the red envelope they'd found in Grace's backpack the previous evening.

"Another note from the resident ghost?" The bartender flashed them his movie-star smile.

Grinning, she glanced between her brother and Noah.

Henry winked. "You tell him."

"Tell me what?" Noah tilted his head. "Did you two find something?"

"Did we ever!" She'd never performed on stage, and until recently, she'd stunk at lying, but she channeled her inner soap-opera star and laid it on thick.

The bartender's expression brightened. "Are you going to tell me what it is?"

"A diamond bracelet." She made a show of scrolling through her phone for the image. "Here. Take a look."

Noah's eyes widened as he studied the photo of the piece. "That's a dime beside the stones?"

"It sure is." Grace put her cell in her pocket.

The man sputtered, "Those stones are at least seven carats...each."

"I tried to google the value of the bracelet but gave up. We'd have to take it to a jeweler to determine the grade of the stones," Henry said.

"Millions." Noah shook his head. "What are you going to do with it?"

"We don't know yet." Grace shrugged. "We haven't had a chance to discuss it with Vince."

"Where is it now?" His voice deepened.

"Someplace safe." She widened her eyes and made her voice come out breathy. They needed Noah to perceive them as clueless kids. "Until we can give it to Vince?"

"We've never dealt with anything like this before." Henry shifted his weight from one foot to the other. "Our mysteries are usually about people pulling pranks or trying to drum up publicity. The Lady in Red..."

"She keeps vanishing into thin air." Grace pursed her lips. "The police didn't find any bullet holes last night. I never thought I'd say this, but what if she really *is* a ghost?"

"As long as the diamonds are real, it doesn't matter if she's the Tooth Fairy." The bartender frowned. "Give it to me. I'll put it in the safe until Vince decides what to do with it."

"That's a really good idea." Grace forced a smile. It wouldn't surprise her to learn Noah was a thief in addition to a traitor.

"If we hurry, we can get the bracelet from Vince's and make it back before the beginning of our shifts." Noah nodded to the door.

Her pulse raced. This was it. The moment of truth. "We don't have to go anywhere."

"Why not?" The muscle above the bartender's jaw tightened.

Henry reached into his pocket and pulled out the bracelet. Knockoff or not, the stones reflected the light like miniature stars.

Noah licked his lips. "May I?"

He set it in his palm as if he were afraid it would shatter. "What do you think?"

"Are they real?" Tilting her head, Grace pretended to study the fake diamonds.

"I think so." Noah glanced at them. "Come with me. I want witnesses when I lock this in the safe."

"Oh." Grace couldn't keep the shock out of her voice. She'd expected him to make up some ridiculous excuse to take the bracelet someplace else or make a break for it. *Was I wrong about him?* "With all the craziness going on around here, I don't blame you."

Henry nodded. "Where's the safe?"

Noah rolled his eyes. "In the freezer, if you can believe that."

Nope, Grace couldn't believe that. She'd seen too many movies where the bad guys locked people in freezers and had no desire to become a Warner-sicle. "Nothing personal, but we'll watch from outside the door."

"I hate the cold." Henry grinned.

"Relax. It's not like I'm going to lock you inside. It's a quirky old building that's had quite a few quirky owners." The bartender laughed. "Come on. I'll show you...from outside."

The twins followed Noah at a safe distance.

Of all the places inside The Wonder Bar he could have taken them, he'd chosen the kitchen. Grace forced herself not to stare at the array of knives and other potential weapons as they walked past the prep area to the freezer.

Noah opened the door and kicked the rubber stopper into place. "The safe is hidden in the back corner."

Yep. Still not going inside. Grace smiled. "We can see you from out here."

He flashed her a smile almost as bright as the cubic zirconias in his hand. "Will you trust me once you see the safe?"

"Sure." Henry chuckled. "But you can't blame us for being cautious. You yourself said the stones were worth millions."

"It's cool. I get it. I mean, who puts a safe in a walk-in freezer, right?" The bartender made his way to the back of the freezer, removed a box from a metal shelf, and exposed what looked like a door to a safe.

Grace exhaled a breath.

"It seems we owe you an apology." Henry ran his hand over the back of his neck.

"A little paranoia is warranted." Noah turned a knob back and forth three times before opening a small door. "But like I said, I'd feel better if one of you witnessed me locking it in here."

No matter which side of the entry she stood on, Grace couldn't get a view of the interior of the safe. She took a step inside, but the angle was off. She'd need to stand beside him to see.

"I'll do it." Henry walked to the bartender but turned at the last minute. "It's not a safe! Run!"

Noah slammed Henry's head against the metal. Hard.

It took her brain a second to make sense of what had happened. Henry slumped against the wall, blood oozing from his forehead. Vince's right-hand man was digging her brother's cell phone out of his pocket. She turned to run for help, but the time she'd spent gawking had cost her.

Noah grabbed her wrist and yanked her back. "Uh-uh-uh. Where do you think *you're* going?"

Rather than panic, Grace fell back on her self-defense training. Lucky for her, breaking free of a wrist hold was the first move she'd learned. She turned toward him, rotated her wrist, and bent her elbow. Jerking free, she punched him in the ear with her other hand.

Noah howled and reached for her again, but Grace saw it coming. She jumped to the side and hurried toward the prep counter and the knives.

"You're going to pay for that." He stalked toward her.

She grabbed the closest knife and held it in front of her with both hands.

The bartender held his hands up. "Even if you escape, do you think I'm going to let your brother walk out of here?"

Grace bit back her words. Getting into a conversation with him would allow him into her head. *Not happening.* She needed every advantage she could get.

"How long do you think he's going to last in there?"

She glanced at the freezer, and her knees threatened to buckle. Noah had closed the door.

He smirked. "Give me your phone. I'll walk out of here, and you'll never have to see me again."

Splitting her attention between Noah and the freezer, Grace tried to remember how long it took before victims of hypothermia reached the point of no return.

"Tick. Tock. Tick. Tock."

Knife shaking in her hands, Grace shook her head. "I need my phone."

Noah narrowed his eyes. "There's a landline in Vince's office and another behind the bar. Don't be foolish. Give me your cell."

He made no sense. Why take her phone when she could still call out? *Think, Grace, think.*

The bartender took a step back, and another, and another. However, the exit was the other direction.

"What are you doing?" Blood whooshed behind her eardrums.

Noah reached the freezer and adjusted the thermostat. "Speeding up the process."

"No!" Still gripping the knife in her right hand, she reached into her pocket for her cell. "Here. Take it."

"I'm not coming near you while you're holding that." He made a circular motion with his hand. "Come around the counter and slide the phone across the floor."

She did as he requested.

Noah scooped the cell from the floor, shoved it in his pocket, and walked out of the kitchen.

Grace ran to the freezer and threw the door open but hesitated to go inside. She didn't know if the bartender had left the building. What would stop him from locking her inside when she went to help her brother? It could be another trap.

"Henry?"

He groaned. "Yeah?"

Grace wanted to weep with joy. "Can you get up?"

"I think so." He pushed himself upright, swooned, and slumped against the wall again. "Or not. A little help here?"

"I'm not sure where Noah is." She glanced over her shoulder and sighed. The bartender was probably long gone, but should she risk it?

"Stay there." Muttering under his breath, Henry crawled out of the freezer and collapsed again. "So cold."

"Stay here. I'm going to Vince's office to call for help."

"No. I'm good." He sat upright. "We stay together."

"You probably have a concussion."

"I didn't pass out. I'll be okay once I've thawed."

A woman gasped from behind them.

Grace turned and locked eyes with the Lady in Red—only she'd traded the flapper dress in for jeans and a sweater. "Please call 9-1-1. My brother is hurt."

"I'm fine." Henry turned toward the woman and gawked. "You."

"What happened?" The redhead glanced behind her as if debating making a run for it.

"Noah Nelson. Is he still in the building?" Grace asked.

"I saw his car pulling out of the lot." She chewed her lower lip. "He did this?"

"Yes, when he stole the diamond bracelet we found." Henry managed to stand.

"You found it?" The color drained from the redhead's face. "And it's gone?"

"Carrie? Where did you go?" Vaughn Villenti walked into the kitchen, took in the scene, and frowned. "What's happened."

"Noah stole the diamonds." She burst into tears. "It's over. I've failed her."

Watching the couple, Henry couldn't help but think he and Grace had made a huge mistake. Then again, the Lady in Red had pretended to shoot up the restaurant the night before.

Grace whispered, "We need to get out of here."

He glanced at the door, then back at her.

She nodded and eased toward the exit.

"What am I going to do? Grandma is getting worse." The Lady in Red's voice cracked. "The diamonds were our last hope."

"We'll find a way," Vaughn said.

Henry did his best to ignore the conversation. Sick grandmother or not, these two had gone about things the wrong way. The illegal way that had ended up scaring people and running Vince out of business...or had they?

"The kid's hurt. We should call for help." The woman turned toward the twins.

Mere inches from making their escape, they froze in their tracks.

Vaughn arched a brow. "Going somewhere?"

Grace positioned herself between Henry and the couple. "Yes. We're going to call the police and report the assault and theft. Then we're calling our parents and going home."

The man smiled, but not a scary *make-my-day* kind of smile. He seemed genuinely amused. "By all means."

Henry brushed his fingertips over his wound. "Maybe I *do* have a concussion."

The redhead wiped the tears from her cheeks. "We aren't the villains in this story."

Grace narrowed her eyes. "No? What do you call scaring people and trying to ruin a man's business?"

"We didn't..." Frowning, the Lady in Red turned to Vaughn.

He pulled the woman to his side. "Why don't we have a seat in the dining room and compare notes?"

"Give me your phone first." Grace held out her hand.

Henry held his breath, waiting for more drama, but it didn't come. Vaughn Villenti pulled a cell from his pocket and handed it to her.

"Don't call the paramedics. I'm okay." Henry's head ached, but he doubted he had a concussion. Besides, he didn't want to take the chance of missing out on what these two had to say.

She frowned. "You really don't care if I call the police?"

"I'd rather speak to my brother, but I'll leave that up to you."

Grace sighed. "I'll call Vince."

The guy's eyes widened. "You know who I am?"

"We recognized you from a photo on Vince's desk," Henry said. "And a pic I took of the crowd on the day of the break-in."

The redhead grinned. "I told you they were clever."

"Not clever enough." Grace dialed the phone.

Vince Villenti walked through the front door five minutes later. He stopped, took one quick look around the room, and walked to his brother.

Henry half-expected him to give Vaughn a right hook, but the Villenti brothers embraced.

Vince said. "It's good to see you."

Vaughn turned his head and wiped his eyes. "Is it?"

"No matter what you've done, you're still my brother."

"I've wanted nothing else for the last six months, but you refused." Vaughn sighed. "Seems we've all been played in more ways than one."

Grace whispered, "I'm so confused."

"Ditto."

Vince glanced at Henry and frowned. "What happened to you?"

"Noah came in after you left. We told him about the bracelet, and he tricked Henry into the freezer." Grace sank into a chair. "Then hit him and took off with the loot."

"Noah?" He turned, walked a few paces, then stalked back. "Noah did this?"

"I'm afraid so." Henry sat beside Grace.

"We'll let the police deal with Noah. He won't get away with this." Vince turned back to his brother. "Will you please tell me what's going on?"

Vaughn draped his arm around the redhead's shoulders. "First, I'd like you to meet my wife, Carrie."

Vince's mouth fell open. He'd likely recognized the Lady in Red. "Wife? You're married to the woman haunting my restaurant?"

CHAPTER TWELVE

Grace felt as if she'd woken up in the Twilight Zone. She and Henry had seen a lot of weird things since they started sleuthing, but the bad guys hadn't turned out to be good guys.

"We should sit." Vaughn motioned to the twins' table.

"We'll give you some privacy." Grace didn't want to leave, but the situation had changed from a mystery to a family matter.

"No. You two deserve to hear what you've been mixed up in." Vince took a seat and smiled like a proud uncle. "This is Henry and Grace Warner, Ethan's twins."

"No kidding?" Vaughn laughed. "Your father is one of the good ones."

Grace grinned. "We know."

Vaughn held a chair out for his wife. "I asked Noah to arrange a meeting between us months ago."

Vince frowned. "Why didn't you reach out to me yourself?"

"Like I said, I wasn't sure you would see me, given our history." He turned to the twins. "Long story short, we were in business together, but it fell apart because of me."

They nodded.

Vince said, "Did you pay my busboy to steal my financial records?"

The man hung his head. "I didn't want the financials."

"You wanted to see the records from the purchase of the business." Vince squeezed his brother's hand. "The Wonder Bar is half yours. I started the process to put it in both our names the day I fired Paul."

Everyone stared.

Henry snapped his mouth shut. "How did you know it was him?"

"The call I made on Paul's phone. I recognized Vaughn's voice instantly." He looked at his brother again. "I would have done it sooner, but you showed no interest."

"I let my guilt and pride keep me away." Once again, he wiped his eyes. "Thank you, Vince. I'd love to work here with you. It's like we always talked about when we were kids—running the Touhys' Wonder Bar."

Carrie interrupted the happy moment. "Noah said he spoke to you about allowing us to search the building for my grandmother's diamonds, but you refused. I take it that was another of his lies?"

"He never mentioned it, or Vaughn." Vince sat back and folded his arms. "Is that why you've been breaking in and destroying the place?"

Vaughn shook his head. "We used the bootleggers' tunnels and the secret passages—"

"Secret passages?" Vince waved his hand. "Never mind. This place never ceases to surprise me."

Vaughn said, "We didn't damage anything."

"Noah." Henry and Grace spoke in unison.

"He must have been searching for the diamonds." Vince turned to the redhead. "The first I heard of any lost treasure was the notes you left for the kids."

"I'm sorry for my part in this. I was desperate to find them. I thought if you wouldn't help your brother, maybe I could scare you into helping a ghost." Carrie dipped her chin. "Vaughn said you had a thing for flappers, especially the redhead in the painting."

Vince shivered. "You had me going. The resemblance is uncanny."

Carrie sighed. "She was my great-grandmother."

"No way." Henry chuckled.

Grace eyes almost bugged out of her head. The woman was distraught for absolutely no reason. If he didn't tell Carrie the truth soon, she would.

"Excuse us for a moment." He stood and motioned for Grace to follow him.

Inside his office, Vince removed a painting from the wall and opened an actual safe, not a weird control panel like Noah. He pulled out a velvet box out and handed it to her. "You do the honors."

"Are you sure?" She peeked inside and smiled at the sparkling jewels. "This will mean a lot to her."

"Which is why you should give it to her. You found them." He walked her back to the table and smiled at Carrie. "Grace has something to tell you."

"Noah stole a knockoff." She handed the box to the redhead.

Carrie's entire face lit. "What?"

"The real diamonds were in Vince's safe." She grinned. "I'm sorry I didn't tell you sooner, but I wasn't sure I could trust you."

The redhead opened the lid and burst into fresh tears. "This was my great-grandmother's. You don't know what this means to my family. My grandmother has Alzheimer's. We're trying to get her into a private facility, but her insurance doesn't cover it."

Henry scratched his jaw. "Is your grandmother Celia Capone-Connors?"

Carrie's hand flew to her mouth. "Yes, but how did you..."

"She came in for dinner."

Grace motioned to the Villenti brothers. "Let me get this straight. Your childhood dream was to own a restaurant built by an infamous gangster family, and one of you married the great-grand-niece of Al Capone?"

Vince leaned close and lowered his voice. "Family lore says my great-grand-father was Charles 'Lucky' Luciano, but that's a mystery for your next visit."

"That explains your fascination with 1920s gangsters." She held up her hands. "But we can't take credit for solving this mystery."

Henry nodded. "We didn't put the pieces together until just now."

Vince shook his head. "You may not have discovered the villain, but you found the lost treasure."

Carrie Capone-Villenti laughed. "And for that, I will be eternally grateful."

Henry put the last of the luggage in the truck. While he hated to say goodbye to the Villenti family, he'd learned a few things about himself during his time in Madison, Wisconsin. One, he wasn't cut out for the service industry. Two, not even the Warner twins could solve every mystery. And three, witnessing siblings reunited after years of a strained relationship had given him a new appreciation for Grace.

Vince met him at the front door. "I wanted to tell you myself. The police caught up with Noah Nelson. He's in custody in Michigan."

While Henry believed in justice, he couldn't help but wonder how anyone could let greed get in the way of friendship. For that, Noah deserved whatever punishment he received. "Thanks for letting me know."

"I hope you had a little fun while you were here."

"Other than getting locked in a freezer, a trip to the hospital to rule out a concussion, and giving multiple police statements, I had a blast."

Grace stepped outside. "I didn't mean to eavesdrop, but I had fun, too. My favorite part was gaining an honorary uncle."

"I'm honored." Vince's cheeks reddened. "Now, how about your first paychecks?"

Henry took the piece of paper and did a double take at the dollar amount. "This is way more than a paycheck."

Grace stared at hers. "We can't accept these. It's too much."

"As your honorary uncle, I insist on contributing to your college funds." Vince folded his arms. "Besides, Carrie wanted to give you both a finder's fee for locating the diamonds."

Henry swallowed. "Did you run this by our parents?"

"They refused." He wiggled his brows. "At first."

Ethan Warner emerged from the house. He took one look at the checks and smirked. "This man doesn't take no for an answer. He threatened to deposit the money into your student accounts once you started college."

Henry chuckled, but Grace seemed perplexed.

"What's wrong?" Ethan clamped his hand on her shoulder.

"It's a lot of money." She turned to Vince. "I don't mean to seem ungrateful, but..."

"I don't plan to have kids of my own. Let me do this for you two." He opened his arms. "The only thing I ask is that you both send me an email now and then to make sure you're following your dreams."

"Like you did." She cracked a grin and hugged him. "Thank you."

Faith Warner walked outside and smiled. "Vince Villenti, you spoil my kids, and you'll have to answer to me."

"Me? Never." He winked.

"Uh-huh." She glanced at her watch. "I hate to cut this short, but we need to go if we're going to make our flight."

Ethan said, "Thanks again for allowing us to leave the fifth wheel here over the holidays."

"It's not a problem." Vince smirked. "But don't blame me if it smells like sausage and peppers in there when you get back."

An hour and many hugs later, the Warners pulled out of Vince's driveway.

With nothing to think about besides two weeks with the grandparents in sunny Florida, Henry leaned his head back and closed his eyes.

Faith turned to the twins. "I have your exam grades."

Henry opened one eye and frowned. "And?"

Grace chewed her lower lip.

"All As, except your B-plus in English Literature." She handed them a stack of papers.

Henry braced himself for questions or a lecture or disapproving stares.

"Good job on the mystery and on your grades." Faith smiled. "Have you given any thought to which urban legend you'll investigate after Christmas?"

The twins glanced at each other and grinned.

Henry said, "We're intrigued by the Villisca Ax Murder House."

Their mother blanched. "Dare I ask?"

"Eight people were brutally murdered in the house in 1912. The police never caught the killer." Grace pulled up the website on her phone. "They offer overnight stays and day tours."

Ethan glanced at Henry in the rearview mirror. "I thought you didn't want anything to do with ghosts?"

"I don't, but Grace and I have a running disagreement." Normally, Henry would have balked at the idea of spending the night in such a place. He'd seen a ghost once and didn't care to repeat the experience.

She nudged his side. "I'm going to prove to him once and for all there's no such thing as spirits."

"And I'm looking forward to being there when she has her first encounter with an entity from the Great Beyond."

"Sounds intriguing." Faith faced forward again. "But for now, the only spirits I'm interested are the ones in the Haunted Mansion."

Henry grinned. "Wait, are you saying you bought us tickets to Disney World?"

Ethan wiggled his brows. "Four-day passes."

"No way!" Grace laughed.

"Nothing like Mickey Mouse and Space Mountain to get into the holiday spirit." Henry rubbed his hands together. "Next stop, Gram's and Pop Pop's, and then the Happiest Place on Earth."

The End

AUTHOR NOTES - CRAIG MARTELLE
WRITTEN APRIL 23, 2019

You are still reading! Thank you so much. It doesn't get any better than that.

I love the "Scooby Doo meets Nancy Drew" tagline for this series, and the stories have done it justice.

The Warners always have their foundation. It's not the house, not the truck, not their friends. It's their family that they always have and can count on.

Even though Grace and Henry are coming of age and starting to stretch their own wings. I thought about this series long and hard. I'm a science fiction guy. I've read thousands of science fiction books. I've written a great number of science fiction stories, but I love Scooby Doo, Nancy Drew, and the Hardy Boys. In the rare times I watch TV, the shows are British murder mystery. Some are cozy. Some are police procedural. And all have a mystery or crime to solve.

I thought I'd try my hand at it and I am over the moon with the feedback I've received from my insider team and others whose opinions I trust and made sure that I was on the right track with these stories. Through Tim Marquitz, I found Kathryn Hearst and she is an all-star! We came up with a series of over-arching plots and tendrils.

There are too many urban myths out there! Everyone is getting in on that action. When we were researching, we came up with worldwide stuff to include, so there we added some travel that doesn't include their custom fifth wheel. We do have a floorplan for that thing, by the way so we aren't making it up. That is a real trailer that someone can and has purchased.

I have a big truck but I'm not sure I'd want to tow a 49-foot trailer behind it.

I would if I had to and my beast could, but I think I won't because I don't want to. I like the comfort of hotels and restaurants which in the end are far less expensive if you don't travel much. If you lived on the road, maybe the big trailer would keep you sane.

The weather in Fairbanks, Alaska where I live (actually, ten miles outside the big city of 30,000 people) has been rather mild this year. We are about 150 miles from the Arctic Circle and it can get brutally cold in the winter. Last year, we had a week of -40F. This year, we had a few days in the -30s, but generally, it's been around zero. As we enter the latter stages of spring, overnight temperatures are still below freezing, but the daytime temps are reaching toward the 50s. We'll have maybe a month of spring before our four months of summer. When it's light all the time (that is coming in less than a month).

It is different living up here. You can't imagine the winter dark compared to the summer light, the cold versus the mosquito clouds. And moose. We always have moose.

Thank you again for joining us on this great ride of storytelling. I hope you were entertained for the time you were with us.

Onward and upward. I have a large number of books in the queue, ready to be delivered as often as they are ready. I think you'll like what you read. *Monster Case Files* has a great deal of fun and excitement. It is Scooby Doo meets Nancy Drew in the modern age.

That's it, now. I'm off to keep writing. There are so many more stories to tell.

Peace, fellow humans.

CONNECT WITH THE AUTHORS

Craig Martelle Social

Amazon
www.amazon.com/author/craigmartelle

BookBub
https://www.bookbub.com/authors/craig-martelle

Facebook
www.facebook.com/authorcraigmartelle

My web page
www.craigmartelle.com

Kathryn Hearst Social

Website & Newsletter
https://www.kathrynmhearst.com

BookBub
https://www.bookbub.com/authors/kathryn-m-hearst

Facebook
https://www.facebook.com/kathrynmhearst/

BOOKS BY CRAIG MARTELLE

Craig Martelle's other books (listed by series)

Terry Henry Walton Chronicles (co-written with Michael Anderle) (also in audio)—a post-apocalyptic paranormal adventure

Gateway to the Universe (co-written with Justin Sloan & Michael Anderle) (also in audio)—this book transitions the characters from the Terry Henry Walton Chronicles to The Bad Company

The Bad Company (co-written with Michael Anderle) (also in audio)—a military science fiction space opera

Judge, Jury, & Executioner (also in audio)—a space opera adventure legal thriller

Shadow Vanguard—a Tom Dublin series

Superdreadnought (co-written with Tim Marquitz) (also in audio)— an AI military space opera

Metal Legion (co-written with Caleb Wachter) (also in audio)—a military space opera

The Free Trader (also in audio)—a young adult science fiction action-adventure

Cygnus Space Opera (also in audio)—A young adult space opera (set in the Free Trader universe)

Darklanding (co-written with Scott Moon) (also in audio)—a space western

Mystically Engineered (co-written with Valerie Emerson)—Mystics, dragons, & spaceships

Krimson Empire (co-written with Julia Huni)—A galactic race for justice

End Times Alaska (also available in audio)—a Permuted Press publication—a post-apocalyptic survivalist adventure

Nightwalker (a Frank Roderus series) with Craig Martelle—A post-apocalyptic western adventure

End Days (co-written with E.E. Isherwood) (also in audio)—a post-apocalyptic adventure

Successful Indie Author—a non-fiction series to help self-published authors

Metamorphosis Alpha—stories from the world's first science fiction RPG

<u>**Monster Case Files**</u> (co-written with Kathryn Hearst)—A Warner twins mystery adventure

<u>**Rick Banik**</u> (also available in audio)—Spy & terrorism action adventure

<u>**Published exclusively by Craig Martelle, Inc**</u>

<u>**The Dragon's Call**</u> by Angelique Anderson & Craig A. Price, Jr.—an epic fantasy quest

For a complete list of Craig's books, stop by his website—<u>https://craigmartelle.com</u>